W9-CEQ-188

BY SAMUEL SHELLABARGER

Biography

THE CHEVALIER BAYARD

LORD CHESTERFIELD AND HIS WORLD

Fiction

THE BLACK GALE

CAPTAIN FROM CASTILE

PRINCE OF FOXES

THE KING'S CAVALIER

LORD VANITY

LORD VANITY

Lord Vanity

by
SAMUEL SHELLABARGER

Little, Brown and Company . *Boston*

COPYRIGHT 1953, BY SAMUEL SHELLABARGER

ALL RIGHTS RESERVED. NO PART OF THIS BOOK MAY BE REPRODUCED
IN ANY FORM WITHOUT PERMISSION IN WRITING
FROM THE PUBLISHER

LIBRARY OF CONGRESS CATALOG CARD NO. 53–7330

FIRST EDITION

*Published simultaneously
in Canada by McClelland and Stewart Limited*

PRINTED IN THE UNITED STATES OF AMERICA

To
Adèle Rouge

LORD VANITY

LORD FAXFY

PART ONE

$\mathcal{V}$enice

I

IN 1757, the Villa Bagnoli, Count Widiman's mansion on the outskirts of Mira, was not the most and not the least splendid of the hundred and forty country palaces between Padua and Fusina, which formed the core of the Venetian summer colony. Innumerable other such palaces lay in the neighborhood of Bassano, Vicenza, and Treviso; but the concentration of fashion and architecture appeared on either bank of the Brenta, where that stream becomes a navigable canal, the Naviglio di Brenta, extending from Stra to the sea. Transforming the flat countryside with parks, gardens and façades, the grandiose estates rivaled each other in magnificence and display. Among them, the Widiman villa could show its baroque front, elegant salons, and spacious gardens, without apology.

It was not for the sake of rural nature that the beau monde of Venice swarmed to the mainland when the short Ascension carnival in May had ended. Like every smart set, in each of its summer resorts before or since, it simply continued the winter's social pleasures on a more lavish scale. Expense rocketed. Gilded coaches replaced the gondola. Along the Brenta, beaux and belles, on sumptuous canalboats towed by horses, visited from mansion to mansion. Stables were busy. People rode or drove of an afternoon to show their mounts and their equipages. In steaming kitchens, servants sweated to prepare the endless meals. Play ran deep around pam, basset, and faro tables. At night, dancing began in frescoed ballrooms; or there was comedy or burletta, for many of the villas had their private theaters; or the music of Scarlatti and Galuppi, exquisitely polished,

3

appealed to more discriminating tastes. And, of course, outside in the formal gardens, between fantastically trimmed hedges of box and myrtle or beside the plash of fountains, couples made love. There were sighs and sonnets. There were hidden arbors, where sentiment could become passion.

It was the kind of life that Watteau liked to paint. It was the end of an age, expending in fireworks the toil and treasure of Venice's thousand years.

On a particular night in August, it had occurred to one of Count Widiman's guests that it would be amusing to dance out of doors rather than in the ballroom; and, as others acclaimed the idea, the Count had affably given the necessary orders. A flooring had been laid down in the garden, where a wide bay of lawn, formed by hedges, looked toward the terrace fountain in the background. Refreshment tables had been spread and resin torches set up. The wavering light gave a sense of mystery; it flattered costume and face as the dancers mingled in chiaroscuro. And approval expressed itself in superlatives.

Only the veterans of the eight-piece orchestra, who had sawed and puffed for a generation to the same interweaving of silks, jewels, panniers, white stockings and red heels, considered it merely another Brenta dance. To the leader, Marco Letta, it was a job that lasted till dawn, was well paid and, therefore, deserved his best efforts; but he preferred the musicians' gallery in the ballroom. Torchlight, to him, did not compensate for the mosquitos that probed safely on his neck. Otherwise, there or here, what difference? Perfume and rice powder, rouge and patches, fluttering fans. So he swung his bow to the tune of *"Sciogli le treccie, madonna"* — he could play it in his sleep — and smiled at the eager face of the extra violin, a young supernumerary to whom all this was still new.

Marco liked the extra violin, named Richard Morandi, for his enthusiasm, which kept up the morale of the orchestra. He was a spirited youth of nineteen, who might turn out to be anything good or bad, but never dull. Marco liked him, too, with the indulgence of an old professional toward a gifted but unsteady amateur; for the fiddling job was only a makeshift to carry Richard through the

4

summer. If Tito-Nani, the second violin, had been guilty of such notes as the extra sometimes produced, Letta would have pulverized him. In Morandi's case, everybody laughed.

And, with liking, mingled a touch of deference. It was well known that Richard might have been a nobleman, if his French Huguenot mother, Jeanne Dupré, and the vague English diplomat who had seduced her in far-off Dresden had ever reached the altar. His nickname *Milòr*, by which he was currently known, and the French *Richard*, that never became Riccardo, testified to his birth. But he had more solid merits than that. He was the stepson of Vico Morandi, composer-director at the San Giangrisostomo theater, who had later married Jeanne. Richard had also been given some schooling by the Jesuits. He stood a peg higher socially than hack musicians because of his function as a part-time actor at the San Luca playhouse; and, though he was not yet a regular member of the cast and did not accompany the comedians on their summer tour, he would sometime belong to that troupe. He had even written a couple of scenarios for the commedia dell' arte, which had been acted last winter at Chioggia. But, as he gave himself no airs on the score of all these distinctions and was hail-fellow with the rest of the orchestra, no one felt jealous.

A nerve-shattering squeak from the extra violin reached Letta, who hissed, "Deh! Can't you keep to the tune?" and received an apologetic grin. Richard's big left hand concentrated on its fingering; he puckered his lips; and "*Sciogli le treccie*" flowed smoothly on.

Letta continued to stare a moment in mock indignation, but he was actually wondering how a boy with an English father and French mother came to be so swarthy. The English visitors in Venice were usually blue-eyed, pink-and-white people. As far as skin went, Richard might have been Spanish. He looked mature for his years; had a big-featured, raw-boned face, large, tawny eyes, and a shock of dark hair, forever slipping from the ribbon at the nape of his neck. The effect was Latin in a daredevil way, and striking rather than handsome. But Letta remembered that he had once met an Irish seaman of about the same type. Apparently there were some dark people in the North.

Having conquered his violin for a moment, Richard was gazing intently again at the dance floor. His expression brought to Letta's

5

mind the first patrician dance he had played at thirty years ago in the Contarini palace. Fiddling had been an adventure then, not a job.

"Psst!" he whispered, catching the eyes of the orchestra. "We'll run into the air 'Anima mia.' Same time."

The tune changed.

But for Richard Morandi, the fashionable world was still unexplored. Of course, he had caught glimpses of it all his life: on street and piazza; in the regattas of the Grand Canal; in the public gaming rooms of the Ridotto during carnivals; in boxes at the theater; before lighted palace entrances, where liveried gondoliers delivered their masters at a banquet or reception. But he had never been so close to it as during the past month in Letta's orchestra. The men and women especially fascinated him. Trained to the theater since childhood, he was an excellent mimic and had a quick eye both for types and individuals. Under the influence of his patron and friend, Dr. Goldoni the playwright, the great man at San Luca's, he had formed early the habit of studying people; for to copy from nature, Goldoni instructed, was the only true method of either the dramatist or actor. And here tonight was a wealth of material.

A snuffbox, thought Richard, should be handled in just *that* way, if he was ever called on to act the role of a fine gentleman. So he would make his bow to a young noble lady with just that poise of leg and sideward sweep of the hands — not too extreme. And so he would bow to an older matron, paying tribute to her age and rank. So he would give his arm. So he would walk, turning out his toes at the proper angle. The actor in him admired the acting of the men and women of fashion. Their manners, he knew, were an exquisite, highly studied art.

And meanwhile, half-consciously, he was on the lookout for interesting characters and hints for plots. It was from casual, undeveloped situations that Goldoni drew his most popular comedies.

For example, this captivating young French countess, Amélie des Landes, whom Richard had often seen during the past month and whom everybody courted. How had she come to marry the seventy-year-old disaster, Monsieur le Comte, with the masklike face, who rarely left his eternal cards and cognac? She was gay and volatile

6

and light as a butterfly, but indeed far from innocent — ethereally cynical, amusingly naughty. She and her husband could be put on the stage in a dozen ways. They were the first cosmopolitan foreigners whom Richard had seen close by. The Countess spoke perfect Italian. It was rumored that she had been educated at a convent in Rome, where her father, an Irish nobleman, and her mother, a French heiress, were prominent at the little court of the exiled Stuart prince.

And there, hotly attending her, was the young patrician, Marin Sagredo, big, handsome and arrogant, the most conspicuous beau on the dance floor. Richard, not for the first time, took note of him for future use. Belonging to one of the great families in Venice, Sagredo was kinsman to most of the others — the son, nephew and cousin of grandees. He had served three years as aide to the Proveditor General in Dalmatia and had brought back some of the savagery of that region; was noted for his recklessness, hot temper and insolence, for practical jokes of the cruel sort, and as a great fancier of women. With the keenness of dislike, Richard watched him now on his high red heels, patronizing and condescending, while everybody played up to him. He wore a white satin coat embroidered with gold; he had gold clocks on his stockings and gold flowers on his crimson waistcoat. His fobs tinkled as he moved. The side rolls of his wig were crisp as spun glass.

Richard's thought, for a moment, became less objective. It was on such occasions — not too frequent, after all — that the consciousness of his birth sometimes ached. Here he was, chinning a violin at two ducats a week or, at best, a despised comico, when, as far as the blood in him went, he might have been the equal of such a gallant. Because his mother had not married her seducer and had so completely broken with him, Richard remained on the far side of a gulf separating him from the pomp and glitter of the world. Of course, he could tell himself that it did not matter, that he did not care about these things; but a youth of nineteen, hungry for living, does care about them, at least now and then. For Richard, the occasional ache represented a rift in himself. Why should he envy Sagredo and the other young bloods, vying with each other in pranks and Parisian clothes, schooling their horses in the manège on the Rio dei Mendicanti, fencing at Cavazzi's salle d'armes, gambling at the Ridotto? He had other more interesting and attainable objects in mind. Think of Goldoni! Think of art and fame! Think of writing plays and burlettas known from St. Petersburg to Naples! Ashamed of envy, he stuffed it down below the level of thought. But the ache was nevertheless there.

He found himself looking at a girl who stood at one side of the dance floor, and gradually Sagredo faded from his mind. As far as he could judge in the light of the torches, she seemed an attractive girl of middle height, dressed very simply in white muslin and without powder on her hair. It was an age when the social world belonged exclusively to married or to older women; but, if this girl was married, she must be a very young wife, hardly out of the convent. It struck him even more that she seemed alone, without an escort or companion. He had been half aware of her for some time and realized now that he had seen no one speak to her, except a couple of the more elderly guests. "Dio!" he thought warmly. "She would be my choice, rather than one of those painted flirts." He liked her fresh, clean look and simple gown, the fact, too, that she did not seem at all conscious of herself and was taking such obvious pleasure in watching the dance. One might have expected the set smile and painful awareness of a neglected girl, but she looked perfectly at ease.

The tune came to an end with a final cadenza; the orchestra broke off for a pause; and the babble of voices rose.

Richard tapped the second violin, Tito-Nani, on the shoulder. Tito was an old hand at the Brenta dances, knew everybody, and picked up all the gossip. "Say, who is that girl in white? There — she's talking with the old gentleman. I haven't seen her before."

The other mopped his forehead. "Can't tell you, Milòr. Pretty, eh?"

"Bellissima."

Lio, the French horn, put in: "Quella piccina? She's the girl that Cate, the maid, pointed out to me. A poor relation of Contessa Widiman's. Daughter of Antonio Venier — you know (or perhaps you wouldn't), the patrician who ruined himself by marrying a ballet dancer in Vienna. Quite a scandal years ago. The family turned their noble backs on him. His wife's dead now. They say he lives in a tumble-down old palazzo on the Frescada Canal. Poor as a louse.

8

The Contessa Widiman feels sorry for the girl. Invited her over here as a treat."

"Unmarried?" asked Richard.

"Of course. Who would marry her? She hasn't a bezzo."

"I didn't mean that. Unmarried girls aren't seen at dances—not of her rank, at least. After all, she's patrician."

"Not according to law, she isn't," said Lio. "When a grandee, like Venier, marries beneath him, his children have no rank."

"But why isn't she in a convent?"

Lio shrugged. "Better ask her, Milòr. Cate says she's had a queer bringing-up. Wants to be a ballerina like her mother. — Dare you to ask her."

"Va bene," Richard grinned, "I will if I get the chance. What's her name?"

"Maritza."

Letta hissed. "Silenzio! We'll take the tune 'Bondì, Marina.' Contredanse time."

The sawing started again. The white stockings and panniers moved to a different rhythm. The girl had disappeared.

"Spaniels!" thought Richard of the neglectful beaux. "Because a girl's poor, because she isn't dressed like a French doll, they freeze her out!" He sympathized with Maritza all the more as her position reminded him of his own. Both of them disinherited from birth; both of them on the wrong side of the gate and peering in through the bars.

But, with respect to the stage, here was a character made to order. Take a girl like this . . .

He fiddled away, lost in plots, until the next pause.

The dance floor cleared. Some of the dancers drifted past to the refreshment table. Sagredo, chatting with his partner, the French countess, paused in front of the orchestra. The lady's gown, sprinkled with tiny rosettes, brushed Richard's knee. He could breathe her perfume light as a gust of jasmine. But the nearness was only physical; as far as noticing him went, he might not have been there at all.

She smiled up at her escort and urged: "Well, well, don't keep me in suspense. There she was in the arbor. And then —?"

Like that of most other Venetians, Sagredo's Italian had a strong

9

local flavor. "Why, then," he said, "I asked her, 'Madama, per favore, why are you so ill at ease?' — 'Because, caro,' she said, 'to be frank, I am troubled by a flea.' — 'Che cossa!' said I. 'Let me assist you, anima mia. Is it on the leg?' — 'Alas, no, mio ben.' — 'Is it on the back?' —'Sior, no.' — Thus, delicately, I learned of what impudence the beast was capable. 'Ah, madama,' I begged, 'am I not your cavaliere servente? Is it not my duty to rid you of this annoyance? I say allow me. Surely you, my love, are unconcerned with bourgeois prejudices.' — We discussed the matter." Sagredo flashed his teeth. "Now, recall, Contessa, that we were alone. What would you have done?"

The Countess parried. "What did *she* do?"

"Oe, madonna, I'm too discreet to answer that. But I'll admit," he leered, "that I was tempted afterwards to take as my private scutcheon a flea rampant on a ———."

"Fie!" She laid her closed fan against his lips, then flicked it open and eyed him over the top of it. "We poor ladies! We poor innocents! How scandalously you men speak of us! I'm trying to blush. What an amusing dog you are!"

The drawl in her voice set him on fire. "But you haven't told me, Contessa, what you would have done!"

She laughed. "Ah, caro Marin, how shall I answer? It's a hard choice between you and a flea. Come, darling, refresh me with an ice and tell me another story."

Sagredo looked doubtful. He spat at random and the jet struck Richard's cheek; but, though absently noticing it, he gave his arm to the Countess. They strolled on.

"Pezzo d'asino!" It was a moment before Richard found his tongue. By that time, the pair were a couple of yards off. As he started up, Tito-Nani's hands clamped down on his shoulders.

"Don't make a fool of yourself."

"By God . . . !"

"He meant nothing."

"Nothing! The swine! I tell you he was looking at me."

"Yes, but he didn't see you."

"You mean I'm too low to be seen, too damned insignificant? Sangue di . . . !"

"Keep cool, Milòr. Whatever the reason, I tell you he didn't see

10

you. What can you do about it? Tear after him in that crowd? Explain that he spat in your face? Demand an apology? Lord! The apology you'd get! Sit still and relax."

Letta, the French horn, and the cello closed round.

Sagredo and the Countess had now joined the group at the refreshment table. Richard glared over at them. Tito-Nani was right. Short of acting the madman, there was nothing to do about it.

I I

OPPORTUNELY, a hamper containing wine, bread and cheese now arrived to refresh the orchestra. Instruments were laid by; the musicians got up and stretched or strolled about. The wine was excellent. Richard's temper cooled off.

Lio, the French horn, who stood with his mouth full, gazing across the now empty dance floor, gulped and exclaimed: "Capperi! There's your girl again, Milòr. See who she's with. The prize of the party, I'll say. Domenedio!"

Turning his head, Richard caught sight of Maritza Venier and a tall gentleman entering the bay from the garden side. Maritza's escort had given her his arm; and as the torchlight fell on the gentleman's handsome costume, Richard swung around to stare. The newcomer stood well over six feet, was broad-shouldered and had a lean, bold face with black, arching eyebrows. Even at a distance, there was something thrilling in the way he moved and carried himself, as if he radiated a kind of vital current. He could not be older than the early thirties, but, in contrast with the youth and simple dress of the girl beside him, he looked double her age.

Richard had never seen him before and wondered aloud who he was.

This time Letta had the answer. "Name's Tromba, I think. The Cavaliere Marcello Tromba. He came this morning. A Neapolitan. They say he's a great traveler and man of pleasure. Knows everybody. I hear he won a big stack of gold this afternoon at faro. The little Siora had better watch out. He doesn't strike me as too safe company for young ladies."

11

Richard had the same impression, but he was glad that Maritza had found an escort.

Evidently the two had been talking about dance steps; for now, with no apparent concern at all for the eyes that at once focused on them, they walked onto the floor and began practising a figure.

"Is it this way, signorina?" asked the gentleman, smiling. He took a step forward, then back, and pirouetted gracefully.

"No," said the girl, "not quite. First, to the side, like this —" her slippers hardly seemed to touch the floor — "then forward and back — così. And così! And così! Then pirouette." Her dress billowed out a little. "There!"

"By God, I have it," said the gentleman. "I remember. You won't have to show me twice." He copied her movements perfectly. "That's right, eh? It's been an age since I danced the furlana."

She clapped her hands. "Benissimo!"

Richard was aware that the whole circle of bystanders — those at the buffet and those strolling about — were now watching. He was aware, too, with a pulse of satisfaction, that the distinguished newcomer had eclipsed Sagredo. If the latter's costume was splendid, Tromba's surpassed it in fashion and cut, was more superbly Parisian. It did not blaze in gold but shimmered in silver. The lines of the cuffs, the more conservative length and flare of the coat skirts, the blue ribbon of an order across the waistcoat, recalled Versailles. If Sagredo was tall, Tromba seemed taller, more graceful. He did not commandeer attention but inevitably became the center of it. As compared with him, the young patrician looked showy and callow.

After a few moments, the couple crossed over towards the orchestra; and, for the first time, Richard could see both of them distinctly. He found Maritza Venier vivid, rather than pretty, and therefore a little breath-taking. What if she had too large a mouth and a short, upturned nose? There was an April lilt about her, something warm and impulsive in her eyes and smile, that made beauty irrelevant or that perhaps could be called beauty in its most subtle form.

"Caro Padrone," said the Cavaliere, addressing Letta, "this very noble lady and I are longing for a furlana, if you will give us one after you and the musicians have rested. I think it may amuse others of the company as a change from the usual dances. Will you be so kind?"

He spoke a polished Italian different from the Venetian dialect. It marked him as a foreigner, but his pleasant voice and manner saved it from sounding affected. Richard was pleased that he had given Maritza a title. The orchestra, as a whole, felt complimented to be asked for a furlana. Though originating in Friuli, it had long since become the Venetian national dance. The Frenchified nobility might cultivate the minuet, allemande, or contredanse, which better suited the costumes and manners of good society; but the true Venetian, grandee or *popolano,* kept as warm a place in his heart for the furlana as did the Neapolitan for the somewhat similar tarantella.

Letta wiped his mouth with the back of his hand and grinned. "Schiao suo, Lustrissimo. That's a request I like to hear. We'll give you as many furlanas as your Excellence and the company can stand. But I marvel that a foreigner like your Excellence should know the dance."

"Oh," waved Tromba, "it's not my first visit to Venice. Besides" — he half turned to Maritza — "with a partner like the Signorina, who wouldn't be able to dance anything?"

"And make it lively, sior," said Maritza, including all the musicians in a smile. "You know, the kind they dance in the campielli. We must show this gentleman a *real* furlana." Her soft Venetian accent that turned *s*'s into *z*'s established a bond between her and the orchestra. "I wish, though, I had a flower for my hair," she added. "It won't be a *real* furlana without one."

Richard was quicker even than Tromba. "If the Lustrissima will honor me," he bowed, "I'll fetch her any flower in the garden. Red? Yellow? Blue? . . ."

"Which do you think, sior?" There was no coquetry in the question. She seemed to want his advice.

"Red, madonna."

"Yes, I think so, too. You're very kind."

At once he was off, his mind torn between some late-blooming roses he had noticed not far from the terrace and a bed of potted carnations further along. But a rose was too fragile for a dance like the furlana, and he had about decided on the carnations when he remembered the crimson camellias at one end of the inner garden. *That* was the flower. He could picture it against the softness of her hair.

A few minutes later, he was back at the dance floor with several camellias for her to choose from. But, by this time, she and Tromba had wandered over to the buffet; and Richard, following, waited in the background. The Cavaliere, already the center of the group, was proposing a furlana as the next dance. The more active and unconventional applauded; the others approved. Tromba magnetized them all.

To Richard, it was absorbing to watch the shift of focus away from Sagredo, who until then had been the dominant beau. He was now slipping down into the ranks. Richard noticed, too, that the ladies especially came under Tromba's spell. They grew unmindful of the other men, appraising the newcomer with thoughtful, enigmatic eyes, but brightening when he looked at them; and his looks included everybody. Clearly he had no special interest in Maritza, who had perhaps been recommended to him by the considerate Count or Countess Widiman. He treated her playfully, a little paternally, and, meanwhile, paid court, one by one, to all the ladies. His technique was marvelous to watch. Richard half forgot Maritza and the camellias as he admired it.

Then at a certain moment, quite definite in Richard's mind, the impartial gallantry changed, narrowed, and pointed in one direction. It was like the poise of a hovering falcon who has chosen its target. Tromba's eyes were fixed on the Countess des Landes. She returned the gaze and wrinkled her nose at him. He smiled. That was all, but the hunt was on. She had not looked at Sagredo in that way.

Tromba merely said: "And you, madame, will you risk a furlana?"

"Why not, sir — if you'll show me how?"

"Alas, I regret. I'm to be shown how myself." He nodded at Maritza.

"I like that!" put in Sagredo, not succumbing easily. "It seems to me I know more about it than a foreigner!"

"Ah, but of course," said the lady. "I had forgotten you, Marin."

"And I suggest," went on Sagredo, taking charge of things once more and glimpsing a chance to regain ground, "that this gentleman — By God, sir, your name escapes me —"

14

Tromba informed him.

"I thank you. That Sior Tromba —"

"Cavaliere," Tromba added.

"Well, then, I suggest that the *Cavaliere* Tromba and —" Sagredo stared at Maritza — "this lady show the steps for the benefit of Madame des Landes and others who may not be familiar with them. It's only right that a Neapolitan should teach us Venetians the furlana. Then, afterwards, we can all join in."

He picked up several of the other young beaux with a glance and all but winked. It was clear that he did not expect much from Tromba. When he, Sagredo, took the floor, it would be different.

There was a murmur of assent.

Tromba smiled. "As you wish, signoria. The Lady Maritza and I will be delighted to amuse, if not instruct, you and leave the finer points —" he lifted an eyebrow at Sagredo — "to his Excellence."

The sounds of tuning up came from the orchestra. Richard had to get back to his fiddle, but he wanted to give the flowers to Maritza. Then, as the group broke up to gather around the dance floor, she came toward him, nominally escorted by Tromba, but, because of the latter's preoccupation with the Countess, momentarily alone.

"I'm sorry to keep you waiting, sior," she said simply. "I couldn't help it. — What beautiful flowers!" She pressed them with both hands against her face and took a deep breath. Then, selecting two of the blossoms, she set one in the V of her bodice and pinned the other behind her ear. "See? Is that right?"

He murmured a compliment.

"Mille, *mille* grazie, caro sior. Will you keep the others for me? I want all of them."

Tromba, turning now from the Countess, added his thanks.

Richard, in a glow, hurried back to the orchestra.

The furlana, being a folk dance, took lots of breath. It involved the whole body, even the head, which sometimes nodded in cadence. The dancers met, parted, circled each other, spun rapidly on their heels; while the music, characterized by its bass chords, stressed the rhythm.

But, though Richard could only catch glimpses through the circle around the floor, he soon felt no concern about the competence

15

of Maritza and her partner. She danced like a bacchante, supple as a willow. Every movement interpreted the dance, expressed its popular features, dramatized it. "A ballerina!" thought Richard. He had seen nothing better on the stage. And, like every gifted dancer, she created an atmosphere. Into the stilted, artificial gathering, she brought naturalness, a breath of joy. The contagion of it set people clapping in cadence, added brio to the orchestra, called forth unconscious *bravas,* as she spun from pirouette to pirouette. And Tromba was no mean second. Vigorous and lithe, graceful as a cat, he had put off conventions for the moment and danced like a Neapolitan *barcaiuolo.* Feline, passionate, a little sinister. Wonderful acting, admired Richard. Or was it entirely acting? But, if Marin Sagredo had expected a failure from Tromba, this was certainly checkmate.

The dance ended in a gale of applause. Everybody, taken by the new game, wanted another furlana. The floor filled with couples or groups, some awkward, some experienced. Tromba appropriated the French countess. Sagredo condescended to Maritza, who had briefly become popular. And Richard, seething, had to admit that the young beau was an excellent dancer.

But stays and high heels, wigs and panniers, not to speak of flabby muscles, could not last the course. The perspiring and disheveled fashionables began dropping out, crowded the refreshment tables. And, after a pause, Letta wisely signaled for a minuet. Its slow tripping began again, to the general relief.

Richard looked in vain for Maritza on the floor, then discovered her, still with Sagredo, at the buffet. Apparently suggesting a stroll in the garden, the latter offered her his arm. They disappeared beyond the light of the torches. If it had been any other man, Richard would have felt happy that Maritza was receiving continued attention. But Sagredo! That arrogant young brute! The extra violin let out so dismal a screech that it jarred Letta to his toes and brought a stream of maledictions from his lips. Fortunately, not long afterwards, Maritza, no longer escorted by Sagredo, once more appeared on the other side of the floor.

And at the same instant, Richard caught sight of another figure, who at once fixed his attention to the exclusion of any one else.

It was Carlo Goldoni.

Richard managed to fiddle but kept gazing across the dance floor at the plump little dramatist talking with Count Widiman and several of the older guests. Goldoni had been spending the summer away from Venice at Zola, the house of his patron, Marquis Albergati, near Bologna. On the way home, he had now apparently stopped off to visit Widiman, another patron. His unexpected appearance delighted Richard not only because of the fondness and admiration he had for him, but it signaled the close of summer, the approaching theater season, the end of makeshift jobs. He could hardly wait to pay him his respects. Dear Papa Goldoni! So modest and famous! It gave a sense of well-being merely to look at him, to know that he was here.

And yet, as Richard watched his old friend, attentive now to Count Widiman, now to another grandee, something of the ache which he had felt earlier returned. It was hard to see his hero at a disadvantage. In the Venetian theaters, Doctor Goldoni was a great person; here on the Brenta, to these noblemen, he was only an entertaining little bourgeois, who had written fashionable plays. This meant patronage and politeness, but not equality. He addressed the people of rank as *Excellence* or *Illustrious;* to them, he was merely *Sior Carlo*. It hurt Richard to notice how much Goldoni himself was aware of the distinction: quick to bow, a little obsequious, nervously rubbing his hands. The pen had brought him as far as it could, but not across the gulf.

Contemptible, chafed Richard, to have such thoughts even for a minute. What the devil was the matter with him? Didn't he believe that generations of men would still admire Carlo Goldoni when all these bigwigs were forgotten? Yes, he believed that. Well, then? Why itch for tinsel? He didn't want it anyway. He hated himself for wanting it. — He hated to remember that Sagredo had spat on him.

The mood vanished at the next intermission when Goldoni, rounding the dance floor, caught sight of his young disciple and, as Richard sprang up, gave him a hug. The good Doctor might not be entirely at ease in such fine company, but he had no trace of the snob.

"Well, Milòr!" he beamed. "Well, well! And how have you got through the summer? And have you turned out any more skits for my enemies of the commedia dell' arte?"

He referred, of course, to the rivalry, grown bitter of late, be-

17

tween the old-style improvised comedy and his own written plays on the French model. Count Gozzi and the Granellesca Academy had just begun the campaign which would later result in Goldoni's self-imposed exile from Venice.

Richard, embarrassed at being singled out from the orchestra and conscious that people were staring, answered in a couple of phrases, which Widiman interrupted.

"And who, Signor Dottore, is this young man? Do I have playwrights in my orchestra?"

It was like Goldoni never to miss the chance of promoting a friend. "Illustrissimo," he replied, "let me present to you one of the most talented youths in Venice, Richard Morandi, stepson of the well-known composer. And let me tell you that his scenario *Captain Harlequin*, which was played last winter in Chioggia, deserves to have been acted by the great Sacchi himself. Can I say more?" But he ran on with a panegyric that stretched the truth a good deal and brought the blood to Richard's cheeks.

Then, while the latter hid his confusion in a deep bow to Widiman, the dramatist added, as an afterthought: "And here's a stroke of luck, Lustrissimo. The boy is heaven sent for our plans, if you agree."

"In what way?"

"He's an excellent actor. Did you not flatter me by asking to see my newest comedy, the one written this summer and played by the Marquis Albergati's guests, *Il Cavaliere di Spirito?*"

"Indeed I did, but it was no flattery." Widiman glanced around the circle which had paused to listen. "How would that please you, signoria: the latest play by our great Goldoni, to be acted by yourselves?"

There was a ripple of applause. "Evviva!" said Tromba.

"Well, then," Goldoni went on, "I have no doubt of the talents of these ladies and gentlemen. But the play needs one professional who knows my methods. And if your Excellence permits, I beg to give a role to Sior Morandi."

Of course, Richard understood this for what it was: a puff to bring him into notice. He knew that Francesco Vendramin, one of the patrician owners of the San Luca playhouse, was a guest at the villa. It might mean a regular appointment for him to that troupe.

18

It was his first big chance. He held his breath for Widiman's answer.

"Anything you like, Signor Dottore," said the Count. And turning to the orchestra leader, "I'm sure you can release Morandi for a time. Neither you nor he will lose by it."

Letta bowed eagerly. He wished the boy luck. "Prego, Sior Conte, prego. At your service."

Happening to glance at the bystanders, Richard noticed that Maritza had joined them. Their eyes met. She gave him a warm smile, as if she, too, was glad.

"And now," continued Widiman to the nearby circle, "shall we complete the cast? I understand there are only six in it and only one role for a lady. Will the Countess des Landes favor us? The best of France and Italy will meet in your acting, madama. They tell me, by the way, that you're a consummate actress."

It was the day of amateur theatricals. Almost everyone had taken part in them one time or another. The Countess accepted without protest, but she did not miss the innuendo of Widiman's remark. "There's no sweeter music than praise, though undeserved, Eccellenza. But God help the lady who isn't an actress in this world of ours."

"And you, Cavaliere?" bowed Widiman.

"Honored," said Tromba.

The golden Sagredo bulked in the foreground. Widiman could not ignore him.

"And your Excellence? I hear that you acted with great applause in an improvised comedy before the Proveditor General at Zara."

Sagredo looked moody, as if he had not been enjoying himself. But his stare at Richard gave a pretext for declining. It said plainer than words that a Venetian aristocrat did not associate with lackeys.

"I beg to be excused, sir."

Richard was pleased. The thought of suffering Sagredo at such close quarters as a play required completely dashed him.

But Amélie des Landes did not intend to lose a fish from her hook. "Ah, Marin!" she put in. "Caro Marin! Not if I ask you?" Her eyes melted; her smile and voice atoned for the dance with Tromba. "Of course you'll act — with me."

He relented at once. "Your slave, Contessa."

19

Richard froze again.

Widiman now invited two other gentlemen, the Signor Brunetti and Captain Beccaria, to complete the cast. The group drifted apart. Goldoni lingered to give Richard a clap on the shoulder.

"I'm counting on you, Milòr. Make a success here, and you'll have a good role this winter at San Luca's."

"How can I thank you enough, Maestro?"

"A small matter," shrugged Goldoni, rejoining Widiman and Tromba.

If only Sagredo were out of it! But Richard braced himself. Sagredo or not, he had a foot on the ladder and proposed to climb.

"Did you keep my flowers, sior?" asked a voice, and he looked up to find Maritza Venier in front of him.

"Madonna, of course." He skirted the grinning orchestra to fetch the camellias from where he had left them.

"You see," she went on, with a finger at her hair, "I lost this one."

"But you kept the other." The crimson blossom still glowed in the angle of her bodice. "That's more important."

"Indeed it is," she smiled. "Close to my heart. Like your kindness." She looked up at him a moment, then gave him her hand.

Confused, he almost forgot to bow.

"Good night and good fortune, Sior Milòr."

III

TO the disappointment of Madame des Landes, who had perhaps expected amusement by playing him off against Sagredo, and to the chagrin of several other ladies, the Cavaliere Tromba now withdrew from the dance in favor of the gaming rooms at the villa, which he may have considered more profitable and less demanding. There he rounded off his lucky streak of the day at faro by winning fifty ducats from Monsieur des Landes, and then, not too quickly, excused himself before the tide could turn. Besides, since des Landes, who acted as banker, had now been reduced to playing on credit and since Tromba preferred cash, the game lost interest.

"You are a prudent young man, Monsieur le Chevalier," said the

Count dryly — he spoke only French — "and you place your bets well. One can see that you have played a great deal." He sipped the last of his cognac and beckoned a servant, who at once re-filled the glass. "Now, I have never been prudent and have never known when to stop. I predict a shining future for you."

No one unfamiliar with des Landes would have suspected that he was drunk; but then few had ever seen him sober. Brandy had no effect upon the polish of his manners or the changeless serenity of his wrinkled old face. People knew, however, that it clouded the memory of his gambling losses, and that he did not welcome re-minders of them. He had fought a good many duels in that con-nection.

Tromba thanked him for the prophecy.

"It may be," added des Landes, "that when I have refilled my purse, you will play with me again. I hope so."

The slate-gray eyes expressed nothing more than usual; but an almost imperceptible edge to the flat voice was not missed by other players at the table. They became elaborately detached, took snuff, or gazed across the room.

Tromba's French equaled des Landes's. He said merely: "Your servant, Monsieur le Comte, at any time — or in any way." By God, if the old devil wanted to pick a quarrel —

Widiman, the perfect host, happened to be passing, sensed the chill, guessed the cause of it, and put in: "Ah, you're stopping, Cavaliere? I'll take your chair. I hope it brings me your luck. Garde à vous, Monsieur des Landes."

And the incident faded. Except that, while shuffling, the French nobleman muttered: "Ah, mm-m, le Chevalier de Tromba, eh? Very clever fellow . . . too clever . . . cela sent un peu la valetaille . . . un peu le filou . . . wonder what name he had before this one . . ." But des Landes's musing fell on deaf ears. Tromba made an excellent impression, had brought letters of introduction from the best quarters. The Count's own reputation was dubious. He had been losing money and did not enjoy losing it. The other players began following Tromba's lead after a deal or two, and the game broke up.

However, des Landes continued to sit at the deserted table, shuf-fling his cards, sipping his cognac, imperturbably drunken, and

"But yes, your Excellence. I have long been intimate with the Siora Morandi. I happen to remember the man's name because it sounds French, unlike most of those English tongue breakers. It was Hammond" (Goldoni said *'Ammond*). "Thomas Hammond. He was a baron, I think, with the title of Marny. Of course, I know nothing about English noblemen."

But Tromba knew about this one. Behind his handsome hawk face, which revealed only what he pleased, interest suddenly blazed. Here was something important.

Lord Marny! Cosmopolitan Europe repeated that name. It was equally familiar to polite circles in Paris as in London, in Spa as in Bath. It had been associated with British diplomacy for the last thirty years, with the Second Treaty of Vienna, the Peace of Aix-la-Chapelle, the shift of England's support from Austria to Prussia in the present war. It was famous in Parliament and in the world of fashion. Marny had reached the top of the ladder: a baron, once; an earl, now, and a Knight of the Garter. He had acquired great wealth by marriage. Tromba remembered seeing a miniature of him in one of the Paris salons: the cold, dark face; the blue ribbon and diamond star. Yes, there was a likeness between him and Richard Morandi.

"Has your Excellence heard of him?" added the playwright.

"I believe I have," Tromba said cautiously. His mind was already sniffing at possibilities. For one thing, he planned soon to visit England. It was the last rich vein in Europe which he had not worked. His stay in Venice would probably be limited. A man of pleasure, without capital save his wits, cannot afford to stay anywhere too long. "But, caro signore," he probed, "I wouldn't expect to find the son of an English milòr fiddling in an orchestra. You'd suppose he'd do something for the boy. Perhaps he has."

Goldoni shrugged. "Nothing at all, though to be fair to him, that's not his fault. It's an odd story."

"Indeed?" With his interest now alert, Tromba maneuvered the other toward a couple of chairs inside the loggia. "Shall we sit awhile? You know, I'm singularly taken by your young friend. He's an attractive lad. Molto simpatico. I'd be inclined to serve him."

"Your Excellence's favor would be a great help," said Goldoni, "especially during the play."

24

"He can depend on it. What were you telling me about Milòr de Marny — not his fault and so on? After all, I suppose it was a casual amour, of no great consequence to a man of his rank. Probably he has several bastards. May find it hard to recall 'em, eh? Often happens."

Tromba spoke from experience. He had sown his offspring across the face of Europe and would not have found it easy to give the number, much less distinguish among them.

"As to that," smiled Goldoni, "I don't know. But this was not a casual amour; it was a grand passion."

"Che cosa!" Tromba's activities required patrons. He needed one in England. Goldoni's statement brightened the prospects of approaching Marny. You could get closer to a man by way of a true romance he has had than a random bawdry. The heart was apt to remember the one and be indifferent to the other.

"Yes," Goldoni insisted, "a grand passion. He proposed to the girl with her father's consent. And I don't believe it was a trick to seduce her. He intended marriage. She was poor but of a good Huguenot family driven into exile at the time of the Revocation. Her father, Richard Dupré, was pastor to the French Huguenots in Dresden. As far as blood went, the match would not have been too unequal. And I tell you, he was in love."

"Anything's possible," agreed Tromba. "Well?"

"Well, sior, of course his family opposed it. They hatched up a marriage for him with one of the old King's daughters by a German mistress, plain but rich to the tune of a hundred thousand pounds sterling. The chief minister — I forget his name; he's dead now —"

"Walpole?" Tromba hinted.

"Yes. Walpole offered him plums in the way of advancement, if he had money to pay for them. On the other hand, he had debts, and his creditors would not be put off. So, he decided as you would expect. However, the Siora Morandi does him justice. He proposed to keep her as his mistress, offered a handsome settlement and the full support of the child she was enceinte with. For my part, Sior Cavaliere, I think he acted like a gallant man; not like a saint, of course, but as well as a man could act in such a pinch. She refused everything."

"La povera!" exclaimed the Neapolitan. "Lunatic, eh?"

Goldoni's knowledge of human nature, expert as far as it went, was bounded by the limits of common sense. He found himself baffled by subtleties of the spirit.

He sighed. "Lustrissimo, I can only tell you what she once told me. That she could not love a man who would break his word and permit his child to be born without a name for a hundred thousand pounds. That she had loved Milòr de Marny and could not live with him on any other terms. That, whatever she did, she would not commit the sin of discounting their love for money; would be tantamount to selling her soul. Romantic notions of the kind. I can't say that I understood them."

Fumbling for his box, Tromba took snuff. "Ah, well. What then?"

"Her family did not know of her condition. It would have disgraced them and ruined her father if she had remained in Dresden. She had a musical training and a pleasant voice, had met Vico Morandi, who was then directing an opera troupe on the way back to Venice from St. Petersburg. She caught his fancy; he took her with them when they left Dresden. So, she disappeared. A day or two earlier, Marny was recalled to England. She has never written him. I don't believe he found out what became of her. Perhaps he judged it better to turn that page."

"No doubt he did," Tromba agreed, "and a sensible man, too. So, she preferred Morandi to Marny and let her son grow up from hand to mouth, when he might have been bred a gentleman. All for the sake of what, Maestro? Can you tell me that?"

Goldoni shook his head. "The Lord knows. Women's crotchets."

The Cavaliere only half listened. His mind was full of charming speculations. From the tiny seed of Richard's nickname, which he had happened not to overlook, might spring up a tree bearing golden apples for his visit to England. Make friends with Richard. Coach him properly. Appear with him in London. Bring him to Marny's notice under favoring circumstances. Tromba seemed to recall that Marny had no children — legitimate at least. Suppose that he still retained bittersweet memories of the old love affair in Dresden. Middle age could often be sentimental about such things. Suppose that Richard took his fancy. Then, by God, what an entrée, what possibilities for the generous Cavaliere who had brought the two together! Tromba's beak of a nose quivered, like a hunting dog's on a hot scent.

But he was not given to counting birds in the bush. Most of all this was conditional. He would have to feel his way . . .

"Again I thank you, Maestro. An absorbing story. The case of young Milòr touches me. I'm strongly drawn to him."

Then, having bid Goldoni good night, Tromba continued on down into the garden and whistled a tune under his breath.

I V

THE Villa Bagnoli retired at dawn and slept till noon. That is, the fair, the gay and honored so retired and slept. The servants had less regular hours, but even they snored for a while on their straw pallets in the mansard. Being servants, they were used to the crowded little cubicles under the tiles, roasting in summer, freezing in winter, and at every season rank with the smell of unwashed bodies. Habit was everything. Animals like them could sleep as well on straw as their masters on feathers — better perhaps.

But, to Richard Morandi, whose lodgings at his stepfather's apartment in Venice, though meager, at least comprised a bed, the sleeping arrangements at the Villa Bagnoli were a considerable hardship. He waked about seven, bathed in sweat, tormented by flies and gasping for air, since it was not the custom of the time to open windows at night. The moist and naked forms of the second violin and French horn, who were packed into the cubicle with him, did not make for refreshment. It was a blue August morning outside, and the tiles of the roof, still warm from yesterday, began radiating heat like the walls of an oven.

After threshing about for ten minutes, he got up, cursing, drew on a minimum of clothes and, with coat and waistcoat under one arm, made his way down the service stairs to the kitchen department in the basement. An outside court, screened by hedges, served as a delivery entrance and contained troughs to which water was piped from the garden fountains. Here a disheveled mob of maids and lackeys were already filling ewers for the guests' bedrooms or smartening up after the short hours of sleep. It was a focal point of babble and gossip.

Stripped to the waist, Richard splashed some water over his face and chest, dried himself on a dubious towel, and waited his chance

27

at a small mirror dangling from one of the hedges. Then, having drawn a razor over the beginnings of a beard, he combed and tied back his hair, slipped on his shirt and visited the outhouse, which hardly differed from a pigsty. Some minutes later, he was ready for the day, and neat enough to gain the favor of a scullery maid, who waited on him in the servants' room off the kitchen. On the sly, she even brought him hot rolls and a cup of chocolate, the breakfast of the gentry, so that he fared like a nobleman.

He had now some hours before him, perhaps most of the day, depending on whether or not Letta claimed him for the early afternoon work of the orchestra. Goldoni's first meeting with his actors in the amateur play was set for five. Richard could accordingly either loiter here or go on a ramble; and with his head still thick from the stuffy mansard, he wanted fresh air. It would perhaps be pleasant to saunter along the towpath of the nearby Brenta, stretch out for a while in the shade of a tree, and catch up on sleep. But, upon emerging through the wall of hedges around the service court, he found the suave serenity of the villa gardens more tempting than the dusty towpath. Fountains and terraces, glimpses of lawn, the delicious contours of trees and shrubbery with the suggestion of leafy walks between them, looked fresh and sweet. Servants or other hirelings were not expected to use the gardens; but, at this hour, they were completely vacant. Then, too, if Richard kept to the side paths, no one could possibly see him from the house. He had no great respect for rules in any case. So, turning right, he skirted the terraces, but paused a moment to look back at the villa before wandering farther.

Nothing could be more elegant and gracious. The tradition of centuries culminated here in architecture and landscaping. It represented wealth, culture and aristocracy. It resembled a perfect apple, flawless in shape and color, a little heavy for its branch. If the core of it was tainted, no sign of that appeared on the skin. Behind damask curtains that reduced the light to rosy-tinted dusk, in appropriately carved beds, their wigs on stands beside them and their costumes in lavendar-scented wardrobes, the slumbering gentry had not yet sufficiently revived from yesterday's pleasures to meet the pleasures of today. Magnificent. Enviable. Richard admired the view and the patrician world it symbolized. He admired it all the more after the servants' quarters to which he had just been subjected. The contrast added perfume to the flowers, grace and spaciousness to the architecture and gardens. He could not help a sigh, as he turned away down a path arched by yoke elms, which led farther from the house.

The white-sanded walk brought him to a little domed pavilion fragrant with verbena. He could lounge here for a while. But it was still too close to the house, and he wandered on past a miniature labyrinth of box hedges toward the remoter end of the garden. There, half enclosed by oleanders, he found a circle of lawn with a stone bench at one side in the shadow of a beech. A marble nymph, shapely and moss-tinted, presided on her pedestal against the hedge. A sundial centered the lawn. Richard, crossing over, stopped to read the Latin inscription: *Horas non numero nisi serenas.* It was a self-contained little cloister, silent except for the hum of bees and a faint stirring of air among the oleanders.

Seating himself on the bench, he let his thoughts wander. What role would be given him in Goldoni's comedy? How would he fit in among his glittering fellow actors? But then, forgetting qualms, he drifted into the future. Everything beckoned there. He was famous like Goldoni, distinguished like Tromba. He made his bow to princes . . . had liveried gondoliers in his service . . . traveled in his own coach . . . was the lion of Parisian salons . . .

A startled *oh* near at hand brought him out of the doze into which he had fallen; and, opening his eyes, he saw first a pair of black slippers, then a white dimity dress, then a droopy garden hat slanting across a vague face. It was not until he had lifted himself dazedly to his feet that he recognized Maritza Venier. A projection of the hedge, which concealed the bench from the path, explained her surprise. She was already on the point of turning back.

"Mille perdoni," she murmured. "I didn't see you. I —"

"Don't," he stammered, "don't go, siora. I'm going on myself . . . must have been asleep . . . stupid . . . excuse me . . ."

Evidently until then she had not realized who he was. Now she smiled and exclaimed: "Why, it's Sior Milòr. I didn't know . . . Bondì, sior. — And you were having *such* a good nap! And I wakened you!"

She looked so morning-fresh in her white dimity that he felt dazzled, and at the same time grubby in comparison. He would have liked to tell her that no awakening could be more delightful, but a compliment would sound impertinent. After a phrase or two, he explained how he happened to be there.

"It's the same with me," she nodded, and at once set him at ease. "It was so hot in our room, and the good Siora Aurelia took up most of the bed. She's Cousin Teresa Widiman's companion. We're on the third floor." Apparently, as a young girl and a poor relation, Maritza was expected to fit in anywhere. Hospitality, in her case, would be the twin of charity. "I don't see," she went on, "why people come to the Brenta for summer; it's cooler in Venice. But, of course, the gardens here are lovely."

A droop in her voice suggested that she was making the best of things. When he asked casually how long she intended to stay, her frankness surprised him.

"No longer than I can help. I'd leave today if I could."

"But why, madonna?"

Her lips balanced between a quiver and a smile. The smile won. "Because I'm homesick. It's a strange feeling. Do you think it's silly?"

He murmured, "Of course not."

"I think it is," she said. "Cousin Teresa was very kind to invite me. I've never been away from Venice before. She wanted to give me a great pleasure. So, I'll stay a few days to be polite. Of course, it isn't her fault. An unmarried girl has no place here. Everybody looks at me as if they wondered why I'm not at home or in a convent."

Richard wondered himself. He recalled last night's gossip about it in the orchestra, and that Lio had dared him to ask her. Now that he had the chance, it wasn't so easy. But she read the constraint in his face.

"You, too. Isn't that so?"

"Well . . ." he hedged.

"Not that I blame you or anybody," she went on. "But Father, who is a very wise man, never would send me to a convent. He calls it an education for sheep. He doesn't like conventions. The main thing, he says, is to be yourself. The trouble, I find, is that

30

most people don't agree with him. They want you to be like everybody else."

To Richard, this line of thought was new, startling, and yet oddly attractive. It explained at once the impression she had made on him last night and was making on him at that moment. Not like other people. He had never met anyone so honest and forthright. The idea of an unmarried girl, neither bold nor shy, talking in this way to a strange man! A man, too, of a much lower social class than hers! Unconventional? Capperi! It certainly was. And fundamentally this challenge to the conventions went deep enough to be appalling. It struck actually at the spirit of the times, the rule of fashion and manners, the whole fabric of society, which depended on conventions. Half shocked, half beguiled, Richard hardly knew what to say.

"When it comes to the furlana," he temporized, "I should think that everybody last night would have wanted to be like you, Zelenza. You were marvelous."

She said eagerly, "You're not just being polite?"

"Of course not."

"Because," she added, "I love dancing. I intend to be a ballerina, like Mother. She even danced at the Opéra in Paris."

Here was another wonder. Instead of keeping silent about the scandal that had rocked Venice, Maritza proclaimed it with obvious pride. Worse still, she planned to repeat it on a bigger scale. That a patrician Venier had married a ballet dancer was bad enough; but that his daughter in turn should become one doubled the offense. Probably she was only naïve, a young girl dreaming of the footlights. Richard wondered if she knew what the dancing career involved beyond skill. He was acquainted with a good many dancers himself, and with the men who patronized them.

"I know you're an actor," she continued. "I heard a little of what Dr. Goldoni said about you last night to Count Widiman. You must have seen a great deal of dancing in the theaters."

"Yes," he nodded, "all my life."

"Then I wish you'd tell me —" she flushed a little — "whether you think I could ever be as good, for example, as Maria Torelli. I saw her once at the San Giangrisostomo. She was splendid. But be honest with me."

31

"That isn't hard, madonna. You dance just as well now as she does." His tongue, slipping the leash, added, "And you're twice as beautiful."

He regretted saying that. She looked down. "Now I *know* you're only being polite — like all the others."

"Zelenza, please believe me."

"And you mustn't call me that. I'm not a *zelenza*. I'm just Maritza Venier."

She half turned and sat down on the bench. For an instant, he thought that he had offended her, and that she did not wish to continue the talk; but she suddenly reassured him with a vivid smile.

"No, Sior Milòr, leave titles and compliments to the Cavaliere Tromba or other such grand people. And I take it back. You weren't being polite. You were just being kind, as you were last night. I ought to tell you how much it meant to me when you brought me those flowers. I was all atwitter."

"You didn't show it, siora."

She moved sidewards on the bench. "Won't you sit down? I mean if you have the time. I've hardly talked to a soul since I left Venice."

The encounter was becoming more amazing every minute. Here was he, a part-time comedian of San Luca's theater, sitting unchaperoned and in private with a lovely girl of seventeen, the kinswoman of Countess Widiman and of half the noble families in Venice. It outraged all the proprieties. If anybody came upon them like this, they would be figuratively skinned alive, and his career at the Villa Bagnoli would be over. He sat gingerly on the bench, ready to spring up at the first footfall on the path. But Maritza seemed unconscious and unconcerned. Annoyed by the droop of her hat, she pushed it back on her head, so that she looked more unsophisticated than ever.

"Hardly anyone," she repeated.

"What about Sior Tromba? You were talking with him."

In view of the Cavaliere's potent effect upon women, it surprised Richard that the name brought no flicker of interest.

"Oh, about dance steps, gossip, clothes — what he thought would amuse me. I don't call that talking."

"But surely you found him pleasant?"

She shrugged. "Cuzì e cuzì."

Richard could not help defending the great man. "I thought he was the most accomplished, most fashionable person there."

"Yes, I suppose he was."

"At least, you must have liked his dancing."

She considered this a moment. "Of course he can dance, if that's what you mean. He's a regular maestro di ballo. But I didn't like his dancing."

"Why not?"

"If you were a woman, you'd know. I felt like a mouse dancing with a great, hungry black cat. He has a way of looking at you — Well, sior, there you are. I didn't like it."

For all his admiration of Tromba, Richard could see what she meant.

"Perbacco! The other ladies liked him."

"Let them," she nodded. "Perhaps I'm wrong."

"And then, there's Marin Sagredo." Richard tried to keep his voice bland. "You were talking with him."

"Oh, dear!" A wave of color crept up her bare throat and across her cheeks. "Meschina me!" Then she laughed. "I'm afraid I talked at him. I was very rude. I called him a baboon."

"*What?*" Richard's heart gave a bound. "You called him that?"

"Yes, it was dreadful. He was very nice after the dance. He actually remembered that the Sagredos and Veniers were related. He proposed taking a walk in the garden. And I was hot from dancing. So, we walked along, and he told me a nasty story. About a flea."

"*No!*" Richard burst out laughing. Evidently the flea had the first place in Sagredo's repertoire when he was alone with ladies.

"Yes, a flea. And you wouldn't laugh if you heard the story. I told him what I thought about it. Then he got still more saucy, and I called him a baboon and left him. Perhaps I called him some other things, too. It's not that I'm finical, sior; but — you know."

Richard recalled how the same anecdote had glanced off from the Countess des Landes's indifference. Gradually Maritza's character was taking form in his mind, a very definite and individual form. He could not think her a prude, or she would not be sitting with him at that moment. Apparently she had scruples that ran counter

33

to the fashionable view. One would expect any young girl to worship the charming Tromba or to be impressed by the magnificent Sagredo. Real scruples. Good God! And she talked of becoming a ballerina! However, the strange part of it was that Richard felt nothing pale or pious about her, any more than April is pale or pious. And there is nothing languid or worldly about April, either. She made just that impression on him.

"But you'll be thinking," she went on, "that I don't like people. Ask me how I feel about Dr. Goldoni. We walked up from the dance together. There's a *real* man."

It was the topic to set Richard off. It led to the theaters, to his own world, to his dreams. He forgot the oddness of being here alone with Maritza Venier; he forgot the Villa Bagnoli. His swarthy face lighted up, and he became his usual unconstrained self, a little too animated perhaps, a little headlong. Theater slang crept out; his language grew less Italian and more Venetian. But, as far as that went, Maritza kept pace with him. They were soon talking the beloved dialect with no Tuscan polish on it. The polite form of address in the third person got mixed up with the direct *vu*, then was dropped. Even *tu* slipped in, and they noticed it only to smile. "Caro ti!" she said more than once. A prude? Domenedio! There was nothing prudish about her.

She had the charm — more attractive in conversation than any other — of eager listening. But she talked, too. He could imagine the bare, faded old palazzo where she lived with her father (whom she called *Sior Pa're*) and a much-quoted middle-aged housekeeper named Anzoletta. Sior Pa're was a poet and had been long at work on a marvelous epic about Venice. It was just as great, Maritza declared, as Tasso's *Jerusalem,* although she didn't quite have the learning to understand it. He had also written some wonderful opera librettos in the style of Metastasio, only better, but had never got around to selling them. It appeared that Sior Pa're, though wise and lovable, did not have the golden touch. But what of that? It was great fun keeping the wolf from the door. A tiny income, the relics of the family fortune, did most of it; and, unknown to Sior Pa're, a conspiracy between Maritza and Anzoletta, whereby needlework was slipped out from the palace and disposed of at a shop on the Merceria, made up the difference. Maritza's outfit for the Brenta had cost a great effort.

34

"Do you like my dress?" she asked, spreading out the skirt a little.

"E come!" admired Richard. "La xe un fior!"

"Well, Anzoletta and I made every stitch. I think it's quite Parisian." She held out a forefinger. "See the needlepricks?" Her hands were small and shapely but looked capable. "As long as I have these" — she turned the palms back and forth — "and good legs, I'm not afraid of Messer Wolf. You wait, sior, you'll see me dancing at the opera yet."

This led back to her stage ambitions. She had been trained by her mother from the age of seven and had kept up the exercises since the Siora Venier's death two years ago. "Father used to play for me," she sighed. "But we had to sell the clavichord last winter, and now I can only hum tunes to myself." The great obstacle to her plans, of course, was Sior Pa're and Anzoletta. She hadn't quite converted them to the idea of herself as a ballerina. But, more important still, she couldn't leave them — not yet. "How could I?" she demanded, "if I'm homesick now, after two days? Still, I believe this," she added, "I believe that if a person wants anything badly enough and hopes and works for it, it will come. Only you've got to want it with your whole heart."

"You think that?" he put in.

"Yes. What you really live for will come. Take you, sior. Don't you want more than anything else to write plays sometime like Dr. Goldoni? Then that —" she broke off. "Don't you?"

"I'm not sure," he hesitated. "I thought so once, but there are other things."

"For example, what?"

"Well, for example, to live and not just write about living. To act a great role in the world. To have power and wealth and a hand in big affairs." He was being a little grandiloquent, unconsciously a little stagy. He hoped to impress her. "You'll say it's impossible; but other poor men have become great men of the world."

She shook her head. "No, it's not impossible, if that's what you really want. Only, you have to make up your mind." She did not look impressed.

"But you see what I mean?"

"I'm not sure I do. Would you call the Cavaliere Tromba a great man of the world?"

"Yes, I would."

"And you want to be like him?"

Richard remembered her feeling about Tromba. "Well, in some ways — his manners, his savoir-faire."

The sparkle in her eyes faded. "I don't think that would be hard. You're an actor; so is he." She asked, a little too casually: "What do you think of *women* of the world — for instance, like the Countess des Landes?"

"I think she's attractive." He felt a rift between them, and challenged, "I suppose you don't."

"Caro vu! But of course I think she's attractive." Surprisingly enough, there could be no doubt of Maritza's sincerity. "She's the most attractive woman I've ever seen. Only — it's strange — she makes me a little sad."

"Good Lord! Why?"

"I don't know."

Getting up, Maritza walked over to the sundial. He followed her.

"Heavens, sior! Look what time it is. Eleven o'clock! And I ought to be paying my respects to Cousin Teresa." But she paused to gaze at the inscription on the dial. "That's Latin, isn't it? Do you know what it means?"

He translated: *"I only count the cloudless hours."*

"I'll always count this hour," she said. "I hope we'll have another talk. A rivederci . . ."

He stood thoughtful awhile after she was gone, the tones of her voice still echoing in his mind. He realized suddenly that it would be hard to wait until he saw her again. Yes, he, too, would always remember the past hour. And yet it had not been cloudless. Something between them — he hardly knew what — had left him ill at ease with himself and, therefore, with her. A very small cloud, but it was there.

V

TO Dr. Goldoni's relief, five of the six actors involved in *Il Cavaliere di Spirito* (*The Gentleman of Good Sense*) turned up reasonably on time at the preliminary meeting that afternoon. The great difficulty with amateur theatricals at a country house, like the Villa Bagnoli, consisted, of course, in luring the actors away from other amusements. Marin Sagredo had not yet appeared; but he was rumored to be somewhere about and, with the Countess des Landes as a magnet, he could eventually be expected. The purpose of the meeting was to discuss the play, distribute the parts, which had been copied out at Zola, arrange for rehearsals and fix an early date for the performance. Luckily the comedy had been written for just such occasion and setting. It was shorter than usual and required no machinery or costumes. With so small a cast, something could be accomplished in three or four days, if the actors could be brought to exert themselves.

"I'm depending most on you, Contessa," Goldini bowed to Madame des Landes. "You're not only our one actress, the lovely center of our play —" the voice of the good Doctor, who had a weakness for feminine charms, sounded mellow — "you're the siren who will persuade the Very Noble Marin Sagredo to favor us with his talents." Goldoni looked at his watch. "I wonder if he has forgotten us."

The place of meeting was the stage in the ballroom, which served equally as private theater for the villa. It possessed a curtain, now closed, and adequate scenery, stacked at present in the wings. For the sake of light and air, the backdrop had been raised; and graceful, arched windows looked out upon the garden.

Amélie des Landes, ravishing in an afternoon gown of striped blue and silver with a dark bodice and tiny fichu cap, tossed her head. She was not a woman to be kept waiting.

"A fig for him!" she said tartly. Her blue eyes lingered on Tromba, propped against one of the windows and absorbed in reading his part; but she also smiled at the two other gentlemen who completed the cast. "Why don't we ask our dear Signor Brunetti or the gallant Captain Beccaria to take Marin's role? They'd each of them do it a thousand times better. Che bestia è quello! Leave Marin to his cards and his horses. They're the sirens for him, Maestro."

Goldoni smiled unhappily. "There might be complications. We don't want to offend his Excellence. Fio mio —" he turned to Richard, who was standing by himself in the background — "see if you can't find the Illustrissimo. Tell him that we are at his service."

But the unpleasant errand was unnecessary; for, at that moment, the garden door burst open, and Sagredo appeared. He was booted, spurred, gloved and otherwise dressed for riding. It was close to the hour of the afternoon *trottata*.

With no word of apology, he addressed the Countess. "Cara madama mia, they tell me you are driving to the Villa Pisani. You will allow me, I hope, to escort you."

She shook a finger at him. "Naughty! Why have you kept us waiting?"

"Oh, did I?" Sagredo did not seem concerned. "Well, what's time in the country? What about the Villa Pisani?"

She glanced again at Tromba, who had not looked up from his reading. "It's very serious to keep me waiting, caro Marin. If you had been on time, now! But, alas, you were not, and I have just invited the Cavaliere here to escort me."

There had been no such invitation, but Tromba was not the man to show surprise. He turned from the window.

"To my infinite honor, Contessa."

Sagredo flushed. "I believe I have prior claims, sir."

"As to that, sir," Tromba smiled, "it seems to me that Madame des Landes should decide."

The young woman's eyes danced between them. "Yes, dear Marin, if you *will* be late, you must accept the consequences. But I understand you're my lover in the play. The Cavaliere's your rival. Perhaps you can make good your claims then. Isn't that a compensation?"

"Depends how the play turns out," sulked the other.

"Well, Marin, we have been waiting for you so that Dr. Goldoni could tell us."

Sagredo muttered something about the bore of learning parts. Tromba put in smoothly: "I'll be delighted to take over your role, if the Countess will accept me as her lover. One of these other gentlemen can have mine." His voice caressed the lady, who spread out her fan and lifted an eyebrow.

"Oho!" frowned Sagredo. "So that's the game, is it? I thank you. But, as it happens, I wish to keep the role myself."

Tromba looked chagrined. "Well, then, shall we get on with the play?" He shot a humorous twinkle at Goldoni. "But remember, Eccelenza, if I'm not the lover, I remain the rival. So take care."

Goldoni did not miss the cue. "If everyone will be seated. Draw your chairs into a circle. It will not take long," he added, rubbing his hands. "A mere outline."

Richard remained standing.

"Sit down, Signor Morandi," Tromba invited. "Here's a chair next to mine."

"Yes, of course," said Goldoni, with a trace of flutter. "My dear boy, of course. After all, you're our chief actor. Do be seated."

He glanced an apology at the others, who, with the exception of Sagredo, murmured affably. It was more than irregular that an orchestra hand should sit in the presence of noblemen — almost as if one accorded that honor to a servant.

On the point of declining, Richard encountered Sagredo's cold stare and at once accepted.

"Thank you."

"By God!" Sagredo rumbled. The Countess laid a hand on his knee. No one else seemed to hear him.

Goldoni hurried to bridge the pause. "And now, with your Signories' permission, I'll describe the plot in a few words.

"Donna Florida, whose part will be acted by our lovely Countess, is a young and charming widow betrothed, before the play opens, to the handsome, dashing Don Flavio." Goldoni bowed to Sagredo, who gave an *ahem!* "At the moment, however, Don Flavio, a soldier by profession, is absent in the wars, and his future wife awaits his return at her country house — shall we say, on the Brenta?"

"Not alone, I hope," put in the Countess. "That would be very dull."

"I quite agree," said Goldoni. "No, madama, not alone. For Don Claudio, a former suitor, whom our superb Cavaliere will impersonate, does not despair of supplanting Don Flavio before the latter's return."

"You see, Illustrissimo!" waved Tromba.

"What happens then?" Sagredo demanded.

"Alas, Zelenza," returned Goldoni, "the lady of our play has not the constancy and character of the adorable actress who takes the role. She is inclined to flirt; she is inclined to look about her."

39

"Shocking!" said the Countess. "I wonder if I can act such a part."

"She is much attracted," the playwright went on, "by a gentleman summering in the neighborhood, a certain Count Roberto, who calls on her as a matter of civility and invites her to view his gardens. He is a man of excellent manners and conduct, who, though not indifferent to the charms of Donna Florida, is honorably aware of her betrothal to Don Flavio and refrains from paying her any other addresses than good breeding demands."

"Something of a stick," remarked the Countess.

"Madonna, perhaps. But he is the gentleman of good sense who inspires the title of the play. It is a role that demands experienced acting to avoid flatness. I have therefore selected Sior Morandi for that part."

Marin Sagredo burst out laughing. "Cospetto! So the fiddler's promoted to count, is he? Good God! Suppose, during the play, I forgot his title and gave him a kick in the breech!"

Richard sat quivering. The rush of blood to his head turned him dizzy. Again, as last night, he was helpless. Sagredo had intended no insult, only humor. One can't speak of insulting a dog by kicking it. Such a remark, from such a grandee, would be swallowed with a grin by most of the poor comedians in Venice. It was meant to be swallowed that way now. Sagredo could not be blamed for Richard's sensitiveness.

In the circumstances, however, he could be blamed for indelicacy, and no one smiled. The Countess, indeed, made a little grimace and studied the polish on her fingernails. Tromba took snuff. Fortunately Richard could see at once that his best retort was silence.

Aware of the chill, Sagredo glanced in surprise from one to the other. His grin faded. He coughed; then, tilting up his chin and patronizing as ever, asked Goldoni, "Well, Sior Carlo, what next?"

The Doctor's hands shook a little, but life had taught him meekness. He cleared his throat. "Ah, yes, as I was saying, Count Roberto treats Donna Florida with civility but does not respond to her flattering sentiments for him. He is unable, however, to escape the jealousy of Don Claudio —" Goldoni smiled at Tromba — "who, aware of the lady's preference, is skeptical of the Count's honorable restraint. And at this point the valiant soldier, Donna Florida's betrothed, returns unexpectedly from the wars. It is unfortunate

40

that the first person he encounters is the jealous and unscrupulous Claudio. — I regret, Cavaliere," the playwright added, "that you should be the villain of the piece. But it is a role susceptible of excellent and even sympathetic acting."

Tromba nodded. "I've glanced through it, Signor Dottore. Excuses are unnecessary. Have you ever remarked that in life, as on the stage, the villain is apt to be more interesting than the hero —" his eyes rested on Sagredo, then shifted to the Countess — "especially to the ladies? Pray continue. I take it that the soldierly Don Flavio is richer in courage than in brains, quicker to fight than to think, and is, therefore, a victim of my wiles — I mean Don Claudio's."

"Sior, yes," said Goldoni. "The Very Noble Flavio believes that valor is everything and that the sword removes any obstacle. He is jealous, choleric and headlong —"

"Wait a moment," interrupted Sagredo.

"— but he is a man," Goldoni persisted, "of the highest distinction, of the most manly qualities, devoted to the Lady Florida and beloved by her, in spite of Count Roberto's temporary attraction. He is the romantic hero of the play."

"Ah," Sagredo approved. "Well?"

"Your Excellence shall hear."

Goldoni rapidly sketched the plot. Claudio-Tromba, intent on winning the lady by any means, accuses her of inconstancy and, in the guise of a friend, prevails on Flavio-Sagredo, of whose return she is still ignorant, to subject her to a test. Flavio will write her a letter announcing his early arrival but describing an ugly disfigurement which he is supposed to have received in battle. Naturally, however, he cannot imagine that such a disfigurement would affect her love for him, and he remains hers devotedly. He would see, Claudio warned, that her loyalty was not proof against such news and Count Roberto's blandishments. The letter is written and presented to Donna Florida.

"What, Contessina," asked Goldoni playfully, "would have been your response? Remember you are betrothed to him."

Amélie's eyes widened. "Affè di Dio, the question surprises me. What on earth could I do with such an ugly man? It would distress me even to look at him. I should send him packing at once."

"Good!" Tromba laughed.

"Traitress!" scowled Sagredo.

"There you are," Goldoni chuckled. "You see how perfectly I've chosen my cast. For Donna Florida takes the same view of it as the Countess des Landes; Claudio is delighted, and Flavio enraged. You can now very well imagine how the play proceeds. Don Flavio discloses himself undisfigured to the lady and denounces her perfidy. He seeks a duel with Count Roberto, who, however, persuades him of his innocence. He actually fights with Claudio, whose treachery he discovers, and but for an accident would have killed him. He again becomes jealous of Roberto. Donna Florida, meanwhile, accuses him of ungentlemanly and unloverlike conduct in writing her the false letter and offers her hand to Roberto. Everyone is at loggerheads. The kettle boils. It is Count Roberto whose tact and good sense provide the solution."

"What solution?" Sagredo grunted. "She marries the fiddler Count, eh? In that case, by God —"

"Not at all, Lustrissimo. Your Excellence and the lady are reconciled, are married. Your future happiness is assured."

"Aha!" relented Sagredo. "Well, that's different. That's as it should be. A very good play, Sior Carlo. My congratulations."

"I thank Your Excellence." The irony in Goldoni's voice was too faint for the other's ears. "There remains, then, only to distribute the parts. Here they are . . . yours . . . and yours . . . and yours. Captain Beccaria, the role of Gandolfo, the lady's factor, can be very entertaining. Sior Brunetti, I regret that the part of Merlino, the servant, offers little scope for your talents. You are most obliging to favor us. Shall we say tomorrow, then, at this hour, for rehearsal?"

"And, mark you, Marin," said the Countess, "if you're to be my lover, you must learn your lines."

"Oh, I'll learn them well enough," Sagredo promised. "We'll have a prompter, of course?"

"I'll do the prompting," said Goldoni.

"Then everything's in order." Sagredo offered his arm to the Countess. "Will you not relent, madama? Will you not allow me to escort your chaise to the Villa Pisani? Remember, this Claudio here is a great rogue."

She shook her head. "But you can escort me as far as my room, caro. I must hurry now to change."

42

With the lady on his arm, Sagredo happened to pass Richard and stopped a moment to laugh.

"Count Roberto, your servant, sir. Don't look so glum. Madonna, how are you going to fall in love with a face like that? I can't understand Goldoni. But, yes, I do. It'll be a comedy in itself to watch the dog acting a nobleman. So, pluck up your spirits, Count. Learn to smile. And take a tip from me. On the night of the play, use perfume. Use plenty of it. Ha? That's a good fiddler."

He gave Richard a playful dig in the ribs with the knob of his riding whip and sauntered on, unconscious of the shadow of murder behind him.

With the exception of Goldoni and Tromba, the others followed.

The Doctor laid a hand on Richard's shoulder. "I'm sorry, boy. I shouldn't have got you into this. But it was well intended. You see, I'd never met him before. He's a most insufferable young beast. If you choose to withdraw, I couldn't blame you. I'll ask Captain Beccaria to take your role."

"No, Sior Dottore —" the smile which Sagredo had invited now appeared, but it had a hooked edge — "I'll not sneak off. We'll see what happens."

"You'll do nothing foolish, Milòr." Goldoni forced a laugh. "Remember, you're the Gentleman of Good Sense."

Richard nodded. He was too angry even to hint at what he had in mind, though his thoughts whispered that some people were worth hanging for.

In contrast with the hot silence, Tromba's voice, when he spoke, sounded cool. His reckless black eyes were probing Richard.

"That's right, young man. Nothing foolish. And you show good spirit in sticking by the play. But I know what you're thinking. There's just so much that human flesh and blood can stand, eh? The damned fellow will go one step too far, and then — Aha, vendetta! I know. There's nothing sweeter. Not even a woman. While it lasts. But listen."

Tromba, who had rolled the manuscript of his part into a cylinder, drew it back and forth between his hands. The diamonds of a blue-enameled marquise ring glittered.

"Revenge is a pleasure that ought to be spun out. Slip your knife into Sagredo? Well, you've had a moment's satisfaction. He's

43

buried with honor; you're broken on the wheel. What's the point? Call that vendetta? Not to my way of thinking. No. But stab his pride, watch him squirm, make a butt of him, enjoy yourself. And you can do just that in this play, if you use your head. Give me a share in it. Between us, we'll turn out something elegant, something in good style. Do you agree?"

"But, gentlemen," put in Goldoni, "I beg. Consider my credit if offense is given to a patrician. What of Count Widiman? And what of our play?"

Tromba laid a hand on his heart. "Maestro, I solemnly promise that your play will have every success, that your credit will not suffer, and that Count Widiman will be delighted. Only trust me. Well, Signor Morandi, shall we join forces in the art of vendetta?"

"I'm not sure," said Richard, "that I know what Your Signory means."

Tromba smiled. "Oh, we'll put our heads together. We'll improvise. I think we can serve up a very neat dish. And, by the way, you must let me supply 'Count Roberto' with the right costume. He needs something extra-fine. You and I are about the same height."

"But, Zelenza —" Richard flushed.

"Also," continued the other, "I beg you will share my room. That's important. If we're to collaborate in this, we must be together. We must exchange ideas. There might be some points I could suggest in regard to your role. You see, I've probably had more experience of people like Count Roberto than you have."

No more roasting at night in the mansard. But especially this opportunity of association with a great fashionable like Tromba. Richard could hardly believe his ears.

"Would Count Widiman consent?"

"I'll arrange it."

"But will your Excellence at least tell me to what I owe your protection, your favor . . . ?"

"Most certainly, my dear boy." Tromba turned to Goldoni. "I promised our good friend the Doctor here that I would be glad to render you any service I could during the play. I'm drawn to you personally. — No, it's the truth, caro Milòr, if I may call you so. — Besides, believe it or not, I'm superstitious. I have a feeling that

our stars may have drawn us together for our common benefit."
Tromba had a far-off look in his eyes, but it was doubtful that they
had in view any star more distant than the one in diamonds on Lord
Marny's coat. "Then, too," he added, "one of my hobbies is cutting
cocks' combs."

He thrust the roll of paper into his pocket.

"Well, I must be off to escort the Countess. " And with a laugh:
"Talk of improvising! I rather believe that she can be persuaded to
give a little spice to our dish."

V I

ON the night of the play, Richard stood wondering at the reflection of himself in the long mirror set up on Tromba's toilet table.
Or was it himself? He had passed through the hands of Count Widiman's friseur and of Tromba's valet. His hair, no longer bunched on
the nape of his neck, was curled, pomaded, and powdered in the
form of a wig. He wore a Parisian suit: rose and gold coat, beauti-
fully flowered waistcoat, dark breeches with glittering knee
buckles, lace at the throat and wrists, diamond studs in the waistcoat. He wore, too, the appropriate shoes, stockings, laced hat, and
court sword — even fobs and a blazing finger ring. Fashionable heels
added an inch to his height. He smelled of attar of roses. Only the
face seemed vaguely familiar; but it, too, had changed from
swarthy to white, with a patch on one cheek to bring out the
pallor. His eyebrows had been trimmed into black arches. What
with his big nose, mouth, and cheekbones, the result was striking.

And, already in his role, he felt an inner change to match the
clothes. He felt elevated, magnificent, and assured. Wait till
Maritza Venier saw him in this glory! They had arranged to meet
in the garden after the play. He had talked with her briefly a couple of times since their parting at the sundial, and she had seemed a
little reserved. But wait till tonight! . . .

Meanwhile, lorgnette in hand, Tromba was eying him from different angles.

"Good!" he approved finally. "You turn out as I expected. Inter-

45

esting, a face to remember, a touch of the devil. That's what takes an audience. Well, Milòr, I congratulate you and a little myself."

"A little! Good Lord!" said Richard. "If I carry this off tonight, your Signory knows that it'll be entirely owing to you."

Indeed, glancing back over the past four days, he could not express his thanks. Tromba's kindness was a perpetual amazement. The Cavaliere had not only shared his room and now his wardrobe with Richard; but he had treated him as a young disciple, discussing fine points of behavior and manners helpful to the role of Count Roberto, drilling him in nuances of carriage and gesture, enlightening his ignorance of the world with precepts drawn from a very crowded experience. If most of these were cynical and rather wicked, they were nevertheless piquant. They smacked of the cosmopolitan beau monde. They had the attraction of new and exotic ideas.

"My dear boy," Tromba said once, "if you will only concentrate on one thought, one thought alone, until you have mastered it, you'll be in a fair way of making the world your oyster. And that's the ruling purpose of every intelligent man."

"What thought, your Excellence?"

"Simply this. To consider anything or any person a humbug until they prove otherwise. And they seldom do. For instance — leaving aside such commonplace frauds as virtue, piety, and that sort of thing, which no one, in private at least, takes too seriously — you've spoken once or twice of a gulf between the classes that prevents you from rising in the world. What a humbug that is! Such a gulf exists only in the minds of sheep and of the shepherds bent on fleecing them. To a man of pluck, it doesn't exist at all. Classes? There are only two: the dupers and the duped. If you take a right view of humbug, you won't be among the latter."

However encouraging this was to Richard's ambitions, he could not accept the main thought.

"But, Sior Cavaliere, I know plenty of honest people."

"Ah, do you? Well, there's no harm in believing them honest, provided it doesn't cost you too much."

"Dr. Goldoni, for instance."

Tromba laughed. "Now, now! You can't tempt me into personalities. I was speaking as a philosopher — and in confidence — for

46

your benefit. Of course, a man of the world should rarely say what he thinks. I hope you appreciate the exception I'm making in your case."

Now, recalling such talks, Richard could not have helped valuing them; if not altogether Tromba's cynicism, at least his cordiality. To be treated as a younger equal and to be favored with the advice of so brilliant a man was a very special honor. It was like being introduced to an exclusive club which he had so far only dreamed of entering. And, after all, upsetting as they were, perhaps more of Tromba's maxims took root in his mind than he supposed. They gave one a sense of superiority to humdrum good people. They were like a fine, rather heady perfume.

But, of course, more impressive than Tromba's teaching was the man himself. He had nothing effeminate or feeble about him. His hard inner core lay close under the veneer. He did not have to swagger about his manhood or hint that he could be a dangerous enemy. The masculine qualities of physical strength and dare were somehow apparent even when he was at his most suave and courtly. A young man like Richard, boiling with life, could not help admiring them.

"I hope," he added, turning from the mirror, "that your Excellence knows how grateful I am."

Folding the lorgnette, Tromba replaced it in his waistcoat pocket. "You confuse me. I never do anything for nothing. As a man of pleasure, I always have pleasure in view. Varied in this case. Our feud with Sagredo, for one thing. By God, isn't it worth some trouble to bait that bull? I don't believe he'll forget tonight. But that's not all of it. There's a pleasure in training people along one's own line. Take a fencing master; he enjoys working with pupils of talent, pointing out this trick or that, polishing their style. Well, my line is action, affairs; in short, the world. And you have talent. Yes, you have considerable talent. No simpleton could act the role of Count Roberto as I believe you will. And if that role, then others more profitable and distinguished. I believe you're cut out for big things, if you learn how to play your cards." Tromba hesitated; but perhaps on the point of something more definite, he said merely: "Who knows, someday I might be asking you for a service in return."

47

"It would be a happy day for me, Zelenza."

"Would it, my friend? — Meanwhile, I'm thinking that your costume needs the ribbon of an order, as a last touch. I don't believe that Sagredo has been decorated. Let's see. What shade? Lavender perhaps."

Walking over to one of his traveling bags, Tromba drew out a small coffer, which he unlocked, then poured its contents on a table. Richard saw a heap of jeweled stars, crosses and other heraldic shapes in a tangle of ribbons.

"Capperi! Has your Excellence all those orders?"

"Obviously, since they're here. Nothing sets off a costume better. I vary 'em to suit my clothes. Then, too, they build up a man's prestige. Women can't resist them."

"But with such a treasure in gems, aren't you afraid of thieves?"

Tromba looked amused. "Lord, no. Thieves aren't so easily hoaxed as people of fashion. The jewels are only paste — like the ones you're wearing. Naturally, you'll keep this to yourself."

"Paste?" A little startled, Richard glanced at the great diamond of his ring, at his studs and buckles.

"Of course," smiled Tromba. "From the Murano glassworks. Do you think I'm Croesus? But don't worry. They're good paste — a lot better than some that's being worn here tonight. And what of it, as long as they glitter? That's the main point. Think it over, my boy; it applies to most things. — Ah, ecco, here's what we want."

He selected a broad lavender ribbon, which he slipped over Richard's head and under his collar to form a contrast with the flowered satin of the waistcoat. A large sunburst of amethysts with a diamond center completed the decoration on the left side of the coat.

"There you are. Effective, eh?"

Eyeing the mirror again, Richard noted how the addition gave depth and splendor to the costume, worthy of Count Roberto's rank.

"May I ask your Signory what order that is?"

Tromba wrinkled his forehead. "I have so many . . . sometimes I confuse them. I believe this one is the Royal Order of the Lilac. It was conferred on me by the Shah of Persia in Baghdad, if that's where he lives. Yes, Baghdad will do. But now" — he consulted his watch — "we'd better be showing up backstage. A little nervous?"

Richard nodded. "A little. Not too much."

"That's right. A little won't hurt. Puts a man on his mettle. But you needn't worry. Madame des Landes will do her part. If you don't pay off Sagredo with interest tonight, call me an idiot — which no one has ever called me yet."

By now, the score against Sagredo had tripled. Richard flamed at the thought of yesterday's rehearsal. The bullying and ridicule would have been past bearing except for Tromba's steadying eye and the Countess des Landes's smiling encouragement. His submission baited the trap into which Sagredo was being led. For the scheme which had been worked out between Richard and Tromba, in alliance with the Countess, was a comedy within a comedy, a practical joke which would not be sprung till the play was actually given and too late for the young patrician to avoid it. So, at the rehearsals, Richard, in his usual drab clothes, had acted Count Roberto's part with more skill than anyone but his fellow conspirators knew. To Goldoni's despair and Sagredo's scorn, he had given a perfect imitation of the clodhopper aping a nobleman. Rumor, fanned by Sagredo, spread through the villa that, if there was nothing else to laugh at in *The Gentleman of Good Sense,* the fiddler Count was bad enough to be funny.

"Good God, Richard!" stormed Goldoni after the last rehearsal. "The thing's a nightmare. I praised you to the skies; I gave you the best puff I could; but here you are as if you had never acted in your life. You seem bewitched. You shuffle your feet, mouth your words, scratch your head. Have you no spirit or pride? Oh, Lord! And Tromba, on whom I really depended shows no more feeling for his part than a post. Sagredo hasn't learned his lines. The Contessa acts well, but she's helpless by herself. I wish to heaven that Count Widiman had never asked for the play. I've about resolved to tell him —"

"No, Sior Dottore," Richard begged. "The Cavaliere and I have profited from your comments. I believe you'll see a different performance from the rehearsal. At least I promise not to shuffle or scratch."

49

Struck by something in Richard's face, Goldoni challenged, "Whose leg are you pulling?"

"Not yours, Sior Dottore, not yours. I'm sure you'll like the play. Don't be concerned."

"I only wish it were over," gloomed the other.

Having let themselves out through a side door of the villa, Tromba and Richard, with long cloaks over their costumes, walked around through the garden to the stage entrance of the theater. Tromba exchanged greetings with several groups of guests, who were strolling about after supper, waiting for the hour of the play. A murmur followed them. Richard overheard: "Who is that other gentleman?" — "Don't know," was the answer. "Never saw him." It promised well.

Tromba chuckled. "There are some famous gossips here tonight. If Sagredo comes a cropper, they'll spread the news. — Well, here we are." He paused with a hand on the latch of the stage door. "Evviva la vendetta!"

VII

THE long, rococo salon, with its frescoed ceiling depicting the glories of the House of Widiman and its frescoed walls bright with "The Rape of Helen" and "The Sacrifice of Iphigenia" in the manner of Tiepolo, contained that evening some hundred and fifty guests. Neighboring villas up and down the Brenta had furnished their quotas of people curious to see the latest Goldoni play. Besides, the Countess des Landes was well known and popular; Marin Sagredo topped the list of beaux; and everybody had met or heard of the accomplished Cavaliere from Naples, who had established himself so promptly in Brenta society.

Under the glitter of the chandeliers, the room, like a jeweled parterre, showed every blending of color. The babble of voices grew momently louder. In the warm summer evening, the air thickened with a steam of perfume kept in motion by the incessant fluttering of fans. People bowed, waved, chatted, with the overtone of vivacity which precedes the opening of a play, and

50

glanced at the still-drawn curtains of the stage. The élite of social Venice were there, all dilletantes of the theater, tolerant of amateur acting and ready to be amused, but quick to satirize. A difficult audience.

Carlo Goldoni, eying the assembly through a peephole in the curtain, felt more nervous than ever. He could expect no good from this evening. The orchestra in their balcony struck up a light air from one of Pergolesi's burlettas. Attendants began snuffing the candles to enhance the lighting of the stage. The surge of voices ebbed toward silence. With a heavy heart, Goldoni gave a signal for drawing the curtains and stepped down into the prompter's box. Though invisible, he seemed to himself in a pillory. The heavy draperies behind him swung apart.

They disclosed the typical salon of a country villa. The factor, Gandolfo, and Don Claudio-Tromba were discovered conversing. The play had begun.

But at the first lines spoken by Tromba, Goldoni felt agreeably startled. There was no trace of the lifeless singsong which had dismayed him at the rehearsal. The voice was warm, modulated, and distinct, the kind of voice, with a touch of humor in it, that captivates an audience. The Martellian couplets, which could be so flat on the lips of an untrained actor, were properly varied with the right cesuras to sound like prose that only occasionally sparkled into rhyme. Excellent! And the voice was the least of it. Tromba had all the arts of gesture and glance which make words dramatic. He had, too, the gift of establishing a sort of confidential relationship with the spectators, of enlisting their favor; in other words, a delightful stage presence. "Perbacco!" thought Goldoni. "If that man hasn't belonged to some good troupe, I've never seen an actor."

To be sure, as a villain, he was too winning. Insensibly the comedy drifted off at an unintended angle. But what of that? Tuned to the vibrations of an audience, Goldoni could tell that this one was fascinated. And, if so, nothing else mattered.

In the following scenes between Claudio-Tromba and the Countess des Landes as Florida, he became even more aware of this curious change. The villain declared his love to the heroine, who rejected him in favor of the absent soldier; but the declaration would

51

have melted a statue, and the rejection sounded like consent. The words were the same that Goldoni had written, but their implication was entirely different. The plot drifted further off line. The actors seemed to be recomposing the play. There had been nothing like this at the rehearsals.

Completely absorbed, Goldoni forgot to turn the pages of his script to keep up with the dialogue; and, when the scene ended, he realized with a start that he had not had to prompt once. He felt an amazed relief. So far, magnificent. Incomparably better than at Zola. Now, if Richard could only act his part as well as the others, the evening would be a success. But with the rehearsals in mind, Goldoni, though encouraged, hardly dared let himself hope. The one actor whom he had sponsored as a professional necessary to the chief role of the play seemed utterly outclassed by these amateurs. Hearing the Count's servant, Merlino, announce his master to Donna Florida, Goldoni braced himself. The first impression was apt to be decisive.

And Count Roberto appeared.

Until that moment, the Doctor had not seen Richard's splendid costume, which had been hidden under the long cloak. He knew only that some clothes had been borrowed from Tromba. Now his surprise echoed the admiring murmur of the audience. If Richard had hardly recognized himself, Goldoni at first did not recognize him at all and half imagined that someone else had taken the role. Moreover, the Count's bearing suited his dress. The sharp critics of the audience would be quick to note the least awkwardness and quick to smile at a goose in fine feathers. But they de-tected no flaws; on the contrary, they found the newly entered player convincing. It was not that he acted a nobleman well, but that, by a trick of art, the audience momentarily did not think of him as acting at all. He *was* a Count Roberto; the scene became real. It became also intriguing. His personality somehow intro-duced a note of mystery, suspense, and dramatic conflict.

At this point, more than ever, when he had adjusted himself in delighted relief to Richard's appearance, Goldoni grew aware of what was happening to his play. As he had written it, the part of Count Roberto portrayed a sensible, virtuous, well-balanced man in contrast to the coquettish Florida, the scheming Claudio, and the

52

hot-tempered soldier, Don Flavio. Only good acting could prevent it from becoming smug and a little dull. But now, though not a word of the text was changed, all the implications had been altered. Roberto threatened to become Count Robert the Devil. His honorable sentiments conveyed an undertone of passion and menace, a hint, too, of conflict within himself. Like a splendid serpent, he held the fluttering little coquette in the coils of his personality. As compared with him, the official villain, Claudio-Tromba, seemed commonplace. And when the act ended with Donna Florida accompanying the Count to view his gardens, a thrill passed through the audience. Imagination escorted them. Many a belle dreamily fanned her hot cheeks; many a beau thoughtfully took snuff.

Then came the applause.

"Canchero!" muttered Goldoni. He felt in a dream. This was his play, and yet it was not his play. He did not know how it would turn out. He had become a curious spectator as much as anyone in the audience. It chagrined him a little, however, to realize how much better this dream version was than the plot he had intended, more exciting, profounder. A great success — there could be no doubt of that — and ironically enough he would receive the credit for it. But what was going to happen? Why had the actors run off with the play? Distractedly he turned over the pages of his unused prompter's script to the beginning of the second act, which followed without intermission.

Then, as Don Flavio-Sagredo entered, the web which had been so subtly spun for him by the others began to appear and with every following scene became more evident and deadlier. So that was it! Goldoni sat on pins and needles, watching each new turn. He was torn between admiration for the artistry used on the victim and dread of the consequences. It was the pillory by ridicule. But suppose Sagredo held Goldoni accountable!

If the comedy had been given as its author intended, the contrast between Sagredo's clumsy performance and the polished acting of the others would have been funny enough. From the rehearsals, Sagredo could not have foreseen that the loutish Richard and the singsong Tromba would be so transformed on the stage as to make him ridiculous. But at least he knew how the play was supposed to go. Now, bewilderingly, the whole plot seemed to have changed, though the lines were the same. His fellow actors said one thing and apparently meant another. He could only stumble on at a loss with what he had half learned, acting his part in ignorance of what the others were about. As a result, instead of the handsome, hot-tempered romantic hero, the audience evidently considered him a butt and, as the play went on, a buffoon. Whatever he did, people laughed. If he had been flexible, he might have made the most of this and accepted it in good part. But he showed his confusion so clearly as to make it obvious that he did not expect to be laughed at. And the laughter became personal. If he sulked, the audience tittered; if he glared, it roared. The idea that a joke of some sort was in progress began to dawn; and, as a crowd is usually on the side of the jokers, a good many of the spectators joined in. Then too, Sagredo's arrogance had made enemies, who could now anonymously pay off their grudge.

Of course the fact that the young grandee had taken no trouble to learn his lines added to the comedy. He was constantly signaling for help from the prompter, the signal being a twitch of the fingers of the left hand, which would have been imperceptible a few times but which was soon detected by the audience. Behind his back, the wits of Venice would tag him with that movement from then on.

In short, Sagredo found himself helpless. He was used to direct action but had no opening for it here. He could not browbeat the audience. He could not vent his rage on the other actors, who kept a perfectly straight face, spoke only their lines, and did not seem aware that he had any cause for rage. Baffled by Richard's transformation in costume and manner, he could not bully him as he had at the rehearsals. His one or two attempts of the sort fell so flat before Count Roberto's urbanity and brought such guffaws from the audience that he dared not repeat them. He could not throw over his role and refuse to act without thereby admitting his failure and making himself still more ridiculous. He was pinned to his role by the public opinion of the social world, which he did not have the courage to defy.

But, as the play went on, as he floundered deeper — jilted by the Countess, cheated by Tromba, patronized by the fiddler Count —

his temperature rose to the boiling point. And when, in the fourth act, the plot called for sword thrusts between him and Tromba, he suddenly decided to turn the tables. Here was a scene where he did not need a prompter, did not need to act, and could be himself. According to the stage directions Claudio-Tromba and Flavio-Sagredo were to draw their swords and exchange a few passes. Then Sagredo, stepping back to avoid his opponent's lunge, would stumble against a chair and fall, leaving himself exposed to his enemy. But Donna Florida, entering in time, would grasp Claudio's arm and thus save the soldier's life. It was a spirited little scene which could be made exciting enough. It offered the fuming Sagredo a chance he ached for. Only he did not intend to stumble or fall. If Tromba got hurt in the bout, so much the worse for him. Sagredo could not help an accident.

It was fortunate for Tromba that the young patrician could not keep murder out of his eyes, and that the first engagement of steel felt too much like the real thing to be trifled with.

"Keep cool, your Excellence," Tromba hissed.

But Sagredo's only answer was a tightening of the lips as he beat, feinted and then thrust.

In his prompter's box, Goldoni sat frozen. The audience, fascinated, held their breaths. If this wasn't an actual fight, it had all the appearances of one.

Sagredo took pride in his swordsmanship, but he soon found that he had met his superior. Indeed, more than once Tromba's blade slipped past his guard but was not driven home.

"Keep it up, Illustrissimo," the Neapolitan whispered, as they closed at one point hilt to hilt, "keep it up. You're giving a fine exhibition. Do that little *enlacement* of yours again, only slower so the people can see it."

And Sagredo, defeated, had sense enough to force a smile. If he could not kill Tromba, he could at least save face by pretending that he had never had such an intention. But he was short of breath and drew back.

The other followed. "Not tired, I hope? — Well, then, it's time your Excellence tripped over that chair."

Unpalatable as this was, Sagredo could see that it offered him the only dignified escape before his inferiority to Tromba became apparent. Renewing the fight with a great show of spirit, he circled around to the chair, stumbled, and fell. The episode was intended to be exciting, not comic; but he fell too hard, and the audience laughed.

"*I have you in my power,*" Claudio-Tromba recited.

Goldoni, not waiting for the signal, prompted: "*No gentleman will strike a fallen man,*" and Sagredo dutifully growled it out.

"*Perfido,*" shouted Tromba, "*hai da morire!*"

Donna Florida des Landes, sweeping in, divinely costumed, laid her hand on Tromba's arm. "*Ah, stay that sword.*"

And the yoke of the cursed play once more settled down on Sagredo's neck. He could only struggle forward raging to the end.

There remained, however, the final scene, which might partly compensate for his earlier trials. The intention of the play was to show a quick-tempered, honest soldier who in spite of his humors remains lovable, and who at last, by the tactful management of Count Roberto, gains the hand of the heroine, to the great satisfaction of the audience. Here, at least, Sagredo could expect a moment of dignity and popularity. But he failed to realize the extent of what had happened. The romantic hero could no longer be resurrected. Though not a word of the dialogue was changed, though Count Roberto placed Florida's hand in his, though every phrase promised happiness ever afterwards, the bubble burst in Sagredo's eyes.

What were those languishing glances between Roberto and Florida during the entire scene? With what a diabolical smile the Count delivered his closing sermon! To whom did Florida des Landes throw a kiss as the curtain fell? If the two other actors had placed a pair of horns on Sagredo's head, the implication could not have been clearer. Fool, oaf, cuckold-to-be!

Conventionally addressing the audience in his last couplet, Roberto-Morandi barbed the point:

> "*Will not true love, indeed, us lovers bless?*
> *My lords and ladies, deign to answer — Yes!*"

The curtains swung to; the ballroom shook with applause, rang with *bravos, bravissimos* and then with calls for Goldoni. One way or another, and whether distorted or not, the comedy was a triumph.

As for Sagredo, he stood speechless, staring at the Countess des Landes and Richard, his fists clenched, his big neck showing red against the white of his cravat. It would be a long time before the humiliation of that night could be lived down. The thousand gossips of Venice would keep it fresh. And as he stared, it was no accident that Tromba entered smiling from the wings to add to his fury.

"You, sir," choked Sagredo, "you and this whoreson —" His eyes shifted back to Richard.

With perfect timing the Countess put in: "Ah, Marin caro, you were superb. I had no idea you're such a genius."

"Madam —"

"Indeed, yes," said Goldoni, a little apprehensive. "Let me congratulate your Excellence."

"You piddling comedian —" He turned again on Richard. "As for you, fiddler, I have a long memory and a long arm. Think that over."

The applause in the ballroom, which had been deadened momentarily by the curtains, grew suddenly loud. Turning his head, Sagredo saw that the curtains had been drawn back again and that he stood raging in full view of the audience.

Advancing to the front of the stage, Goldoni bowed, then beckoned the actors to stand beside him. Each in turn received an ovation.

But Sagredo was no longer there.

Dropping back, the Countess des Landes seemed to be taking someone by the hand, someone invisible, whom she led forward. To this unseen actor, she made a deep curtsy, while Tromba and Richard bowed to him.

It convulsed the house.

VIII

FOR the first time in his life, popularity lifted Richard Morandi to the stars. It was too sudden and excessive not to be bewildering. He could not help feeling dazzled and a little drunk at the reception that greeted him when, drawn along by Goldoni and Tromba, he walked down with them from the stage to mingle with the audience.

There were compliments by the dozen — but not only compliments. Several gentlemen presented him with their snuffboxes in token of esteem, and one of these was filled with gold pieces. A very lofty lady, who belonged to the great house of Tron and who hated Sagredo, gave Richard her hand to kiss and a jeweled pin of some value. The eminent Francesco Vendramin, Jupiter of San Luca's theater, to whom Goldoni at once made a point of introducing him, spoke handsomely of his merit and promised the long-desired contract. Others, more vaguely, offered their services. Women caressed him with their eyes. He felt that every hope had been fulfilled at once. He was both a great actor and a man of fashion. It did not occur to him that this kind of thing was like the first uncorking of a champagne bottle, froth and bubbles which are soon over.

So, keeping up the role of Count Roberto, he shook hands, exchanged bows and compliments, expressed his thanks in different ways, and flattered himself that no courtier at Versailles could have done better.

Meanwhile, with one corner of his mind, he expected that Maritza Venier would be among those who congratulated him and was faintly disappointed that he did not see her. He could have spared twenty of the other ladies for one admiring look from her. But no doubt she was already waiting for him at the sundial, where they had arranged to meet after the play. The idea brought a glow. To meet her there, no longer in his scrubby clothes but in this costume, on the crest of this triumph, would be the real crown of the evening. It was like an old fairy tale, with himself as the prince.

The crowd in the ballroom had begun thinning. People drifted out for refreshments or for cards or to take the air in the garden. Servants were again lighting the chandeliers and lining up chairs on the sides for the dance which would begin later. In a moment now, he would be able to disappear.

But he reckoned without Count Widiman.

"My dear young friend," said the latter, when Richard made his final bows on the point of withdrawing, "you don't mean to leave us, I hope? We demand your company tonight. You will consider yourself as much my guest as anyone here. I know that it will add to the pleasure of all to have Count Roberto among us."

The group of men and women, comprising Goldoni and the other actors, murmured cordially.

"You see they will not be denied," continued Widiman. "Until now, Signor Morandi, you have been so beset with admirers that I have been unable to express my own appreciation of your acting and my thanks to Dr. Goldoni for selecting you. Please accept this very small evidence of my gratitude." And waving aside Richard's attempt to thank him for the plump purse he bestowed, "Pray do not speak of it. — Cavaliere," he added to Tromba, "will you keep this young gentleman under your wing a little longer? I think you should sponsor him to the company this evening."

"No, per Dio," put in the Countess des Landes, "*I* will. You forget I'm madly in love with him. We must make the most of time before my husband Don Flavio gets back from the sulks." And to Richard, "Your arm, Signor Conte."

"What of my arm?" Tromba protested. "Am I to be left out? Are we going to start the play all over again?"

"No," she smiled, "just continue it."

A ripple of jokes followed.

Richard gave the Countess his arm. It took more savior-faire than his to extricate himself. But, instead of pride at the honor, he felt trapped as he walked with Amélie des Landes and the others down the length of the room and so out among the groups of guests beyond. What of Maritza? And yet surely she must understand that he had been detained; she would wait for him a little while. He would be able to break away in a few minutes.

But it did not prove easy. There were more people to greet. The Countess desired an ice, a glass of champagne, insisted on his drinking with her. And as they drank, her eyes suddenly held his. It was an odd, veiled look, half shy, half bold, piquant as the wine itself. Inevitably, his pulse quickened. She had marvelous expressive eyes, dark blue but in the light of the candles almost black. He had caught that look in them during the play and had considered it part of her role. Now he would have been a blockhead if he had failed to see the personal invitation.

"Ah-h!" she said, lowering her glass. "You can pour me another. I feel in the mood tonight. I intend to be tipsy. No, no, not drunk — there's no fun in that. Superbly tipsy. You know. Drift, feel, burn. Let's be tipsy together. Fill up your glass, mio ben."

And once more the challenge of her eyes compelled an answer in his.

It was typical of her, as it is of some women, that every physical attribute became sensually provocative. Her shapely fingers around the glass, the curve of her forearm where the lace fell back, the tiny patch on her chin, the insolence of her breasts half revealed, half hidden by the low décolletage, each stirred a man's blood. In another woman, the same details might have been disregarded. The Countess's personality gave an electric charge to everything about her. Even the faint huskiness of her voice, its slight drawl, was exciting.

She remarked: "Ah, *mio* signore, do you know that you're handsome? Yes, quite handsome. — Please! Some more champagne — and for you, too. But I must have a macaroon first. Look, we'll share this one." She bit the macaroon in two. "Open your mouth. There!" Her finger drew along his lips. "What a pity you don't speak French!"

He answered by dropping easily into that language. It was the one he used constantly with his mother.

"Tiens! Then you do speak it?"

"Mais oui, madame."

She broke into rapid French and at once changed slightly, becoming, if anything, more vivid. "Now we can talk. We can extend ourselves. Italian's musical — yes, but sentimental. I hate sentiment. I like clarity even when it's naughty. Where did you learn French?"

He explained, but she only half listened.

"Well, my mother was French too, and my father Irish. And what the devil am I? And what are you? And what does it matter?" She raised her glass. "Shall we drink to the Island of Cythera and a pleasant voyage there?"

A laughing voice put in: "Yes, but not without me, by your leave. There's a toast and a voyage I won't be left out of — not with you on the quarterdeck, madame." Tromba's hawk face loomed over the little table where they were seated near the buffet. He drew up a chair, poured himself some wine. Although smiling, he seemed to Richard a little put out. "Or is three a crowd on that trip?" he added.

"Not at all," said the Countess. "I'm sure you're an excellent sailor, Monsieur le Chevalier."

She clinked glasses with both men and gave both the same glance. But at once Richard felt himself eclipsed. He felt, too, an odd relief in spite of the lady's charms. His brief experience as a man of the world was not up to navigating such waters. And some moments later, when Tromba proposed a game of faro before the dancing started, he again tried to excuse himself.

The tall porcelain clock in one corner of the dining room showed that at least three quarters of an hour had passed since the close of the play. He hardly dared hope that Maritza would have waited so long for him. But at least, if he hurried now to the appointed place, he would have done his best.

"And so, with your permission, madame —"

"My permission, nothing! I need you to bring me luck. This is your lucky night, Monsieur le Comte. I require your attendance, unless — Ah, I see." She drew an obvious conclusion and laughed. "Le petit coin, eh? Well, in that case, I release you to the claims of Nature. But return at once. I'll not make a bet till you do. À tantôt!"

Following the side path of the garden, Richard avoided strolling couples here and there and finally reached the distant circle of lawn around the sundial. But he found it empty, as he expected. There was only the marble nymph pallid in the moonlight, only the rustle of leaves among the oleanders.

Short of breath and his head swimming a little from the champagne, he stood awhile glad of the cool air and the quiet. Gradually the voice of Amélie des Landes, the thoughts of her, faded in his mind.

The gold in his pockets, the success he had had, the promised contract at San Luca's, seemed less important now. If only he had been able to keep the appointment with Maritza, what might it have led to in the future! And yet the time with Amélie des Landes had passed very quickly, had seemed very pleasant. After all, he could have met Maritza if he had really cared enough.

He walked back to the house, took up his role again, and rejoined the Countess and Tromba at one of the faro tables. To the profit of Madame des Landes, who copied his bets, the flood tide of the evening still held. His coins on the layout almost invariably won — even against Tromba, when the latter acted as bank.

"You see!" the Countess exulted. "You're better than a gold mine. All I need is to hang on your luck. Didn't I tell you how it would be! One more bet, and then shall we dance? Harken! The violins! I'm sure they'll give us a minuet."

But even though Richard now felt tipsy to the point where nothing mattered, the evening had lost its earlier sparkle. It was like a room where some of the candles have burned out. He found himself tripping through a minuet with Madame des Landes. Then other partners claimed her. He danced a quadrille with two gentil-donne and a young blood of the Renier family, who would not have looked at him earlier in the day. During an intermission, he climbed to the musicians' gallery, chatted with his old friends of the orchestra, told them the good news of the San Luca appointment, and drank too much of their red wine.

Consciousness began breaking into fragments, some vague, some vivid. He was dancing again with Amélie des Landes. Her rank and the fact that she was perhaps twenty-three to his nineteen had become indifferent. Suppose they were to slip out into the garden. The thought of being alone with her . . .

Marcello Tromba strolled in from the gaming tables. He stood looking at them, waiting till the end of the dance. It would be hard to get away from him.

Then, happening to glance across the room, Richard saw Maritza Venier.

She was seated in one of the small gilt chairs next to an older woman, probably Countess Widiman's companion. How long she had been there, Richard could not tell. In his present foggy state of mind, she simply emerged.

Amélie turned her head to follow his gaze. "Ah, la petite Venier. Pity no one asks her to dance. She's good at that. Do you know her?"

"A little."

The Countess's eyes deepened a moment, then looked away. "I'd like to be that age again . . ." she smiled.

At the first pause, when Tromba had replaced him, Richard crossed the room and made his bow to Maritza and her companion. In spite of his drinking, he felt more than a little unsure.

"Siora Aurelia Benito — Sior Morandi," she said formally, presenting him.

The role of Count Roberto, which had availed him so much all evening, began to show cracks at this point. He found it hard to keep up the fashionable pose with her.

"I was hoping —" he began. "May I have the honor of a dance, madonna?"

She shook her head. "Thank you, no. I'm not dancing. — By the way, let me congratulate you on the comedy. You were excellent."

Her eyes were direct and clear as ever. It would have been hard to define the difference in her manner, but there was a world of difference. For some reason, he felt stripped of his borrowed clothes and paste jewels.

At another time, he would not have referred to their thwarted meeting in the presence of Signora Aurelia, who probably knew nothing about it; but at the moment he didn't care.

"I expected to see you after the play, siora. I was detained for a time. Then I looked for you —"

"Indeed? Well, sior, I waited. When you didn't come, of course I knew that you were — detained."

"A thousand excuses! I can't tell you —"

"La bela cossa!" she interrupted, stressing the Venetian accent. If she had frozen him, if she had looked hurt, it would not have been so bad; but she only seemed indifferent and a little amused. "There's no cause for excuses. I didn't mind waiting at all. Since then, I've had a pleasant evening admiring you as a man of fashion."

"I don't believe I understand." But he understood perfectly.

"No?" she said. "Well, it's not important." And as the music struck up again, she added: "Don't let us detain you. Good night. And, again, congratulations!"

If a door had been closed in his face, the dismissal could not have been more definite. The two ladies nodded to his bow. He could only drift away. He tried to do this with dignity, but staggered a little as he walked.

DRUNKENNESS uses any fuel to promote itself. High and low spirits alike demand another glass and another. But gloom has the one advantage over elation that it tempts a man to drink alone and spares him the ridicule of making an ass of himself in public. It was fortunate, then, that Richard's drunkenness took a dismal turn at this point and got him out of the ballroom. Whatever the customs of northern Europe, intoxication had no place in Italian society and was considered unpardonable. The truth is that Richard himself had so little experience of it, especially in the wake of champagne, that he hardly knew what was happening to him. Dizzy and morose, he wandered away from the dance, finally reached the buffet, and drank a couple of more glasses.

Maritza's recent words gave the pattern to his thought. *Acting the man of fashion,* he brooded. Given the special favor of prancing here for a night in Tromba's Parisian suit. Clown of the villa. People winking at each other behind his back. Shabby comedian! Capering after Madame des Landes! Getting hot about her! Poor cub! How Maritza Venier had seen through him! How different she was in point of reality from the others! And what was he? A sham. And now a sot.

He had reached the stage where every idea turns black. What the devil was the matter with him? Why should a simple young girl like Maritza burst his bubble and put him in this humor? Was it because he had actually fallen in love with her? In that case, the more fool he — and even so he had made a mess of it.

Several people, strolling up to the buffet, spoke to him civilly; but in his present mood every smile was a sneer and every word, a prick. He murmured an answer and tried to look as if something of consequence called him away, then forced his unsteady legs to walk an imaginary straight line out into the hall. Thank God, here to the left was an empty card room. Entering it, he slumped down on a chair at the end of a long faro table, with the layout of spades painted on the green cloth.

He was now almost completely drunk. The paneled walls of the room, with gilded cupids romping along the cornice, tipped up and down, merging with the frescoed ceiling that showed Venus asleep and a prying satyr. The long mirrors blurred and swam.

What happened then did not have to make sense or stand in any apparent connection with anything else. Indeed, it hardly surprised Richard to be facing an old gentleman seated at the other end of the table whom he had been too foggy to notice when he came in. The old gentleman had a bottle of cognac at his elbow and was dealing himself a hand at cards. His face looked waxen; his bushy eyebrows gave him the appearance of an owl. Stopping absently to taste his liquor, he became aware of Richard, then gave a start; his slate-gray eyes widened; he sat staring and lowered the glass to the table. It was as if he found himself in company with an apparition.

Somewhat nettled, Richard stared back. At the same moment, he realized vaguely that this was Count Hercule des Landes, who had been pointed out to him once.

"Grand Dieu!" breathed the latter finally. "Dammy, but I'm amazed! My dear friend! God curse me if I'm not glad to see you!" He tried to get up, but sat down hard and drew a hand across his forehead. "It seems a long time. Welcome, cher Milòr, welcome!"

In Richard's condition, this was too much to untangle. He was certainly not the Count's dear friend, and yet des Landes knew his nickname. He shook his head. The old gentleman was drunk — no doubt of it — drunk as an oyster. They were both drunk together.

He answered in French. "À votre service, monseigneur. How do you happen to call me Milòr?"

"Isn't that what you're usually called?"

"Yes."

"Why do you call me monseigneur?"

"Isn't that your title?"

Des Landes waved his hand. "Mon cher ami, do not let us become involved with words. It's always confusing. I perceive you are drunk. So am I. Our natural state when we're together. And what of it? Have a drink."

He shoved the bottle and a glass along the table. Richard filled up. They sat vacantly smiling at each other.

"I hope you've kept well?" said the Count.

"Very. And you?"

"Not bad, Milòr. A twinge of the gout, a touch of the gravel. No trouble from women à force de précautions. But, speaking of them —" des Landes's eyes lit up, he raised his glass — "à la chère petite Lulu, eh! Your wench and mine! The sweetest trull on earth!"

Though completely in the dark, Richard drank as proposed.

"Yes, indeed," the Count added, wiping his mouth, "that must always be the first toast between us." He smacked his lips. "We've fought over the hussy. We've diced for her. Now yours, now mine. A real bond between us. Quelles cuisses sympathiques! Quelles fesses adorables! Remember that night at the Opéra? Ho-ho!" Hiccups stopped him. "Passe la bouteille."

Richard complied. The cupids on the cornice were swinging in wider arcs. He focused his eyes on the Count, who was staring again.

"But, curse me, she's dead," des Landes whispered suddenly, "dead long ago. And — come to that — why, ventredieu, you're dead, too, aren't you? Seems to me —" He broke off. "What is this? Where am I? What place is this?"

"The Villa Bagnoli."

"Never heard of it. Aren't you dead?"

Richard had some trouble with his tongue. He got out: "If you'll only tell me who you think I am, I'll tell you whether I'm dead or not." It didn't seem quite right, but it was the best he could do.

Des Landes frowned. "My poor Charles, you're pretty fuddled. Dammy, when a man forgets his own name, he's in a bad way. Now, listen," he went on. "Make an effort. You're Charles Hammond, Baron Marny. Called the *Black Baron* because you're so cursed dark. Aha! Cela te rafraîchit la boussole? You don't have to gape over it."

Richard's scalp prickled. There was a tinge of nightmare in this. He knew little enough about the family of Hammond; but he knew that his grandfather had been Charles Baron Marny, nicknamed the Black Baron. Obviously Hercule des Landes had been a crony of this nobleman. Obviously, too, Richard bore a strong likeness to him. Or perhaps the latter was not only drunk but dreaming.

"Dead a long time," Richard muttered.

"À la bonheur!" said des Landes. "It's all I wanted to know. Makes no difference. A trifle anyway. Must confess it seems to agree with you." He kept pinching his forehead and shaking his head, as if trying to clear it, but finally gave up. "You're an odd fish, Milòr.

By God, I love your company. We've had fun together, eh? You old scoundrel! You old Seven Sins! I never knew a sweeter devil. Must come from being a Stuart. Am I right, Fitzroy?"

"*Stuart?*" Richard mumbled. "Thought you said *Hammond.*"

"Fi donc!" Des Landes sagged to one side of his chair but straightened himself. "Why d'you pretend with me? Everybody knows that Milady your mother, God rest her, side-stepped with His Majesty. A good thing, too, for the family fortunes. But if they didn't know it, ma foi, all that's necessary is to look at you and a portrait of King Charles. Pity he didn't live to see you. You might have been a duke. It's no disgrace to be a royal bastard. Quite the contrary."

Richard lifted his glass. "To all bastards!" he said thickly.

Des Landes drank and nodded. "I may be one myself. The late Count took a large view of things, just like the late Baron your legal father. And right they were. Why stew about nothing? If there's one man I despise, it's the jealous pedant. That can never be charged to me. I tell any wife of mine: 'Madame, you have my name; I have your dot. Good! We have no further claims on each other except a regard for appearances. Amuse yourself, and I shall do the same. If God blesses our union with offspring, I shall be duly grateful and pay you my compliments. Adieu then, ma vie, until we meet again.' That, Milòr, is the only polite and sensible philosophy."

Richard inquired: "Have you been married more than once?"

"God, yes. Strange you've forgotten." Des Landes began counting and pressed a thumb down on the table. "Annette de Roche-martin — 100,000 livres. Not bad, eh? Gave me two sons. The last killed her." Down came the index finger. "Gabrielle de la Popeli-nière — 200,000 livres. The best I've done with any of them. Roturière, but rich. Died of smallpox." He pressed the middle finger next to the others. "Marie des Charmettes — only 25,000 livres. Won her at cards from her father, the Marquis. Big mistake. She lived a long time. Had some daughters, who are now in a convent. I couldn't afford to marry 'em off. As it was, my sons ate me up, until they were both killed at Fontenoy."

The Count fell silent, tapping uncertainly with his ring finger. "Parbleu!" he hesitated. "It's odd how names slip. The present Countess . . . 50,000 livres. Good to look at. Une fausse maigre.

The King had Boucher paint her in the buff for his little apartments at the Trianon. And, confidentially —" Des Landes winked. "Well, enough said. What's the name? Aymée . . . Annabelle . . ."

"Amélie," Richard suggested.

"You're right, by God. Amélie de Clancarthy. Trust you to know the name of my wife when you forget your own. But be careful, mon vieux Charles. Take a tip from me. She's the Devil's first cousin. Quite as bad as I am. We're most congenial. Know her father?"

Richard shook his head.

"A mad Irish Jacobite. Stuck to your kinsman, the Stuart Pretender. But clever, too. Feathered his nest with one of the de Bussy heiresses. Only trouble is, that dot's about spent. Money goes fast."

Doubtless by an association of ideas, des Landes's eyes wandered to the sunburst of amethysts around the diamond on Richard's coat. "Fine decoration you've got there, Milòr. What order is it?"

Increasingly Richard found talk a burden. "Don't remember," he mumbled.

"Where'd you get it?"

"Shah of Persia."

"Damned joker! Real stones?"

Loyalty to Tromba exacted a quibble. "What do you think?"

Des Landes chuckled. "Paste. Remember that ring you paid me your losses with at Chantilly? Cré Dieu! What a swindle! Two carats of glass."

Even in his befuddlement, it occurred to Richard that his grandfather and the Count must have been two rogues of the same kind.

"But no matter," des Landes went on, "I'd have done the same in your place. Anyway, we settled it, like gentlemen, on the field of honor. A good fight, and let bygones be bygones." His eyes rested again on the decoration. "How much do you value it?"

"Thousand livres," Richard gave the first figure that came to him.

"Dear at a hundred," snapped the other. "However, I'll dice you for it at that figure."

"Don't care to play." It was too complicated to explain the

ownership of the decoration. Besides, by now the room was becoming a merry-go-round — cupids, frescoes, mirrors, and the Count himself. Richard planted his elbows on the table to keep from falling off.

"Of course you'll play," cackled des Landes. "Never saw you refuse a wager yet. Or put up a hundred livres, if you please. I don't care." From one of his side pockets, the Count produced a dice box, which he rattled invitingly, though in doing so he began to slump under the table, and it took an effort to straighten up. "Only, we've wasted enough time. Dammy, a man's got to play or he'll die of boredom."

Mechanically Richard found some of the coins he had won at faro and clapped them down. Might as well — whether he was the Black Baron or not. Part of the merry-go-round had become a seesaw, now rising, now falling.

"Ho!" said des Landes. "I see you're in funds. Tant mieux. You can cast first." He slithered the box along the table.

"Where's your money?" Richard asked.

"Money? Let's see . . ." The Count felt in his pockets and shrugged. "I seem to be unprovided at the moment. Purse upstairs. You can have my note."

Richard was not so drunk as that. "No, thanks."

The other glared. "Foutre! You deny me credit for a scurvy hundred livres? You question my honor? By God, in that case —"

"What then?" Richard's mood, having covered most of the scale, now turned hot. Meeting des Landes's stare, he gathered up his coins.

"You know what then. Sacredieu, monsieur, I think I have a thrust that will teach you manners! Or, if you want pistols —" But the Count's love of play outbalanced his wrath. He looked uneasily at the disappearing coins and contrived a smile. "Mon vieux Charles, why do we always have to quarrel? There's no profit in it. I tell you I'm unprovided. But remember Mademoiselle Lulu. Remember the last time we diced for her?" He brought up a reminiscence in detail. "So, what do you say to Amélie? You don't get a king's mistress every day for a hundred livres."

Fighting nausea, Richard shoved back from the table and tried vainly to stand up.

69

"What's matter, Milòr?"

"Sale maquereau!" Richard got out before his native Venetian took over, and he ran on in waterfront terms that did not need to be translated.

"Aha!" said the Count.

Somehow struggling up, he found his sword hilt, his face more masklike than ever. Then an odd change came over him. Like a marionette when the strings are no longer pulled, he sat down with a jolt and began to slide gently under the table. The lace at his throat bent up a moment above the edge. There was a last glimpse of his yellow face, and he disappeared.

Richard sat gazing at the vacant chair.

Then a broad-shouldered lackey who had evidently been biding his time in the corridor entered, moved the table, and, lifting his master up in a practised grip, conveyed him out of the room.

A clock somewhere struck the hour of three.

X

MUCH later that morning Richard awakened with a splitting headache and corresponding remorse. He vaguely remembered reaching his cot in Tromba's dressing room by the aid of the Cavaliere's valet, who had also doubtless undressed him. Now, managing to get up, he held his still curled and pomaded head in a basin, drank a quart of water, and lay down again, though not to sleep. Characteristically, when the hammering behind his forehead eased a little, repentance took the form of an idea for a comedy, in which he would be the harlequin and laughingstock. Even the title came to him — *The Sham Gallant* (*Il Finto Galante*). It would be bitter to write and funny to look at. He would not spare himself a single lash. Per Dio, he would flay himself. The characters were all there: Maritza, the Countess, Tromba, des Landes and himself, the dressed-up booby showing off. He had only to point it up a bit, and the thing was done. It would be his penance, his amends to himself. Man of fashion! Cacasangue! He never wanted to hear the term again.

After a while, with a certain satisfaction in his old clothes and

70

darned stockings, he got dressed, tried to tie his hair back in the usual way (it would take some time to wash the grease out of it), and looked over the proceeds of last night. But even the three silver-gilt snuffboxes, Madonna Tron's pin, and a hundred and nine sequins in cash, brightened him chiefly with the thought that he could now afford to get away from the Villa Bagnoli and back to Venice. It was an easy trudge to Fusina, an easy ferry from there across the lagoon to the Angelo Raffael landing on the Giudecca Canal. "Home!" he longed. "And may the Devil continue to enjoy the beau monde with my compliments!"

Some time later, at Tromba's prescription, two cups of black coffee and a glass of brandy enabled him to stand the sight of the Cavaliere, fresh as ever, breakfasting in bed on chocolate and rolls. But, even so, Richard turned his eyes away when Tromba, dunking a well-buttered crust in the thick fluid, plopped it into his mouth and began buttering another.

"My dear boy," said the Cavaliere, motioning him to a chair beside the bed, "your performance last night was beyond praise—up to a point. A small point since only I observed it. But a man of fashion —" Seeing Richard wince, he broke off to ask what was wrong.

"Nothing, Zelenza. A touch of headache."

"Exactly. As I was saying, a man of fashion must learn how to drink. You may not believe it, but I took no more than three glasses all evening and, so, could finish the night with a very fine woman to our mutual contentment. That leaves a man relaxed and in good appetite. Whereas, liquor —"

"The Countess — ?" Richard swallowed his question but not in time.

Tromba smiled. "You can hardly expect me to answer that, figliolo mio. A man of breeding never names his conquests until he's old enough to write memoirs, and then it doesn't matter. But I'll tell you this time with chagrin that it was *not* the adorable Amélie. *There's* a nymph who likes to drive men mad with her hide-and-seek. It seems to me that she actually had more of a penchant for you. But I don't intend to give up. Which reminds me of another matter."

Tromba poured himself a second cup and buttered a third roll.

"At the dance last night," he went on, "I could not help noting

71

that you addressed yourself to the little Venier girl. No accounting for tastes, my dear boy. If she's the kind you like, *avanti* and welcome. But I also noticed that she cut you pretty short; that you then left the ballroom, went on drinking, and did not return. I'm no mind reader, but one and one equals two."

"Let me explain —"

"Another time," said Tromba. "I simply want to make this point. You seem to be in love. When a man of fashion is rebuffed, he does not slink off. He retires, smiling — to renew the attack later, and if necessary, again and again. Believe me, at last the fort will be taken."

"I don't understand, Lustrissimo. I'm in no position to marry the Siora Maritza."

"Marry her? Lord save us! Who spoke of marrying? Who in his senses would marry a girl as poor as that? My dear boy, at times your simplicity disturbs me." Tromba shook his head but added: "However, don't be concerned. I guarantee you'll grow out of it. The long and short of what I wanted to say is this. As far as manners are concerned, the bearing, address — in brief, the externals — of a man of fashion, you've learned an amazing lot in a few days. I suppose your skill as an actor accounts for it. You give every promise of distinction. But what you and I must now work on is something more fundamental: the purpose underlying manners, the philosophy of success."

Twenty-four hours ago, Richard would have been charmed by Tromba's compliments and delighted by the prospect of his continued instruction. Now, with a bad head and a fuzzy mouth, he felt indifferent to both. The idea of distinction in the lofty circles that included the old Count des Landes was considerably wilted. The thought, too, of hanging on somehow at the Villa Bagnoli revolted him. But the Cavaliere had been generosity itself, and he did not wish to seem unappreciative. So, he suggested that, having been given the freedom of the Villa last night on a footing with Count Widiman's guests, he could hardly return to fiddling in the orchestra.

"Of course you couldn't," agreed Tromba. "I had no thought of it. I herewith appoint you, caro Milòr, as my confidential secretary. You will continue to share these rooms, and I shall supply you from my wardrobe. — For God's sake, throw away that filthy suit you have on; it no longer fits your condition. — You will thus have a respectable position here, and when I leave in a few days to visit Senator Grimani near Stra, you will accompany me. We'll return to Venice in October and lodge at the Grimani Palace."

"But my contract at San Luca's —"

"Think no more of it. You are now promoted from comedian to man of affairs. You see, dear boy, I have resolved to make you my associate. It's the first time I have ever taken such a step. Your performance last night decided me. I think we shall be very useful to each other."

"Your associate in what, Zelenza?"

Richard had often wondered about the *affairs* to which Tromba rather obscurely referred. What business carried him up and down Europe, sojourning now in one capital, now in another, flitting from spa to spa, the intimate of ministers, generals, and grands seigneurs, at home everywhere? Was he the agent of some prince? How did he manage to live on such a big scale?

Tromba answered: "My associate in pleasure, Milòr. Isn't that an attractive profession?" He emptied his last cup and pushed the breakfast tray to one side. "Let me explain. Pleasure is the mainspring of life and pleasure is my business. But the kind I like costs money. So, in various ways, money must be got. That offers excitement, and excitement also gives pleasure. As my associate, then, you would share both in the end and the means."

"What means?"

"Good Lord!" Tromba smiled. "They're so many that it would take too long to number them. Gaming's obvious. I don't cheat at cards, but I know how to play. The institution of lotteries is often profitable. Occultism's another line."

Richard asked: "What is occultism, your Signory?"

Tromba coughed. "How shall I define it? It has been my fortune to travel much in the East. I have learned many of those secret arts which give to the Magi their supernatural powers. I am familiar with the cabala. I can foresee the future, summon the dead, restore youth, command demons, enlarge jewels, and the like. I shall communicate this knowledge to you, but it takes study and practice."

73

Richard might still have some illusions, but he had not grown up in theatrical circles for nothing. Besides, he had heard the claims of too many carnival fakirs to be impressed.

"I see," he nodded.

"No, my dear boy, you don't see at all. You are thinking of vulgar charlatans you have known — Professor This-or-That on his platform at a fair. You have no idea of the difference when a Cavaliere Tromba reveals some of his science to the proper people at the proper time and place. The approach, the effect, and the rewards are all of a higher order. But I find that occultism is best employed in connection with some other project, such as I am engaged on at present."

Tromba broke off, rearranged his nightcap, which had shifted to one side of his shaved head, and gave Richard a sharp glance.

"It's a confidential matter. If the state Inquisitors —"

"You can depend on me, Zelenza. Surely you don't imagine that I would repay all your kindness by betraying you."

"No, I don't believe you would," said Tromba. "Besides, you have more to gain by holding your tongue. Well, then, have you ever heard of the Freemasons?"

Richard's eyes narrowed. Of course he had heard of that society, which was then spreading through Europe. Unlike the Anglo-Saxon parent organization, it had taken a turn on the Continent toward free thought and radical politics. Banned in Austria and Russia, it was looked at askance in Venice and other Catholic states and, because of the mystery surrounding it, was popularly considered a menace to church and society. But Richard had heard it favorably spoken of by Goldoni, who inclined to the liberal side, and he was, therefore, interested rather than shocked by Tromba's question.

"Zelenza, yes," he answered.

"Well, my boy, I am a Freemason. But I find that ancient and honorable order limited in various ways. It is my purpose to extend it by including Eastern occultism older than the Pharaohs, and I am at present founding lodges with that end in view. The mystical powers acquired by belonging to this new order are beyond price. As its founder, I am the benefactor of all the initiates, and their gratitude is valuable. Several of the patricians here are much interested. Perhaps you're beginning to understand what it means to become my associate."

Whether Tromba himself believed in the mystical powers of the new sect would have been impossible to tell from his expression. His face was grave, his voice convincing. But Richard, with his present headache, felt no attraction to occultism. However dished up, it looked like quackery. The contract at San Luca's, the thought of writing *The Sham Gallant*, seemed a good deal more solid and, at the moment, more desirable. Besides, he was shrewd enough to wonder at Tromba's offer. Remembering the latter's philosophy of humbug, he felt certain that altruism did not wholly account for it.

"A great honor, Lustrissimo," he said. "But why me?"

Reading his thought, the other chose to be frank. "A sensible question, Milòr," he nodded. "I might tell you how much I loved you, but I hope you would not be taken in by it. I'm making the proposal, of course, because I believe you would be of profit to me, not here in Venice — here you would simply be continuing your studies in the art of success under my direction — but in England."

"In England?" Richard exclaimed.

"Yes. A rich and promising country. I intend to visit it after leaving Venice, and, I hope, together with you. Dr. Goldoni has told me the story of your birth, that you are the son of Milòr the Count — they call it *earl* there, I believe — of Marny, who is one of the leading noblemen of that kingdom. You're his only son, so far as I know. It would be my object to establish you in his good graces. In that event, your fortune would be made, and I would obtain the introduction I need to the best circles there. I might even expect a more tangible reward. Until last night, I had my doubts of the game; now I'm convinced that you can win the stakes. A most glittering career. There's the plan in a nutshell. And I deserve your thanks."

But to Tromba's surprise, Richard shook his head. "My thanks, indeed, Zelenza, though I'm afraid it won't do."

"In God's name, why not?"

"Because Mother and I have never turned to Lord Marny for help, and I wouldn't do it against her wish."

"Look, man." Tromba launched into a description of the career open to Lord Marny's son. Illegitimacy didn't much matter. A purchased seat in Parliament covered that drawback. There was the foreign service, the army, the court, a rich marriage. There was wealth, distinction, fashion. "Instead of being a door mat for people like Marin Sagredo, you could hold up your head with any of them. Instead of scurrying for a living, you'd be independent. Do you mean to tell me that you'd give up all these advantages for the sake of farfetched sentiments?"

Richard could see no use arguing the point. "You can call any sentiments farfetched that aren't connected with money."

"And how about me?" Tromba continued. "Only last night, you were abounding in gratitude. If I asked you for a service, it would be the happiest day of your life. Well, fortunately, I know how much that kind of talk is worth."

"But, your Signory, this doesn't depend on me. It involves my mother."

"Persuade her, then. I suppose she's not an imbecile."

"I'll talk it over with her, Zelenza."

"When?"

"Tonight."

"So you're set on returning to Venice. What of the employment I offered you?"

"Give me leave to think it over."

"Ah," said Tromba. And at that point suddenly his frown cleared; he even smiled. Whatever his shortcomings, he knew human nature. Let the young fool go back to Venice, spend the windfall he had picked up here, feel the pinch again. He would not forget the glowing alternative that Tromba had outlined for him. Every jog-trot day would remind him of it. But he would soon forget his present headache and calf-love affair, if that was the trouble. Then, too, there was something else that would incline him to England, something which the Cavaliere had foreseen and to a certain extent had helped along.

"Well, my boy, you must do as you please. Think it over. There's no hurry. I don't expect to leave Venice until Lent. We'll see each other from time to time, I hope. And please remember that I'm very much your friend, whatever you decide regarding England."

Richard, whose sense of indebtedness to his patron was beginning to take the latter's part, thanked him warmly.

Tromba added: "It's hard for me to believe that a youth of your spirit, abilities, and prospects, will be permanently content with small beer instead of burgundy. But, if so, make up your mind that you'll have to drink it somewhere else than in Venice. Has that occurred to you?"

"Somewhere else?"

The Cavaliere smiled. "Of course. Unless you keep hidden. And the stage at San Luca's is just about as public as the Piazzetta. I hope you don't imagine that the Very Noble Marin Sagredo is going to forget last night. Our vendetta was too complete for that. Or do you think, because we made an ass of him here, that he's beneath your notice?" Tromba wagged a long forefinger. "When you meet him again, Milòr, it won't be in private theatricals, and it won't be a battle of wits. Every advantage will be his. You can't have the thing both ways; you can't be a poor comedian and at the same time a match for the leading young magnifico of Venice, if he chooses to pay off his grudge. Take my word for it. I hope it's a word to the wise."

Since the victory of last night, Sagredo had about slipped from Richard's mind. The thought of him now in this sober morning-after brought something of a chill. The report was that after the play he had left in a rage for one of his family villas near Mestre and so out of the Brenta neighborhood. But he would certainly be back in Venice for the winter season. Tromba did not exaggerate the dangers connected with that return; they were very real and worth considering. Their present effect on Richard, however, was defiance.

"I'll not be chased out of Venice by him!"

Tromba shrugged. "Lucky if you're not chased out of life. Still, it's your problem." He pulled the bell rope for his valet and tossed the sheet back from his muscular legs. "Time to begin the labors of the day. Since you insist on leaving, good-by with my blessing — whatever that may be worth."

At Fusina later, Richard missed the public ferry to Venice, and rather than wait for the next, indulged himself at no great cost in the luxury of a private boat. It was soothing to recline on the cushions of the little cabin, as the boatman sculled him across the three-mile lagoon. Memories of the Villa Bagnoli drifted far behind him. His birthplace, the millennial city, drew nearer. It had never seemed to him so beautiful. With half-closed eyes, he watched its domes and campaniles mellowing in the gold of sunset. Bells faintly sounded the Angelus. From far away, over the hushed water, he caught the notes of a familiar song from some *peota* returning laden with merrymakers who had spent the day on the mainland. The tune became words in his mind.

> *Roma xe grande, e xe Venezia bela;*
> *Roma xe santa, e xe Venezia bona . . .*

It was like a welcome home.

The towers rose higher against the saffron sky. He could almost hear the murmur of the city. He would soon be gliding between the ancient walls again, past the Giudecca, past St. Mary of Salvation, into that great harbor of St. Mark, thronged with the ships and banners of the world. Instinctively he crossed himself. The thought, inarticulate enough, hovered in his mind that he had been dreaming awhile and was now awake. The world of the Brenta seemed like the feverish vision of an unsubstantial masquerade.

XI

RICHARD'S mother, Jeanne Morandi, had been thinking of him on that late afternoon, when the sound of an opening door and of his familiar footsteps in the entry of the apartment brought her hurrying from her room.

"Richard! Mon trésor!" Her face reflected its former beauty at that moment.

He half lifted her from her feet, swinging her back and forth. "Petite Maman! Well, here I am again!"

A torrent of exclamations carried them out of the vestibule before Jeanne could ask: "But, Richard, what's happened? You were to be two months with the orchestra — until October. Is anything wrong?"

"Wait!" He swept her over to the table of the salon. "Just

78

wait!" Down came a heavy purse, which he opened, spreading out the gold coins. "There!"

"But, Richard . . . !"

Down came the snuffboxes. "There!"

"Mais, chéri!"

"And there!" He handed her the jeweled brooch of the Signora Tron. "A little present for you. Isn't it pretty? Don't you like it?"

She stared at the gems, bewildered. "It's beautiful. But how . . . Won't you explain?"

He enjoyed teasing her. "Where's Babbo?" It was the nickname for his stepfather.

"Out for supper," she said absently.

"And have you good news," Richard asked, "from Julio and Carlo?" These were his half brothers at school in Padua.

"Yes, very good. — Why do you plague me like this? I demand to be told —"

But at this point, Nana, the bouncing little maid of all work, hurried in from the kitchen to greet Richard, and Jeanne's curiosity was again put off.

"And now," she burst out, flicking angrily at the objects on the table, "if you don't answer me and explain how you got these things, I'll think you're a robber."

Then at last he plunged into the story. But there was so much to tell, to describe, to be told over again, that it took him through supper. And afterwards on the small balcony of the apartment, which overlooked the little square of St. John Chrysostom, they had only begun to talk.

A hot summer night, smelling of ancient walls and streets, languished between the surrounding houses. Though in the center of Venice, not far from the Rialto and the Merceria, it was a quiet neighborhood at that hour, since the Piazza of St. Mark and other open or waterfront sections of the city attracted most of the population. A shimmer of moonlight brought out the silhouette of the nearby church, the scattered chimney pots along the roof line of buildings, and the distant bulk of the San Giangrisostomo theater, not yet named Malibran. The balcony was deep enough to be private from the street, two floors below, and from neighboring balconies.

79

Half reclining on a chaise longue, with Richard in a chair beside her, Jeanne exclaimed: "I want to hear it all again! Just *who* is the Chevalier de Tromba? You haven't told me exactly."

Richard hesitated. It seemed odd, after the companionship of the past week, that he could hardly answer her question. "A gentleman of Naples," he said. "He has brought letters from the Cardinal de Bernis and Monsieur de Voltaire. He's protected here by Senator Grimani and other big people."

Richard wished that he felt as convinced about Tromba as he sounded. Their conversation that morning had left him uncomfortable. By his own admission, the Cavaliere was plainly an adventurer. However, let him be what he might, he had been generous and frank with Richard; and the latter had promised to respect his confidence. He had even promised, hopelessly enough, to discuss the English venture with his mother. This was as good a moment as any.

"By the way, when Monsieur de Tromba leaves Venice, he plans to visit London. He invited me to go with him."

"Why?" Her voice was suddenly tense.

"You see, he learned about my father from Dr. Goldoni. It seems that Milòr de Marny is a great man in England, much greater and richer than he was years ago. He has no children. Monsieur de Tromba would like to bring the two of us together."

"Why?" It was a frozen syllable.

"To be honest, the Cavaliere wishes an entrée in England. Aside from that, he thinks it would make my fortune."

After a silence, Jeanne asked in the same compressed voice: "What answer did you give him?"

"I said that I could do nothing without your permission, that I would talk it over with you."

Another pause. "My permission isn't necessary, Richard. You're grown now. You can decide for yourself."

Leaning forward, he covered her hand with his. "Petite Maman! I answered him that way because I expected you to say *no*. Then I wouldn't have to argue about it. What could I do in England? You and the people I care for are here. Besides, I want to write plays and I want to act at San Luca's. Money isn't everything. Why should I hang on to Lord Marny now, when we've gotten along without him all these years? Ridiculous!"

At once the tension was gone. Her hand relaxed. "What a tease you are! You actually frightened me. Of course I say *no*. Of course it's ridiculous. And I think you ought to be wary of that man Tromba." Her thought evidently drifted off. "So Monsieur de Marny's grown rich and great and has no children. Well, he chose riches and greatness. One can't have everything. I suppose he's content. — But tell me more about the Brenta."

Naturally Richard brought up Marin Sagredo. To Jeanne's amusement, he gave a lively account of the vendetta; and, as he was not above dramatizing himself, the story lost nothing in his telling of it.

"Still," she commented, "it would be serious if the young man bears a grudge. But perhaps he'll forget; perhaps he's too proud to notice you. I hope so. Otherwise —" She broke off.

"Otherwise, what?"

It startled him that she echoed Tromba's opinion. "You'd have to leave Venice — for a while. The patricians are masters here. I don't believe I've told you that Babbo has been asked to conduct the opera at Bordeaux next year. If we go, you could go with us. There's the Italian Comedy in Paris. It's time you saw more of the world, Sagredo or not."

"I don't intend to run away from him."

She did not debate this but said quietly: "No use crossing bridges. The theaters won't open for two months. Probably by that time Monsieur de Sagredo won't remember that Richard Morandi exists. — So, you were Count for a night and danced with that charming Madame des Landes? Was she very pretty? What did she wear?"

As he talked, it struck Richard all at once that his disgust with the fashionable world had, like his headache, waned a good deal since morning. In comparison with the present surroundings — the stuffy little square, the jumble of middle-class houses — the Villa Bagnoli took on glamor again. He could smell the jasmine of Amélie des Landes's dress; he remembered the enchantment of her eyes in the candlelight over the champagne glasses; he recalled the glorified image of himself in Tromba's mirror. Even the raffish close of yesterday evening, the Count des Landes and himself at the seesawing table, began to seem more amusing than blameworthy, though he did not tell his mother about it. Perhaps, after all, he

81

had been a fool not to stay on with Tromba. The next six weeks in Venice were apt to be dull.

So, his descriptions of life on the Brenta were glowing enough. It was not until afterwards, and then with a casualness which did not escape Jeanne, that he asked:

"By the way, Mother, do you happen to know anything about the Antonio Veniers? He seems to have married an Austrian ballerina."

She nodded. "Yes, of course. Twenty years ago, everybody in opera knew of Hélène Venier. She was a great dancer. I met her when she first came to Venice as a bride. Her husband married her in Vienna. She's dead now, I think. A lovely woman. — Why do you ask?"

"I met her daughter, Maritza Venier. She was visiting the Widimans."

Jeanne did not need to be especially perceptive to catch something on the wind. Richard's voice was too carefully impersonal.

"Ah? Did you like her?"

"Very attractive. She dances well, too. Hopes to become a ballerina like her mother."

"Indeed?" Jeanne feigned indifference.

A pause followed. Then, in the darkness, her eyes quickened when he added: "She's different from any girl I ever met. So unconventional."

Jeanne said skillfully: "Pert, I suppose? These modern girls cheapen themselves."

He forgot his mask. "I don't mean that at all. There's nothing cheap about her — and nothing pert. I meant unconventional in being sincere and frank and just herself . . . I meant . . ."

Flushed into the open now, he ran on at length, while Jeanne speculated.

She said skillfully again: "And so you fell in love? Well, mon cher poulain, it's not the first time. You're always in love with one girl or another. There was the little Annetta Bari at San Luca's, and there was Maria Fontanelli of our troupe, and Bettina — "

"Please!" he broke in. "Please! That was entirely different. It isn't right to speak of them and Maritza Venier in the same breath. They're just ordinary girls. She —" He sought in vain for the right word. "Well, for one thing, she's a patrician."

Having now learned enough, Jeanne became serious. "And who

are you — if you're really in love? Have you thought of that? Don't you see —"

He interrupted. "We're both poor. Her mother was on the stage. She wants to go on the stage herself. No, I *don't* see. And, besides, as regards birth —" What he had found out last night from des Landes was too good to keep. He swelled a little. "Mother, did you know that my grandfather, Baron Marny, was really the son of King Charles of England, and that I'm the spit and image of him? Did you know that?" Omitting the drunkenness, he told her something of his talk with the Count.

It surprised him when she answered coolly: "Yes, I knew. Your father showed me a miniature once of the Black Baron. You're very like him. He was a great rascal, I believe. And I know the rumor that he was a son of the King. What of it, Richard?"

"What of it? Well, if so, I should think that my blood was just as good as the Veniers'. You spoke as if —"

Reaching out, she laid her hand on his knee. "No, I didn't mean that. I meant your position in the world. You say she's poor. What have you to offer her? Do you think she cares for you?"

The question brought Richard down to earth. He had let the topic carry him too far, and now managed a smile. "You've put your finger on the sore spot there, Mother. No, she doesn't care for me at all — just the contrary."

"Why?"

Embarrassed, he told her of the neglected meeting and described the rebuff Maritza had given him in the ballroom.

"And in spite of that, you're still in love with her?"

He shrugged. "Don't worry. I'm not a fool. You're right. I have nothing to offer her. Only, I'd like to see her again and explain . . ." His voice dropped off.

"Better not," said Jeanne. "Better keep to your Annettas and Bettinas for a while, mon cher. This Mademoiselle de Venier sounds like a nice girl. You're not old enough to think of marriage. Take my advice before it's too late, before you're too much involved."

She opened her fan brusquely. For a minute, only the click of it was heard.

Her thought reached a point at some distance from Maritza Venier.

"Will you do me a favor?" she asked impulsively. "It's important."

"Of course I will, if I can."

"You can and you must. You must try to put that talk with the Comte des Landes out of your mind — the Black Baron and the rest of it. You have better ancestors to think of. Will you promise?"

"Bon Dieu!" Expecting a different request, Richard laughed. "I don't take that seriously."

"I hope not. Be sure you never do. Will you promise?"

He was glad to humor her. "I promise. But how did you happen to think of it?"

She hesitated. "I hardly know. It came to me that it's sometimes dangerous to give life to the dead."

XII

THE motives that govern youth are not always clear to youth itself. Richard had returned to Venice fired with the idea for a play which, by ridiculing his own folly that night at the Villa Bagnoli, would be good for his soul and at the same time amuse the public. But somehow the theme, or rather his zeal for it, faded during the next week. Instead of getting to work, he mooned a good deal, sauntered about, purchased a new wardrobe, and spent time at the coffeehouses on the Piazza. He felt that he needed a holiday. He felt, too, much more a man of the world since his experience on the mainland. The idea for the comedy was excellent, but it would lose nothing by being kept in reserve. Actually the thought that Maritza Venier by now was back in Venice occurred to him much more often that *The Sham Gallant*. And yet it did not occur to him that the very thought of Maritza might have more to do with the mooning and the wardrobe and the holiday than anything else.

For, whether she was back or not, what difference did it make? He felt sure that she despised him and, this being so, he ought to take his mother's advice and forget her. He ought to forget her in any case. As Jeanne had pointed out, the prospect was hopeless. He had nothing to offer even if somehow he made his peace with Maritza and contrived both to meet and commend himself to her father. He could only dangle and pine. No, it was hopeless. He must not be a fool. But if he loitered so often along the Merceria and other busy streets or if, at the coffeehouse, instead of reading newspapers, he preferred to watch the passers-by under the arcades of the Piazza, it was not just the shops and the people that accounted for it. Soon or late, every Venetian passed through that section of the city. What harm if he had happened to catch a glimpse of her? And if finally, out for a stroll one afternoon, he found himself at the Rialto, it meant nothing that he turned in the direction of San Tomà and the Frescada Canal. As well walk there as anywhere. It was only incidental that he would see where she lived. But he had dressed himself up too fine for a summer walk through Venice.

From the Rialto, one reached the San Tomà district by way of the Campo San Polo, then the Frari, and then a short, narrow passage south. To Richard, it was a relatively unfamiliar quarter, and he asked his way more than once until finally, threading an alley-like street, he paused at the near end of a bridge that arched the Rio Frescada. Here a three-story brick building on his left formed an angle with the street and the canal. Since, though time-worn and crumbling, it was obviously a private house, whereas the one at his right across the alley served for shops and lodgings, this must be the Venier palazzo which had been described to him.

On the street side, it was dour and unrevealing enough. Only a squat service entrance broke the expanse of the wall. But the canal front of it, viewed from the arch of the bridge, made a wholly different impression. Its long façade, the Gothic doorway, balconies and windows, mirrored in the water beneath, ensured its right to be called a palazzo. In contrast, facing it across the thirty-foot-wide canal, rose the wall of a building converted into a warehouse, blank except for the tightly shut loading doors and lofts.

As compared with the closeness of the street, it seemed cooler here. An emerald shadow cast by the palace darkened the water down from the bridge; and a slight curve of the canal at that point formed, as it were, a separate nook in the closely built quarter, which gave a sense of retirement and almost of solitude. To this, the weathered brick walls of the palace, the crumbling tracery of its windows, the cluster of decayed mooring posts, draped in sea-

85

weed, that stood lapped by the canal at one side of the main doorway, contributed. It was a spot haunted by the peace of age,
twilight and seclusion.

Richard leaned absently against the parapet of the bridge. So
here it was, the place where Maritza Venier lived. But the sight of
it did not seem to bring her any closer to him. On the contrary,
he found it difficult to reconcile his thought of her with the
medieval remoteness of the old building, its air of tattered dignity,
the half-effaced coat of arms above the arch of the portal. Indeed,
at the moment, he could hardly believe that it was inhabited by
anyone. It gave the feeling of emptiness. Not a sound came from
within. The lower windows had been boarded up, and those above
them looked vague and vacant. One could gather that the heavy
door between its wasted stone columns had not been opened for a
long time.

Perhaps, after all, no one lived here, and he had mistaken the
street. The Venier palazzo might be further up or down the canal.
Trying to make out the actual arms on the scutcheon above the
door, he found it impossible to read the worn carving at that distance, and so, turning back across the bridge, he walked along the
fondamenta, or stone coping of the canal bank, which led to the
marble landing block in front of the entrance. From that point,
the almost obliterated crest was perfectly visible. No, there had
been no mistake. The famous bars of the Veniers, familiar to any
Venetian, were still faintly apparent across the weathered shield.

And now what? He gave up deluding himself about the good
clothes he was wearing and the real object of his walk. The hope of
seeing not only Maritza's house but, somehow or other, of seeing
Maritza herself had to be acknowledged — as well as his disappointment that the better half of that hope seemed impossible. He
stood vainly looking up at the empty windows and balconies.
Not a sound, not a flicker of life. For a moment, he felt an insane
impulse to lift the heavy ring-knocker hanging from the mouth of
a bronze lion's head on the door. But the notion was too mad to
be indulged. Unconventional as the Veniers might be, they were
not unconventional enough to allow an almost complete stranger
to call on the daughter of the house, even if Richard had been in her
good graces. He would have to give it up and trudge home again, fine

86

clothes and all. There was no use kicking his heels any longer here. Of course later he might try the expedient of a serenade, hire a gondola and some musicians. But he was on no such footing with Maritza as that. Then, too, it meant the reversal of his decision not to make love to her. And yet — to hell with prudence and pretenses! He suddenly admitted to himself that he was damnably in love with her.

Standing with his back to the palace and staring absently across the canal, he became gradually conscious of a small object in the water, which at last drew his attention. Too big for a rat, it turned out to be a young puppy, which had no doubt drifted down under the bridge and, swimming feebly, was scratching in vain for a purchase on the vertical stone foundation of the warehouse. That it had been destined to drown was shown by the string trailing behind its neck, from which the weight had dropped off. But this fate had been only delayed and was now closing in.

Richard viewed the struggle with rising concern. He had a natural fondness for dogs and in his boyhood had fought many a battle with fellow street urchins to protect some tortured cur that had fallen into their hands. It was one of his recognized weaknesses, perhaps deriving from his own insecurity. The Venetian small boys had poked fun at him for it but had learned to respect it. Now at once he became involved in the puppy's distress; for if the little creature could not be detached from that impossible landing place, it was surely finished. Stooping down, he whistled and called, hoping that the puppy would swim over so that he could fish it out. But the frantic scratching went on. Unless some casual gondola appeared, he had no way of reaching the little dog except by going into the water after it himself. And yet here he was in a new suit which had cost him ten sequins. He glanced rapidly up and down the canal, but no boat was in sight.

Maladetto! . . .

The puppy fought on, scrabbled against the wall, disappeared, then in a last spasm managed to come up.

"Coraggio, piccino!" Richard shouted. Off went his hat, coat and waistcoat, cravat and shirt. He added his shoes to the heap, stripped off his stockings, and slipped into the water. After all, if his nankeen breeches were ruined, it would be no great loss.

87

The distance was not more than ten yards, but he arrived only in time to grasp the limp little animal, which resigned itself to the big hand closing over it. The question then arose what to do next. He could not climb out on this side of the canal, which was lined by the warehouse. On the other hand, it might not be feasible to regain the bank in front of the palace, because it was low tide and the water level made it difficult for a swimmer to catch a hand-hold on the coping. The best plan was to swim up to the bridge, where a couple of steps led down to the water.

But turning in that direction, Richard found that he was no longer alone. The whistling, calling and splashing had made more noise than he realized. To his astonishment, the door of the palace stood open and, more amazing still, no less a person than Maritza herself was watching him from the landing block.

Evidently she had not recognized the half-naked swimmer with his hair plastered flat on his head and a puppy in one hand. She called heartily: "Bravo, sior! That was gallant of you. Is he all right? Swim over here and hand him to me. Then I'll help you up." But a face like Richard's was unmistakable. Her voice faded out. She stared. "You? Sior Morandi?"

Richard would have liked to sink from sight. To be meeting her again this way, almost stripped, bobbing about in the dirty canal, and burdened with an absurd puppy was so unromantically the reverse of anything he had pictured that his thought collapsed. As he swam nearer, he managed to get out: "I'm sorry . . . I didn't know . . . please excuse me . . ."

A little flushed, she kneeled on the landing block and, reaching her arm down at full length, took the puppy from Richard's up-stretched hand. The little dog trembled and dripped beside her on the pavement.

"Poveretto," she said, patting it. Then, reaching down again, "Now for you, sior. Take hold."

He hesitated. "Thank you. I'll swim up to the bridge."

"Don't be silly. — There!" Her hand felt capable and firm. "Now!"

Ordinarily nothing would have been easier. A tug on her part, an extra kick on his, and he would have caught the edge of the coping. But neither of them counted on the slipperiness of the land-

88

ing block. His weight drew her forward; her knees slid on the worn marble; he heard a despairing *Santa Maria!* and down she plunged on top of him.

They both went under, came up sputtering.

"I can't swim." Her arm clamped itself about Richard's neck and submerged him again.

"Take it easy," he puffed. "Put your hand on my shoulder."

At once her arm relaxed. Her face was streaked with hair and water, but she managed to smile. "La perdoni . . ."

"Perdoni?" he returned. "It's all my fault. Clumsy fool!" Complete humiliation swept over him. He told himself that this was certainly the end. A grand finale! Nakedness and the puppy were bad enough, but dragging Maritza into the canal left nothing to add. There could be no forgiveness for that in earth or heaven. "Che gonzo!" He threw in other phrases of choice Venetian.

"Sior!" she reproved. "Hush! How are we going to get out?"

A hurry of footsteps sounded from the palace doorway. An aggrieved voice rose, calling on the saints. Looking up, Richard saw a broad-shouldered, middle-aged woman, her cap over one ear, seething down at them.

"Misery! What's happened? My poor darling! Is he trying to assassinate you? Aha! Bandit!"

Maritza put in: "Quiet, Anzoletta. He's not a bandit. Stoop down and give us a hand, but don't slip. — And look out for the puppy."

"What puppy?"

"There — in front of you."

With a disgusted glance at the shivering object, the woman leaned over and caught Maritza's hand. A pull of her stout arm, a push underneath from Richard, shot the girl up like a cork. A second later she was on her feet.

"Thanks, Anzoletta. You're better at it than I am. Now help Sior Morandi."

"How! You know the fellow?"

"Of course I do. It's Sior Morandi, the gentleman I told you about, at the Villa Bagnoli — remember? — Count Roberto."

"Count Roberto, indeed!" Anzoletta kept a watchful glare on

Richard. "He looks like a Moor and a pirate. With my own eyes, I saw him pull you in."

Maritza protested. "No, he didn't. It was just an accident. Please hurry!"

Dubious and reluctant, Anzoletta gave the needed tug, and Richard clambered to a sitting position on the coping. He hardly dared stand up. The cotton breeches, grown almost transparent with their soaking, clung to him like tights and offered little concealment. His one thought now was to snatch up the rest of his clothes and vanish at the first possible moment.

Fortunately Anzoletta, whose alarm had turned to scolding, concentrated on Maritza at the moment and left Richard in the background.

Look at that dress! A ruin. Did they have money to throw into the canal? But this was the least of it. That a girl of family, a girl of rank, the daughter of his Excellence Antonio Venier, should run out of doors bareheaded to throw herself at a strange young man, and he naked at that — it was such behavior as Anzoletta had never seen the like of! It was behavior that deserved an old-fashioned whacking. And Maritza could make up her mind to it!

The housekeeper of the Veniers spoke the dialect of Friuli and looked as if she belonged to the class of well-to-do peasants on the mainland, but no doubt she had spent most of her life in the Veniers' service. Her tone of authority indicated that she had gradually become the incarnation of that family, its mainspring and dictator. Brown-eyed, square-faced, she radiated energy and, just then, indignation. Richard felt sorry for Maritza. The girl stood downcast and dripping under the lecture.

"And worse still, there you stand catching cold . . ."

At this point, an inquisitive gondola drifted by, but the boatman prudently confined himself to stares. Anzoletta lowered her voice until he was past.

"And now in with you! Fraschetta! I forbid you to touch that smelly little dog!"

But Maritza picked up the puppy and cuddled it. "Cara . . ." she coaxed.

"Well, get into the house at least."

"And Sior Morandi? We can't leave him out here."

Richard put in: "Don't think about me, madonna. Again, please forgive —"

Anzoletta cut him short. He was amazed at a sudden relenting in her eyes. "Of course you'll come in. You can dry off in the kitchen. If we do that much for a dog, we can do it for a human. I won't have you on my conscience."

She propelled Maritza not too gently toward the door, but the girl turned to nod at him and again smiled. It was the smile she had given him that first night in return for the camellias.

"Well, are you coming?" Anzoletta demanded from the threshold. "Hurry up. Don't forget your things."

So induced, Richard gathered up his clothes and, conscious of his nudity, slunk, rather than walked, through the doorway. A trickle of water followed. Romantically considered, his entrance into the Palazzo Venier could hardly have been sorrier. Still, one way or another, here he was.

The door closed with a boom behind him.

XIII

AS in other mansions of its age, the front door of the Palazzo Venier opened upon a vaulted passage, or *entrada,* that led into a central court around which the mass of the house was built. Here an outer staircase supported by Gothic arches and flanked by a richly carved parapet rose to the second floor. In the middle of the court, like a marble hub, stood the inevitable well resembling the huge capital of a column and bearing the arms of the family on its sides.

At one time, in the days of the merchant princes, the palace must have been a very splendid dwelling. Remnants of its past magnificence were obvious in the fine and spacious proportions of the courtyard, in the delicate arches of the second-story arcade that gave access to the rooms on that level, and in the exquisite, though worn, sculpturing of column and architrave. But the dilapidation of the building which had been so apparent on the outside was equally advanced here. Occasional weeds pushed up between the flagstones of the court; some windows of the upper

91

floors had lost their panes and showed various makeshifts for keeping out the weather; lizards sunned themselves on the fallen brickwork that lined the base of the walls. It was a crumbling and neglect that implied poverty as well as age.

Maritza had withdrawn somewhere to change and had taken the puppy with her. Conducted by Anzoletta, Richard crossed the courtyard to the kitchen, a vast stone-paved region with blackened beams and a cavernous hearth which might once have turned out banquets for a hundred guests. Now only the embers of a tiny charcoal fire gave a point of light in the dusk.

"Put your clothes down there," said the housekeeper, indicating a rough-hewn oak table. "And you'd better wash yourself off well in that tub. You'll find some buckets of fresh water next to it. The canal's pretty foul at low tide. And a lunatic you were to go swimming after that dog. What made you do it?"

Shamefacedly, Richard explained.

"More heart than head," observed Anzoletta. "Still, I don't know that it isn't more to your credit than the other way round." Richard could see that it was hard for her to conceal the warm kindliness under her crusty manner. "I suppose what you need now," she went on, "is breeches. While you're washing up, I'll find you a pair of his Excellence's."

She brought him a clean but well-worn towel and disappeared.

It was a cold bath in the clammy twilight. Richard rubbed himself hard afterwards to get warm. Luckily he had slipped on his shirt and was drying his hair when Anzoletta returned; but that he still lacked a good deal in point of dress did not seem to trouble her.

"Here," she said, holding out a garment. "His Excellence insists that you wear these. They're pretty elegant — the best black silk. He's only used them on great occasions — the last time at the Siora's funeral."

Richard thanked her and handled the breeches reverently, but he began to have misgivings when he drew them on. They had surely been elegant once, but they were cut for a smaller and shorter man, and time had so frayed the material that it seemed unlikely to hold against any new stress. He pointed this out tactfully to Anzoletta, with the private thought that he did not want to be blamed for damaging an heirloom.

"Well," she decided, "it can't be helped. Wear them anyway. I doubt if his Excellence will need them again, and they'd fetch nothing if sold. I'd have brought others, but the truth is —" She left the truth unrevealed. "Even if they tear," she added, "I hope they'll cover the essentials."

Moving warily, Richard hoped so, too. The breeches did not come to his knees. He rolled up his stockings to meet them, but the margin of contact was slight and needed watching. Luckily the long skirts of his plum-colored coat would cover a good deal.

And now at last — what with the coat and his flowered linen waistcoat, frilled shirt, snowy neckcloth, white stockings, and silver shoe buckles — his handsome new clothes came into their own. His black hair ribbon had lost its crisp bow and dangled a little; but, except for that, no sign of the canal remained. Anzoletta, visibly impressed, righted her cap and smoothed out her apron.

"I didn't know you were such a fine gentleman," she conceded. "You mustn't mind what I said outside there. You'll have to admit that you weren't looking your best."

"I hope not," said Richard. Half from vanity, he drew out one of his recently acquired snuffboxes, which he offered with a bow. "Do you take tobacco, Sior' Amia?" Even if Anzoletta had not been the Veniers' prime minister and major-domo, there was something about her which demanded politeness. But he had been a little too forward in calling her *aunt*.

"*Siora* is enough," she corrected, and then sugared the reproof by accepting a pinch of snuff. "Excellent. Real Seville. It's been a long time since I had any. And I thank you."

Richard took a pinch himself with the reflection that their relations had been very deftly established. Anzoletta was favorable tentatively and up to a point, but she did not fully commit herself.

"His Excellence," she went on in the manner of one speaking for a sovereign, "invites you to have coffee with him and the Lady Maritza in the roof pavilion." And with a view perhaps of dashing any too-hasty ideas on Richard's part, "As I told him, it was only proper under the circumstances, much as he hates to leave his desk."

"I hope it isn't too great an intrusion, siora."

"No, not that. It's what he calls the Muses, whatever they are. Once pry him loose, and he's happy enough. But you've got to

93

pry him. So, if you'll take a seat on that bench or wait in the courtyard . . ."

Leaving Richard to his thoughts, she sparingly added a few charcoals to the fire, set a coffeepot to boil, and assembled some odds and ends of china on a pewter tray. Richard watched her absently. He was more than a little nervous about the approaching meeting with the Veniers. What would come of it? Was it to be a beginning or an end? Would he be able to re-establish himself with Maritza? What kind of man was Antonio Venier?

"How did you happen to be outside our palazzo?" queried the housekeeper suddenly, with a shrewdness which was not lost on him.

Improvising, he mixed some truth in the reply. On an errand in San Tomà parish, he had happened to cross the Rio Frescada and had stopped to admire the Palazzo Venier, all the more as he knew that the Lady Maritza lived there.

"And do you always dress so fine when you walk through the city?"

"I had a call to make." But the woman's shafts were falling too close for comfort.

Anzoletta removed the pot from the fire and transferred it to the tray. "You're sure her Excellence knew nothing about it? She's spoken of you more than once. Looks rather pat to me."

"Indeed not, siora."

There was one comfort in this catechism: that Maritza had spoken of him, and, it seemed, not too disparagingly, or the woman would not have suspected connivance on her part.

Once more Anzoletta adjusted her cap, then lifted the tray.

"Let me carry it," Richard offered.

"I should say not! Guests in our palace don't carry trays. But you can open the door for me."

So, embodying in herself a vanished retinue of servants, Anzoletta marched rigidly out into the courtyard, and Richard followed.

"Mind the steps," she cautioned at the foot of the outer stairway. "They're broken in places."

It was not only the steps that were broken. Along the arcade of the floor above, Richard stumbled once or twice on the pave-

94

ment, from which tiles had worked loose. Here and there, as they passed, he glanced through the windows of unfurnished, tomblike apartments, with the frescoes half peeled off from a wall or ceiling. One could guess that the furniture had been sold piece by piece to pay debts or meet living expenses. The place had that forlorn look about it.

Pausing in front of a door at the foot of an inside staircase leading to the third story, Anzoletta knocked.

"Zelenza, coffee is served." There was no answer. "Coffee, Zelenza!"

"Go away," came a muffled voice. "Leave me in peace. Va via . . ."

She knocked again. "We have a guest, remember. Sior Morandi. He awaits your Excellence."

A sound, very much like a groan, issued. "Yes, yes. One moment. My respects to the gentleman . . . One moment."

She shrugged. "There you have it. The Muses. Let's go on up. I think he'll be along presently. If not, I'll come back and fetch him."

She led the way to the third floor, which contained another file of vacant rooms once occupied by servants, and then up a last short flight to the vacancy of the roof.

Emerging into the glare of afternoon from the twilight below, Richard stood dazzled an instant, half-conscious of the city spread out below and around him.

"Finalmente!" exclaimed a nearby voice. "Sior, you certainly take time to dress!"

An *altana*, or open pavilion built of tiles, lay several paces distant across the roof. In the doorway stood Maritza, her wet hair covered by a tightly bound scarf, with the puppy, a ball of yellow fur, in the angle of one arm.

Richard put on his best manners and made his best bow.

"The most devoted servant of the Siora."

Dropping him as deep a curtsy as the encumbrance of the puppy allowed, she copied his greeting.

"The most humble servant of Sior Morandi."

He flushed and stiffened. It reminded him of her mockery in the ballroom of the villa. They seemed to be back at that point, as if the adventure in the canal had never happened.

He forgot manners and blurted out: "Why are you offended, madonna? What's wrong?"

"Nothing. I suppose it must be hard to get over being Count Roberto."

"You don't like Count Roberto?"

"I like Sior Milòr better. I don't think Count Roberto would have jumped into the canal to save a little creature like this." She glanced warmly at the puppy. "A fop doesn't do that kind of thing." Then suddenly her expression changed. Her eyes quickened and danced. "And I'm sure Count Roberto wouldn't be as much concerned not to offend me as about keeping his stockings up."

Richard looked down. A widening zone of bare thigh showed between breeches and hose. Worse still, his elaborate bow had started a gap in the frail silk, that ran several inches up. Good God! And he had been displaying his manners in that condition. Plum-colored coat above, disgrace below. With a strangled sound, he stooped over and jerked the stockings into place. It seemed fated that whenever he came near Maritza something ridiculous or humiliating happened.

Anzoletta, who had understood nothing of this but had listened with growing disapproval, now came to his defense and swung into action like a ship of the line.

"Sior Morandi," she said, advancing into the altana and setting down the tray with a thump on the small center table, "I hope you'll forgive this vanerella, who seems to be bent on disgracing herself and the family. I have tried to teach her politeness, but you see the result. — As for you, povera gnocca," Anzoletta continued, turning a full broadside on Maritza, "are not even you ashamed? Che sesti! Has a guest ever been so received at the Palazzo Venier! The gentleman greets you courteously; you make fun of him. He asks how he has offended you; you call him a fop —"

"No, Anzoletta, I didn't."

"Permit me to believe my own ears. And then, to cap everything, you laugh at his dress. Is it his fault that your father's breeches are too short for him? Is that a topic for a lady? Do ladies point and jeer at such things? I marvel at you."

"I didn't point." Maritza's face was crimson. "I'm sorry! Sior, I'm very sorry! I didn't mean . . ."

96

Now that the tables were turned, Richard sympathized with her. "Of course not, madonna. I'm happy you like me better than Count Roberto. But, really, I didn't intend . . . I wasn't trying . . . I mean I'd do anything to please you." He broke off again. "I'm afraid these stockings just won't stay up."

"Puffeta!" said Maritza. "As if it mattered!" She explained to Anzoletta. "You don't understand. Sior Morandi and I had a little — a disagreement at the Villa. He was so grand and popular, that I thought . . . Well, I was cross and not very nice to him. So just now, when he made me such a fine reverence and talked about *devoted servant*, I couldn't help making fun again. It's a little mixed up . . ."

Richard had the feeling of a boatman who, having barely squeezed past the reefs, enters harbor. He would avoid those particular reefs, he decided, from now on. As far as Maritza was concerned, the man of fashion could be dropped from his repertoire.

Anzoletta glanced back and forth between them. "Mixed up, indeed! You're too young to be having disagreements with gentlemen at country houses. You're too young to be cross and saucy. You should wait for that till you're married. I never did approve of your going alone to the Villa Bagnoli. And I was right."

Fondling the puppy, Maritza drew fire in another direction.

"Don't let that dirty little dog lick your face," continued the woman, "What do you intend to do with him?"

"You mean with Bapi? Don't you think *Bapi* is a good name, Sior Milòr?" And when Richard nodded approval, "We need a watchdog, Anzoletta."

The housekeeper did not intend to submit without an effort. "Tolè," she declared, "you can choose between that dog and me. I have enough to care for without that."

"Darling! I'll take care of him."

"Nonsense! I've heard that before."

"I promise."

"Your promises! Who will clean up after this Bapi? I, Anzoletta. See, a puddle on the floor already. Which brings fleas. Haven't we fleas enough?"

"But, cara, a few more . . ."

"And who will feed him? I, Anzoletta."

97

"Vecchia, no. I'll feed him myself."

"That's what *you* say."

"Cara ti . . ."

The pleading was irresistible. Anzoletta succumbed. "You see how it is." She turned to Richard. "A spoiled minx."

"Exactly!" put in a voice from the doorway. "So much for Maritza!" Richard looked around, half startled, at a figure entering the pavilion. "You're Sior Milòr, I believe," said the newcomer with a smile very much like Maritza's. "I've heard of you often since my daughter's return from the Villa Bagnoli. It is a pleasure to welcome you. I am Antonio Venier."

XIV

AS Richard returned Venier's greeting and sat down at the coffee table with him and Maritza, a quality in his host's manner put him immediately at ease. Venier looked about fifty. He had a short and slight, though well-proportioned, figure. The mark of recently removed spectacles crossed the bridge of his nose. Because of the warm day, he had left off his coat, retaining only the long waistcoat, which was half unbuttoned across his shirt. But, for all that, the whiteness of his linen and his well-tended hands gave him a distinguished appearance. Remarkable, too, was the vivacity of his brown eyes, changeable, vivid and extremely eloquent.

From the rescue of the puppy, with laughter on Venier's part and apologies on Richard's, conversation turned naturally to the latter's meeting with Maritza at the Widiman villa.

"My daughter tells me," said Venier, "that you are a musician, an actor, a writer of plays and a friend of Carlo Goldoni's. For so young a man, I call that a great deal. Few at your age have so many titles of distinction."

"Except for Dr. Goldoni's kindness," Richard answered, "they are titles without the distinction, your Excellence. As to music and me, the less said the better. As to acting and writing, perhaps some day —" He finished the sentence with a shrug.

Maritza put in: "Sior Pa're, he's just being modest. Dr. Goldoni himself told me all about the play that Sior Morandi wrote called

Captain Harlequin. He said it was the best commedia dell' arte he
had seen in a long time. And, of course, everybody at the villa
went mad about the way he acted Count Roberto."

"Except you, madonna," Richard observed.

She colored a little. "Well, you know I admired it. I told you so.
It was only — But please don't let's talk about it any more."

"I should say not!" exclaimed Anzoletta, who sat knitting in the
background. "She's been very pert, your Excellence."

"No doubt," Venier agreed. But it was natural with him to keep
a guest at the center of conversation. "Are you writing something
now, Sior Morandi?"

It struck Richard that here was an excellent chance to put *The
Sham Gallant* to use. "As it happens, I am," he answered, supplying
the will for the deed. "And I think the plot, at least, is unusual. It
occurred to me at the Villa Bagnoli."

"Tell us about it," urged Venier.

"Please!" said Maritza, leaning forward.

What Richard told, with a due substitution of names and comic
exaggeration, was of course the story of himself on the Brenta. As
he portrayed them, the characters of Maritza, Tromba, the
Countess, and Sagredo, could hardly be identified by Venier and
Anzoletta; whereas almost at once Maritza gave him a sharp
glance, then smiled, then bit her lips. Under the guise of fiction
and keeping a steady face, he could pay Maritza, as Rosaura, the
heroine, all the compliments he wished, and she could do nothing to
stop him. On the other hand, while ridiculing himself as Harlequin,
the Sham Gallant, he pleaded his own case. The complications of
the plot had been well enough thought out; and, as he described
them, the actor in him took over. Venier was delighted; Anzoletta
held her sides. Maritza, vexed, pleased and embarrassed, could not
keep from laughing, too. In the end, Harlequin, having been sufficiently baited, exposed, and made fun of, received his sentence
from the charming heroine.

"Bravo!" Venier applauded, while Anzoletta echoed him.
"Comedy in the best tradition, Sior Morandi."

Only Maritza, drawing imaginary lines on the table with her
forefinger, said nothing.

"How do you like it, madonna?" Richard asked after a moment.

Her smile had its own special meaning. "I think you're very clever, sior. But I don't like the heroine. I think she's stuck-up, the way she treats poor Messer Harlequin." And Maritza smiled again, enchantingly this time. Whether *The Sham Gallant* ever got written or not, it had been successful.

Conscious that Venier had kept him too much in the forefront of the talk, Richard now sought to step back. "Would it be indiscreet, Zelenza, to ask about your own work? I understand that you are writing a great poem on Venice, but Siora Maritza did not tell me enough. Comedies are such froth compared with —"

"Not at all," put in Venier hurriedly, "not at all. I wish you'd explain to me why the Granellesca Academy is so much at outs with Goldoni."

"Isn't that always the way!" Anzoletta interrupted. "Ask the Lustrissimo anything about his own writing, and he's off, like an eel. Who cares about the What-you-call-it Academy?"

Maritza joined in. "It's true, Sior Pa're. Why do you behave like that?"

"Behave like what?" Venier looked unhappy.

"I told him it was an epic poem," she insisted. "Was that right?"

"No, not entirely . . . philosophical rather . . . But, Sior Morandi —"

"In the manner of Lucretius?" Richard asked.

"No, a philosophy of history. Very long-winded. And now let us —"

"No!" said Maritza. "What do you mean by a philosophy of history?"

Venier sighed. "The causes underlying events, piccina. The forces of life and death in nations. Our Republic of Venice has had its day, has reached the end. But our age everywhere is closing. *Why?* That's the theme."

Out of respect for Venier, Richard did not smile, but the terms seemed extravagant. What end had Venice reached? Her empire might have shrunk since the days of colonial greatness, but it still persisted on the mainland, on the coasts across the Adriatic. Her fleets were still a power in the Mediterranean, and her ships penetrated every ocean. One had only to look out now over the sparkle of the city to feel its continued, immemorial life. The unbridled

100

horses still proclaimed the spirit of Venice above the portal of St. Mark's. The lion stood guard upon his column in the Piazzetta. On Ascension Day, the gilded Bucentaur carried the Doge in state to the annual wedding of the sea. Richard thought of the wealth and display he had seen on the Brenta or here in the city, the pomp and lavishness of the all-powerful patricians. An end of Venice? And what about mighty France, imperial Spain and Austria, bustling England? It all looked pretty solid.

"The end?" Richard repeated.

"Yes. But call it what you like: the last phase. All signs point to it."

"What signs does your Signory mean?"

Venier hesitated. "I'm a philosopher, not a preacher. But let me ask you a question. What is the official religion of Europe?"

"Why, sir, Christianity of course."

"And would you call that the *actual* religion of Europe — I mean the faith by which men live and for which they are willing to die?"

Unused to such discussions, Richard could only blink.

"Well, then," said Venier, "put it this way. Do most people practice Christianity nowadays or do they practice worldliness?"

"The latter, sir; but hasn't that always been so?"

"Yes, but with a great difference. It's a question of degree. Christianity did not become the official religion of Europe merely on the strength of lip service. Such words as charity, repentance, and honor once had a real meaning. They reflected an integrity, a spiritual core, which has vanished. And I am one who holds that the spirit is more than meat; that a man, a nation, a millenium, grows and is strong, or declines and perishes, in proportion to the spiritual content of each. But when nothing spiritual remains, what is left to man but the worship of vanity? Lord Vanity rules our present world. — But these are deep waters."

Deep indeed, thought Richard, who was very much at a loss.

"Didn't you have a letter yesterday from Monsieur Diderot in Paris?" suggested Maritza, proudly intent on drawing out her father. "You know who Monsieur Diderot is, Sior Milòr. He's writing an inclopedia."

"Encyclopedia, cara," murmured Venier.

"Well, anyway, he's a very learned man, and he agrees with you, doesn't he, Father?"

"Yes, in part. At least he prophesies the end of France, as we know it, within the next generation."

"But how?" Richard exclaimed. The idea of this was even more incredible than the end of Venice. The power of France, the prestige of France, overshadowed Europe. "Surely," he added, "England and the King of Prussia aren't doing so well in the present war as to bring that about. Besides, France is allied with the Empire, and the Empire with Russia."

"Not by war," said Venier. "Diderot means revolution. There's too much misery in France, too much corruption, and too much new thought, for the present state of things to last. But revolution is contagious. It will not be confined to France; it will spread through the world."

The click of Anzoletta's needles sounded a moment. "Do you believe in revolution, Zelenza?" she asked suddenly. He took so long to answer that she glanced up from her knitting.

"No," he said at last, "for revolution mixes too much falsehood with too little truth. Like war, it sells its soul for a mirage. But like war, too, and like other plagues, it clears the ground for the future — perhaps a better future, who can tell? I'm always doubtful, though, of bad means to a good end."

He smiled reminiscently. "When I think of revolution, I somehow identify it with a strange fellow I used to meet around Venice fifteen years back. He was secretary to the French ambassador, Monsieur de Montaigu; but he was too thin-skinned to hold the position long and gave it up. Since then, he's done well in the literary way. I hear he's quite a lion in Paris. A Genevan by the name of Rousseau."

"I think I've heard of him," put in Richard. "He wrote an intermezzo called *Le Devin du Village* that Dr. Goldoni admires."

"Yes," nodded Venier, "and an essay on the arts and sciences which was much talked about. He dabbles in music, education, government, or what you will. He's one of Diderot's encyclopedists. But the point of mentioning him is that he has the kind of ideas which cause revolution." Venier shook his head. "To my mind, he's a thoroughly detestable fellow. And yet that makes no difference. For thoughts are like fire that can burn down a city, no matter who thinks them."

Maritza drew her chair closer to the table. "What ideas, Sior Pa're?"

"A few excellent ones. I confess that Monsieur Rousseau had something to do with your education or lack of it, fia mia — though perhaps it would have been the same in any case, because your mother and I were natural rebels." Venier turned to Richard. "Of course you've noticed that my daughter has no bringing-up at all, that she's a perfect barbarian according to genteel standards. No savoir-faire, no polish. Look at her now with her elbows on the table!"

Maritza removed them and tried to look chastened. It was the moment for a compliment; but before Richard could think of the right words, Anzoletta expressed herself on the subject of *Monsù* Rousseau. She could see no advantage in being a barbarian and ignorant of polite customs. How often she had pointed this out to his Excellence and to the dear dead Siora! How often she had worked upon Maritza herself until her hand was numb! To no purpose. And all because of said Monsù. She could well understand that he was the apostle of revolution.

Venier leaned back with relief at being out of the conversation. But he did not escape; for when the gale was over Maritza again asked: "What ideas were those, Father — I mean the ones you liked?" And Richard seconded her.

"Well," continued Venier, "for example, when he used to discuss the silliness and bother of most of our conventions — how contrary they are to nature and how much more honestly we could live without them — I agreed with him. — Yes, Anzoletta; you can say what you please. — Furthermore, when Monsieur Rousseau urged that emotion, that warmth of heart, should not be stifled by prudence and reason, I agreed with him, too. Then, besides, he had a novel conception of beauty, which has meant much to me as a poet. He finds grandeur in mountains and desert solitudes, in aspects of nature which have always seemed merely forbidding to man. And he is right."

"Why do you call him detestable, then?" Maritza objected.

"First, because of his personal self, which is vain, sickly and

103

unbalanced. He is forever wronged and a martyr. He is a petty man of mean passions. But this would not be important if he were not so dangerous. For he has great persuasiveness; and the world is full of men like him, men with a grievance, to whom he tells not the truth but what he and they like to believe. That's what I meant by the falsehood back of revolution. He preaches, for instance, that all men are equal."

"Aren't they," said Maritza, "in the eyes of God?"

"Perhaps. Only God can say."

Richard suggested: "I remember reading somewhere, your Excellence, that laws should be the same for everybody without respect to rank. Doesn't Rousseau mean that?"

"Yes, in part. But he uses words recklessly. To the poor, the ignorant, the envious, and the oppressed, equality is sure to have the meaning that one man is as good as the next, deserves as much as the next; that there are no superior, no inferior, men. Which is nonsense. But the lie is so flattering, offers such promise, that the multitude is sure to welcome it. It is apt even to replace the religion that we have lost. There's the fire which will consume our age. But when it has leveled everything, fire burns itself out, and so does a lie."

"Does your Signory think —"

Venier raised his hand. "No, I beg. You've had enough of my opinions. What I really think at the moment regards supper. I hope you will join us, Sior Morandi, if you are free."

"*Please* do," Maritza urged.

On the point of gratefully accepting, Richard stopped short at a warning sound from Anzoletta. It was half a cough, half an urgent clearing of the throat. It signaled distress.

Venier laughed. "What! No supper, Anzoletta?"

"Lustrissimo, not much."

"La bela cossa! We have soup?"

"Yes, a little."

"Put water in it. Bread?"

"Thank God, yes."

"Well!" . . . Venier's tone expressed opulence. "Wine?"

Almost at the point of tears, Anzoletta burst out: "Your Excellence knows that we have only the little half bottle that was left from dinner."

"Ample!" he declared. "Do we need a barrel? Water is again indicated — and temperance."

Richard put in: "I thank your Signories, but the fact is I'm engaged . . . I must . . ."

Maritza laid a hand on his arm.

"You see!" Venier smiled. "We won't let you off. Don't lead me to believe that you scorn our menu. Soup! Bread! Wine! Friendship! — Maritza, help Anzoletta carry up the banquet. It's after sundown. Let's feast here under the stars. And while you're making ready, I'll show Sior Morandi the palace."

XV

THERE was not much to see, after all; but each empty apartment and dim gallery, indeed almost every stone, it seemed to Richard, had its story; and Venier, fond of the past, mingled fact with legend, as they strolled about. However, it was the study that detained them longest. Unlike the other rooms, it contained a clutter of odds and ends, an inundation of books, a vast writing table littered with manuscripts, broken quills, clay pipes and tobacco crumbs, that stood beneath one of the high Gothic windows now pale in the light of evening.

At the writing table, Venier displayed the manuscript of his poem, a bulky pile of closely written folio pages.

"But it must be a vast work, your Excellence," Richard exclaimed.

"No, what you see here are seven versions of the same theme. I am now beginning the eighth."

"Has your Signory any idea when you will finish it?"

"Not the least. Probably never. I've already been working on it fifteen years. Besides, I should never dare publish it. The Council of Ten finds any idea of political change treasonable. — But here —" a sudden thought occurred to him, and he dragged out another sheaf of manuscript from under a pile of cascading books — "is something else."

In spite of the dim light, Richard could make out a heavily inked title — *Theseus, an Opera* — and recalled that Maritza had spoken of librettos which her father had written. It was a form that Rich-

105

ard knew more about than philosophical poetry. His interest quickened. Turning over the pages, he saw another title, *Oenone*.

"I wrote those long ago," said Venier, "at the desire of my wife. Indeed, we wrote them together. Maritza has told you, I believe, that the late Siora Venier was a ballerina. She was very accomplished, very beautiful." His voice shook suddenly, and he paused. "She withdrew from the stage when we were married, but she always looked back to it. So these plays were written."

He made a pretense of stacking up the tumbled books.

"Would you permit me to read them?" asked Richard.

Venier nodded. "Sometime, if you have leisure, I should value your opinion. The style is romantic, rather high-flown perhaps; but I used to believe the plays had merit. My wife designed the ballets for them. She and Maritza would go through the figures and imagine themselves dancing at the San Giangrisostomo. It was pretty to watch . . ."

If the plays had been the heaviest Latin tome on the surrounding shelves, Richard would have been charmed to read them because of the pretext they offered of returning to the Palazzo Venier. He expressed his sense of obligation at the privilege and hoped that his Excellency would allow him to read them soon.

Venier had found a tinderbox and was lighting his pipe when Maritza, appearing at the door, announced supper.

"No, Sior Pa're, you can smoke afterwards. The soup is hot, and so is Anzoletta. Please come at once."

"Between the two of them," sighed Venier, "I have no more to say than a post."

He waved Richard to precede him. And the three of them climbed up again to the roof pavilion.

By this time, the suave Venetian evening had deepened. There was no moon as yet, but the stars grew momently brighter and more far-flung. An aromatic breath from the sea replaced the stagnant air of afternoon. The city lanterns, one of the glories of Venice in that age of relatively unlighted streets, spread a glimmering network through the darkness. And, here and there, music, the chief expression of the city, could be heard along the waterways, voices alone or in harmony blending with guitars and violins. The tones, dispersed through distance, did not assert themselves;

106

they were, rather, a muted vibration, faint as the scent of flowers. On the roof of the Palazzo Venier, one felt remote and yet not separated from the city, which awakened from the drowsiness of day to greet the night.

Supper, thanks to Anzoletta's resourcefulness, did not prove too meager. Afterwards Richard, afraid of outwearing his welcome, moved to leave and was more than happy to be persuaded to linger. They sat grouped about the doorway of the pavilion, the shadowy distance in front of them, Venier with his pipe, Anzoletta at one side. Maritza, seated on a cushion, sometimes leaned her head against her father's knees. Bapi, the puppy, now completely at home, lay curled next to her, his little eyes sleepily phosphorescent in the dusk.

"Did Father show you his librettos?" Maritza asked, when conversation once more involved the stage. "I think they're lovely. And the ballets! Sior Milòr! They would be ravishing."

Richard answered that he had seen and looked forward eagerly to reading the plays. He asked whether they had been brought to the attention of any opera director or composer.

"Oh, no," said Venier, releasing a careless puff of smoke into the night. "As I told you, they're rather personal. I don't want strangers thumbing over them. Of course they'd have to be adapted to music, cut here, rearranged there. It would be distasteful to me. Besides, I have no contact with the theater."

Anzoletta spoke from the shadows. "But isn't an opera libretto worth money, Sior Morandi?"

"Yes," Richard said. "Perhaps a hundred sequins. Well-known authors, like Metastasio or Goldoni, get that much."

"A hundred sequins!" breathed Anzoletta. "Cospettonaccio! Zelenza, did you hear that? We could live six months on a hundred sequins!"

"We can live as it is." Venier's voice sounded abrupt and at the same time uneasy, as one who knew from experience where this kind of talk would lead. "I won't go peddling my work, I won't expose what is sacred to me for money."

"But, Lustrissimo —"

"Anzoletta, we have a guest. Please —"

"I don't see what a guest has to do with it," she retorted. "We

107

don't pretend that we're well off. We couldn't pretend if we wanted to. The truth is we have just enough to keep us alive. That may do for people of our age, but what of Maritza? What of her future?"

"Che roba!" put in the girl. "Don't bother about me."

"I do bother. I shall continue to bother, since his Excellence is above such trifles. Here are two hundred sequins possible, a year's keep — not to mention what might be earned by writing other plays. But no, his Excellence won't peddle his work; it's too sacred to sell. He prefers to write poetry for himself."

"Please!" murmured Venier.

"No, Zelenza, let the truth be said while it's on my tongue. I think you're deceiving yourself with this sacredness. That's not the main point. Other great poets haven't been so squeamish. The fact is it's easier to live with books than take knocks from people; it's easier to write than sell; it's easier to think grand thoughts than do disagreeable jobs. But the time comes when everybody with a flat purse has to spit soft and swallow bitter, as the saying is. There! That's how I think, and you can call me impertinent if you wish."

The pause that usually attends outspokenness followed. Venier cleared his throat, sucked at his pipe, crossed and uncrossed his legs. Richard felt embarrassed for him, but at the same time he could see that Anzoletta had hit the mark.

"Spuar dolce, e inghiotir amaro — yes, a true saying," returned Venier after a moment. "And you're right about the rest of it, Anzoletta. How long has it been since I paid you your wages?"

Indignation sounded. "If your Excellence means that I was thinking of myself —"

"I meant nothing of the sort."

"Or that I serve this family for wages, it's time I returned to my village."

"Nonsense! Don't be so prickly. It's only that while I dream in my room, you and Maritza do the dull jobs that keep me from being a poor barnaboto living on state alms. You drudge and skimp for nothing —"

"Except love," snapped Anzoletta.

"And I permit it," Venier ran on. "I permit it. There's nobility! There's pride!"

108

"Oh, Jesus!" the other exclaimed. "I shouldn't have spoken. I didn't mean to hurt you, caro Lustrissimo benedetto. Think no more of it. I'm only a fool."

"No, you were right. . . ."

Remembering Richard's presence, he broke off, fingering his pipe. Maritza leaned her head back against his knees.

"Papà caro! What a fuss about nothing!"

He drew his hand back and forth over her hair. "Perhaps I could find a director," he said, "who would consent to read my librettos. But don't you see that I'm not the kind of man who could ever sell anything? It will be better to give up this house. There'll be something left over when the mortgage is paid. Only, where could we go . . ."

Meanwhile, an alluring idea had been developing in Richard's mind. He recalled that when he had last seen his stepfather, Vico Morandi, the latter had been in one of his black moods with regard to the coming opera season. There were some old favorites on the list; but the Venetian public craved novelty, and the composer-director had found no librettos to please him. Here, then, might be an opening. But if not, Richard, as Venier's agent, could peddle the librettos from theater to theater. He knew his way around in those circles and he had a ready tongue. Besides, he felt sure that he could count on Goldoni's influence. Naturally, everything depended on how good Venier's writing really was; but at least — and this was the compelling part of the idea — Maritza would know that he wanted to be of service.

So, interrupting at this point, he suggested the plan. He would consider it a great honor to be entrusted with the manuscripts. Of course he could not be certain of disposing of them.

A moment of rapt silence followed.

"You really mean that you would do this?" said Venier in a low voice. "You would be so kind? I call that the act of a true friend."

Maritza exulted. "You see, Sior Pa're! It won't be long now before all Venice is talking about you. Who can say that Bapi didn't bring us luck!"

And Anzoletta breathed a long-drawn "Siestu benedetto! . . . Two hundred sequins!"

The bear, Richard reflected, was being skinned before it was

caught. He knew what it took to squeeze money out of directors'
purses. But he kept these misgivings to himself. Maritza was already at the première of *Theseus* in the San Giangrisostomo. They
would be given a box. Anzoletta must buy herself a new dress.
Venier, happy at being left in peace as far as the plays were concerned, indulged in one more pipe. As long as dreams were in order,
Richard paid court with a new one of his own.

"And the ballet?" he put forward. "It would be wonderful,
madonna, if you would consent to dance. For every reason, it would
be an added attraction. You know how your mother the Siora
Venier designed it; you know all the figures. Isn't it the proper
occasion for you to make your debut? Suppose I sell the librettos,
would I be permitted to suggest this to whoever buys them?"

The response exceeded anything he could have hoped for. There
was a breathless pause. Maritza sat bolt upright. "Caro ti! *Would
you be permitted!*" She sprang to her feet, hands outstretched toward Venier. "Sior Pa're! I beg. Sior Pa're, you won't refuse . . ."

"Nonsense!" put in Anzoletta, but mildly, it seemed to Richard.

"Sior Pa're! You won't refuse, you *will* let me dance?"

"Yes," Venier answered at last. "Your mother would have wanted
it. How could I refuse?"

At once she was on his knees, her arms about his neck, her face
pressed to his. "Papà carissimo, I'm the happiest girl in Venice."
Then, standing up again, she hugged Anzoletta. "Oh, vecchia,
think, *think!* You'll dress me for the ballet. You'll stand in the
wings when I'm on stage. You'll watch me dance at the San
Giangrisostomo."

Finally she turned to Richard. "Sior Milòr, I can't tell you . . .
I can't thank you enough . . ."

For a moment, almost as if alone, they stood facing each other in
the vague light, the glimmering distance of the city around them.
She did not need to thank him; she would not have needed to speak
at all. Something more intimate than words passed between them,
something that each would always remember and that words or
even a touch would have diminished.

But the fear that attends too sanguine hopes already descended
on him. What now if he failed in regard to the librettos? After all,

110

the chance of success was not much more than slight. But, by God, he would not fail; he would not even think of failing. He would move heaven and earth rather than disappoint Maritza. No knight ever went out to do battle for his lady with a fiercer resolution than Richard felt about the sale of *Theseus* and *Oenone*.

However, Anzoletta helped him a little at that point. "Of course we're all grateful to Sior Morandi. But don't count birds in the bush, Maritzetta. Though I know —" her voice appealed to Richard — "that he'll do his best."

"You can be sure of that, siora."

"*Sior' Amia*," she corrected. "*Siora* isn't enough *now*."

XVI

VICO MORANDI, Richard's stepfather, belonged to the class of people who are vehement about everything. He had the sensitiveness of an artist, but he had also the build, vigor and appetites of a small black bull; so that life for him was a series of impulses usually tense and often explosive.

On this hot afternoon in his study, he felt explosive about the librettos that Richard had thrust on him several days ago and which he had neglected to read in spite of his stepson's pestering. He considered it a damned bore. Librettists in general were a vile race, and he expected nothing from Venier, though he was vaguely curious as to what the patrician husband of the once celebrated Austrian ballerina, Elena Klähr, had written. But, since it had to be, he at last smoothed out the manuscript of *Theseus* on his desk, drew up a chair, put on his spectacles, and, after a grunt or two, began reading.

At such moments, in spite of irritation, the best of him gradually came to the surface. He thought in terms of art. Scenes were visualized; characters lived. He could hear the recitative against the monotony of the continuo instruments. Aria cadences stirred vaguely in his mind. Also he read from three different angles: how the play affected him personally; how it fitted in with the singers and resources of his theater; how it would suit the public.

As might be expected, this poor Venier did not know much

about opera construction. There was his first soprano in a long recitative and aria practically at the beginning of the play, before the pit had settled down and while the loges were filling. What prima donna or leading castrate would submit to such an infliction? There were also nine characters in the piece instead of the customary seven. Well, that wasn't fatal . . . But here an important aria had been given to an inferior character, an infringement of their rights which would set off rebellion among the principal actors. Apparently, too, Venier did not know that the three leading singers must each have five arias: two in the first and second acts, and one in the third. He did not even know that two arias cantabile and two arias di portamento must not follow each other. And, glancing forward to the end, Morandi groaned. What a finale! No provision made to bring all the characters upon the stage; recitative where there should have been the chief airs; no scope allowed for a proper mingling of adagio, allegro, andante, amoroso, which must conclude the opera. Venier had followed dramatic and logical rules. But they were nonsense in a performance intended merely to display the talents of a group of singers. No, from the standpoint of conventional opera, *Theseus* would not do. Turning to *Oenone,* he found the same faults.

Morandi sighed and took snuff. He was sorry. The verses sang; the plots were gripping; the arias, which, according to the Metastasian model, summed up each foregoing scene, were fresh and lyrical. Venier was surely a poet, and the artist in Vico acknowledged this. It was likely, too, that the public would have been pleased. But Italian opera, at that point, existed not for the public, let alone for the composer or dramatist, but for the singers. Their whims, prestige, and rivalries, were the paramount consideration.

Morandi was more than sorry. He sat brooding about his servitude to foolish conventions and silly virtuosi, until, as usual, he caught fire. Why was he born in such an age! Why could he not have lived in the great days of Monteverdi and aristocratic music! Hell's fury blast the Neapolitan pimps who had sold out art to a set of fashionable castrates concerned only in showing off the range of their effeminate voices!

Well, there was nothing he could do about it. But today at least, he would give himself the treat of reading good poetry. Richard's praise of Venier's style was justified. Metastasio himself did not write better. Vico plunged again into *Theseus*.

But with him, reading of the kind easily transposed itself into music. For example, this lyric of Ariadne's:

> *Riposo dolce, pace innocente* . . .
> (Sweet repose, innocent peace,
> Happy the heart that holds you ever . . .)

deeply moved him. Tears crept into his eyes. At once a melody, tentative at first, then more assured, fitted itself to the words. His nostrils widened; his thin lips tensed. The music, growing louder in his mind, passed to his throat. He hummed a bar or two, nodded, stood up, and, taking *Theseus* with him, drifted over to the clavichord.

The melody now transferred itself to the instrument, took wings, developed variations in the da capo repetition, suggested the proper accompaniment. Already Vico was thinking in terms of his orchestra. He was thinking, too, of his leading castrate soprano, Serafini. By God, this was the aria for him! How he would fill his lungs and send those unnaturally high, thrilling, perfect tones through the house! Wait till Serafini heard this. He would clamor for it.

Aware from experience that melodies sometimes escaped unless written down, Vico reached for a pen and a blank sheet of paper beside the clavichord. But, dipping furiously, he found no ink in the well. Too intent to explode, he fetched ink from his desk, scribbled at top speed, broke one quill and snatched another. So! That tune would not get away from him. And, being now in fettle, he leafed rapidly through the libretto to another aria which had struck him. The melody for it flowed into his mind.

He had been suffering from an imaginative drought, but all at once this seemed to be over. The floodgates of music swung open. He could again create. Something in Venier's libretto had brought release to his inhibited faculties. Surely it ought to be possible to adapt this play somehow to the stage, rules or no rules.

But these were side thoughts. He was busy dashing down notes on paper or tinkling them out on the clavichord . . . D-flat; no,

B-flat, a diminished seventh . . . ta-ta-ta-tà . . . The goddess Minerva was descending on a cloud to right the wrongs of the heroine, Ariadne, and restore her to Theseus. She sang an aria di portamento of great dignity. It would be like this. Vico struck some chords and chanted: "*I bring from heaven the answer to your prayers* . . . Ecco là!"

"I hope you do, Babbo," said a quiet voice in front of him. "I hope you realize by now that *Theseus* and *Oenone* are the only possible operas for the coming season. It ought to be obvious."

And, looking up from the keyboard with a start, Vico found Richard, his elbows on the clavichord case, eying him across the music rack.

For an instant fury at the interruption sent the blood to Morandi's head and blazed in his eyes. But almost at once it faded out. He had affection for Richard, not unmingled with regard for the latter's theatrical talents. They were on easy, humorous terms with each other. Besides, Vico had reached the end of his vein for that time. So, he merely grinned and struck a final chord.

"It's a gruesome thing, fio mio," he complained, "to be faced with that black phiz of yours at the end of a hard day's work."

Richard filled a glass with red wine from a nearby carafe. "Here, drink this, Babbo, and you'll feel better."

Morandi tossed it off, held out the glass to be filled again, drank more slowly this time, and smacked his lips.

"Well, my boy," he remarked, "those librettos aren't bad." But remembering that Richard wanted to sell them to him and that praise on his part was poor tactics, he hedged at once. "Though of course they won't do for the stage. You know that."

Richard glanced meaningly at the scribbled pages of music on the rack.

"I'll admit," Vico hurried to explain, "that I found the verses good. They even suggested some airs which I've been jotting down for the pleasure of it. But, as operas for the San Giangrisostomo —" he smiled and shook his head — "they're very amateur."

Looking about for another wine glass and not finding one, Richard tipped the carafe to his lips, took a pull, and, swinging up a chair, sat down. He was just as unconcerned as Vico and an equally good bargainer. He could sense that his stepfather liked the librettos and that, after some passes, he would offer the least sum possible. But a small sum wouldn't do. He had recklessly mentioned two hundred sequins, the top price, to the Veniers, and he must come as near that figure as he could. To obtain such a price would take a miracle of persuasion.

"You mean, Babbo, that the Very Noble Antonio Venier hasn't dotted all the *i*'s and crossed all the *t*'s of your opera conventions. For instance . . ." Richard expertly ran through the list of technical defects that Morandi had noted. "And what of it? Any libretto has to be adapted. There's nothing in these that couldn't be tailored to fit by the average theater hack."

Vico looked doubtful. "I'm not so sure. It needs skill. I don't know offhand of anyone I could turn to."

"What about me?"

The other considered this and nodded. Richard had a facile pen and knew the requirements of opera. "Possibly — if you would."

"Well, I will. — So, then?"

"Tell me, fio mio, how much of a cut are you getting from Venier?"

"Twenty on the hundred," Richard lied promptly. To have told his stepfather that this was a labor of love would either not have been believed or would have led to too elaborate explanations.

Morandi stroked his chin. He let his expression gradually soften. At last he said: "My boy, really I don't want these librettos. But I'm fond of you; I'd like to do you a good turn. And perhaps, between us, we could do something worth while." He hesitated. "I'll tell you, figliolo. For your sake, I'm willing to pay fifty sequins for the two manuscripts. Fifty sequins. Your work thrown in, of course. That means ten whole sequins for you. A fat little sum. Almost picked up, you might call it. Well" — Vico rubbed his hands — "what do you say to that?"

The decks were now cleared, and action could start. Richard's craggy face showed appreciation.

"Very kind of you, Babbo, very kind. Unfortunately it's impossible, but I thank you."

"*Impossible?*"

"Yes. The Very Noble Antonio values his work at a much higher figure and, I think, properly. He demands two hundred se-

115

quins for the manuscripts and forbade me to sell them at a lower price. So, there you are."

"Two hundred sequins?" Morandi balled his fists and lowered his head. "Did you say *two hundred sequins?*"

"Yes, the usual price for a good libretto. Venier knows that; so do you; so do I."

"The price of a Metastasio! The price of a Goldoni! This fellow's unknown."

"No, he isn't, Babbo. You're wrong about that. Antonio Venier is more apt to fill a theater than either of them. Scandal of his marriage. Patrician who gave all for love. Two passionate plays by such an author. It won't take much to set the coffeehouses and coteries humming about him before the opera's put on."

Remembering Venier, Richard had the grace to wince secretly, as he talked. Nothing could be more offensive to that retiring gentleman than such promotion. But, thank God, with good management, he would never hear about it. And the plays had to be sold.

"Two hundred sequins!" Vico snorted again.

"And here's another point," Richard went on. "Consider the ballets. Designed by the Siora Elena Venier herself. The dancer who stirred all Venice when she became the wife of Antonio Venier! How that will add to the interest of the opera, when the report gets about!"

"You didn't tell me of the ballets," said Morandi.

"Didn't I? Well, so it is. But that isn't the best of it by a good deal."

He paused, smiling contentedly, and paused so long that Vico growled, "What do you mean?"

"I mean," said Richard, "that I've found a ballerina who would pack the theater if the opera offered no other attractions at all. She has consented to make her debut either in *Theseus* or *Oenone*. I'm speaking of Maritza Venier, daughter of the Siora Elena and of the Very Noble Antonio. I hope I don't need to point out what an appeal that will have."

Morandi knew the Venetian public well enough to see at once the value of such a sensation. It would revive and enhance the former scandal, but, except from the standpoint of the ultraconservatives, in no objectionable way. It was not seditious; the Council of

116

Ten would not ban it. Antonio Venier had paid for his folly. If his untitled daughter chose to become a ballerina, it was not illegal. The Venier clan and other patricians might frown, but they were also apt to be curious. The fashionable ladies of Venice, with their lovers and attendants, would be sentimentally thrilled. The middle classes, envious of their betters, would exult and flock to the theater. Finally, Vico remembered that his patron, Michele Grimani, proprietor of the San Giangrisostomo, had always spoken well of Venier. But two hundred sequins!

"Who has ever seen her dance?" the director grumbled.

"I have — at the Villa Bagnoli, and so did everybody there. She was splendid. Magnificent! Listen, Babbo. You'll have to admit that I know a dancer when I see one. I've seen the best. And you can take my word for it that Maria Torelli or Ancilla Campioni herself is no better. Besides . . ." He explained how Maritza's mother had trained her especially for these ballets. "So you see how it all fits in."

Morandi gave ground a little. "I'll admit that what you say puts a different light on it, Richard. But I can't go to anything like two hundred sequins. That's final. I'll give you a hundred — my last figure."

This was the crisis. Except at San Luca's, which specialized in comedy rather than opera, Richard had no such connection with the other theater directors as he had with his stepfather. If he declined to sell here, he might fail to sell anywhere, in spite of the waiting and wirepulling that would be involved. On the other hand, the scribbled notes on the music rack showed interest in the librettos. Besides, Richard had casually learned from his mother that Grimani had given Vico ample funds for any such purchase. It was not that the director lacked money, but that he intended to buy cheaply and to keep the difference for his own profit. But above all, what disappointment at the Palazzo Venier if Richard returned with only half of the expected price! Naturally a gambler, he decided to plunge now.

"No use, Babbo. My hands are tied. The illustrious author was very firm about the price. His dignity, he said, would not permit him to dispose of his work for less than the amount usually paid to Metastasio or Goldoni. I'm sorry. I was hoping that these two operas would be your masterpieces, that they might even bring

117

back the great days of the San Giangrisostomo. But I understand how it is. You have to economize, what with the new San Benedetto drawing the public. Still, a success would have been a feather in your cap if you move to Bordeaux."

Morandi frowned; his eyes smouldered. But it was true that the Grimani theater had lost its pre-eminence in the last two years. His own management hadn't been successful. The appointment at Bordeaux was a saving of face rather than a promotion. He was a talented but not a great composer or director, although he did not admit that. He had simply never been lucky. He needed a success at this point.

Richard tightened the screws. "So, I'll see what I can do at the San Benedetto. I think Galuppi will be interested."

The name of the famous composer, his dominant rival, overflowed Vico's cup. He sprang to his feet, kicked a chair, and demanded to know why everything musical in Venice had to be consigned to that everlasting mill. Galuppi! Galuppi! Galuppi! Were there no other musicians on earth?

"But, Babbo —"

"Hold your tongue!"

Vico flung over to the window and, leaning against one side of it, stood majestically with folded arms defying the injustice of life.

On an inspiration, Richard got up and began looking through the notations to *Theseus* on the music rack. He stopped at one point, stretched out his hand, and played the treble of a few bars.

"Beautiful, caro!" he admired. "Enchanting! Baldassare Galuppi couldn't do that."

"Ha!" growled Morandi.

In a low, pleasant voice, Richard sang:

> "*Riposo dolce, pace innocente,*
> *Felice il cuor . . .*"

"You can have the money," Vico shouted. "By God, it's well spent if I can keep those verses from being mauled by that tinkling jackass from Burano! There are two operas, at least, that Galuppi won't compose."

"Bravo!" Richard exclaimed. He strode across the room to em-

118

brace his stepfather. "Caro paregno! You couldn't do a wiser thing. These operas will crown your reputation. They'll immortalize you. They'll break Galuppi's heart. In the future, people will speak of you and Scarlatti, you and Porpora, you and Monteverdi."

It was a touching moment. Vico's eyes smarted; he blew his nose.

But after the right pause, Richard murmured, "When can I expect payment?"

"When you've finished the work of adaptation. Of course that's included in the price. As it is, you're getting forty sequins of easy money. How long will it take you?"

Richard did not cavil. He had done so much better than he could have expected that he was content to let the other get away with this little finesse.

"I'll start at once. Probably I'll need four or five days."

"Va bene. The desk is yours. I've an appointment now at the Caffè del Berizzi." Vico put on his wig and coat, took up his cane. He did not consider Richard more of a rascal than most people, but he judged it prudent to add: "Naturally, I'll expect Venier to sign a receipt for the money, as well as an understanding that the sale is void unless his daughter Maritza appears in the ballet."

"Naturally," agreed Richard, trying to keep his voice level. But when the door had closed, he gave a puff of satisfaction that fluttered the sheets of music on the rack.

The success was almost unbelievable. He stood picturing his return to the Palazzo Venier and could paint it in the brightest colors. So bright they were that he lost his head a little and, to the amazement of the Siora Binetti at her window across the court, he took a few dance steps here and there that looked very much like a jig.

XVII

DURING the next five days, Jeanne Morandi often shook her head and smiled, as Richard labored early and late over the Venier manuscripts. But she did not speak to him on the subject of the head-shakings or smiles. She had had her say on the evening of his return from the Brenta and must let it go at that. In the meantime, she brought him his meals and got him to bed, though with some difficulty, at a not too unreasonable hour. She even pretended to believe the fiction that the motive of his hard work was the commission to be paid by Venier. That made her smile as much as anything else.

On the evening of the twelfth day since his visit at the palace, Richard handed over the revised manuscripts to his stepfather. There were a few additional changes that Vico wanted; but, in high good humor, he paid out the two hundred sequins, drew up the papers to be signed by Venier and Maritza, and insisted on Richard's drinking a bottle of wine with him as a flourish.

The finishing touches on *Theseus* and *Oenone* took a part of the following morning. Richard was at work on them in his room, when Nana, the maid, wide-eyed and with a letter in her hand, flung open the door.

"A gondolier brought this," she gaped. "He's waiting outside for an answer. A tall old man . . ."

Gondoliers were the usual messengers in Venice, but Richard did not often receive messages. The zigzag, unformed handwriting of his address on the outside was unknown to him; the paper itself looked unusual, as if it had been a flyleaf taken from some book and not too skillfully folded. At a loss, he pried off the blob of wax with his fingernail and spread the sheet open. But glancing beyond the thicket of writing at the signature, he made out the initials M. V. It took him a puzzled moment before he identified them.

A letter from Maritza!

He could not read it with Nana staring at him. "Run along," he told her. "Say to the man I'll be out presently."

His eyes turned back to the page. The handwriting wavered, the spelling defied rules; but she wrote just as she talked, and he could hear the tone of her voice in every word.

"Caro Amico, I've never done such a thing as this in my life. It's very improper, but I don't care. If you knew how I've been waiting for a word from you about Father's librettos! The thought of dancing in one of the ballets is too exciting to ever come true; but I'd rather hear the worst than not hear anything. Twelve days! Surely it wouldn't take Sior Vico Morandi that long to read the manuscripts. I suppose he has and doesn't like them. I suppose you've taken them to some other director, and that you don't want to discourage us. But caro Milòr, (I just can't go on calling you *sior* all the time), don't be concerned about that. I want you to tell me frankly how matters stand. So, if this finds you home, will you please come with the messenger, Padron Zorzi Rosso, to his gondola, where I'm waiting. Padron Zorzi is Anzoletta's cousin and my old friend. I've seduced him to do this. Father and Anzoletta must never hear of it — especially not Anzoletta. Woe to me, if she did! But I couldn't wait any longer. La vostra buon amica. M. V."

Richard kissed the letter, then got to his feet a little dizzily and hurried into his waistcoat and coat. How much more thrilling and wonderful this was than the call he had pictured for that afternoon! To see Maritza alone! To tell her the great news before anyone else! To sit with her in the *felze* of a gondola, just the two of them together! By God! By God! . . . He stuffed the little canvas bag of sequins into one pocket, Maritza's contract into another, crossed over to the door, remembered that he hadn't brushed his hair, turned back to the mirror, headed again for the door, remembered his hat in time and caught it up. He was dressed in a nondescript old suit, but that didn't matter now. He sailed through the apartment, muttered vaguely about a business appointment to his mother in the salon, and dashed out to join Padron Zorzi on the stair landing.

Gondoliers have a sharp eye for people, especially if, like Zorzi Rosso, they have spent a long life in that calling. Zorzi had heard a good account of Richard from Anzoletta (in fact he knew all about the projected sale of the librettos) or he would never have let Maritza wheedle him into promoting such a rendezvous. As to anything that concerned his dear little Zelenza, Zorzi was respectability in person. But, for all that, he resolved to judge for himself. Richard might easily be one of those smooth rakes, of whom Zorzi had known plenty, who made an art of corrupting young girls under a show of good offices. But the short walk with Richard from the Morandi apartment to the Rio Crisostomo, where he had left his gondola, completely reassured him. Smooth rakes wore wigs; they would rather be seen dead than appear out

121

of doors in their own hair and with such a hat. Smooth rakes did not have an ink stain on the middle finger. They did not look so flurried and pleased, were not so coltish. It was lucky for Richard that he had not had time to dress.

"A good lad," thought Zorzi, warming up to his companion and hard put to keep up with him. "I hope your Worship has good news," he said confidentially, when they had gone half a block.

For a moment startled at the other's inside knowledge until he recalled the lines of Maritza's letter, Richard nodded. "The best. The very best, Padron. I was going to call this afternoon on his Excellence. But, you know, I think I'll pretend at first that it isn't so good, just for fun."

The man's eyes twinkled. "Benissimo! Makes it all the better afterwards. Fine! Will the little Siora dance? That's what she wants to hear."

"Yes. At the San Giangrisostomo, this carnival."

"Viva Dio!" exclaimed Zorzi. "*There's* one opera I wouldn't miss for a hundred doppias. I think her mother will come down from heaven to see it." Thawing entirely now, he clapped Richard on the shoulder. "Bravo!" And pointing, "There's the gondola."

They could see the top of it above the embankment near the bridge. Zorzi became at once the impersonal boatman and dropped back a pace behind Richard; but he exchanged nods with one of his colleagues, who had been asked to keep an eye on things while he was gone. Maritza could imagine herself on a breathless adventure; actually she was very much guarded and chaperoned.

The curtains of the little cabin were closed when Richard came up. But they were at once pushed aside, and Maritza in spite of all conventions stepped out. She wore the usual mask, of course, the usual black cloak or *bàuta*, and a little three-cornered black hat. In such circumstances as these, no Venetian girl of family would have appeared without them. The mask was respected in Venice when almost every other propriety had ceased to be respected. But a masked lady did not pop out from the cabin of her gondola, stand in full view, and eagerly hail her approaching cavalier.

"Ecco là! Bondì, Milòr. I was so afraid you weren't at home . . ." But she was scanning Richard's face; and, at the half-somber look which he contrived to put on, her voice fell away. She gave him her hand, drew back into the cabin, and sank down on the cushions.

"I suppose . . ." she faltered. "I'm afraid you haven't very good news . . ."

He seated himself next to her. "Well, madonna . . . ."

There was silence while Zorzi maneuvered the boat out into the canal. Her lips quivered below the mask. The sculling oar took up its rhythm.

"Then your stepfather didn't like them!"

"There were objections."

The morning sun lay full on the cabin. She exclaimed suddenly, "These hot things!" and tossed aside her hat, cloak, and mask. The disappointment in her eyes was already too much for Richard. His hand stole to the contract in his side pocket.

Zorzi, watchful of conventions, directed from the poop: "If the Siora unmasks, she must draw the curtains."

Richard carried out the order. It was a delicious, dizzy moment to be so close to her in the curtained space.

"And now," she went on, "you have taken them to someone else."

"Not yet. Perhaps . . ."

She leaned her head back and turned it away slightly. "Yes, of course. As I wrote you, it was too wonderful . . . I suppose things don't happen that way . . . not that easily. But one can't help . . . You see it would have made such a difference . . ." Her voice blurred. "Now I'm being silly."

She straightened up with a smile, then looked down startled at the sheet of paper on her knees.

"What's this, Milòr?"

Richard felt contrite. "I ought to have given it to you at once. This wasn't the time for an act. I suppose I just can't keep away from stage business. Please forgive me."

She was reading the paper. Her lips silently shaped the words. "Dio mio!" she breathed. "Dio mio! . . ."

He dropped the plump little bag of sequins into her lap.

"But, Milòr . . ."

"And here . . ." He handed her the receipt to be signed by her father.

Still dazed, she read half aloud: " 'I, Antonio Venier, hereby acknowledge to have received . . . it being understood that my daughter . . . in the ballet . . . that this clause is essential to

123

the sale . . .' " She drew her finger across her forehead. "But then
. . . but then!" The words rose in a crescendo. "It means —!" She
sat speechless a moment, gazing at him, her eyes dilated. "I think
you are the cruelest person! I think you're — Oh, Milòr, I *am* so
happy!" She read the contract again. "Me!" she whispered. "*Me!*
At the San Giangrisostomo!"

Springing up, she turned, flung the rear curtains aside and, half
leaning out, called to the stern: "Zorzi! Zorzi! It happened! Everything! The librettos! Me — a ballerina! At last! Zorzi! But you
mustn't breathe a word of it at home. I'll pretend to be just as
surprised as they are. Promise!"

The gondolier rose to the occasion. Suspending his stroke, he
waved his left hand in a flourish and abounded in joy, amazement
and benedictions.

"Please take us somewhere on the lagoon —" she went on, "towards the Lido. There's so much to talk over."

"Yes, and will the Siora either put on her mask or draw the curtains!"

Once more screened from curious eyes, Maritza settled herself on
the seat. "And now tell me everything, Milòr, just as it happened.
But no play-acting. I still think you're dreadfully cruel."

It cannot be said that Richard's account of his dealings with
Vico Morandi was strictly accurate. The inducements which had
led the director to pay the full price were left out. The campaign
to be launched in the coffeehouses, the value of scandal as an attraction to the public, did not have to be mentioned. To the
credit of Richard's modesty, if not of his candor, Maritza could believe that he had done nothing except prevail on Vico to read the
manuscripts. Afterwards everything had gone of itself. Even the
work of adaptation was barely touched on.

When they had finished with this, the absorbing plans for that
evening had to be discussed: how Anzoletta would first hear the
news; how she would then call Maritza, how the three of them
would proceed to Venier's study. And afterwards, perhaps, they
would celebrate by dining out somewhere — in one of the semipub-
lic gardens of the Giudecca or at Murano. And the menu. Sior
Pa're loved *polpettinò*; Anzoletta, roast sausages. Turbot was the
best fish in September. How strange it seemed to be rich! . . .

124

The gondola threaded the colorful shipping of the harbor, glided under the sharing figureheads of merchantmen, under the gilded sterns of mighty frigates. The shadows of them momently darkened the little cabin. A smell of tar, spices, and of Eastern cargoes, hung on the air. Now and then snatches of outlandish tongues reached them. And finally there was only the empty lagoon, bright in the morning haze, and the gentle lapping of water as they drifted with the tide.

But now Maritza, with the theater contract on her knees, felt the first pangs of stage fright. How could she ever face those tiers of boxes, that vast pit, the sea of faces, the critical, Argus-eyed public? She already felt weak in the knees. How would it be on that terrible evening, probably no more than three months off? Richard, comparatively an old hand, reassured her. Of course you were scared — you never entirely got over being scared — but once you were on the stage something happened. You found yourself doing twice as well as at rehearsals. The ballet master, Monsieur d'Aubry, would see to that.

Maritza was full of questions about Monsieur d'Aubry and about that season's troupe at the San Giangrisostomo. It was her first experience of theater gossip. She enjoyed the new terms, the slang, the professionalism.

Richard took care not to dampen her enthusiasm and described the San Giangrisostomo company in as favorable colors as possible. But, reviewing them name by name, he began to feel uncomfortable and even a little panicky. It dawned on him more and more that in trying to please Maritza he had done her perhaps the worst disservice possible. He did not mention the vulgarity, the jealousies, the morals, above all the defenselessness of theater women and especially of dancers; the thick, rank air of dressing rooms; the leering fops in attendance; the necessity and the cost of patronage; the dirty scandals. Some imp in his mind called up one detail of the sort after another. And there sat Maritza in her simple cotton dress, unsophisticated as a spring dawn, romanticizing the theater world! What would happen when the first damned roué . . . Richard turned hot and cold.

"What's wrong?" she asked. "You look troubled about something."

125

"Well," he hesitated, "it's a different kind of people from any you've known. A lot of things go on that you won't like. You've never been backstage, madonna. It's not the same as front, and you spend most of your time there. Perhaps you'll find it hard —" he paused for the right word — "a little coarse. You oughtn't to imagine it better than it is."

Impulsively her hand closed upon his a moment and set his heart racing. "Caro ti! Don't worry," she laughed. "I'm not made of porcelain. Most girls aren't, really. They only pretend. I suppose you think that because I've been brought up so much alone I don't know anything about life. Well, I do. Mamma was a ballerina — she told me how things are. Anzoletta doesn't mince words, either. No, I won't be shocked. And I can take care of myself. Marin Sagredo found that out, remember. If you don't like dirt, it's my belief that it won't hurt you."

Richard's hand still burned from the brief contact with hers. In the case of any other girl, this would have been an invitation. But instinctively he knew better than to so consider it.

"Besides," she was saying, "you'll be at San Luca's. It isn't far from the San Giangrisostomo. We'll meet often. You can advise me about things. San Luca has a ballet. Maybe sometime we'll even be in the same theater. Oh, Milòr! Caro! That would be wonderful! . . ."

Yes, he was not so poor at dreams that he had not long since pictured that — and a much more radiant sequel.

But now they talked about the coming season. She had never had more than glimpses of the carnival. Suppose they slipped away some night after the close of the theaters, mingled with the crowd on the Piazza, went to the Ridotto? She turned on the seat to face him, her eyes shining with excitement.

"Oh, magari! What fun! Is it a bargain?"

"Per Dio, a bargain!"

And then, for no reason at all, they fell silent. She flushed a little and looked down. He felt awkward but divinely happy. It was just a moment; it takes no longer than that to turn a page. When she raised her eyes, there was a new light in them — and doubtless in his, too, for she looked down again.

Zorzi Rosso warned from the stern that the Siora should be getting back if the errand she was supposed to be doing at a shop in the Calle dei Fabbri was not to be suspected at the palace. So, they retraced their way across the harbor. By the time they parted at the bridge on the Rio Crisostomo, the thought of the approaching evening absorbed them again. The precious papers and the bag of sequins were once more in Richard's pockets for the official surprise later. Maritza put on her cloak, hat, and mask; but she smiled "A rivederci" and let him hold her hand to his lips longer than farewell required. He returned to the apartment on wings. It was the happiest day of his life.

And, to crown it, a letter had arrived from Dr. Goldoni, who was still with the Widimans. No doubt it confirmed the San Luca appointment. Perhaps Richard would even learn what his opening role would be.

He broke the seal. "Listen, petite Maman," he said to Jeanne. "I'll read it to you." What a day this was! His eyes leaped down the page.

"Richard, has something happened?" she demanded. "Why don't you read it to me?"

But he was still gazing at the paper, his face drawn. Then, sitting down, he said, "Here, read it yourself."

In the silence, as she read, phrases of the letter mingled with his own thoughts.

". . . The Very Noble Marin Sagredo has made it clear to his Excellence Francesco Vendramin that if you appear at San Luca's or in any other theater of Venice, he will contrive such unpleasantness that the play must fail. And his Excellence does not dare . . ."

Yes, it was easy to hire disturbers in the unruly, restless playhouses. No management dared invite that kind of thing. Recourse to law to protect an insignificant actor against the House of Sagredo? Absurd!

". . . My dear boy, I believe the very noble gentleman will not stop at this. You should leave Venice at once. There are other cities in Italy . . ."

And Maritza? And the golden plans of an hour ago?

Jeanne replaced the letter on the table. "You must come with us to France."

But Maritza was in Venice. Any other place seemed impossible. Then he thought of the approaching evening and rallied. Nothing must spoil that.

He snapped his fingers and, springing up, embraced his mother. "Who cares about San Luca! I can do other things than act. It'll take more than Sagredo to get me out of Venice now. But isn't it funny?" He thought of the two letters that bracketed the morning. "Why does a man always have to keep his fingers crossed?"

XVIII

TO the average Venetian, the three months from early September till the end of autumn were simply a change of season. To Maritza Venier, glancing back, they seemed a decade. That morning with Richard on the lagoon, though unforgettable, looked immensely far off, like a point viewed through the big end of a telescope. It belonged almost to another life.

Why, at that time, she had not even met Monsieur d'Aubry, not to speak of a hundred others who were now her daily companions; had not worked in the ballet master's treadmill; had not been initiated into the patter and outlook of the dancing profession; had not coped with the spite of veteran ballerinas who saw a newcomer promoted to the leading part in the *Theseus* ballets. She felt much older, hard and worldly-wise as compared with the ingénue of September.

Of course she had started off with a big lead over the usual beginner. Naturally gifted, she had also been thoroughly trained by her mother. Monsieur d'Aubry could teach her little about the fundamentals of dancing. She began, too, with the prestige of her father's rank and her mother's professional fame. The kinswoman of patricians and the daughter of a celebrity like Elena Klähr had a very different rating from the ordinary little figurante. Then, too, there was Richard, who, as Vico Morandi's stepson, knew everybody backstage and could smooth the way for her. And there was Anzoletta, nicknamed the *Warship*, an unfailing chaperon and bodyguard. But more important than anything else, perhaps, was Maritza's own temperament, good-humored and natural. She was friendly but not intimate, played no favorites, did not flirt, indeed seemed indifferent to men, with the exception of Richard. Naturally enough it got around that there was a serious understanding between them; and this, premature as it was, blocked one form of jealousy.

So far, then, she had made a good start. Monsieur d'Aubry prophesied great things for her. "I warn you," he remarked to friends more than once, "that, barring accidents, she will be a great dancer. Yes, it would not astonish me if sometime you saw her —" he paused for effect and then expressed the ultimate — "as a première danseuse at the Opéra in Paris."

And meanwhile, Vico Morandi, with the speed that marked composition at that time, had finished the music for *Theseus*. Giovanna Casatti would sing Ariadne; Serafini, of course, had the title role. The ballets designed long ago by Maritza's mother had been similarly set to music and rehearsed. Gossip, not altogether spontaneous, predicted success, revived the romantic scandal of Venier's marriage, puffed Maritza, whetted the curiosity of the public in salon and coffeehouse.

Anonymous sonnets, celebrating Maritza in the fashion of the day, were printed and circulated. They were not too bad to have been written by various prominent people, and guesses at their authorship ranged from very noble patricians to very clever abbés. Richard, who turned them out at dead of night, took good care to be unidentified with them. As advance publicity for Maritza, they would have had no point unless fashionable names could be tagged to them. Among others, that of the Cavaliere Tromba, now elegantly installed at the Grimani palace, became prominent. Since unmistakable allusions to the Villa Bagnoli appeared in the sonnets, since people remembered that he had danced with her there, and since more than once he had been present at the ballet rehearsals, his authorship seemed not unlikely. That he denied it meant nothing; denial was to be expected.

Of course, by one hand or another, the leaflets reached Maritza. They were in good taste, hinted at nothing personal, expressed only admiration for her dancing, and hailed the new Terpsichore of Venice, attended by Fame, Fortune and the Graces. At first she made fun of them a little, but was immensely pleased.

129

"Richard, do you swear," she would say, "that you don't know who writes these things?"

"Of course I swear."

"So, you don't know who it is? Word of honor? Because the first one I thought of was you."

"Good God!" he exclaimed, resisting the temptation to confess. "If I wrote about you, madonna, I'd try to be original at least. I'd leave out the gods and nymphs — all that old ballast."

She colored a little at the expression in his eyes and changed the subject. "What I wonder at is all this to-do about Father and me. They tell me we're even talked of in the coffeehouses. How does it happen?"

Richard could have told her a good deal. Ripples of interest, launched in various quarters, had built up a wave of expectation that would fill the theater on the opening night of *Theseus*.

"It's the pride of the city in itself," he explained. "A Venetian author, composer and ballerina. The name *Venier* has a good deal to do with it. People love to talk. And a good thing, too, for the success of the opera."

She sighed. "I suppose you're right. I've been learning here at the San Giangrisostomo that the success of art has little to do with art."

But this was before she heard the gossip that linked the sonnets with Marcello Tromba. She faced Richard with it in her dressing room after a rehearsal. They were momentarily alone, since Anzoletta, who had had several clashes with prowling gentlemen, stood guard outside the door.

"I won't have it," Maritza said. "I don't want my name connected with him."

Richard had seen a good deal of Tromba since the latter's arrival in Venice from the mainland. Balked of employment at San Luca's and for the time being at loose ends, he found the Cavaliere's patronage flattering and agreeable. It gave a sense of security to have such backing against the continued threat of Sagredo. Besides, he was fascinated by the arts — legerdemain, ventriloquy, and magic — to which Tromba, an adept in the whole field of deception, was playfully introducing him as a gifted and diligent pupil. It delighted Richard to exhibit each new accomplishment at the Palazzo Venier.

130

"I give you my word that his Excellence did not write a line of those sonnets."

"How do you know?"

"I asked him about it," Richard invented. "There'd be no point of his lying to me. You can't prevent gossip. But what's wrong? I can't think of a single name in Venice that would be more flattering to you. He's the lion of the season. There isn't a gentildonna in town who wouldn't be charmed if he wrote verses about her."

"Here's one," Maritza put in firmly.

"But why?"

"You know very well. You know what his reputation is. The Great Gallant. I heard enough of that at the Villa Bagnoli. The kind of man who never thinks of a woman except in one way. I could feel it when I danced with him and when you've brought him here to the theater. Rating us all through that French lorgnette, like an expert at a sale. Mention a girl in connection with him, and people wink. That's what makes me angry about this. Isn't there something we can do?"

He shrugged. "Deny it of course. But there's no offense in the poems. My word! They're correct and distant enough. Meanwhile, it's a stroke of luck that people think Tromba wrote them. It puts you in the fashion. It's just the right cachet for a ballerina at her debut."

"You mean it's the right cachet to be considered the choice of a popular rake?"

"If you're not his choice," Richard flushed, "and don't intend to be, what's the harm? It makes you interesting to the public; it brings people to the theater."

She faced him, square as a rock, "I think that's cheap."

"Listen, cara," he said, a little ruffled. "You've chosen the career of dancing. You want success. That means winning the public, making it love *you*, not just your dancing. And people don't love prudes. It's the same in opera or drama. The stage is the stage. Perhaps anything that caters to the public has to be a little cheap. It's the way the world is."

Maritza retorted: "Says Count Roberto? I thought we had shelved him, Milòr, but he seems to be with us again. I'm not a prude because I don't want people connecting me with Marcello Tromba. It's simply that I hate sham and do have scruples. Of

131

course a girl oughtn't to go on the stage if she wants the reputation of a nun. Nuns don't do entrechats and show off their figures. But a girl doesn't have to be a scheming little timeserver, either."

"Doesn't she?" put in Richard. "Up to a point, she does."

"What point?"

He found no ready answer to that. The argument was carrying them afield, as arguments do.

"Look," she went on, "if I succeed, it won't be thanks to people like Marcello Tromba. I'll please the public — yes; but I won't have any other patron. Would you like to wager?"

"Of course not. I hope you won't." It was a gallant boast; he loved her for it. She would not need a patron, he thought, because she would marry him. Otherwise, the idea of a ballerina, independent of husband or influential lover, making her way in the corrupt theaters of the time, was sadly ridiculous. His mother could have told her a good deal about that. He could not help quoting a little stiffly: "Just the same, madonna, you may find it hard to live with wolves if you won't run with the pack."

They left it there, each a trifle out of tune with the other, each aware of an obscure antagonism and disturbed because of it. Later, they made up, of course; or, rather, because the issue between them was so indefinable, they pretended that there was none. And yet, for some reason, this particular disagreement, like a pebble in one's shoe, kept on nagging; and they seemed unable to escape it.

But such things were trifles compared with the awesome approach of that towering event scheduled for late November: the first night of *Theseus* at the San Giangrisostomo. For Maritza, everything referred to it — the fading summer; the rains and chill of autumn; fire on the hearth; warmer clothes; the bells of All Saints'; the more frequent masks on street or piazza, forerunners of carnival — everything marked the passing of time toward that evening of crisis. She felt eager but more often terrified. And terror grew, as the days dwindled to a fortnight, then to a week, then to only a day.

XIX

IN an orchestra stall which his valet had been holding for him, Signor Mario Caretti, newly arrived in Venice, savored the splendor of the San Giangrisostomo theater. Here, he proudly reflected, was a fitting temple for music; and here, as he looked around at the gathering audience, was a musically civilized public — how different from the stodgy Britons and tone-deaf Frenchmen, among whom, of late years, his lot had been cast! He foresaw a delightful evening and happily polished the glasses of his lorgnette. Even the thought that he would soon be returning to London did not depress him at the moment. He had still a couple of weeks and would make the most of them.

A diplomatic representative of the King of Sardinia and condemned to long periods of residence abroad in the cold northern capitals, Caretti passionately enjoyed his brief recalls to the music and color of Italy. Business at the court in Turin never detained him too long. He always managed a round of pleasant pilgrimages to other centers, to the opera in Parma or Milan, to the theaters of Florence and Bologna (once even to Naples), where he relieved his pent-up hunger for Italian music and Italian acting. In this roving banquet, he always kept Venice for dessert, a final enchantment and satiety, to tide him over another stretch of exile. In Venice there were seven great theaters; there was opera every night during the season; there was symphony of instruments and voices at St. Mark's and other churches, at the four musically renowned conservatories for young girls, not to mention the numberless private accademias.

But this round of pleasure was not altogether self-indulgent. For diplomatic and personal reasons, Caretti gladly combined it with small services. If Lord So-and-So in London desired a capital piece of Italian painting for his new house, if Lady Such-and-Such yearned for Venetian glass or Parma perfume or Florentine majolica, Signor Caretti did his best to oblige them. He hoped, during the present round, to accommodate his ingenious friend Mr. Garrick, manager of Drury Lane Theatre. The latter had earnestly begged him to keep an eye open for possible talent to meet the English demand for new faces and voices in Italian opera and had commissioned him to act in his interest.

Thus far, Caretti had found no one who, if free, had promise enough to meet Garrick's requirements. But Venice was a rich field. He had heard good things of tonight's singers, Giovanna Casatti and the male soprano Serafini. Perhaps he would have luck tonight. The thought added to his sense of expectation.

Standing up, his glasses poised, he surveyed the expanse of the theater. It was one of the largest, containing well over fifteen hundred people. Five tiers of boxes rose above the orchestra to the shadowy ceiling. They were richly gilded, and inset medallions at regular intervals gave another touch of magnificence. The interior, as a whole, looked vague because of the meager lighting common to all Italian playhouses of the time; but individual loges stood out sharply in the gloom, bright with their own candles, displaying a group at cards or taking refreshments. Scattered here and there at various levels in the obscurity of the house, these vivid glimpses seemed to hover like images cast by a magic lantern. And since, by custom, nearly everyone in the boxes wore cloak and mask, each separate group looked weird and unearthly.

Having gazed enough, Signor Caretti sat down, ready for the overture. An attendant applied his taper to the footlights. The orchestra leader entered, took his place at the harpsichord, nodded to the musicians, and the first movement began.

An opera lover of even the next century would have been amazed, bewildered, and more than a little offended by the musical drama which the audience that night considered in perfect taste.

Caretti found the costuming admirable. Theseus appeared in a feather-duster helmet, curled wig, brocaded doublet, silk stockings and flowing mantle. Ariadne, garbed in the latest fashion, wore a train so heavy that it had to be carried at all times by two little blackamoor page boys. The other mythological characters showed a like hodgepodge of fancy and Parisian styles.

As for the music, the singers of course entirely eclipsed the composer and orchestra, let alone the librettist. The handsome verses over which Venier had toiled served merely as a thread of recitative on which to string arias. And the longer these lasted, the better. In the libretto, which Caretti consulted by the light of a penny taper purchased at the entrance, the action covered most of the

134

space; but, in point of time, the arias at the end of each scene took four times as long. They were the vocal gymnastics which the audience most wanted to hear. They re-created and covered up Morandi's original melodies with improvised coloratura, with shakes and runs so prolonged that the orchestra could lean back and take snuff, when it did not hover in the background with a haphazard accompaniment. And the effeminate voice of the castrate Serafini, supple and powerful beyond the reach of any tenor in the future, outsoared the highest notes of Signora Casatti and brought down the house. And other, less eminent, singers had their chance at an aria. Occasional duets, but never a chorus, varied the concert. Meanwhile, of course, wonders took place on the stage. Lightning flashed; thunder pealed; demons rose from the underworld; gods floated down from Olympus; Medea made a grand impression in her dragon chariot; and the scene shifted in every direction. Finally, with Theseus and Ariadne in the depths of despair, attended by a climax of arias, the first act closed amid flattering applause.

So far, Caretti decided, the opera could be termed a moderate success worth several repetitions. Realistically, however, he did not consider it better than average. Morandi was not the equal of Hasse; Venier did not excel Metastasio. As for the singers, Caretti, with his friend Mr. Garrick in mind, found them capable but mediocre — certainly not worth the salaries paid in England, nor worth presenting to a public that still recalled the peerless Faustina and Farinelli. No, he would have to look further.

And now came the ballet, as an intermezzo between acts. It would doubtless be a leaden affair and much worse in its kind than the opera — indeed contemptible to anyone who had seen ballet in Paris. For, prejudiced as Caretti might be in favor of Italy, he had to admit that Italian dancing could not hold a candle to the French. So, leaning back at this point, he exchanged remarks with a neighbor and then, as the curtains once more parted, sat picking his teeth.

In keeping with the nature of the opera, it was supposed to be a dance of nymphs and shepherds; but the nymphs, of course, were modishly dressed young belles, and the shepherds wore costumes to be envied by the gallants in the boxes. The object was not only to entertain but to furnish a pattern of graceful dancing, which could

135

be imitated, if never equaled, by the amateurs in the audience. Passepieds, gavottes, allemandes, minuets, furlanas. tambourins, and chaconnes, would follow each other. If, here and there, entrechats and pirouettes were introduced, they would serve merely as garnish. The dresses of the ballerinas, made of flowered silk, damask, or brocade, would inspire imitation as well as their steps. Skirts were little shorter than those worn at a ball or fiesta. And yet the gentlemen's opera glasses did not go unrewarded by neat ankles, décolleté charms, and now and then even by a shattering glimpse of lovely calves.

Unaware of Monsieur d'Aubry's work, Caretti noted with surprise that the ballet of the San Giangrisostomo had improved since his last visit a couple of years ago. It was still provincial by Parisian standards; but it actually looked French and was not unpleasing. He lifted his lorgnette for a closer view.

Then, as the others drew back, leaving the prima ballerina alone at the center of the stage for a pas seul, Caretti's eyes opened and his lorgnette became rigid. During the rest of the ballet he did not lower it again.

One of life's sudden events faced him, though at the moment he was too absorbed to realize it. He found this girl simply delicious to look at, and he could not look at anyone else.

She seemed so fresh and young, so vibrant, as she stood poised a moment on the threshold of her dance. Perhaps a little frightened, but if so, the more appealing. Caretti felt a pang of personal suspense. Then she relaxed to the music, like a swallow upon the air, and he forgot concern in artistic enjoyment. He had seen the great Camargo on the Parisian stage before her retirement six years earlier. The thought of her now came vividly to his mind. Here was the same sparkle and lightness, the same mysterious projection of personality across the footlights to enamor an audience and to infuse it with a spirit of gaiety. But Marie-Anne de Camargo had been relatively old when he had seen her; this girl was young, and youth gave her its special aura. Yes, she pleased him infinitely — infinitely. He took an odd pride in the applause that now burst out increasingly through the theater, as if confirming his opinion of her; but he felt, too, an obscure jealousy that she had so many admirers. Spontaneous *bravas* and *benissimos* spread like wildfire.

She finished the tambourin she was dancing, with a flicker of entrechats. But the orchestra leader, sensing the will of the audience, signaled an encore. And now, caught up by the applause, she danced like the spirit of carnival itself, showing her gratitude to the public with an unfeigned happiness that endeared her all the more, imparting to everyone her own delight. And the house answered with a roar of admiration, fell completely in love with her, replied to her deep curtsy, as the dance once more ended, with a fervent tossing of kisses, salvos of clapping, an immense rumble of *evvivas*. Thenceforth, even in the composite figures of the ballet, all eyes were on her. And, at the end, one united voice called her before the curtain.

Viva Maritza Venier! Siestu benedetta! . . . Benedetto el pare che t'ha fatta!

"There," exclaimed Caretti's neighbor, when the ovation had died down, "is a twenty-four carat ballerina. I don't believe that the Campioni herself ever had more applause. It's a feather in our caps, sir, to have been present at her debut — something to talk about, eh?"

"Indeed," Caretti murmured vacantly. "Yes, to be sure."

The other ran on: "She's certainly robbed her father tonight of his laurels. — Though I'll wager he doesn't mind. There he is up yonder in that loge. Looks pleased, doesn't he? — It's a good opera — yes, a worthy opera. But the ballet — that, sir, was straordinarissimo, maravigliosissimo . . ." He piled on superlatives. "Am I right?"

"Entirely," Caretti agreed.

He did not want to lose the vision he had had by gossiping. He wanted to lean back in the semidarkness and let the rose-clad figure of the girl go dancing through his thoughts. What witchery of gesture! What perfection of movement! The radiance of her smile! The expressiveness of her hands! She had worn a little coronal of pale rose that matched her dress — and her youth.

He was middle-aged, a man of forty, a bachelor, and a very correct diplomat. Thus far, his career and dilletante passion for the arts had left only a small and casual place for women in his life. But now, from some unsuspected depths in himself, rose the ferment of spring, a new or at least a forgotten sensation. It restored briefly the climate of twenty-one.

The opera had resumed. The lungs of Signora Casatti vied with

137

the lungs of Pietro Serafini. Kings, queens, and heroes sang arias. Invisible machinists pulled ropes. It all passed unnoticed by the diplomat from Turin, who was lost in dreams. He returned to Venice only when the opera closed with a grand finale in the form of a ballet. And as Theseus and Ariadne, happily reunited, witnessed the dancing of their joyful subjects — a graceful minuet, a romping allemande, a sprightly chaconne — they shared the storm of applause that greeted Maritza's final pas seul and could imagine, if they pleased, that the tribute was for them.

"Questa! Questa!" shouted the public, demanding a repetition when, according to custom, the title of another opera was announced for next time. "Give us the same!" And, "Viva Maritza Venier!"

But Mario Caretti did not wait. He was already shouldering his way out and around to the stage door, where a tip would give him access to the coulisses. Even so, there were others in front of him and at his heels, a throng of young dandies, who unmasked to pay court to the new divinity. With practised assurance, he made his way forward to where she stood, the radiant center of a jubilating group, including her father and a broad-shouldered peasant woman. Caretti knew that she would soon be whisked off to celebrate the triumph of the opera somewhere. But he did not intend to forgo a few words.

She kept curtsying to compliments, shy and a little overwhelmed, but her smile was adorable. "Serva," she murmured "Grazie, sior . . . your servant . . . your servant . . ." Applause still continued far off beyond the curtain.

Then, at last.

"Mario Caretti," he bowed. "An ambassador from London to the most exquisite dancer I have ever seen. The great Mr. Garrick of Drury Lane presents his homage to Maritza Venier and the offer of a most flattering engagement. If I could wait on you tomorrow . . ."

Confused, she did not understand. "London? Mistair Garreek? Of course . . . if you wish . . . tomorrow . . ."

A dark young gentleman, whom she greeted excitedly as Milòr, now pushed in front of Caretti.

But tomorrow . . .

Yes, thought the gentleman from Turin, making his way out of the theater, Garrick could congratulate himself. A salary twice the size of any Maritza could hope for in Italy would be a bargain from the standpoint of London. And certainly she would not refuse such an offer, with the prestige connected with it.

But actually Garrick was only a front for Mario Caretti himself. He imagined next year and found London transformed. Intimate pictures hovered in his mind. Himself as her benefactor. Himself with the privilege of her dressing room at Drury Lane. Himself with Maritza at Ranelagh or at Richmond on the Thames, when spring in England brought back lilacs and blue skies. Himself . . .

X X

ST. STEPHEN'S Day, that marked the official opening of the carnival, had come and gone. And now the season when Venice lived most intensely was well past the middle of its course, quickening in tempo towards the climax of Shrove Tuesday. The public gaming rooms of the Ridotto grew more packed; the gold on its tables multiplied. The private *casini*, those jaunty little rendezvous of wealth and fashion, so much less formal than the great palaces, hummed with guests of prodigal hosts. Costumes and masks and mountebanks thronged the streets. The two hundred cafés of the city functioned day and night; its theaters and inns reaped the annual harvest; its two hundred thousand population went more or less mad. It was the season of folly and, therefore, welcome to those who exploited folly. Among them, Marcello Tromba made the most of it, both as to pleasure and profit.

Reviewing his sojourn thus far in Venice and on the mainland, Tromba had every reason to be content. He had been lucky in love and at cards; had contracted valuable friendships; had founded two separate lodges of the occult Masonic order which he was promoting; and, in this connection, had called up phantoms of the dead, practised the Cabala and given startling proof of supernatural powers — all for big fees. Now, as the trusted adviser and almost the adopted son of rich, old, doting Senator Grimani, he blazed in the forefront of the beau monde, had an apartment in the Grimani palace, a gondola of his own, a *casino* near the Piazza, and the handsomest mistress in Venice. Though people still called him Cavaliere, it was well understood that this was only the screen of a much greater foreign title, one of the most exalted in fact, which reasons of state and a point of honor required him to conceal. Speculations about it ranged from grand duke to royalty itself. Tromba fed the rumors with an expressive silence.

As a result of all this, though he spent much, he saved a good deal and laid out his money in letters of credit. He was prepared for instant departure. He knew from experience that good fortune did not last and could turn sour overnight. He knew also that the spies of the state would be on his traces, no matter how secretly he maneuvered. The heirs of Senator Grimani were bitter and alert. The dry realists of the Council of Ten cared nothing for mysterious titles or mystical powers; but they viewed with interest some proposals which Tromba had made for a new kind of state lottery, and would perhaps overlook his other activities for a while.

However, he had a sharp nose for danger. Thus far, though he kept sniffing the wind, he detected nothing too ominous. Probably he could stay out the carnival. But in case of an emergency, his plans were made. He knew all the exits from the palace. A gondola with two good oarsmen awaited him day and night in one of the obscure canals. Swift horses were stabled for him at Mestre. He had dispatched his more prized belongings there. And beyond Mestre, beyond the Austrian frontier, he looked toward England, his next venture.

It was in this connection that he found it worth while to spend so much time on Richard. For he had spent time, too, with John Murray, the British Resident in Venice, pumping for information about Lord Marny; and the more he considered this approach to his operations in England the better he liked it. So, he kept dangling the bait in front of Richard, convinced that he would soon hook his fish. It had to be soon or never.

"Magnificent, my dear boy!" he exclaimed one late morning in his apartment at the Grimani palace, when Richard, for the fun of it, had been running through some of the parlor tricks which he had learned from his patron.

The reason that Tromba had taught them was twofold. They

140

amused his pupil, and amusement fosters liking in return. But, with a really profound insight worthy of better uses, Tromba felt that tricks of the sort might gradually, under his guidance, condition Richard's mind to other more profitable tricks. It stirs a man's vanity to fool people, and vanity has a big appetite. Between parlor magic and the art of deception on a grander scale, the transition was logical, when a few childish scruples had been eased out of the way. En route to England and upon arriving there, Tromba did not want a companion with a queasy conscience.

"Magnificent, my dear boy! Your hand work is flawless. I know what you're doing and have a quick eye, but dammy if I could catch a single movement. As to the patter — superb! Though that's natural with an actor like you. It's a good stroke, your mixing in ventriloquism with the different tricks. Surprises an audience to the point where you could steal the coats off their backs. I'm delighted with you."

Delighted himself at the praise, for Tromba was an honest critic, Richard tossed a final disappearing coin into the air and shook his head. However, he had reason for pride. In addition to the usual card sleight of hand, he had mastered other tricks involving watches, dice, coins and handkerchiefs. He had learned the use of invisible inks; had a firm grasp of the optical delusions produced by mirrors or by magic lanterns, whereby Tromba performed some of his wonders. He had shown great aptitude for ventriloquism. Above all — and here his acting served him — he had acquired the magician's manner, the knack of diverting attention and of faintly hypnotizing an audience.

"I'm glad you're pleased, Maestro."

"Yes," the Cavaliere nodded, "and, for that reason, I'm all the more horrified that a man of your parts and your cleverness should be so lacking in common sense."

"As how?"

Richard expected another plea in favor of England. But Tromba this time approached the subject from a different angle.

"Oh, every way. For example, that you haven't so far condescended to take my advice in regard to a fencing master. What with your reach, eye, and quickness, you would have been well along by this time and a match for most people. As it is, you're simply trusting to luck. Do you think that the noble Marin Sagredo will be satisfied with shutting you out from the Venetian stage?"

"He's had plenty of time, if he intended anything more. I've passed him once or twice on the street. He didn't seem to remember me."

"Wait," smiled Tromba.

A knife appeared suddenly in Richard's hand, so suddenly that it seemed to have materialized out of nothing.

"I *am* waiting."

"Don't show off," snapped the other. "That's a proof of what I mean. You're too clever to be such a fool. If you knew how to use a sword, you could defend yourself like a gentleman. If anyone got hurt, you'd still have a case. But use that thing, and you'd have none at all. There's no one who could put in a good word for you. Do I make myself plain?"

Richard balanced the knife across his forefinger. "Why expect the worst, your Signory?"

"*Why?*" Tromba repeated. "Because I know human nature. It's my favorite crystal ball. And I can foretell, just as certainly as tomorrow's sun, what Marin Sagredo will do when I leave Venice. Indeed, he would have already done it, if I had not let drop in certain quarters that he would be required to settle with me personally for any attack on you."

Richard moodily still balanced the knife. "What do you think he'll do?"

"Oh, he's famous for his jokes. They're not very subtle. You might or might not survive one. He always has a pack of toadies with him."

"Well, then, against numbers, how would a sword be better than a knife?"

"Aside from the reason I've given you," returned Tromba, "which relates to the law, a good swordsman can hold people at arm's length and gain time. A knife means close quarters, and there you're lost if you have two or three against you."

Without sleight of hand this time, Richard returned the dagger to its sheath inside his coat.

"I think you're trying to scare me, Zelenza."

Tromba said impatiently: "There's no need for heroics. I know you have pluck enough. I'm talking about common sense. Don Quixote is no hero of mine. What will you do when I leave Venice? Kill Sagredo, perhaps? And then what? Whereas you have an obvious career open to you by coming with me — though I'm perfectly frank in telling you why I'm interested."

So, they were back to the crux again, with one more valid argument pointing to England.

"Besides," added Tromba, slipping another fly on the hook, "does Maritza Venier in London mean nothing to you? I should think that would be tempting enough by itself."

He was justified in considering this the decisive trump. It startled him when Richard shook his head.

"She's not going to London."

"What do you mean?"

"I mean she declined Caretti's offer. She's on contract next year at the San Giangrisostomo. Her father doesn't want to leave Venice, and she wouldn't leave without him."

Tromba's black eyes bulged. "Name of heaven! After the success she had! Turn down three times the biggest salary she could ever hope for here! Turn down the chance of a lifetime! Her father must be mad. He ought to take her to London with him. She'd make a comfortable living for both of them. There's no future in Venice. By God, what a selfish old fellow! If I were she —"

He broke off to consider an idea that suddenly occurred to him, while Richard, not for the first time, chose to drop the subject of the Veniers. For all his cleverness, Tromba could never understand them.

"My dear boy," the Cavaliere went on after a pause, "Have you no imagination? Don't you see what an opportunity this offers you?"

"Opportunity?"

"Yes. A golden opportunity to show your manhood and devotion. Am I wrong in believing that you love this girl? Will you permit her to let such a piece of good fortune slip by because her father chooses to rot on here in his tumble-down palace? Of course you will not. This is the turning point of her career; her future depends on it. Only you can help her."

"Honestly," Richard put in, "I have no idea what your Excellence is talking about."

The Neapolitan vivacity which Tromba usually had well under control boiled up at this point. "Good God! Do I have to show you the nose on your face? Why, take her with us to England. Get her away from that old codger. Believe me, a little proper urging is all she needs."

Richard shrugged. There was no use explaining colors to a blind man. The values in life that Maritza and her father entertained had no existence for Tromba except to laugh at.

Tromba mimicked the shrug. "Well, if that's the only answer you have, God pity you!"

"What do you mean by *proper urging?*" asked Richard in order to say something.

"What do I mean? How often have I pointed out to you that your dangling, romantic attitude toward a lusty, spirited girl like Maritza Venier is an insult to her and a disgrace to you! Girls are all the same. They long and don't dare; they're hungry but can't show it. It's the duty and pleasure of men to bring them out. The way you act, one would think you're a virgin yourself. Why, by now she ought to be in the palm of your hand and go to England with you as a matter of course. But it's not too late. You're showing her the carnival tonight. Make the most of it. That's the *proper urging.*"

"In brief," said Richard stiffly, "you mean seduce her?"

"Lord!" exclaimed Tromba. "What an ugly word for beatitude. Call it rather a jaunt in Paradise." He broke off with a stare. "My dear boy! Have I said anything to offend you?"

Richard felt ashamed at his own pique. After all, Tromba merely expressed the fashionable point of view, and he had expressed it before. But this time the calculating ruthlessness of it, as applied to Maritza, seemed a profanation. Richard's dark face turned a shade darker.

"It happens," he said, "that I have a peculiar respect for Maritza Venier and don't choose to discuss her in those terms, that's all." To defend himself against the aspersion of being a ninny, he added: "I've jaunted enough, as your Signory puts it; but she and I are on a different footing. There's such a thing as honor."

144

"I believe there is," agreed Tromba, with a sudden frost in his voice. "And I believe that no one has found it healthy to challenge mine. So I don't know that it's necessary for a young man to remind me of it." He let a few seconds pass. Then his expression changed, like that of a doctor with a testy patient. "But we won't quarrel, Milòr. Have it your own way and dangle on, if that's what you like. Nay, more, I'll even apologize to you on one condition."

"No need," Richard disclaimed. "I only wanted —"

"Ah, but there is," the Cavaliere insisted, "if I've unwittingly stepped on your chaste toes. Be the judge, but be frank. Tell me honestly if what I have just suggested for your happiness hasn't occurred to you, too, not once but often during the past months. If it hasn't, I most humbly beg your pardon. Well?"

"Well?" he repeated.

"If you mean I'm not a saint," Richard floundered, "of course I'm not. One can't help thoughts. One can't help — you know, Zelenza. But between thinking and doing —"

"No, my friend," Tromba interrupted. "The highest authority's against you there. Perhaps you've read that he who lusts after a woman in his heart has already — eh? And because I put into words what you turn over in your mind, you talk to me about honor. Pshaw! — Look, caro. Be a hypocrite as much as you please, if it serves your purpose. But never be a hypocrite with yourself."

"I didn't intend to be. I meant —"

"Yes, yes. I understand. Let's drop it." Tromba fished in the pocket of his waistcoat and drew out a small object which he tossed across the table. "There you are. Catch."

It was a bronze key. Richard looked at it, puzzled.

"To the door of my casino," Trombo explained. "I shan't be there tonight. You know where it is on the Calle del Ridotto. You may find it convenient for the lady, if she wishes to retire somewhere during the evening, or even for a tête-à-tête when you've had enough of the Piazza crowds. A caretaker keeps the place heated. There's wine on the buffet . . ."

The offer was tempting. Tonight had been set for the mild escapade of showing Maritza the sights of carnival, which she had so far only glimpsed under the rigid wing of Anzoletta. They were to

145

visit the Ridotto, make the round of booths and cafés in front of St. Mark's, mingle with the vast frolic of other masks on the Piazza. Their costumes were ready. Anzoletta had even consented to waive chaperonage this once in favor of youth and the season. Richard had planned refreshments at one of the cafés. But how lordly it would be, and out of the ordinary, to show Maritza the interior of such a smart casino with its gildings and pictures! Yes, and how delicious to sit there awhile with her before a fire in the salon! Thought slipped the leash at once. He caught himself up sharply. No, he would not give Tromba that satisfaction.

"Your Signory, a thousand thanks. But we shan't be out late. There'd hardly be time to avail ourselves of your Excellence's kindness . . ."

Still smarting from the other's shafts, he found it best to leave out the impropriety of taking Maritza to a suite of empty rooms. He wanted no more jibes on the subject.

"Ah, well," returned Tromba, "keep the key anyway. You can return it tomorrow. One never knows how an evening will turn out. My dear Richard, I insist."

He got up a little absently and, not for the first time that morning, crossed the room to one of the long windows opening on a balcony that overlooked the Grand Canal. Across the balcony railing, one could see the opposite palaces, with their mooring posts and gondolas.

Yes, the same nondescript, rather shabby gondola, with drawn shutters, was still tied up in front of the Tiepolo palace. It had been there now for several hours — just an ordinary hack gondola, undistinguishable from a thousand others. But Tromba did not like those drawn shutters that might conceal a watcher covering the Grimani entrance. Instinct, as much as anything else, whispered an alert.

It was a corner room, with side windows on the narrow Rio San Luca. Crossing over, he peered down at an oblique angle. Yes, about a hundred yards up the canal lay a similar gondola, that might be watching the side exit of the palace.

Hm-m! Well, the uncertainty could be cleared up soon. He would be going out in a few minutes. If either of the two boats followed him, he would know what was brewing. And then? Fortunately no arrest was probable before night; the State Inquisitors liked darkness. He gave a pale smile. Secret police were the same everywhere, blundering idiots.

"What amuses your Signory down there?" asked Richard, getting up in his turn.

"Nothing of consequence, Milòr." Tromba took snuff and whisked off some particles of it from his waistcoat. "By the way, it occurs to me that I may leave Venice before the end of carnival. My safety may require it. As you know, the government here takes a prejudiced view of Freemasonry. There are certain indications that I might not even have time to bid you farewell. In that case —"

"But your Excellence!"

It was not quite a bolt from the blue. Richard, though he had kept away from Tromba's occult operations, could guess pretty well what was going on, and that what had happened elsewhere in the adventurer's past might happen here. He had no illusions about his mentor. That had been one of the chief stumbling blocks in regard to England. But, for all that, this news was sudden and upsetting.

"I had no idea . . ."

"One of the smaller vicissitudes," smiled Tromba, "if it should occur — which is by no means certain. However, in that case, as I was saying, you can always reach me during the next two months at the sign of the "Black Eagle" in Munich. I shall then leave for England. And I hope with you. I hope so for both our sakes."

He laid his muscular hand on Richard's shoulder. "You think I'm a rogue, Milòr. It's a term that has no meaning for me. No, I'm a corsair. I take the solid goods life offers and enjoy them while time serves. When time is out, I shall not whimper." His hand closed hard. "By God, Richard, wake up. Stop cheating yourself with dreams. Stop the shilly-shally of right or wrong. Empty words, both of them. Decide to live. You want love — well, reach out and take it. You want place and pleasure — let Marny pay for them. It's as easy as that. Or else, what? You will indeed wake up someday, having never lived, old and sorry and on the edge of the grave. — There, curse you, is my last sermon for this time. I hope you'll remember it — at least tonight."

147

"No," he waved, as Richard once more tendered the key of the casino. "Tomorrow will do; or if by any chance I'm not here tomorrow, keep it to remind you of a pleasant evening or, in case you're a fool, of what might have been. You can take your choice."

X X I

COLD and the threat of rain that night did nothing to dampen the revels of the city. From its farthest outskirts to the center of jubilee on St. Mark's Square, Venice presented the spectacle of a merrymaking bedlam. At an hour when the rest of Europe snuffed candles and put on nightcaps, its myriad lamps burned brighter, its crowds grew denser, and the tumult of its masquerade had just begun.

Dressed as Harlequin in spangles and a black mask, arm in arm with Maritza, whose Columbine hat brushed his cheek, Richard shouldered a way for them both through the throngs on the Merceria up towards the Great Square. All the shops and cafés were open. The rays of window lamps or street lights fell on the drifting jumble of costumes, like an animated crazy quilt of a thousand changing colors. Dozens of other Harlequins and Columbines, Pierrots, Pierrettes, Brighellas, Pantaloons, Tartaglias — all the masks of comedy — gypsy girls, Spanish dons, bandits, Papal Guards, Silenuses on donkeys, clowns on hobbyhorses, Turks, Moors, Chinamen . . . Horns tooted, bagpipes squealed; gusts of confetti settled down on every kind of headgear; sugar bombs burst. Mingled with the typical Venetian smell of oriental wares displayed outside the shops was the odor of oranges, roasted .chestnuts, and fried delicacies being consumed by the crowd.

"Having a good time, Maritzetta?" asked Richard, pausing in a recess between two shops, which gave them momentary relief from jostling.

"Am I? Isn't it *fun*, caro!" She gave his arm a squeeze, her white mask with its red painted cheeks tilted up at him. "I've never had such fun. Though it's going to hurt to sit down. The way I've been pinched! But I've boxed plenty of ears."

He returned the squeeze. "Columbines at carnival ought to wear

148

armor. Gran' Dio! Wouldn't it be a good joke if you wore some kind of pin arrangement under your skirt, like a thistle! That would give the pinchers a start. Look. I'll have one made for you the next time we go out."

"Perfect! Do, please — for the Mardi Gras. But we'll have to start courting Anzoletta. She said it was to be only this once. She's such a tyrant."

"You wait," Richard boasted. "I'll talk her over."

"Milòr —" she pointed to a booth across the street that was selling slices of roasted pumpkin — "I do love zucca baruca, don't you? Let's have some."

"At a kiss a slice," he returned. "Is it a bargain, Siora Columbina?"

"Well," she hesitated, "I'm hungry, and I don't wear pins on my lips, Messer Arlechino. But I want four whole slices."

He took his pay in advance and stole another kiss for good measure. Then, with his arm around her waist, they shoved across the street to the booth, ate the hot *zucca* with relish, and afterwards inched along toward the Piazza.

But they could not pass one shop window, or rather enclosed shrine, where a crowd of worshipers, chiefly women, gaped at the "French Doll," the renowned Piavola de Franza. She was beyond doubt the most influential lady in Venice, a life-size mannequin imported from Paris and showing the latest fashions in dress of the Rue Saint-Honoré. Other saints might receive prayers and candles, but none was adored with such *ahs* and *ohs* of admiration and such intense scrutiny. She, or replicas of her, made a royal progress each year to all the capitals of Europe. She brought to the masses of women who could never hope to see far-off Paris one eye-filling token of French elegance. She exacted the homage of dreams and sighs, dressmakers' bills, utter obedience.

"Isn't she lovely, Richard?"

The French Doll stood graciously inclined in a half curtsy.

"Why can't Italian women ever dress like that, Milòr?"

"But they do."

"No, they try, they copy. But with the French, every gown is different, personal as a sonnet. That can't be copied. Ah, Paris! Mother used to tell me so much about it. I wonder if I'll ever go there."

"Of course you will." He remembered his talk with Tromba. "It's only a step from London."

"And London?" She smiled and shrugged. "Now, don't spoil our evening. I had to refuse Sior Caretti's offer. — Look at that girl on the shoulders of the satyr. She doesn't care how she shows her legs . . ."

Detaching themselves from the French Doll, they were soon at the lofty gateway under the Clock Tower, which gave entrance to the Piazza; and the bronze giants above them banged out the hour of eleven. Here, under the looming shoulder of St. Mark's, one looked out upon an ocean of people, fringed by the lighted arcades and cafés on either side. The noise of the multitude rose and fell; but always, as an undertone, sounded the infinite tramp of feet upon the pavement, a vast murmur deepening the surface roar of fifty thousand voices.

Skirting the fringes of this sea of costumes, they reached the booths on the Piazzetta in front of the Ducal Palace. Torches flared, acrobats tumbled, Irish giants outdid Hercules. Here was a puppet show; there, a dancing dog; there, Dr. Anonymous in person dispensed elixirs, salves, and pills; there, a magician wrought wonders, to the amusement of Richard, who could have duplicated most of them; there, a fortune teller whispered Maritza's future to her down a long speaking tube. And fauns, buffoons, Pulcinellas, Moors, nymphs, and Scaramouches danced the furlana on a platform. The bobbing lanterns of gondolas moored along the landing resembled footlights of some fantastic stage; while near and far on the shadowy lagoon, sparks of wandering boats, a gush of fireworks, strains of music, showed carnival overflowing from the land and established on the water.

Then, too, there was the Molo, that broad landing on the flank of the Palace, where comical and fearsome beasts were kept: the most whimsical monkeys, two live elephants, lions, bears.

But the sights of carnival would not have been complete without a glimpse of the famous Ridotto, two blocks off near the church of San Moisè. It was well past midnight when Richard and Maritza joined the stream of masks surging up the broad stairway of the gaming palace, while others at their left drifted down.

150

Here, in contrast to the tumult outdoors, one was struck by the silence. People spoke in hushed voices; amusement at the Ridotto required decorum. The succession of splendid rooms on the second floor contained sixty tables adapted to every purse. There were the small games, where a few sequins changed hands, and the big games involving thousands. As if to assure that all was fair, only patricians acted as bankers. They wore no masks or costumes but they were dressed, befitting their rank, in the traditional long dark gown or toga. Often representing financial groups, they won or lost gravely, imperturbably.

But people did not have to play. There was plenty of space for sauntering through the elegantly paneled rooms or for chatting with other masks. One vast apartment was known as the Big Room; another, reserved for those who, having lost everything, wished to compose themselves, was called the Room of Sighs. Everywhere chandeliers of gilded bronze shed the mysterious, flattering light of candles. The air had a perfumed warmth. The distinctive sound was the shuffle of cards and ring of coins.

"You know," said Maritza, "I like it better on the Piazza. This is all very splendid of course . . ." She broke off, then added: "Don't you think it's uncanny somehow? As if there were fever around, something mad. Don't let's stay too long. — Look, there's that Pierrot again. I've noticed him several times this evening."

"Don't you want to bet a lira or two?" Richard asked. "You might win."

She shook her head. "No, thanks. You try, if you want."

He risked a ducat in a small game and promptly lost.

"There you are," she nodded. "Now let's go. We can't either of us afford to waste money — not in that stupid way, at least. Come on."

Richard's funds had dwindled a good deal since the Villa Bagnoli, and he did not protest. But they stopped at one of the big tables on the way out.

Here the gold lay in heaps, and people pressed close. Most of these serious players, men and women, did not wear costumes, but only the usual white, beaked mask, long cloak and cocked hat over the black head scarf. The patrician banker, who sat at

151

one end of the faro table, had been jotting down some figures on a tablet, but he now looked up, preparing to deal.

In the quiet, stuffy room, it was like an apparition, because so unexpected. Richard found himself facing Marin Sagredo.

The young grandee's immaculate wig showed particularly white against the sable of his robe. His big, arrogant features dominated the table. A diamond flashed as he handled the cards.

"Place your bets, sioria."

But during the pause, while coins were being spread on the layout, it seemed to Richard that Sagredo was looking straight at him. The black Harlequin mask, of course, prevented recognition, and yet the insolent eyes gave an impression of drilling through it. Then, as they shifted slightly, Richard perceived that Sagredo was looking not at him but at someone behind him and, glancing around, discovered the chalk face of the Pierrot at his shoulder. Doubtless Sagredo's stare had meant nothing, or perhaps he had known who Pierrot was . . .

"Please come," urged Maritza in a low voice. "It's so close in here."

"Tired, cara?" Richard asked, as they descended the great stairs.

"A little, perhaps. That brute Sagredo . . . Let's rest awhile, have a sherbet somewhere. Didn't you mention going to the "Regina del Mare" on the Piazza?"

"Yes, or any one of the cafés. If we can only find a table . . ."

A group of masks hanging around the entrance below gave the first warning of a new complication. Through the doorway came a wet gust from outside.

Rain!

It was not a drizzle but a steady pelting that might last for some time. One could only wait it out here. The baffled masks at the door were deciding, one by one, to return upstairs. Maritza stood eying the vague downpour in the street.

"Well, madonna," said Richard, "there's nothing for it. We can find a place to sit in the Room of Sighs. Well named, isn't it?"

She drew her arm through his and pressed closer to him. "I don't mind getting wet. There must be some café pretty near. I don't like this place . . . and Marin Sagredo . . ."

"We couldn't get inside a café now. All the street crowds —"

"Or find a gondola."

"That's even harder. But, look . . ."

The rain made a great difference. It was no surrender to take advantage of Tromba's casino under these circumstances. Either that or remain here. Richard made the proposal with a clear conscience, but he conceded a hint about the impropriety of it.

"Pooh!" Maritza exclaimed. "As if I cared! It isn't the first time we've been unconventional, is it? I've always wanted to see one of those casini. You say it's near?"

"Just half a block."

"Marvelous! We'll make a dash for it. Ready?"

The Pierrot from upstairs, who had also been appraising the weather, smiled at them.

"Going to be brave?"

"Yes, Sior Maschera," said Maritza.

"Well, good luck! I'm staying here."

But, oddly enough, in spite of the rain, he followed a few steps down the street and watched the hurrying figures plunge into a nearby doorway. Then he re-entered the gaming house and once more climbed the stairs.

XXII

SOME casini, as the name implied, were small, isolated houses; but, generally speaking, the term *casino* meant a luxurious apartment, one of several in the same building. Their charm was their privacy, as compared with the vast, inconvenient palaces. The accent was on elegance, comfort and expense. These pieds-à-terre were owned or rented by wealthy fashionables of both sexes. They were a feature of Venice no less typical than its music and regattas.

Tromba's casino occupied the second floor of a house in the Calle del Ridotto, where Richard and Maritza, a little out of breath from their dash through the rain, now pulled the bell cord and gave the Cavaliere's name to a sleepy concierge eying them through the wicket.

The man opened at once. "But yes. His Excellence sent word that company might be expected. I have seen to the fires. You will

153

find a candle at your left, as you go in. Or do you wish me to light up for you?"

Being informed that this was unnecessary, the custode then bowed them toward the marble steps leading up through the stair well and returned to bed.

"If this isn't exciting!" breathed Maritza, as Richard self-consciously turned the key in the lock of the richly paneled door. "It was a wonderful idea to come here. People are always talking about the casini. Now I won't have to look so dull and ignorant."

It crossed Richard's mind that probably no other girl in Venice would have displayed such an attitude at that moment. He could never quite get used to Maritza's complete naturalness and unconcern.

In contrast with the damp chill of the stair well, it was blandly warm inside, which gave an immediate sense of well-being. The mingled scent of rose and violet, faint as dried petals, permeated everywhere. There was the odor, too, of silken hangings and well-waxed floors. From the side hallway, connecting the length of the apartment, one entered at once a spacious salon in the French style, comprising the whole width of the house. Seen by the light of a single candle and by the glow of a coal fire in the grate, it gave a shadowy impression of glass and gilding, graceful furniture, vague and occasional paintings. Then, as Richard lighted here and there the candles of the side sconces, details of the room stood out: pendant crystals of the chandeliers, the tall mirror of Murano glass above the mantle, delicate upholstery, damask curtains at the windows, exquisite scrollwork on paneled walls and cornice, glint of silver on a buffet. The nymphs of several paintings looked exuberantly nude, but they did not exceed the prevailing fashion of Watteau and Boucher. It was the Villa Bagnoli again, only on a smaller scale and more exactly Parisian.

At one end of the room, Maritza, who had taken off her wet mask and hat, stood with her back to the grate, while Richard made his round of candle-lighting.

"Lovely!" she admired. "What perfect taste! Look at that darling harpsichord over there with the roses painted on it . . . And the light blue of this sofa, Richard! Ca de dia! How wonderful! It must be just like the Faubourg Saint-Germain — if that's the way

154

to pronounce it. I wish I spoke French . . . But you know, it doesn't remind me at all of the Cavaliere Tromba. It's too feminine for a man like him. He didn't furnish it, did he?"

"No, I think he rents it from one of the Dolfini who was long in Paris. After all, Maritzetta, it's women who set the fashion, not men."

"Yes," she nodded, "Sior Pa're makes a great point of it in his poem." She broke off. "Dear Sior Pa're! I wonder what he'd say if he knew where I was. I don't believe he'd mind. But Anzoletta! Woe's me! It would be terrible . . . I think that's enough candles, don't you? It's prettier when there are not too many. — Aren't you going to take off your mask?"

"Perbacco! I'd forgotten it."

He untied the lacings and emerged in his own countenance; but the spangled green, red and yellow costume, with its long breeches, kept him still very much a harlequin.

"Come over here and dry yourself," she went on, making way for him at the hearth. And, as he joined her: "But do you know who this place *does* make me think of? From the very moment we came in . . . Why I could almost expect her to walk through the door any minute."

"Who, cara?"

"The Countess des Landes. She belongs in a room like this. Do you know what became of her?"

"Oh, she went back to Paris. The Cavaliere Tromba heard from her once, I think. Matter of fact, she lives in the Faubourg Saint-Germain." Yes, the jewel-box apartment recalled her; but she seemed remote, half effaced by time. He said absently: "How far off it all seems now, doesn't it, cara ti! I mean last summer, the Villa Bagnoli . . ."

"Years," she murmured. "So far off. Do you remember . . ."

"Do you remember . . ."

Thought glanced back and forth between them. Gradually they fell silent without being aware of it, aware only of standing close together in the warmth of the fire, with the pelting of the rain outside.

Then, on an impulse, almost unconsciously, he drew her to him and kissed her.

"Maritzetta!"

"Dearest!" she said, returning his kiss.

In the silence, the fall of the rain sounded louder.

Then, trying to copy her usual voice but failing to keep out of it a new undertone, she murmured: "We've hardly looked at the casino. Aren't you going to show it to me?"

"Yes, of course."

He took up a candle and opened the door of the adjoining room. It was a large boudoir rich in hangings and mirrors, deliciously warmed by a coal fire in the grate of a marble chimney piece. On one side stood a vast dressing table furnished with all the clutter of silver boxes and crystal vials that fashion required. On the other opened an alcove containing the wide, canopied bed, its azure curtains gathered to a peak under a golden cupid. From above the mantel a copy of Boucher's "Mademoiselle O'Murphy," or rather, in its bolder emphasis, a variant of that painting, centered the boudoir and, as it were, enforced the theme of the ribald ceiling medallions with their scenes from Ovid. Prone on a couch, the naked and robust contours of the French king's pretty mistress dominated the room, were reflected in the panel mirrors that lined it, and proclaimed the place for what it was, a temple of Venus.

Used to the light conventions of art, Maritza found Mademoiselle O'Murphy well painted but amusing.

"Ecco la bella bionda!" she smiled, standing in front of the canvas. "Isn't she free and easy! I know it's the fashion, but don't you find her a *little* too plump, Richard? I do."

"Yes," he admitted, more embarrassed and less objective than Maritza.

"No doubt of it," she went on, "I can tell you that a few months with Monsù d'Aubry would trim her down. You can see she's never been a ballerina . . ."

Then, suddenly confused, Maritza broke off, flushed, and turned away. That would not have happened some minutes ago.

But it was the mirrors that especially fascinated her. The walls were paneled with them; and as the room was octagonal they showed the human figure from every side.

"Can you imagine people being so vain! Always looking at them-

156

selves. Why, Richard —" she had walked over to the alcove — "they even have a mirror hidden in the bed canopy. Why should they do that? It's mad. They can't look at themselves when they're asleep. Or . . . or . . ."

Her voice stammered into silence. It showed that the purpose of the mirrors had been half guessed. Richard stood fiddling with a silver box on the table. The blood pounded at his temples, and yet strangely at the same time he resented the too patent implications of the room.

"My poor dress!" she complained. And he knew it was to cover up the uneasy pause, though actually the Columbine frock which had begun the evening so gaily looked spattered enough. "I'm all over confetti and sugar flour. — And I simply *must* wash my hands."

He opened a door on the right that disclosed a cabinet with ewer and basin.

"I'll wait for you in the salon."

He withdrew with the feeling of having somehow scored on Tromba. Then, finding another dressing room down the corridor, he cleaned himself up, and returning to the salon laid out some refreshments from the buffet on a small table in front of the fire. Whether by the Cavaliere's special instructions or because the casino was always kept provisioned on the nights of carnival, there was a decanter of malmsey on the sideboard, together with cold fowl, meat pâtés, and confections under separate silver covers.

And how different now from the surcharged atmosphere of the boudoir to sit and chat together in this more conventional setting, with the table at their knees and facing the glow of the fire! It was quiet and cozy and companionable, putting them once more at ease with themselves. Now, too, for the first time, they could talk about their new relationship. But, side by side on the small blue sofa, they interrupted talk very often.

Always forthright, Maritza accepted the change wholeheartedly.

"Is it possible to be so happy? Caro mio, is it possible! Now, at least, one thing's settled. You can't leave me in Italy and go to England."

"Unless you go with me," he said.

"Go with you?"

157

"Yes, you know I can't stay in Venice. I have no future here. But in England, I think my father, Lord Marny, would help me. You'd have your engagement at that big theater Sior Caretti talked about. We could be married. Listen, cara, don't you believe —"

"No." She laid a forefinger on his mouth. "I *don't* believe, I *won't* listen."

"But why not?"

"Because I hate Lord Marny."

"You don't know him, Maritzetta."

"Yes, I do know him. At least I know enough about him from what you've told me; how he deserted your mother and *why* he deserted her. I'm glad I had to refuse Sior Caretti's offer, because that might have given you another reason for going to England."

"Of course it would have," he interrupted, "But still, I don't see —"

"How blind you are! Don't you see what I am, as far as Lord Marny is concerned? If he accepts you, would he accept me any more than he did your mother? An Italian ballerina of no consequence. You know how I love Sior Pa're and Anzoletta. But I'll go with you anywhere except England. We could join any troupe you like. Do you doubt we can make a living? Of course we can. Only not England. Not Tromba and Lord Marny and that old ghost of a Black Baron you keep thinking of! No, no, no! Is that settled now? For good?"

"For good," he repeated. "And buried. I don't know why you even argue about it. All you have to do is to lift this little finger —" he stopped to pay tribute to it — "and say do this or that. Nothing else matters with me."

"Well, I'll only lift it this once . . ."

Loud and startling as a pistol shot, though at first they could not identify it, came a sound from the corridor. The moment shattered like a bubble of glass. They sat upright and tense, listening. Then again. It was a sharp knock on the outer door. And again.

"I'll see who it is."

Richard crossed the room.

"Yes?" he said, having reached the door.

A muffled voice from outside answered: "Word from the Cavaliere Marcello Tromba. Open, please. It's urgent." And the unseen knuckles rapped again.

It flashed upon Richard that probably Tromba's forecast of an early flight from Venice had proved correct. He opened at once. But instead of the single messenger —

A rush of men bore him back into the vestibule. He wrenched free of them and reached the salon. They were six in all, wearing white, beaked masks, long cloaks, and cocked hats. As they pressed toward him, he retreated toward the fireplace, where Maritza was standing. Like gigantic crows, they paused in a semi-circle three or four yards off.

With his mind on Tromba, Richard thought at once of an arrest. Perhaps they connected him with the Cavaliere . . .

Then the tallest of them plucked off his mask.

The bold features of Marin Sagredo stood out from the black cowl of his bàuta.

"Well, fiddler Count," he grinned, "we come to the last act of our play at the Villa Bagnoli. Or shall we call it an epilogue?"

XXIII

UNTIL it arrives, no man can know how he will face a deadly and sudden danger. And that the danger threatening him was deadly enough, Richard could take for granted from the moment when Sagredo unmasked. But now, if he had had time to think at all, he would have been amazed at the cold fury that mastered him to the exclusion of any other feeling. Without knowing it, he became actually a different person. If the Black Baron Marny was looking for reincarnation, he found it at that moment.

No doubt the involvement of Maritza contributed to this, but not altogether. It was equally Sagredo's insolent, leering face. Anger, however, did not take an uncontrolled form. It did not impair speech or dull the brain.

"Your Excellency," said Richard in a deliberate voice, "seems to forget not only manners, which is nothing new, but that this is the Cavaliere Tromba's casino. I wasn't aware that he had given you the freedom of it."

Expecting all the signs of fear, if not of panic, Sagredo had the startled look of a mastiff suddenly bearded by a cock. It took him a moment to find his tongue.

159

"Good God!" he choked. And then, with a glance to his companions, "You see what I mean, gentlemen? The poor beggar is so swollen with conceit and has been so pampered that he's actually mad. He has no idea who he is or who his betters are. Well, we must try to cure him. — As to your master, Tromba," he flung at Richard, "you needn't be concerned about his casino. He won't be needing it again. He's being lodged from now on, with other swindlers, at the expense of the State."

So, it appeared that the blow had fallen, and Tromba had been caught. This explained, too, Sagredo's boldness. Evidently he had learned of the proposed arrest and could therefore write Tromba off as Richard's protector. But how had he known where to close in? Richard's visit to the casino had been casual and improvised. As it happened, the unmasking of one of the other men at that moment answered this question. The white countenance of the Pierrot, not yet wholly free of make-up, emerged.

Conscious of Richard's stare, the man identified himself with a smirk. "Our paths seem to cross, don't they?"

"Don't they?" said Richard in the same drawl. "I'm glad to see you out of costume, Messer Rat."

But it was Maritza who now opened fire, and the unexpectedness of it once more caught Sagredo off balance.

"You coward!" she burst out. "Wait till I publish this in Venice! The magnificent Marin! Laughingstock of the Brenta! Hot for vengeance — after five months, when he thinks it safe! Girds on his sword, hires enough bullies, lies his way into a private apartment! And now, per Dio, struts and swaggers! Marvelous, you hero! Admirable!"

The words slapped his face back and forth. He stood convulsed. And she took a step toward him, head up and eyes blazing.

"Well, Don Flavio, strut on! Have you forgot your lines again?"

Extending her hand, she gave the twitching movement of the fingers which had been his appeal to the prompter on that miserable night of the play and which had dogged him ever since.

With a fraction of his mind, Richard both exulted and wondered at her. She had learned more than dancing in the rough school of the ballet. No spitfire of the backstage could have been more devastating.

160

"Sior Morandi, your arm," she added. "We'll let these prowlers explain themselves to the watch."

For an instant, it almost seemed as if her boldness had carried it. The astonished rufflers did not move, except the one who stood directly in Maritza's way and who actually drew back a little. But she and Richard had not taken two steps when Sagredo barked out, "Mind the doors!"

A couple of the men drew their swords and blocked the exits of the room. Temperature leaped up. The young fashionables who attended Sagredo did not like being called hired bullies or referred to as rats. They were only out on a lark which concerned the chastisement of an impudent upstart who had got above himself. Indeed, they rendered all noblemen a service by making an example of him. Originally Maritza had no part in their plans; they intended no physical harm to her now. She was a popular ballerina and could call herself a Venier. But, from their standpoint, she had sunk to the level of this lackey and deserved no special treatment.

"Madonna!" bowed Sagredo, elaborately polite. "I thank you for your compliments. Schiavo della siora! But let me reciprocate. A little prude who rebuffs a gentleman and then gets caught spending the night with a scullion is hardly entitled to publish anything, is she? I think *I'll* do the publishing. Your venerable father will undoubtedly enjoy it."

"Toco de carogna," she cut in, "you can spare yourself the trouble. He'll learn from me what happened. Do you suppose I'll hold my tongue because —"

"No," he growled, "probably not. An opera jade has no reputation to lose. And yet I don't think you'll breathe a word of what happens to your pretty Harlequin. He'll get the treatment I once saw given in Dalmatia to a puppy of his sort. He won't die of it but he won't be the same afterwards. Stir up the fire, Lucio; we can use it. You have the whip and the little knife? Good. Now, friends, do me the favor to strip him." He drew his sword and swung forward, the blade poised. "I don't believe he's Jack-fool enough to resist."

It was disconcerting that the fellow Morandi still looked unimpressed. His six feet of height equaled Sagredo's. His swarthy, irregular face and broad shoulders, the tight-fitting Harlequin cos-

161

tume that half revealed the muscles of arm and thigh, gave him both a bizarre and a formidable appearance. Sagredo's "friends" hesitated.

Richard eyed the motionless point of steel an instant — it was two feet from his body — then turned to Maritza.

"Madonna, you hear this very noble gentleman. It's better for you not to see what may happen. — Surely, your Excellence —" he glanced at Sagredo — "will permit the lady to return home? You have no vendetta with her."

"I'm not so sure of that," snapped the other. "But in any case we'll have no alarm given until we've finished with you. She can go to the other end of the room, if she likes, and stop her ears."

Maritza seethed: "Listen, galioto. You have two of us to deal with, remember that!" She wondered a little at Richard's docility and at his compressed, altered voice.

"You see," Sagredo grinned. "She wants to look on; she likes to see her lover in the buff." But he gave a nod to the ex-Pierrot.

The latter, closing in from behind, pinioned her arms and drew her back. She struggled furiously a moment and screamed, "Aiuto! Aiuto!" The man clapped his hand over her mouth. Another gagged her with a scarf. Almost at once, bound hand and foot, she was carried to a sofa at the rear of the circle.

Richard felt relieved. In the oncoming action, he would have one anxiety the less. But intercepting a more imperious glance from Sagredo to his followers, he exclaimed: "Siori, one instant! I beg you to listen. Permit me to show you something."

His dramatic, wide-flung gesture held them back.

"Siori," he went on in the style of a stage harlequin, "you propose to amuse yourselves with me, is it not so? Let me add to your amusement. Among other talents, I have those of a magician. It might entertain you to see —"

"What gammon's this?" Sagredo fumed. "I said strip him."

"One *little* moment, your Excellence. Let me show you how I can pluck things out of the air. Ecco! You see my hands empty; my sleeves offer no concealment. Behold!"

In spite of themselves, they paused to watch him. A new intentness grew in Maritza's eyes, and a new suspense. She recognized the patter of his showmanship, but she would not have recognized his voice.

162

"Behold! And yet, while Messer Pierrot sneers and the great Sagredo frowns —" was there a second's shift of attention? — "behold, you see a knife."

It was a needle-sharp little dagger with a gilded hilt, that seemed almost to take form in Richard's hand. A start of alertness shot through the group.

"Drop that, by God," roared Sagredo, "or you'll find —" It would spoil everything to be forced to spit the rascal.

"But of course, your Signory," the arresting voice went on. "What could a little knife do against your sword, with the point already at my guts? Don't be troubled. I shall now make it vanish or rather reappear. In the ceiling perhaps? Then you can strip and whip me and so on. Look . . ."

Inevitably, unconsciously, they followed his upward glance, aware, too, that his hand was empty. They did not catch the lightning fling of the other hand. A sword clattered down, a shocked cry split the silence. Every eye was now on Sagredo, clutching at a sudden gilded object on his breast.

"Ecco!" said Richard. "Not the ceiling, after all."

He caught the crumbling Sagredo long enough to pluck out the knife, then flung himself against the nearest man, sent him sprawling, and in the next breath slashed desperately at the scarf that bound Maritza's ankles. The confusion gave him a moment. She was on her feet . . .

A couple were bending over Sagredo. The man on the floor scrambled up. The two others sprang at Richard, who took the blow of one sword on the thick of his arm, answered it with his fist, but could not have avoided the second had not his assailant, swinging down with a cut, forgotten the chandelier. The blade, tangled in the strands of pendants, brought a shower of crystals on the man's head; and in the same instant Richard, swinging Maritza along with him, vanished into the vestibule. It took a brace of seconds before the flurried pursuers could follow; and in that time he reached the outer door, jerked it open — then stopped dead.

He stood face to face with a solid group of men outside.

Someone struck with a sword hilt from behind . . . He went down, but the blow did not completely stun him. It reduced what followed to a kind of phantasmagory.

163

He was in the salon again, giddily leaning against the wall. His breath came in gasps. He had manacles on his wrists. A stream of blood oozing across his forehead half blinded him, though he managed to dab it away with his sleeve. The room seemed full of men, but one dominated all the others. Dizzy as he was, Richard recognized the long red cloak which distinguished the most dreaded man in Venice, the *capobargello* or supreme police official, who bore the title of Capitan Grande. It was he who made the more important arrests at the command of the State Inquisitors. His name was Mattio Varutti. But how did it happen that Capitan Grande could be here? How had he known so immediately of an obscure fight in a second-floor apartment?

Then, dazedly, from the talk around him, Richard became aware of what had happened. After all, the circle closing in on Tromba had not yet caught the fox. Since he was not at the Palazzo Grimani, he might possibly be found at his casino. It was a mere chance which had brought the Inquisitors' agents there at that instant.

"And lucky, too," remarked Capitan Grande, with a side glance at Richard, "for their Excellences have this fellow on their books. He's been too thick with Tromba for his own good. — You!" Varutti's big fist closed on Richard's collar. "Where's your friend? You were with him yesterday morning. Speak up! You'd better. What with this murder on your hands, you're in pretty deep . . ."

Richard could only shake his head.

"By God," growled the other, tightening his grip, "we'll have it out of you. Do you want to spend the night on the rack?"

But he broke off at the hurried entrance of a wigless, half-dressed physician, who had been summoned from a neighboring house.

Attention now centered on the blue couch, to which Sagredo had been lifted; and with the opening up of the group Richard, still dizzy, caught sight of Maritza, half outstretched in a chair across the room. Her face was dead white; her eyes were closed. He started toward her, but one of the two men guarding him shoved him back against the wall.

"Stay where you are. You needn't bother about the Siora. She'll come around."

Black points danced in front of Richard's eyes. The transforming

164

anger of a few minutes ago had vanished, leaving him sick and weak and nerveless. He had killed a man, he was in the grip of the law, he was utterly lost.

The physician stepped back from the sofa. "His Excellence is still breathing . . . God alone knows . . . We must put him to bed here. He can't be moved . . ."

Vaguely Richard saw them carry the sagging body into the next room. An incongruous picture of the bloodstained Sagredo on the canopied bed with the gilded cupid crossed his mind. He leaned faintly against the wall.

Capitan Grande paused at the side of Maritza.

"Checo," he directed one of his men, "as soon as the Siora is able, conduct her home. Show her every consideration. And have regard too for the Very Noble Antonio Venier. He'll learn what happened soon enough, but it's none of our business to peach on his daughter. — As to this fellow, we'll take him to the Pozzi."

These were the famous prisons, nicknamed *Wells*, in the Ducal Palace.

XXIV

HE was lodged, not in one of the lowest cells of the Pozzi, which, being underground, were never free of sea water, and where the inmates lived, like frogs, on ledges above the reach of the tide, but in one of the upper cells, which was merely black and fetid and verminous. No doubt he owed this indulgence to the policy of keeping him alive both for examination and for the gibbet.

They tortured him that same night and again later, but not extravagantly. Venetian justice used restraint in this direction. A touch of the rack, but only enough to stiffen him for some days and not to the point that required resetting of the bones. A session with the screws that merely lamed his hands until the thumbnails righted themselves. It was essential to find out at once whether Tromba was still in Venice and, if so, where? But the expert examiners soon decided that Morandi had nothing to conceal. Then too, messages next day reported that the adventurer had crossed the Austrian frontier. Nor did the prisoner evidently know as much about Tromba's Masonic activities as the Inquisitors themselves. That he did know and readily revealed the Cavaliere's magical tricks betrayed his intimacy with the charlatan and prejudiced his case, but the knowledge of legerdemain was not illegal.

These, after all, were minor matters. He had enough against him, on his own account, to hang ten men. However, the attack on Sagredo involved no mystery that required the probe of torture. So, except for a couple of appearances before the Tribunal, he was left in the darkness with his desperate self.

Marin Sagredo kept lingering on; and until his death or recovery occurred, Richard's fate could not be determined. If Sagredo died, his assassin would perish more terribly than if he lived. There was that much difference. And, indeed, if he lived, a gleam of hope remained that Richard might live too, that the Tribunal might show mercy. So, the wretched merry-go-round of nightmare went on continually day and night.

Richard's friends stood by him loyally at this time. The prison system of the day permitted and, indeed, almost required charitable assistance to prisoners. Bribes to the jailor for better fare and better treatment were one of the latter's most important perquisites. With a sufficient bribe, visitors could even be smuggled in for a brief interview through the bars.

His mother spent all she could rake and scrape for the purpose; so did Maritza, whose visits were always a godsend. It was a consolation that Antonio Venier and Anzoletta appeared more than once with assurances of faith in him and with their implied acceptance of his and Maritza's new relationship. Dr. Goldoni came several times, and Vico Morandi.

Then, at last, one day Father Procolo, the prison chaplain, brought him the decisive news. Since this time the priest entered with the turnkey and a lantern, Richard guessed that it boded something of importance and, springing up from his pallet, stood waiting tensely.

"You will rejoice to hear," said Father Procolo, "that his Excellence the Very Noble Marin Sagredo has been pronounced out of danger."

"Indeed?" muttered Richard.

"I have to report that his Excellence has besought the Tribunal for your life."

"*Marin Sagredo?*" Richard gasped.

"Yes, and, what's more, successfully. Considering such an attempt against a patrician, the utmost you could have expected was a merciful death by the garotte. Instead, I am informed that when you are summoned before the Tribunal tomorrow, a capital sentence will not be imposed."

Richard could hardly believe his good fortune. The days and nights of suspense were over.

Father Procolo hesitated. "You have been saved from committing murder, my son. You will continue to live . . . I wish I could speak to you of complete pardon. But, after all, that's impossible. The Tribunal could not overlook . . ."

"Of course not," said Richard. He had every reason to expect a year or two in prison. "Do you know what their Excellences have in mind?"

The other ran his tongue over his lips. "The galleys," he said, "for life."

Richard stood rigid, with clenched fists, while the awful realization spread through his mind. Worse than any agony of death at the hands of an executioner. Infinite degradation. Prolonged torture until the end. Galley slave for life!

X X V

RICHARD was assigned to the *Generalizia,* a state galley anchored at Malamocco five miles down the lagoon, and so named because it belonged to the service of the Proveditors General of Dalmatia, who had their headquarters at Zara on the opposite coast of the Adriatic. It was even now being readied for the first voyage of the year, which would take place about the beginning of April.

In a half stupor, he sat chained among several other galley recruits under guard of a warden, as the freight boat sculled by a convict ferried them down from the city. Like the other prisoners, he kept blinking in the unaccustomed daylight. He was chiefly conscious of a leaden emptiness tinged with dread of what lay before him.

Behind were the hopeless adieus of the last two days since his sentence by the Tribunal. Lifers in the galleys were practically never released; and in Richard's case the entire influence of the Sagredo family would be against any possible pardon. Lifers, too, never left their ship, except to be housed in slave pens when the vessel was careened, or for rough fatigue work on the wharfs. All of this, most of it unspoken, had been understood at those farewells in the prison.

With her stern against the Malamocco wharf, the *Generalizia*, low and lean in the water, pointed outward in the blue lagoon, like a gigantic black water beetle. She was a hundred and fifty feet long by forty-odd broad and, like all galleys, had only one deck covering her six-foot-deep hold. Along this, four feet apart, were ranged the rowers' benches; so that, except for the high cradle-shaped stern and the small forecastle, practically the entire surface space of the ship formed the slaves' quarters. A long projecting beak, used for ramming in naval engagements, and resembling that of a swordfish, stuck out from the prow. In preparation for the sea, the vessel had already been careened and tallowed, but the three masts that carried her lateen sails, to the relief of the rowers in favorable weather, had not yet been stepped. Near by, down the wharf, another galley, the *Conserva*, used as an escort to the General's ship, was being similarly put in shape for the voyage.

As the freight boat drew up to the quay, it entered an uproar of labor, for the six hundred slaves of the two galleys were busy returning to its place in the hold the ballast of small stones which had been removed and thoroughly washed on the wharf. This was done by means of wicker baskets passed from man to man, from wharf to stern, and so ultimately down the hatches. Speed was exacted; the baskets were heavy; the sun beat down. There could be no pause in the rhythm, no excuse for a poor grip or a faulty footing. Grunts, oaths, the clanking of chains, rumble of stones in the hold, frantic raking down there to level them out, roars of the overseers, blended to form a miserable, harried din.

The warden in the prow of the barge flung a painter to someone on the jetty.

"Out with you!" he barked to the recruits. "Look alive! Step along!"

Still unaccustomed to their fetters, Richard and his companions

168

stumbled up the steps to the wharf. But at that moment something went wrong with the ballast loading. A basket crashed on the gangway to the stern, a cascade of stones plunged into the water. Apparently someone had missed his grip. Then, at a volley of oaths from a nearby overseer, the offender dropped out of line, which immediately resumed its work, and came slinking to the guard who had summoned him.

He was a thin little man, naked except for his loose canvas breeches, and with leathery skin tight on his bones. His shaved head and low stature gave him the look of a wizened boy in comparison with the burly warden and heavy-set Turkish slave, who evidently acted as helper.

"Padron . . . I didn't do it on purpose . . . Padron . . . I couldn't help . . . I kiss your feet . . . Not again, for Christ's love! Not again . . . I beg . . . I beg . . ."

"Horse him," nodded the warden.

The Turk grasped the slave's wrists, turned and heaved him to a dangling position, as one carries a sack, then leaned forward to bring the victim's shoulders more horizontal beneath the lash. And, at a glimpse of the slave's back, Richard felt sick; for the man had evidently been whipped recently, or rather flayed, and showed an angry, ridged pulp from neck to waist. Upon such a surface, the least touch would be painful; but the *aguzino* now exerted himself on the wretch with a whip of cords weighted at the ends.

Thin screams rose above the noise of the loading. The victim's dangling legs, with a length of chain between the ankles, jerked up and down, like a swimming frog's.

Nauseated, Richard turned away only to find himself facing a bear of a man who had come up behind him.

"Ho!" said the fellow, sizing him up with a practised eye. "Don't like it, eh? Makes you queasy? By God, you'll go through worse than that if you don't watch yourself, you whoreson!"

In a sick haze, Richard stared at his interlocutor, a man of middle height but deep-chested and broad-shouldered to the point of deformity. A silver whistle or pipe, hanging on a long string around his neck, proclaimed him the chief aguzino. He wore a red cap — red being the color of the galley — perched on a thatch of black hair.

169

"Yes, I'm Luca Buranello," he continued. "You're Morandi, are you? The rogue who stabbed the Very Noble Marin Sagredo? I'm happy to have you with me." He showed his yellow teeth. "Now get on over to the barracks. We'll put you in uniform."

Dragging their chains, Richard and the other new arrivals shuffled on to a square, low building at the end of the wharf. From the corner of his eye, he noticed that the flogging of the culprit had stopped, and that a speculative group stood about an inert figure on the pavement. But he was concerned now for himself.

In a big, unfurnished room that smelled of sweat and dust, the newcomers were relieved of their irons long enough to strip, and were then examined like any other work animals. It was a brutal process of thumping and fingering, performed by a couple of sub-wardens under Padron Luca's direction. Every part of the slave's body that could offer concealment of any object whatever had to be searched. A superficial estimate of his freedom from too contagious disease had to be formed, and his physical strength appraised. The naked bodies were shoved here and there.

Padron Luca rated them tentatively. This man could start as Number 3 on Number 5 bench; that one as Number 4 on Number 7. That little weakling wasn't worth his chains; put him as Number 6 on Number 34. Another, who had evidently been recommended as a musician, was exempted from the oars and reserved for the ship's band of drummers and trumpeters. Struck by Richard's height and physique, Luca reckoned that he might be developed into a stroke oar or *spaliero,* when he had been taught the duties of it. Meanwhile, let him serve as Number 2 on Number 6 bench.

Their examination over, the slaves took their turns on a low stool; and the galley's barber, another convict, shaved their heads without benefit of water. The shaved head together with the leg chain was the badge of their calling. But there were differences. The Turks, or prisoners of war, retained a long tuft of hair on the top of their scalps; the criminals who were condemned for shorter periods of service than the lifers grew mustaches.

Clothing was then issued: two shirts; two pair of canvas knee breeches; a red coat reaching to the knees in the form of a poncho; a loose red cap; an overcoat of rough cloth, made like a nightgown and extending to the feet, of use in cold weather or as a blanket at

170

night. This completed the slave's summer wardrobe, except for shoes, issued by the warden to work parties on shore and returned by them when they came back aboard the galley.

The convicts now slipped on their breeches; spare garments were stuffed into individual sacks, which would be stowed on board; and a guard replaced the leg and wrist irons. By this time, the cowing process was well under way. Cuffed, kicked and bullied, the wretched slaves stood listlessly awaiting the next affliction. That Richard had been especially singled out for the roughest treatment was apparent. The blows, shoving, and fingering, carelessly harsh in the case of the others, were intentionally so when it came to him. The devil in Luca's eyes made it clear that the warden was goading him to an outburst which would justify some outstanding punishment.

"Here, you Polo," he directed one of his assistants, who was putting on the fetters, "I want the extra-heavy for that swine. He needs taming. We'll soften him up."

But through it all, to Luca's evident disappointment, Richard controlled himself. At the moment, impassiveness was the only retaliation in his power. It compensated a little when Luca muttered: "Al corpo de Dio, you're a tight-lipped bastard. I know a snake when I see one, and I know how to break its back."

The new slaves were now ordered on board the galley; and the dejected group, picking up their sacks, shuffled out on the wharf. Richard's chains, weighing fifty pounds, made walking hard; the ankle irons began chafing into the flesh. In spite of his efforts, he lagged behind and, for the first time, felt the bite of an overseer's cat on his bare shoulders — a stinging, excruciating pain that set him scrambling ahead to avoid a repetition of it. But the aguzino followed him close.

The taking in of ballast had now ended, and the slaves had been assigned to various jobs: some of them at work on the sails, others mending the canvas tent that was raised over the deck at night, others preparing and suppling the new cordage. Apparently, too, the high-built stern, which contained the captain's quarters and some crowded accommodation for officers, was being given a thorough washing down; for there was much noise of scrapers and scrubbing.

Coming aboard from the gangplank, Richard edged along a nar-

171

row passage between cabin and bulwarks and found himself facing the half-filled benches that extended forward to the *rembate* or parapets of the forecastle. The *corsia,* a gangway three and a half feet wide, rose somewhat above the rowers and furnished the only means of passing from one end of the ship to the other. There were twenty-five benches on either side of this raised walk, which was enclosed and served also to hold the tent canvases and the few belongings of the slaves. It gave protection, moreover, to the hatchways and to the apertures for the masts when, as often happened, the deck of the low-lying galley ran with water in rough weather.

Up and down along the corsia, whip in hand, patrolled three aguzini, having the slaves beneath them in convenient reach. The near ends of the ten-foot benches were set in the oaken sides of the corsia casing, while the farther ends fitted into a thick timber called the *posticci,* where the oars were fixed and which formed the lower section of the bulwarks. The latter supported a broad rim or bench used by the seamen and soldiers of the galley, who would otherwise have had insufficient room on the crowded deck.

Assigned as Number 2 on Number 6 bench, Richard now scrambled down from the corsia at that point; and his leg irons were at once locked into position. He found the bench itself not too uncomfortable. A rough upholstery of sackcloth stuffed with flocks was covered with cowhide reaching almost to the deck, so that the entire bench resembled a long traveling trunk. Below it, at the right distance, extended the *pedagna,* or footrest, which, among other uses, served to keep the rowers' feet dry when the deck was awash.

Three of the six convicts at Number 6 had been drawn off for other duties; but Richard found a couple of his future associates at work with packthread and needle on a section of the galley tent. Under the eye of the aguzino, they did not look up while the newcomer was being chained to the bench.

"Here you, Zanetto," snapped the guard. "Set him to work. Give him something to do."

With the weight of the extra-heavy irons on his wrists, there was little that Richard could do except to hold the canvas taut while Zanetto sewed. But when the warden had turned away,

172

the soundless stream of obscenity that served the convicts as communication began. It was so much like ventriloquism that Richard caught on to it at once. The lips barely moved, but the hiss of words sounded distinct. In the course of it, Richard identified himself and learned who his companions on the bench were: Asouf, a Turk, as Number 1; then, on the other side of Richard, Zanetto, a naval deserter, as Number 3; then Bastian, a pickpocket, Number 4; and Bepo, condemned for banditry, Number 5. It turned out that Number 6, Tofolo, was the slave who had been recently flogged. Richard learned that he had been thrown afterwards into the forward cabin of the hold, where he might die or not. At the moment, only Zanetto and Bastian were present. The slaves on the benches before and behind were also named.

Zanetto knew a surprising lot about everyone, from the *Sopracomito,* or Captain, the Very Noble Anzolo Ruzzini, to the ship's boys.

"Favorite of Padron Luca's, aren't you?" he hissed, with a glance at Richard's fetters.

"Call it that."

The other leered. "You're luckier than you know. I can tell you something . . ."

But whatever it was had to be put off. Luca roared behind them at that moment: "Who set this cockroach to idling here? We need hands aft. Unchain him and send him along."

So, Richard joined the harassed gang of house cleaners in the stern and was put to emptying and filling pails of water for those who were scrubbing out the officers' quarters.

With a heavy bucket in each hand, he clanked back and forth between cabin and bulwarks or lowered pails to those who were working in the captain's room below deck. It was stuffy in the crowded stern and hot outside; sweat blinded him; his heart began pounding. Then the worst happened. He crumpled suddenly at the entrance of the stern in a sick faint, and the water he was carrying sloshed off along the deck.

He came to under the anguish of Padron Luca's cat, which brought him also to his feet; and he stood dizzily guarding his face from the blows that continued to pelt down. His stomach turned. Half falling, tripping over his chains, he staggered to the bulwarks and vomited. But the warden did not let up with his whip.

Like a tortured animal, Richard whirled on Luca, flailed at him with his chained arms, yelling an oath, and at once was dropped to the deck by the warden's fist.

Now, at last, the whipping stopped, to be followed by an ominous silence. Several of the guards closed in, awaiting the inevitable sequel. Richard's crime was obvious even to himself. He had struck at and cursed the chief petty officer of the ship. This entailed the bastinade, the most dreaded of naval punishments; and a soundless whisper of what was coming passed through the galley.

Luca now blew the call to assembly on his silver pipe. The hands who had been working in the stern and those in the prow trooped out and stood attentive. For the bastinade was an execution conducive to general morale, which it behooved everyone to watch. The big Turk, named Galafas, who had helped in the earlier flogging, presented himself for orders, the huge muscles of his naked torso standing out, the long lock projecting from the center of his shaved head. At a word from Luca, he jerked Richard up and propelled him, more dead than alive, toward the middle point of the corsia.

Half-dazed, Richard was lifted from his feet by Galafas, and found himself lying on his face across the corsia, his wrists and ankles gripped by convicts on both sides of it. Above him stood the Turk armed with a heavy rope-end attached to a handle. Ten or twelve blows of this sufficed to render a man unconscious. But that did not put an end to the flogging; thirty blows for light offenses; forty, fifty and up to a hundred for more serious ones. In such cases, however, few recovered, or they lingered on permanently crippled. For a crime like this, the cowed spectators reckoned, a maximum penalty was certain.

Padron Luca made a short speech for the benefit of his audience, recalling the attempt at murder which had sent Richard to the galleys and which had been now repeated against Luca himself.

Then he gave the order: "Su! Avanti!"

The first blow of the thick rope-end, descending with all the force of the Turk's two arms, resembled that delivered by a heavy but rather supple club. It was jarring and frightening as well as

174

unbelievably painful. It compressed the lungs; it brought out a cry of astonished agony and raised a weal an inch thick. To endure a second seemed impossible, but down came the rope again and again . . .

The slaves holding Richard's ankles and wrists had need of all their strength. Even so, his body arched itself on the corsia, heaving up and down. Flashes of inconceivable pain skewered him. And then all at once the sunlight went out. He seemed to be plunging head first into blackness. The jar of the twelfth blow meant nothing, and his muscles went limp.

At that, to the onlookers' surprise, the aguzino called a halt. "Va bene," he growled. "We'll keep the rest of it till another time. He won't get to hell so cheaply. You, there," he called to the surgeon barber of the galley, who stood waiting on the corsia, "do your job."

The job consisted in rubbing the wealed back with a mixture of strong vinegar and salt, which prevented gangrene and at the same time revived the patient with a new kind of torment. Richard regained a sort of delirious consciousness, in which he seemed to be grilling over a slow fire; but he did not know what was actually happening around him until several hours later.

Then he found himself once more chained to his bench, crouching on the footrest with his head against the seat. It was in this posture that the slaves took what sleep they could when the galley had been commissioned for the summer.

Night had fallen, and the tent had been raised over the vessel, though the open sides of it permitted a circulation of air. The curtained beds of the aguzini had been set up on their standards above certain of the benches; but those officers had not yet retired and were taking the air on the wharf, except for one who kept watch, patrolling back and forth along the corsia. Profound quiet reigned; for the slaves had been ordered asleep, and no one dared break the silence. Only here and there sounded the uneasy rattle of a chain.

"Water," Richard muttered.

"Drink this," came the toneless voice of Zanetto at his ear — "with Padron Luca's compliments."

It was a bottle of sour wine. Richard drank greedily.

"Wasn't I telling you how lucky you are?" Zanetto added.

175

A suppressed groan answered.

"No, davvero. I mean it. It's got around that that young blood you stabbed has a bargain with the Chief. He's to keep you on the hooks but keep you alive. Understand? That's why you got off with twelve today when another would have had eighty. If you die, his pay stops." Zanetto composed himself to sleep. "So, I think you'll live a long time."

XXVI

DURING the next two weeks, the galleys *Generalizia* and *Conserva* continued to be fitted out for the voyage. Masts were stepped and rigged; the long, slanting yards, each twice the length of their respective masts, were hoisted; stores, artillery, and ammunition, taken on; sails, canvases of every kind, and cordage, readied; the deck and all quarters, washed down. It required back-breaking work for the slaves from morning to night. Rowing itself would be almost a relief.

Meanwhile, there appeared, too, the rest of the ships' complement, who had been on leave or otherwise assigned during the winter. These included, for each galley: twenty-six seamen to handle the sails; twenty-five free rowers who replaced the sick or the dead among the slaves; petty officers, such as pilots, steersmen, boatswains, coxswains, and the like, having to do with the sailors and the two ship's boats; a commissary, in charge of stores; a chaplain, a surgeon, a master gunner; and, finally, a company of one hundred Morlacco soldiers, with their officers, returning to Dalmatia. In all, about two hundred men, which, together with the three hundred slaves, made a total ship's company of nearly five hundred. Among the last arrived several of the galley's chief officers, two lieutenants and an ensign. There was also a handful of passengers, young gentlemen volunteers posted to regiments in Dalmatia, and a couple of government officials with dispatches for the Proveditor at Zara.

At last the day of departure arrived. The Captain, the Very Noble Anzolo Ruzzini, came aboard to a ruffle of drums and flourish of trumpets, well executed by the ship's convict band. The

176

Morlacco soldiers, lining the bulwarks, presented arms. Every officer, in his appointed place, saluted. The slaves, dressed for once in their red coats and caps, their hands on the oars, gave a united *ho!* of welcome at a note from Padron Luca's pipe. The Banner of St. Mark was unfurled at the stern.

Remote as a god, the Captain, a lean, hard-looking young man, gave the order to cast off. The chief aguzino's pipe twittered *ready!* His threatening gaze embraced the benches. His pipe shrilled *go!* And fifty oars dipped as one.

Cannon salutes roared from the prow and were answered by a squadron of sailing ships of war, anchored near by. The galley *Conserva* now dropped in astern, flying all her bunting. From the standpoint of the waterfront, it was a gallant show.

For the slaves, however, shut in by the bulwarks, it was no show at all. With one foot on the pedagna and the other braced against the bench in front, they stretched their arms and bodies forward to bring the oar over the backs of the next rowers, who were in the same position; then, raising the heavy thirteen-foot end of the oar, which was hollowed into handles for a better grip, they flung themselves back together upon their bench, straining every muscle. And this effort of three hundred men at fifty oars in perfect time sent the long galley skimming down the lagoon. The timing had better be perfect. Three aguzini, distributed along the corsia, intently supervised it.

As the vessel headed south, Richard caught one far-off glimpse of Venice under the April sky, a faint mirage. But there was no time for gazing. Forward, *back;* forward, *back.* Without pause. Steady as a pendulum. Forward, *back.* Teeth set, muscles aching. The unaccustomed clothes stuck to the body. Breath grew shorter. Here and there, one of the weaker convicts faltered, was expertly touched up by a warden to the right pitch. Forward, *back . . .*

However, before rounding into the strait of Malamocco, that divides the long strip of land protecting the Venetian Lagoon and leads to the open sea, a pause was made. The slaves were ordered to strip. Off came the dress-parade uniform, red caps and coats, the last stitch, in short; the garments were stowed away; and the slaves reverted to their usual nakedness when at the oars.

So lightened, they took up their toil again; but, once through the Malamocco passage, when the first heave of the sea lifted the ship, and their oars found less regular purchase, they had some luck. The wind being favorable to sailing, oars were shipped; and the seamen now took over. The great yards were lowered; the triangular sails, attached and hoisted; and the ship assumed a different rhythm. Thus, for some hours, the human engine rested, until an afternoon calm once more required its efforts.

A galley was not a seagoing, but rather a coastwise vessel. It was this fact which had more or less confined it to the Mediterranean and which, as time passed, was gradually shelving it. Accordingly, though in a straight line the distance from Venice to Zara was less than two hundred miles, the *Generalizia* and *Conserva*, following the Adriatic coast and anchoring at night in convenient harbors, required twelve days for the voyage.

As it progressed, several slaves collapsed, could no longer be revived by the rope-end, were left to the chaplain. At almost every harbor, a burial party carried someone ashore, since it was not the Venetian custom to bury a man at sea. The empty places were filled by the free oarsmen.

On the third day out, Padron Luca, his heavy face more lowering than usual, stopped above Richard's bench, ordered him unchained by one of the guards, bade him put on his shirt and breeches and come along.

"The Captain wants you." He added in a mutter: "God knows why. Watch your tongue, if you know what's good for you."

Conscious of the stares focused on him, Richard clanked aft at the heels of the aguzino, and so into the sanctum of the stern, where the Captain alone had the luxury of a cabin.

Anzolo Ruzzini sat behind a table, with a freshly brewed cup of coffee in front of him.

Padron Luca saluted. "The convict Morandi, Zelenza."

"Very well. You can withdraw."

"He is a violent man, your Signory. Is it safe . . ."

The immense distance between a patrician captain and a chief petty officer showed in Ruzzini's tone. "I said *you can withdraw.* Do not make me repeat a command twice. Close the door and resume your station on the deck."

"Schiao," murmured Luca, vanishing, as if his big frame were a feather puffed away by the cold voice.

Then, for a long moment, the Captain eyed Richard, who stood passively, his hands at his sides, the heavy chain between them.

Ruzzini took a sip of coffee. "Well, Count Roberto, we meet again."

Startled, Richard looked up. The clear-cut face now seemed vaguely reminiscent. But meeting the hard blue eyes, his own fell.

"I had the pleasure," Ruzzini went on, "of seeing you act that part at the Villa Bagnoli. I had a few days' leave at the time. You gave an excellent performance and made a jackass of Sagredo. I take it this is the result?" But as Richard said nothing, he rapped, "I asked you a question."

"Yes, Zelenza, this is the result."

The Captain's next remark was still more unexpected. "You are a friend, I believe, of the ballerina Maritza Venier — indeed, as she tells me, more than a friend." The effect of this was so plainly shattering that Ruzzini did not wait for an answer. "I must inform you that she sought me out in Venice before we sailed. She had learned that you were assigned to this ship. I was told — truthfully, I believe — what occurred that night when you stabbed Sagredo. She begged me to show you what favor I could."

To hear Maritza spoken of in this hell affected Richard so deeply that, for a moment, he struggled to control himself.

Noting it, the Captain went on: "I shall tell you what I told her. I am no friend of Marin Sagredo's. I don't like bullies. No doubt you acted in self-defense. But the knife is no proper weapon. It is the weapon of bandits and assassins. If you had used a sword, none of this would have happened."

It was Tromba's opinion almost word for word. How often and how bitterly Richard had regretted his neglect of it!

He could only answer: "I had no sword, Zelenza. I was outnumbered six to one. I did what I could . . ."

Ruzzini shrugged. "A good fight, I'm told. But there you are. The Tribunal sifted the case and condemned you. It is not my business nor my desire to criticize their Excellencies. You were condemned to the galleys for life; and so it must be, as far as I'm concerned. I told the Siora that. On the other hand, I'm prepared

179

to do what I can for you. Those extra-heavy chains, for example — were they put on before or after you attacked the aguzino?"

"I did not attack him, your Signory. That is, I hardly knew —"

"Answer my question. I've been told about that 'attack.'"

"They were put on before, Zelenza."

"Aha! That wasn't the way I heard it." Evidently the Captain had been looking into matters. "For what reason were they put on?"

"I know of none, Vossioria."

A tight smile showed. "I think I can guess the reason. And as long as I'm aboard this ship, I'll protect you from it. We'll have no outside grudges paid off here. Besides, I know Padron Luca." Opening the table drawer, he took out some small coins to the value of about a sequin and knotted them in a coarse handkerchief. "Here, take this. Buy extra rations from him. He likes that. I'll let him know where the money came from."

Richard tried vainly to express himself.

"Don't thank me." The captain kept his rigid expression. "You're indebted to the Siora Maritza. I'm simply discharging a promise I made her. Within the limits of discipline and of your sentence, I'll look out for you. But nothing more, understand?"

He finished his cup, wiped his lips, then called the sentinel on duty outside. "Anselmo, reconduct the convict. When he's been chained, send Luca to me."

And so, between one hour and the next, Richard was promoted several circles higher. The heavy irons were replaced by the lightest chain — with what unspeakable relief! He treated his fellow slaves on the bench that evening to cheese and wine. The aguzini no longer singled him out for their blows. Some days later, he became one of the spalieri or stroke oars, a position of some importance that carried a few scudi a month and better rations.

But the grind, however relieved, went on. He still sweated on the bench, still crawled with vermin, still smarted under the wardens' lashes when the command was for speed and the rowing had to be forced.

The stay at Zara was brief. When the dispatches and supplies for the Proveditor had been landed, and when the places of the dead slaves had been filled by a new batch of convicts from Dalmatian prisons, the *Generalizia,* unattended this time by the escort galley, headed north again homeward bound.

And then, almost at once, the ship's fortunes changed. Winds were contrary, thus multiplying the demands on the rowers. In a half gale, among the islands southeast of Pola, the vessel all but went aground and received damage to her hull that would require expert repairs at the Arsenal in Venice. Worst of all, malignant fever broke out among the exhausted crew and decimated it. The Captain himself was stricken and had to be taken off finally at Rovigno. Straightway the shift of command to his subordinate made itself felt through the galley. The thinned ranks of the slaves suffered more than ever. The return voyage took twenty-one days.

At length, exhausted, shattered, demoralized, the *Generalizia,* after an absence of two months limped through the Porto di Lido and came to anchor in the great basin of the Arsenal ship-yards. The slaves, pending repairs on the vessel, were transferred to an ancient barracks once used for prisoners of war, and could look forward to rough labor ashore during the next weeks.

That same night, Padron Luca, whose duty it was to inspect the manacles of the convicts, paused for a word to Richard.

"Well, Moro —" the nickname *Moor* belonged naturally to a swarthy man — "Well, Moro, it's a pity that Captain Ruzzini's no longer about, isn't it? I think a certain other very noble gentleman in Venice will be wanting to look at you one of these days, and I intend to put you in shape to please him."

XXVII

ALTHOUGH the Ascension spring carnival, which consoled Venice for Lent, was three weeks past, the city gladly welcomed any pretext for another festival. Important saints' days, anniversaries of all kinds, were enough to promote regattas, attract crowds, and set off fireworks. Some such occasion, on a specially grand scale, seemed to be in progress after *Generalizia's* crippled arrival at the Arsenal. At night rockets soared up above the Canal of St. Mark, strains of music sounded, and the vast rumble of people.

181

"It can only be a foreign prince or ambassador," Richard whispered to his chainmate, Polo, a young Dalmatian outstretched beside him on the floor, as the distant fireworks showed one night through the square, barred windows of the crowded barracks room. "At the end of May, there's no saint big enough to account for it. Look at those rockets! Jesus! I'll bet it's splendid on the Piazza tonight. I'll bet they've had regattas and processions all day."

"Tell me what it's like," breathed the slave. "Please, Moro. I've never been anywhere but Zara. You make things so real when you talk about them. If they hadn't sent me to the galleys, I'd have enlisted as a soldier. Then perhaps I'd have seen Venice. Now —" He did not embroider on the hopelessness of the *now*. "Tell me," he repeated.

"Why, Polo, it's like this . . ."

On the score of experience and physical strength, Richard was wealthy as compared with his chainmate, a pathetic, simpleminded waif who had been condemned to the galleys for some minor offense. At least, Richard had lived; he had something to remember. Polo could hardly be said to have lived at all. Born in some kennel of Zara and existing from hand to mouth until the law had sent him to the oars, he was perhaps seventeen years old. The voyage had broken him; he would not last much longer. The bond between him and Richard was not only the chain, but a doglike worship, on one side, and pity, on the other.

"It's like this, Polo. Imagine the Grand Canal — I've told you about it — palaces and palaces, all finer than the finest at Zara. Great people on the balconies, which are hung with brocades and cloth of gold. Everybody in their robes and jewels. Such beautiful women, Polo! Such a crowd! You can hardly see the water for the gondolas. And there comes the regatta. One barge after the other, each patrician family outdoing the next. Tableaux! Gods and goddesses. Perhaps the Contarini show Apollo on Parnassus, with the Winged Horse, the Nine Muses, and Fame. Or the Corrers show the Triumph of Valor. Or the Mocenigos show the Garden of the Hesperides; or the Querini, the chariot of Venus, drawn by doves . . ."

"I don't understand, Moro. But it doesn't matter. It sounds like a picture of heaven."

182

"Heaven couldn't be finer, fio mio. And then there are the processions on the Piazza. The guilds of the city, the six Schools, the nine Congregations, the girls of the four conservatories. — What voices they have! Like angels! — And there come the canons of St. Mark's and St. Peter's, the senators, the patricians, the Patriarch, the Doge himself. And just imagine the torches, statues, banners, spears, gold and silver emblems. Just imagine the fifes and trumpets and drums and bells."

"Christ!" breathed Polo.

"And there's your foreign prince or ambassador, and everything's done in his honor."

"To think you've seen all that!" the other marveled. And after a pause, "I suppose your Siora mother will be seeing it now."

Richard stared up at the ceiling. "No, she'll have had to leave with my stepfather for France. I'm sure she isn't in Venice."

"But the beautiful ballerina you've told me of, Moro — she'll be seeing it." There was no answer for so long that the slave added, "Are you angry with me for speaking of her, Moro?"

"I'm not angry. I was only thinking."

"Perhaps she knows that you're here," Polo suggested. "Perhaps she would even come to the Arsenal and you could see her."

"Don't talk nonsense," snapped Richard. Then he laid his hand on Polo's arm. "I didn't mean that. Only there's no use fooling one-self."

A sigh answered. And after a pause, "What's the Garden of the Hesper you mentioned — if that's the right name?"

"Call it Paradise. Do you know what that is?"

"Not very well . . ."

A guard's voice from the end of the long, stifling room lined with naked bodies rumbled: "By God! Is one of you bloody swine talking?"

After that, there was only hot silence, the whine of mosquitoes, the subdued clank of a chain as someone shifted in his sleep, and the remote sounds of the festival.

While the repairs on the *Generalizia* were being made, the slaves were set to rough labor beneath the dignity of the *arsenalotti*, or skilled Arsenal workmen, who ranked as the most privileged guild in Venice. The convicts unloaded heavy lumber from

183

barges, crushed stone for ballast, repaired embankments, and the like. As usual they worked in pairs, coupled together by a long chain from ankle to ankle. Each wore a hook at the belt, supporting a section of the chain, which would otherwise have been too hampering. The guards oversaw the various gangs.

Luca attended to Richard himself. It was a daily torment, now denying him water in spite of the heat, now inventing special degradations, now imposing the heaviest tasks, and all to the tune of lashes and oaths.

But some of the ill-usage had to be shared by the young slave Polo. It was impossible to set Richard to some back-breaking job and exclude his chainmate. And Polo did not have the strength for it, though Richard took as much of the work as possible on his own shoulders. At last, on a certain morning, when they were carrying a two-hundred-pound weight of lumber between them, Polo collapsed on the hot pavement of the shipyard.

At once Luca was there, his cat flailing the unconscious body.

Richard put in: "Lay off him, Padron. Can't you see the boy isn't up to this work?"

The other turned on him with a bellow.

But at that moment, one of the foremen of the Arsenal, running up, shouted: "Get your men in line. Drop all work. Everybody at attention! Their Excellences . . . They've brought the foreign count to show him the Arsenal. Hurry . . ." And he ran on, spreading the news.

"Cospetto del diavolo!" Luca fumed. He yelled orders to the other guards. Then, in a panic of haste, he unlocked the chain coupling Richard with Polo and, grasping the latter by the shoulders, dragged him out of sight behind a low heap of stones. There was need of hurry, for the front of the distinguished cortege had now come into full view, strolling leisurely along the docks. "Get into line over there," he gestured to Richard. "And fix your chain to look as if it's linked to the next man."

The various gangs of convicts now stood drawn up, each near the work they had been engaged in. "Fold your hands in front!" hissed the guards. "Dead still, all of you!"

It was to have been expected that the foreign guest would sooner or later have been shown the Arsenal, which for centuries had been one of the glories of Venice. But apparently this unannounced visit was being made on the spur of the moment. The great dockyards, which in time past had launched fleet after fleet for trade or war, now shared the decay which had overtaken the dying state. There was not much to see in the Arsenal any longer — only the setting and birthplace of vanished armadas. A hundred and fifty years before, the great basin had contained a fleet of two hundred galleys ready for the sea. Now only a handful remained. The thousands of workmen, who, in the days of Lepanto, could build and launch a ship in twenty-four hours, now were numbered only in hundreds. The vast warehouses that had contained every article necessary to a vessel, from the smallest screw to the highest mast, lay bare and empty. Like the rest of Venice, the Arsenal had long since begun to live on memories.

Gazing over at the still distant group of visitors, Richard could see the "High Admiral" of the Arsenalotti, as the chief of their guild was called, pointing out things to a tall gentleman in black, while others of the escort put in a word now and then. These included the chief officers of government. Among them Richard recognized the long red robe of Capitan Grande, symbol of Venetian law.

From the corner of his mouth, Richard shot a toneless whisper to the slave at his elbow. "Who is the foreign count anyway?"

But the question had to be relayed on down the line. The answer came after a minute. "They say he's a special ambassador from England."

Richard felt a pulse of interest. If he had listened to Tromba, he might have been in England by this time.

"What's his name?"

"How would I know?"

The cortege drew nearer. They were all officials. Some of them belonged to the Council of Ten. There was the Procurator of St. Mark's . . . But Richard could not take his eyes from the English visitor, tall, dark, very much of a grand seigneur. He carried a long ebony cane with a gold pommel and used a lorgnette to follow the pointing of his guides.

But the face . . .

It was strangely familiar, though Richard knew that he had

185

never seen him. Disturbingly, uncannily familiar. It brought a quickening of the heart, a mad wonder . . .

Suddenly a guard hissed: "Attention now! . . . Their Excellences . . . the Conte di Marny . . ."

Richard's consciousness focused to one vivid point. His father! This great lord whom Venice delighted to honor — his father!

The Englishman was opposite the slaves, about twenty feet off. His finely modulated voice, speaking perfect French, could be heard distinctly. He addressed the Procurator.

"Et ces gens, votre Excellence?"

"Convicts, monseigneur, from the galleys, at work in the Arsenal."

"Ah, indeed?"

He glanced carelessly and looked away. In a moment he would be past. It was now or never — a heaven-sent, incredible chance . . .

To the horror of everyone, a half-naked galley slave, carrying his chain, was seen to dash forward out of the line and sink on his knees in front of the ambassador. It was so shocking, so unheard of, that the guards, for an instant, stood motionless.

Richard spoke rapidly in French the first words that came to him. "Monseigneur, I am your son by Jeanne Dupré. I beg you to save me."

There was no time for anything more. Luca, bounding forward, already had him by the throat, shaking him back and forth. Other guards hurried up.

Lord Marny's poise was justly celebrated. He looked unruffled, though slightly annoyed, drawing back a pace.

"The fellow must be mad."

"Monseigneur . . ." A chorus of apologies sounded. "Pardon . . ." Black scowls on the part of the officials followed the guards, who were hustling Richard away.

"One moment, please." Marny's voice sharpened. "Stop those men. I beg leave to point out something, though doubtless, to gentlemen of your Signories' sagacity, it needs no mention."

He paused, while his dark eyes, still bland but with a hint of ice, dominated the group. To Richard, whose guards had stopped at a word from Capitan Grande, the phrases of courtly French had the incisiveness of a death sentence.

186

"The convict," Marny went on, "should have been under control. As regards myself, it is a trifle of no moment. But an offense to the dignity of the King, whom I unworthily represent, is no trifle, and my office does not permit me to overlook it."

It was true, a little rigid, perhaps, but very true. An ambassador plenipotentiary, the other self of the prince who accredited him, had every right to insist on such a point.

The Procurator of St. Mark's, who, as an officer of the Republic, came second only to the Doge himself, bowed low.

"Monseigneur, I am more afflicted by what has occurred than you. If your Excellence will but condescend to state what measure of satisfaction would be acceptable, consider it already offered."

At once Marny relaxed, smiled, returned the bow. "Far be it from me, Monseigneur de Saint-Marc, to make difficulties about so trifling an affair. Your courtesy has already effaced it. However, if I might suggest — ?"

"At your Excellence's service."

"Then it would seem to me that if this slave were consigned to the Ducal Prison and there straitly examined on the charge of lese majesty, to be dealt with afterwards as the crime deserves; and if the warden, who should have prevented him, were well punished for negligence — the matter might be considered closed, to the infinite honor of Venice."

The Procurator turned to Capitan Grande. "You have heard Monseigneur de Marny's desires. See that they are executed."

"I thank your Signory." The Englishman was all graciousness. "By the way, may I have the name of this convict — for my report?" He waited for the information.

"Ah, Richard Morandi. — And now, may we resume our inspection of your famous Arsenal? To one of a seafaring nation, like mine, the very name inspires reverence . . ."

They drifted on. Padron Luca, who, understanding no French, had not caught the implication to him of Marny's *desires*, tightened his grip on Richard's arm. "And now, *you* —" But he broke off at a touch on his shoulder.

Capitan Grande used the phrase which, during the centuries, had brought so many Venetians before the Council and to their deaths.

187

"Their Excellencies wish to see you, Luca Buranello — and you, Richard Morandi."

The warden cried out: "God! But I'm innocent, your Worship. I've done nothing. It isn't my fault if this dog —"

"Their Excellencies will determine your guilt, Luca Buranello."

Beckoning his archers, who closed in, the Officer of the Red Robe himself accompanied the prisoners.

In a leaden apathy, Richard followed his guards. As it happened, he was brought to the same cell of the Pozzi where he had first been imprisoned. The same turnkey received him. He stretched out on the same pallet.

There gradually he realized that this meant the end. But the idea of death no longer appalled him. He could stand anything but the living death of the galleys. At least, that was over.

As the hours passed, he thought more about Lord Marny than himself, the suave, experienced face, the imperturbable ruthlessness. How adroitly he had freed himself forever from the vilifying bond with a galley slave! Dead men do not talk and are soon forgotten. Because he had made an issue of it, the Tribunal would act quickly. There might be whispers, but he was too great a personage to be affected by them.

On the whole, Richard felt that he had no right even to hate his father. If as a young man, long ago, Marny had sacrificed love in the interest of personal advantage, could a foolish weakness be expected of him now? For the sake of this very mission to Venice, he would not dare to incur the disgrace of acknowledging such a son. He must repudiate him sharply and finally. No, Richard had to admit that the appeal to his father had been an insane impulse. As Marny had said, he must have been mad.

XXVIII

THAT day passed, and the next. The turnkey entered with the usual ration of bread and water, carefully inspected the prisoner's chains, and went out. Richard asked him once if he would take a message to the chaplain, Father Procolo; but the man said curtly:

188

"I have the strictest orders that you are not to see or communicate with anyone."

Richard lay in complete darkness, sometimes asleep but more often in a waking dream, disconnected, almost passionless, except for the lingering dread of what certainly awaited him. Perhaps he might not even be brought before the Tribunal. People often merely disappeared in prison. It was the most secret method.

Then, on the evening of the second day, the door opened, lanterns showed, and the turnkey unchained him from the wall staple. The time had come. Richard braced himself as well as he could.

"The Tribunal?" he asked.

"No, you will not appear before their Excellences."

"Am I to have no priest, no time to —"

"No."

With the turnkey and two guards whom he vaguely remembered as torturers' assistants during his earlier examination, Richard followed the windings of the corridor. He walked mechanically, a cold emptiness at the pit of his stomach. It seemed a long way. At last the turnkey threw open a door, and Richard's worst fears were justified. The room was cloudy with steam. He caught the glimmer of fire under a huge vat from which dim figures were drawing water. They were pouring this into another tublike container that was being stirred by the phantom of a man evidently in charge of operations.

Richard's manacles were removed from his wrists and ankles for the first time in months. He was stripped naked. The turnkey said, "I leave him now with your Worship," and went out. The phantom, who had been bending over the container, answered, "Very well." Then turning, he approached Richard with what seemed gallows humor. "The bath is ready."

And, at that, Richard knew what it was to go mad. For he recognized the man as a well-known barber on the Piazza, a Monsù Golimbert.

The phantasmagory went on. The water was hot but not boiling. He was being rubbed with soap, then afterwards with towels. In the next room they helped him into black satin breeches and white stockings. He was shaved . . .

189

"But what is this?" he kept asking.

"I think that's evident," said Golimbert.

"But why?"

"I don't know. We're obeying orders."

"What's to be done with me?"

"I have no idea. His Excellence did not say."

"What Excellence?"

The other hesitated. "A great official."

"But, Monsieur Golimbert, you know me. I'm —"

The Frenchman laid a firm hand on Richard's mouth.

"I don't know you. None of us know you."

They put him into a shirt of fine cambric, chose a neckcloth with lace beneath it, applied a mouche to his chin, tried on several wigs and made a selection.

In the end they showed him his reflection in a long mirror. It was the first time he had looked at himself since January. From the appearance of the other galley slaves, he had been able well enough to imagine his own. But there was nothing of the galleys in this elegant figure that recalled the role of Count Roberto — yes, in the hands, perhaps, which all the scrubbing and manicuring had been unable to refine. He looked, too, much older, the hollows and bones of the cheeks more pronounced, the mouth and eyes harder. Remembering his face six months ago, he wondered if his self had changed to the same extent.

Golimbert now handed him a long cape, a laced hat, and a mask.

"There you are," he said. "If clothes make the man, I think what you were has disappeared."

By this time, the dream impression had given way to a no less mysterious reality. What was the point of it all? What would be the next development?

"I seem to be going out," Richard smiled, with a glance at the hat.

But Golimbert was not to be drawn. He answered with a shrug, then summoned the turnkey, who had been waiting outside.

Once more Richard accompanied the jailer down the winding corridor, but in what direction he had no longer any idea. It seemed odd to be walking without chains, and he found it hard to adjust his gait.

"Where are you taking me?" he asked.

"To the west portico, Vossioria." His clothes had evidently won him a title.

"Am I to be free then?"

"Sior, no. I'm handing you over to someone else."

A moment later, Richard found himself in the open air and could see the glimmering of the Piazza lights.

"Is this the gentleman?" asked a voice from the shadow, and a masked figure came forward. "Very good, you can leave him with me." When the turnkey was gone, the voice turned French. "Your humble servant, Monsieur Hammond."

Utterly confused, but catching a glimmer now of the truth, Richard answered, "My name's Morandi."

"No," returned the voice, "I think you're mistaken. — I beg you to put on your mask. So! That's better. — Morandi, mon cher monsieur, will not be seen again. He has been disposed of in the prison. It is better to forget him."

"May I ask who you are?"

"Of course. I am Jean Martin, Milord de Marny's French secretary. I am directed to bring you to him. He is expecting you."

XXIX

RETURNING from a ball at the Palazzo Contarini at an early, though not too early hour — it was one o'clock — Lord Marny relaxed in the library of the sumptuous apartment which had been assigned him in the "Procuratie Nuove." That is, to the valet, who brought him his gold-brocaded dressing gown, and to the footman, who set a decanter of dessert wine on a small table beside his chair, he gave the usual impression of serenity and of taking his ease after a busy day. It was a habit with him to read awhile before retiring, and he now asked for the volume of Crébillon which he had begun the night before.

Bob Brown, the footman, one of the staff which he had brought with him from England, lingered a moment.

"Will there be anything else, m'lord?"

"No, except this. I will see Monsieur Martin at once when he

191

comes in — and the gentleman with him. Bring another wine glass."

"Very good, m'lord."

"Then you can go to bed." Marny added, with a smile. "These late Venetian hours must be a trial to you, Bob."

"Not so bad, m'lord, though it must be said Eyetalians do turn night into day. We manage better in England, sir."

"No doubt," agreed Marny. "Well, we won't be here much longer." And he opened his book.

But when the servant had gone, he did not read. Instead, filling a glass from the decanter, he sat tasting the wine, his eyes vaguely on the portrait of an old Venetian, set in a panel of the opposite wall. And yet even now, though unobserved, his practised features expressed only an amiable insouciance that bore no relation at all to the eagerness, curiosity, and suspense behind them. He had long since reached the point of a complete divorce between feeling and expression. Tonight, however, an occasional impatient twitch of his right foot set the diamond buckle twinkling.

Like his friend Voltaire and others of the same school, Lord Marny took a detached, unflattering view of human nature which did not exclude himself. Human nature was a compound of frailties, vices and inconsistencies. If a man used his will and his reason, he could cover these up under a decent exterior, control them somewhat and endeavor to keep them out of sight; but he could not hope wholly to eradicate them. For instance, who of Marny's friends or enemies would dream that so rational a man, so disciplined, so worldly, could ever indulge himself in memories which were as weak as they were absurd, could regret a lost happiness which, if he had been foolish enough to pursue it, would have ruined him? But so it was. And, aware of this infirmity, he could not help it. In the long, dusty pageantry of his life, there had been one radiant, tender, irrational interlude, to which his thought at times returned. He remembered it now, as always, with a sigh.

That the slave at the Arsenal had appealed to him in the name of Jeanne Dupré was decisive. Years ago, he had deserted Jeanne herself for what he considered compelling reason; but since then, she had become a symbol of his youth. He had long realized that she was the only woman he had ever loved. Compared with her, the homely heiress he had married or the random conquests of idle hours were only means that served his ambition, vanity, or pleasure. They had no purchase on his innermost self. She alone haunted him. Her name, spoken aloud after the silence of so many years, had the force of a master word.

But it was not only her name that moved him. It was the amazing, soul-stirring fact that he, baffled by childlessness so long, had actually a son, a son, too, by this single, unforgettable romance of his life. It had seemed a derogation of his great success, almost a judgment upon him, that he had no child. He had secretly smarted under the sense of incompleteness, had secretly envied his more fortunate friends. Now suddenly he was dazzled by the knowledge of his own paternity.

Not that more than a hundredth of all this had occurred to him during that brief instant at the Arsenal. But one of Marny's gifts was quickness of wit. Jeanne Dupré. A son by her. Possibly. But he must not compromise himself and he must gain time. He must also protect the boy from punishment while he investigated. If the slave were an impostor, let him hang; if not, Marny could take the proper steps.

Looking back, he congratulated himself on playing his cards well. The clever and energetic Monsieur Martin had covered the case thoroughly. Though the Morandis were no longer in Venice, Dr. Goldoni, together with the chaplain, Father Procolo, supplied all the information necessary, not only as to Richard's mother, but regarding the crime which had sent him to the galleys. The rest had been easy. As British ambassador charged with concluding a trade agreement beneficial to Venice and another one involving common action against the Barbary pirates, Lord Marny had only to make a small personal request to have it granted. He and the pertinent officials were all men of the world. Nothing could have been more amiably confidential. Venetian justice was served and the Sagredo claim met by disposing of the galley slave, Richard Morandi, in prison. The proper passport was issued for his lordship's near kinsman, Richard Hammond. Marny could rely on their Excellences' discretion in the future; his son's Venetian past was obliterated.

Yes, he had played his cards well. He was content, too, that Jeanne had left Venice. For every reason, that was fortunate.

Whatever his regard for her, he did not deceive himself about her opinion of him. Her silence during the years, when she could so easily have communicated with him — at least with respect to their son — spoke for itself. Afraid of very little on earth, he would have found it hard to meet her. Besides, they had both altered, both grown middle-aged. There was no use disturbing one's memories . . .

At last, he caught a murmur of voices, the sound of footsteps. Though his expression did not change, his pulse quickened a beat. He set down his glass on the table.

From the doorway at the far end of the room, Martin said, "Mr. Hammond, my lord," but, as had been arranged between them, he did not enter. Lord Marny got up and stood facing the tall, dark figure who approached him.

And at that point, he needed all his self-control to repress a start. For it seemed to him momentarily that his own father, dressed, to be sure, in the latest fashion, but otherwise unchanged, had been released from the portrait which hung in Marny House and was coming down the room toward him. The resemblance was so close that for an instant it excluded any other thought. His glimpse of the convict at the Arsenal had not prepared him for it.

Richard dropped to one knee. "Monseigneur!"

"Mon cher fils!" smiled Marny, lifting him in a short embrace and relishing his use of that phrase for the first time. "Let me assure you that you need no documents to prove you are a Hammond. Your likeness to your grandfather is most amazing. Has anyone informed you of it?"

"But yes, milord, my mother has spoken of it."

"Has she, indeed?" said Marny lightly. He recalled showing her his father's miniature. "Well, be seated, my dear boy." He waved Richard to a chair and resumed his own. "I hope you forgive my odd reception of you day before yesterday at the Arsenal. You will admit . . ."

He ran pleasantly on, explaining his motives and the steps he had taken. He was famous for his charm, turning the full force of it now on Richard. The situation required a light tone to put the young man at his ease and to avoid committing Marny himself until he had determined what kind of son this was. He had no intention of playing the fool. If Richard were a rogue or a dull, commonplace dog, he would provide for him accordingly; if he had parts, that was another matter. So far, the boy looked promising. Martin's report, derived from Goldoni, indicated talents above the average. Personally, he now made a good impression, had an attractive manner, carried himself well.

Yes, promising. And, with that, a vista opened up which at once caught the Earl's imagination. At fifty-five he had passed the summit of life, was aware in himself of approaching age, felt lonely at times. What if this boy were fit to become his younger self, his confidant, the inheritor, not of his title, alas, but of his ambitions and career? To one of great talent, illegitimacy offered no barrier that could not be surmounted.

"In short, mon cher Richard," he was saying, "as a Venetian, you are dead; as an Englishman, I wish you long and prosperous years. How does it feel to die and come to life? I have always been curious about Lazarus."

Richard looked down. "I wish I could tell you, milord. I wish I could thank you . . ." It was impossible to express himself. He felt dazed and unreal. "Perhaps sometime I can do better, monseigneur."

Marny gave a negligent wave of the hand. "My dear lad, if your merit equals my expectation — and I have no doubt it will — I shall consider myself indebted to you rather than the reverse. Believe me, it has not been my fault that hitherto you have had no proof of a father's very natural affection. I was not even aware of your existence. May I ask why you never made yourself known to me?"

In some embarrassment, Richard answered with a question. "I take it, milord, that you have not seen my mother? She is perhaps no longer in Venice. You see, the galley has just returned from Zara, and I have no news —"

"Of course not," Marny put in. "No, to my infinite regret, I have not seen her. She left recently, I believe for Bordeaux, with the very worthy man she married." Richard did not miss the disdain of that reference. "So it was she who prevented your writing me?"

"She was opposed to it, monseigneur. She did not —" it was hard to be tactful — "she did not believe that you would welcome —"

"Nonsense!" smiled Marny. "She knew very well that I would

195

welcome it. Say, rather, that she did not wish to give me that satisfaction. Your mother, my dear Richard, is a very singular woman, singular in her pride and her resentment. — Not that I blame her," he added graciously. "The fault was altogether mine. But there is such a thing as charity." Unpleasant as it was, Marny now decided to clear the air once and for all. They could not go on evading the subject. "I fancy you've only heard her side of it?"

"No, milord, she has always been fair to the motives that governed you at that time."

"I warrant not," exclaimed Marny, taken somewhat aback. "She could not have helped justifying herself. Let me put it this way . . ."

He put it very well and logically, with a touch of sentiment, a touch of humor, condescending a little. Why, after all, should he defend himself to this boy? Why, as he spoke, did he have an odd impression of futility? The world, this; the world, that. He used the term a good deal. As if he thought it proved something; as if he did not know perfectly well that it proved nothing, except the choice he had made between the world and other values.

"I have always entertained," the Earl concluded, "a deep regard for your mother — let me add, a deeper regard than for any other woman. That I did not choose to renounce the world for her sake is the only fault she can urge against me." He knew this to be an equivocation, but it was well phrased. "So, I hope you perceive that I hardly deserved her inflexible severity, in so far, at least, as it concerned my share in you."

A ring glittered on Marny's well-shaped hand as he reached out to the decanter and filled their glasses.

"May I ask," said Richard, after a sip or two, "what my own position is — in Venice, I mean? There are some friends —"

"I thank you for reminding me," said Marny. "Your position here depends on the parole which I have given to the very obliging Inquisitors. Remember, *your former self is dead*. Dead men do not ordinarily walk abroad or communicate with friends. I have promised their Excellencies that you will remain incommunicado in this apartment until you leave it as one of my suite — at night and masked. A matter of only a few days, I hope. Between you and me, I detest this foolish operatic city."

"But, monseigneur, Dr. Goldoni must know the truth about me from Monsieur Martin."

"Not at all. Martin posed as a traveling Frenchman, an acquaintance of your mother's in Bordeaux, who sought news of you. Neither the good Doctor nor the chaplain, whatever his name is, knows anything else. Martin is a very able man."

"But does it mean that I am never to communicate with anyone I have known — with my mother, with —"

"That would be too rigorous," smiled Marny, "though, in a way, I wish it were possible." He leaned back thoughtfully. "No, but not for some time, my dear Richard, and then most discreetly. Let the mists gather over your unknown grave in the Pozzi. You will admit that it would not improve whatever figure Richard Hammond may make in the world, if he were identified with an ex-galley slave. Let's see. I shall present you as having been brought up in France. Your French is excellent . . ."

Richard felt a surge of revolt. Maritza? She was here in Venice. Could he tamely ignore her and sneak away without a word because of Marny's parole? He could rely absolutely on her silence.

"But there is one friend, milord, a lady, whom I must communicate with."

To his astonishment, Marny answered: "Ah, yes — the dancing girl, I suppose. Goldoni spoke to Martin about her. Toujours la femme, eh?"

"She belongs to one of the noblest families in Venice," Richard said hotly. "Her father is Antonio Venier."

The other did not seem impressed. "Dancing girls have no families, though I confess they're sometimes attractive to young men and old fools. However, my dear boy, don't be concerned. You couldn't communicate with her here. I understand that she and her father have left Venice."

The news was a thunderbolt. "Left Venice?" Richard stammered.

"Yes. And I believe as a result of your friend Sagredo's intrigues. What a doddering old state this is with its terrors and tyrannies! It seems that Venier dabbles in letters. He foolishly read some poetry of his to a distant kinsman of this Sagredo, who denounced him to the Tribunal. The poem was seized, found treasonable. He was banished a fortnight since. I take it he's all but a beggar and must live by his daughter's legs — forgive me for the equivoque."

Richard's cheeks burned but he managed to hold his tongue.

197

Marny added: "Goldoni says she had no choice but to enter a strolling troupe destined for Florence or Milan, I don't know which."

It was easy to fill in the gaps of this account. Richard remembered how Venier himself had pointed out that the beloved and much rewritten poem on Venice would not please the government. Probably it was Goldoni with his wide connections who had secured a place for Maritza in one of the traveling companies. Money would be scarce, and it took both time and money to restore relations with Caretti in London, even if that were at all possible.

"You look positively stricken," observed Marny, fingering the stem of his wine glass.

"We are betrothed, monseigneur."

The Earl's black eyebrows went up. "Indeed? I was unaware of it. My congratulations! My regrets that Mademoiselle should suffer the inconvenience of exile. But what then?"

"I must find her, milord, if you permit."

Marny's languid, smiling face showed nothing of his disappointment. He took a few sips, touched his mouth with a handkerchief, and eyed Richard indulgently.

At last he said: "Far be it from me, young man, to constrain you in any way. You have my permission to do as you please. Nay, more, you may count on my assistance up to a point. I consider it fortunate that this subject presents itself now, so that we may at once understand each other. It might have been very distressing if later your betrothal and Mademoiselle had crossed the very different plans I had in mind for you. Because, frankly, such a marriage is incompatible with any of the more shining careers."

He took snuff and lightly brushed off the jabot of his shirt.

"You have, therefore, a vital decision to make," he went on, "which, as far as I am concerned, will be irrevocable. You must choose between two utterly opposed ways of life. Embarked on one, you may regret but you cannot pursue the other. Do you follow me?"

"I think so, monseigneur."

"Good. But I shall put it in plain terms. Nothing will be easier, when we are once beyond the Venetian frontier — I travel by way

198

of Turin and the Cantons — than for you to become Richard Morandi again. In that case, I shall give you a moderate purse and my blessing, and you can set off in quest of Mademoiselle. I shall also give you the advice to keep thereafter at a safe distance from Venice for the sake of your own neck, and I shall warn you that the stigma of the galleys is not easy to remove, though doubtless the charms of Mademoiselle may compensate for it. If I do not believe that they will compensate permanently for all the squalid details and vexations of a shabby career, you must forgive me. I have no faith in the lasting qualities of honeymoons."

"In other words, milord," put in Richard, "you would be through with me."

"Well," Marny said, "after all you could not expect me to take much pride or interest in your affairs." He suppressed a yawn. "Now consider the other alternative. Suppose you decided to remain Richard Hammond."

He kept his detached, good-humored expression, but he played the game very carefully at this point.

"In that case, you would accompany me to England. You would agree, not to forget Mademoiselle Venier but, for some time, to look around you under my guidance and, during that time, to entertain the idea of a brilliant and ambitious future rather than of marriage. Believe me, there are worthier and more virile objects of a young man's attention. I make no promises. You are perhaps wholly unfitted to the business of the world. I shall study you critically and shall be frank in my verdict. But I am much deceived if you are not capable of something more respectable than the role of Harlequin and the claptrap of the stage."

His face now obediently grew more serious, with the proper tinge of sentiment.

"My dear boy!" He rested his hand lightly on Richard's knee. "It is pleasant to dream, though I avoid dreams that have no promise of accomplishment. Believe me, it is not so with regard to your future. Let us dream, then, that you are capable of greatness. How much more worth while to be a peer among the masters of men than a slave subject to tyranny and injustice! How much more worth while to enjoy the security of power and esteem than to live defenseless and on sufferance! Haven't the galleys enlightened you as to this? Would you return to a life where that sort of thing can happen? I hope not."

While Marny spoke, Richard's thought, much nimbler than words, supplied the text with illustrations from the galleys. He had been freed from them by a miracle. Incur the smallest risk that that might happen again? Choose to be one of the little people who were open to such brutality, when he could put himself forever beyond the reach of it? Live as a vagabond actor or needy playwright groveling for patronage, under the stigma, as Marny put it, of having served in the galleys?

"Par Dieu, monseigneur, you are right!"

"Of course I am," nodded Marny. "I shall exert myself in your favor, and I demand a like effort on your part. I am sure you'll decide wisely."

"The decision has been made, milord. You will not find me ungrateful; I hope you will not find me incapable."

For once, Marny showed the growing warmth he felt. "My word on it, Richard, I shall not. I'm persuaded that we think very much alike, that we have more than the bond of blood between us. I think we understand each other."

PART TWO

XXX

IN spite of the war between England and France, and their allies, which had now been in progress for several years, it did not rouse suspicious gossip, much less hostility, that Amélie des Landes, though wife of a French nobleman, should spend some weeks at Bath without her husband during the autumn season of 1758. Amélie was Irish on her father's side and could claim the highest English connections. Besides, Mr. Pitt himself, who was in Bath at the moment, not only countenanced but received her more than once at his own house. If a Secretary of State could overlook her nominal nationality, everyone else could do so.

Therefore, bewitching as always, radiantly chic and very much the fashion, Amélie, in the words of the infatuated Mr. Nash, adorned Bath with her presence. And so, on a late October morning, she opened languidly lovely eyes to the light that filtered through dimity bed curtains in Mrs. Hodgkinson's highly select boardinghouse close to the Abbey.

The Abbey was much too close. She might have slept an hour longer except for the chimes that welcomed the equipage of every new visitor to Bath and were now bing-banging, it seemed, just over her head. She considered the custom a dreadful bore and would have shifted her lodgings from Orange Grove to a less stylish, though quieter, section of town if her projected stay had been long enough to warrant the trouble. Now, drowsily annoyed, she waited for the chimes to stop. They had similarly wakened Monsieur Coco, her parrot, who, from clucking and grumbling, finally shrieked *Merde!* at the top of his lungs.

"Precisely, mon amour," she approved. "C'est le mot juste."

Then, as the bells and the parrot subsided, she let her thoughts drift: back over yesterday, forward over today, and still further along to her happy departure for France a month hence. With few exceptions, she hated everything in England: the coarse men, the frostbitten women, the universal smugness and idiotic prejudices. Especially she hated this watering place with the dull routine of baths, Pump Room, shops, stuffy breakfasts and tea parties. She hated the balls twice a week at the Assembly Rooms, where, until livelier country dances began, a suffocated crowd sat for two mortal hours, watching one gawky couple after another go through the same minuet to poor music.

Of course, Amélie was too well bred to voice criticism; she appeared ravished with England. Besides, now and then one did encounter really polite people with a French training, or some foreign adventurer from the Continent, polished enough to flirt with; or a good-looking country squire worth tormenting. But above all, England was rich; it exuded money — at the gaming tables, where Amélie could hold her own even with professionals, at conferences with a minister who exchanged broad guineas for French secrets — and for the sake of money she could swallow quite a few pills. Then too, while selling France to Pitt, the Countess gathered data on England to be sold later to the Duc de Choiseul — especially with regard to this expedition against Quebec. She had no conscience at all in the matter, no national prejudice. Nor was she unusually mercenary. She thought only in terms of extravagances that money would buy. To acquire it was worth a couple of months' boredom.

She now pulled the bell cord for her morning chocolate and, comfortable in bed, reflected happily on the wretched women parboiling themselves at that moment in the King's Bath. It might be fashionable, but such a regime was not for her. She had an exquisite deshabille; and now and then before the eleven o'clock breakfast she paid her respects to the waters by appearing in the Pump Room for a few sips, to the dazzlement of her beaux.

Chocolate finished, she submitted to the long ordeal of the

toilet at the hands of her two maids, Stephanie and Babette. In Paris, this would have been enlivened by masculine callers bringing the latest scandals and the newest epigrams. It was the hour of gossip and flattery, an hour of titillation devoted to the fine art of accidentally revealing and promptly veiling charms that skirt and bodice would soon conceal. But this was sober England and Mrs. Hodgkinson's. The gorgeous Monsieur Coco, whetting his beak on a pumice stone and now and then cracking a seed, was therefore the only male creature present. A cynical bird with a salty vocabulary, he upheld his sex and lent a note of gallantry. An admiring *O-la-la!* at proper moments encouraged the skill of Stephanie and Babette. His *tiens-tiens!* and *Oh, la belle poule!* paid homage to Amélie.

At last, sufficiently made up and arrayed for the earlier part of the day, the Countess entered her boudoir, where a neat coal fire tempered the chill of the season, and settled herself in a chair near the hearth. At a sound of voices from the next room, she looked a question at Stephanie.

"As I already told Madame — Mistair Pickerly, Milord Ferrers. They have been waiting a long time."

The Countess shrugged. "Bon Dieu! I forgot." She glanced at the window. It was a leaden, overcast day threatening rain. "No, no, no!" she rebelled. "I can't, I won't. It's no weather for a walk. They afflict me with their bad French. They glower at each other. I haven't the courage today. Get rid of them, chérie. Say I'm ill. Say how grieved I am. If anyone else calls, let me know. And, meanwhile, bring me my letters."

It was the usual packet of invitations, billets-doux, and appeals. She opened them with little interest, though sufficient not to hear the footsteps of the departing gentlemen, whom she had again forgotten. Then, glimpsing an envelope addressed in a well-known hand, her eyes quickened. Here was something different! She drew it out from the other letters, which she discarded, and took pains in breaking its seal.

It came from Lord Marny in London and must have been carried by one of the government couriers. It should have been brought to her at once, for a letter from Marny had a special rating. A privy councilor and close to Pitt, it was thanks to him that she found

203

herself in England, that she was so well paid for her political disclosures and could look forward to continued payments on her return to France in the secret employ of the British government. They had met before the war in several of the Paris salons, where Marny, who was then ambassador, had distinguished her with his attentions. Subsequently they had exchanged civilities by letter and were on a sprightly, cordial basis. Marny had a keen eye for people, how they could be used and approached. Amélie's veiled contempt for Englishmen in general did not apply to him. He might just as well have been a French as an English statesman. She stood somewhat in awe of him, all the more as he had now become her actual paymaster.

Opening the letter, she could look forward to a graceful French style that Monsieur de Fontenelle himself would not have disowned. Marny was always urbane and amusing. Usually, too, he had a motive in writing that was of practical concern to her.

"Mon Enchanteresse," she read (his pet name for her was the Countess Circe), "Where do I find you today? How occupied and disposed? If I intrude upon any game of yours where diamonds or hearts are trumps, then lay me aside, I beg, but not too long; for I would mingle my congratulations on your certain victory with the laments of the conquered. To one who, like me, madame, has been long a captive of your charms, it is consoling to reflect that that fate is shared by all who cross your path, a consequence not of their weakness but of your power. The chains of a divinity are worn with honor. Nay, in all truth, I am so persuaded of this that I come to sue you for a special grace: to confer the dignity of your chains upon one more servant, to enroll him with me in the happy company of your slaves."

So, it was a letter of introduction. Some acquaintance of Lord Marny's arriving in Bath. His friends were usually worth while.

"He, at least, is young," the letter continued, "and, therefore, apt to be a more profitable servant than I, whom age prevents from offering the only fire proper to your altar. Still, though I envy, I do not grudge him youth; for, to be frank, I have grown to consider him a newer version of myself. In brief, madame, I solicit the favor of your magic for my son. Let me explain . . ."

"Saprelotte!" muttered the Countess. "His *son!* Mais, que diable que diable!" It was odd that she, who heard everything, had never heard of Marny's son. One could assume that any man of pleasure had begotten casual offspring; but here was a son whom Marny evidently sponsored. And she had not heard of him. Strange!

Her eyes romped down the page. Richard Hammond. Educated on the Continent. His mother a woman of good birth. Some fine phrases about that. . . . Brought to England in June, since when he had been living at the Earl's country seat in Kent, learning English, preparing, too, for the foreign service and a small post which had been promised him at one of the German courts. Now the crucial step remained. He must be socially baptized, not, indeed, as Marny's son — though that would be understood — but officially as a distant relative whom the Earl took pleasure in favoring. Shepherded by his father, he would first make his bow in Bath, which was less formal than London.

The letter continued: "I own, madame, to fondness for the lad, but I cannot be charged with a blind partiality. Anyone, I believe, would allow that he has strong parts and native charm, is of good stature and carriage. I own myself vastly pleased with him. But in one respect I am fearful, and therefore especially seek your aid. It appears that sometime before his arrival in England, the boy fell in love with a girl of no fortune — a dancing girl, to put it bluntly — and, indeed, offered to marry her. You smile? You give that charming lift of the shoulder, which I so well remember? But, of course, one smiles at such a moon-calf trifle. I would think of it no more than you except for the strong impression he seems to retain of it. Upon my word, the silly affair lingers with him. Leave it to time, you say. And, in truth, so I did until recently, when by pure chance I learned from the Sardinian Resident, Monsieur Caretti, that this same dancing girl would shortly appear at Drury Lane. As yet, my young man is uninformed of it, but he will hear soon enough.

"Do you now catch my drift, Countess Circe? Will you indulge my petition? Who can escape your enchantments if you choose to exert them! What slave of yours could even remember another mistress! In brief . . ."

Amélie leaned back smiling. In brief, the Earl was pandering for his son. It did not, it could not, cross her mind that she had already met Richard Hammond. Marny went on to explain that he would take good heed not to prepare the boy in advance for a meeting which must seem casual if it was to avoid the suspicion of parental scheming. He would not even speak of the Countess des Landes to Richard. Let the boy imagine that her favor toward him was wholly inspired by himself. So would her arts be most effective. For already the Earl implied that he took her co-operation for granted. Beneath the incense and phrasing, Amélie knew well enough that the petition was a command.

It did not occur to her to refuse. Even if Marny had not added the none too subtle hint that he would pay a thousand pounds to see young Richard in the Countess's toils, she would not have refused. She was too beholden to Marny now and in the future. Besides, he asked for nothing that Amélie was not disposed to grant. In the dullness of Bath, it would be amusing to divert herself with a youth who spoke French, save him from a cheap entanglement, correct his manners, introduce him to the gay science of gallantry. Smiling, she felt a tingle of anticipation.

She was glancing at the complimentary close of the letter, which assured her that within three days Lord Marny hoped to reach Bath and would crave the honor of declaring himself in person her humble, obedient servant, when Stephanie, entering, announced the Marquis de Corleone — or did Madame again desire to be excused?

"Polissonne!" returned Amélie in high spirits. "You know very well that I'll see an old friend like the Marquis." She spoke loud enough to be heard in the next room. "He's the only man in Bath I love. Show him in here at once."

"*Love?*" a voice echoed on the threshold. "Did I hear *love,* madame? Then at last —"

"I repeat *love,* monsieur. But it's a word of nuances."

"It has only one, Eccellenza, when I think of you."

The tall, very elegant caller had prominent black eyes, a hawk nose, and swarthy cheeks; for, though Tromba might change his title, he could not change his corsair features. Deeply inclined over the Countess's hand, he raised it to his lips, held it there devoutly, then flashed her a burning look before stepping back.

It was inevitable that Tromba, having reached England two months before, should soon drift to Bath. He had lacked the carefully prepared entrée to England that had served him so well in other countries. His warmly desired approach to Lord Marny through Richard had come to nothing with the latter's sentence to the galleys and subsequent death (as he had heard) in prison. Actually, he might have put off working the English vein until a more favorable time, had not a series of scandals in Munich launched him on the road again and made the Continent too hot for him. But, once in England, he could find no better field than Bath. The place swarmed with sharpers more or less plausible; gaming was its chief industry. The social informality, upon which Beau Nash so much insisted, offered a man like Tromba the chance to worm his way among the rich and the fashionable. So far, he had been confined, not unprofitably, to cards; but he looked forward to a wider scope later.

That he should have happened upon the Countess des Landes in Bath was a piece of luck for both of them. They could relax with each other. He spoke perfect French and made love with the Latin fire. It entertained her to fence with him, hold him off, and yet keep him in spirit.

"How is Monsieur de Corleone today?" she teased. "That's right, isn't it, mon cher Marquis? You have such a wealth of names."

"Not with you, madame," he smiled. "Let it be only your Marcello."

He looked so ardent that she turned away, seated herself, and spread out her dress.

"Have a chair then, my own. What were you doing last night?"

"Oh," he said absently, withdrawing speculative eyes from the Countess's figure, "playing loo with blockheads. Gainful but tedious." He glanced at the drizzle that was beginning outside. "To the devil with this climate and Bath! I've never yawned so much in my life. That's the chronic disease in England, the yawns. Don't you agree?"

"Practically. But why did you come to England in that case?"

He sighed. "Expiation for my sins, I suppose. And you, Eccelenza?"

She said cryptically: "To pay for future sins, monseigneur." Then with a real but no apparent connection, "By the way, Lord Marny's arriving. He's good company. Do you know him?"

Tromba's eyes lighted up with interest, but he shook his head. "No, as it happens."

"He has his son with him," Amélie went on, "a natural son, of course, but evidently a favorite. That surprises me. He's kept the secret pretty well — or perhaps you've heard?"

The other controlled a start and managed to look blank. By God, suppose he had shown up with Richard, when another boy, dear to the Earl, was in the saddle! What a fiasco that would have been. The collapse of those plans was a stroke of luck after all.

"No, madame."

"Well so it is. *A distant cousin,* you see. Brought up abroad. To be known as Mr. Richard Hammond."

"*Richard?*" exclaimed Tromba.

"Yes. Have you met him?"

With a man like Tromba, discretion was second nature. He had learned vaguely of Richard's death in prison, and that was all. One could not jump to conclusions, but the name Richard was striking.

"How old is Mr. Hammond?"

"About twenty, I gather."

"Hm-m. He's been long in England?"

"Only since June."

"Peste! And brought up abroad?"

"So it appears." Discreet herself, Amélie chose not to mention the letter. "You seem interested."

The word hardly expressed Tromba's excitement. He had not heard of Marny's embassy to Venice. It was fantastic that this Richard Hammond and the deceased Richard Morandi could be one and the same. On the other hand, the Christian name and other circumstances fitted. He was about to unburden himself to the Countess and remind her of the young actor at the Villa Bagnoli, but thought better of it. They would both learn the truth soon enough. No use starting pointless gossip, if the two Richards were not the same.

"I believe," he said thoughtfully, "that I have met a Richard Hammond somewhere. Possibly not. I'm curious to see him."

Amélie, recalling her role of Circe, observed, "I'm rather curious myself."

XXXI

ON that same morning, as it happened, while Madame des Landes
and Tromba-Corleone were discussing him in Bath, Richard Hammond emerged from the imposing doorway of Marny House on St.
James's Square in London, prepared for a walk. That for once he
was unattended by Monsieur Martin, or by his own special tutor,
Mr. Stanton, or by his valet, Harry Briggs, or by any of the other
mentors or menials with whom his father had surrounded him for
the past five months, gave him a sense of being let out of school. It
marked, too, the next phase of the training that Marny, logical
in all things, had decreed for him.

"My dear boy," the Earl had declared at their last interview the
night before, "you begin to shape well. When I consider what you
have accomplished since our meeting in June, I am more than
gratified. To speak in terms of your former profession, you have
been learning a role infinitely more difficult than any on the
stage and you are halfway toward mastering it."

Richard thanked him for the praise, aware, too, of his father's
insight. Marny could have spoken of learning a new profession or
way of life, but *role* perfectly expressed it. Only here there could
be no intermissions, no dropping back into one's own familiar self.
That self had to be suppressed until only the stage self remained.
It had cost many an ache of head and heart.

"Let's see," continued Marny. "With regard to English, I'd say
you've learned the *tune* of the language, though you still owe
something to grammar and enunciation. For God's sake, Dick, pay
heed to your *th*'s and don't roll your *r*'s. However, that will come.
— Also on the credit side, an acquaintance with native customs
and attitudes, which are no doubt silly but must be complied
with. You can bark out *sir* or *madam* like a true Englishman. You
can be stiff or engaging with the proper people at the right time.
Mr. Stanton assures me that you fence well and have a tolerable
seat on horseback. All these are trifles, of course, but essential to
your figure in the world. As to serious studies for your post abroad
— Puffendorf, the *Ius Gentium,* and so on — I learn from Monsieur
Martin that you have worked solidly and to good effect. The
Jesuits in Venice must have been sound teachers. — Now, I call this

an excellent showing in five months. What, then, remains to be done?"

Marny, who was a noted speaker in the House of Lords, retained at times something of the orator in private, especially when, as now, a topic passionately interested him. But beneath the formal manner, Richard could feel the warmth of what, though it would have shocked the Earl to admit it, could only be called love, something wistful and appealing. It drew him to his father in spite of the latter's unemotional pose. Love for love.

"Obviously," the Earl went on in answer to his own question, "you must now practise what you have learned. You must try your role on the public. Monsieur Martin and Mr. Stanton will withdraw. I shall continue to watch you from the wings, so to speak, and advise you if necessary. You will make mistakes, but you will learn more by them than if you had someone always at your elbow. We leave day after tomorrow for Bath, an absurd place in many ways but a good one for your debut. Lady Marny, as you know, has been there for some time. By the way, it would not be amiss if you brought her a small gift — a fan, a snuffbox. Such attentions please her . . ."

It was with this errand in mind that Richard now walked down the steps of Marny House into the expanse of the great square. He liked Lady Marny, who was a plain, simple old woman with a thick German accent. Starved of everything from her husband save faultless politeness, she had welcomed Richard as bringing a faint echo of romance to her otherwise dull age. That the romance had not been hers did not matter.

Considering London and the season, it was a fine day. A bleary sun showed through the haze, and the air was not too raw. Making the most of it, nursemaids with their charges, dressed like infant belles and beaux, strolled sedately on the footway around the enclosure lined by noble residences. On the small pond in the center of the square, two privileged children were being rowed back and forth by a footman wearing a laced hat.

Unconsciously Richard sighed. He had not been long enough in England to forget the colors and animation of Venice. The poor little boat on the pond depressed him, as did the solemn, self-conscious children. Then a private coach rattled in from Charles

210

Street with a splash of surface mud from the pavement, and he forgot himself long enough to damn the driver in fiery Italian before taking stock of his breeches. Mr. Stanton would not have been pleased.

"Chair, sir! Chair!" came from a stand of chairmen at the corner, who had seen the mishap. And naturally he ought to hire a chair. He was too well dressed for a walk eastward. But he hated the cramping leather boxes and their stale smell.

"No, tanks," he said, walking resolutely on and remembering the *th* too late, but repeating, tongue between teeth, "No, *th*anks . . . no, *th*anks . . . Sanguenazzo!"

Entering Pall Mall from the south end of the square, he turned left. It was of course the new and aristocratic section of London, built largely since the Great Fire of 1666. Indeed, except for the continuity of streets and houses, it hardly belonged to London at all. It was a city of nobles and country gentry centering about the Court. Wide districts separated its regularly laid out squares from the congestion of London proper. To one used to the mellow age of Italian cities, it looked stark and modern, as well as semirural; for there were many gardens, and the open country lay close by. But as Richard came closer to Cockspur Street, the noise and traffic thickened, and the roar from the east thundered. By the time he had reached the Strand south of Covent Garden Market, he was in the thick of a din and jostling hardly less than that of Cheapside itself.

Though he had driven up to London from Kent several times in the past months, he still found the tumult of the streets outrageous. It seemed to him that noise was the chief aim of the population. On the footpaths, set off from the rest of the street by posts at regular intervals, fifty kinds of hawkers, male and female, bawled their wares or services every few feet. It was a clamor announcing all the articles used in a household from brick dust to cat's meat. A clanging of hand bells backed the shouting. Bellows menders, chair menders, knife grinders, ragpickers, old-clothes men, vendors of fruit and vegetables, almanacks, ribbons, scissors, brooms, coal, firewood, spigots, buckles, old shoes and so on, proclaimed themselves. Chimney sweeps on the housetops, bootblacks on the pavement, apprentices in front of shops, yelled in chorus. Mean-

211

while, almost drowning out the human roar, carts, wagons, coaches, vehicles of all sorts, with iron-rimmed wheels screeching on the gritty flagstones, jolted along splashing mud from the central gutter or tangling with each other.

Having crossed the street on one of the causeways, he found his shoes covered with mire and let a bootblack repair the damage. There was a legion of such urchins on the London streets, armed with their three-legged stools, tin kettles, and other implements. A pedestrian might need their services ten times a day. While the boy worked, Richard gazed north across the Strand. Here, in addition to the great market, lay the theater district. He could see an occasional bill displayed of Covent Garden or Drury Lane. It was in the latter that Maritza would have appeared if she could have accepted Mario Caretti's offer.

He thought of her, as usual, with a mingling of shame and defeat. Looking back, he knew that he should have done his utmost to communicate with her. He should have announced his escape from the galleys and explained why he had accompanied Lord Marny to England. That he had not done this was sheer cowardice, however valid the reasons for secrecy might have been. But it was a hard letter to write, and he had put it off then and later on one pretext or another. It was hard because, however phrased, it represented the choice he had made. He had had no difficulty in writing to his mother in Bordeaux, but Maritza was altogether different.

Where was she now? Perhaps in Parma, perhaps in Florence . . .

"There you are, sir. Thank'ee, sir," concluded the bootblack, and Richard continued on to the notion shop which had been recommended to him before setting out.

Here the proprietor, in silver buckles, white stockings, and wig, welcomed purchasers on the threshold; and when he had learned who Richard was, made a point of serving him in person. Master Brooks had had the honor of Lady Marny's patronage for years and knew her taste. Since the gift was intended for her, he ventured to believe that he had exactly what Mr. Hammond required. In the end, Richard chose a gold snuffbox, newly brought from Dresden, with a porcelain miniature of the King of Prussia on the lid.

"I happen to know, sir," advised Brooks, "that her ladyship has a peculiar veneration for our ally the gallant Frederick. She is a lady of deep sentiment. Observe the liveliness of the portrait. You could do no better, sir. And cheap at ten guineas . . . I thank you."

Facing the return home, Richard this time weakened to the thought of a sedan chair and desired that one be fetched for him. Then, accompanied by the obsequious shopkeeper, whose manner gave notice to passers-by that this was no common patron, he crossed the footpath to the waiting chairmen.

"Marny House," Brooks directed in a loud voice. "Mr. Hammond, your servant, sir."

"Richard!" exclaimed a suppressed voice near by. "*Richard?*" It was more of a gasp than a question.

On the point of entering the chair, he turned to find himself facing two women, who had stopped a few feet off. Because of their unfamiliar dress and partly, too, because of his own stupefaction, he failed to recognize them for a second. Then he stood thunderstruck. They were Maritza Venier and Anzoletta.

Maritza was staring at him. "*Richard? Caro mio?* Ma non è possibile. È morto!*" — And the woman beside her echoed a like wonder in the single word "*Milòr!*"

He went toward them mechanically, but already his first surprise and happiness was yielding to confusion and an almost panic embarrassment.

"Maritzetta!"

Luckily one of the chairmen interrupted. " 'Ere, sir. 'Ow about it? Do you want us or not?"

He gave the man a coin and then turned back again.

"I don't understand," Maritza stammered. "We heard you were dead. The Captain Anzolo Ruzzini himself wrote that you had died in the Pozzi. I can't believe it's you . . . here . . ." The first stiffness showed in her voice. "Un gran sior! *Mistair 'Ammond!* And not a word from you! How . . ."

People jostled them back and forth. It was impossible to talk on the narrow footpath. Fortunately the entrance to the "Fountain," a well-known inn on the Strand, lay only a dozen yards off.

"I'll explain, madonna. What happiness to see you and Sior' Amia! . . . Che gioia! . . . Let's go in here out of the crowd . . ."

His arm under Maritza's, he guided them through the archway

213

that led into the inn yard. But, stealing a sideward glance, he noted the rigid line of her jaw as well as Anzoletta's thoughtful expression and dreaded the coming interview.

Once inside the inn, he ordered a private room and a token bottle of wine. At last they were seated at a small table.

"But you, cara —" he clung to every minute of delay — "how do you happen to be in London?"

"Oh," she said absently, "it's natural enough. I wrote to Sior Caretti. He kindly spoke for me to Mistair Garrick. I'm to dance this winter at Drury Lane."

"And his Excellence your father is here?"

She nodded.

"I hope he's well."

"Quite well, thank you."

Anzoletta put in brusquely, her homespun Venetian waking echoes in Richard's mind: "He's not well at all, and you know it. He has a weakness here." She patted her breast. "He misses the palazzo, he misses Venice. And who wouldn't in this ugly town!"

"Are you comfortably lodged?"

"Yes," said Maritza.

"Did you have a pleasant voyage? Was it from Holland? I suppose so because of the war."

"Yes," said Maritza.

It struck him suddenly that her first breathless curiosity about him had disappeared. While he uttered polite phrases and put off explaining what could not be explained, she did not urge him to explain. It struck him, too, that she looked older; not less attractive, but with the shadows that hardship and experience lend to a face.

"I would have written you," he began, "if I had known how. You had left Venice when we got back from Dalmatia. I didn't know where you were."

"Dr. Goldoni knew," she murmured.

"Yes, perhaps. But I couldn't communicate with him. You see, officially I was dead. It wouldn't have been wise —"

Anzoletta interrupted. "Tell us what happened — all of it. We saw you last in chains at the prison before they sent you to the galleys. Afterwards, nothing. Except Captain Ruzzini's letter. We were in Bologna then. What a grief on top of everything else!

And yet we comforted ourselves that even death was better than the galleys. We might have spared our tears, fio mio. *Well?*"

When his story was finished, Richard felt that he could not have told it better. They listened, absorbed. Surely Maritza must understand what the compulsion had been, and that he could not have acted otherwise. Relieved, he emptied his glass and brought it down on the table.

"So, you see, it was a miracle, siore. When I think of the galleys, I thank God and Milòr Marny who saved me from them. And now it's another miracle that we're together again, cara mia."

He did not intend to be insincere. And yet the warmth he expressed required a shade of effort. What of Lord Marny? What of his own plans? It may be unromantic to balance such things for one moment against love, but he could not help being aware of them. And, unconsciously, perhaps a trace of qualification showed through, even when he added,

"Carissima mia!"

"Don't!" said Maritza suddenly. Her frank, brown eyes met his.

"Don't what, madonna?"

"Pretend."

No, evidently she had not understood in spite of all the skill he had used in explaining. Her eyes were too level and he could see the hurt in them.

"How *pretend?*"

"I mean this." Her voice shook a little. "We were engaged to each other that night at the casino. We were to be true to each other always — or so I thought."

"Ma certo," he put in, "of course."

"The galleys made no difference to me, Richard. If we had never met again, I should still have waited and hoped. Didn't Captain Ruzzini tell you how I went to him?"

"Yes. It's impossible to thank you —"

"I don't want thanks; I want you to know how I felt. Now, suppose — suppose I had been in your place, had been released from prison, wouldn't it have been you before anyone else, you above all, I would have tried to reach, let you know about me —"

"I told you why I couldn't, Maritzetta."

"I don't see why you couldn't. You've been here for months.

You could have written . . ." Abruptly her manner changed. "Perhaps you did. Oh, Richard, I'm sorry. Did you write?"

He was tempted to lie but faltered, "No, you see —"

"Why not?"

"All sorts of reasons." Being in the wrong, he grew angry. He would not be hectored. "Only, you wouldn't understand."

"Indeed?" Her temper rose with his. "Then, let me show you that I do understand. All sorts of reasons? There's only one true reason, and it's this. You want what Lord Marny has to give you. You have always wanted it. From the first day we met. To be the big gentleman, to play the big role. And now it's yours. And nothing must stand in the way of it. There's the reason, Milòr."

"You're pretty hard." He pushed his chair back from the table.

"Yes, the truth's apt to be hard, but it's still the truth. Do you think I'm blind? Do you think, at this very moment, that I don't see how embarrassed you are to have Maritza Venier turn up out of the past? She doesn't fit in. She isn't acceptable to Lord Marny."

The very fact that her shafts, one after the other, hit the target incensed him still more. The truth, as she had said, remained truth; but she did not temper it with the charity which he thought he had a right to expect.

"Very well, siora," he froze, "if you choose to consider me only a timeserver and hypocrite, that's your affair. You hint that I intended to withdraw from my engagement to you —"

"Hint?" she cut in. "I despise hints. Of course you intended it. Or, rather, you preferred to forget about it. Isn't that plain? Can you deny it?"

"In other words, you think me a villain?"

Reaching out, Anzoletta laid her hand on Maritza's. "Eh, via, cara ti! You don't mean half of this."

On the point of a retort, Maritza checked herself. "No, I don't think of you like that, Richard. I never could. Only be frank. Admit that you have changed your mind. It's not dishonorable."

"I have not," he maintained.

She got up, and, absently lifting her cloak from the back of the chair, drew it around her shoulders. "Then I have. You'll make no sacrifices on my account. I want no condescension from you. Lord Marny needn't be concerned."

He stood facing her, equally hot and inflexible. "Who spoke of sacrifices and condescension? I did not. You saddle your own thoughts upon me and then charge me with them. If you think I'm changed, siora, consider yourself. I have different memories of you. In the future, I hope —"

"The future?" she interrupted. "What future? You are free of me, and I am free of you. Come, Anzoletta."

The old woman looked from one to the other. "Children!" she begged. "Fia mia —"

Maritza cut her short. "Tasè. We've had enough words. We'll leave Mistair 'Ammond to his future."

Vaguely Richard was aware of her tilted chin and the straight lines of her cloak, as she passed him.

XXXII

ALTHOUGH Lord Marny disliked vulgar ostentation, he none-theless believed in upholding his rank, as a matter of policy. The world, he was apt to remark, accepts you on your own terms, and it would not have occurred to him, when traveling, to omit those features of wealth and dignity that impress the world. He traveled like other eminent noblemen. Six horses, with three postilions, one to each pair, drew his soberly gilded coach. His coronet showed on the door panels. Two footmen perched behind, and several armed and mounted lackeys served as outriders. This not only assured him deference but safety on the road. He would have the best rooms in inns and did not need to fear highwaymen.

It took some minutes of bustle and clatter in the chill dawn before luggage had been stowed away and the cortege was ready. Hoofs beat a tattoo on the pavement, harness jingled, grooms busied themselves. Then the steps of the coach were let down; Marny, followed by Richard, got in, while the footmen stood at attention; the steps were raised again; the door was closed; the footmen swung to their perch. And, with a final prancing, the journey started.

It was a hundred and five miles to Bath from Hyde Park Corner, which at that time marked the western limits of London. Such a distance required two days of travel unless one chose to arrive late at night. Marny could easily recall when it had taken a day longer, and when coaches, plodding through the mud, had been lucky to average three miles an hour. Now the improvement of the roads had more than doubled that speed. In fact, on certain stretches, one could make a furious eight or even ten miles.

But a pace like that was out of reach during the first stage between Hyde Park and the villages of Knightsbridge and Kensington. Along here, after its brave start, the carriage floundered hub-deep from mudhole to mudhole through that zone of mire which had formerly proved one of the chief defenses of London. And here, too, the outriders, closing in, kept alert; for the district almost equaled Hounslow Heath itself as a haunt of robbers. The horses strained; the springless coach, suspended on its straps, jolted and swayed.

"I can hardly blame you, Dick, for looking solemn," observed Marny with a side glance. "But, like purgatory, this won't last forever. The road improves at Hammersmith. I hope you took the precaution of a first breakfast before we left. Your man should have seen to it. It's ill traveling on an empty stomach."

Richard assured his father that Briggs had indeed seen to it, and he then made an effort to brighten up. He wanted no probing into the gloom which had weighed upon him since yesterday's quarrel with Maritza. Anger, or rather the self-justification he found in anger, still colored his thought of that meeting, which, of course, he had kept to himself. He had spent the better part of last night re-arguing the case in his own favor.

But the Earl was in too good spirits that morning to mind his son's moodiness. At White's the evening before, he had won heavily at cards against a young Virginian of the Fairfax family and was richer today, as he put it, by two thousand acres and a hundred niggers on some stream called the James — wherever that was.

Richard exclaimed at the size of the stakes.

"Too deep by far," Marny agreed. "Though not unusual at White's. I've seen many an estate change hands there. But the young fool was heated; he forced me to the wager. As it was, I stood to lose twenty thousand pounds, and I doubt if the prop-

218

erty's worth that figure. Now I'm saddled with the task either of administering or selling it." He gave a sudden smile. "Suppose I deeded the place and the problem to you? By God, I shall, if you continue to please me. It would give you a nest egg of sorts. We'll think it over."

Richard murmured appropriately, but he wondered about young Mr. Fairfax and asked how such a loss had affected him.

The Earl's dark, almond eyes, which had softened for a moment, turned hard. "It remains to be seen. If a man risks more at the tables — or in life, for that matter — than he can afford to lose, he must take what comes. Let him show his manhood or blow out his brains. If the latter, 'tis one fool the less. We must all swim or sink in this world. I waste no sentiment on flinchers."

With a final plunge, the horses gained the better pavement outside of Hammersmith, and the coach rolled haughtily past the "Red Cow" with its vast stables on the outskirts of the village. Here the animation of the road began, for the inn marked the end of the first stage out of London and supplied horses to all the public coaches to Bath, Bristol, Wells, Bridgewater and Exeter.

Here, too, Lord Marny, who missed no occasion to improve Richard's knowledge of England, began to comment on places, customs and people, as they drove along. He talked well and found Richard an attentive listener.

This village, for instance, beyond Hammersmith, was Turnham Green, where the King's men and Cromwell's had clashed a hundred-odd years ago, and where Marny's great-grandfather had been left for dead. And here, at the "Old Pack Horse" in 1696, the Black Baron himself, together with Sir George Barclay and other Jacobites, had vainly plotted the death of William III.

"They had a commission for it," Marny went on, "from the exiled King, James Stuart, who was in France. But most of them were apprehended; six were hanged. Your grandfather, who was then young and unmarried, saved himself to the coast by good luck and good horseflesh. He spent the next years abroad and did not win his pardon till Queen Anne came to the throne in 1702. Strange," the Earl added, "that a line of such unthrifty princes as the Stuarts could inspire such devotion. The Hammonds, to mention only our family, gave them their lives, wives and fortunes in this world, and their immortal souls in the next. For I have no

219

doubt they went to hell with them. Luckily I was born too late for such folly." He paused a moment. "Yet I can understand something of it from knowing my father, who, of course, was a Stuart in all but name. It's droll indeed how much you resemble him."

This was a burning topic with Richard. "What manner of man was he, my lord, if I dare ask?"

"Why not?" smiled Marny. "But, upon my word, I hardly know how to answer. He had all the natural qualities that appeal to youth: high spirits, humor, dash and heartiness. He died before I was grown, and I have only the warmest memories of him. Perhaps they color my affection for you. But sentiments of the kind should never warp our judgments. Looking back now, 'tis frankly impossible not to admit that, like all the Stuarts, he was a considerable rogue, faithless, fickle, lecherous and bloodthirsty. In spite of his attractions, I hope your likeness to him is only skin-deep."

Faithless and fickle. Somberly appraising his own character, especially now in view of the breach with Maritza, Richard found too many traits in common with his grandfather to derive much comfort from the Earl's hope.

"Do you have faith in heredity, my lord?"

The other took snuff. "Yes and no. The same faith I have in a pack of cards. Only here the pack's unlimited. Consider how many ancestors we have. I, for example, inherit the dark Stuart complexion but am otherwise more like my mother, who was cool, practical and self-controlled. Nature, you see, deals the cards, and any combination can turn up." He broke off to point carelessly through the window. "Well, here we are at Hounslow Heath."

A whiff of carrion supplemented Marny's pointing. In the foreground of the desolate landscape stood a gibbet with the tar-blackened remains of a man dangling from it in irons. Not far away, against the skyline of a low hill, another gibbet showed a wisp of bones light enough to be set in motion by the wind and swaying like a fish on a hook. Then, as the coach proceeded, other gallows loomed up by the roadside, more frequent than milestones. What with these gloomy objects and the overcast autumn day, Richard had never seen a drearier country. Furze bushes, swampy pits high with bulrushes, ugly little mounds covered by rank grass, stretched off into the distance.

220

Here, in spite of gibbets and posses, the highwaymen followed their calling and had done so for generations. Here Moll Cutpurse had ridden; and the great Duval with his squadron, a hundred years back, had brought off many a prize. Here, more recently, Dick Turpin had flourished. Here Dr. Shelton, leaving his scalpel, had operated with a pistol. And there were "Gentleman Harry" Simms, John Everett, Tom Lympus, a dozen others, whom Lord Marny named on the long stretch over the heath. Indeed, he confessed to suspicions that his own father the Baron, when a young man, had run a course or two here, being prone to devilment and debts.

At Cranford, where they stopped to breakfast at the "Berkeley Arms," Richard, still unused to obsequiousness on the part of innkeepers and with the memory of the galleys still vivid, could again admire the advantages of grandeur. One of the mounted servants, riding ahead, had announced the Earl's coming. Everything was in readiness, from the landlord, bowing at the coach steps, to the table laid for two in the finest private room and his lordship's own people in attendance. Other travelers could wait, even an Indian nabob, whose gaudy equipage in the inn yard paled before the coronets on the arriving coach. The place belonged to Marny. And everybody stared as he and Richard entered, noting the resemblance between them, admiring, too, their bearing and London fashion and bland assurance. So noblemen were expected to carry themselves.

For Richard, the great road that day was not merely a succession of villages, each with its inn and jail, its stocks and whipping post, across the level land of Middlesex and Berkshire. Nor was it merely a chapter on England past and present. It became rather an interpretation of life on the part of Lord Marny, an interpretation with which Richard was expected to conform.

They put up for the night almost exactly halfway between London and Bath at the "Pelican" in Speenhamland close to Newbury. It was a house of excellent cheer and corresponding charges, which Quin the actor had celebrated in a well-known jingle:

The famous inn at Speenhamland,
That stands beneath the hill,

May well be called the Pelican,
From its enormous bill.

Here, although fifty miles and the worst half of the journey remained, one was already aware of Bath. Fine carriages, either going or coming from that resort, filled the inn yard; and good company, the house itself.

In the hallway, Marny stopped to greet warmly a tall, slender young man in brigadier's uniform, whom he at once invited to supper. Richard did not catch the name but gathered that the officer had just returned from America, since Marny referred to him as the "hero of Louisburg." He had thin, sensitive features and wore his red hair undisguised by powder. He accepted the Earl's invitation, looked forward to drinking his health, exchanged bows with Richard, and walked on.

"A great favorite of Pitt's," said Marny, "but I think too young for his rank. I doubt if he's much over thirty."

"The name escaped me, my lord."

"Oh — James Wolfe. He's much praised for his conduct last summer in Canada, where he was second to General Amherst."

The supper was interesting on more counts than one. It afforded a glimpse into another world very different from Lord Marny's. Something greater was apparently on foot than the fashionable circles of St. James's realized: England approaching her hour of empire, unleashing her hoarded strength on distant oceans and continents, in India, in America. Wolfe, Celtic and imaginative, consumed by an almost romantic military ardor, conveyed somehow the tang of that remoteness and of that future. Still young enough to dream, the poetic strain in him flashing through now and then, he stirred a kindred faculty in Richard.

And, charmingly polite, Marny encouraged him, kept his glass filled, drew him out. As the evening passed, Wolfe grew more impassioned. At one point, he remarked to Richard:

"I marvel, Hammond, that a young man of your build and kidney, with red blood in his veins, should be content to linger in England and squire ladies, when history is being made overseas. Why not buy a commission in the army? If you desire a cornetcy or even a lieutenancy in my command, I'll arrange the matter. And, by God, I promise to show you action."

"Ah, but, General," put in Marny — and there was ice in his voice — "Mr. Hammond has no thought of lingering in England. A foreign post is being offered him. Or do you hold that history is made only in the wildernesses of America? If so, I beg to differ with you. Where on earth, sir, let me ask, is history not being made?"

Wolfe reddened. "A just reproof, my lord. I ask your and Mr. Hammond's pardon. I spoke heedlessly, being much devoted to my own profession . . ."

"The more honor to you!" Marny interrupted, raising his glass. "Such devotion is a rare article, sir. England owes Louisburg to yours. Permit me again, in all admiration, to drink your very good health."

But when the punch bowl was empty and the young General had retired, Marny yawned. "What a hotspur! I like you to meet all kinds of men, Richard, and to study them — even such enthusiasts as Wolfe — so that you may learn to use both their talents and their weaknesses. For men will be the tools of your career. I trust, however, that you will avoid too much enthusiasm yourself, a fatal infirmity."

No doubt this was true, but something in Richard answered with a sigh.

Late next day, after a toilsome journey through Savernake Forest, Marlborough, and the Wiltshire Downs, they crossed into Somerset and, from Box, descended the slope of the hilly amphitheater that encloses Bath. Beneath them, the town, half gilded by sunset, huddled within the embrace of the Avon. Gentlemen showing off their mounts, and ladies, their equipages, crowded the road. Then at last the coach threaded its way through the gaily thronged little city to the Earl's residence on Pierrepont Street. A furor of welcome rang out from the Abbey chimes.

The Countess des Landes, returning from an afternoon promenade, sent one of her footmen to inquire why the din was greater than usual; and, being informed that Lord Marny had arrived, gave special heed to her evening toilet.

XXXIII

NOTHING could have seemed more casual than that Marny, strolling next day with Richard on the fashionable North Parade and stopping to greet one or another of his acquaintance, should happen upon Madame des Landes, similarly strolling with Lady Mary Coke and Mr. George Selwyn. That the Earl had called on Amélie the evening before to arrange such a meeting could not possibly have been suspected.

"And let me present," he said nonchalantly, after the usual compliments, "my young friend Mr. Hammond, who has recently —"

But here he broke off in amazement at the startled expression of both Richard and the Countess.

"Gran' Dio!" she exclaimed, lapsing into Italian. "Am I dreaming? Is it possible? Il Cavaliere di Spirito? The Villa Bagnoli? Ma, che roba è questa!"

"Vossioria!" Richard stared. "Contessina!"

Marny cleared his throat. "You seem to know each other." It took effort to keep alarm out of his voice. And it might well cause alarm that, presenting his son to the world of fashion as a young man properly brought up on the Continent, he should at once stumble upon a person who had known Richard in the discreditable past. "I had no idea that your ladyship —"

Though more pleasantly, Madame des Landes was no less surprised than Marny. That the latter's son, upon whom she was to use her wiles, should turn out to be the attractive young actor she had flirted with on the Brenta seemed incredible.

"Know each other!" she repeated, turning back to English. "Why, my lord, we're intimate friends. I had the pleasure of acting with Signor — with Mr. Hammond last year in a play at Count Widiman's near Venice and utterly lost my heart to him. He took the leading role. Count Roberto, wasn't it, Mr. Hammond? And I was Donna Florida. But tell me," she dashed on, "how this happens. I didn't know then —" on the point of an indiscretion, her veteran tact saved her — "that I should have the happiness of seeing you in England," she finished.

Richard, who had now recovered himself and could see the danger of a word out of turn, said meaningly: "My plans for England were not then formed, madame. Besides, as I recall it, you did not speak of England yourself."

At once Amélie could guess what she did not entirely grasp and put in the right touch. "Well, sir, in any case, welcome to Bath. Lady Mary, we must take Mr. Hammond under our wing. We must flaunt him through town. He's a most accomplished person. I remember he speaks perfect French. Your arm, sir," she invited. "Nous avons tant à nous dire."

And preceding the rest of the group, she and Richard joined the other saunterers along the Parade. The rapid lilt of her native language detached itself from the background of English voices.

"Perfect French, indeed, my lord," observed Mr. Selwyn, following with Marny and Lady Coke. "I'm properly impressed."

"His mother was French, sir. He has been long abroad."

Though still at a loss, Marny felt relieved. Since he had never encouraged Richard to discuss the Venetian past, which was best forgotten, he had no more than heard of the Villa Bagnoli and of what had happened there. But apparently, to judge by the Countess's references, Richard had distinguished himself in some way. He reflected, too, that this must have occurred before the degrading episode of the galleys, and that Amélie des Landes, who had spent the past year in France, was most probably ignorant of that unhappy event. If so, the boy would certainly not be fool enough to blurt it out. Therefore the preposterous coincidence of their meeting did no harm that a few adroit explanations to Amélie would not cure. Marny could count on her secrecy for a good many reasons, and she seemed more than well disposed toward Richard.

Luckily the Earl could not hear her remarks at that moment, as her arm tightened gently against Richard's, and her perfume recalled that night long ago on the Brenta.

"But, mon ami, can you guess who's here and who will be as delighted as I am to see you? Mon Dieu, que c'est bizarre! The three of us in Bath of all places! Guess."

"I have no idea, madame," said Richard, once more on the alert. "Who do you mean?"

"Why, Don Claudio himself — your special friend Monsieur de

225

Tromba. Only, for God's love, don't call him that. He's now the Marquis de Corleone."

"Tromba!" Richard echoed.

"Yes. You don't seem pleased. Why not?"

"But I *am* pleased," he faltered, thinking of Marny.

"No, you're not. And why? Did he know then that you were Mr. Hammond?"

"He had some notion of it."

Amélie recalled her conversation with Tromba several days ago and wondered that he had left her in ignorance about the young man they had both known at the Villa Bagnoli. It would have been so natural to mention him. Why, too, had Lord Marny somehow conveyed the impression that Richard had been brought up in France at his charge and under his direction? Brought up? Rubbish! She remembered now that Richard had played in Count Widiman's orchestra and had been a part-time actor patronized by Goldoni. Then it suddenly occurred to her that Lord Marny had been on a brief embassy to Venice last spring. That was the answer. The Earl had finally decided to acknowledge this son of his and naturally did not wish to have all the facts known. Amélie's quick mind, darting here and there, had now pieced a good deal together. But she still did not understand Tromba's silence.

"Well, mon cher," she ran on, "you will soon be meeting the Cavaliere or, rather, the Marquis." And, allowing her gloved hand to close on his arm, she added shrewdly: "It's one of the charms of such old friendships, isn't it, that each one knows too much of the other to be at a disadvantage. If you greet him as Corleone, he would be an imbecile to forget that you are Mr. Hammond."

Richard got the point and laughed. "You are adorable, madame. What you say is so right. But doesn't he feel at a disadvantage with you?"

"Oh," she smiled, "if I went around divulging what I knew about my friends, I should have few left. It's much more entertaining to watch Tromba at work than to warn people against him. He knows that he amuses me and counts on my discretion." Her eyes teased and melted in a side glance. "As can you, Monsieur Hammond."

He took fire at once. "I wish I could count on more than that, Comtesse."

Since the break with Maritza, he was in an apt state for catching fire. If nature abhors a vacuum on the physical plane, she abhors it equally on the emotional. A woman of half the charm and half the skill of Amélie des Landes would have found him responsive in his present doldrums; and, if so, how much more this beauty who had set his heart fluttering once and whom he had always remembered.

"More than that, mon ami?" she repeated.

"Yes — on your favor, on your partiality."

She chose to be direct. "And why not, nom de Dieu! Have you forgotten Donna Florida, Count Roberto? Didn't she wear her heart on her sleeve for you?"

"Only in Goldoni's play, alas."

"We could always continue it impromptu, Mr. Hammond." She let her smile and her eyes enchant him. "Are we so dull that we need Dr. Goldoni to write the lines for us?"

The blood was pounding at his temples; but, in view of the North Parade, he kept a light tone. "If you're serious, madame, I can't wait for the next act to begin."

"Hasn't it already begun?" She broke off. "It certainly has. Speak of the devil! What did I tell you! Here's your rival, Claudio, now. But, in the name of heaven, see who he's with!"

Among the fashionable throng on the Parade, Tromba's graceful figure was easily the most distinguished. As he had once shone among the beaux of the Brenta, so he shone now among the beaux of Bath. No English tailor could vie with the elegance of his Parisian costume; no laced hat was cocked at such a fetching angle; no one could equal his assured lordliness. People made way for him and for the elderly woman in a wheel chair who was being pushed along by a solemn footman in livery. His attentions were all for her, and he had not yet seen the Countess and Richard. But the latter was startled to recognize the woman in the chair as his stepmother, Lady Marny. She seemed blissfully absorbed in Tromba and would have passed by with her escort, had not Amélie blocked the way with a curtsy.

"Good morning, madam. Monsieur le Marquis, your most obedient. And have you left off greeting your friends, monsieur?" She gave emphasis to her voice. "I believe you know *Mr. Hammond.*"

Then Tromba's black eyes widened. The next moment, to the edification of onlookers and the astonishment of Lady Marny, he clasped Richard to his breast in a stately embrace, kissed him on both cheeks, and exclaimed rapidly in Italian: "My dear boy! What happiness! You remember *di Corleone,* I hope! Ah, what a benediction!"

Several paces behind and closing in, Lord Marny had trouble maintaining his usual pleasant impassiveness. Now that the reef of the Countess des Landes had been safely met, he certainly did not expect another apparition from Richard's past to raise a new problem. Such bad luck twice in a morning was an outrage. "What the devil!" he muttered.

"Odd's life!" remarked George Selwyn. "Mr. Hammond must have been damned popular on the Continent. All the foreigners seem mad about him."

"I don't believe I know the gentleman," said Marny, expertly appraising Tromba from the near distance.

"An acquaintance of the Countess des Landes's, I think," put in Lady Coke. "At least I've seen them together at the assembly."

"Di Corleone. A genius at cards," Selwyn added. "I dropped fifty guineas to him night before last — all in my best French, too, for he speaks little English."

Marny looked a question, to which Selwyn shook his head.

"No, I don't believe he cheated. But from all appearances, it seems to me that Lady Marny ought to be able to inform your lordship about him."

"Yes, egad," the Earl nodded, and threw in a quip. "You behold in me, sir, a budding Othello. The man's too handsome by half. Has my lady been tripping while I was in London?"

Since nothing was better known than Marny's polite indifference to his wife, who had served him only as a financial milch cow since their marriage, his remarks raised the smile he intended. And, with that, they joined the group around the wheel chair.

Introductions followed. "My love," said Lady Marny in her thick German accent, "you must meet the Marquis di Corleone. We fell into talk this morning in the Pump Room, when I was taking my fourth cup of water. And, d'you know, he advised against it. Since then he's been telling me of a cure for the vapors used in Egypt.

Also of other remedies and elixirs I never before heard of. A most learned and talented man, my lord. I vow he almost encourages me to believe that I may recover my health."

There was nothing the matter with Lady Marny, except boredom and imaginary ills, but it would have been cruel to suggest such a thing.

The Earl bowed, and dropping into French, "Votre serviteur, Monsieur le Marquis. Are you perhaps a physician?"

With just the right seasoning of amused hauteur at being connected with a humdrum calling, the other answered: "No, milord, I have no claim on Aesculapius. As it happened, I once served the King of the Two Sicilies on an embassy to the Sultan and on that occasion returned via Cairo, where I spent some time. As you know, the medical practices of the East are little understood in Europe. Being of an enquiring turn, I picked up some scraps of science from a learned hakim which I have used with benefit ever since."

"How interesting!" said Marny.

"And, my lord," put in his wife, "isn't it odd that the Marquis knows Richard!"

Tromba was quick to remark: "Why odd, milady? Madame des Landes can bear me out how many people of the first fashion knew Mr. Hammond last summer a year ago on the Brenta and were much taken with him. But I own that he and I were especially close. Let me say that I was drawn to consider Mr. Hammond in the light of a younger brother and took pleasure in furthering him among my Venetian acquaintance. Indeed, at one time we shared the same apartment — eh, Richard? — for even Count Widiman's palatial villa was full to overflowing."

As far as it went, this was balm to the Earl's soul. In presenting his son to Bath, he had wished to convey the idea of a rich Continental experience not only appropriate to the Hammond name but of value socially and in the foreign service. The remarks of Corleone, supported by those of Amélie des Landes, in the presence of such a gossip as George Selwyn were priceless for Marny's purpose and exceeded anything he could have hoped for. By evening, the story of Richard as socially distinguished abroad would be well launched. But since Marny knew that the story (whatever

229

might have happened on the Brenta) was altogether false, he could not help a chilly sense of uneasiness. That the Countess promoted his game, he could understand. But what reasons had Corleone for chiming in with it? Who was this Corleone? Lord Marny, an expert in people, could tell an adventurer when he saw one, in spite of dress and manners. Though the vulgar phrase *on pins and needles* could hardly be applied to him, he was more than eager for a word in private with Richard. He hated this fencing in the dark.

It impressed him, however, that Richard played up to the Marquis without embarrassment. In Marny's book, poise was the greatest of all virtues.

"It would be utterly impossible to express my gratitude to your Excellency," Richard was saying in polished French. "And I believe that no one who has not enjoyed the Marquis di Corleone's favor can conceive the generosity of it. Why, my lord," he added, turning to Marny, "I am indebted to Monseigneur not only for the condescension that rendered my stay on the Brenta so pleasant, but for his repeated courtesies in Venice. I owe him even for the loan of his casino at the last carnival."

It was a handsome *quid pro quo* in return for the Marquis's testimonial to Mr. Hammond. But it was more than that. Catching a sudden intentness in Richard's eyes, Marny at last began to see light. He had been well informed about the casino episode, however vague he might be with respect to the play at Count Widiman's. The fight which had sent Richard to the galleys had taken place in a casino loaned him by someone — not Corleone. By God, he had it! A charlatan named Tromba, who had escaped from Venice that same evening. There still remained a good deal to clear up, but Marny had now been given the right lead.

So this was Tromba! And he had to be handled with gloves. Like Madame des Landes, the Earl at once understood that Corleone had something to conceal. But exposure, in the case of a hardened rogue, would not be so fatal as to a young man with the Foreign Service in view. Therefore, blackmail in one form or another could be expected. How much of it would have to be endured depended on whether Tromba had learned about Richard's sentence to the galleys. There was a slight chance that he had not.

No hint of reserve appeared in Marny's cordial thanks to the

Marquis for his kindness to Mr. Hammond. "We must be better acquainted, monsieur. I hope you will favor me by calling at my house on Pierrepont Street. It will delight me not only to welcome the benefactor of my young kinsman, but to enjoy the conversation of so eminent a traveler. And I am sure that Lady Marny —" he included his wife with a smile — "will desire to know more of those occult remedies which you were good enough to recommend."

"I assure you, milord," Tromba bowed, with the relief of a man who at last swings into the saddle, "that I crave no higher distinction in England than to be numbered among the admiring servants of yourself and Countess Marny."

There were other compliments. The group strolled on to the end of the Parade, where it paused to consider the day's program. It pleased the Earl that Richard already seemed fascinated by Amélie des Landes. That, at least, promised well.

Apparently she and George Selwyn were both taken up that evening by Lady Huntingdon, who had formed a party to hear the celebrated preacher John Wesley at a room on Avon Street. Lady Huntingdon was too great and militant a person to be easily denied. During the past fifteen years, she had coaxed and bullied her fashionable friends into evangelistic meetings and had procured for Methodism whatever social standing it possessed. A scrawny, self-righteous woman, filled with a devouring solicitude for other people's souls, she pursued big game, the lords of Vanity Fair, and now and then snatched a brand from the burning. Woe to the sinner from whom she had wheedled a promise to hear one of the Methodist divines, if that promise were broken. It was much better to endure a sermon than Lady Huntingdon's rage.

"But why not come with us?" Amélie pleaded, with a special glance at Richard. "There's much more safety in numbers. You wouldn't want to lose Mr. Selwyn and me to heaven, would you? I'm more susceptible to religion than you think. Long ago, I almost became a nun. They say Mr. Wesley doesn't preach very long. Besides, think how it would please Lady Huntingdon." She added casually, "I hope you would escort me home afterwards, Mr Hammond."

Richard bowed his acceptance. Lady Coke declined. She disliked

Lady Huntingdon and would have nothing to do with her conventicles. Tromba excused himself on the score of not understanding English and a compelling appointment at cards. But Lady Marny was all enthusiasm. She *adored* Mr. Wesley and Mr. Whitefield. It comforted her to hear them. They had such beautiful voices and nice hands. She enjoyed a meeting like that more than the opera.

"Won't you join us, my love?" she begged her husband. "It would so encourage dear Mr. Wesley and dear Lady Huntingdon."

To Richard's surprise, his father promptly consented. "Why not? Everything's worth doing once. The fellow's a madman, of course, but *usefully* mad. He inspires the lower classes to decency, labor and contentment. I do not hold with the railers at religion, who are more apt to be coxcombs than not. It seems to me that France could do with a few Wesleys at present and with fewer Rousseaus." He smiled at Amélie with an implication that did not escape her. "You may count on me, then, madame, and I will count on you."

But once at home with Richard, Marny sought information about the Brenta affair and Tromba; while, on the other hand, Richard withheld nothing but the now sore topic of Maritza.

"You say," probed the Earl, "that this Cavaliere, or whatever he chooses to call himself, knew of your relationship to me?"

"Yes, he learned of it from Dr. Goldoni."

"And that he urged you to accompany him to England, so that he could exploit that relationship?"

"Yes."

"I would have welcomed you. Why didn't you come?"

"For the reasons I have already given your lordship. My mother opposed it for one thing . . ."

As always on the rare occasions when Jeanne was mentioned between them, now again Richard felt indecision, a trace even of feebleness, on the part of his otherwise imperious father.

"Yes," muttered the Earl, "to be sure. Well . . ." Then, after a pause, "Do you think Tromba knows that you were sent to the galleys? There's the sore point. For people are governed by words, and the term *galley slave* is not a pretty one."

Richard nodded. "It's likely that he learned of what happened from his correspondents in Venice. Probably until now he considered me dead."

"And so . . ." Marny fell to musing. After a while he summed up. "We shall have to countenance the rascal, give him an entrée, let him pluck some geese. So be it. I fancy, with enough rope, he'll hang himself. And I may be able to speed the day. Meanwhile, though without offending him, I hope that you'll not appear too much in his company, for he will stink in the end. However, if you can't destroy such a fellow, embrace him for the time being. No half measures will serve."

"I wish that your lordship were clear of me," Richard burst out. "Why should you risk embarrassment on my account! It would be easier —"

An unwonted ray lighted up Marny's cold face. "Pshaw!" he put in. "You forget our family device, *Ut volo, As I choose.* I'd risk more than embarrassment for you —" the next words were almost inaudible — "my son."

XXXIV

AS compared with the smart quarter of Bath surrounding, and north of, the Pump Room, Avon Street was relatively shabby and thus appropriate to the small society of Methodists who maintained a meeting place there. For the most part, they were lesser tradesmen, mechanics, farm laborers, and domestic servants. To the handful of gentry whom the efforts of Lady Huntingdon recruited on special occasions, attendance in the naked upper room, filled with people of this sort, had a spice of novelty and almost of adventure. It was an excursion out of one's own caste: a condescension on the part of some; a pretext for ridicule or trifling on that of others. But often it implied curiosity in regard to the Wesleyan movement itself. For undeniably Methodism, with the religious excitement it inspired, was pervading England. To be generally well informed, one ought to know something about it.

Tonight Lady Huntingdon beamed at the exceptionally fine catch she had made among her reprobate friends. To have actually brought a railer like Selwyn and a foreign coquette like Madame des Landes within firing distance of Wesley was a triumph in itself, and she had not let them out of her sight on the way to the meeting room. Her sister, Lady Fanny Shirley, and Lord Chesterfield's elderly sister, Lady Hotham, also appeared, together with several beaux, who had been lured the more easily since it was not a ball night. But when the Earl and Countess Marny entered, accompanied by the tall, dark young man who was such a striking proof of his lordship's wickedness, Lady Huntingdon's pale fish-eyes glowed, her flabby face lighted up, and she hastened to seat them in the front row. Her one regret now was that she could not expose such a gathering to the shafts of George Whitefield, whose theological views she considered sounder than Wesley's. But, after all, in the case of thumping sinners like these, one did not have to split hairs.

Meanwhile, the humble and grubby part of the audience on the back benches could thrill at the presence of the nobility and rejoice in the Lord, who included even these mighty ones under sin as well as Tom, Dick and Harry. Sharp eyes would watch the effect of the sermon on them. There would be no end of speculation and comment afterwards.

Richard managed to seat himself next to Amélie, who gave him a look as of one martyr to another and whispered in French: "Mon Dieu, what a supper I had at Lady Huntingdon's! Religion for soup, religion for meat, religion for dessert. Mon cher, me voilà farcie de religion, comme une oie de châtaignes. Poor little Amélie, who used to be so gay! Now I'm only a saint. And that fine Monsieur Selwyn! He's lost all his tail feathers. So have I. How do you like me en quakeresse?"

In deference to the occasion, she had put on a somber gown and wore a white ruffled cap over her powdered curls. The piquant lines of her face seemed to Richard more provocative than ever, and suggestively bare, in the absence of rouge and patches. Except for her beauty, no woman in the room showed a more demure appearance. But, whether by chance or design, she had selected a fan for the evening that needed expert handling. On one side, it was modest enough, with an innocent pastoral scene in quiet colors; but the reverse showed a belle in a swing, who disclosed much more than her ankles to an admiring gallant bent on pushing her higher and higher. This the Countess flashed at Richard while languidly fanning herself, but at the same time kept her expression angelic.

"Scoffer!" he whispered. "Hypocrite!"

"Why? — Oh, you mean this?" She flashed the lady at him again. "No, my dear Richard. Never! If I had been a hypocrite, I'd have brought along a black mourning fan with a tombstone on it. That would have been hypocritical. This is just an antidote."

"Against what?"

"Fanaticism. — Hush! Here comes the executioner."

A short, frail-looking man in a black gown with white lappets at the collar made his way along the side of the room to the low platform. His loose, slightly graying hair almost reached his shoulders and ended in a faint curl. What with this and the fresh-colored, sensitive features, he recalled a portrait Richard had seen of the poet Milton. Seating himself next to a reading desk crowned by a Bible, he awaited the signal for the first hymn and gazed serenely at his audience. Though doubtless aware of the noble recruits in the front row, he did not seem more conscious of them than of the crowded benches behind. Indeed, he included everyone in the same calm and benevolent regard.

"Nice-looking," breathed Amélie. "He reminds me of Père Thibaut, my confessor at Saint-Germain-des-Prés, a dear man."

"How are you going to explain this to Père Thibaut?" Richard murmured. "Attending a Protestant meeting! You're a good Catholic, aren't you?"

"I'm a Catholic," she shrugged. "And you?"

"Vaguely. But I haven't been to confession for a long time. Maybe I'm a Protestant now. Anyway, you're guilty of a mortal sin."

"Don't," she pouted. "You aren't Lady Huntingdon. Consider Monsieur Wesley. Have you noticed his eyes?"

Increasingly Richard had felt the power of them. They were unusually penetrating, though at the same time with the clear directness of a child's. One could not meet them easily.

A precentor consulted his tuning fork, gave the tone, and some young men and women launched out on a hymn set to the melody of a popular Scottish ballad. It was catchy and sentimental, but the voices flatted a good deal. Glancing to the left, Richard observed that his father, who sat on the other side of Lady Marny, covered a smile with his handkerchief as he blew his nose.

The singing stopped. Wesley, after a brief invocation, opened the Bible. And at that point, as far as Richard was concerned, the mood of the evening began to change. It was not so much the speaker's compelling voice as an emanation of his personality that wrought the change and sobered trifling. Levity at once seemed feeble and forlorn in the presence of a dedication like Wesley's, in the presence, too, of the values he represented.

Choosing his text from the Sermon on the Mount, he read a few verses. To Richard, who knew them only in Latin, it seemed that he was hearing them for the first time.

"Lay not up for yourselves treasures upon earth, where moth and rust doth corrupt, and where thieves break through and steal: But lay up for yourselves treasures in heaven, where neither moth nor rust doth corrupt, and where thieves do not break through nor steal . . . The light of the body is the eye: if therefore thine eye be single, thy whole body shall be full of light: but if thine eye be evil, thy whole body shall be full of darkness. If therefore the light that is in thee be darkness, how great is that darkness!"

"The eye is the intention," Wesley continued: "What the eye is to the body, the intention is to the soul . . . This eye of the soul is then said to be single, when it looks at one thing only; when we have no other design, but to 'know God and Jesus Christ whom He hath sent' . . . 'If thine eye be' thus 'single,' thus fixed on God, 'thy whole body shall be full of light' . . . all thou art; all thou doest; thy desires, tempers, affections; thy thoughts and words and actions. The whole of these shall be 'full of light'; full of true, divine knowledge . . ."

In the churches of Venice and at his Jesuit school, Richard had heard sermons on this theme before, but Wesley had the gift of making it seem both new and ultimate. He spoke with an authority lacking to the urbane, rhetorical *abbati* in their lofty pulpits. Why? Because of his own absolute singleness of purpose. It occurred to Richard, who had been given an outline of the preacher's career at supper by Lord Marny, that behind Wesley's voice, behind the

236

thoughts he uttered, amplifying and authenticating them, lay the thousands of miles on horseback up and down England, lay the hardships, dangers, courage, poverty, effort, and persecution, of the last twenty years. Whatever he said was backed by that sanction. His power derived not only from believing but from living his doctrine. It was the power of Paul of Tarsus or Francis of Assisi or Loyola.

And gradually, as he listened, two ideas took form in Richard's mind. First, that Wesley was speaking out of a world immeasurably distant and different from that represented by the fashionable front row, a world that admitted no compromises with the ambitions, pleasures and values of the beau monde, a world of antithesis to everything that most men lived for. But, second, and terrifying, that Wesley was speaking to him, Richard Hammond, personally. For what did the sermon deal with but Richard's lifelong vacillation between this and that, yea and nay, one purpose and another? What did it deal with but his present scramble up Lord Marny's ladder at the cost of everything else? Or so it seemed to him, while no doubt others in the room applied the sermon to themselves.

". . . If thine eye be not singly fixed on God, 'thy whole body shall be full of darkness.' The veil shall remain on thine heart . . . Yea, if thine eye be not single, if thou seek any of the things of earth, thou shalt be full of ungodliness and unrighteousness . . ."

If thou seek any of the things of earth. Amélie had closed her fan and held it so tightly gripped in her lap that the knuckles of her hands stood out. For the preacher spoke to her. Poor old simple Lady Marny wept and dabbed at her eyes, dimly conscious that he spoke to her. And here and there, a choked *amen,* an inarticulate muttering, sounded in the room, as others realized that he spoke to them.

Not Lady Huntingdon, however. If anybody had the single eye, it was she. And being thus above reproach, she could not be affected by the sermon, except pleasantly, as an indirect tribute. Nor could George Selwyn. Tedium had brought him to such a point of collapse that he looked like a petrified fish and sat with vacant eyes fixed on a point above the preacher's head. Nor could the sermon penetrate to Lord Marny, although no one appeared more solemnly edified. He listened, to be sure, because he had no patience with absence of mind in himself or others. But the words simply confirmed his opinion of Wesley as an extravagant madman whom no one of sense could take seriously.

". . . Hear ye this, all ye that dwell in the world, and love the world wherein ye dwell? Ye may be 'highly esteemed of men'; but ye are 'an abomination in the sight of God'! . . ."

Marny nodded. Well, well!

". . . How long shall your souls cleave to the dust! . . . When will ye seek only to 'lay up treasures in heaven'; renouncing, dreading, abhorring all others? . . ."

"When the rivers run uphill, honest John," thought Marny.

". . . O who shall warn this generation of vipers to flee from the wrath to come! . . . Not those who court their favor or fear their frown . . . But if there be a Christian upon earth, cry aloud . . . show these honorable sinners the desperate condition wherein they stand. It may be that one in a thousand may have ears to hear . . ."

The Earl could not deny that Wesley had very fine hands and used them well — an excellent thing in an orator. He must call Richard's attention to it. Indeed, he could very well bear it in mind for himself in his next address to the Lords. That graceful, vibrant gesture of appeal. Capital!

The sermon rose to its climax. No doubt of the man's sincerity and real passion. No doubt of the emotional response of his listeners.

". . . Thou art to die! Thou art to sink into the dust . . . And the time draws on: the years slide away with a swift though silent pace . . . You feel in yourself sure approaching decay . . . Now what help is there in your riches? Do they sweeten death? . . . Will they prevent the unwelcome stroke or protract the dreadful hour? Can they deliver thy soul? . . . Can they restore the years that are past? . . . Or will the good things you have chosen for your portion here follow you over the great gulf? Not so . . ."

Compunction worked strongly in the audience. There were groans and weeping. Marny found the bench hard and crossed his legs in the opposite direction. Then, happening to glance toward

Richard, he felt a pulse of uneasiness. The boy sat with his fists clenched, apparently lost in the preacher. 'Fore Gad! A pity! The boy was too much inclined to enthusiasm. It was a weakness that must be taken seriously. Marny should have been warned by that experience with Wolfe at the "Pelican." He must speak to his ally, the Countess des Landes, about it. A woman of the world —

But catching sight of Amélie's profile beyond Richard's, he could not credit his eyes. An unnoticed tear rolled down the curve of her cheek, followed by another. Zounds! Amazement turned bitter. Was *she* going soft, too! *She* of all people! Why the little jade! Who had no more principles than a butterfly! Who had sold herself one way or another ever since hatching from the convent! Who was now selling her country to Pitt without a second thought! Understandably enough on a rational level, but not precisely à la Wesley. There was woman for you! Undependable, feeble-minded! He had always heard that madness was contagious, but that Amélie des Landes could swallow stuff like this and weep over it passed belief.

With a shrug, Marny stared back at the platform. Then second thoughts consoled him. Women enjoyed melting; they snivelled happily at the play or opera. Did that transform their natures? Devil a bit. Would the tearful old wife next to him be any the less self-indulgent because of her sobbing here about heavenly treasures? He would believe that when he saw it. And Amélie des Landes? Pshaw! *One in a thousand,* Wesley had said, and he was right. Marny considered the estimate extravagant. This sort of thing was like the emotions of drunkenness, expansive while they lasted but gone the day after.

The sermon ended. "'By patient continuance in well-doing, seek' thou 'for glory, and honor, and immortality.' In a constant, zealous performance of all good works, wait thou for that happy hour when the King shall say . . . 'Come, ye blessed of My Father . . .'"

Lord Marny was the first to compliment the preacher.

"Sir, a most commendable address and one to be long remembered by its fortunate hearers. The milk of the word, Mr. Wesley, the milk of the word! What I like about you, sir, is that you don't water it down. That's the proper physic for the poorer classes, where I understand your labors are beginning to show fruit. Upon my credit, most gratifying. Bring the rogues to their knees, hey? Teach 'em their duty to God and man? An incalculable benefit to the entire kingdom, sir. — Do you take snuff?"

Wesley declined, his clear eyes meeting the Earl's unrevealing ones. "I would, my lord, that the labors you speak of could show more fruit among the favored classes."

"Believe me, they will, sir," Marny evaded with a smile. "Don't be cast down. Egad, you're doing very well as it is. What fairer fruit" — his bow embraced the hovering noble ladies — "could you desire than these adornments to the Household of Faith? Quality always surpasses quantity, Mr. Wesley." His glance twinkled at Amélie, who turned away. "Madam," he added to Lady Huntingdon, "pray enroll me among the subscribers to the new chapel which I hear you intend to build. No doubt you can set down Mr. Selwyn, too, for a handsome figure — hey, Selwyn?" And in farewell, "Ladies . . . Mr. Wesley, your devoted servant." He gave his arm to his wife. "My love — "

Between the benches of the humble folk, who waited standing until their betters had left, he walked out, affable and benevolent. The Great Revival would go on, to the regeneration of England. Mad as it was, he wished it well, to the amount of ten guineas or, say, fifteen. He planned a sprightly letter on the subject to his lifelong acquaintance Monsieur de Voltaire.

"Ah, the good man!" rejoiced an ecstatic old woman, as he passed. "If all the gentry was Christian like him! God bless you, my lord!"

"I thank you, madam."

And so out of the room and down a steep flight of steps to the street, where the chairs were waiting. But he lingered for a word with Richard. The latter continued to look much too solemn.

"Why, you young dog," smiled Marny, after Madame des Landes had been handed into her chair. "What ails you? Are you off to a funeral? Aren't you conducting a pretty woman to her lodgings?"

"I'll be home directly, my lord. I'll bid you good night there."

"You'll do nothing of the kind," the Earl snapped. "You'll make the most of this occasion, like a sensible fellow. *Home directly!* By Gad!"

STEPHANIE, the Countess des Landes's personal maid, had been instructed to set out cake and wine and to stir up the fire in preparation for Madame's return that evening with a gentleman escort. This was usual enough. But what surprised and, indeed, almost startled the girl was the evident seriousness of both the Countess and the tall young man who accompanied her. No laughter, no badinage, none of Madame's usual sparkle. Even Monsieur Coco, the parrot, who woke up and sleepily cursed, did not amuse her tonight.

"Take him into the next room, Stephanie," she directed. "Then leave us and close the door."

Intensely curious, the girl eavesdropped awhile, but she could hear only an indistinct murmur.

"You were good to come up with me," Amélie was saying. "I had to talk with someone. I don't want to be alone with myself tonight . . . Like a scared child . . . Silly of me. I'm not often afraid." She stood in front of the hearth, staring down at the coals, her two hands gripping the edge of the mantelpiece and her forehead pressed against it. "Are you ever afraid? It seemed to me, up in that room, you felt like me — a little anyway. Bon Dieu, I wish I could forget his eyes! What did you make of what he said?"

"Probably the same as you, madame — if you were afraid."

She turned to face him. "Really? You aren't making fun? I hope not. I want someone who understands."

"Lord!" he muttered. "Who am I to make fun?"

He was too preoccupied to notice how the tone between them had changed since their meeting that morning. It was just as different as her naked face compared with the fashionable make-up that she usually wore. The conventions of speech and manner dropped off.

"Then you do understand how I felt, with his eyes through me, as if I were made of glass. Talk about Judgment Day!"

"Yes, I know what you mean." He sat down absently, his big hands, developed by the galley oar, clasping his knees. "Truth's pretty frightening."

"Truth about what?" she murmured.

241

He shook his head. "Oh — what's in the Bible, what Wesley said . . . I kept thinking how far apart heaven and hell are."

"So did I." She took a step toward him. "Just that. Too far. Infinitely. And so . . ." She fell silent. "What help?"

"I think he made that clear enough," Richard said.

She did not answer to this, but, after a long pause, seated herself near him. Her eyes, dark in the candlelight, seemed larger than before. She sat nervously plucking at the silk of the chair arm.

When she spoke again, his thoughts had drifted so far that he did not at once follow her.

"Corbleu!" she said bitterly. "What would he have! Did I make myself the daughter of parents who had no love for me? Did I shut myself up in a convent of noble brats who could think and talk nothing but gallants? Did I hand myself over at fifteen to an old satyr like des Landes? Could I help what followed? Did I give myself passions and the thirst to enjoy them? Tell me that, Monsieur Wesley. Ah, if all you could have known was the court at Versailles and people of fashion, what of the single eye then? What of God's justice and the great darkness?" Her voice fell away. "But no . . . I didn't mean disrespect. I'm a silly moth reproaching the sun. Only, why should the sun reproach me? Is it wicked to ask that, Richard?"

He shrugged. "I don't know. He spoke as if one could change — didn't he? — begin over again."

"Yes," she burst out. "And I don't believe him. Not for myself. I know what I'm not able to do. Tonight, I'm afraid — yes; in a panic, like someone who wakes up to find herself buried alive. I'm fluttering against the coffin lid. But tomorrow I'll forget. Soon I shan't flutter any more, even for Monsieur Wesley. In the end, I can hope to be like Milord de Marny. He isn't troubled by nightmares. How he would laugh, if he could hear us!" She added in another tone: "You're so different. How old are you?"

"Close upon twenty-one."

He found himself aware of her hands, the shapely beauty of them. And yet a moment past, he had not thought of her physically at all.

"Why, that's nothing," she exclaimed. "You're still a boy. I con-

242

sidered you older. You're free to change and begin over again."

"Are you so old, madame?"

"Practically middle-aged. Twenty-four, and nine years married. A woman's soon old. If my little girl had lived" — she drew a quick breath — "I'd be a grandmother before very long. But she died — fortunately, I know."

He felt the masculine, outgoing sympathy, so prompt at twenty-one — and so misleading — for a beautiful woman's distress. It veiled in ideal colors something much more elemental. Tonight, at least, Amélie did not wear her aura of countess and cosmopolitan belle; she was simply lovely and forlorn. The emotional experiences of the evening had brought them straightway more intimately together, and on a deeper level, than would have been possible in months of fopperies. Because one emotion, however inspired, can lead rapidly to others.

She seemed to close a door in her mind and asked abruptly: "Tell me, Richard — why don't you go back to that girl you're fond of? What if she doesn't fit into Lord Marny's plans? Do you want so very much to fit into them yourself? At least it would be a first step toward —"

"How did you know?" he asked, startled by the reference to Maritza. "What girl?"

On the point of betraying Marny's letter, Amélie thought better of it. "Why, the girl at the Villa," she said easily, "the one who danced so well. I heard she intended to go on the stage. You were much taken with her. What was her name?"

"Maritza Venier."

"Just so. But perhaps you did not see her again?"

"Yes, often. We became engaged. That's over now."

"Why?"

"We grew apart, I suppose."

So, Lord Marny's fears were groundless after all. Though she did not pause to consider it, Amélie felt a lift of personal satisfaction.

"Is Mademoiselle still in Venice?"

"No, in London. I saw her there recently. She does not care for me." He added after a moment, "Nor I for her."

Amélie surmised that the Earl did not know of this, or he would

243

have told her. Perhaps it was only a lovers' quarrel. And yet, for some unanalyzed reason, she preferred to accept Richard's statement at face value.

"What did you mean by *a first step?*" he demanded.

"I mean toward beginning over. We were talking about that."

He said nothing for a while. The qualms of conscience that Wesley's passionate sincerity had evoked were somehow becoming fainter. The unworldly vision of the sermon had begun to fade like some cloud pattern. For the cost of such a vision, if it is to be retained, had to be faced; and he found it too great a cost. He was not the first to write off that sort of challenge with a sigh.

"To do as Wesley bids," he returned finally, half to himself, "one has to be more of a hero than I am. Tonight I can see what he means; I can admit that any other life seems cheap and trivial as compared with his and of great men like him. But I'm already hanging back. I'm simply not the stuff saints are made of. You see how it is."

In spite of herself, she could not check the sudden throb in her voice. "Yes, we understand each other. How strange that seems! Do you know, I never talked with anyone like this — hardly with myself. Ma foi, when I think of the others! The everlasting pretense! But you —" She stopped and smiled. "You're still a boy. You can still be sincere. I can't tell you what that means . . ." She paused again, as if she had been led too far. "You speak of hanging back. For what, Richard?"

"For you," he answered. And, in the silence, he got up and stood with his hands stretched toward the fire. "You're so very beautiful."

She shook her head. "I wonder if you know what I am. You will find out soon enough, but then it may be too late . . . I want to be honest with you."

He walked over to her. "I'll be honest with you first. Do you know what *I* am? Do you know where I was when Lord Marny came to Venice? In the galleys. What do you think of a galley slave?"

"The galleys?" she repeated, staring up at him.

"Yes. I may be a boy, as you say. But no one stays young in hell."

To his surprise, the confession that cost him so much to make, knowing the infamy attached to the word *galérien*, only surprised her. There was no sign of repulsion.

"But, Richard! What ever did you do?"

"Tried to kill a man. You knew him — Marin Sagredo. I wish I had. How does that jibe with saintliness?"

"Sit here." She took his hand and drew him down to a cushioned tabouret beside her knees. "Tell me what happened."

The other-worldly trumpets were very distant now. Amélie's expressive eyes, thoughtfully intent or dilating with interest as he talked, the curve of her half-parted lips, the warm nearness of her, absorbed him. And on her side, too, the trumpets were forgotten, though the emotional agitation they had stirred up sought its outlet in another form.

"Canaille!" she exclaimed of Sagredo. And her eyes filled at the description of the galleys. And impulsively her hand closed on his arm, as he told of the scene at the Arsenal. But she asked repeatedly about Maritza — indirectly, with elaborate casualness, and yet returning to the point. Why had Richard not written? What had been said in London? She told him that she considered Maritza to blame. A cold girl, doubtless; one who valued her own pride and hurt vanity more than anything else. Whereas, though Amélie did not need even to imply the comparison, Richard here found warmth and understanding and heart.

But her jealousy was hardly conscious. She thrilled to the discovery of a new need in herself, a new desire. Something remained of her first despairing response to Wesley's appeal: a sense of loneliness, a craving for sincerity, an intimation of love, passionate, to be sure, but not wholly sensual. Her need answered his.

"So, you see how it is," he concluded. "Though the Lord knows why I should trouble you with all this. Probably we have Mr. Wesley to thank for it. Then, too, I get so tired of acting Mr. Hammond. It reminds me of the old days in Venice, when I was playing Harlequin and could hardly wait to get off the stuffy mask. I should think the Countess des Landes would expose such a fellow."

She put her hand on his arm again. "Will you forget the Countess? Will you call me Amélie?"

"But, madame —"

"Amélie," she persisted.

The word echoed through his mind. He repeated it slowly. "Then you forgive me?"

"For what?"

"For being what I am."

"Come!" she said with a kind of tender sharpness. "You know that's nonsense. We must be ourselves with each other. Talk of *forgiving!* Look, Richard." She leaned closer. "If you've been in the galleys, I've been in the Parc aux Cerfs, the King's pleasure house at Versailles. I don't know which slavery is worse, except that a mistress of Louis XV gets richly paid for her services. And speak of masks. What of mine with these English respectables? Lady Huntingdon! My God, when I could tell her of horrors that she wouldn't even understand! But let's console ourselves. Most people wear masks — even Lady Huntingdon."

"At least," he said, "mine is off with you."

"And mine with you. Listen," she went on eagerly, "suppose we could keep it like that — just you and me, whatever we are with others. Suppose we could have that understanding between us. It would be so new and different from anything I've ever known. I'll try, if *you* will."

"Try?" he wondered, lost in the fascination of her eyes and voice, his senses aching for her. "It won't be difficult."

"And it won't be easy," she returned — "at least for me. Perhaps I'll be ashamed sometimes not to wear a mask. I'm very wicked, Richard — call it damned, if you like — and damned souls don't change. That's what I meant earlier. But I promise not to lie to you about myself, if I can help it. Promise that you'll do the same for me. Is it a bargain? Only, think before you answer."

He took both her hands between his. "And what would you think of me, Comtesse —" . . . "Now, now!" she put in. — "Amélie. — What would you think if I sat here thinking?"

"I'd consider you very wise."

"There's a fib already."

"Yes," she admitted . . . "But you haven't answered."

"Is it necessary?" He raised her hands to his lips. "Yes! . . . A thousand times! . . . Yes! . . ."

"All for my hands?" she murmured. "The rest of me is jealous. . . . But wait! No, wait! We must drink to our agreement." He stood on fire, as she got up, brushing the folds from her skirt. "Eh bien, voilà! I've stopped fluttering already. I told you I would. Remember the last time we drank together? I wish this was champagne instead of claret."

"It'll be champagne," he said, walking over to the table that Stephanie had prepared, "just as soon as it touches your lips."

"Ah? So, it hasn't taken you long to discover my secret. Yes, I'm a witch. Very cruel and cunning. I tried to warn you. But now it's too late. Beware of my arts."

He was pouring the wine. "Really? Why *beware?*"

"Monsieur Wesley could tell you why," she answered in a low, hot voice. "He would be right, mon amour perdu. But what then?"

From the table, he glanced over toward her. The sober dress, which had suited the first part of the evening, now looked like masquerade. Debonair, a little flushed, she seemed on the point of a dance step.

"Why, then," he smiled back, "forget Monsieur Wesley."

She shook her head. "Not at all. We owe him for introducing us to each other as we are. We owe him for Richard and Amélie. Poor Monsieur Wesley! I'll join Milord de Marny in a subscription. — Stop! How can my magic work if we don't use the same glass? Were you only flattering me? Hand it here . . ." She took a sip. "There you are — taste. Don't tell me I failed."

He drank, and held the glass up to the candlelight. "Fail? Could you ever fail? On my word, champagne for the gods! Compared with this, what poor little wine we had at the Villa Bagnoli!"

"Yes," she nodded, keeping up the game, "this time I used my strongest charm. Why, it not only turned claret into champagne but Richard Hammond into a connoisseur. Perhaps you could even tell me from what vineyard the wine comes."

He drank again, as if trying it. "Not from France."

"No? Where, then?"

"You know, I believe from your own vineyard on the Island of Cythera."

"Richard! You're almost a courtier . . . Richard! . . ."

247

He held her close, their lips together a long time. Passionately. Her body yielding.

Then she leaned back a little in his arms, lifting her face and eyes.

"True," she breathed. "Cythera. We drank to a voyage there that night at the Villa. Ah, mon bien aimé, we witches are all prophetesses. But I'll tell you a secret. This is the first time I've ever really loved . . ."

A passing watchman called the hour of one. Stephanie, awaiting Madame's pleasure until she could retire, listened sleepily outside the door. Then, hearing no voices, she lifted the latch and peered in. The room was empty, but the gentleman's hat and cane still lay on the chair where he had placed them. So, she had misjudged the spirits of Madame and Monsieur after all. Anyway the evening had ended in the same routine. Yawning, she snuffed what remained of the candles in the parlor and boudoir, gave a shrug at the closed bedroom door, but paused a moment beside Monsieur Coco's perch in the boudoir before extinguishing the last candle. She had neglected to cover his stand for the night.

Rousing himself, the bird cracked a seed. "Putain," he chuckled.

"Hush," whispered Stephanie, as one realist to another. "You mustn't say what you think in this world, petit frère. Go to sleep."

About the same hour, Lord Marny, who had risen late from cards, consulted his watch and asked a servant if Mr. Hammond had returned.

"No, my lord, I believe not."

To the man's surprise, his master looked unusually pleased — "Ah, well. These young dogs, eh, Thomas!" — and walked upstairs with a smile.

He could congratulate himself on his own perceptiveness. Human nature ran true to form. He had not misplaced his confidence in Amélie des Landes, who well deserved a thousand pounds. Richard was henceforth safe. He would profit from this affair, be saved from romantic nonsense, acquire the tone of good company.

"How large a dividend," thought Marny in his nightcap, "a little foresight pays!"

XXXVI

IT must be allowed that no blackmailer ever operated with more delicacy, cordial consideration, and avowed regard for a victim, than did the Marquis di Corleone-Tromba in his relations with Lord Marny and Richard Hammond. Beyond admitting, with the utmost sympathy, that he knew of the injustice at Venice under which his dear young friend had suffered, and that no one could realize better than he *how all-important it was to keep the fact secret,* he gallantly avoided any threat whatever. Men of the world understand each other. It would have been crude to elaborate on vulgar social prejudices against convicts, however innocent they may actually be, or to suggest that His Majesty would never appoint an ex-galley slave to represent him abroad and, indeed, would harbor the keenest resentment against Marny for even proposing it. The maxim *A word to the wise* disposed of the matter.

Nor did Tromba exact anything in return for secrecy. It could be assumed that the Earl would be delighted to countenance a nobleman of Corleone's rank and Mr. Hammond's benefactor. So well-bred a man as the Marquis, so infinitely agreeable and distinguished, would not shame Lord Marny at his own table nor in the fashionable circles to which he might present him. Indeed, rather, such a glittering protégé would reflect credit on his sponsor.

In terms, then, of blackmail, nothing could have been less painful than this. Tromba did not expect to pluck Marny. If he plucked Marny's friends and even drew a couple of feathers out of Lady Marny's rich plumage, it was still a cheap bargain for his lordship. When the plucking was over, and the Marquis faded from England, as fade in the end he must, the Earl could point to his own wife as a victim and confess that for once his astuteness had been at fault. No serious harm in that.

Besides, except in a case of jealousy or vengeance, Tromba was not ill-natured. For Richard especially, he had as much real liking as a man of his sort could be expected to cherish for anyone, a kind of master-for-pupil fondness. Of course if he had known of Richard's affair with Amélie des Landes, and that the favors which had so far eluded his expert advances were bestowed on a novice, he might have felt less benevolent.

As it was, however, on the pleasantest terms with everybody, he rode the flood tide of fortune during the next two weeks, his sails swollen with the prosperous wind of Lord Marny's endorsement, and not a cloud in the sky. He could now give full rein to his genius. *"Mundus vult decipi,"* he liked to quote — "the world wishes to be deceived, and deceived it shall be." In the fine art of tactfully prepared and alert imposture, he could rank with such masters as Saint-Germain and Cagliostro.

Almost at once, he became a lion at Bath, especially among the ladies. He shone in Lord Marny's salon, was received by Mr. Pitt, and opened an Assembly Ball with the exquisite Lady Coventry. His social accomplishments made any party a success.

". . . My dear," (to a newcomer) "you must meet the Marquis di Corleone. Quite the most talked-of man in Bath. A warm friend of the Marnys, you know. So affable, so truly genteel. A pity he speaks only French. To walk alone with him, I vow, is a test of virtue. No impropriety, of course — he's most restrained — but what sensibility, my love! One feels tempted to swoon for the pleasure of being revived by him. They say he's traveled much in the Orient and dabbles in magic, though he smiles it off. In any case, I do know that my Lady Marny is quite restored by remedies he advised. They say he's Grand Master of the Rosicrucians or some such order . . ."

As might have been expected, the men, eclipsed by these attractions, were less favorable. Intolerant of foreigners on principle, they condemned the ladies' partiality for a tripping Italian, marquis or not. He was too versatile by half, and therefore suspect. They did not care for his damned graces and insolent assurance. They did not relish the implied or outspoken comparison on the part of a spouse or sweetheart between his accomplishments and their own limitations. What if sturdy British manhood did not shine and caper, it had bottom and beef.

But another, more solid, grievance took form. It could not be denied that Corleone had devilish odd talents. It began by his amusing some company with a few parlor tricks, about which he jested as much as anyone. But he never explained them; and, together with his cryptic references to the East, they gave the impression of a man to whom these things, indeed, were trifles, but who, if he had wished to divulge it, had knowledge of deep and occult matters beyond the scope of ordinary people. Then, too, consider the precious elixirs which had rejuvenated Lady Marny and for which other afflicted women were clamoring. The good doctors Oliver and Peirce pooh-poohed them, but they could not deny the cure. Her ladyship no longer required a wheel chair or complained of headaches, backaches and constipation. At a ball night in the Lower Rooms, she even danced a minuet with Corleone, to the edification and envy of other old ladies. But why, then, did the Marquis not publish his wonderful nostrums for the benefit of all sufferers? The answer was simple but disquieting: the cost.

"What cost, Musher di Corleone?" asked the rich Lady Cavendish in her awful French. "The cost makes no difference to me. What's money compared with a sound head! Is your remedy good for the migraine?"

"Undoubtedly, madame."

"Then send me a vial of it tomorrow, dear musher. And no more nonsense. Even if it costs fifty guineas."

"Alas, madame, I must decline."

"But why, nom de Dioo?"

"I repeat, the cost, madame. If I had more than a tiny flacon reserved for my own use, Madame would honor me by accepting the vial she desires without cost. But to concoct the amount you mention from the necessary ingredients would require twenty times fifty guineas, and that is beyond my means. I am no merchant, Milady Cavendish, and do not sell the secrets which have been entrusted to me. Madame will recall my intimate relations with the family of Hammond. I could do no more than share with Milady Marny the small quantity of the elixir I possess."

"What ingredients, musher?" the old woman asked eagerly.

"That is a part of the secret, madame, and I prefer not to discuss it. But I may hint that Cleopatra, an adept in Egyptian lore, undoubtedly knew it, and that something of its nature is revealed by that incident where she dissolved pearls for the delectation of Anthony. As you are aware, all precious stones have singular and different properties."

"Do you mean — ?"

251

"Nay, madame, I must beg to be excused."

But Lady Cavendish suffered tortures from migraine and gave him no peace.

The upshot of this was never quite clear. Certain it is that for some time her ladyship felt astonishingly well. And it is also certain that a pearl and diamond collar belonging to her estate had disappeared when the latter was inventoried after her death. But time had lapsed, and nothing was proved. She owned, however, to certain of her friends that she had prevailed on the dear Marquis to supply her with a few drops of the elixir, and that he had administered them privately over several days. He had a charming method of stroking her forehead with his fingertips and of making odd passes of the hands in front of her eyes, after which she seemed to waken from a profound sleep vastly refreshed.

Rumor had it that Corleone's good nature was similarly prevailed on by other ladies, with equal results. No one in Bath had heard of Franz Mesmer, who was only twenty-seven at the time. But mesmerism did not begin with him, nor did the nervous diseases that charlatans exploited.

And yet, if this had been all, the head-shaking gentlemen would have been less concerned than they actually became. They had much more to disturb them. What of the Marquis's knack in fortunetelling, that amounted to clairvoyance and intimated a devastating knowledge of family secrets and private affairs? He divulged none, but he came so close, with so insinuating a manner, that it prickled many a scalp and brought out sweat at night on the brows of wakeful sinners. If Corleone happened to be a blackguard, he had a gold mine here; and the sinners knew it. Or what of reports that he had raised the dead at intimate gatherings of favored admirers? Worse still, a growing secretiveness and air of mystery, apparent among certain dowagers, piqued curiosity to madness and launched rumors of all kinds. Some held that the Marquis's pleasant house and garden, which he had leased on Orchard Street after moving from the "Bear," was the scene of orgies in the nature of a Witches' Sabbath. Others, led by Lord Bolton, who had knocked the admissions out of his wife, spoke of a Rosicrucian lodge for women, called the Priestesses of Isis, devoted to occult practises under Corleone's guidance.

In any case, the ground swell of masculine suspicion rose higher. One might have supposed that, with all the beef and bottom on one side, and only a tripping Italian on the other, the annoyance could have been dealt with at once in a straightforward, manly fashion. But it was not so easy. Aside from Lord Marny's and the muscular-looking Richard Hammond's support, a good deal about Corleone himself discouraged roughness. He had a quiet, often languid manner, but he conveyed somehow the impression of a tiger. No use talking horsewhips to one who seemed likely to do the whipping; or pistols to a man who smilingly, on one occasion, shot the spots out of cards at twenty paces; or swords to the best fencer at the salle d'armes. Hired bullies could be had; and once, indeed, a gang of roughs, whether hired or not, attacked the Marquis on his return at night from the gaming rooms. But they fared so badly in the scuffle that it was a pity of them, and the couple of wounded left on the field were hardly worth hanging.

So, the Marquis continued to flourish, admired by the ladies, dreaded by the men, and altogether cock-a-hoop.

"Groundwork, my dear boy," he explained confidentially to Richard, "mere groundwork. First dung, then sow, then reap. The analogy is imperfect, because even now I'm not doing badly; but I shall do much better. Reputation is everything, and mine is spreading. After Bath, London. There's Golconda."

Mindful of rumblings in the coffeehouses, Richard queried: "How far can your reputation spread without bursting?"

"That remains to be seen," Tromba nodded. "I admit your metaphor of a bubble comes pretty close; for that, as some poet has put it, is what a reputation is. I've tossed off a good many in my time, big and small. But, with good luck, this ought to be the biggest yet." He pursed his lips, as if on the stem of a pipe, and spread his hands to indicate size. "More colorful and grandiose. The point is, Richard my boy, I toss them off; I don't wait till they burst in my eyes." He added, suddenly: "How ill-conditioned people are! Instead of considering me as I am, a benefactor, a blessing upon society, they backbite and persecute."

It must be owned, greatly to Richard's discredit, that Tromba amused rather than shocked him. Culpable as he might be, the charm which he had exerted in Venice hung on.

253

"Benefactor!" Richard murmured. "Blessing upon society!"

"What else?" exclaimed Tromba. "Do I not cure diseases? Revive the old? Comfort the sorrowing? And relieve boredom in a thousand different ways? Is that no benefaction? I say it is. But, in return, what do I meet? Slander, malevolence, and always, at last, tyranny. Saint Christopher! It's too much!"

They were in the billiard room of the house on Orchard Street; and, at this point, the Marquis, selecting a cue, made a difficult carom shot in perfect style.

"Yes, it's a shame," said his guest, "that people don't like being fleeced."

"Say rather —" Tromba studied his next shot — "that they don't like paying for what they get. Am I to expect no reward? Well, it happens that I not only expect but intend to have one."

And he fell to practising his game.

From their association in Venice, Richard had a general notion of his unscrupulous friend's methods. He knew that visions of the departed, spirit voices, and the like, in dark, hushed rooms, were the result of a masterly combination of concealed mirrors, magic lanterns, and ventriloquism, properly spiced with the superstitious awe that Tromba knew so well how to induce. He was aware, too, how the Marquis performed his feats of fortunetelling and clairvoyance — a mixture of shrewd character-reading and information derived from various sources in various ways. But his medical cures — apart from the elixir, which Richard knew was a very fiery and perfumed liqueur — remained mystifying. And on that subject, Tromba, who was usually open enough with him, seemed evasive.

"My dear Richard," he would say, "there are tricks in this trade which can be done without knowing how one does them. And there are tricks that some people can do and others not. I discovered long ago, in the case of a girl I was courting, that, if I fixed my eyes on her intently, it had an effect not unlike that of a serpent on a bird. Awake, she seemed asleep. I found out that at such times I could put ideas in her head which lingered afterwards. Since then, I have used the same method for different purposes. Most of our ills are imaginary. Assure a woman in a trance that she's well, and well she will be when she comes out of it. It's as simple as that." He heaved a sigh. "If the damned thing could only be used in all cases! I tried it not long ago on the adorable Countess des Landes; but she only enquired if I was going into a fit. Corpo di Dio!"

Richard could make nothing of all this and put it down to a not unreasonable desire on Tromba's part to keep some of his secrets to himself.

But there was another trick in regard to which the adventurer could offer no explanation and seemed no less puzzled than anybody else. It came up one evening at the lodgings of Madame des Landes, when the Marquis and Richard had escorted her home from the Assembly Rooms. Amélie, who was skepticism itself as to Tromba's magical powers and rallied him gaily about them, had been exercising her wit on the subject, when he drew a leather case from his pocket and presented it with a bow.

"Very well, lovely scoffer, tell me what you think of that?"

The case, which was about six inches square, had gilded cabalistic signs stamped on it. Otherwise it resembled the usual shallow box used for containing a necklace.

"A present? For *me*?" she dimpled. "Dear Marcello!"

"If you desire it, madame."

"I'll wager, some of your false diamonds, more beautiful than the real."

"No, not diamonds."

She opened the case and looked blank. It contained a very bright round disk of metal.

"Just a mirror?" she said, disappointed, raising it to a level with her face. "And not a good one at that. I can't even see myself in it."

"Hold it close to the light, madame, and keep your eyes fixed on it for a short time. Perhaps you will see something, perhaps not. To be frank, I've never seen anything in it myself, but others have. I don't understand the properties of it. I don't know what you will see. Do you wish to try?"

"Of course. I love your naughty little tricks, Marcello."

"Madame, on my honor, if it is a trick, it will be yours as much as mine."

"Mystifier!" she laughed; and then, bringing the disk under a candle, she followed Tromba's instructions.

"Nothing at all," she shrugged, "except that it hurts the eyes."

"Please — a moment longer."

"Nothing . . . but wait . . . yes . . . sapristi!" If she was acting, she did it well. Her face became more intent. Suddenly her eyes widened in a look of unfeigned horror. She uttered a low cry. The mirror dropped to the floor. "Richard . . ."

He supported her half fainting to the couch. She looked ghastly, fighting against the loss of consciousness. "Mon flacon . . ." she murmured. Tromba found the smelling bottle in her small kerchief-bag and held it beneath her nose. Gradually she showed color again, opened her eyes, and drew a hand across her forehead.

"Stupid of me . . ." The look of horror returned. She pointed at the fallen mirror. "Take that thing away. Let me never see it again. Marcello, you're the Devil himself. But tell me it was a trick. Tell me how you contrive —"

"Madame, I swear." Tromba dropped to one knee beside the couch. "Believe me, I contrived nothing. I would cut off my hand rather than distress you. It is only a metal disk brightly polished. Whatever you saw was a thought which took form, as happens in sleep."

"Please, please," she begged. "Say it was a trick, and I'll forgive you. How could I have such thoughts?"

"What frightened you, madame? Don't brood upon it. We'll laugh at your nightmare."

She said faintly: "A crowd of dreadful people . . . an old woman's head carried on a pike . . . the face was mine . . ."

They all laughed in the end. It was impossible and absurd. But Tromba could not be brought to confess that he had anything to do with it.

XXXVII

AND then, as the autumn season at Bath drew toward its close, with the Marquis di Corleone riding high, a disquieting contretemps befell him. That in a career like his such mishaps were familiar and inevitable did not make this one less awkward on the eve of his biggest harvest.

Summoned by an urgent note to the Orchard Street house, Richard found Tromba in a brocaded dressing robe pacing up and down his bedroom. The note had indicated that the Marquis, feeling indisposed, desired the attendance of his friend; but no signs of illness appeared on his dark face. He merely looked annoyed.

"Gran' Dio! What's wrong?" asked Richard, laying aside his cloak and hat. "I expected to find you in bed."

"Bed, nothing," snapped the other. "Though you'll kindly spread the news that I'm out of sorts. Which is true enough. Damn Caretti!"

"Who?" For a moment, the name meant nothing.

"Mario Caretti, the Sardinian Resident in London. You ought to remember him well enough from Venice. He's the patron of your ex-flame."

Richard stiffened. Though he had never met Caretti, he did not like him — nor the word *patron*. "What about him?"

"Well, he's here in Bath. And — what may be of interest to you — he's brought the ballerina and her father with him. I had a glimpse of them on Stall Street, though luckily they didn't see me."

Here was news that once would have set Richard's pulses galloping. Now, passionately involved with Amélie des Landes, he found it only vexing. After all, he had nothing to dread from the Veniers' knowledge of the galley episode. In spite of the break with Maritza, they would be the last people on earth to betray him. But Bath was a small place. Likely enough he and they would meet somewhere, he forced to exchange civilities, which they would all find difficult.

He explained that he was unacquainted with Caretti and added: "I don't see why you're troubled about him, either. Does he know you?"

"He does not."

"Well, then?"

"Well, then, this. He may be harmless. But he's a foreign Resident, which means that he's in probable correspondence with his colleagues elsewhere. Now, as it happens, I had some trouble with the Sardinian Resident in Munich. It concerned his wife, but that's beside the point. He's a jealous old codger, with no understanding for gallantry; and I'd have called him out, had other circumstances not compelled me to leave the city. He's responsible for that, too, damn him! — a perfect relentless old fury. I think he knew I had thoughts of England. It's one of the reasons I became Corleone before shipping from Holland. There's a good chance he did not inform Caretti, but I'm afraid he has."

"Even so," Richard argued, "why should he identify Tromba with the Marquis di Corleone? There are other Italians in England. You told me once that such a marquisate exists, and that your papers are in order."

"Of course they're in order," put in Tromba. "I challenge anyone to discover the least flaw. Whatever one does should be well done, especially forgery. But still . . ." Tromba shook his head and nipped at the side of his thumb. "Caretti's familiar with forged papers. If he has my description from his confrere in Munich, he'll suspect the truth. But let your ballerina friend point me out to him in the street as Tromba, and the game's up. So, I must play ill for a time and keep out of sight. He plans to leave, I think, in another week."

"How do you know that?"

The other shrugged. "Good Lord! Do I need to tell you again that I hire shrewd servants and pay them well? It appears that the old man Venier is ailing, and that the doctors ordered him to Bath. His daughter and the old warship of a maid are attending him. No doubt Caretti's footing the bill, and he came along as escort; but he has to return to London. His mistress, the ballerina, will not make her debut at Drury Lane until late December. Let her stay on here, as far as I care. With Caretti out of the way, she'll not trouble me. Our paths won't cross."

"Mistress?" flared Richard. "What right have you to call her that?"

"Well, isn't it evident?"

Richard boiled up but controlled himself. There was no answer he could make to Tromba's remark. It seemed justified as far as appearances went. And yet he could not think of Maritza in that way.

"I refuse to believe it — that's all," he said.

"Please yourself."

Returning to the subject at hand, Richard objected: "But when you go to London, Marcello, you'll find Caretti there."

"Yes, but London's a big city. I can avoid him. He moves in the literary, artistic set, which has no attraction for me. Anyway I can take the chance. In Bath, there's no doubt at all: I can't help meeting him unless I lie low. Now, here's a service you can render me. Keep your ear to the ground, listen to the gossip. If he knows anything of me, he'll probably talk. If he does, the rumors will spread like wildfire. Then I shall know what to do."

"And what will that be?" Richard asked, with the side thought that Lord Marny would not be ill pleased if Caretti delivered him so cheaply from the Marquis.

"I have two choices." Tromba held up his index and middle fingers; he bent one of them down. "I can disappear. And that, I assure you, I don't intend to do at the first shot. Later no doubt. But I have too many rich irons in the fire to leave them forthwith because of Caretti. — Or," he bent down his other finger, "I can silence him."

"How?"

The temperature in the room seemed to have dropped in the last moment.

"Why, then," Tromba went on, "*he* will have two choices. He will listen to sense and publicly retract any damaging statements he may have made — I think a signed letter in the *Bath Journal* will do — or he will hold his tongue permanently for a most compelling reason."

"You mean — ?"

"I mean this, my dear boy —" the other's manner had grown gentle, almost silken — "that, although I'm a very peaceable, patient man and suffer fools gladly in the way of business, some dead fools have learned the danger of meddling with my affairs. Reprisal is a luxury I sometimes indulge in at whatever cost." He flashed a smile. "But don't look so concerned. I hope it won't come to that, Richard."

XXXVIII

TO Lord Marny, the seclusion of Orange Square or Grove, snugly shut in on all sides by houses and buildings, offered a soothing retreat toward the end of the morning. He had, he thanked God, no ailments that required him to parboil in the baths or to fill his stomach with detestable water in the Pump Room. At the age of fifty-five, the animation of the North and South Parades or similar strolling places no longer attracted him. But in Orange Grove, shadowed at one angle by the walls of the Abbey, he could take the air around the obelisk; or, following the line of houses, he could saunter past the "Cross Keys Inn," the various fashionable lodginghouses and residences, drop into Mr. Frederick's bookshop, and finally come to rest in Mr. Morgan's Coffee House for a glance at the newspapers or a random chat.

In the coffeehouses, especially at Bath, formalities ceased; people did not have to be introduced; and all ranks were on an equal footing. Lord Marny, who did not have to be concerned about his rank, except when it was directly challenged, enjoyed casual meetings and conversations. He could often, in this way, obtain glimpses into walks of life, such as art or the stage, industry or farming, which his own pursuits did not usually afford.

On this particular morning, while scanning the *Journal* and the *Advertiser,* he found himself peculiarly attracted and intrigued by a distinguished-looking elderly gentleman at the next table. An expert in people, he at once formed certain conclusions. The man was a foreigner both by the cast of his features and the somewhat different cut of his well-worn clothes. He was afflicted with a tight, dry cough and looked ill as well as poor. Probably, concluded the Earl, an exiled Frenchman of rank, a *philosophe,* to judge by his thoughtful forehead and eyes. It was a type that vastly appealed to Marny, as representing the ultimate in civilized values.

Absorbed in the latest French gazette from Holland, the gentleman seemed unaware of Marny's appraisal. But, finally, laying aside the paper, he encountered his neighbor's gaze and smiled.

"A pleasant day," said the Earl, paying him the compliment of assuming that he understood English, though with a shrewd suspicion that he did not. "And yet 'tis somewhat chiller than one would expect in Somerset before winter."

The gentleman bowed and again smiled, with a deprecating movement of the hands. "Hélas, monsieur, je suis navré . . . I no spick English, sair."

"Je disais, monsieur . . ." Marny dropped into French and repeated his remark, while the other's eyes kindled with pleasure at the familiar tongue. There followed graceful regrets, excuses, and compliments. As he had surmised, the foreigner was evidently a person of fine breeding, with all the manners of the great world. But in one respect, Marny's estimate had missed; he was not French, though a very slight accent in no way impaired his command of that language. An Italian, thought Marny, with a touch of disappointment, for he preferred the French. But he had known very great gentlemen of Italy who were the peers of anyone; and, indeed, within a few minutes, he so warmed to the conversation and felt so drawn to his new acquaintance, that the point of nationality entirely faded.

Starting from an item about the current war between Prussia and Austria in the Hague gazette, talk ranged over the whole political field in Europe. Though himself an authority on this topic, Marny was immensely struck by the Italian's scope of information, his accuracy and historical learning. What impressed him still more were the latter's profound reflections on the course of history, his philosophical interpretation of it.

"I take it, monsieur," he probed, unable at last to contain his curiosity about the gifted foreigner and leading tactfully from the general to the personal, "that, like me, you have engaged in political and perhaps diplomatic affairs."

"No," smiled the other, "I assure you that, except for a year or so of foreign service, as a young man, my life has been bookish and secluded. Your extreme politeness endows me with a virtue which I must disclaim." On the point of leaving, he beckoned a waiter, then added to Marny: "It has been a rare pleasure, monsieur, to converse with you, all the more as my own lack of English keeps me so usually tongue-tied. Perhaps sometime again —"

But the Earl did not choose to let it go at that. "Indeed I trust so," he put in warmly. "It is in the hope of soon renewing our conversation that I take the liberty of presenting myself. You have possibly heard of me. My name is Marny."

He was surprised at the other's somewhat startled expression, which did not so much indicate deference to a celebrated statesman as a more personal response. But at once the stranger controlled it.

"Who has not heard of Milord de Marny?" he bowed. "But, as it happens, I have known of you more intimately than by public report. You are the father, I believe, of a young man whom I count among my very dear friends. It was with inexpressible joy the other day that I learned through my daughter of his escape by your help from Venice. Perhaps Richard has spoken of us. I am Antonio Venier."

Marny's thought covered various emotions during the next few seconds. But, for all his dismay, he kept an impenetrable front and returned Venier's bow.

"My son has indeed spoken of your Excellence and of Mademoiselle de Venier in the warmest terms of grateful affection. I am most honored to make your Signory's acquaintance. But I did not know that you were in England."

"We arrived three weeks ago. Thanks to Monsieur Caretti's generous offices in her behalf, my daughter is to appear this winter at Drury Lane. It surprises me that Richard, if he happens to be with you, did not speak of meeting her in London."

"Damned underhanded dog!" thought Marny of his son, at the same time shaking his head with a pleasant smile.

"And yet it's understandable enough," Venier added. "They quarreled, I gather, and spoke their minds, as young people will. My daughter, milord, has too small a regard for realities, and your son, perhaps, has too much."

Assuring himself that no one in the coffeehouse could overhear them, Marny hitched his chair closer. It was a relief to learn that Richard and the ballerina had quarreled. Youth has a right to its secrets, and he erased the word *underhanded* from his mind. He could take comfort, too, that Richard was now deep in the toils of Amélie des Landes. But these Veniers had too intimate a knowledge of his son's past, would have to be tactfully managed.

"Realities?" he queried.

"Yes, in the worldly sense of material things. Personally, like my daughter, I lean in the opposite direction and admire realities of a different kind. But how easy it is to comprehend that a young man, released from the living death of the galleys by nothing less than a miracle, should embrace what your Signory can offer him! I pointed out to Maritza that we cannot require our friends to be Don Quixotes, but that therefore they need not cease to be friends."

"Precisely, dear sir!" exclaimed Marny with enthusiasm. "I do not know if your Excellence is aware of my plans for Richard. They are plans, let me add, with which he is fully in accord. When I say that a post of Resident at one of the German courts has been promised him by the Duke of Newcastle, subject only to the *pro forma* consent of His Majesty, it will indicate the career I have in mind for him. He will obtain more creditable posts. He will enter Parliament —"

"No doubt," Venier interrupted, with the faintest touch of impatience. "I can well imagine, Monsieur le Comte, that your favor and his own merit will carry him far. And, with submission, I may be permitted to say what your own delicacy would find embarrassing, that marriage with a penniless girl who follows the profession of a public dancer would prove utterly ruinous to those plans." He hesitated a moment. "I ask you to believe, milord, that I am not without common sense or, foolish as it is, a certain pride."

Marny was quick to approve. "Indeed, as your Excellence so charitably observes, there are those other considerations." And, taking the opportunity to insert a wedge at this point, he added: "Besides, I understand he's at present very well with a certain fine woman of fashion here."

"Ah?" said Venier with apparent indifference.

"On the other hand," Marny went on, "I know he is devoted to his friends, among whom in chief he will always be proud to reckon your Excellence and, I am sure, if she will forgive him, Mademoiselle de Venier."

"I hope he will," the other replied earnestly, "I long to see him again. He will ever be welcomed by me. Pray tell him so, milord; and, with respect to my daughter, assure him of what I believe he knows, that she is too generous to cherish a grievance, when time has once removed the smart of it."

The Earl expressed his handsomest appreciation of this attitude. He enquired of the circumstances which had brought Venier to Bath, regretted his ill-health, and noted with secret satisfaction that Caretti was responsible for the journey. A man did not go to such trouble nor incur such expense (even in the form of an advance upon Maritza's salary at the theater) without something, or the expectation of something, in return. Probably the ballerina, for all her father's naïveté, was too happily preoccupied by now to

263

feel much animosity against a former lover. Then, having carefully taken the address of Venier's lodgings on Trim Street, Marny promised that Richard would hasten to pay his respects at once, and placed himself personally at his Excellence's command for any possible services.

In the end, he would have felt more pleased with his diplomacy, had he not committed a slight blunder.

"I need hardly point out," he observed, "that any unguarded reference to my son's confinement in the Venetian galleys would be most unfortunate. Every step has been taken to disassociate him from that affair. Until he is well established in the world, the report of it might ruin him."

Venier answered with a trace of coolness: "The warning is quite unnecessary, Milord de Marny. People of honor do not make unguarded references to secret matters which affect their friends. You need not feel that my daughter or I would be gossips — or delators — under any circumstances."

The Earl hastened to apologize for the remark, which he ascribed not to the faintest misgiving in regard to Venier's discretion, but to his own over-anxious solicitude for Richard. And the two gentlemen parted with renewed civilities.

"I own," Marny asserted later on in the day, after reporting this conversation to the astounded Richard, "that I was much taken with Monsieur de Venier. You have, therefore, my permission to call upon him. Indeed, more than that, I expect you to do so. It is both good policy and good manners."

"Good policy?" Richard repeated.

"Yes. Consider that your future is to some extent in the hands of these people. I assume that your sentimental affair with Mademoiselle is over." He broke off. "Am I right in that?"

Richard nodded. "However, it would be painful —"

"Painful, nothing. I'll be bound she cares no more for you at present than you for her. Make a friend of the girl and insure her silence. A mere civil gesture is all that's needed."

"I can rely on Maritza in any case," said Richard.

The other smiled. "You think so? Very well, then, all the more reason to be on good terms with her. I'll waive *policy*, if you please;

but I insist on *manners*. And let me add that time is the essence of politeness. The sooner you call the better. Nay, I'll take no denial."

Obviously, for whatever reason, the visit must be paid, though it was more of an ordeal than Richard liked to face. It would not be easy to weave the broken threads of the past into a new relationship; not easy to forget or — what was still worse — to pretend that he had forgotten what had been between them.

But, though Richard had foreseen that he could not avoid meeting the Veniers in Bath, it struck him as preposterously ironic that Lord Marny, of all people, should insist on that meeting.

XXXIX

"ANZOLETTA cara, how can I face it? Sior Pa're should not ask it of me."

Dressed for the night, Maritza leaned her head back against the woman, who was leisurely combing out her hair. The combing served chiefly as a pretext for mothering and endearments, for Maritza had been brought up to wait on herself. But at times, such as tonight, when her spirits were at low ebb, she took comfort in Anzoletta's fondling.

"And yet he's right, cara," the woman said gently. "For old times' sake. And he's right, too, that you shouldn't leave things at sixes and sevens between you and Milòr. To what good? If you love him, will it help that you pretend to hate him?"

"But I do."

"Ah?" returned Anzoletta. "Is that being frank with yourself, piccina?"

"I am frank."

There was no use arguing at the moment. "Well, then, you should be too proud to show him that he has hurt you."

The comb passed slowly several times down the length of hair.

"No, I'll be out when he comes. He can talk with Sior Pa're."

"That's as you decide, of course." But a few strokes later, Anzoletta added: "You should meet him because of your father,

265

alma mia. It would so much please his Excellence. Don't you think you ought to, for that reason — especially now?"

Maritza half turned her head. "You think Papà's seriously unwell? You think —" Her voice tightened.

"Now, now," soothed the other. "He's unwell, to be sure. But you say the doctors are hopeful. These things are in God's hands. It serves nothing to torment yourself."

"This foul climate!" Maritza exclaimed. "The cold and damp! No wonder he's ill. I wish we had never left Italy. How I wish it! I should have kept on in the Bologna troupe. At least Father had people to talk with. He could get news from Venice. Here he's like a lost soul. And," she added passionately, "so am I."

"Mo che! Wait till the season in London opens. Think. It's only a month now. Then you'll be dancing again." It was the infallible comfort. Anzoletta could feel the girl relax. "You'll show these stiff English what dancing is. Remember the nice things Mistair Garrick said to you at the trial and his compliments and thanks to Sior Caretti. You will have a triumph. It's hard to idle and fidget, cara ti."

"I hope you're right," Maritza agreed. The comb had been replaced by the brush. She half closed her eyes. "At least I'll be able to pay our debts to Mario Caretti. I know what people think. And I have to endure it because of Sior Pa're — the doctors, everything. And I have to endure . . ."

"What?" said Anzoletta after a pause.

"Oh, what Sior Caretti thinks, too. There's no use pretending he doesn't. I've tried to be frank with him. I tried to persuade him not to come with us to Bath. He's been very considerate. But I know what he expects in the end — from a ballerina. The trouble is . . ." She stopped until Anzoletta again prompted her. "The trouble is I didn't dare be too frank. I couldn't offend him, because of Father. We had to get that advance — more than I could ask of the theater. And so I have to overlook . . . I have to pretend a little . . . and I'm ashamed."

"Puffeta!" retorted Anzoletta, the realist. "'I'll tell you what the trouble is, my love, and always has been with you: spinning things too fine. Keep a good conscience, I say, but grow a thicker skin. You can't travel without picking up dust. Take Sior

Caretti, now. You'll pay him back to the last soldo. You'll be civil with him, as you ought to be. If an old bachelor like him wants to languish and imagine (of course I can see that, too) — well, it isn't your fault. And as for what other people think—" here Anzoletta divided the torrent of hair before braiding it — "you knew what they would think before you went on the stage."

"Yes," Maritza hesitated, "I suppose I didn't mean *people* exactly — not the public. That's to be expected. I suppose really . . . really . . ." She gave a little shrug of surrender. "I meant what Richard thinks of me."

The other suppressed a smile. "Why should you care, as long as you hate him?"

"I don't . . . how can you say such a thing! . . . you know I don't. You know how much . . ."

Bending down, the woman pressed her lips to Maritza's hair. "I know. I know. But then, all the more you should see him. You can pay too much for pride."

So, next morning when Richard's valet called with a note from his master, requesting the honor of being received that afternoon, or otherwise at their Excellences' convenience, the man returned with a cordial answer; and Maritza spent the intervening time in a half trance. Though as a rule heedless of the mirror, today she fluttered back to it, as the five o'clock hour came closer, giving little touches to her dress or hair that no one else would notice. And yet, standing in front of it, she was not absorbed by herself but by little glimpses of the past involving her and Richard, one scene replacing the other against some background of Venice, until she forgot the mirror and drifted away.

Then, when it was near the time, she joined her father in the impersonal little sitting room of their lodgings.

"It's good of you, Maritzetta," he smiled, putting down the book he was reading, "to humor me about this call of Richard's. I know you find it hard. But forbearance is one of life's dignities. It will honor you; it may even help him. Resentment would do neither. And he needs help."

"Why do you say that?" she asked. "Milòr de Marny has given him everything."

"Except a purpose, fia mia. And a man without one is lost. He had a creative purpose once in Venice with Goldoni. But that's over. Someday he may find another to replace it. Until then —"

"But, Sior Pa're, didn't you mention the foreign career, Parliament? Isn't that purpose enough?"

"For an Englishman like Marny, yes. The truth is, Richard as yet has no country. He takes over Marny's interests for lack of his own, but I wonder if he has much heart in them. I imagine he's very poor, Maritza. That's why he needs his friends."

"After turning his back on them?"

"All the more for that reason. What is the good of friendship — or of love — if it is not unalterable?"

She sighed. "Caro, doesn't it take years to learn that philosophy?"

A knock at the outer door of the apartment interrupted. Maritza felt a moment of tenseness like that which precedes a first appearance on the stage. She spread out her dress, seated herself. Venier got up, smiling, and started to cross the room. They could hear Anzoletta hastening to open. But the voice that greeted her, though familiar enough, was not Richard's. They had time only to exchange a glance of dismay when Mario Caretti entered.

At once Maritza, even more than her father, could see what this ill luck meant and realized that she ought to have provided against it. But, absorbed in the thought of Richard's call, she had simply forgotten that Caretti might drop in at this hour. Now there was nothing she could do to remedy matters. If Caretti was there when Richard arrived, they could have no intimate talk of any kind. Worse still, the man's very presence would add to the appearances against her. She would be unable to make clear what her relations with Caretti actually were. As far as the opportunity of this afternoon went, it was doomed at the outset.

For Caretti evidently intended a long call and made himself at home with that hint of ownership that Maritza increasingly disliked. He was a very correct man, a little prim and old-maidish; and his role of gallant did not fit him easily. In formal company of his own age, he made an excellent impression, as a cultivated, aesthetic person of good taste and good sense; but when he acted the part of beau to a girl twenty years younger than himself, he looked self-conscious, overarch and a trifle silly. His greeting this afternoon to Antonio Venier was more careless than usual. He turned at once to Maritza; while the older man, feeling himself excluded, withdrew to his chair across the room.

"And how is our bellissima ballerina today?" Caretti simpered, jackknifing over Maritza's hand, which he held too long to his lips. "Did we do our exercises this morning? Are we keeping our beautiful legs in shape for the debut? I hope so. That will be my evening of glory as well as yours, madonna."

She forced a smile and waved him to a chair, at the same time seating herself as far away as possible.

Noticing her constraint, he raised a playful forefinger. "Now, now! We seem out of sorts; we seem under a cloud. Are we unwell?"

"A touch of headache," she said, detesting his middle-aged babytalk, all the more as he looked so pleased with himself.

Yes, she reflected, his tone had changed considerably from the earlier deference he had shown her in Venice. It reminded her too much of the cuddling manner used toward theater girls by their gentlemen. She especially resented his apparent neglect of her father. What would Richard think of such conduct when he came? But perhaps (it occurred to her with a wild hope) something had happened to prevent him; perhaps he would not come.

"Well, no headache, I'm certain," Caretti was saying, "that a cup of coffee won't cure. I hope we're having coffee today in the good Italian fashion. It's such a relief from English tea. Tasteless stuff and so very binding." He broke off. "Someone at the door? Are you expecting a caller?"

The atmosphere in the room had suddenly become electric.

"A young Englishman we knew in Venice," put in Venier. "A Mr. Hammond."

"Indeed?" Caretti felt annoyed. He had looked forward to a cozy chat with Maritza. Then, too, it did not take much to rouse his jealousy. He could see that Maritza had forgotten him and was all eyes for the door opening from the passage. "Of the well-known family?" he added. "Lord Marny —"

"Yes," said Venier — he had got to his feet with a smile of welcome — "yes, the same."

A hearty voice reached them from outside, addressed to Anzoletta. "Sior' Amia, cara! You won't refuse me a kiss. There! There!"

"Intimate," thought Caretti. "And very colloquial Venetian." He fancied, too, that he heard whispering. Evidently Anzoletta was warning Hammond of another caller in the sitting room. And, as the door opened to the tall, elegantly dressed young man, the news had apparently displeased him, for a faint look of vexation showed on his face.

At once Caretti scented a rival. He was alert to the repeated embraces between the newcomer and Venier, the latter's obvious pleasure, the use of Hammond's first name, the flush on Maritza's cheeks and the expression of her eyes, that contrasted with an odd kind of awkwardness. Here was no casual acquaintance but one on close terms with the Veniers, far closer than those enjoyed by Caretti. The Sardinian felt himself an outsider. He became aware, too, of the constraint his presence was imposing; but, with a jealous obstinacy, he refused to budge. He had the first place here. He sat tight and half-consciously patronized more than ever.

Why had Maritza and her father never mentioned this fellow? An Englishman who spoke the Venetian dialect like a native? An Englishman who could pass for a Spaniard? But then, recalling Lord Marny, Caretti could see the striking resemblance between them. So *that* was it. Like most people, Caretti had not known that Marny acknowledged a bastard. Yes, that was probably it. And yet this conclusion did not lighten Caretti's jealousy very much. From the silver buckles on Mr. Hammond's shoes to the perfect fit of his modish wig, he looked a young man of fashion. He made Caretti feel passé.

"And how is Bapi?" the newcomer was asking Maritza, though his tone somehow conveyed the idea of embarrassment. "When we met in London, madonna, it slipped my mind to inquire. Such an old friend, too. He's bigger, I imagine?"

So! They had met in London!

"Enormous," she said. Caretti could not understand the conflicting notes in her voice, conventional and yet with a stifled undercurrent. "So yellow, Richard, and *so* ugly, with a wart on his nose. It broke my heart to leave him in Bologna. He's staying with a friend of mine there. I'm to have him again when I get back."

270

"And *who* is Bapi, my dear?" probed Caretti, not to be left out. "Someone I should know?"

"My dog, sior. A puppy that Mistair Hammond saved from drowning in our canal and gave me. — How wet you were, Richard!" A truant warmth slipped past the conventional guard.

"And how wet *you* were! Remember how Anzoletta scolded us?"

"Yes, and —" She checked herself. "Yes."

Caretti noted the uncomfortable pause, and that their eyes avoided each other. He asserted himself. "From your speech, signore, you seem to have been long in Venice."

The other replied coldly, "Some years."

"You speak perfect Italian — but perfect."

"I thank you."

It strengthened Caretti's suspicions of a rival that, if he resented Hammond, the latter evidently resented him as much. A mere friend of the Veniers would have no reason to act so aloof.

In a tone of proprietorship, Caretti said to Maritza: "I'm surprised, my sweet," (he had never called her that before, and the word startled her) "I'm really surprised that you have not spoken to me of this good friend of yours in England. I have the honor of knowing his great kinsman, Lord Marny. Why did you not introduce us in London? I'm always so glad to meet one of your acquaintance." He raised the playful forefinger again. "Ah, naughty Maritzetta! Baronzella!"

The familiarity of this, with what it implied, turned her crimson. Her eyes blazed. "I'm unaware, sior, that I need to account to you for my — acquaintances."

The finger stupidly persisted. "Ah, ah! We're hot-tempered today, piccina!"

On the point of an explosion, Maritza managed to suppress it. Nothing she could say now would correct the impression that Richard must have formed of her position with Caretti. The little endearments, the simpering manner, the flicker of jealousy underneath, must all have confirmed it. She could read her sentence in Richard's evasive glance as he turned to Venier.

Fortunately, at that moment Anzoletta entered with the coffee tray; and the topic could be overlooked. But Caretti obstinately held the floor.

Conversation limped. Maritza sat hot-eyed and silent. Venier's attempts at general subjects prompted dissertations by Caretti. But suddenly, without any warning at all, the hobbled, frustrated talk stumbled upon danger.

"Speaking of Venice," said Caretti, "did any of you happen to know of a certain impostor there who called himself the Cavaliere Tromba?"

He was looking at Venier. The latter nodded. "Yes. In fact I met him." About to add something, he stopped. "Why are you interested, Sior Caretti?"

"Met him?" repeated the other. "Oho! Now, that's excellent, excellent! And you, Mr. Hammond, did you also know him?"

Very much on the alert, Richard said guardedly: "Yes, I knew a Cavaliere Tromba."

"Benissimo! A tall, handsome rascal, posing as a man of fashion — prominent features, dark skin?"

Richard shrugged. "The Cavaliere Tromba was certainly a man of fashion. Why do you call him a rascal? Do you know him?"

"Not I, thank God! But I've learned enough about him from my colleague Signor Giovanni Luzio in Munich. Why I call him a rascal? Didn't he leave Venice to avoid arrest?"

"A good many have left Venice for that reason," said Richard. He exchanged a glance with Venier. "And they have not been rascals. I believe that the charge against Signor Tromba was Freemasonry. Or do you consider that a crime?"

"If it is against the law," Caretti pronounced, "how else would you consider it?."

Venier smiled. "Then writing a poem about Venice which is displeasing to the government is equally a crime."

The other flushed. "Your Excellence is pleased to quibble. You know I did not mean that. The case against Tromba is very different. Aside from his Masonry, he is a cheat, a forger, a charlatan . . ."

Hoping that the subject would be dropped, Richard said nothing. But Venier asked again: "You haven't yet told me why you are interested in the man."

"Because" — elation sounded in Caretti's voice — "I have reason to believe that he is now in Bath."

"In Bath?" echoed Venier.

"Yes. Signor Luzio wrote me that he was bound for England. Today, at the coffeehouse, I heard of a Marquis di Corleone who tallies with the description of Tromba both as to appearance and behavior. If it's the same fellow, I intend to expose him. Perhaps you, Mr. Hammond —"

Heedless of bad manners, Richard stood up. His skill in acting served him well. No one could have looked more indifferent to the subject under discussion, though actually he felt like a man on a powder keg with the burning fuse close to the touchhole. He had only a second left. If he waited for the inevitable question, he was trapped. To deny that he knew Corleone, or to deny that Corleone and Tromba were one and the same was equally impossible, because the lie could be so easily disproved and would make matters worse. On the other hand, to admit the truth meant a betrayal.

"Beg pardon, signore," he said carelessly. And to Venier, with a bow that included Maritza: "Your Excellences will forgive me, I hope, if I take my leave . . . an errand or two for Milord de Marny . . . With your permission, I shall look forward soon again . . ."

"But, Mr. Hammond," Caretti persisted, "let me ask —"

"By your leave, another time, signore. At present, as you see —" Richard glanced at his watch — "I'm pressed for time. A great pleasure. Servo umillissimo . . ."

"Hm-m," said Caretti, before the door closed, "our young friend seems rather abrupt."

But jealousy outweighed Tromba in his mind; and he stood staring, when Maritza, defying appearances, followed the caller out into the passage.

"I want to have one word with you, Richard, one real word."

"Yes, madonna."

They were facing each other close to the outer door. Now that a real word needed to be spoken, how could it be uttered? Pride and modesty both prevented it. Maritza could not say: "I am not Caretti's mistress. I love only you; I shall always love only you." That was the real word in her mind; but they had grown too far apart and time was too short for her to express it.

"I wanted . . ."

"Yes, Maritza?"

She gave him her hand. "Can't we be friends, Richard? Can't we forgive each other?"

He raised her hand to his lips. "I'm the only one who needs forgiveness."

He meant to be honest, and yet his honesty did not imply love. Friendship, yes. But forgiveness did not turn back the clock, did not cancel what had happened since Venice; it could not quench his fever for Amélie, or remove the aftertaste that Caretti had left with him.

She said: "Then whatever it is, is forgiven."

If he could have taken her into his arms at that moment, there would have been no need of words or explanations. The miracle of reversing time might have happened. But when he only answered, "You are so good to me, cara," she drew her hand away, stepped back a little, and smiled.

"Then it's understood; we are friends."

"God knows I am yours," he said — "always. Anything I could ever do . . . anything you could ask of me . . ."

"Thanks," she said, opening the door. "I'm very happy . . . I'll remember . . ."

He went away haunted by the look in her eyes.

X L

IF Lord Marny had not been engaged for supper that evening, Richard would have first consulted him on the problem of Caretti versus Tromba. But, since he was not available and no time could be lost, Richard decided at once to let Tromba know of the recent conversation at the Venier lodgings. The adventurer ought to be warned that the cat, so to speak, was almost out of the bag.

He found the Marquis on the point of sitting down to table in the gray-paneled, candle-lighted dining room and was invited to join him. But, beyond listening to a brief account of the meeting with Caretti and complimenting Richard on his skill in avoiding the Sardinian's questions, Tromba put off any discussion until after supper. It was one of his principles, he observed, glancing at the two lackeys, never to spice food with business.

274

"So, let the Signor from Turin wait, my dear boy. We'll attend to him in good time. I believe this filet de sole merits your attention."

That evening he was more scintillating than ever. Though he had planned to sup alone, he wore clothes fit for the Assembly and looked his best. The candlelight sparkled on the false diamonds of one of his decorations, kindled the gems of the blue-enameled ring on his left hand, flattered his dark face and the recklessness of his eyes. Story followed story, chiefly about women and ribald enough. Burgundy followed hock. He ate with gusto and kept plying Richard with food. "A little more of the capon, vecchio mio . . . Try this venison now . . . Your health, caro!"

"You're in good spirits tonight," said Richard, returning the toast.

"Yes," Tromba nodded, "and that I owe entirely to you. From what you tell me, it looks as if my retirement is about over. I hate inaction, and I've put in three dull days. It will be good to be stirring again. But we'll discuss that later."

It was not until dessert had been served, and they were alone, that Tromba, pushing back a little from the table, observed: "Now tell me about Caretti. What kind of man is he? I've no more than seen him, remember — once in Venice and the other day here."

Richard described the self-important, precise diplomat in no flattering terms.

"Jealous?" smiled Tromba.

"No, but I don't like him. Reminds me of a conceited, round-eyed schoolmaster."

"That's bad."

"Why?"

"Because schoolmasters are apt to be rigid. They don't know enough of the world to believe in compromises." Tromba sipped his wine. Finally, he said, "The only thing for you and me, Richard, is to take the bull by the horns. We must call tonight on Signor Caretti."

"Call on him?"

"Yes. You were clever to dodge his question about me this afternoon, but you can't go on dodging it. And I don't intend to skulk here while he spreads his reports. Expose me, eh?" Tromba gave a short laugh. "We must give him a chance to keep quiet. If we call tonight, perhaps it won't be too late."

"But what —"

"Look, Richard. I'm thinking of you and Milord de Marny as well as myself. You both vouched for me, and I'm not ungrateful. The trump that Caretti thinks he holds over me is that Corleone and Tromba are the same man. Very well, I intend to admit the charge even before he makes it, and certainly before he can prove it by confronting me with Venier or the ballerina. That will exonerate you and your father. For if the Marquis di Corleone in Venice chose to call himself by one of his other names and titles, that was his affair. Certainly the practice is not unusual, nor is it a crime. Do you follow me?"

"Perhaps."

"Benissimo. Now the chief complaint against Tromba in Venice was Freemasonry, and that isn't a crime either, at least in England. Well, then, what is left of Caretti's trump except the letter from his whoreson colleague in Munich? But Munich is far off, and all the farther by reason of the war. It would take a long time to prove Luzio's charges against a nobleman of my rank who is sponsored by Milord Marny. Perhaps Caretti can be induced to see that — schoolmaster or no."

Richard nodded. "Yes, but what if the Venetian Resident in London backs him up?"

"No fear," waved the other. "He's inclined to Freemasonry himself. He's under obligations to my old friend and patron Senator Grimani in Venice, who gave me a letter to him. Lastly, while in London, I took the precaution of winning his I.O.U. at cards for five hundred pounds. A mere piece of paper unless he proves unfriendly."

"I see."

But Richard saw more than that. He saw the quicksand into which his and Marny's fear of blackmail on the part of this brilliant rogue had led. And that fear had derived from the venial first dishonesty of concealing Richard's past in view of the foreign service. He saw how prolific and embarrassing even an innocent lie becomes in the scheme of things, how hard to manage even by a man of his father's astuteness. And yet lies of one sort or another were the currency of this fine world in which he was now involved. They were the warp and woof of it. He felt a sudden panic, like a

276

fly in a web, to tear himself loose; but the strands were many and very strong.

"Why do you want me to call on Caretti with you?"

Tromba shrugged. "You must suit yourself about that, of course. I should think you would want to. Certainly I intend to call, and I shall have to refer to your meeting with him. Wouldn't it look more manly and straightforward if you simply brought us together and left the rest to me?"

Making the best of a bad business, Richard could not deny that this was so. With his hearty dislike of Caretti, he did not want the man to consider him a sneak or a coward. That decided it.

"Very well," he agreed.

Tromba consulted his watch. "It's now half-past eight. We have time for a game of billiards before going over. He lodges not far from the Veniers on Trim Street. My servant tells me that he keeps early hours; but ten o'clock ought to be soon enough."

A glint of something in his too languid manner caught Richard's attention. "I hope you intend no violence, Marcello. If you do, I wash my hands of this."

Getting up from table, the other stretched himself like a great cat.

"Not tonight, Richard. Don't be concerned; he'll be given his chance."

Ushered by Caretti's landlady into the small parlor of his two-room lodgings, they did not have long to wait before the opening of the street door below and a sound of footsteps on the stairs announced the occupant's return. Richard had given their names to the landlady, and she had apparently informed Caretti of their presence; for he did not look surprised upon entering, though his greeting to Richard was chilly enough.

"Ah, Mr. Hammond. Your servant, sir." He did not seem to have caught the name of the other caller and turned a questioning glance on Tromba, who stood tall and dark in front of the mantelpiece. But he had too accurate a description of the latter not to guess almost immediately who it was. His head went up; his expression changed from startled to rigid. "I don't believe I know this gentleman."

"The Marquis di Corleone — Signor Caretti," said Richard in Italian. "I informed the Marquis at supper of our conversation this afternoon. He desired to meet you."

As compared with the stature of his visitors, Caretti, though of average height, seemed overshadowed by them. No doubt he could feel the menace that the call implied. But he did not flinch.

"Conversation?" he repeated. "I recall that you took singular pains to avoid it. And I now begin to understand why."

"Yes," said Richard, "you were about to ask me a question which the Marquis had best answer for himself."

Caretti pursed his lips. "I hope he can answer it satisfactorily. I hope —"

He was cut off by a laugh from Tromba. "You do, eh? Why, my little magistrate!" He laughed again. "Suppose I'm not here to answer satisfactorily or otherwise, but to drop you a hint, what then?"

"I don't like your tone. There's nothing —"

"Stop arching your eyebrows," put in Tromba. "It annoys me. And learn this. Your likes have nothing to do with the matter."

"Indeed?" Caretti turned toward the door, but the sudden grip on his arm stopped him. He could not help wincing.

"Marcello!" Richard cautioned.

"Che cosa? I'm merely attempting to alter Signor Caretti's frame of mind. He seems to mistake the object of my visit. Instead of considering it a kindness —"

"Release my arm," choked Caretti.

"— he struts," Tromba went on. "He plays the judge. He assumes that I am here to 'answer satisfactorily,' conciliate perhaps. Gran' Dio! What an error!"

Caretti had courage of a sort, but it did not help him at the moment. He was not trained to physical encounters, where the conventions are of no use, and he shrank from them. Under Tromba's black stare, he looked pasty and daunted.

"What's your purpose, then?"

"That's better," nodded the other. "Are we to be kept standing like lackeys? I suggest we sit down."

"As you please," said Caretti.

The three men seated themselves. Tromba crossed his legs, drew out his snuffbox, and took a pinch.

"To begin with," he said, "you made use of an expression today in respect to me that no man of honor can let pass. You spoke, I believe, of *exposing* me. Is that correct?"

Caretti swallowed before answering, but he did not evade. "Yes, if you are the same person as an infamous Neapolitan sharper known in Venice and Munich as Marcello Tromba. Otherwise, no. Otherwise, I beg your pardon."

"Of course I'm Marcello Tromba and I'm also the Marquis di Corleone. I use both names. How do you know that I'm infamous and a sharper?"

"I have your record from a man of unquestioned honesty and my old friend, His Sardinian Majesty's Resident in Munich, Giovanni Luzio."

"And you accept his word, without proof, against a man of my rank, who has been honored by the Earl of Marny's favor and who has been received into the best circles here?"

Caretti had by now recovered himself from his momentary shrinking. Who was he, a member of the corps diplomatique and of a good family, the official representative of the House of Savoy in London, to be bullied by this cheap scoundrel! He arched his brows again.

"I am informed that it is one of your talents to insinuate yourself everywhere into the best circles in order to swindle them. I am not surprised that you have been successful here. As for Lord Marny, I rather suppose" — he glanced coolly at Richard — "that Mr. Hammond has had something to do with it, I hope as your dupe; I should regret believing that he is your accomplice."

"You see, Richard," smiled Tromba, "you are becoming an infamous sharper, too."

Richard again thought of the quicksand. Step by step deeper. He felt increasingly uncomfortable. He was certainly not Tromba's dupe. Did that make him his accomplice? The charge came pretty close.

"Don't twist my words," Caretti was saying. "I'm not concerned with Mr. Hammond."

"By God," drawled Tromba, fingering his snuffbox, "how right you were, Richard, in describing him as a schoolmaster! It's too bad for him that he isn't dealing with a schoolboy. — So, you intend

279

to expose me, Signor Professore? Give me a touch of the rod, eh?"

Caretti's voice shook. "I intend to publish my colleague's letter."

"Why?" Tromba sounded genuinely curious.

"Because I am a man of honor, and, as such, it is my duty to warn innocent people, many of them my friends, to beware of your tricks. They can then do as they please, but my conscience will be clear. Let me add, however, that you are already in no good odor, to judge by what I heard today at the coffeehouse. I think your stay in England, Messer Marcello, is about over."

To Richard's surprise, Tromba nodded. "Yes, you may be right." Then he threw in smoothly, "And what about *your* stay in England, Signor Residente?"

"I don't understand."

"No, I suppose you don't," Tromba purred. "It's odd that a man of your age and calling should be so dull. Amazing, really." During what followed, he kept his voice silken, though it was all the more ominous because of that. "We come now to the object of my visit. I want you to understand."

He had been opening and closing the lid of his snuffbox with his thumb. He now snapped it shut and returned the box to his vest pocket. In the silence of the room, the click sounded clear and definite.

"I wonder," Tromba went on, "if your esteemed colleague in Munich, while transmitting my record, as you put it, failed to explain what kind of sharper I am. One would imagine" — he mimicked Caretti's tone — "that a man of honor would think it his duty to warn innocent people, among them your very innocent self, that they had more to beware of than my tricks, before saddling them with a quarrel against me. Did he do that?"

Half bemused by the gentle, sultry voice, Caretti said nothing.

"I don't think he was very kind to you, Signor Residente, though doubtless your devotion is such that you are eager to take up his vendetta. But you must have no illusions. I shall not sneak away because of your 'duty' and your 'conscience.' And I tell you plainly that if they cross me in any fashion, you are a dead man."

The very quietness of this doubled its effect. The ticking of a clock on the wall, the footsteps of a passer-by in the street below, seemed to prolong the pause. Richard found himself staring at the hearthrug.

At last Caretti managed to get out. "So, you're threatening me!"

"I'm glad," said Tromba, "that the idea begins to penetrate."

"You seem to forget that there's law in England."

"No, I even remember a law against slander. You are so dull, Signòr Residente, that you compel me to think for you. If you publish Luzio's letter, you will be publishing the unproved slander of an unknown person against a man who has, after all, some standing in Bath. You will be traducing not only me but Lord Marny and Mr. Hammond. Had you thought of that? However, don't be concerned. I have no intention of puttering with lawyers and judges. After a fashion, you see, I'm a man of honor myself and am so considered here. There is an unwritten law which requires satisfaction in cases of this kind on the field of honor."

Caretti braced himself. "Do you think I'd give satisfaction to a bandit like you?"

"I don't think about it at all," smiled Tromba. "You might prefer to be flogged, with all that would mean to your health and your social position. That's for you to decide."

"Flogged!" Caretti's hands shook; he steadied them by gripping the arms of his chair. "I'll have you bound over to keep the peace."

"Bind away," Tromba returned, "but don't imagine that that will save you." He glanced at Richard. "Speak of the rod! Picture the schoolmaster breeched. If he survives, it will take some living down here — and in Turin."

With an obvious effort, the other almost kept the quaver out of his voice. "You ruffian! I'd like to know how an attack on me would profit you. When that letter is published, your wings will be clipped whatever happens."

"True," said Tromba, "I don't deny it. And, therefore the pleasure of vengeance, Signor Residente — a very great pleasure. There's my profit."

He stood up suddenly, towering above the man in the chair. "I leave you to think it over. If you have sense, perhaps you'll conclude that to forget me and to avoid meddling in what does not concern you is a small price to pay for living. If you're an ass, as I greatly fear, you may let 'duty' and 'conscience' dig your grave for you. Only don't make the mistake of doubting that I mean what I say."

Perhaps if Richard had not been present, Caretti's response might have been different. But to be browbeaten in front of his supposed rival, who might report the scene to Maritza, was more than the gentleman could accept. The sting of it upset his judgment and spurred him to one of those grand gestures which at the moment seem worth what they cost. He intended to have the last word and to make it a round one. Getting up in turn, he stood facing Tromba.

"I do not need to reflect. I refuse to be muzzled by a villain like you. That letter will certainly be published, and I shall do all in my power to show you up for what you are. Your threats can make no possible difference with regard to that, I assure you. And now I shall ask you and your *friend* to take yourselves off."

It could not be denied that this sudden defiance struck Tromba off guard. He had no reason to think that the issue would be joined so promptly. For a moment he stared, but it was only for a moment.

"So!" he exclaimed. "Well, well!"

Something in his voice, a slight movement of his body, alerted Richard, who closed in. But almost at once the tension relaxed.

"Very good," Tromba added. "Be a fool to the end. Let's be going, Richard. He's had his warning."

Caretti should have stopped there; but, pleased by the effect he had made, he was tempted to strike a final attitude.

"And I'll test one of your threats now," he went on. "You talk about satisfaction, as if you deserved the treatment of a gentleman. Well, on second thought, and to cut your comb, I'll give you satisfaction, if you want it —" he should not have added — "which I doubt."

This time Tromba's black eyes rounded in sheer amazement. Then he burst out laughing.

"Good God, Richard!" he exclaimed, when he had got his breath. "The longer one lives, the more one marvels at the unexpectedness of human nature; it can't be fathomed." And to Caretti, "Spoken like a man, my little schoolmaster! I congratulate you. — So, the letter will be published?"

"Certainly, in any case."

"Then, to avoid delays, I ask for satisfaction now. Richard, you will act for me in this. Perhaps Signor Caretti will kindly refer you

282

to one of his friends, with whom you can arrange the articles of meeting."

It was Caretti's turn to be taken aback. He had not expected to pay for the grand gesture at once. Indeed, with his momentary bravado over, he began for the first time to realize what it entailed. Henceforth, as the hours passed, he would have leisure to meditate on this more and more. But under Tromba's challenging stare, he could only agree.

He cleared his throat. "Yes . . . Captain Hugh Miles. He lodges at the 'Bear.' "

"Right. Captain Miles it is. You have the choice of weapons. It's your affair, but you'd better take pistols. You couldn't match me one minute with the sword. I have two inches reach on you."

Caretti looked blank.

"You understand of course," Tromba continued, his eyes keen, "that not one word or hint of the duel is to be given to anyone. We're all honorbound on that point. If there should be an interference, it could only mean one thing. I suppose you're aware of it."

Caretti said nothing.

"Eh?" prodded Tromba. "Or are you already hoping for an interference?"

"No," said the other, "no, certainly not."

"Then, until day-after-tomorrow morning, Signor Residente. And now, as you so civilly put it, we'll take ourselves off."

Tromba tossed his cloak over one arm and put on his hat. But when he and Richard were at the door, he turned with a flash of teeth.

"Keep your hand steady, schoolmaster. For if you miss, I won't."

XLI

IN the cold dusk that preceded sunrise the next day but one, Richard, with a case of dueling pistols under his cloak, walked over to Tromba's house on Orchard Street. He found a hackney coach and driver waiting outside, and two riding horses equipped with saddlebags in the charge of the Marquis's Italian servant. Before he could knock, Tromba, who had evidently been watching from one of the windows, came out, booted, spurred and muffled in a long traveling cloak. Under the black cocked hat, his face looked unusually somber and hard.

"You're leaving at once — afterwards?" Richard asked, keeping his voice down.

"Yes, or not at all."

It was the duty of a second to be cheerful. "No doubt about that."

"No, I expect not," said Tromba: "but it's bad luck to take things for granted. Anyhow, I sent my portmanteaus ahead yesterday. They'll be on the ship."

"From Bristol, I suppose?"

Tromba shook his head. "Bristol's too obvious. There may be a hue and cry. I'm not telling you where I'm sailing from, so that you can honestly say you don't know. Ireland, first; then, somehow to Paris. I've arranged a new entrée there with the Countess des Landes. A lottery venture this time. We'll go snacks."

Knowing Amélie, Richard was not surprised. Women of fashion often had a finger in business.

Tromba turned to glance up at the house which represented his career in Bath. "Well," he muttered half to himself, "it was a good run while it lasted. I can't complain. But, God, what I might have done except for this ass from Turin! Cacasangue!" For an instant, he looked the portrait of Satan gnashing his teeth. But the grimace passed. He forced a smile. "You know, Richard, I wouldn't take ten thousand pounds for the minute of pure joy I expect within this hour. You have the tools with you? Right. Let's be going."

They climbed into the hackney coach. The servant, mounting one of the saddle horses and leading the other, followed. In a straight line, it was no long distance across the lower end of town to that expanse of open country beyond Milk Street, not yet built upon and known as King's Mead Fields. But there was no through street, and the drive took some time.

The demure house fronts, still dim in the twilight, drifted by. To Richard, shivering with the cold in spite of his cloak, and taut as a fiddlestring, they seemed like the vague background of a

284

dream. He could not shake off the sense of unreality that pervaded everything: himself in the dank coach, a case of pistols on his knees; the impassive Tromba beside him, indistinct in the darkness; the dead end of their errand, which drew steadily closer. It had no connection with familiar, reasonable life. He found himself longing for sunrise. Perhaps it would be less fantastic then.

"You seem depressed," his companion remarked suddenly. "You're the deuce of a second. You ought to liven me up with a joke or so, take the edge off my nerves. I'm the one to worry. Instead, I'll have to bolster *you* up." His gloved hand closed on Richard's knee. "But don't bother. I'm happy as a bride. Often I've had to fight in cold blood — not much fun. But today — ah!" He drew a long breath. "My one regret is that it couldn't be swords. You can take longer, play your man."

"You suggested pistols yourself," Richard answered in order to say something.

"Yes. Point of honor. Give the poor puke every advantage."

Not much advantage, thought Richard, recalling a sweepstakes that Tromba had won last week with a pistol from some of the young bucks — and, aside from skill, his icy nerve and assurance. He imagined Caretti driving to the rendezvous in a very different state of mind.

"Perhaps he'll back down, Marcello. Suppose he does?"

"It's too late," said Tromba. "I think his statements are already in the press. They'll be read today by everybody in Bath. But," he added, "I don't think they'll be read by him. — You know, that gives me an idea. I've been considering where to hit him. Look. I'll lay you ten pounds, to be paid immediately afterwards, that I shoot out one of his round fish-eyes. Are you on?"

"God, no!" Richard said.

The gloved hand closed again on his knee. "Take it easy, boy. I ought to have more sense. Lord! I remember how I felt before my first fight. Nervous as a colt. Empty stomach and all that. You'll get used to these things." He changed the subject. "By the way, give my compliments to the Countess. Explain why I couldn't bid her farewell. You might add" (Richard could imagine the wink accompanying this) "that in Paris I'll expect an entrée in every sense of the word."

285

The coach turned off from Milk Street along the dirt road that crossed King's Mead Fields.

"Stop here," Tromba called through the window after several minutes. And when they had got out, "We'll walk the rest of the way. Tell the coachman, Richard, to wait for you. He mightn't understand my English. Tell him I'm out for a horseback ride."

Richard conveyed these directions to the driver, who grinned and winked.

It was now much lighter. With the saddle horses following, they made their way left for some distance among low bushes and at last came out on a stretch of meadow along the river.

"They're not here yet." Tromba scowled. "If that damned bastard should give me the slip, I'll hunt him down though I hang for it."

But a minute later, they caught sight of a group approaching from farther upstream. The two men in front were Caretti and his second Captain Miles. They were followed by another, evidently a surgeon, carrying his bag, and by an officer in the uniform of Miles's regiment, who had been called upon to act as umpire. At the same moment, light from the eastern hills swept across the meadow and brought out long shadows on the grass.

There was a flourish of hats, an exchange of bows. Glancing at Caretti, Richard noticed his colorless face and harried eyes. Probably he had not closed them last night. He moved jerkily and kept his hands clamped behind his back. It was a plain case of will versus fear. If he flinched now, if he played the coward, he would never live it down; his accusations against Tromba would be nullified by his own disgrace. He looked at Tromba, met the latter's cool smile and turned his head.

Captain Miles presented Major Whitlock, who asked as a matter of form whether the gentlemen were resolved to pursue their quarrel and, being assured that they were, read the brief agreement as to procedure, which both had signed. Then he expertly examined the pistols, had a word of praise for their balance, and proceeded to load them, driving home the charges with delicate, firm strokes of the small ramrod.

Strolling up to Richard, Miles said in a low tone: "Never saw a worse funk than Caretti's in my whole life. Thought he'd swoon before I got him here. Had to dose him with brandy. I hope to God he'll last the course. Look at Corleone now — cool as steel. He may be a rogue, but he's a topper."

Tromba was exchanging views with Whitlock in French on the subject of pistols. Caretti stood looking at the river.

"Very well, gentlemen," said the Major, holding both weapons out by their long barrels, "if you please."

Caretti snatched one of them, holding it stiffly down at arm's length. He was white to the lips.

"Relax, sir," murmured his second. "Easy!"

Tromba tossed his cloak and coat to Richard before taking the weapon. He made a fine, tall figure in his powdered wig and black riding boots.

"You will stand back to back," rehearsed Whitlock. "Then, as I count them, you will each take ten paces, about-face, cock, and, when I give the word, fire as it pleases you."

Painfully tense, Richard found himself siding with Caretti, in spite of his dislike for him. There was something infinitely more significant, more human in his struggle than in Tromba's hateful nonchalance. However much a victim of the code and of his own self-esteem, Caretti at the moment outranked the other. Strange that Tromba's career in Bath had not been cut short by one of the men of beef and bottom, but by a physical inferior.

There was, of course, one remaining hope. They might both miss their aim; or a wound, if inflicted, might not be fatal. In either case, honor would have been satisfied, Tromba would have lost . . .

"One, two, three, four . . ." Whitlock counted.

Caretti walked like a mechanical puppet which has been wound up. Tromba might have been strolling down the length of a drawing room.

"Ten!"

They both turned. The cocking of the pistols seemed unnaturally loud. The outstretched arms went up.

But then, whether because of nervousness, confusion, or intent, Caretti, without waiting for the word of command, fired.

Tromba reeled back a step under the impact of the bullet, which had struck him in the right shoulder, but he did not fall. A splotch of red leaped out on his shirt, and he clapped his left hand to it with a grimace. At the same moment Whitlock roared to Caretti, "God damn you, sir! There's no excuse for that."

The Sardinian, his pistol lowered, gazed vacantly at Tromba.

Captain Miles groaned in disgust. Richard sprang forward. But he had not taken three steps before Tromba motioned him back. "Little harm done, fio mio . . . We haven't finished . . ." And transferring the pistol to his other hand, "I can shoot just as well with my left. Major Whitlock," he constrained himself to English — "you have not give the word."

"Fire!" barked the officer. And hardly under his breath, "I hope you drill the rogue."

Then slowly Tromba raised his left arm.

The last of Caretti's courage was spent. The pistol dropped from his hand. He stood cringing a moment, then flung his hands out against the motionless weapon that faced him. "No!" he cried, and half turned.

The shot crashed. He spun around, plunged forward, and lay jerking a few moments. The flesh had had its way after all, and the spirit had failed. It was well, after this, that he did not have to face the code and his own shame.

While the surgeon and Miles bent over the prostrate figure, Whitlock came forward. "Monsieur di Corleone, my compliments on a fine performance. You're a gallant man, sir. Dammy if I ever saw anyone carry himself better. I hope you ain't badly hit."

Tromba shook his head. "I thank you, no. Forgive me if I speak French." He moved his right arm, though his lips tightened. "Not serious. Missed the bone, I think." Then, as Miles came over, he glanced at the body on the grass. "How about *him*?"

"Dead twice over," said the Captain. "Through the brain. An elegant shot, that. Something to remember, by Gad! Left hand, moving target, and all. My respects, sir." He kicked at the turf. "Christ! What a shabby end! Fancy getting it from behind. Faugh!"

Tromba was smiling. "It's a pity you didn't take me on that bet, Richard. You'd be ten pounds in pocket. But then I didn't expect to shoot him on the wing. Ask the surgeon for some brandy, will you? I'm losing blood."

When the brandy was brought, he paused before drinking and raised his cup. "To the Signor Residente! Our accounts are now settled." He glanced at Richard. " 'Duty' and 'conscience' have been satisfied. Don't be too severe in your report of him, gentlemen. A flash in the pan? Granted. But I marvel that he flashed at all. Think it over. You'll find he did better than his best. Carve that on his tombstone."

It was very handsome of Corleone, Miles and Whitlock agreed afterwards. Scoundrel or not, they would give a glowing account of him that night over a punch bowl to other gentlemen at the "Bear." If he left a stench in Bath, he left also a name for manhood that carried far in sporting circles.

Having now unflinchingly submitted to the attentions of the surgeon, and with his arm in a sling, he rejected all protests that he should not ride in that condition. He had his ship to meet at an unspecified port, preferred a saddle to jail, and would manage very well. Then in a final flourish, he presented his case of pistols to Whitlock as a memento of the occasion, and Richard helped him to his horse.

Muffled in his long cloak, he sat looking down a moment, like a black hawk on the point of flight.

"A rivederci, caro vecchio. We'll meet again, I hope. My thanks to you; my duty to Lord Marny. Tell the ballerina I wish her better luck with her next patron." A final bow to the other gentlemen. "Adieu, messieurs."

He spurred his horse and set off at a gallop, followed by the servant. Richard caught one glimpse of his cocked hat above the bushes, then briefly the thudding of hoofs.

"A damned game fellow," observed Miles.

Jolting back alone in the hackney coach, Richard thought chiefly of Caretti, who had tried so hard to be brave and had not lasted the course. It made no sense. But, after all, did anything make sense in the crazy world? Yes, Tromba's jeering epitaph — *He did better than his best* — made sense.

XLII

IT needed all of Lord Marny's prestige to outface the storm of censure that Caretti's published charges against Corleone and the latter's flight from Bath called forth. If Marny and that dubious son of his had not sponsored the counterfeit Marquis, no one would have been taken in by such an evident sharper.

In public, the Earl adapted his bearing to his critics. If they were his inferiors, he haughtily ignored them. If they were of his own rank, he treated the matter with amused chagrin, as a devilish shrewd joke on himself, and acknowledged that he and Richard had been more deeply bitten by Corleone than anyone else. But in private, he spent a good many somber hours.

"As far as it touches me," he told Richard, "I don't care a fig. Let the dogs bark. Their fury lasts no longer than their love. They'll come wagging their tails to my next assembly in London. 'Tis you I'm concerned for, and, egad, more than concerned. Checkmated's the word. I wish I could see the next move." He added gloomily: "If you only hadn't acted as the scoundrel's second! That put the final seal on it."

Richard once more explained his reasons, and his father once more admitted the point of them.

"Yes, I suppose there was nothing you could do. He had the whip-hand. But it was damned unfortunate. Here's the latest development. You're not only finished in Bath but in London."

He drew out a letter from his pocket and handed it to Richard. Its anonymous author warned that a copy of it would appear in the next issue of the *London Public Advertiser*. Written as a short essay, it was entitled "The Black Baron Returns," and, sharply satirical, it identified a certain Mr. H——d, the reputed son of a noble lord, with his profligate and unlamented grandfather. After pointing out Mr. H——d's amazing likeness in appearance and character to the late distinguished ruffian, it gave a lurid account of his association in Bath with a notorious Italian cheat, the so-called Marquis di Corleone. This had now ended in a murderous duel and the tragic death of Signor Caretti, a respected member of the corps diplomatique.

The article concluded: "We learn that the nefarious Mr. H——d is to be offered a glittering post at one of the German courts, where he will have suitable scope to discredit England and employ his talents for chicanery. Such a man is selected to represent his country abroad! And yet there remains a hope that even if the Duke of N——l, with his well-known powers of digestion, should be content to swallow the knave, His Majesty will consult his own honor and that of the nation before subjecting both to the outrage of this appointment . . ."

Richard returned the letter to his father. He ached too much already from the snubbing he had received in Bath to care a great deal. "I didn't know I was quite so depraved."

Marny shrugged. "I believe I can guess who wrote that. He's aiming at me, of course, through you. But there go our plans for the Foreign Service. I don't mean on the strength of that squib alone but of what it represents. Dear friends of mine at Court will take pains to bring it to the King's attention. Newcastle wouldn't dare even to submit your name. It was enough to get over the hurdle of your illegitimacy; this is an impasse."

He looked so defeated that Richard laid a hand on his shoulder. "I beg you, my lord, don't be cast down. It makes little difference what I do."

"It does to me," returned Marny. "I conceived of reliving my career in yours and improving on it. I must own that this offered me some amends for growing old. Call it a new stake in the game, of which I had begun to tire. — But a plague on the dumps!" He straightened himself and showed his usual thin smile. "I have seldom failed in a purpose; I won't fail now. You're close upon twenty-one. I'll see to it that you are brought into Parliament. And that's something beyond the power of king or minister to prevent, for I hold the Borough of Ashford in my pocket. You'll make your mark yet. Only, meanwhile . . ."

He fell to musing, then looked up. "There may be something in this. You remember the Virginia estate I won from young Fairfax. It needs to be dealt with, one way or another. Suppose you looked into it as my factor. A six-month absence from England would be no bad thing. By the time you are back, this fracas will have blown over. You could speak with authority on colonial matters, which are growing in importance. What d'ye say?"

Richard hesitated. "Give me leave, sir, to think it over."

"Well, do so," said the Earl. "The worst thing in life is to have no plan at all."

But, as Richard paced his room before going to bed, the thought of Virginia did not attract him. What did he know or care about

291

tobacco or negro slaves? Indeed, at the moment, he cared little enough about anything, except perhaps to cease being a charge on Lord Marny, to strike out for himself. But where? How? He didn't know. He had made a sad hash of the role which his father had groomed him for, and he was sick of the fine world anyway. Better than Virginia would be to slip back to the Continent and pick up the threads of his old profession. Yet this, too, seemed impossible.

He found himself thinking of Maritza. On the afternoon following the duel, he had written her, attempting to explain his part in it, beseeching her not to think too ill of him. It had been a long letter straight from the heart. His man Briggs had delivered it. She had not answered. Then his thoughts turned to Amélie des Landes.

It was fortunate that the unconventional Countess did not give one snap of her fingers for the world's opinion, Tromba's wickedness, or Caretti's death. She took pleasure in being seen everywhere with Richard, at the Assembly Rooms, in her coach, or along the Parades.

"But, ma'am," exclaimed Lady Mary Coke, "have you no thought for your reputation? Don't you know that people are talking, and that Mr. Hammond is the blackest of black sheep?"

"Why, ma'am," returned Amélie, "in the interests of happiness, I have long since kissed my reputation good-by. As to people, what else do they do but talk, even in their sleep? And, ma'am, the blacker my sheep, the more I love them. They're so much more amusing than white ones."

"Including the Marquis di Corleone, I suppose?"

"Him especially. I believed you shared my taste for him."

"Before he showed himself to be a villain, madam."

"Ah," said the Countess, "your simplicity intrigues me. If it's sincere, I must pity you. But since I prefer to think it is not, pray join me in a pinch of snuff."

She laughed over this afterwards to Richard and nicknamed him her Black Sheep or *Noiraud*.

"Come, Noiraud, tell me all over again about the duel. I attended one once — by stealth, of course — which was fought in my honor between Monsieur de Lusignan and Monsieur de Vrouvrières. Swords, that time. Pauvre Jean-François fut tué. Quite fascinating. So, Monsieur Caretti shot first. And then?"

Richard rather suspected that her callousness was put on in order to cheer him up.

"Don't look so tragic," she begged, when he had once more described the fight. "You say he was over forty. A man of that age has lived long enough — a woman, too, for that matter. I've often pointed this out to Monsieur des Landes. He doesn't agree with me, except as to women. Think of all his duels and my bad luck! Think of all the *young* men he has killed!" Her head drooped. "Well, I'm sleepy, Richard. Carry me off to bed, and I'll wake up."

However, Amélie would soon be lost to him. Her stay in England was about over. Indeed, she confessed that she had spun it out on his account. He felt increasingly alone.

On her side, she refused even to talk about parting. "Isn't it bad enough when it comes, without grieving beforehand? *Me*, I refuse to grieve. I say to myself, 'There's still a week.' I'll say, 'There're still some hours . . . some minutes.' And then . . . and then . . ." Her voice faded. "Richard, I do love you."

"If it wasn't for the cursed war!" he burst out.

"Miséricorde!" she protested. "Don't kick that bandbox. It holds my best hat. — Yes, the war. But afterwards? . . . I won't talk about it, Noiraud. S'il te plaît! Only remember that you're seeing me off in Bristol. That gives us one more day than a week — and one more night."

Soon after this, returning one afternoon to Pierrepont Street, Richard found a letter from Maritza. He was in no hurry to open it. The fact that she had taken so long to answer him did not promise well for its contents. And, when he finally broke the seal, the formal Italian *Signore* — not the intimate *Sior* of the Venice days — warned him of what was to come.

He read: "After all, it seems best to write you, so that there may be no misunderstanding. I do not accept your explanations of the share you had in Signor Caretti's murder, to use the only proper word for it. On the night before the so-called duel, Signor Caretti wrote me a full account of his interview with you and your friend Tromba. He did not expect to survive and wished me to know the truth. The letter was delivered to me on the morning of his death. That a bandit like Marcello Tromba should bully, threaten and finally kill a man, is understandable enough. But I did not suppose that you were a ruffian or the backer of ruffians.

"One more word. In spite of what you may have imagined, my relations with Signor Caretti throughout were those of friendship and involved nothing more. I have not altered my principles and I shall not alter them. I hope you have not become too cynical to believe this. — Maritza Venier."

Oddly enough, when he had finished the letter, he felt no anger, such as had followed their quarrel in London, only a dull acceptance. He could see very well how he appeared to her, how he had appeared to Caretti; and, in his present mood, he viewed himself in the same light. The closing paragraph especially touched him on the quick.

Then impulsively he put on his cloak again and took up his hat. Too much out of the past remained. He could not leave it like this. He must see her now, while the mood was on him and before flinching or pride could invent pretexts for not seeing her at all.

Twilight had fallen, as he walked north. Here at last was Trim Street, and he began looking up at the houses. Number 5. He recalled absently that General Wolfe lived here. The figure of the red-haired, intense young officer crossed his thought. Suddenly he paused. What was it Wolfe had said about purchasing a commission in the army? By God, of the possible solutions to his present quandary, he had not thought of that. The army. A career that he could make his own, that would probably take him out of England, that would relieve Lord Marny of future embarrassment for him. He stood pondering a moment. It seemed to answer everything. Then, with a lighter step, he continued on to the Veniers' lodgings.

Anzoletta opened, but at the sight of him looked dismayed.

"Milòr! I regret . . ."

"I know, Sior' Amia. But I have to see them."

He pushed by her gently and opened the door of the small living room. The woman followed him.

At the sound of his voice, Maritza and her father had risen from their chairs beside the table lamp and now stood facing him.

"Why did you come?" she breathed.

"I had to come — after reading your letter. You could not think worse of me than I do of myself. I wanted you to know that, madonna —" he included Venier — "your Excellence."

"Richard . . ." she began, then stopped.

"I must thank you for coming," Venier put in. "It means a great deal. You've made it possible for us to meet again in the old way. It was generous of you to come. But it's hard to talk now. Later, yes. We're returning to London tomorrow. Will you call on us there?"

"If I go to London, your Excellence. You see, I may enter the army. In that case —"

"The army?" exclaimed Maritza. "But your post abroad? I thought —"

"No, that's finished."

She took a step toward him. "What do you mean?"

"There isn't much to tell. The world agrees with you about me, and the world, too, is right. So, there's no chance of an appointment. I'm glad of it." He broke off. "You may remember the scenario I wrote once back in Venice — *Captain Harlequin*. I'm going to try that role for a while."

She said wistfully: "Do you always have to be an actor, Richard? Does everything have to be a role with you?"

He realized for one vivid moment that she had touched upon the flaw of his entire life.

"Perhaps," he shrugged. "At least, I'm not acting now."

"I know that." She gave him her hand. "So, when we do meet again —" her eyes suddenly filled — "we can be — friends."

A few minutes later, he knocked at Wolfe's door, and, being informed that the General was at home, asked for a word with him.

That evening he broached the news to Lord Marny.

"You might have consulted me," said the latter, but he looked thoughtful.

"No doubt I should, my lord. Even so, I wanted to take this step alone."

"I can't say I blame you," muttered the Earl, "the way my own plans for you have addled. — How did Wolfe take it? He knows the gossip in town."

"We reached an understanding. As to my share in the duel, he thought nothing of it. He owned that he would have acted in the same way. Besides, my lord —" Richard could not help a smile — "he needs officers. Commissions are for sale. I gather that service in Canada is not too popular."

The other said dryly: "Very likely not. But the cost? A lieutenancy, is it? Commissions aren't cheap."

"You've made me a most generous allowance, sir. I've saved a good deal. I —"

"Rubbish!" exclaimed Marny. "If my son enters the service, he shall do so on a proper footing. You'd starve on a lieutenant's pay." He was silent a moment, then nodded. "So be it? On the whole, I think you could do worse. Nay, I'm not sure that you could do better. Make this campaign with some credit, and your slate is clean. Then —" The old ambition leaped up. "Why, then, Parliament. And we'll see if the King could refuse you a post. When do you join your regiment?"

"My lord, in ten days — at Portsmouth. It's the point of assembly. I don't know when we sail."

"Egad," said Marny in high good humor, "the more I think of this, the better I'm pleased. I'll call on Wolfe tomorrow myself and discuss your commission. Spare nothing on uniforms. I'm doubling your allowance."

XLIII

AT the "Bush" inn on Corn Street in Bristol, Richard admired as much of his new uniform as a small glass, supplemented by another mirror in the hands of his man Briggs could show him. It was the first time he had put it on except at the tailor shop in Bath, where it had been hastily turned out during the last few days. He found it magnificent: the scarlet coat and regimental facings, white waistcoat, crimson sash over the right shoulder, fawn-colored breeches and black boots with brown turnovers, the high cocked hat with its edging of gold braid. It added another inch to his already tall stature.

"Very becoming, sir," approved Briggs, adjusting the glass. "Very martial, sir."

Richard grinned. "I hope so. I don't even know how to keep step, much less the difference between *Make ready!* and *Present!* Never fired a musket in my life. Competent foot officer, Briggs."

"I dare say they'll put you on to it at Portsmouth, sir. There's few of the gentry know much at first. I'll warrant your Honor learns as well as any of 'em. — Shall you wear your sword tonight?"

"Yes. *Grande tenue,* as the French say. All the trappings."

His sword, gold-hilted, was a fine weapon, presented to him at parting by Lord Marny. The belt fitted stiffly, and it took Briggs a moment to find the proper hole for the tongue. Then, more self-conscious than before, Richard again consulted the glass. Splendid! As far as costume went, this last touch left nothing to be desired. But costume, he reflected, was the least of it. Before going on the stage, he had to live himself into his new part.

"You can take the evening off, Briggs. I'll have supper with Madame des Landes, of course. I won't need you later."

Well informed and well trained, the valet murmured, "Very good, sir."

"And have everything ready in the morning — post chaise and luggage. Madame's packet sails with the first tide. When I'm back from the ship, we'll leave at once for Portsmouth."

Then, with a final glance at the mirror, Richard went out and followed the winding inn corridor, up and down steps, toward Amélie's rooms.

This was the big moment. For the sake of a surprise, neither he nor, at his urging, Marny, had told her anything of the new commission and of his army plans. During their ride up from Bath that day, he had worn his usual civilian clothes. She would be seeing him in regimentals for the first time, and he had pictured her amazement in different ways.

Replying to his knock, a remote voice bade him enter, and he crossed the sitting room to the door beyond. Seated with her back to him at her dressing table, and clad in nothing but a negligee, the Countess, under the hands of Stephanie and Babette, was having her hair powdered. A perfumed haze floated in the room.

Expecting him, she did not turn but said merely, "Ah, te voilà,

297

mon cher! A little moment till I've finished —" But one of the maids, seeing only his red coat, gave a scream; Monsieur Coco, the parrot, squawked in chorus; and Amélie caught the reflection of Richard's uniform in the mirror. Clutching her gown together, she sprang up and faced him in hot indignation. Only a great lady could use her tongue with such blistering authority.

"Damn your impudence, sir! What d'ye mean by this intrusion! Will you be gone at once! Or, by God —" Her voice stopped short, her eyes and mouth rounded. "Richard!" she breathed. "Nom du ciel! What's the reason for that masquerade? You almost frightened me to death."

"You didn't sound frightened," he retorted. "You singed my hair off. *That* was a greeting!"

"But those clothes, Richard! Why are you dressed like that?"

"Lieutenant Hammond, at your service, Comtesse."

"Trêve de plaisanteries!"

"No joke at all. Didn't we agree that as long as the war lasts, we won't be able to meet? So, I've decided to end it — destroy armies, capture citadels — with the sole purpose of waiting on you soon again. Don't you think I look like a field marshal?" He turned to the maids. "Don't you, Stephanie and Babette?"

"Monsieur est superbe . . ."

Amélie's eyes were still round. "I don't understand . . . You're such a fraud . . ."

"I'm not. Listen —"

"No," she interrupted. "Wait till I'm dressed. I must have clothes on to receive an officer of the King." She made a slight curtsy. "If you please, monsieur, withdraw to the next room. Je suis à vous dans quelques instants."

Knowing what a "few instants" in Amélie's parlance meant, Richard objected. "You don't usually banish me like that."

"No, but I don't admit strange gentlemen to my privacy. I'm not acquainted with Lieutenant Hammond."

"You're cruel. We haven't many instants to waste."

Her glance entreated. "Va t'en, maraud! I'll hurry."

She kept her word. He did not have to wait more than a half hour before the door opened and she entered in a loose-fitting gown of black velvet, half parted over the silver of her bodice and panniered skirt. The tiniest symbol of a lace cap nested on her hair. She wore a collar and strand of pearls. A gust of fragrance attended her into the room, where one of the inn servants was now laying the table for supper.

"Always exquisite!" Richard bowed.

"Well, Monsieur le Lieutenant, I refuse to be outdone by you. Scarlet and black go well together — yes? Now, I demand an explanation."

He told her of the circumstances which had led to his commission, and at last she believed him.

"Of course, it makes me love you more than ever," she declared. "What woman can resist a soldier? Why is a uniform so attractive? The old story of Venus and Mars, the only god she ever loved. But don't get hurt, mon petit Noiraud — at least not disfigured. I want my men whole. Like Donna Florida in our play. Remember?"

"Indeed, I remember. She was very heartless."

"But perhaps you won't leave England," Amélie went on. "I hope not. Do you think you will?"

"Yes, we're to be sent to Louisburg, then to Quebec."

"Ciel!" she murmured, "So far away — beyond the world . . . Mon pauvre! Shall I ever see you again?" She put her hand on his arm but then smiled. "Quebec? Tiens! I have a kinsman there, a cousin of my mother's — That makes us what? I'm so poor at relationships. — The Marquis de Montcalm. He has been often at our house in Paris. I'll give you a letter to him."

"Probably," said Richard, "I shan't be on calling terms with the French general."

"True," she admitted. "War's so silly. But you never know. You might meet him. In that case, give him my compliments and tell him I love you."

"Madam is served," announced the waiter; and they sat down at the small table in front of the fire.

They had reached the point of last things: the last meal together, the last night. The shadow of parting overhung even Amélie's gaiety. Do what she would, it sounded brittle and sometimes even tremulous. Pauses grew longer; sentences, begun, were apt to be unfinished. On the threshold of tomorrow, they could not ignore tomorrow.

"How long will you be in Ireland?" he asked.

Since communications with France were interrupted because of the war, her homeward route had to be circuitous. Having kinsmen and, indeed, a small estate in Cork, she had chosen that approach rather than through Holland.

"No longer than I can help," she said. "A few days with relatives near Kinsale. They've found a smuggler who agrees to land me somewhere on the French coast — Brest probably."

"Marcello Tromba's in Ireland. Do you expect to see him?"

She shook her head. "No, but he's coming to Paris. Did he tell you about our lottery scheme?"

"Yes, and of course I'm jealous."

"Why? It ought to be profitable. He's terribly clever. Why are you jealous?"

"You ought to know."

Preoccupied, she looked absent a moment, then smiled. "Oh, that! Well, why not? You won't be there. C'est un très bel homme. You don't expect me to live like a nun while you're plodding around Canada. I must have *some* pleasure — Tromba or another."

"Amélie!"

She shrugged. "That's so like a man. Always possessive. Did I ever promise to be faithful to you, Richard? Fidelity and I never went through the same door. I promise to love you, though. Love's different. Don't look so grim. Please! Not tonight. Do you want me to break our agreement and lie to you? Of course I shall, if you frown."

He could not help smiling. "No, our agreement forever! I love my witch as she is."

"You'd better, because I can't change myself." She leaned back. "Sometimes I wish I could. Remember the night we heard Monsieur Wesley? How long ago it seems and not quite a month. But what a month, mon bien aimé!" Her low voice thrilled in the room. "Would I exchange it for heavenly treasures? No. Let me have a heaven to remember when I'm 'old, beside the fire.' How are those verses of Ronsard's — *Quand vous serez bien vieille, au soir, à la chandelle* . . . ? I forget. They end something like this — your name instead of his: *Richard m'aimait du temps que j'étais belle.*" She repeated the last words: "'. . . loved me in the days when I was beautiful.' The only trouble with that heaven —"

Suddenly she burst into tears.

Getting up, he crossed over to her. She pressed her face against his coat.

"The only trouble is that it's past."

"No," he said, "we'll have it to look forward to — soon, after the war. Can't you use some of your magic to speed the time?"

"I'll do my best." She straightened up. Then, with an effort: "Besides, it isn't past. There are hours yet." She made a little grimace at the table. "But I've had enough of this bad supper. Haven't you? Puddings! Bon Dieu, how I hate puddings! Nasty stuff. And how they swell the hips! I'm leaving just in time. I've begun to oscillate. You must have noticed . . ."

She rattled on from one topic to another.

Afterwards, when the table was cleared and the servant gone, Richard drew back the curtains of a window; and they stood, he with his arm around her, looking out at the night. A low moon silvered the broken roof lines of the medieval city still contained by its ancient walls, and, beyond the jumble of houses, showed a nearby forest of masts rising from the floating harbor. A smell of ships filtered in on the air through the drafty casement. Some church bell struck nine.

"By the way," he said, "I have a favor to ask. If we didn't understand each other so well, I wouldn't dare. It's for Maritza Venier."

"Indeed!" she stiffened. "I hate that girl. Well, what can I do for her?"

"Have you any influence at the Opéra in Paris?"

"I know the directors, Rebel and Francoeur. Of course I have influence."

"Enough, do you think, to get her a place at the Opéra when this season in London is over?"

"Perhaps. A small place, yes. Mais, que diable! Why do you ask? What's your interest in her? By God, if I thought . . ."

His arm tightened. "Amélie! Don't tell me you're jealous, yourself?"

"It's a woman's privilege, Richard. But go on. Twist the knife. Why do you want this place for Mademoiselle?"

"Because of Caretti. Without his backing, I don't think she'll find it so easy in London. She doesn't like England. Paris has always been her dream. Her mother danced at the Opéra. An invitation

301

from the directors there would mean everything to her — even if it was only a small place. You see —" he hesitated — "I've behaved shabbily. I'd like to feel that I'd done something to make amends."

Amélie smiled. "Do you want her to know that the Comtesse des Landes procured her an invitation for your sake? I suppose not."

"Lord!" he exclaimed. "If she ever knew! She's proud as Lucifer."

"Very well then, we'll keep it a secret."

"And you'll do this for her?"

"Yes, I think it can be arranged."

She drew away and stood a moment looking up at him, half fondly, half amused. Then with a light laugh, "Do you know why I love you so much, Richard? You're such a boy, in spite of your stature and red coat. You're so unspoiled, in spite of Lord Marny and me. Promise me something. I can't tell you how much I mean it. Promise that you won't change, won't grow suave and smooth and false. That's the only sort of man I've known. Hypocrites! I pay them in their own coin. But with you — Promise . . ."

"I'll never change toward you, Amélie."

She was all caprice again. "Words! Just words! I want more than that. Don't think you can get off so cheaply. What presumption! On the eve of parting, ask your mistress to promote her rival, with the calm assurance that she's fool enough to do it! Very well! But, in return, à nous deux, mon ami. By morning, I expect to have no doubt that you love me more than anyone else in the world . . ."

Because of the fog, her little hooded figure on the quarter-deck of the packet looked already distant, though, from where he stood on the quay, only a few yards separated them. Now and then she called down to him some vacant trifle, such as people use at parting, and he answered in the same way. Her last kiss in the small cabin below deck still burned on his lips. That had been farewell; this was only a fading echo.

But they did not hear the order to cast off, the thud of the tossed ropes. Suddenly the distance widened between them. The fog thickened. He heard her voice but not the words, only his name, and called in reply. Then, nothing but the mist.

He stood for a while, staring into it, and at last turned back toward the inn.

PART THREE

Quebec

XLIV

TO the Rt. Hon. the Earl of Marny from Major General Wolfe
HEADQUARTERS OF MONTMORENCY IN
THE RIVER ST. LAWRENCE
Aug. 31, 1759

MY LORD,

I take the occasion of dispatches transmitted herewith to Mr. Pitt, concerning the progress of His Majesty's arms in the present campaign, to write your lordship a brief account of Mr. Hammond, pursuant to the promise I made before setting out last February from Portsmouth. The pressure of affairs and latterly my own indifferent state of health, must plead for your lordship's indulgence that I have so long deferred the execution of that promise. Your lordship will no doubt learn from Mr. Pitt or my Lord Holdernesse, as well as from Mr. Hammond himself, what our difficulties have been, and what small hope of success they afford during that part of the campaign which remains. However, as far as time serves and as far as I am able, the most vigorous measures will be employed for the honor of His Majesty and the interest of the nation. But, to the subject in point.

It is with great satisfaction that I am able to commend Mr. Hammond both as a man and an officer. Though he has had no occasion as yet to distinguish himself above others of his own rank in the Forty-seventh, he is certainly the inferior of none and the superior of many, in the performance of his duties and in personal conduct. By close attention and by modeling himself upon seasoned officers, he learned in an astonishing short time not only the niceties of drill and military forms, but even that air and carriage which is not usually acquired short of several years in the army. He is well liked both by the officers and men of his regiment. Indeed, Lt. Col. Hale, at present in command of the Forty-seventh, is especially fond of Mr. Hammond, takes pleasure in his company, and has more than once assigned him to the duties of an adjutant.

Trivial accomplishments, if joined to real merit and a manly bearing, are not seldom of value to a young officer. Mr. Hammond's skill in music, his dexterity with tricks of legerdemain, which, indeed, would do credit to a juggler by profession, have afforded much entertainment, with a corresponding effect upon his own popularity. For instance, today as I write, he has been granted leave to visit the lazaret at St. Francis on the nearby Île d'Orléans in order to entertain some of our poor fellows there who were wounded in the recent action at Montmorency. And I recall with pleasure that, when I had occasion ten days since to invite to supper a few French ladies of condition who were temporarily our prisoners, Mr. Hammond, by his proficiency on the fiddle and his complete command of the French tongue, lent an easiness to the company which might otherwise have been lacking. His knowledge of French, which, to be frank, he speaks with greater perfection than English, is of capital value here in Canada and has proved repeatedly useful for the interrogation of prisoners or deserters. With this talent in mind, I propose shortly to employ him on a mission of some delicacy, which, if successful, may be of considerable benefit to His Majesty's arms. But, as the plan is still undetermined and, in any case, awaits Mr. Hammond's consent, I shall not burden this letter with a particular account of it, leaving to him the satisfaction of acquainting your lordship with its outcome.

So far, then, I have nothing but good to communicate of Mr. Hammond. I am sensible, however, that this, gratifying as far as it goes, does not fully answer the question uppermost in your lordship's mind and relative to which you did me the honor to desire my opinion. Should Mr. Hammond continue with His Majesty's forces after the end of the present campaign? Should he devote his life to the profession of arms? That, as I recall, is the subject of chief concern to your lordship.

In regard to this, it is still too early for a final judgment; and, in any case, I make no claim to be an oracle. Events may easily reverse my present estimate of Mr. Hammond. But, since you require frankness, my lord, I must tell you plainly, in spite of everything I have above wrote, that I do not believe he should seek his career in the army. This, I am well aware, must seem a *non sequitur* to your lordship, in view of the many excellent things I have been happy to relate of him. Nor can I give a reasonable basis for such an opinion. It is a sentiment merely, but one derived from considerable experience of young men in the military service. I feel that Mr. Hammond excels as an able actor excels, but that the passions and subject of the play do not touch him personally. The cause of England, for which we fight, the science of war, the zeal for promotion, none of these, in my opinion, animates him. He is intent on a brilliant performance convincing to his audience, nay, I dare say, convincing to himself. But, with submission, I do not think that in private he regards himself as a soldier. Briefly, then, his heart does not seem to me engaged by any of those objects which ordinarily attract a man to the career of arms; and in the circumstances, I should consider unfortunate his choice of that profession.

Let me hasten to add that I believe Mr. Hammond to be wholly unaware of this disposition in himself, and that his superior officers, notably Col. Hale, would most sharply differ from me. Let me add, too, that I have a warm personal regard for Mr. Hammond. However, I submit these reflections for what they are worth in the hope that, though tentative, your lordship will do me the justice to believe them dictated by the great truth and respect with which, my lord, I have the honor to subscribe myself your lordship's humble, obedient servant,

Jam. Wolfe

X L V

"AND so, schentlemen and frien's —" for the delight of his hearers, Richard put on as thick an accent as possible — "being very 'ongry, I have swallow', as you obsairve, seex eggs, shell an' all. Dey lie now togedder in my belly." He rubbed that portion of him.

"But, goddam, messieurs, I begin to regret . . . I begin to feel de pains . . ." Prolonged contortions, so comical that the bandaged audience roared. "Why I such a dam fool? 'Ow I relieve myself? Up or down? Neider way is proper in dis company . . ."

"I sees 'ee, lieutenant," put in one of the grenadiers out of a bloody clot of rags covering most of his face. "I sees 'ee — how you got a egg cupped in your left hand. You don't fool me, sir."

Richard had been waiting for that and blustered: "Tom, you rogue! I deespise your suspeecions, sair! Schentlemen, I appeal. Dis man 'ere tink I play tricks. Well den, look! Voilà!" He held up both hands completely empty. "Dis man make fun of my deestress. Ah, schentlemen, I ask pardon. I relieve myself . . ."

With a hideous gurgle, Richard's throat swelled; his cheeks puffed out; he appeared to draw an egg from his mouth, another, another . . . It was so lifelike that the faces of his audience writhed in sympathy. Oaths rumbled. On the pallet-covered floor of the little church of Saint-François, which had been turned into a lazaret, some of the wounded who had been unable to drag themselves into the circle surrounding Richard craned and stared. The torment of the flies, the stench of the place, was forgotten. A surgeon who had been stooping over a man in one corner shook his head, drew a blanket over the face of his patient, stood up, and stared himself.

"Ah-h-h!" Richard gave a happy sigh. "Dass better! Schentlemen, 'owever 'ongry you are, I beg you not to swallow eggs like dat. See 'ow much lighter dey are outside dan in . . ."

He was juggling the six eggs in a bewildering circle. But the circle thinned. One egg after the other vanished.

"Who take my eggs? After de trouble I 'ave to acquire 'em from Madame Brunneau's 'en-roost at Montmorency! I suspec' dis rogue, Tom." He drew an egg from the grenadier's pocket, and one from his ear, amid the hoots of the gathering. "And dis scoundrel, Jack." A couple came out of the soldier's empty sleeve. "And Sergeant Wilkins, I'm surprise' a man of your rank . . ." Two more were recovered from the amazed Wilkins.

An unexpected woman's voice from nowhere put in: "Always was a rascal, sir. That's why he 'listed. Wait till I gets him when he comes home!"

"But who are you, ma'am?" Richard stammered, while everybody's eyes sought the origin of the eerie voice.

"He knows who I am — the false wretch! Bell Buckley of Salem, what he got into trouble at the quilting party and left with twins, sir. Wait till I catches him!" The voice ended in a screech.

"'Tis a damned lie," fumed Wilkins, a New Englander of the Royal Americans. "I've never been to Salem. I don't know the slut."

The voice amended: "Well, now, I may be mistook, sir. I've been so often in trouble. But, sure, 'tis one of them egg stealers you're a-talking to, sir."

Vast merriment. Richard's ventriloquistic efforts had brought out the sweat, and he swabbed his face.

"I'll lay you a sovereign," drawled a young Virginian named Carter, who was an ensign in Wilkins's regiment, "that those are trick eggs, suh, weighted to suit, and you dassn't show us the insides of one of 'em. Nobody can juggle raw eggs like that."

"I won't take your money, sair," returned Richard. "I only ask, if you're wrong, that you'll eat 'em. Is it a bar-gain?"

"Done, suh." The ensign, who had been hit in the leg, hobbled a couple of steps forward on his crutches and shook the magician's hand.

"Now, give me room, schentlemen. Obsairve veree close." Richard took up a grenadier's miter-shaped cap and leaned it top down against a low stool. "I scorn base trickery, my frien's. More hones' dan me, you will not fin' in de King's forces. Obsairve . . . I break de eggs." At least the latter were honest. One after another, he broke all six and emptied them into the cap.

"Glad it ain't mine," muttered a tense voice. "What a shockin' mess 'e's makin' of it!"

Richard turned to Carter. "Be'old, Mistair Skeptic."

"You win," said the ensign. "But, dammy, I insist on cookin' 'em."

"No, sair," Richard bowed. "Permit *me*. I prepare you one lovely omelette." He stirred vigorously with his wand inside the cap, muttering strange words. "It cooks, it cooks. Almos' it is ready. Ah, finalmente! Ecco! Voilà! Be'old!" He reached into the cap. "But what is dis . . ."

With a comically horrified expression, he began pulling out a string of objects tied together: a woman's garter, a ship's pennon, a dead mouse, a twist of tobacco, a dog-eared broadsheet, a half-dozen nails, a battered pipe . . . On and on . . .

"Ah, schentlemen, what a omelette! . . . I mus' 'ave use' de wrong charm . . . An' poor Mistair Cartair, 'e promise to eat it . . . But 'ere . . . what's dis? . . ." So quick were his hands that, seeming to emerge from the cap and not from the skirts of his coat, a good-sized bottle appeared. "At leas' I give 'im someting to drink it down wit'. I believe 'e'll find it prime grog. Perhaps 'e share some of it wit' you. Mistair Cartair, sair, my compliments."

This was the grand finale. All eyes were on the coveted bottle in Carter's hands and did not see the swift substitution for the magical cap of one exactly like it.

A deep bow. "Schentlemen, I t'ank you for your patience."

The voice of Bell Buckley sounded for the last time. "Give him a cheer, mates, and to hell with him!"

Amid the roar of applause, and while one of the grenadiers, reaching for the cap, stared nonplused at its innocent emptiness, Richard picked his way out of the church between the sprawled figures of many too stricken for entertainment. Some lay quiet, some moaned, some lay twisting their heads from side to side. The fetor of excrements and blood and sweat and gangrene blanketed the place. The stench of war. The wreckage of war. The cost of an attack that had blundered. It recalled vivid memories of the galleys. Only, physically at least, this was more horrible.

Half nauseated, he stood gulping in the clean country air outside.

"Damn good of you, Hammond," said one of the surgeons, who had followed him, "to give these poor chaps something to take their minds off themselves. Can't tell you how much they look forward to your visits."

"How many are there?" It was a relief to drop the exaggerated lingo of the sorcerer and speak naturally again. Richard's accent had grown much less foreign in the months since Portsmouth. "Seem more than ever."

The surgeon stopped his pipe with a dirty thumb and used his tinderbox. "They keep dribbling in. Skirmishes here or there. Now and then a hit from the French batteries. But the bulk's still from Montmorency. We've a hundred odd here, packing them in, as you see; and there's close to two hundred and fifty more in other lazarets. What a mad venture that was! Landing head on against the works of the whole damned French army. There's not an officer has a good word for it. In my opinion, Wolfe that day lost well-nigh all the credit he gained at Louisburg. I heard Brigadier Townshend say himself . . ."

He went on discussing the passionate topic of the disastrous attack on July thirty-first against the French redoubts on the Beauport side of the Montmorency. True, the Louisburg Grenadiers, the storm troops of the army, landing on the beach from small boats, had lost their heads, had failed to wait for the battalions advancing to their support from beyond the foot of the falls, had plunged on in a helter-skelter, though heroic, charge, which had crumbled under the French fire to the tune of four hundred and fifty killed and wounded. True, also, an unsuspected shoal in the river had slowed up the landing boats. And the change of tide had shortened the period left for attack. But, with every allowance, the operation seemed as ill advised as it was ill executed.

"Ah, well," the surgeon concluded, voicing the widespread frustration, "I dare say we'll hang on a week or so longer and then slink off with our tails between our legs. They tell me Admiral Saunders is running out of patience. Summer's about over. Amherst doesn't arrive. What's to be done with a handful of troops against three times our number — all the more as the Mounseers stick to their trenches? And right they are. Let me tell you, sir, with no disrespect to our generals, they're schoolboys to Montcalm. That's my opinion." He took a few angry puffs. "I only wish I had more laudanum for my poor bastards."

Still sickish from the closeness of the lazaret, Richard half listened. He had heard all this a hundred times since the Montmorency defeat: the growing discouragement of an army which had set out with high hopes, only to see them wither week by week during the fruitless siege of impregnable Quebec. The spirit of soldiers and seamen was still excellent; they were still eager to dare the impossible. Only the impression hardened from day to day that they faced the impossible. They were too few; the cliffs were too high; the enemy was too strong, and winter, too near. Another futility in the long annals of war, wasted treasure, wasted lives.

"You look peaked yourself," added the surgeon. "You ought to have sampled your own grog."

"No," said Richard. "But I'll take the air awhile. The lads who rowed me over went foraging for apples. You're better off for fruit over here than we are. I've an hour to kill. Your servant, sir."

He made his way down to the point of the island at no great distance from the church. Then, having washed out the magical grenadier's cap in readiness for the next occasion, he stowed it away in an inner pocket, stripped off his coat, and, seating himself against a tree, gazed down the river.

From here, no trace of the war could be seen — no ships, no redoubts, no smoking ruins of the lower town, which had been leveled by the British guns at Point Levi and Pointe-aux-Pères; above all, no cluster of haughty, unchanging spires that marked the unattainable upper town — only the golden haze of August on the water, a hint of gold along the nearer shore line, and, far away to the left, the lovely slopes of the Laurentian mountains. It was one of those extremely rare moments of solitude, unmonopolized by the crowding of people and camp routine, that permitted a man to catch his breath and realize himself.

Mystery. Vastness. Canada. America. Another planet. How far away in time, distance, and all the formal tapestry of life, from ancient Europe! This month last year, thought Richard, he was at Audley Court, Lord Marny's estate in Kent, studying Grotius, Puffendorf, and the *Ius Gentium*, studying even harder the intricate conventions of fashion; but an outsider on the fringes of a class to which he did not belong. This time two years ago, he was on the Brenta, hovering mothlike on the fringes of that same class, but equally without belonging. There was this, at least, about the emptiness of America, that he belonged here as much or as little as anybody else . . .

Then, too, it could be said for the present expedition that the man of fashion played no part in it. Here, other virtues than sophistication were admired. Here, though rank and birth counted for something, they did not count for much as compared with fortitude and courage. There were fops among the officers, but foppishness did not promote them. And here, though selfishness and vanity were often crass enough, they were sometimes eclipsed by bigger motives: comradeship, esprit de corps, the well-being of the army, devotion to England. It was good to discover this other side of humanity, good to be associated with it, good to recognize the change and deepening in himself. Only . . .

Only what the devil was wrong? He had made a success as Lieutenant Hammond. He could swear that he had made a success. Only the other day, Colonel Hale had promised him the first vacant captaincy in the Forty-seventh. Why, then, did he avoid looking forward to years in the service? Why did it really matter so little to him whether England snatched Canada from France or not? Why did the work of war itself appear so increasingly hideous and idiotic — the human wreckage in the lazarets, the devastation of the countryside, civilian suffering, aimless destruction? Perhaps because England, except nominally, was not his nation. He had no nation. But somehow the excuse failed to satisfy him. One could be a professional soldier without patriotism. The trouble was that he had no compelling mainspring, like art, in the case of Goldoni; or thought, in that of Venier; or religion, with Wesley; or pleasure, with Tromba; or military ardor, with Wolfe. No unifying principle. He remained a dabbler, an opportunist. Why? He could not find the answer.

He fell to thinking of Wolfe, conscious that his admiration for the young general had been the mainspring of whatever success he had had, and not of his alone but of the entire army. What a miracle leadership was! A spiritual emanation independent of anything visible, infinitely pervasive, infinitely powerful. It was this that gave soul and purpose to the expedition. But Wolfe was dying — so the report went. The fever which had stricken him after the fight at Montmorency, added to the chronic diseases of a constitution undermined by a lifetime of hardships, was more than his frail body could stand. It was said that the General himself recognized this, though he made light of it. He would spend himself to the last. And then? Why, it was the final act of a drama, ending in defeat or victory — probably defeat. The curtains would close. The actors would scatter. What meaning did the army have for Richard then? He smiled at his own habit of thinking in terms of the stage. Captain Harlequin!

And from association to association, his mind wandered on through the golden haze of the river . . .

Curious (it occurred to him) how much more often these days

he remembered Maritza Venier than the passionately adored Amélie. It was doubtless, he reflected, because he could picture Maritza among the surroundings of the camp or in the vast distances of America, whereas the Comtesse des Landes did not fit into them at all. Maritza, with her self-reliance, her freshness and courage, belonged essentially to the New World; Amélie reflected only the Old. In the last letter from Lord Marny, who wrote him by every ship that brought dispatches, he had learned that: "Mademoiselle Venier is now, I understand, called to the Opéra in Paris, where I wish her every success, principally because of the worthy man her father . . ." So, Amélie had kept her word. Richard wondered how Maritza was faring now in the Mecca of her hopes.

An odd creaking sound that approached through the trees caught his attention; and he looked around to see the young Virginian ensign, Carter, swinging himself along on his crutches.

"Mind if I join you, suh?" greeted the latter. "The air in that church is too thick for me. Glad this is my last day of it. I can hobble just as well around camp as here. — Well, did I speak up at the right moment of your show, as you asked me?"

"On the dot," said Richard, giving the other a hand in sitting down. "It helps a magician to plant questions like that. How did the grog taste?"

"Excellent," Carter answered — "what there was left of it when the bottle got back to me. — But, suh, please accept my compliments on those tricks of yours. Lawdy, how I wish I knew some of 'em! I can picture myself in the taproom of the 'King's Arms' in Williamsburg and the company a-starin' and a-gapin'. You couldn't teach me a few, could you — especially the cyard tricks?"

He spoke in a soft, pleasing drawl very different from others in the Royal Americans, who were chiefly New Englanders.

"All tricks are simple," Richard said, "when you know them. But it takes time until you learn the knack and until your hand is quicker than the eyes of the people watching you. Everything's in that. Look me up at your leisure if our regiments are close by, and I'll show you what I mean."

"Where did you learn 'em yourself? — if it's not an impertinence, suh."

312

"In Italy. I grew up there."

"That accounts for your accent. But Hammond's an English name."

"My father is English." Richard changed the subject. "You're from Virginia. Do you know of a river called the James?"

Carter repressed a smile. He drew out his pipe. "As it happens I do, suh. We have a plantation on the James. I was born there."

"Indeed! Why, then, perhaps you've heard of a Mr. Fairfax — Mr. Eustace Fairfax?"

The other nodded. "Aye, he has a fine place called Meriton in Prince George County. But he's been much in England. I don't recall having seen him. Our plantation is considerably farther down the river in Norfolk County."

Richard could see no point in announcing Fairfax's loss of Meriton to Lord Marny, and observed merely that he had heard of Fairfax in England.

"Yes," said Carter, "I reckon he considers himself a Britisher. Now, it ain't that way in our family. The more I see of Englishmen, suh (no offense), the happier I am to be a Virginian. That's what I am and nothing else, a Virginian. Let me tell you . . ."

What he told was new to Richard. Apparently a queer independence was stirring in the colonies. They no longer considered themselves the pensioners of England. They resented patronage, social or political; thought of themselves increasingly as Americans. A curious ferment.

Carter drifted on to a homesick account of the far-off Southland, its climate and fertility, horses and hunting, pretty girls, easy hospitality, the balls in Williamsburg. Yes, and there were lands opening up in the West that Carter wanted to look into.

"I'd like mighty fine to show you Virginia, Mr. Hammond, when the war's over — bring you acquainted with my family and friends. They'd sure make you welcome. Think it over, suh. Don't judge of America till you've seen Virginia."

But the sun was lower. The men of his platoon would now be waiting at the skiff, Richard hoped, with a good store of apples. He took leave of Carter, promising to consider a visit to Virginia. It was a polite evasion that cost him nothing.

313

As the boat rounded into the river, the panorama of war again opened up: the British entrenchments, guarding Wolfe's camp eastward of the Montmorency; the French divisions spread out between that stream and the walls of the city; the sentinel spires of Quebec, overlooking everything. Here and there the red patch of an English flag showed, or farther off and harder to see, the white lily banner of France. A rattle of drums, a distant bugle call, announced the changing of a guard. The huddle of British masts on the other side of the Île d'Orléans came into view. And now and then a roar sounded from the batteries at Pointe-aux-Pères, with an answering puff of dust from the ruins of the lower town.

Back to duty again, back to the siege.

The boat dropped downstream to avoid roving shots from the French floating batteries above the Montmorency, and landed at the extreme east of the British lines. But hardly had Richard entered the encampment of the Forty-seventh, which lay closest to the river, than a headquarters' orderly hailed him.

"Mr. Hammond, I've been kicking my heels here for the last half hour. You were expected back earlier, sir. The General desires your attendance at once in his quarters. I repeat *at once*, sir."

For a lieutenant to be summoned personally by the Commander in Chief was so exceptional that Richard had no idea what it portended. Side by side with the orderly, he made his way between the lines of tents, the long shadows of the two men slanting behind them away from the setting sun.

X L V I

WOLFE'S quarters were at the extreme west of the camp in a small whitewashed stone farmhouse at no great distance from the Falls and thus almost within reach of the French guns, which were separated from the British lines by only the narrow Montmorency. A modest little house, with a single chimney, a ground floor and attic, it overlooked the steep slope down to the North Channel of the St. Lawrence and, beyond that, the long shore line of the Isle of Orléans. Its position seemed to Richard characteristic of Wolfe, who was always at the point of danger in attack or defense. A couple of scarlet grenadiers, stiff as ramrods, precise as clockwork, patrolled the front of the house. Otherwise, nothing else distinguished it as headquarters.

Having been challenged by the guards and passed at a word from the orderly, Richard found himself in the close, farm-smelling interior, of which the rooms at right and left served as offices for staff business, and was directed to the foot of a ladderlike stairway at the chimney-end, leading to the attic. Careful of his head, he ascended this and emerged into a dim space lighted by dormer windows on the south side and extending the length of the house. In front of one of the windows, a ship's hammock, evidently Wolfe's bed, was slung from the naked rafters. Farther along, toward the end of the attic, he vaguely recognized the General, seated with another officer at a rough table.

"Yes?" said Wolfe, looking up. "What is it?"

"Lieutenant Hammond reporting, sir. I was informed —"

"Right." The General's voice, though firm, sounded a trifle faint. "Pray come here, sir. I have something to discuss with you."

Richard had not seen the Commander in Chief for some days. Now, owing partly to the wan evening light, he was struck by the notable change in him. Always slender, Wolfe had grown pitiably thin, his uniform too big for his shrunken body, his nose, from which forehead and chin sloped back, more prominent than ever, his eyes larger and sunken. Aside from his recent fever, he had suffered much of late from his chronic affliction of the gravel, and the lines of pain were sharp at the corners of his mouth. He looked more like a man at the point of death, or a specter in uniform, than the responsible head of an army. Perhaps, too, his infirm appearance was heightened by contrast with the ruddy-faced, broad-shouldered officer at table with him. This was Colonel Guy Carleton, the Quartermaster General, one of Wolfe's intimate friends, a strict disciplinarian, but nonetheless popular because of his energy balanced with humaneness and common sense. Thirty-five at the time and actually three years older than Wolfe, he looked younger, his physical robustness emphasizing the other's invalidism.

Richard bowed to both officers and hoped that he found the General better.

315

"Well enough to do business," said Wolfe, "and that is the main point. By the way, Hammond, I wrote Lord Marny today about you. Before leaving, I promised to let him know how you got on. It gratified me to be able to give an excellent account."

"He will be most grateful, sir, as I am," Richard bowed again.

"But I did not summon you here," Wolfe continued, "merely to inform you of it — except that you may wish to write him yourself. Dispatches for England are leaving with a sloop of war on the second. — There's another matter. You may be seated, sir. Draw up a chair."

Completely at a loss as to what the matter might be, Richard obeyed; but for a minute the General eyed him in silence, with the air of a man who had not yet decided how much he ought to say. Reticence was a trait of Wolfe's which had become especially marked on this campaign, and even the brigadiers were often in ignorance of his plans till the moment of their execution. Gossip ran rife in the small army; there were leakages to the enemy through prisoners or deserters; and what people did not know they could not communicate directly or indirectly to Montcalm.

"The subject is most secret," he said finally. "Whether or not you undertake what I am about to propose, I require your word of honor that you will inform no one of this interview while you are in Canada."

Richard earnestly assured him on this point.

"I have selected you," Wolfe went on, "for two reasons: your complete mastery of French and because I consider you a man of resource and intelligence. No other of the young officers will do; I cannot afford to detach one of higher rank for the purpose. It is a mere shot in the dark and has only the barest chance of success. If you decline the undertaking, we must give up all thought of it. On the other hand, if you accept and have luck, it should prove of benefit to other plans I have in mind."

"Sir," Richard said, "you have only to command me."

"No, I do not choose to command in this instance. The affair is beyond the line of your duties and should be entered upon, if at all, gladly and with fervor. I shall not take it ill if you decline. Briefly, the scheme is this. I propose that you allow yourself to be captured by the French."

"Captured?" Richard echoed.

"Yes. It means that, as an officer, you will be brought before the Marquis de Montcalm himself for questioning. This in turn means that you will be able to convey to him certain information."

"False, perhaps?"

"No, I don't request a gentleman to lie even to an enemy. Misleading, yes; but the truth as far as you know it. You could say, 'I have heard on good authority,' or 'It is rumored,' or 'I am inclined to believe' — which would be true enough, for I intend now to hint to you certain plans actually under discussion, one of which may be indeed attempted. If I withhold others, that is my affair, not yours — or Montcalm's. So give heed."

Once again Wolfe hesitated, as if selecting his words.

"On the advice of Brigadiers Townshend, Moncton, and Murray," he went on, "it has been decided to break camp here, beginning tomorrow, and withdraw our forces to the Isle of Orléans and the South Shore. But if the Marquis de Montcalm should think to attack us during this operation, he might fall into a trap, and he has need of caution. Now this withdrawal, sir, does not mean that we have given up all thought of attacking below the town. If Montcalm should sensibly weaken his forces between the St. Charles and the Montmorency rivers, this might indeed be the proper point for a coup de main; and our ships will keep alert to probe any such weakness. I confess, however, that the Brigadiers strongly urge an attempt twelve miles or so above the city in the neighborhood of Cap Rouge. I have acquiesced in the plan, and I am so reporting to England. We have seventeen ships at anchor upstream, with a sufficiency of flat-bottomed boats. Our troops have only to march west from Point Levi along the South Shore and embark under cover of the fleet."

"But, sir," put in Richard, "isn't Monsieur de Bougainville on guard in force at Cap Rouge? Or so I have heard."

Wolfe nodded. "Yes, but where is the enemy not on guard at every practicable landing place on the North Shore? The Marquis de Montcalm is too old and able a soldier to leave any point open. Ours is a choice of difficulties, sir. The truth is this campaign has little prospect of success. Our casualties approach a thousand. Disease spreads. The season advances, and we have so far accomplished nothing of consequence. Men and officers grow restless. We must be out of the St. Lawrence within the month. But an expedition of this size demands that before leaving we make at least one effort for the honor of His Majesty's arms. That is my duty, and I shall be held answerable for the consequence of it, as for everything else."

Answerable indeed! Richard could well imagine the storm in England which would greet the failure of such an expensive campaign. And Pitt would also be answerable. He had promoted the young General above many higher-ranking officers. He had backed the gamble with a vast national outlay, the flower of the British army, seventy-odd sails of the fleet. Such failures overturn governments. As for Wolfe himself, what would the glory of Louisburg avail him in the face of the national disappointment, the criticism of his own officers, the defeat at Montmorency, the ultimate inglorious withdrawal? One could hope that death would spare him some of the shame. But even in death he would know that he had failed.

"All of this," Wolfe continued — "I repeat *all* of it — you could let drop to the Marquis de Montcalm and to other French officers, not as derived from me, of course, but as the result of what you have heard or observed. And note that all of it would be perfectly true. Moreover, you would not fail to comment on the state of my health, which is indeed ruined and offers little hope for the future."

Richard stared. Why should the General wish to expose his weakness to Montcalm? Worse still, why should he point out to him the brigadiers' plan against Cap Rouge, and also the possibility of a renewed attack below the city? It seemed both aimless and suicidal. And yet there was something in Wolfe's manner that recalled a chess player who makes a move incomprehensible at the moment to anyone looking on.

"I — I understand, sir. You desire all of this information to reach the Marquis."

"Yes —" a pale smile showed on the other's lips — "and much good may it do him! If you consider what I have told you, Hammond, you will observe that it amounts to little more than he will learn from his outposts or surmise for himself fairly soon. But if,

318

on the strength of it, he chooses to hold firm below the town and to reinforce the Chevalier de Bougainville at Cap Rouge, God's will be done." Wolfe exchanged a glance with Carleton, then added: "Well, Mr. Hammond, will you undertake this mission?"

"Of course, sir, if you believe I am fitted for it."

Indeed, as far as it concerned him personally, Richard felt elated. He was tired of the camp routine, the drills and inspections, the babble at officers' mess, the aching tedium of the siege. To be released from all this on a venture that Wolfe seemed to consider important and one that depended on his own wits came as a godsend.

"I can think of no one else so well fitted for it," answered Wolfe. "I've heard you're something of an actor, as well as a juggler. That's the kind of skill you'll need in this affair. For, pray consider, the information you bring to the Marquis will depend for its effect on your manner of conveying it. He is too much a fox to be easily misled. There must be nothing implausible about your capture. Your replies to his questions must seem inadvertent, the result of simplicity and not of design. If he suspects the least artifice, your game is up. In short, you must act a convincing part and sustain it throughout. I leave the invention of it to you."

"Should I give him my parole, sir?"

"No, you might possibly be able to escape and should not commit yourself. As an officer, you will perhaps be less rigorously confined than if you were a private. Then, too, you'll be lodged, as are other of our men, in the common prison, which is back of the Intendant's Palace and hence outside the city walls. You have therefore a slight chance. If our attack fails, and we leave the St. Lawrence, you could give your parole then. The issue will be decided in ten days. That, of course, is not for the ears of Monsieur de Montcalm."

So, barring escape, thought Richard, if the attack failed, he would be left behind to a Quebec winter and indefinite captivity. Not if he could help it, by God!

Wolfe continued: "I'll inform Colonel Hale that you are detached for special duty and drop him a word as to the nature of it. You may consult with him on how best to give your capture a natural appearance. Lose no time; by tomorrow night, you should be in the hands of the French. I like your spirit, Hammond. Whatever happens, I shall not forget it. — Well, good luck to you, sir, and God bless you."

Richard stood up, with a word of thanks. Then, having bowed to the General and Carleton, he found his way through the almost dark attic to the stairs. But the last impression of Wolfe that he took with him was altogether different from the first. A dying man, perhaps, but nonetheless invincible. His last effort against Quebec would be an outpouring of that force which it had been said could move mountains. And Richard had no intention of being left out of it, if escape from the French was at all possible.

Money, he reflected, was a sovereign opener of locks everywhere; and he had a small store of gold guineas in reserve. But how to conceal them on his person? The Indians or Canadians, who would no doubt be his captors, searched their prisoners and appropriated what they could find. Indeed, it was by no means certain that he could even retain his scalp.

Then he recalled that Tromba had once shown him a pair of traveling boots designed for carrying gold or jewels. The soles revealed no opening device. Unless one knew the manipulation of the heel that permitted the layers of leather to be taken apart, like a trick box, there was no means of discovering the shallow inner compartments, short of cutting the soles to pieces. Yet the mechanism was not beyond the skill of an average shoemaker.

There was an excellent cobbler in the Forty-seventh, and Richard proceeded to confer with him at once. As a result, the man worked most of that night.

XLVII

THOUGH for Wolfe, about to break camp east of the Montmorency, there was only a choice of difficulties, each of them pregnant with defeat, it could hardly be said that his great adversary Louis de Montcalm, quartered in the manor house at Beauport, regarded the future with much more confidence. He held the advantage of position, numbers, and climate, but his advantage stopped there. He did not have, indeed, to contend with a hostile population, impregnable cliffs, and the advance of winter, yet even so, his difficulties were no less heavy. They were the limitations inherent in the French cause itself: the weakness, stupidity, and corruption of his own people. His chief problem was the dead weight of an outworn and decomposing human tradition, which he was pledged to defend and somehow drag along. And that tradition, centering around the vapid, handsome Louis XV in far-off Versailles, represented the only order he knew or loved. Therefore, like many another hero of lost causes, he could only make the best of it and put his trust in God.

For him, it was a choice of vexations. He had not even the supreme command of his army. He was the one eminent soldier in New France, distinguished in the Italian wars, the victor of Oswego and Ticonderoga; but he stood second, by the very terms of his commission, to the civilian Governor General, Marquis de Vaudreuil, a conceited, incompetent, jealous man, bent on thwarting him. Technically, at least, he commanded only the three thousand regulars from Old France, while more than three quarters of his army — the *troupes de la marine*, the Canadian militia — depended on Vaudreuil. In influence, too, he stood only second, or perhaps third, to the all-powerful rascal, François Bigot, the King's Intendant, who held the purse of Canada, enriching himself and fellow sharpers on its contents. No help from France, cut off by the British navy and absorbed in the European war; friction between Canadians and Frenchmen in the army; opposition of the Governor; financial chicane — Montcalm found himself balked everywhere by the human factor.

He had the advantage of numbers; but what were mere numbers compared with the disciplined British troops and fleet splendidly officered, keen for empire, backed by an intelligent government and wealthy nation! Among the French, there was one unifying force, hatred of the invaders; and this Montcalm made the most of to keep his motley army on foot. He had also a handful of capable lieutenants, de Lévis, de Bougainville, de Bourlamaque, and others. Above all, he had himself, his experience and fame of leadership, his singleheartedness, unfaltering courage, and devotion to the King. Perhaps these values, combined with the strength of position, would suffice to turn back once again the British tide.

Perhaps. If so, to God the glory and to someone else the task of withstanding the next tide. For the haughty ships would return . . . They would return. Well, let them. It was sufficient for Montcalm to have held Quebec in his day and generation.

Thoughts of the sort crossed his mind as he stood warming himself at the fire in the comfortable living room of the manor house. August had been hot, but September had set in damp and chill, so that the crackling birch logs at the end of a day were more than welcome. His clothes steamed a little; his worn riding boots showed flecks of mud; for he had been out as usual inspecting the mile-long entrenchments between Quebec and the Montmorency, keeping an eye, too, on the British camp and fleet, where he had observed a sudden new activity. This would probably take him out again tonight. Indeed, during the last month he had not once undressed, alert to any call; for with an antagonist like Wolfe, he could expect the unexpected. So, he multiplied his vigilance. Wherever the Englishman struck, he would be there to meet him.

The strain told, however. He had begun to feel the weight of his forty-seven years. A robust man, with the compact build of the southern Frenchman, with the fire, too, and vivacity of the South, he still feared no labor; but, after all, he was middle-aged . . .

Sinking into a chair, he stretched out his hands toward the hearth, relaxing in thoughts of home. It would be sun-baked summer still in Languedoc, with its dusty olive trees and vineyards. They would be close upon the vintage now at his dear Château de Candiac near Nîmes. He hoped the harvest would be good. He hoped that Monsieur le Curé of Vauvert, the Château village, was not forgetting to celebrate a weekly Mass for him, as had been promised. He had need of Masses. But chiefly his reflections dwelt on the little circle at home: his mother, wife and children. He was a devoted family man. Reports had reached him that one of his daughters had died. Anguished, he did not yet know which it was. "It must be poor Mirète," he pondered, "who was so like me and whom I loved so much." The others, thank God, were prospering: his son, the Chevalier de Montcalm, a colonel; another daughter well married . . .

A knock at the door recalled him to Canada. "Entrez."

"Mon Général," one of his aides reported, "an English officer, a lieutenant, was today taken prisoner beyond their camp in the direction of Ange-Gardien by a party of Canadians and Indians. Do you wish to examine him yourself?"

"How was he taken?"

"Apparently he was out reconnoitering with one platoon. The English are no match for the Canadians at that work. They were all but surrounded when one of our savages gave the war whoop. The detachment broke and ran. This officer, who showed more courage than sense, covered the retreat, if you could call it that, and was cut off. He put up a good fight against several of the Indians until Pierre Laurent the Canadian closed in and saved his scalp. It was a near thing, I understand."

"His name?"

"Richard 'Ammond. Something like that."

"Regiment?"

"Lascelles's Forty-seventh."

"Hm-m. A regular, then. They generally use the Rangers for reconnaissance. Where is he now?"

"We have him here, monseigneur."

"Well, fetch an interpreter, and show Mistair 'Ammond in. He may tell us something, though I doubt it. Englishmen are apt to be close-mouthed."

"You will not need an interpreter, mon Général. The man speaks perfect French. He might even pass for a Frenchman. Makes a very agreeable impression."

Montcalm's black eyebrows lifted, his aquiline face sharpened. "Ah-hah? Does he so? I'm the more curious to see him. I hope he was blindfolded after crossing our lines."

"But yes, mon Général."

The Marquis shifted his chair to face the door and waited thoughtfully. A regular. Spoke French. Could be taken for a Frenchman. Pleasant impression. Hm-m. Montcalm was not born yesterday. He knew all the tricks of war.

"The prisoner, mon Général."

"You can leave us alone, Marcel, but stand at the door."

Montcalm's sharp eyes missed nothing of Richard's appearance, his height, build, well-made uniform, powerful hands, dark features. Certainly not English, but not altogether French. Perhaps Italian or Spanish. Queer.

"Approach, Monsieur le Lieutenant," he beckoned. "Permit me to ask if you are English by birth or merely serving with the English. Your aspect isn't quite — shall we say? — Anglo-Saxon."

"Perhaps not," said Richard, "and yet — By the way, have I indeed the honor of addressing the Marquis de Montcalm?"

"I am Montcalm."

"Why, then, monseigneur —" the lieutenant's courtly bow and perfect French were alike notable — "let me present the homage of my father, Milord de Marny, who informed me, before we parted, that he had once the extreme pleasure of meeting your Excellence in Paris when he was ambassador there."

"Marny!" exclaimed the other. "*You are his son?*"

"On the wrong side of the blanket, monseigneur. But he is good enough to acknowledge me."

The General's manner, crisp until then, unbent. He recalled Marny's family name of Hammond, and could see the likeness between him and the young prisoner. He recalled, too, the gossip that linked Marny with the House of Stuart. To a French nobleman, royal blood, however derived, was venerable.

"The side of the blanket, monsieur," he said cordially, "is in my opinion of small consequence compared with the character and parts which I am prepared to believe you possess. Indeed, though an enemy, I esteem Milord de Marny — as who does not? We met — let me see . . . yes, in the salon of my distant relative, Madame des Landes."

This was an opening that Richard had not anticipated, but he made the most of it. "Which reminds me," he said, "that I have another pleasant duty to perform with respect to your Excellence. Madame des Landes has been visiting in England, where I had the privilege of her favor. She most graciously charged me to give you her compliments and tendres amitiés, if I should have the occasion of conveying them."

But this seemed too pat for Montcalm, and it revived his suspicions. What was Amélie doing in England after the declaration of war? How did a casual prisoner happen to have so many recommendations to him? It began to look like a pattern. A clever rogue could easily catch at that reference to the salon in Paris and develop it.

"Indeed?" the General said dryly. "A charming woman and at

324

one time beautiful. Unfortunately a brunette shows age more quickly than a blond. She has fine dark eyes, however, and delightful manners. Twenty years ago, she was a reigning beauty. I hope she is well."

Unconscious of the trap, Richard stared. "Alas, monseigneur, you have evidently another lady in mind. Twenty years ago, Madame des Landes was still in the nursery. She could hardly be called a brunette . . ."

As an honest man, Montcalm felt embarrassed. But he was not quite satisfied.

"What is the Christian name of the Madame des Landes you refer to, monsieur?"

"Amélie, the wife of Comte Hercule des Landes, whom I had also the honor of meeting two years ago in Italy. She told me that her mother was in some way related to your Excellency. Her father, I believe, was an Irish nobleman."

There was no question about the authenticity of this. Montcalm had even heard of the des Landes's visit to Italy. He forced an uneasy laugh. "Amélie, to be sure." And, getting up from his chair, "Monsieur, I beg your pardon. I hope you will forgive the small ruse on my part. Since you are completely unknown to me, I wished to test your acquaintance with my kinswoman. There are a good many rascals in the world. — Pray be seated. One can hardly speak of welcome in these circumstances, but at least be assured of my consideration."

Richard expressed his thanks, but Montcalm's finesse put him doubly on his mettle. The Frenchman would be no easy dupe.

"Tell me about your capture," added the Marquis. "I trust you were not badly treated."

"No, monseigneur, I retained, as you see, my scalp and my clothes. Your savages were less than polite, but" — he glanced at the swollen knuckles of one hand — "we reasoned together."

"Ce sont de sales messieurs," agreed the General, who had no love for his Indian allies. "God knows I have had my trials with them. But how does it happen that regulars of the Forty-seventh were out on reconnaissance? I would have expected Rangers or Light Infantry."

This, Richard knew, was the beginning of his real test; and here flawless acting became necessary. Montcalm had probably accepted Lord Marny and Amélie des Landes, but that did not mean that he was off guard or uncritical of the prisoner. His black eyes looked innocent but were nonetheless shrewd. To act the part of a blockhead, Richard decided, would be no less suspicious than to show himself too clever. He must improvise a character somewhere in between: a young lieutenant, the son of a wealthy nobleman, rather spoiled, fashionably superficial, bored with the army, where he was killing time until he could enter Parliament — in short, something of a coxcomb or, in French, a *petit maître*, like many of the subalterns in Montcalm's army.

So, with regard to the reconnaissance, he declared that God alone could answer for Colonel Hale, who took pleasure in hardening his men by needless exertions of all kinds. For what could be gained by tramping around in the woods save wet uniforms and muddy shoes? Anyone knew that the Canadians were there without reconnoitering. It seemed to Richard especially uncalled-for today, since everybody would have work enough breaking camp tomorrow. But so it was in the army. However, Richard was glad the men had got off and, except for the pleasure of this interview, he wished he had himself, as the Marquis could well imagine . . .

Breaking camp. This, if true, was big news. It would account for the activity which Montcalm had observed through his glass during the day. But nothing in his face showed particular interest, nor did he at once guide Richard back to the point. Like a good host, he encouraged him rather to talk about himself, his prospects in England, likes and dislikes. He interrupted only to call for a bottle of wine, which he hoped Monsieur 'Ammond would find to his taste, and then with charming courtesy drank to the latter's health and Lord Marny's. Under such mellowing influences, the lieutenant's tongue wagged faster. If Englishmen were usually close-mouthed, this one was an inexhaustible spigot, emitting froth for the most part but with here and there a speck of gold.

Yes, likely enough, thought Montcalm, Wolfe's brigadiers were beginning to champ the bit. Likely enough, if the English struck camp at the Montmorency, they were either lifting the siege or preparing one last effort. The concentration of ships above the town, including ships of the line and flat-bottomed boats, gave support to the young fool's unconscious hints of a major attack building up against Cap Rouge or Pointe-aux-Trembles. If so, excellent. De Bougainville was on the alert. He had troops and batteries enough to contain it. Even in the event that a landing was forced at great cost, there were still miles between the shattered remnants of the attack and the walls of Quebec. On the other hand, Montcalm did not fail to draw the inference, from a remark or two, that this might be only a feint to put him off balance, and that the real attack might fall below the town if he weakened his defenses there. Why should he weaken them, unless Bougainville were defeated? No, let the English strike upstream at Cap Rouge or downstream at Beauport, they would be equally well received.

All this, he astutely gathered, crumb by crumb, from a mass of nonsense and unrelated chat. He found it tedious but repaying. On the whole, he had not learned one tenth so much from any other prisoner.

"I grieve, Monsieur 'Ammond, that General Wolfe is in the state of health you describe. He is a brilliant soldier. I shall defeat him, if possible, but I would not have his illness deprive me of that credit. You admire him, of course?"

"Ah, but extravagantly, monseigneur," Richard said. "Who could help admiring him! I protest it's heartbreaking to see him so infirm. Nobody thinks there's much hope for him."

"Don't they?" returned Montcalm. "Well, then, mark my words. A man of that kind does not flicker out. He'll end like a thunderstroke. I don't deceive myself."

"C'est bien possible," murmured Richard. And, with livelier interest, "By the way, I hope that the Quebec ladies I had the pleasure of meeting are well — Mesdames Duchesnay and Magnan, among others. Delightful! Pray, monseigneur, give them my compliments."

"Freluquet!" thought the Marquis, but he smiled. "So you were the gallant who entertained them so well at General Wolfe's supper? On the violin, I believe?"

"Yes." Richard looked embarrassed. "Of course no man of fashion ought to admit a knack for the fiddle. Rather silly. But I learned the hang of it in Venice. The ladies seemed to enjoy a few airs I played them of Scarlatti and Galuppi. Do you like music, monseigneur?"

"Now and then." Montcalm suppressed a yawn. He was tired of

327

Hammond. That the scatterbrained young lieutenant played a fiddle put somehow the final stamp on him. Besides, he had been pumped dry.

And yet, suppose (the idea occurred suddenly), suppose he was not the fop he appeared. Something about him, some hint of experience — his big hands, perhaps, his irregular dark face — clashed with the foppish impression. If he was not a fool, what a spy he would make, with his knowledge of French and plausible giddiness. In that case, he would be glad to give his parole and would feel no compunction about breaking it.

The Marquis suggested: "Unfortunately, monsieur, we must now discuss the terms of your detention. Disposed in your favor as I am, I would make them as generous as possible. If you will give me your word of honor not to escape nor commit any act of hostility against France until the end of the war, you would be permitted some freedom within the city of Quebec. Under *act of hostility*, I naturally include any uncensored communication with the enemy. But of course you know the laws governing parole and the consequences of breaking them." Montcalm's thought added: "I shall keep an eye on you more than you suppose, my musical young friend."

Unexpectedly Richard shook his head. "I thank you, monseigneur, for your condescension, but I can't avail myself of it, at least while our army is in Canada. You will easily understand why."

"Frankly, I don't," said the General, though he felt relieved. "There's nothing dishonorable about a parole. I had no hesitation in giving mine to the Austrians when I was captured at Piacenza."

"Yes, Monsieur le Marquis, but the other British officers in your hands have either not been given that privilege or have declined it. I know some of them personally: Captains Grow, Mayors, Holborn, Mr. Stadford, for instance — good fellows, all of them. How would I look, free and at ease by your Excellence's special favor, while they sit in prison? No, no, monseigneur, it would reflect on my honor. I must beg to be excused."

"As you please," said Montcalm, now completely reassured. "Of course, you compel me to severity. You will be housed in the common prison, since there are no other facilities. However, I shall do what I can for your comfort there. And now, by your leave . . ."

He called for his aide, on duty outside, and when the latter entered: "Monsieur 'Ammond refuses to give his parole for reasons of sentiment which are much to his credit. You will therefore conduct him in person to the prison, Marcel. But I especially desire that he be assigned to the best available quarters and receive the treatment of a gentleman recommended to me both on the score of his birth and connections. Please look to it. — Monsieur 'Ammond is the son of Milord de Marny, at one time ambassador to France. Farewell, monsieur, or rather au revoir, for I shall hope to renew our conversation at a later time."

Accompanying the aide, Richard breathed a sigh of relief. His mission had been well launched.

But, once more alone, Montcalm stood pondering the information that had been given him. How much it was worth, he would know soon enough. If the enemy actually broke camp at the Montmorency, it would tend to authenticate Hammond's other slips of the tongue. Then the Marquis could get off a dispatch to Bougainville and stand ready alike at Cap Rouge and Beauport. With the unscalable cliffs along the river, there could be no other alternative. Yes, it looked like the beginning of the end. He would hold Quebec. And to God the glory!

XLVIII

AS compared with the cell he had occupied in the Pozzi at Venice, Richard found his room in the Quebec prison almost luxurious. Built into the thickness of the wall, it was long and narrow, fourteen feet by eight. But it overlooked the interior court from an upper window; and, unlike other British prisoners, who were crowded nine to a cell and slept three in a bed, he had his quarters to himself. Besides, these were reasonably free from vermin, all the more as a miraculous gold piece made a servant of the jailer, who cleaned the place and provided extra rations, books and candles. Except for the window bars and the gloom of the prison, it would have been a decent enough billet anywhere.

Distractions, too, of different kinds, relieved the monotony after a day or so. It did not take long for the news to spread that the son of a well-known English statesman had been captured. That he was *très sympathique,* a young officer of distinguished manners who spoke perfect French, and that Monsieur de Montcalm had shown him extreme politeness. The Governor General de Vaudreuil, not to be outdone by his subordinate, summoned Richard for examination to the Palace. The Intendant, Monsieur Bigot, attracted by the fame of Lord Marny's wealth, like a rat to cheese, called on the prisoner and offered him civilities. The Quebec ladies whom Richard had entertained at Wolfe's supper now returned the compliment with a social visit and trifling gifts of table delicacies. And all these notable people were alike impressed by his good breeding, lack of English reserve, and his amusing small talk. They were pleased also to gather that the British army was discouraged and about to raise the siege after a last demonstration either at Cap Rouge or Beauport. Then, too, the prison doctor, Lambert, who enjoyed gossip, called daily on the pretext of some bruises that Richard had got in his struggle with the savages. And the jailer, struck by his prisoner's evident importance, often dropped in to pass the time of day.

These contacts were not only entertaining but informative. They disclosed piecemeal the misery of Quebec, half in ruins from the English batteries, short of food, impoverished by the war for a long time to come even if it succeeded in resisting capture. The Canadian militia, drawn from the farms and urgently needed at home for the harvest, chafed at the service and were prone to desertions. Homesteads and hamlets had been here and there burned at Wolfe's orders in retaliation for civilian hostility. The plight of women and children, taking refuge with their livestock in the forests, grew daily worse. Richard could sense, too, the friction between Vaudreuil and Montcalm, which represented the cleavage at every level between the French regulars and the colonial population. He could smell the corruption that permitted Bigot to keep a fine table and entertain lavishly in spite of the siege. On the military side, he learned the disposition of Montcalm's forces below the city and upstream at Cap Rouge. He heard some talk of posting the Regiment of Guienne on the plateau west of Quebec, but nothing came of it. Because of the cliffs, no attack could be delivered there.

Some of all this would perhaps be of interest to Wolfe if it could be conveyed to him. But, rack his brains as he might, Richard could think of no way of escape. The doctor and jailer, though friendly, were honest. The smallest nibble at corrupting them, if it did not succeed, would alert suspicion and render escape doubly impossible. The prison was well built and well guarded. The methods he had heard of in famous escapes of the past did not apply here. Those prisoners — such, for example, as Giacomo Casanova, who had broken out of the Piombi in Venice three years ago — had had plenty of time to make their plans. But Richard knew that he had only ten days and these were rapidly slipping by. At the end of a week, he was no closer toward solving his problem than at the beginning of it.

Meanwhile, he picked up rumors of the British operations, which seemed to be following the pattern that Wolfe had indicated. The camp on the Montmorency had been struck and the troops shifted to the Isle of Orléans. It was believed that most of them were still there, though detachments had been observed marching upstream along the South Shore. This pointed to an attack at Cap Rouge or Pointe-aux-Trembles. And certainly the British ships were active in that direction, drifting up and down with the tide, as if probing for a landing place, while Bougainville, equally alert, kept his troops on the march abreast of them. It might be only a feint, however, to divert attention from Beauport, below the town, which had been Wolfe's favorite point of attack from the beginning. The major force of the fleet lay opposite Beauport, and probably the greater part of the army. So, Montcalm held firm east and west.

To Richard, at his wit's end, it began to look as if he were out of action, whatever happened. The English would deliver their blow and most likely be repulsed. In that case, they would sail off, leaving him indefinitely in Quebec. It was a bleak prospect that set him pacing his cell, concocting schemes of escape which he realized were impossible. Worse still, he could see no point in the sacrifice imposed on him. If he could have felt that he had accomplished anything of value in his talk with Montcalm, he would have faced a long captivity with some cheerfulness. But why send him to inform the Marquis in advance of plans which the latter could see developing with his own eyes? Wolfe had hinted that the information might be misleading, and Richard recalled the General's cryptic reference to other plans which he did not choose to mention. There was some hope in this. And yet what other plans could there be? The possibilities were limited by the few landing places along the north shore of the river.

Footsteps outside, the clash of the jailer's keys and grating of the lock, interrupted these reflections one somber afternoon eight days after Richard's capture. He had hurriedly caught up a book and seated himself, when the door opened upon Monsieur François Bigot followed by the obsequious jailer. It was the second time that the all-powerful Intendant had called on him, and Richard showed himself duly sensible of the honor.

Bigot was an ugly, pimply-faced man in the late fifties, who revealed the fox in spite of hail-fellow manners; but he had a sharp intelligence, energy and practice of the world that somehow made him impressive. This side of him vaguely recalled Tromba, and the thought of the Cavaliere flitted through Richard's mind as he exchanged compliments with his visitor.

"I was wondering," said Bigot, "how prison life is agreeing with you, Monsieur 'Ammond, and wished to satisfy myself that you are well treated."

"Thanks to good Monsieur Jules here"— Richard nodded at the jailer — "and in great part, I'm convinced, to your own favor, Monsieur l'Intendant, I'm not only well treated but pampered."

"At least, I see you have books," remarked the other, picking up the volume that Richard had laid down. "I read very little myself. But, tiens! Here's one I *have* read. La Rochefoucauld, eh? There's a sound writer. Looks at life in the nude — the only way to look at it." He turned over a page. "Hm-m! Take this: *There are few chaste women who aren't tired of their trade.* Ha, ha! What could be truer?" And, putting the book aside, "Well, I'm glad you have no complaints, Monsieur 'Ammond."

"Except for the confinement, none at all."

"And that," Bigot retorted, "is your own fault. If you hadn't refused your parole, you'd be out and around Quebec now." He gave a leer. "I can think of certain ladies who regret it."

Richard sighed. "You flatter me. But I believe I explained —"

The Intendant laughed. "Bah! Scruples of sentiment. You must be a rich man. Sentiment's the one luxury I've never been able to afford." He glanced at the jailer. "You can leave us, Maître Jules. I'll let you know when my visit with Monsieur is over."

His complete authority showed in the man's subservience.

"As Monseigneur wishes," he murmured, and bowed himself out.

Richard waved Bigot to the single chair in the cell and took a seat on the bed. He wondered about the motive for this repeated visit. That it had a personal point, rather than interest in the prisoner's comfort, could be taken for granted. The thought of Tromba recurred, and, with it the shadowy stirring of an idea.

"I'm amazed," he said, disregarding the interruption, "that there's anything which Monsieur l'Intendant Bigot is unable to afford — even sentiment. I had a glimpse of your palace the other day" — he nodded in the direction of that building, which stood in front of the prison — "when I was summoned before Monsieur de Vaudreuil. Its appointments are really splendid. And I hear wonders of your country house, l'Hermitage. The King of France must be a generous master, Monsieur Bigot."

Since the King's generosity consisted in having been well plucked by his Intendant, there was some irony in this that Richard carefully concealed.

Visibly pleased, the other took snuff, but he shrugged modestly. "Generous indeed. Besides, some of my private investments have turned out well. No, I've not done badly. But, after all, I'm a mere worm compared with your great father, Monsieur 'Ammond. What a fortune he must have!"

It occurred to Richard that Bigot had referred to Lord Marny's wealth during his first call. Evidently it was much on his mind. If so, it might be useful to find out why.

"Yes," said Richard, "very considerable, I believe."

"Come," Bigot smiled, "more than considerable. Finance is my profession. I've heard him spoken of as one of the richest peers in England — and that means something."

"I suppose it does."

"Have you any idea what Milord's income amounts to?"

There were various ways of answering this impudent question. Richard could truthfully profess ignorance, or he could play down Marny's wealth; but, if he wanted to learn what Bigot really had in mind, he had better play it up.

Multiplying the probable figure by ten, he said carelessly: "Oh, I imagine in the neighborhood of a million livres — perhaps more."

Since the French and English livre had two very different values, Bigot, though impressed, put in: "You mean French, of course."

"But no, monsieur, English, of course — pounds sterling."

The Intendant gasped, his sharp rat-eyes goggled.

"One million pounds sterling! Twenty-five million francs! But that's fabulous. That's — You must be wrong."

"No, I think not." Richard now dived into fiction. "You see, in addition to his very profitable estates in Kent, he has coal mines around Newcastle, receives handsome rentals from his properties in London, and has largely invested in the East India Company. He owns, too, immense lands in Virginia, which, by the way, he has offered to me. No, I should think his income far exceeds the figure I mentioned, though, of course, I can't be sure."

"Twenty-five million francs a year!" Bigot repeated in the hushed voice of adoration. "Twenty-five million . . . God! Think of it! Think of it! . . ."

But now the tenuous idea, so faint that Richard had barely been conscious of it, suddenly took form in his mind. He had been a dunce. He began to see the problem of his escape through Tromba's eyes. Would the Cavaliere waste time on hairbreadth schemes if his tongue and his wits could help him? He would not. Being just as unscrupulous a shark as Bigot, he would play on Bigot's hunger.

"Yes," said Richard, "my respected father has a sound philosophy. Let me add, entre nous, that I completely share it. He takes an enlightened view of life which, I imagine, Monsieur Bigot, resembles your own. He is not avaricious, but he knows the value of money in terms of pleasure and in terms of power. How often he has instructed me on that point! 'My dear boy,' he says, 'remember the proverb *If money leads the way, all paths are open.'*"

"A profound thought," nodded Bigot reverently.

"Yes," said Richard, with a mental blush for the lie, "the first Latin he ever taught me was *Quaerenda pecunia primum est; virtus post nummos.*"

"What does that mean?"

"Get money first; virtue comes after. Do you agree, Monsieur Bigot?"

334

"Emphatically — but confidentially, mon cher monsieur. I would not choose to publish it, nor would Milord de Marny, I reckon. Grand Dieu, what a man! Twenty-five million! I wish I had the honor of his acquaintance."

Richard leaned forward. "You take the words from my lips. I wish he had the honor of yours. The profit to you both might be incalculable. My father is always alert to new openings. Suppose you pointed one out to him here in Canada — something to do with the fur trade, for instance. A secret partnership, eh, Monsieur Bigot? Your experience, his money. By God, between the two of you . . ."

The Intendant's eyes glittered; his lips were moist. Possibilities loomed, a whole new horizon of chicanery.

"I see," he muttered, "yes . . . Only —" he shook his head — "this damned war."

Richard nodded. "But it won't last. You know very well that England will take Canada in the end, if not this time, then next year or the next. Consider her mastery of the seas. Consider the New England colonies. You're cut off; they're growing. And when Canada falls, it would be useful to have a friend in England."

It might have occurred to Bigot that the frivolous young lieutenant was showing an unexpected shrewdness, but he had his own affairs to consider.

"What are you suggesting, Monsieur 'Ammond?"

"Merely the idea that a man of great intelligence and cool judgment like yourself might wish to play safe."

"In what way?"

"Why, this. When the forthcoming English attack is repulsed, as it probably will be, and the fleet sails, let it carry a message from you to Milord de Marny. Make him a business proposal. Offer him an attractive investment. Ma foi, he'll think twice before declining it. By God, what do you lose? If Canada remains French, you're still Intendant but with new funds to draw on. If Canada falls, you have a secret partner and powerful friend at court to urge that Monsieur François Bigot's vast experience would be of use to the new government. It's as simple as that."

The Intendant gave a twisted grin. "You're a bold man, monsieur. In other words, you're suggesting treason."

"Call it so if you like," Richard smiled. "I had the impression that we were speaking in confidence and that we both held the same belief in the importance of money."

"And how to convey such a proposal?" the other bantered, as if no more than amused at the notion. "Would Admiral Saunders agree to carry a letter from me to your illustrious father, even if I were fool enough to put my name to it?"

"There's the trouble, Monsieur Bigot," Richard admitted. "Of course, if I didn't happen to be penned up here when the fleet sails, I should be glad to offer my services. As it is, there doesn't seem to be any other way. A pity. The idea was interesting."

Bigot dropped the amused manner. "Why should you be glad to offer your services?" he probed. "What assurance would I have —"

"None, monsieur, none — except, to be frank, my own profit. Surely I don't need to explain that if I put Milord de Marny in the way of a good thing, I wouldn't lose by it. He's rather fond of me. I could expect a handsome mark of his favor. Perhaps — who can tell? — he might allow me to conduct this affair for him. And you and I know, Monsieur l'Intendant —" Richard gave a slight wink — "that even the handling of money is profitable. However, why discuss it? Here I am in your comfortable prison."

Bigot chuckled. "I can see you're a regular fellow, Monsieur 'Ammond; I have rarely met anyone so congenial."

"Je vous remercie, Monsieur Bigot. May I return the compliment?"

There was a pause while the Intendant offered his snuffbox to Richard and then refreshed himself. His face was a study of blandness underlaid with cunning.

"I agree it's an interesting thought," he said finally. "If Milord de Marny would care to place funds to my account for the purchase and sale of goods, I could promise him a hundred per cent on his money, for, as it happens, I control the market in Canada. The transaction could be made through the Hopes of Amsterdam, who will answer for me and with whom details could be discussed. On the other hand, if Canada falls to the English, I should be governed by circumstances. I am internationally minded, Monsieur 'Ammond. I have grown devoted to this people, and certainly no one knows better than I how to get the most out of the colony. You could hint as much to your father."

"I could, indeed, Monsieur Bigot, if I wasn't detained here." Under a show of resignation, Richard felt tense. The shark was sniffing the bait. "Unfortunately," he added, "London is three thousand miles away. But, among other functions, aren't you the Minister of Justice in Canada?"

Bigot did not pretend to misunderstand. "Yes, of civil justice. You are a military prisoner, and, as such, not under my jurisdiction. I confess, without underestimating you, that if a lieutenant of foot were restored to the English army, it would seem to me of no military importance. But that is outside my province. I could not meddle with it. I should be open to criticism. Monsieur de Montcalm is no friend of mine."

Richard nodded carelessly. It would not do to seem eager, though he knew well enough that Bigot, with the Governor General in his pocket, could meddle with anything he pleased.

"Well, then, there we are, Monsieur l'Intendant. As my father has often pointed out to me from his own experience, a noble scheme is often blocked by some trifling detail. — Speaking of Monsieur de Montcalm, you must admit that he's a great soldier."

"I admit nothing of the kind. He should have fallen on the English when they broke camp at the Montmorency. He missed a great occasion there."

"It's conceivable," murmured Richard, recalling one of his "slips" when talking with Montcalm, "that General Wolfe may have foreseen the possibility, and that the Marquis avoided a trap."

But Bigot was not interested in strategy. He returned to the topic in hand and gave Richard an intent look. "It all depends on how much you wish to rejoin your regiment."

"Does it, monsieur?"

"Yes. You have money. I know, because your jailer had a small debt to me which he repaid with an English gold piece."

"I have a few coins," Richard nodded, "that I keep in a secret pocket. Your savages overlooked them when I was captured."

"A few coins go far in Canada," said Bigot. "Well, then, you have money. No doubt you have courage. Perhaps you will have opportunity. Need I say more?"

"You mean Maître Jules? Dr. Lambert?"

"Certainly *not*," Bigot coughed and apparently changed the subject. "I'm concerned that you're so closely shut in here. A young man needs exercise. I'll see what can be done. An evening stroll under guard in the neighborhood of the prison might be arranged. I'll provide the guard."

Richard's thought sang hosanna. The shark had taken the hook.

"How can I thank you enough, Monsieur l'Intendant?"

"De rien, de rien. Let me assure you again of my esteem. Twenty-five million francs a year, you said? Grand Dieu!"

Bigot stood up. There were further compliments. But at the door he turned back.

"Remember the name I gave you in Amsterdam?"

"Hope, I believe."

"Right. Thomas and Adrian Hope. The profit, one hundred per cent at least. I say *at least*. Remember, too, Monsieur 'Ammond, that if by some chance Wolfe's attack should not fail, François Bigot is a valuable man."

"I'm not likely to forget it, Monsieur l'Intendant."

The door closed. Richard felt that Tromba would have been proud of him, but he had a bad taste in his mouth.

XLIX

IN the vague but lively expectation of escape that Bigot had left with him, Richard made the most of such time as he might still have in prison to bring his dossier of information up to date for the benefit of Wolfe. He enriched the jailer with another gold coin and begged Lambert to drink a bottle of wine with him, when the doctor called the same evening. Adroitly, he pumped them both, imagining that Wolfe would be especially interested in any forces west of the city, since those east of it were fully known.

But he added little to what he had already learned. For double assurance, there was a post of a hundred men and a battery of four guns that guarded an insignificant little cove called the Anse du Foulon a mile and a half upstream from the city; beyond this lay a couple of other posts and some cannon at Sillery. Otherwise, Richard could hear of no detachments short of Bougainville's pickets eight or nine miles along. And actually none were needed; for the English did not have wings, and the towering cliffs east of Cap Rouge put any landing in strength out of the question.

This fact was emphasized by a casual remark of the honest doctor's, who happened to be discussing some of Bigot's clique, Cadet, Varin, Péan, and other exploiters of the King and the colony.

"Or take Vergor," he said, "There's another prime rat."

"Who's Vergor?" Richard asked.

"The poltroon who commanded at Beauséjour in Acadia and sold it out to the English in '55. He was court-martialed and should have been hanged. But he's a crony of Bigot's and the Governor's. They got him off, restored him his rank. Only they couldn't get Monsieur de Montcalm to give him a charge of any consequence. The Marquis has put him where he can do no damage at least."

"Where's that?"

The doctor gave a puff of amusement. "In command at the Anse du Foulon. He might as well be guarding a windmill for all the importance it has. He's the joke of Quebec. But trust a rat like that to make the most of anything. He's supposed to have a hundred men, yet I understand he lets half of them off to work their farms provided they work his. There's Bigotry for you," added Lambert, with a laugh at his own pun.

Yes, thought Richard, Quebec needed no guards east of Cap Rouge.

This talk with the doctor took place on the evening of September eighth. During the whole of the ninth, Richard held himself in readiness for the first indication that the opportunity Bigot meant to give him was at hand. He reviewed and analyzed the Intendant's obvious hints. Certainly Bigot would contrive matters so as to be free of suspicion himself. He would furnish a guard who would take Richard out for an airing, and that guard would be corruptible. This covered the Intendant's reference to money and opportunity. After that, no doubt, Richard would have to depend on himself. He reasoned that the airing in question could only take place at the end of the afternoon close upon nightfall. Bigot had mentioned an *evening* stroll. Once free of the guard, Richard had only one route to follow. He must round the city on his left and head west until he came somewhere within swimming distance of the British ships operating in the direction of Cap Rouge. The much shorter distance from the mouth of the St. Charles to the South Shore was blocked by the concentration of French troops below the town.

As the afternoon drew to an end, he felt increasingly on edge. He had shifted the gold from his shoes to his pockets in order to have it in readiness and also to make walking easier. But night came; the turnkey brought him his supper; and that day could be written off.

Perhaps Bigot needed time to select the proper guard. Perhaps he had been busy with other affairs. Or he might have changed his mind. Or again he might have decided that there was luck in leisure. He had no special reason for haste. But to Richard, tossing on his bed and weighing one possibility against the other, time was crucial. Tomorrow, the ten days mentioned by Wolfe would be up. The English attack might be lanched; and if it were repulsed, Bigot might be planning to let Richard escape just in time to rejoin the defeated army before it sailed. There was one encouragement. It had rained steadily for the past two days. Such weather was apt to hold up operations.

Monday, the tenth, dawned equally wet. The tense hours dragged by; the afternoon light faded; it was night again, and not a sign from Bigot. The ten-day allowance had now completely expired.

Maître Jules arrived with supper and stopped to chat. To Richard's added frustration, he reported increasing activity up at Cap Rouge, where the English ships were drifting up and down with the tide, keeping poor Monsieur de Bougainville's troops continually on the march. But signs of preparation had been noted, too, in the ships opposite Beauport.

"Let them play-act as much as they please up the river," grinned Jules. "Monsieur de Montcalm is on to their tricks. He knows that their main force is down here, and he's not budging. The English don't trouble him as much as slim rations. But I hear that grain boats are expected day after tomorrow night from Monsieur de Bougainville's camp, if there's no battle before then."

This had no interest for Richard, but he said absently: "You'd think they'd send grain across country — what with the English ships in the river."

Jules explained that that would take too many wagons and horses;

340

that the flat-bottomed boats ran no risk if they kept close in shore and drifted down in the darkness with the ebb tide. "We've never lost one of them yet."

He broke off to observe: "Monsieur is not eating tonight. Monsieur seems depressed. No doubt it is want of fresh air, as Monseigneur l'Intendant remarked the other day when he had been calling on Monsieur. He talked of furnishing a guard to take Monsieur out for a walk of an evening, since, of course, earlier in the day it would excite too much comment."

Richard hoped that his face did not betray him. He managed to answer carelessly: "Yes, Monsieur l'Intendant was very civil. I hope he hasn't forgotten."

"By no means. But naturally Monsieur would not wish to go out in the heavy rain we've been having. I expect by tomorrow . . ."

So *that* was the reason — the stupid weather! Richard's airing had to seem natural, and nothing would look more peculiar than to take a stroll in a downpour. Damnation! What with the attack gathering at Cap Rouge, tomorrow night would probably be too late.

He forced himself to sound languid. "Well, Maître Jules, the way I'm beginning to feel, fresh air and exercise would even be worth a soaking. If it's at all possible tomorrow, I'll be more than ready."

The jailer expressed the hope that it would be possible and took his leave.

That night Richard slept in snatches broken by the ominous, unhurried march of the rain.

Tuesday, the eleventh, offered no better than the preceding days. Rain all morning. But then, by midafternoon, a letup, though with heavy clouds and the threat of more rain at any moment. Richard fretted up and down his cell, dreading the next downpour, hoping against hope. Twilight began to gather about five. The rain still held off. Then at last he heard the welcome sound of footsteps approaching outside.

Maître Jules was pleased to inform Monsieur that the guard provided by Monseigneur l'Intendant awaited him at the courtyard entrance. Since it would very possibly start raining again before Monsieur returned, the jailer offered him his own overcoat and hat, but not only for reasons of the weather. Monsieur Bigot had graciously suggested that it would cause the English lieutenant less embarrassment if his scarlet uniform was not in evidence when he took his airing outside the prison. This was thoughtful indeed, because, by hook or by crook, Richard would have had to secure some disguise before heading across country; and the necessity had been much on his mind.

He had expected one guard; but he found two, lounging pipe in mouth on either side of the door leading into the courtyard. They were typical Canadian militiamen: broad-shouldered country fellows, dressed in little better than token uniforms, and each showing a strain of the Indian. One wore a battered felt hat and the other, a fur cap. They both carried muskets and knives.

"You know Monseigneur l'Intendant's orders," the jailer told them. "You are to walk where Monsieur the prisoner wishes, but you are not to enter the city nor leave this neighborhood. You are to return Monsieur here within a half hour."

The men growled assent and shouldered their muskets; Richard placed himself between them; the trio marched across the familiar courtyard and passed the sentry at the outer gate into the area that separated the prison from the Intendant's palace. Beyond this they emerged into the Rue St. Nicholas and turned downhill toward the harbor.

By now, dusk had fallen; and, what with the threatening weather and the supper hour, the street was almost deserted. Steep behind them rose the city with its walls and houses, casting a deeper gloom than elsewhere. In front, the shacks along the water already showed an occasional light.

Meanwhile, Richard for the first time realized the actual difficulties facing him. In his cell, it was easy enough to minimize them; but now that he had the promised chance he hardly knew what to do with it. Had Bigot in any way prepared the guards for an offer on his part? If so, they gave no indication of it, but trudged along taciturn and sullen. Language was another difficulty. They spoke a patois that Richard could hardly understand, though they grasped his French. Then, too, harder than anything else, was the time element. He had only a half hour in which to make his proposal, bribe the two men (if they were open to a bribe), and set off. Yet, tramping along in this fashion with two complete strangers, he could think of no way to broach the subject.

He asked them where they came from and gathered that it

was from some point east of Ange-Gardien. He queried about the harvest but learned only from monosyllables that it was good enough if there were any people to gather it. Weren't they tired of the war? Didn't they want to go home? They grunted and spat. He had heard that many good fellows were deserting and, indeed (drawing on his recent talk with Dr. Lambert), that some officers, notably Captain Vergor, let their men return to the farms. Didn't they wish they belonged to Vergor's company? More grunts and spitting.

Richard could think of nothing else but a flatfooted proposal, win or lose, when the clouds opened again, the rain poured down, and there was nothing for it but the inadequate eaves of a shed. The disgusted guards considered it time to turn back.

"Messieurs," said Richard in desperation. "I have a better idea. Isn't there a grogshop close by? We could all do with a drink, couldn't we? Maybe this will let up in a few minutes. Then we can go back. We'll be soaked through if we try it now."

For the first time, the men brightened. Yes, at the Veuve Étienne's around the corner — and many thanks to Monsieur.

It was a mean little pub, serving the waterfront, which lay a hundred yards off. Fortunately, at the moment, it had few guests; and Richard moved to a table in the farthest corner. Copying his guards, he ordered apple brandy, which a girl poured out for them in small glasses.

"Leave the bottle," he told her.

"Your money first, monsieur. That will make all of two francs."

He had had one of his gold pieces changed in the prison and now paid her an écu. "Keep the extra franc, m'amie."

She went off enchanted, and he was quick to note the impression that his liberality had made on the two militiamen.

"À votre santé, messieurs."

They emptied their glasses, which he refilled and kept refilling. The liquor was white and raw and burned like fire.

"That hits the spot, hein? That makes a man forget the rain."

"Vive Dieu, but yes. Monsieur says well."

The guards were visibly thawing. One of them filled his pipe, lighted it from the table candle, and leaned back. The other put oil into his grin.

"Monsieur is rich. Two francs for the eau de vie, a franc for the girl. Sainte Vierge! It's more than I earn in a month. No wonder Monseigneur Bigot is fond of Monsieur. He has a fine nose for money, that one. Pierre and I couldn't understand why a prisoner was given such favors, but now we can guess. We hope that Monsieur will have a few sous for us."

This was the opening that Richard needed. He had no time for finesse; the half hour was about up, though the guards, with three quarters of a bottle still in front of them, had forgotten time. It continued to pour outside. At the prison, Maître Jules would probably assume that they had taken shelter somewhere and would not be too much disturbed for a while.

"Drink up," said Richard, filling the other's glass. "If you're a sensible fellow, this is your lucky night." A coin rang on the table. "Do you know what that is?"

Both men reached for it, but the last speaker got it first.

"A franc piece?" He rubbed it between his thumb and forefinger. "No, it's a half sou," and added glumly, "Merde!"

"Hold it up to the light."

As the other brought the coin close to the candle, his jaw sagged. He sat staring. After a moment, he whispered, "Gold? Is it gold?"

"Give it here, François," growled the pipe smoker, and then in turn he twisted the coin, with the strange yellow gleam of it, in front of the candle. "Gold," he repeated in a hush of adoration. "A louis d'or. I saw one once at Monsieur le Curé's. Twenty francs in gold! What is that worth in sous?"

"Four hundred at least," breathed François, calculating. "Probably much more, because it's gold."

Richard detached the piece from Pierre's fingers.

"No, my friend, an English guinea is worth twenty-six francs at least and closer to thirty. That's six hundred sous." One by one, he rang three more guineas on the table. "There you are — twenty-four hundred sous. A tidy sum, eh?"

"A fortune!" François gasped.

The men had forgotten even to drink. They sat dazzled by the wealth in front of them.

Richard added another four guineas. They were doubtless unnecessary, but he considered escape cheap at eight guineas. The guards had almost stopped breathing.

"So, Messieurs, you have now four thousand, eight hundred sous before you. You have also a choice. You can return tonight to your farms, your wives and your children, as rich men. In that case, I shall leave you to finish the bottle and bid you farewell. *Or,* after bringing me to the prison, you can return to your barracks with empty pockets. In that case, let me add, I think Monsieur Bigot will consider you blockheads, as shall I. But the decision's yours."

There was no hesitation at all. Two calloused paws reached for the gold. Each of the men bit and examined his four coins before pocketing them.

"Monsieur knows," murmured Pierre, "that the Regiment of Guienne is encamped along the St. Charles. Perhaps we could guide Monsieur."

Richard shook his head. In the open country, he had more to fear from such guides than from the soldiers.

"It will not be necessary." He raised his glass. "Again to your health, messieurs, and good-by."

"To yours, monsieur — and bon voyage."

A moment later, secure from notice in his borrowed overcoat and hat, Richard slipped out into the almost complete darkness of the rain.

L

STRICTLY speaking, Quebec was no city, but a town of little more than twelve thousand, penned by its walls within the eastern tip of the long plateau that edged the St. Lawrence. Richard could therefore easily round it by proceeding northwest for a distance and then up the steep slopes of the Côte Sainte-Geneviève, which formed the northern side of the plateau. This would bring him out on the high, rolling plains west of the town. Here were a couple of roads, of which he must take the one nearest the river leading to the village of Sillery. After that, he would have to be guided by circumstances. If he were not prevented, an eight-mile walk would bring him in the neighborhood of the British ships upstream. Otherwise, he could always swim the St. Lawrence to the South Shore and perhaps connect with one of the English detachments which had been reported near the mouth of the small Etchemin River on that side.

Topographically, then, his task was reasonable enough. But he had to be alert to possible pursuit, and, worse still, he had to make his way in the pitch darkness through completely unfamiliar country. Above all he must avoid stumbling into any outpost or random party, whether French, Canadian or Indian. He did not speak the local dialect, and the very fact of a stranger wandering alone at night in such weather would be more than suspect. He decided, however, that the rain helped rather than hindered him. It discouraged pursuit and was apt to keep people indoors.

After hurrying on for a quarter of a mile, until the houses thinned out, he stopped behind a thicket to get rid of the telltale scarlet uniform under his overcoat, and stripped to his shirt and breeches. Into the pockets of these he transferred the rest of his money. Then, less encumbered for walking and less open to immediate discovery if he were held up, he put on Maître Jules's drenched garment again and pushed ahead.

Soon a faint blurring of bivouac fires showed in front and to the right, indicating the encampment of the Regiment of Guienne along the St. Charles. To avoid possible sentries on the outskirts of the camp, he kept well to the left against the steep slope of the plateau, feeling his way past an occasional house and stumbling through underbrush or garden patches. Finally, judging that he had passed the walls of the town above him, he turned to the left and made his way uphill over what seemed to be pasture land, strewn with boulders. Here, in the end, by great luck he found himself on a path and could make some speed. But an hour and a half had gone by since leaving the Veuve Étienne's before the position of a few dim lights in the city and the feel of the ground under his feet showed that he was on a level with Quebec. At this rate, groping through the darkness, circling houses and settlements, tangled in corn fields and thickets, it would take him at least another four hours to reach the neighborhood of Cap Rouge. His feet were clumps of mud. The jailer's heavy coat weighed like lead. Out of condition from his ten-day confinement, he already felt tired and winded.

At the moment, he must, if possible, find the Sillery road by crossing the plateau toward the river. But, in the thick darkness, he could only do this by guess, since the handful of lights he had first noticed in the town now disappeared behind a rise of land. However, he kept as straight a line as he could, and at one point came out on what seemed to be a road. This might or might not be the one to Sillery; but if not, it would bring him to Sainte-Foye at a considerable distance from the St. Lawrence. Fortunately he pushed on and after another blind half mile stumbled into a second road. Here, by feel rather than any other indication, he judged that the river lay ahead of him and therefore turned to the right.

The first part of his escape was now successfully over. He had only to trudge ahead, avoid the hamlet of Sillery and the post on guard there, rejoin the road farther west, and then take to the river before reaching Bougainville's encampment. With no clear notion of the time, he reckoned that it must be after eight. The rain still fell, but with luck he ought to reach one of Admiral Holmes's ships before midnight. He had gathered that a half-mile swim at that point would be enough.

Poor as the road was, it seemed luxury compared with his floundering walk across the fields; and, having scraped some of the mud from his shoes, he pressed on at a relatively good pace. By this time, he discounted pursuit: the rain and the night were both against it. He could rely, too, on Bigot's good offices, though doubtless these were limited in the case of an escaped military prisoner. Listening intently now and then, he could hear no sound of approach behind him. So, all was well. He pictured himself reporting next day to General Wolfe.

"Halte!" yelled a nearby voice out of the blackness. A dark lantern suddenly flashed in his eyes; there was a rush of feet on either side of him; hands gripped his arms.

"C'est bien lui, le fripon!" shouted the voice.

Absorbed by the thought of pursuit from behind, he had stupidly forgotten that parties of men taking a short cut through the city could block the roads ahead of him.

On sheer impulse, he fetched the lantern a kick that knocked it out of the bearer's hands, and at the same instant wrenched himself loose from the soldiers who had gripped his arms. His fist cracked against someone's face. He plunged from the road into what seemed to be a thicket at the left and struggled forward, gaining perhaps fifteen yards on the disorganized patrol. They now crashed behind him with shouts and oaths.

But the thicket proved to be a corn field, the tall stalks lashing him, plucking at his ankles, the furrows tripping him, as he floundered through. He could not run in his overcoat and stopped an instant to fling it off. Then on again, tugging his feet out of the wet earth.

However, it was no less difficult for his pursuers, who had to keep on his traces with only their ears to help them. By the time he was through the corn field, he had gained another fifteen yards. He now found himself on meadow grass, and dashed blindly along in the pitch darkness with no idea where he was going, except that by luck he had plunged left from the road and must therefore be approaching the river. With renewed yells, the party behind him broke into the open. Perhaps the white of his shirt could be dimly seen, for a pistol shot crashed and the bullet whistled near by. He bounded forward, remembering the hundred-foot cliffs somewhere ahead of him which he had once seen through a glass from the South Shore. The thought of suddenly dropping from this almost perpendicular wall was even more appalling than capture. He ran with his arms outstretched in front and narrowly missed colliding with a tree. Rounding it, he caught himself just in time, one foot in the air, the other on the edge of what seemed to be a drop. Here were the cliffs, and the hue and cry was closing in. He could not run along the curving brink of an abyss which he could not see. Desperately he lowered himself over the edge, slid down a yard or so, clutched at a bush, dug his toes in against a rock, and lay there prone at a sixty-degree angle. The chase passed above him, then, twenty paces further on, came to a sharp stop.

"Qui vive?" challenged someone. They had evidently encountered a sentry. "Halt or I fire!"

The pursuers identified themselves. No doubt they were asking the man on guard whether anyone had run past him. Farther along, other voices could be heard coming up. Richard thanked his stars that he had stopped in time. This must be Captain Vergor's post at the Anse du Foulon. A moment later he would have plunged into the center of it.

But his respite was short-lived. Footsteps were trooping back along the edge of the cliff.

"I tell you I saw him," someone panted — "a patch of white anyway. It disappeared around here. I'll bet he's lying low somewhere."

"Here comes a lantern," said another. "We'll have a look."

And Richard could now see against the trees above him a bobbing glimmer of light hurrying along from the direction of Vergor's encampment. He did not have a minute to lose. He would be in plain sight as soon as anyone held a lantern over the edge. He could either give himself up or continue down the cliff. There was no other choice.

Heart in mouth, he held on to the bush with one hand and reached for the stone at his feet with the other, then let himself down another two yards. The stone gave way; he started sliding, but came to a halt against a second bush. The noise he made set off a chorus of yells.

"Le voilà . . . le voilà . . . sacredieu . . . attends . . ."

The rays of the lantern showed vivid at the rim of the cliff, probing downward. Apparently the men caught sight of him.

"Hah . . . salaud . . . le voilà!"

A musket roared, then another.

A voice shouted, "Where's the path to the water?"

The reply came, "Up there, but look out for the abatis . . ."

A third musket went off.

So there was a path down the face of the cliff. Richard must get to the bottom before they could cut him off. He let go again and half crawled, half slid backward, digging in with fingers and toes, clutching at the dwarf undergrowth, now able to control his speed and again slithering helplessly. At one point, his legs shot out over a vertical drop. He managed to grip the edge of it, and lowering himself to arms' length could feel the continued slope under his feet. But the momentum carried him on face downwards at a hopeless pace. His legs were again in the air. He could not stop himself and catapulted over another drop, with the thought that this was the end, only to land heavily three feet beneath in a shallow pool of water.

For a few moments, he lay not so much stunned as incredulous that he had actually made the descent. He felt also as if he had been drawn over a gigantic washing board, and every bone ached.

But he had no time for reflection. His pursuers, following the path down to the little cove under Vergor's post, that lay a hundred yards upstream, would shortly be upon him if he did not take to the river.

Pulling himself together, he ripped off the shreds that remained of his shirt, together with his military gaiters, and finally his shoes. Then, retaining only his breeches, for the sake of the money in their pockets, he felt the cold of the water on his legs as he staggered out among the rocks along the shore.

Suddenly, from the right, came shouts and a scrambling of feet. He could see, too, the bobbing of a lantern. Again someone fired aimlessly into the dark. Crouching down, he tripped and reeled a yard further, then sank to his shoulders in the water and struck out, though at the same time the cold almost took his breath. He had last swum in the mild water of Venice; this seemed a different element. But it also revived him, cleared his head, and brought a fierce exhilaration. By this time, the men had reached his clothes and stood cursing on the shore.

To be free and in the river, however, did not mean safety. After a minute or two, he realized that his biggest effort lay ahead. No English ships were reported at this point. He must swim the river, and he had only the vaguest idea of the distance — perhaps a mile, perhaps two. Moreover, he could not swim it in a direct line because of the tide, now setting upstream. Where this would bring him on the South Shore, God only knew. In the complete blackness, he could see nothing and could only swim blindly stroke upon stroke.

A quarter of an hour of this, a half hour, perhaps less or more; he lost all notion of time. The first exhilaration of escape disappeared. He now felt merely the sense of cold and utter loneliness verging on panic. If he could only have seen what progress he was making or what distance he had yet to cover! But, for any help of that kind in the thick darkness, he might as well have been in mid-ocean. Already tired from the earlier efforts of the evening, he could not go on swimming indefinitely. But relaxing to float and catch his breath, the cold set him on again. What if his muscles cramped? What if he went down in the inky, hostile water? He found himself struggling an instant and realized that he had no chance at all

350

unless he kept such thoughts out of his mind. What was he doing here in the black river at the world's end? Unreal, fantastic, a dream. Men were only straws in a whirlpool of invisible, mad forces that had no purpose and no end . . .

How long had he been in the water? An hour? Two hours? He felt suddenly exhausted, went under and, in a last effort, managed a few more strokes. Then miraculously his feet struck something solid . . . though how he dragged himself out on the shore he never knew.

He came to his senses, coughing, with a throat on fire and a blinding light in his eyes.

"What'd I tell you!" said a voice in English. "Live and kicking. That rum would raise the dead. Give him another tot, mate."

Someone clicked a flask against Richard's teeth and poured. He exploded in another cough, then gradually became aware that he lay in what seemed to be a clump of black gaiters, and, lifting his eyes farther, saw the scarlet coats that topped them.

"Where am I?"

Exclamations answered. "By God, he's English!" — "Thought he was a Mounseer!" — "Where you are, mate? Why, they call this place the Etchemin River, and lucky for you we camped here to-night. You'd have been stiff by morning. Who're you? What happened? Drop off a ship or something?"

"No, swam the river." By now he recognized the regimental facings of the Royal Americans. He sat up. "I'm Lieutenant Hammond of the Forty-seventh! Who's in command of this platoon?"

The gaiters and scarlet coats stiffened.

"Mr. Walker, sir."

"My compliments to Mr. Walker. Pray report me to him and say that I am returning from a special mission to Quebec by the order of General Wolfe."

L I

THE decks of H.M.S. *Sutherland,* lying south of midstream off Cap Rouge, were as immaculate and orderly as the decks of a ship of the line ought to be. They breathed discipline, from their scoured planks to the ramrod stiffness of the marines on guard and the professional alertness of officers and sailors.

But to Richard, waiting for his interview with General Wolfe, something in addition to the usual snap and smartness of a man-of-war was evident. The air tingled with purpose. Footsteps rang louder and quicker; commands had a sharper bite; aides with dispatches put off or arrived; the cutter and long boats of the ship were being readied; signals parleyed with the signals of neighboring vessels. And behind the screen of ships, veiling their movements from French observation on the North Shore, he watched a gathering of barges, each capable of holding fifty men; while near by on the South Shore could be seen an occasional red-coated detachment, such as the one that had picked him up last night. Not only the fleet but the army was astir, especially upstream in the direction of St. Nicolas, where he understood the main force had assembled. Certainly the supreme effort of the campaign was pending on this forenoon of September twelfth. Thanks, perhaps, to the hampering weather of the past few days, which had held up operations, he had managed to arrive just in the nick of time.

Keeping out of the way as much as possible, he felt ill at ease in the improvised uniform which had been put together for him by his hosts of last night. As compared with the natty ship's company and the well-groomed orderlies, he looked ruffianly enough. His sleeves were three inches too short; coat and waistcoat gaped; his neckcloth was past laundering; his gaiters lacked several buttons. Above all, his escape had left him haggard and battered. He was conscious of amused stares as he waited, and the aide, a Captain Smith, who finally beckoned to him remarked:

"Sir, I leave it to your own discretion whether you care to face the General in such disorder."

Richard flushed. "Sir, I believe that General Wolfe desires an immediate report whether I am in disorder or not. If I am wrong, he will inform me."

"As you please," said Smith icily and, opening the door of the large cabin in the stern, announced: "Lieutenant Hammond of the Forty-seventh reporting, sir."

But the reception accorded to the newcomer took Captain Smith very much aback. Apparently in the bustle of the morning he had failed to understand the special nature of Richard's business. Wolfe, who was seated in front of the semicircle of windows, sprang to his feet.

"Hammond! Egad, sir, I did not expect to see you again this side of Lethe." He turned to the aide. "You did not inform me that Mr. Hammond was waiting. You spoke carelessly of some officer of the Forty-seventh. You must learn to be definite and plain. Now, see that we are not interrupted for the next half hour on any except the most urgent business. I have important matters to discuss with this officer." And as the door closed, he added: "By the Almighty, you look as if you had gone through the wringer, Hammond. I don't believe that you'd pass inspection by the fine ladies of Bath, eh?"

Richard excused himself for his appearance and explained it.

"Pray don't waste time on trifles," said Wolfe impatiently. "You'd be equally welcome in a breech clout. Be seated. Let me hear what happened in detail. Details are more important than generalities."

To Richard's relief, Wolfe seemed in better health than at their last interview. He was still appallingly thin, but he looked more vivid and alive. And yet, on second thought, he gave the impression not so much of renewed strength as of intensity, an upflaring of the spirit rather than the body, like the lengthened flame of a candle before it expires. No doubt the impending action accounted for it. Instead of the sick man at Montmorency, he was now again the mainspring and focal center of the English effort — of the humming ships that lined the St. Lawrence, of the battalions poised on the South Shore. It almost seemed that an emanation of him set the red standards snapping on the sterns of the men-of-war. The brand-new uniform he had put on added another touch of dash and gallantry.

"You saw Montcalm?"

"I did, sir, and I believe he obtained all the information you gave me. I believe, too, that he considered me only an ass."

"Bravo!" said Wolfe. "When he failed to attack us on our withdrawal from Montmorency, I guessed that you had warned him. I hear, besides, that he has reinforced de Bougainville at Cap Rouge. Again, bravo! And a third *bravo* that you managed to escape. I never expected that. But now tell me, did you happen to learn anything behind the enemy's lines?"

Richard had given much thought to what he would say on that

353

point, and he described tersely the conditions in Quebec and in the French army, on short rations and plagued by desertions and rivalries. He enumerated the regiments and their positions. The best of them were at Cap Rouge with de Bougainville, who was also well supplied with stores and artillery. He felt that this would be of special interest to Wolfe in view of the planned attack in that direction; but the General merely nodded.

"What about the defenses between Quebec and Cap Rouge? Did you learn anything of them?"

Richard smiled. "That there are none, sir, or at most trifling. The Regiment of Guienne was to have bivouacked on the Plains of Abraham, but it is still in camp along the St. Charles."

"How do you know?" There was a slight tenseness about the question.

"I passed that way last night."

Wolfe seemed to relax. "However," he said, "there appears to be a post of some sort at the Anse du Foulon. At least I could see the tents there through my glass."

Richard congratulated himself that he happened to know so much on this point. "Yes, supposedly a hundred men under Captain Vergor. But I doubt if there are more than half that number. He's a slack officer with worse than a poor reputation. I understand that he lets his men off to their farms, providing they work on his. He was given that post, I believe, because he can do no harm there. The cliffs are guard enough."

"Ah," said Wolfe. "And beyond that?"

"A nearby battery called Samos, some men and cannon at Sillery; together with the posts of Remigny and Douglas along the cliffs. Beyond them — de Bougainville."

"Odd's life!" Wolfe exclaimed. "You've exceeded my estimate of you, Hammond. But tell me how you escaped."

Richard explained his negotiations with Bigot.

Wolfe laughed. "I think you've missed your vocation. You should have been an actor." Then, struck by the embarrassment on Richard's face, he added quickly: "A jest, of course. You've turned out to be an excellent soldier. What happened then?"

But when Richard told of crossing the plateau west of the city, Wolfe stopped him.

"The terrain? What idea did you form of it?"

"As far as I could tell, sir, open for the most part but with scattered corn fields and thickets. There seems to be a rise of some sort not far from the city gates, for the lights I first saw disappeared."

"Yes," Wolfe nodded, "it shows on my map as the Buttes-à-Neveu. But you would say that the terrain is open enough — not too many thickets and corn fields?"

"No, meadow grass in general."

"Good. Then I suppose you proceeded to some point beyond Sillery?"

Richard shook his head. "I was held up by a party which had been sent in front. I managed to break away. Actually I got no farther than the Anse du Foulon and came down the cliffs there."

"The *Anse du Foulon!*" echoed Wolfe in a whisper so intent, so electric, that Richard almost started. "You came down the cliffs at the *Anse du Foulon?*"

"Why, yes, sir, and then swam across."

There was a long pause of complete silence.

"This is most important," Wolfe said finally. "Pray describe every feature of it."

Richard did so, wondering at the General's absorbed attention.

"The sentry? How far was he from the main post?"

"Two hundred paces, perhaps."

"And how far was he from where you went down?"

"Another two hundred paces."

"You found the cliff steep, but is it so steep that twenty-five resolute men could not climb it?"

Amazed at the question, Richard took a moment before answering. He said at last: "No, sir, I believe not. It would be easier to climb than to descend. There are plenty of bushes and rocks to serve as hand holds. It could be done."

Probably the General was thinking of some raid, though why he should select the obscure Anse du Foulon remained puzzling.

After another pause, he said abruptly: "Mr. Hammond, what I am about to tell you is known to no more than a half-dozen officers in the entire expedition. I am informing you of it simply to jog your memory as to any detail which might be of service.

Have I your promise of absolute secrecy until after the event?"

Richard assured him earnestly that he had.

"Then, listen." Wolfe leaned forward a trifle. "The attack has been planned for tonight at the Anse du Foulon. De Bougainville will be drawn farther upstream by a feint off Pointe-aux-Trembles. Montcalm will be pinned at Beauport by a similar feint on the part of Admiral Saunders. The barges with three thousand troops or more will drift down with the ebb and rendezvous at the Anse du Foulon —"

"But good God, sir!" Richard could not help interrupting. The madness of the scheme dazed him. If it was hazardous enough for twenty-five men to scale the cliffs, what of three thousand? "But, sir —"

"Listen. Everything depends on the first detachment. If they can gain the cliff and hold Vergor's post in check, they will be closely followed by units of the Light Infantry. If Vergor is overwhelmed and the Samos battery silenced, the path down will be cleared of obstructions, and the rest is easy. Our one advantage consists in taking the enemy off guard. What you tell me of Vergor's post is encouraging. On the other hand, if you and I are wrong, if the sentries are alert and if the edge of the cliff is held by a hundred or even by fifty determined men, our first detachment will never reach it. In that event, the entire plan must fail, and we shall draw off. I would not risk the army in an utterly hopeless attack. We must have incredible luck to succeed. But the effort should be made. Now is there any trifle, *anything* you remember that could be of help?"

So, this was the *other plan* which Wolfe had left undisclosed that day at Montmorency. This was the point of what had seemed to Richard his foolish mission. He could now understand the strategy of the past two weeks to keep Montcalm and Bougainville widely separated, each engaged at his end of the line, then strike between them at a point weakly defended because it was deemed impregnable. The brilliancy of the idea equaled its daring. Success depended on a hundred trifles, but success gave promise of complete victory.

Richard sat lost in admiration. "Marvelous, sir!"

"Keep that word for tomorrow," said Wolfe sharply. "But answer my question. Can you think of anything at all that would be useful for me to know?"

Combing his brains, Richard could recall nothing that he had not already reported. Then suddenly he stiffened.

"Indeed, sir, yes. And, if true, it's important. I heard at the prison that grain boats are expected downstream tonight from Bougainville to Quebec. They must be stopped, or our own barges will be discovered."

Wolfe's face showed his concern. "Lord! I'm glad you remembered that. Yes, they must be stopped." He fell to musing, then exclaimed: "Perhaps we're in luck. No sentinel along the cliffs tonight will be surprised to see barges on the river. We'll impersonate those boats. And, if challenged —" he broke off, smiling. "You have a perfect French accent, Hammond. Are you willing to go with me in the first barge?"

"Willing, sir? You could do me no greater favor except one."

"What's that?"

"To allow me a place among the first up the cliffs. After all, I know them better than the others."

Wolfe demurred. "You've had your share of hard knocks. Frankly, you don't look up to more of them. Those men may very well be sacrificed."

"And yet, sir, I beg. If I have given any satisfaction —"

"You have indeed. And if that's your desire, so be it. I'll inform Captain Delaune, who's in command of the detachment. Let me say further, Mr. Hammond, that a statement of your services will be this day transmitted to Colonel Hale with a recommendation of promotion — in case I should not live to see to it personally."

"Heaven forbid such a case, sir."

Wolfe's angular, boyish face was impassive. "As to that, Mr. Hammond, I'm indifferent one way or the other, provided I shall have been of use to England. — That, sir, is the chief concern of all of us."

He got up, closing the interview.

As Richard stood once more on deck, looking out at the gathering barges, Montcalm's reference to Wolfe crossed his mind and, with it, a sense both of fear and exaltation. *A man of that kind does not flicker out. He will end like a thunderstroke.*

357

THE late evening of September twelfth promised fair with something of a moon; but as the hours before midnight passed, it grew darker, though the stars remained dimly visible.

In the thirty or more crowded barges, moored between the line of Admiral Holmes's ships and the South Shore, there were seventeen hundred men. These formed the first division, which would be followed by the rest of the available troops after an interval. But the men in the bateaux did not know this, did not know anything except that they were to attack somewhere on the long line between Pointe-aux-Trembles and Beauport. It might very well be the latter. In contrast with their numb inactivity as they waited cramped and silent in the boats, all hell seemed loose downstream, where Admiral Saunders's squadron, pushing in as close as the shallows allowed, flamed and thundered against the French redoubts below the city. They could not see much of the demonstration that kept Montcalm and his battalions alert all night to repel the threatened landing. But the continued flash and violence of the guns indicated that it was no usual bombardment. Perhaps when the swift ebb tide set in, the boats would be drifted down there.

And yet the General's orders which had been circulated during the course of the day did not point to Beauport. According to them, the troops were to land "where the French seem least to expect it." The first body ashore was "to march directly to the enemy and drive them from any little post that they may occupy." There were instructions, too, about forming on "the upper ground," then marching on and endeavoring "to bring the French and Canadians to battle." This might mean any place except where the enemy was now concentrated.

Only the occupants of the first barge, the twenty-four volunteers of the Light Infantry who were to lead the attack, had an inkling of something more. They had offered themselves with enthusiasm for what they knew must be a desperate risk from the very terms in which it had been proposed: "that if any of them survived, they could depend upon being recommended to the General." And they had expressed their thanks for the honor he did them, assuring him that "his agreeable order would be put in execution with the greatest activity, care and vigor in their power." That the Light Infantry had been so honored probably meant a climb, and a climb could only mean the cliffs. Putting two and two together, they knew a little of what Wolfe expected of them.

It was a cold night, and colder in the boats because of suspense and darkness, the remote pounding of the guns, the stringent silence. Time itself seemed frozen, like the cramped bodies on the thwarts, so closely packed that no movement was possible. Squeezed between Captain Delaune and Captain McDonald of Fraser's Highlanders, Richard could only ease his position by leaning forward or back a little and by flexing his feet to avoid numbness. A spectral quality pervaded everything. It might have been a barge of ghosts on the Infernal River, ghosts who had lost their voices and could express themselves only in faint whisperings.

Two hours passed, until midnight, for it took time to embark seventeen hundred men and warp the barges into their proper sequence, regiment by regiment. Compared with this tense waiting, Richard found his ordeal of the preceding night almost easier, as effort demands less of a man than passive endurance.

At moments, the sense of unreality which he had felt while swimming returned. Was it actually himself in the crowded barge? What mysterious weaving of cause and effect had brought him to a distant war that did not concern him? If this or that, in his own past and in the past of countless others, had not happened, he would not be here. Was it the result of chance or of some infinite pattern so vast that the human mind dared not contemplate it? He grew dizzy at the thought and found himself pondering another problem. It was untrue, after all, that the war no longer concerned him. It had become identified with Wolfe, who sat near by in the prow of the barge, muffled in his cloak, and waiting like the others. What was the source of the strange power that certain men possessed to magnetize and inspire. Singleness of purpose, perhaps, singleness of dedication . . .

He felt McDonald's elbow against his ribs, and, following a tilt of the Scotsman's head, glanced up at the towering bulk of the *Sutherland* above them. A light now showed in the main topmast shrouds.

" 'Twill na be sae lang noo," came the whisper.

Almost at once a stir began, a louder lapping of water, a faint movement of oars, as barge after barge, gliding down the line of vessels, assembled close to the flagship. Some minutes of this. Richard kept staring up at the point of light on the mainmast. Then rapidly another lantern rose above the first. A rope thudded somewhere. At once the hull of the ship dropped away. On either side, there was now only the emptiness of the river, and behind, the sense of a spectral column following on the ebb.

Wolfe, who sat next to Delaune, was speaking to him in a hushed voice. Probably last-minute instructions, Richard thought, or to make sure that the tactics upon landing were understood. But then, struck by the odd cadence and listening more intently, he realized with a start that the General was reciting verses. He began even to catch a line of them here and there . . .

Of such as wandering near her secret bow'r . . .
. . . .
The breezy call of incense-breathing morn . . .

They were vaguely familiar, and suddenly Richard could place them. They recalled his tutor Mr. Stanton, who had given them to him to memorize when he was learning English. They were from Mr. Gray's celebrated *Elegy*. And now, aware of what was being spoken, he could follow it.

The boast of heraldry, the pomp of pow'r,
And all that beauty, all that wealth e'er gave,
Await alike th' inevitable hour: . . .

. . . .
Can storied urn or animated bust
Back to its mansion call the fleeting breath?
Can Honour's voice provoke the silent dust . . .

The words fell like drops of lead. They expressed the hour and occasion, the procession of phantom barges down a phantom river. Good God! What if the seventeen hundred others knew that their commander in chief was leading them on in this mad enterprise to the tune of an elegy! But they would not know. These were the musings of his private self detached for a moment from his duty and mission.

"Yes," he concluded, "I would rather have written those lines than take Quebec . . ."

Guided only by their steering sweeps, for the tide and current together gave speed enough, the barges now veered off from the protection of the South Shore and approached midstream halfway toward the Anse du Foulon. They could take their bearings from the light of the sloop of war *Hunter,* which had earlier dropped anchor at a certain point, though, to avoid suspicion, well upstream from the cove itself. Crossing astern of the ship, they entered suddenly the profounder darkness below the hostile cliffs and also the critical stage of the venture.

Along here was the first of the lookout posts, commanded by a Captain Douglas, whose sentries, if they were alert, might easily become aware of the dim line of boats crossing the river and now drifting past them. The men in the barge sat rigid and almost breathless. Yard by yard, yard by yard. But no challenge came. Luck! What luck! They were beyond the point of danger and could breathe awhile. The French, blinded by their own security, had seen nothing. Between here and the Anse du Foulon remained only the Remigny post further down. But there was no reason to believe that the sentries there —

"Qui vive?"

After hours of silence, the sudden cry seemed to reverberate. It stiffened every man in the boat. Richard could see vaguely the white-uniformed figure on the shallow beath, could hear the cocking of a musket. The barge drew closer in. Everything depended on that moment. A shot would alert Vergor's post at the Anse du Foulon; and if so, the element of surprise upon which the attack depended would be lost. The attack itself would be impossible.

"Hammond!" prompted Wolfe.

Richard found his voice. "France!" he called.

"Of what regiment?"

"La Reine." This was known to be one of Bougainville's battalions.

But the man on the beach, though expecting the grain boats from Cap Rouge, did not seem satisfied. Perhaps something in the shape of the barges, perhaps the number of them disturbed him.

"Why don't you speak louder?"

"Sacrebleu!" Richard hissed in French. "Tais-toi! Can't you hold your tongue? You see that English ship out there. You want us to be heard?"

The man lowered his musket. After all, if, together with grain, Monsieur de Bougainville was sending reinforcements to Monsieur de Montcalm, what sentry would risk exposing them to the English guns? And that reinforcements might be needed could be imagined from the bombardment which had been going on earlier against Beauport. So, the man kept silent, and history took its destined course.

But there was no relaxing again. Though still unsuspected, the leading boats of the column were now approaching their objective, where the supreme hazard would be met. Here were the quiet waters of the Anse du Foulon, the almost perpendicular cliffs, the decisive moments.

Rounding the cove itself, the barge put in beyond the rock, which stood at its eastern tip; for the ascent had to be made downstream from Vergor's post and beyond the beat of the sentinel on that side. That the men, chilled and cramped from hours on the thwarts, could get themselves ashore in absolute silence was a chance in a hundred. And yet, weighing every movement, they achieved it, helped by the indefinite sound of the river itself and by the noisy rush of a torrent in a nearby ravine. Meanwhile, close in, the next barges, with the supporting Light Infantry, waited.

But never had the attempt to scale the heights seemed more impossible than now. There was scarcely room on the narrow beach for the twenty-odd men who were to spearhead the attack. Though cool and determined as ever, Wolfe himself, staring up at the vertical wall of underbrush and rock, acknowledged in a low voice to Captain Delaune: "I don't think we can by any possible means get up here, but, however, we must use our best endeavor." And to the men, "So up with you as best you can."

Delaune's orders were to signal if or when he reached the top and before attacking Vergor's post. A detachment of the Light Infantry would then storm the winding path leading up from the Cove du Foulon, so that the French would be engaged on both sides. Other companies of the Light Infantry would follow at the heels of the first party up the face of the cliff. Wolfe himself remained temporarily behind to direct the landing.

"Up with you! Up with you!" The whisper passed from man to man.

Richard hoped to be first, but he was at once outdistanced by Captain Donald McDonald. The wiry Highlander scaled the first few yards like a serpent. Behind him, the others, each for himself, their muskets on their backs, climbed as best they could.

But it was no scrambling, heedless race. Everyone shared the same responsibility for silence. A dislodged stone might start a miniature avalanche, attracting the notice of a sentry; the failure of a handhold and crash of a body would be heard a long way. Foot by foot, testing every step, the party struggled upward.

Now that the actual crisis had come, Richard was aware only of the effort itself, the need of quiet, and the immense chance of discovery. Personal fear had no part in it. That likely enough the summit would soon be lined by muskets racketing down at the men clinging to the cliff, that there might be a last futile struggle at the top, did not occur to him nor probably to anyone else. It was the first shout, the first shot, announcing failure, that he waited for as he hauled himself up from rock to rock and bush to bush.

Perhaps twenty minutes passed on the hundred-foot wall, perhaps less. The distance was not measured in time, but in the hammering of the heart, the strain of muscles, the intensity of suspense. He could hardly credit it when his hand gripped the root of one of the tamarack trees at the summit and, with a final heave, he found himself on level ground. McDonald was already standing there, together with five or six others. And as yet there had been no hail from a sentry. But with every second other figures were gaining the top and closing in.

Then, at last, came a faint *qui vive!* three hundred paces away.

"Wait," said McDonald. "We'll play for time, but make ready to fire." And he strode off toward the sentry. Richard could hear him answering "France!" to the challenge. He had served on the Continent and knew some French. No doubt, for as long as possible, he would take advantage of the darkness to palm himself off as someone from Quebec on an errand. But, what with his accent and the suspicions of the sentry, the ruse could gain only a few moments.

However, not much time was needed. The first party had now all reached the summit, and behind them, thick and fast, came others of the Light Infantry. In some way that Richard never learned, McDonald managed to spin it out a minute, two minutes. Then, a cry, a shot, a racing of feet.

Someone, perhaps Delaune, yelled: "Come on! Double quick now! And give a cheer, men! Give a cheer, by God! Fire when you see the tents!"

At that point, the silent, deliberate night broke into uproar, a confusion of detached impressions. Shouting. Running. Discharge of muskets. Richard tripped over a rope and found himself among the tents of Vergor's post. But the half-awakened enemy had fired hardly a volley before taking to their heels. The worthless Vergor himself was brought in wounded. His men were chased out of the neighboring corn field. After the rigors of the climb, the rest of it had been absurdly easy.

Uninterrupted, however, the noise, the pelting of impressions went on. Near by came the roar of cannon as the Samos battery, in a last gesture, opened up on the barges now flocking into the cove. A brief attack silenced it. On the winding path down to the river, Richard tugged and sweated to clear away the sharpened logs mingled with branches that formed the abatis. Already in single file, platoon by platoon the regiments were flowing up. Now and then came a sputtering of fire in the middle and far distance as the scattered French posts along the river were overrun. He was aware suddenly of many ships' lights below him on the water, where Admiral Holmes's squadron, having dropped downstream, brought supplies for the landing and more troops. A vast animation of voices and oars in the twilight of dawn.

Then all at once, he realized that it was day. Scarlet coats everywhere, tartans of Highlanders, the familiar regimental facings, companies forming up, sergeants barking orders . . .

A heavy hand crashed on his shoulder. He turned to meet the wide grin of Colonel Hale.

"Well, by God, here you are, Hammond. And damned glad to see you. I hear you've done well. But don't stand idling. Your company's over yonder. Pray report to Captain Gardiner at once."

"Where's the General, sir?"

"Gone ahead to reconnoiter the terrain. We're to march within a few minutes. Kennedy's on the move already. Hear the drums?"

And now oddly enough for the first time, Richard felt the thrill of what had been accomplished. The long night and uncertainty were over; the heights had been won.

L I I I

THE blow at Vergor's post had been struck an hour before dawn. It was not until eight, and with a considerable regrouping of detachments, that the English line of battle had been formed across the plateau. Wolfe had only forty-eight hundred men in all upon the heights that morning, and of these, seventeen hundred secured the landing place, acted as skirmishers against the Canadian and Indian sharpshooters on the left and right, or were held in reserve. So the scarlet battle line itself, that stretched between the Valley of the St. Charles on the left and the Valley of the St. Lawrence on the right, was pitifully thin.

It consisted of two ranks, the files standing about three feet apart, with forty paces or more between the separate battalions. These, in order from the right, were the Thirty-fifth, drawn up on the slope of a little hill that served as anchor for that flank, then the Louisburg Grenadiers, then the Twenty-eighth, the Forty-third, the Forty-seventh, then Fraser's Highlanders, then the Fifty-eighth. At right angles to the last, arrayed *en potence* and therefore facing front and toward the left to protect that flank from attack up the Côte Sainte-Geneviève, stood the Fifteenth and two battalions of the Light Infantry. A thousand paces behind the center, the Forty-eighth Regiment and further battalions of the Light Infantry were held in reserve.

But to Richard Hammond, with the fusil, or light musket, of his rank in hand and concerned with the evolutions of his platoon until the Forty-seventh reached its final station, the order of battle meant nothing. He could see only a narrow section of it, aware of the Highlanders on one side and of the Forty-third on the other,

365

with the still vacant ridge of the Buttes-à-Neveu in front. Close behind this, but out of sight, lay Quebec.

Having become once more only a cog in the precise discipline of the infantry, Richard took pleasure in noting that the men of his platoon were glad to see him again. Fellow officers chaffed him about his makeshift uniform; but word had got around that he had distinguished himself on his mission, and there was an accent of esteem behind the joking. Used for the past two weeks to the less rigid French, he found it bracing to be back in an English regiment with its inflexible emphasis on details. The men might have spent last night in the bateaux, but that was no excuse for deviating more than necessary from regulations. Once on the heights, the eagle-eyed sergeant major and his noncommissioned officers put a stop to any laxness. Hair had to be neatly tucked up under the miter-shaped caps, every gaiter properly buttoned, the coat-skirts uniformly looped up for marching, the crossbelts and pouches, the frog that supported the bayonet, the knapsack and haversack, water flask and cartouche box, duly adjusted. As the battalion marched down the Sainte-Foye road, sergeants called the step, the sergeant major watched the intervals, every musket sloped on the left shoulder at exactly the same angle. "A sorry sight, sir," observed Judson the sergeant major. But, except for a small difference in spit and polish, Richard's less practised eye could see no difference from the drills at Portsmouth.

It would be a fine day. After a few early showers, the sun was shining, the blue sky spread, and all the colors of an autumn morning flamed. Mingling with these, the red coats of the infantry, the tartans of the Highlanders, the regimental colors, the glint of steel down the line made a grand show. Best of all were the high spirits of the troops. Behind them lay months of dawdling and frustration, camp routine, recent confinement in the ships. Now, miraculously, they stood under the walls of Quebec, no longer at an unbridgeable distance but within musket range. At last they would have their day. And they were all veteran regiments, the flower of the English army, proud of their officers and their colors, proud especially of the young general who last night had achieved the impossible.

But would Montcalm accept the challenge? Would he fight?

Wouldn't he choose, rather, to shut himself up in the town and wait until Bougainville had learned of the landing and brought up reinforcements, thus taking the English between two fires? One couldn't be sure at first. There was no way of knowing what went on in the city or in the French camp at Beauport.

"One thing's certain, though," said Captain Gardiner, munching some ship's biscuit that would have to serve as breakfast. "The Marquis has had the surprise of his life, and I'll wager the whole French hive is humming. I've been told that the city walls won't stand a bombardment, and we'll soon fetch up enough guns from the fleet."

"But not before de Bougainville would be on our backs," Richard objected. "He has two thousand regulars. His vanguard ought to be here by noon at the latest."

"Mark my word," returned Gardiner, "the Frogs are pretty excitable. What's more, I'll lay you ten guineas to one that they don't know our numbers. A good many of us are hidden by the terrain. It's odds they consider this only a raid in force. Their thought will be to sweep us over the cliffs before more of us can come up. Look yonder."

He pointed to the low ridge in front. Beyond its crest could be felt, rather than seen, a gathering of troops. Now and then the tip of a flag moved along, or half figures of men appeared, and more frequently small parties emerged, staring at the British line.

"What'd I tell you?" asked Gardiner. "Besides, the Marquis may be a Frenchie, but he's a gallant old fellow. He won't refuse a dare."

And soon it was evident that Montcalm would fight. Skirmishing grew heavier on the English left, where a small wood filled with sharpshooters commanded Brigadier Townshend's position on the Sainte-Foye road. Skirmishers, too, under cover of little hillocks and patches of underbrush, were thrown out against the center and right, to be met in turn and driven back by several platoons of the Forty-seventh. A brass six-pounder, which had been hauled up at the Anse du Foulon, banged away from the right with good effect on any formation that appeared above the crest of the Buttes-à-Neveu. Here and there a French gun answered.

One could feel a sort of crescendo in the scattered fire, a tensing before the supreme moment of attack. It was completely unlike the impression that Richard had formed of battle from steel engravings. No serried squares of infantry, no prancing of horsemen, not much artillery, no theatrics. But a great deal of landscape, meadow, coppice and corn field; several scattered houses on the left, with puffs of smoke issuing from the windows; a sputtering of fire on the flanks; now and then distant shouts; a growing excitement covered up by elaborate sang-froid. More than once, when the French skirmishers had been thrust out against the center, men had been hit at no great distance from Richard. He could hear the impassive orders of the sergeant. "Numbers Six and Seven will remove Number Four to the rear! Close up to three paces!"

A wounded man was groaning somewhere behind. "Christ! . . . Christ! . . . Christ! . . ."

But no one looked around.

A ball whistled close and passed harmlessly.

"Lucky there ain't more of us," said a voice. "Hard to hit, we are."

"Silence in the ranks!" roared Captain Gardiner. "Sergeant Jones, take note of that man!"

Then several platoons of Captain Smelt's company marched out against the skirmishers. There was an exchange of firing. The French retired. The wounded were helped back, though a few patches of red remained on the ground. The tense waiting continued.

A stir went down the line. A distant voice shouted "Attention!" and started echoes from point to point, which brought muskets to the shoulder at the correct slope and turned officers into rigid statues at the proper intervals.

It was Wolfe with a couple of his aides. He came to a stop not far from Richard and faced the battalion. Evidently he had been hit slightly, for a bloodstained handkerchief bandaged his wrist. Otherwise, he looked transfigured. Last night's mood of elegy had been replaced by an almost incandescent elation. He had won the heights; the goal of battle, so long delayed, was close. His spirit burned higher at each moment. The sun kindled the scarlet of his new, though severely plain, uniform, glittered on the leather of his kneeboots with their brown tops. Every detail of him became

vivid in Richard's mind: the black cockade, which was the only orna-
ment of his hat; his unpowdered reddish hair tied in a long queue;
the waist belt on the outside of his red coat, with a frog holding a
bayonet but no sword; the light musket slung on his back. He wore
a black band on his left arm in mourning for his father, who had
died since he had left England. But especially the triangular, imperious face of the General, which Richard could see in profile, expressed the lilt and expectancy of the day.

"Men of the Forty-seventh," he said, his voice level and distinct,
"we have succeeded in bringing the enemy to battle. We may expect his attack. I desire everyone to load with two bullets for the
first volley. You will fire at forty paces, and not one pace before,
whatever the provocation. This is of chief importance. Officers
will measure the distance and delay the order to present until the
enemy approaches it. The order to fire will be given only when he
reaches it. Is that understood? The discharge must be close, not
scattered. Every man will select a target; there must be no aimless
firing. When the first volley has been delivered, you will reload, advance, and again fire. When the enemy breaks, you will charge."
He paused a moment, then added: "I repeat the orders you have
already received. Officers and men will remember what their country expects of them. You will be attentive to commands and resolute
in the execution of your duty. Good luck and God bless you! Colonel
Hale, I expect Lascelles's Forty-seventh this day to add to the
credit it won at Louisburg."

He glanced up and down the line. His cheeks showed a faint
color; his eyes sparkled. No flight of rhetoric would have so much
impressed the battalion as this proud, dry directive. Then, with a
nod, he strode off to repeat his instructions to the next regiment.

But now, shortly after, the crest of the Buttes-à-Neveu, some
hundreds of yards off, came alive with a surge of white uniforms
and standards. As a gesture, the English line moved a short distance
forward, then halted, musket on shoulder.

It was different over there on the ridge, where the white fleur-
de-lis banners and the quarterings of regimental standards tossed
over tangled columns. In general, the Canadian detachments
seemed to be in front of the regular battalions; and their less ordered ranks gave the impression of an armed mob rather than of

369

disciplined troops. Besides, the little brass cannon from Wolfe's right worked like mad with its discharges of grape and added to the confusion.

But, for all that, the regiments on the hill were no mean enemies. Some of them were among the oldest in the French army. They not only outnumbered the British by a third, but they had beaten them again and again at Oswego, at Ticonderoga. In the center, Richard could distinguish the famous white Cross of Béarn with its alternate quarterings of orange and red — a veteran regiment if there ever was one. And there was the green and philamot of the standard of Guienne; the blue, red, yellow and green of the Royal Roussillon; the red and blue of La Sarre; the purple and red of Languedoc. Moreover, if the English craved battle, the French craved it no less. One could feel across the distance their passion and defiance. A constant movement went on; an angry hum rose from the battalions in contrast to the British immobility and silence. They stood now in three wide columns about six deep. The firing of sharpshooters on both wings of the armies grew heavier.

Suddenly an officer on a black horse rode along the French front. Montcalm! He was haranguing his men with the fierce exuberance that they understood. He had led them to repeated victories; he would lead them to one more. He raised his sword above his head. Doubtless those master words *France* and *the King* were spoken. A roar of voices answered, rolling down to the rigid English line. And even there no one would have denied him esteem as a great soldier and a great nobleman.

Colonel Hale nodded to Major Hussey, who rapped out: "The Forty-seventh will load! Double charge!"

In perfect rhythm six hundred musket butts thudded on the ground, six hundred jaws bit out two bullets, six hundred ramrods tamped down the charge, six hundred mouths spat the bullets into musket barrels. The ramrods shot back into their loops.

"Fix bayonets!"

The sunlight danced along facets of steel.

"Shoulder your muskets!"

Six hundred arms dropped in unison along six hundred thighs. Forty yards were now paced off, and markers set up.

"It won't be long now, Mr. Hammond," said Ensign Dunlop in a queer, breathless voice.

He was only sixteen and showed some yellow fluff on his brick-red boy's face. Trying hard to set an example of coolness, as an officer should, he had something in his eyes that reminded Richard of Caretti on the morning of the duel. Spirit versus flesh, again.

"Scared, Dunlop?"

The boy gulped. "A little."

"Who isn't?" Richard grinned. "I'm shaky myself."

"You don't show it, sir."

"Because I'm an actor, Dunlop." He caught himself. "Like everybody else, Colonel Hale included. They're all scared, but they're all acting a part. The main thing is to act it well — with polish, d'you see? Overdo it a little. Think of it that way."

Dunlop stared, but he smiled. "Thank you, sir."

"Yes," thought Richard, applying his advice to himself, "polish is the word."

Firing on the left grew in volume almost to battle pitch. A detachment of the Light Infantry which had been thrown against a similar body occupying the woods on that flank was seen falling back in disorder. But word flew along the line that it was only a feint to draw the enemy on. If so, the trick was effective.

A shout rose from the Buttes-à-Neveu. Slowly at first, the massive columns began to move down the slope, then quickened to a charge, but almost at once fell into confusion as the Canadian front ranks started firing and, in their fashion, dropped to the ground in order to reload. The French regulars, unused to these tactics, faltered, lost the first impetus of attack, and fired in their turn as they came on.

Ragged and largely out of range as the volleys were, here and there a motionless figure in the British line dropped. A French cannon posted on the crest gashed at various points. But not a shot was returned. The scarlet line stood with shouldered muskets. A mighty blow struck the ground close to Richard, plastered him with earth, ricocheted, and left Private Hill a bloody pulp some yards off. Instinctively Richard made a movement in that direction.

"I'll thank you to keep your place, Mr. Hammond," called Major Hussey, who happened to be looking. "You have no permission to stroll about."

"Close up to three paces," intoned a sergeant. "Dress to your right."

The rigid line adjusted itself. Richard resumed his position in front of the platoon, kept his eyes front. "Polish," he thought again.

The French were now much nearer, their ranks bent and tangled, firing at will but blindly. One could see their white gaiters and little three-cornered hats, the flicker of their bayonets. Their quick step became a run. But still the English stood motionless.

It took neat timing. The Regiment of Béarn was close to the forty-pace limit.

"The Forty-seventh will make ready!"

Like clockwork, muskets swung to the required position; firing mechanisms clicked in unison.

"Present!"

Six hundred muskets were leveled. But a pause followed even then. It was in this fraction of a minute that the numberless hours at drill, the savage, pedantic discipline, bore fruit. Along the entire center of the British line, muskets were leveled; but not a finger twitched, though the oncoming wave had now resolved itself into individual faces, tense mouths, staring eyes. Had Colonel Hale lost his tongue . . .

"Fire!"

The roar was like a single cannon shot.

Smoke blotted out everything but not the order "Load!"

In the fog, Richard was dimly aware of his own ramrod in cadence with the others.

"The Forty-seventh will advance ten paces! March!"

"Left! . . . Left! . . ." from the sergeants.

"Halt!"

"Make ready!"

"Present!"

"Fire!"

The smoke, which had thinned a little, shut in again, began shredding out. Between the rifts appeared an utterly different scene. No longer the passionate, charging ranks, but tangled, unquiet bodies on the ground, and behind them daunted men, staggering back, on the point of flight. No troops in the world could have withstood those two close volleys at that range. They were a turning point in history.

"Charge!"

372

And now the British automatons became individual men. They could forget drill, forget sergeants, forget discipline, and unleash themselves in one glorious, elemental lust. There was no fight left in the stunned French battalions as the huzzaing scarlet line surged into them, only a desperate impulse to escape. Run, run, get away somehow from the furious bayonets, the clubbing of musket butts, the barbarous red killers; save themselves somehow from the nightmare men in gaudy skirts and with hairy legs, bounding among them swinging heavy double-edged swords. For the Highlanders dropped their muskets, raised their slogan, and took to the claymore.

Madness seized Richard, as it did everyone else. He plied his bayonet, used his musket as a club, exchanged blows with occasional fugitives, found himself now among the Highlanders, now with elements of the Forty-third, or again with the Forty-seventh.

The English line dissolved into scattered units, some shooting, some stabbing, herding the French toward the city walls or, in a vague movement left, toward the northern edge of the plateau, down which the beaten enemy was streaming in the direction of the St. Charles and the pontoon bridge connecting with Beauport.

But Richard had no notion of time or locality, only of pell-mell pursuit and killing and the kaleidoscope of unrelated glimpses. Now, he could see one of the town gates, choked with white uniforms, and in the midst of them a hatless man on a black horse, seemingly carried along by the torrent. The man, slumped forward, was being held in his saddle by a grenadier on either hand; and his side dripped blood. It flashed upon Richard that this was Montcalm, stricken, perhaps dying; but at once the kaleidoscope shifted to another pattern. Here, further along, was the St. John Gate, with the nearby clump of woods where Canadians had rallied in an obstinate stand that gave the French remnants time to reach the valley below. Here the battle eddied for a while until the gallant band was overborne and the wood swept clear.

Victory! Victory! Complete! Decisive! There could be no question of that. Leaning breathless against a tree Richard could look back over the battlefield, alive with British redcoats, but dotted here and there with twisted bodies and castoff equipment, the refuse of battle. Now that the firing had slackened, he could hear another sound, pitiful and tormented, the cries of the wounded, that mingled with shouts of men trooping back to their regimental standards. And now that the lust was satisfied, he felt burned out, indifferent and half sick. Near him, face downwards, lay the body of a French soldier, a mere boy, of about the same age as young Dunlop, his little white queue sticking up under the three-cornered hat. He glanced at his own bayonet and gagged . . .

Then, to steady himself, he thought of his hero, the General. What glory! What triumph of faith over despair, of purpose over difficulties, of spirit over flesh! The battle had that much meaning. He could imagine Wolfe's elation at this supreme moment and looked forward to the next glimpse of him.

Over yonder were the colors of the Forty-seventh. He made his way toward them and met Captain Smelt with half a platoon headed in the same direction. They looked oddly somber and dispirited.

"Well, sir, a creditable performance," said Richard, after joining them. "The General will be pleased."

Smelt turned on him with a stare. "Great God, sir! You mean you haven't heard the news!"

"News?" Richard echoed. "What news?"

Smelt's heavy face puckered. He looked away, cleared his throat. "Why," he began — "Why, dammy, sir, the General was killed in the first charge. Shot through the breast. I had it from a man who was with him. Lived long enough, thank God, to know of the French rout. Said . . . he said he died content."

Richard walked on mechanically.

"Bottom's out of everything," Smelt added.

"Yes," Richard muttered, "yes . . ."

An aide hurried by. "General Townshend's compliments. The Forty-seventh will form line immediately . . ."

L I V

ON September eighteenth, five days after the battle, Quebec, abandoned by the army, which alone could have defended it, surrendered. The banner of France drooped down from the Château St.

Louis, and the red banner of England was raised. What remained of the garrison marched out with the honors of war, drums beating and matches lighted, followed by their baggage, but they marched as prisoners of war on parole, to be conveyed to France.

Meanwhile, the great Montcalm slept in his humble grave in the chapel of the Ursulines; and marines stood guard about the coffin of James Wolfe on H.M.S. *Sterling Castle.*

Meanwhile, too, awaiting possible attack from the now rallied enemy under Vaudreuil, Lévis, and Bougainville, the British army camped on the battlefield. The dead had been buried; tents had been brought up; redoubts and batteries, constructed. Generals Townshend and Murray kept anxious watch, but the French had had enough for that season.

On the night of the city's capitulation, Richard, now a captain, was summoned to the headquarters tent of the Forty-seventh. He reported with a heavy heart, for everyone knew that Colonel Hale had been appointed to carry the great news to England, and that he would be sailing tomorrow. This meant the parting of the last link that bound Richard's affections to the army. Wolfe's death had left him nerveless and apathetic. In the dreary aftermath of the battle, he realized that he was no soldier, that admiration for the lost General had given him a brief incentive which was now extinguished. So far, he had acted the part of an English officer creditably enough, but he had no interest in continuing it. Courage, comradeship, and self-sacrifice were realities; it was good to have known them; and yet the savageries of war, the petty dullness of army routine, seemed a wretched framework for them. With the departure of Colonel Hale, who had been his chief friend and patron, he could look forward to a lonely winter of garrison in Quebec, a renewed campaign in the spring. To what purpose? The final conquest of Canada. What the devil did he care about that!

"Sit down, Dick. I've something to tell you." Leaning back from a camp table, with last-minute papers in front of him, the young Colonel — he was only ten years older than Richard — beckoned the latter to a stool. "You've heard that I'm leaving?"

"Yes, sir, and I can't say how much I regret it."

"Well, here's the point. In the first place, as I've told you, General Wolfe sent me a communication on the twelfth describing and commending your recent services. He desired your promotion — that's been attended to — and urged me to interest myself in your favor as much as possible — though, egad, that don't take much urging."

Richard murmured his thanks, which Hale interrupted.

"Wait! In the second place, I'm associated on this voyage with Captain Douglas of the navy, a worthy man but dull as they make 'em. I want some entertainment. You've never taught me those card tricks of yours. In brief, how would you like to come along?"

"Come along?" Richard repeated, openmouthed. "Good Lord, sir —"

"Yes, and I believe you could tell the bigwigs in London more about the French side of this campaign than anyone else. I don't need to point out that you would profit by it, and that Lord Marny would be pleased."

Richard sat dazed, staring at the other's manly, smiling face.

"Come, sir," Hale bantered. "I hope I don't have to persuade you. General Townshend has given his permission."

"Sir!" Richard exploded. "I wish I could find words to tell you — to express —"

"Then don't. See to your packing. We sail before dawn with the ebb tide."

PART FOUR

Paris

L V

BONFIRES flamed through England. Universal jubilation greeted the marvelous news that reached Portsmouth on October sixteenth. The King, as Mr. Walpole put it, had so many addresses of congratulation that he could have papered his palace with them. Pitt, the Great Commoner, whom defeat might have tarnished, rose to new heights. Quebec fallen and with Quebec the whole of Canada almost in the English grasp. But not Canada alone — Louisiana, the vast, little-known American hinterland from the Lakes to the Gulf. What glory! What horizons of empire! Dramatically, too, Wolfe's earlier dispatches, foreboding failure, had arrived only three days before the announcement of victory, and the recent gloom added flavor to success. Indeed, so happy was the nation that it could afford the luxury of sorrow for the dead hero.

It had been a wonderful year. In India, Clive had won the victory of Plassey. In Africa, Senegal and Gorée had been captured by England, and Guadeloupe in the West Indies. In Europe, the French were driven from Hanover. In America they had yielded Ticonderoga and Crown Point, Fort Niagara and Fort Duquesne. But now, more splendid and far-reaching than anything else — Quebec!

To the bearers of such tidings went the first laurels, the first outpourings of exultation. And these were no mere couriers, but officers representing the army and navy, themselves participants in the immortal battle, heroes in their own right. John Hale, promoted to full colonel and well on his way to a generalship, was commissioned to raise a new crack cavalry regiment. Captain James Douglas, who had commanded the *Alcide,* received knighthood and five hundred pounds from the King. As for Richard Hammond, Lord Marny could be counted on, when plums were falling, to see to it that he did not miss his share.

Richard had the honor of a personal interview with the half-blind, grumpy little sovereign at St. James's, an interview that lasted a full half hour. George II could not hear enough about "dat great victory" as he expressed it in his heavy German accent. He liked soldiers anyway and took a marked fancy to Captain Hammond, gave him a purse of a hundred pounds, and observed "dat dis was only a token of someting better later on."

But the plums that Lord Marny sought for Richard were not to be found so much at the Palace as at 10 St. James's Square, across from Marny House, where Mr. Pitt held court. Captain Hammond was directed by the chief minister to give a detailed account not only of military operations but of his own secret mission to, and escape from, Quebec. Colonel Hale, always his friend, had taken care that Wolfe's memorandum of Richard's services should reach Pitt. The latter, indeed, pointed it out among other papers on his desk.

"You are fortunate, sir, to have merited the praise of such a man. It will be remembered to your lasting credit. I am informed that you do not wish to continue actively in the army. Why not?"

Faced by the imperious eagle beak of the minister, by the arrogant eyes and personal splendor of him, which was somehow independent of his sober dress and bushy wig, Richard had never felt so awe-struck by any human being. As Wolfe had been the mainspring of the Quebec expedition, here was the mainspring of England, the architect of empire, perhaps the greatest man of his age. Though he seemed benevolent enough, his effect on the young captain was too overpowering for comfort.

Richard explained that his tastes were not military, that his father desired him to enter Parliament and to follow some civil employment, perhaps abroad; that he hoped, however, for Mr. Pitt's interest and would consider his advice not only an honor but a command.

"Well put," said the other, visibly pleased. "As to soldiering, you may be right. Your services to General Wolfe show parts that can be better used than in the army, though your conduct there was pretty enough. It is likely that I can offer you employment more suited to your bent than a military post, and presenting a more ambitious future. Lord Marny and I will discuss it. Meanwhile, remain on the army list. The rank of captain, provided it has been well earned, as in your case, adds stature to a young man."

With a view to the future, Lord Marny also escorted Richard to Leicester House, where he paid his respects and described the recent campaign to the Prince of Wales, soon to become George III, and the Prince's favorite, Lord Bute.

Then, too, there were calls on the Duke of Newcastle, Lord Holdernesse, Lord Hardwicke, other notables. There were routs and assemblies at great houses. There were fashionable suppers, appointments of all kinds. And everywhere Captain Hammond, as one who could tell at first hand of Quebec, as one whom the King, the Prince and Mr. Pitt, had favored, was a center of attention. Who now could reproach him with Corleone, Caretti and the scandal in Bath? The very ladies and beaux who had snubbed him there were the first to claim his acquaintance. In short, he was much the fashion, gamed at White's, danced at Mrs. Cornelys's in Carlisle House, appeared now with one, now with another reigning toast at Drury Lane or Covent Garden.

These were the days when Lord Marny looked ten years younger. His pride took a new lease on life. He delighted to be seen in public with Richard, aware that people commented on the likeness between them. Above all, he could now give ambition for his son free rein. No barriers any longer; a choice of beguiling schemes to be weighed. He no longer faced old age alone. In a sense, he was no longer old. His self, projected in Richard, could renew its faith in worldly values which had begun to stale. Vicariously, in imagination, he breathed again the perfume of withered vanities and found it still intoxicating.

At Christmas time, nonchalant as always when making a gift, he presented Richard with a deed for the Virginia land now managed by a factor and worth two thousand pounds a year. But, as if that was not enough, he added two thousand more to Richard's allowance. "Funds," he declared, "are a *sine qua non* to any considerable figure in the world — such, thank God, as we can now expect for you. I will have no son of mine hampered in that respect. When all has been said, nothing glitters like gold."

So, the autumn of '59 made way for a new decade. In late November, to overflow the national cup, Admirals Hawke and Saunders crushed the navy of France in Quiberon Bay. In December, Richard Hammond could view himself as a young man of means and consequence. For him, as for England, the year ended with the brightest prospects.

He would have been a fool or a sage if so much good fortune had not affected him. Looking back, he found it hard to identify the part-time fiddler in Marco Letta's orchestra, the understudy harlequin of Venice, with Captain Hammond of St. James's Square. Although conscious still of playing a role, it was one that he had mastered. He could act it flawlessly, without effort. And now that he had tasted success, he wanted more of it.

In such a frame of mind, he returned home one January evening to find Lord Marny absorbed in front of the library fire, legs outstretched and hands tipped together under his nose. Except for the firelight and a candelabra on the center table, which cast vague glimmerings on the shelves and cornice busts of the spacious room, the place was dark. Only the glow of the fire outlined Lord Marny's face and wig in a kind of chiaroscuro.

"Hah, Richard," said the Earl, rousing himself. "I happened to be thinking of you. Join me, and we'll think of you together."

Taking a chair on the other side of the hearth, Richard stretched out his hands toward the fire. "The gentlemen at White's send their compliments, sir. They regretted your absence."

"Luck?" asked Marny.

"Fifty guineas. I recouped myself on the last deal."

The other smiled. "Naturally you did. This is a season when you can't lose. Your tide's on the flood. A propos of that, I was again talking you over today with Mr. Pitt. I believe he has something to your taste. I was thinking of it when you came in."

At once Richard knew that this was no casual chat. "I'm heartily glad of it, sir. I can't go on dawdling."

"Nonsense!" said Marny. "You deserved some leisure after Quebec. And to become known in London is no waste of time. Still, a young man needs employment. How would you like to go to Paris?"

Paris! In view of the war, the suggestion was startling. "*Paris,* sir?"

"Yes. I consider some acquaintance with Paris indispensable to the career now open to you. After all, in certain respects, it remains the hub of the world. Aside from that, you would go on business; you would be of service, perhaps, to the ministry here. Mr. Pitt, let me say, is particularly impressed by the conduct of your mission behind the enemy's lines at Quebec. He does you the honor to propose a similar mission, though of greater consequence, at Paris. That he selects you is no small compliment." The Earl added with gusto: "By Gad, nothing could have pleased me more. I've sifted the matter and see only good in it. Even if you fail — which may be expected — you'll gather experience; if you succeed, your entire future's made."

"But the war?" put in Richard. "How can an Englishman show himself in Paris? And what mission . . ."

"We'll come to that," Marny interrupted. "As to your first question, the Duc de Choiseul and the Comte de Saint-Florentin are old acquaintances of mine. We've had dealings in the past; I've done them some favors and can expect a small one in return. If I desire a young kinsman (they'll be informed how close the kinship is) to finish his education in Paris, the seat of all courtliness and good breeding, they'll be flattered. Of course, you would not embarrass them or yourself by appearing in public as Richard Hammond. You would call yourself Monsieur d'Amond, a gentleman of French extraction from The Hague; and your papers would bear you out. But, furthermore, if I hint to Choiseul of your closeness to Pitt and that any remarks on the subject of peace he might favor you with would not be wasted, he'll be very much your servant. For in the present state of France, peace must be had on almost any terms; and even a twig of olive is worth cultivating."

"In brief, my lord, I'd be an agent in disguise, though also accredited?"

"Precisely," nodded Marny. "They have similar agents here on a like footing. 'Tis a common practise at all times, whether in war or peace. No nation could conduct its affairs otherwise."

"And my mission would be to explore possible terms of peace?"

"Ostensibly, yes; actually, no. France, beaten on all the seas and continents, hungers for peace. But we of Mr. Pitt's persuasion know that England can only secure the fruits of her victories by decisive war. What are those fruits? The final elimination of France as a colonial power; the undisputed dominion of the seas, and therefore of world commerce, by England. There you have Pitt's objectives in a nutshell."

"But, in that case, my lord, why even a twig of olive?"

Before answering, Marny thoughtfully took snuff and flicked off a couple of grains with his handkerchief.

"Because war is expensive," he said finally, "and, hence, in the long run, unpopular. Consider the rising costs of it. To cover the sums required, loans have been raised in the amount of twenty-two million. People as a whole are shortsighted, Richard. Hardships of the moment loom greater than future empire, which they may not live to see. At present Pitt rides high on the crest of last year's conquests; but the itch for peace grows, and political opponents will make the most of it. For lack of one last effort, we may forfeit the great prize. It will be your mission to discover a convincing pretext for continuing the war."

"Such as what, sir?"

"The duplicity of France, Richard. Suppose that, while broaching peace, she is secretly preparing to renew the war at her own time and with increased resources? Suppose we have undoubted proof of it? Would not that silence our peacemongers? For who but an idiot would forgo our present advantage, to be caught short later?"

"I see," Richard murmured. "And there are reasons to believe in French duplicity?"

"Good God!" exclaimed the Earl. "Don't be naïve. In foreign affairs, double-dealing is the one constant factor. 'Tis the life breath of them. Why else do statesmen exist save to bubble one another for the sake of their countries? Reasons? You shock me. Consider Choiseul, who has one of the shrewdest minds in Europe. He holds poor cards at the moment; but, given the chance, he'll mend his hand. If we did not know that he held an ace up his sleeve, we'd be fools not to assume it."

"An ace, sir?"

"Yes," said Marny. "Spain. She's been long asleep, but Choiseul hopes to waken her. The new king, Charles III, remembers he's a

Bourbon; bleeds for the woes of his French cousin in Versailles; bleeds still more, under Choiseul's pricking, at the danger to Spanish colonies in America if the French colonies are lost; views England (correctly enough) as the common enemy of both Bourbon states. Pitt's agents are many and keep him well posted. We believe there's a rapprochement on foot between Paris and Madrid which will end in a formal alliance, but we must have proof of it in time to scare off a premature peace. To furnish that proof would be your mission."

Nothing simpler! thought Richard sarcastically. Were his father and Pitt mad? What did he know of the infinite complexities in European politics, of the maneuverings and personalities that controlled them? What did he know about superlative espionage? How could he, a stranger in Paris, be expected to penetrate the secrets of Choiseul?

"Well?" Marny prompted. "Are you not flattered?"

"Too much so. I'm afraid your lordship and Mr. Pitt overrate me. I have no acquaintance with foreign affairs. How would I proceed in Paris? Where would I . . ." He dropped the question with a shrug. "You'll admit there are difficulties."

Though he considered laughter ill bred, for once Marny laughed. "You put it mildly, sir. You can call them impossibilities if you like — though I hope they're not. Still, the difficulties you're thinking of needn't trouble you. Now, mark. You'll go first to The Hague and spend some time there with the British minister, General Yorke. He knows as much of the present posture of affairs as anyone. He has dealings, too, with the French ambassador, Monsieur d'Affry, and will bring you acquainted with him. Between the two of them, you'll be well instructed when you go to Paris. So much for that. But, once there, don't imagine that you'll act alone. You'll present yourself to another British agent, who will see to it that you're properly launched."

This began to make sense. In itself, the thought of Paris was intoxicating. Amélie was there. Maritza, too, occurred to him. She was dancing at the Opéra.

"I understand, sir. I'm most indebted to you and Mr. Pitt. At least, I would do my best. Is it indiscreet to ask the name of the British agent you mention?"

Marny laughed again. "Not at all. In point of fact, your relations with said agent had considerable bearing on your appointment."

"My relations with him?" Richard stared. "Do I know the gentleman?"

"The lady, sir," Marny corrected. And with an arch look, "Egad, I wish I knew Madame des Landes as well as you."

"Madame des Landes?" Richard breathed.

"None other. The divine Amélie. She's been in the pay of His Majesty's government for some time. And at no small figure. But worth it. We heard of de Conflans's sailing through her, and the size of his fleet. Admiral Hawke did the rest. However, she remains Amélie, and that means in debt. I suppose she's equally in the pay of Choiseul. We're on our guard against that. And, therefore, you can easily see why you were selected for the mission."

"I'm afraid I don't," mused Richard. He found this new aspect of Amélie hard to accept. That she had no morals in the usual sense, he knew; but it was somehow different to serve as traitor, and perhaps double traitor, for the sake of money.

"Why, isn't it obvious," said the Earl, "that she would be less likely to betray you than anyone else we could send? Isn't it probable, on the contrary, that she will do her best to promote your designs and exert herself to your advantage? She's very partial to you. Sentiment's paramount with a woman. And in this case, we need her devotion. She has great influence and the best connections."

"Clever!" Richard thought, but without enthusiasm. He could see now why he, of all men, fitted the task in Paris. There was no favoritism about it. Far from being mad, his father and Mr. Pitt were simply artists in intrigue, opposed to other artists; and in that cold game expediency ruled.

He was silent for so long that Marny asked what ailed him.

"Nothing, my lord. I was considering what finesse one needs in foreign business. Perhaps, too, I had thought better of Madame des Landes."

"Odd's life!" snapped Marny. "Surely you don't think worse of her on such finicking grounds. If she were French by birth, there might be room for cavil; but she was born Irish, bred in Italy, and married to a profligate thrice her age, who is her only link with France. Patriotism in her would be sham. Besides, my dear boy, what do you expect from a woman of rank and fashion? Spartan principles? Gad! Such a woman lives to please and be pleased. There's her function. And that takes money." He broke off, smiling, then added: "In the career you're embarked on, Richard, keep what scruples you must, but, for God's sake, don't look for any in women. Their motives are love and vanity. Apply yourself singly to those, make a deft use of them, and you'll seldom miscarry. What's more, if you don't take women seriously, you'll never be disenchanted. Pray remember that."

"I shall remember it, my lord. — By the way, will the Countess be expecting me?"

"Of course — and impatiently, I warrant. You lucky fellow! I wish I were young again." Marny sighed. "It hasn't escaped you, I hope, that the old Count des Landes won't live forever, nay (what with his vices), that he'll soon be called to his reward. Have you given thought to it?"

"I have not, sir."

"Well, do so, I beg. The Countess des Landes would be as good a match as a young dog like you could expect. Your birth precludes any fashionable marriage here. On her side, I wager, she'll have little fortune left; and that means few takers in France. But her rank and experience of the world would enhance your credit. I'd make good her dowry. When the time comes, you'd have my blessing. What d'ye say?"

To the Earl's disappointment, Richard said merely that both the suggestion and his lordship's generous interest did him too much honor; that if the time ever came . . .

"Forgive me," Marny interrupted. "I thought 'twould please you."

"Immeasurably sir."

But they left it at that.

"At least," Marny went on, "I can assume that you welcome the flattering employment that Mr. Pitt offers you."

"It is impossible to express my gratitude, both to your lordship and his Excellency."

LVI

FOUR months later, at the inn in Beauvais, his last overnight stop on the road from Holland, Richard put in some time over his already well-studied map of Paris. For every reason, it was important to know the city as well as possible before plunging into it. He had heard all his life of the Louvre, the Palais Royal, or the Tuileries, but it was a different matter to find his way in imagination from that center to the Marais quarter in the East or to the opposite Faubourg Saint-Germain.

Not for the first time, the roundish shape of Paris reminded him of a spider's web. On the map, he could follow its growth from the tiny Ile de la Cité through ever widening circles of ramparts to its present vastness. The spinning of the web had taken two thousand years. It embraced the rise and fall of polities with the creeds that animated them; it represented billions of human lives; it connected the Caesars with the Bourbons, the Druids with the Encyclopedists, the dawn of history with this most modern second of May, 1760. But the ageless spinner lived on. Rome had dwindled with the centuries, but not Paris. Richard traced the present limits of the city along the great boulevards that now half encircled it, forming an elegant driveway and promenade between ranks of trees with convents, mansions, and cafés scattered behind them. Beyond these, beyond the gardens of the Tuileries and the Place Louis XV, or, crossing the Seine, beyond the quarters of the South, lay, for the most part, open country. And yet even there filaments were reaching out. Perhaps, north of the boulevards, the very vineyards of Montmartre would someday disappear in the network of the city. And here to the west, the magnificent new park with its superb avenue, which had been named the Elysian Fields, might someday be enclosed by the expanding web. And there, across the river, the dome of the still recent Invalides, the mass of the just completed École Militaire, now beyond the suburbs, stood as lonely forerunners of inevitable growth.

Richard wondered how the map of Paris would look two hundred years later. It was hard to imagine a greater, more splendid city than this, with its population of nine hundred thousand, its countless palaces, gardens, squares, shops, theaters, convents, churches, public buildings, its multitude of streets. Compared with it, Venice was a little town; London, though big enough, a smoky hodgepodge. Here was the humane center of the world, toward which all eyes were turned, from which all Europe, humbly aping, derived the arts of life. And tomorrow at this time, thought Richard, he would be in Paris.

Turning to the window, he stood for a while breathing the spring air. But he was unconscious of the inn at Beauvais. His months of training at The Hague had already grown dim. He was absorbed by tomorrow.

Yes, a spider's web, infinitely vibrant and glittering. He would soon be one of the million gnats tangled in its filaments, pulsing to the current of its intense life, and ecstatically so; for spring and love and adventure beckoned to him from Paris. And above all he was young.

Early on the following afternoon, his post chaise, having threaded its way through the unregulated stream of vehicles that filled the busier streets on the Right Bank, crossed the Seine, followed the Quai Malaquais a short distance, then, turning right into the Rue des Petits-Augustins, deposited Richard at the fashionable Hôtel de Luxembourg.

As befitted a young gentleman of Holland, traveling for his pleasure, one of the better suites at four hundred livres a month had been reserved for him by the Dutch embassy. Indeed, the ambassador, Monsieur van Berkenroode, in person had visited the hôtel-garnis to assure himself that Monsieur d'Amond would be well lodged. Therefore, the proprietor and his wife showered civilities on the new guest, conducted him to his rooms, and put themselves entirely at his service. Monsieur desired his own valet? Several would present themselves tomorrow for his selection from the *bureau de placement*. Monsieur needed a private coach while in Paris? The proprietor would himself call at the *remise* and obtain one of the most elegant, complete with coachman and footmen. Until tomorrow, alas, he hoped that Monsieur d'Amond would condescend to the servants of the hotel, who would be devoted to his orders. A public conveyance could be summoned in a little moment. An excellent barber would at once be called.

A little dizzy with new impressions and glad to have finished with the long jostling of the post chaise, Richard gave himself over to the barber while his boxes were being unpacked and a suit for the evening laid out. It was pleasant, with nice-smelling soap on his face, to lean back under the hands of the expert. His bedroom opened on a little walled garden at the rear of the house, and a linden in the center of it softened the light. Through the long window breathed the pungent, enticing odor of Paris.

The man chatted civilly. Yes, Monsieur was perfectly right. The Rue de Varenne lay at no great distance. One had only to follow the Rue Jacob to the Rue des Saints-Pères, then turn left to the Chemin de la Justice, then right to the Rue de la Chaise, then left to the Rue de la Planche, then right . . . But Monsieur would, of course, take a fiacre. No gentleman would expose himself to the spattering of the streets . . . The Hôtel des Landes? Naturally everyone knew of it. A princely residence, one of the finest in the new quarter. Opposite the Hôtel de Biron, close to the Couvent des Récollettes. So. Monsieur was paying his respects at the Hôtel des Landes? The barber grew reverential. Only the haute noblesse inhabited the Rue de Varenne . . .

At last, shaved, powdered, and perfumed, Richard was valeted into attire suitable for such a call. He wore a maroon-colored coat, with his best lace at the wrists and jabot, his finest brocaded waistcoat and snowiest wig. His fob and knee buckles glittered. He carried a cane with a gold knob. Finally, the hotel lackey handed him his hat, with its edging of white plumes, and draped a long cloak on his shoulders. Tall and splendid, he was now Monsieur le Chevalier d'Amond; for in a land of titles like France, it would be ridiculous not to adopt one.

His dress somehow recalled the scarlet uniform of Lieutenant Hammond in Bristol, the paste jewels of Count Roberto on the Brenta. Here was another costume. He half shrugged. What was the world after all, or the life of a man, but a sequence of costumes? Sometime, he could write his memoirs in those terms. It was an amusing notion. Waiting below for the fiacre, he took a pinch of snuff.

But once in the carriage, behind a clip-clopping horse, he could think only of Amélie. He had thought of her a good deal more than of anything else during recent months. If she had seemed remote and out of place in Canada, a thousand trifles every day in the fashionable circles at The Hague had reminded him of her. How would she receive him? Had the passion of a year and a half ago faded? He was a little surprised that no welcoming note from her had been left at his lodgings. Perhaps she had not been informed by the Dutch embassy that he would arrive on the third of May. Perhaps, too, because of his known mission to Paris, she was being discreet. Perhaps something else . . .

There was a good chance, too, that Amélie would not be at home. He ought to have informed himself . . .

The city suddenly thinned out into the Faubourg Saint-Germain. Streets were straighter and wider. Mansions of the nobility, called *hôtels* to distinguish them from simple houses, stood somewhat apart from each other, proud and massive, with courtyards in front and formal gardens behind them. Here, too, as everywhere else in Paris, were convents and religious establishments. But all was of comparatively recent date, reflecting the tide of fashion which had shifted from east to west in the last sixty years. Gilded coaches rolled by, with bewigged footmen behind and a bewigged coachman in front. Through their windows Richard caught a glimpse of arrogant profiles. Here and there, at the gateway of some mansion, flunkeys gossiped. A convent bell sounded the Angelus.

Then, without warning, the fiacre turned into the courtyard of a fine house, and Richard's heart sank. The place was alive with coaches, while others waited along the street. There could be no doubt that Madame was at home, but at home to a number of people. Yes — damnation! — it must be her *jour de salon*. The idea, so long entertained, of a first meeting in private, had either to be given up, or he must drive back to his lodgings.

He was in two minds what to do, when the fiacre stopped in front of the imposing entrance, and a liveried servant, opening the carriage door, stood waiting for him to get out. Caught unprepared, he did so, and the die had been cast.

"That will be one livre," said the driver, adjusting the fare to Richard's clothes. "Does Monsieur desire me to wait?"

"Yes . . . No, I'm not sure . . ."

The driver pocketed his money. "As Monsieur wishes."

"On second thought, yes. Please wait . . ."

The fiacre got itself out of the way of a grand coach rolling up behind it with a clatter of horses and much agility of footmen leaping down from their perch. The liveried servant hastened to make his reverence before the coat of arms on its panels.

Still confused, Richard walked into the house to be received by another flunkey, who took charge of his cloak and hat. A third bowed him toward the great stairway leading to the second floor.

Like several mansions in the quarter, the Hôtel des Landes had two wings, facing each other across the courtyard and connected by the central body of the house. It was three stories high, including the mansard. In a worldly ménage like the des Landes's, Monsieur le Comte no doubt lived in one wing, and Madame la Comtesse, in the other.

By this time, Richard had recovered himself and walked leisurely up the stairs. Used to great houses in London and The Hague, it was not the magnificence here that disconcerted him but rather the loss of a first tête-à-tête with Amélie. Once resigned to that, he adjusted himself to what could not be helped. And, after all, this was an event of importance which he had often anticipated. It would be his initiation into the Parisian salon, which, more than any other French institution, molded the thought and manners of Europe. Here was the fountainhead of urbane life. He had also his mission to consider and must be concerned with it from now on.

Upstairs, a hum of voices drew him to the right, and he gave his name to the tall footman posted outside an open door. The man bowed, waving him in, and called out,

"Monsieur le Chevalier d'Amond!"

LVII

RICHARD'S first impression was of height and color. Against the pale walls of the long room, with their moldings and inset panels above doorways, against the high arched windows, with their rose-silk hangings, the costumes of men and women formed vivid patches of scarlet, azure, green, saffron and every other shade. Tall mirrors added space and multiplied the gathering. There were perhaps thirty people present, but separated into small groups: one at a table where *thé à l'anglaise* was being served; others, seated or standing in conversation; another about the harpsichord. Over there, a couple played cards, while several bystanders looked on. So large was the room that one had no sense of crowding, and yet the various groups did not seem isolated. Then, as details emerged, Richard noticed the typical flaming red on the women's faces in contrast to the whiteness of their coiffures. He was aware of the ribbons, stars and crosses of the gentlemen; the polished, assertive lilt of French voices . . .

And almost at once, he caught sight of Amélie, who at the sound of his name excused herself to some guests and came sweeping toward him. But almost at once, too, he could feel the complete difference between now and eighteen months ago. Her eyes and lips smiled; her curtsy was not too formal; yet somehow she made it plain that he was nothing more than a pleasantly remembered acquaintance.

"Monsieur d'Amond! What joy to see you at last in Paris! It's most civil of you to call. I hope your journey from The Hague was not too fatiguing. How time flies! We met, I believe, two years ago — or was it three?"

He could put this welcome down to play-acting; but, surely, as he bent over her hand, the faintest pressure of her fingers could have taken all the chill from it. He looked, too, in vain, for a signal of any kind in her smiling eyes.

He adopted her manner. "No, madame, no more than a year and a half since I had that honor."

She made a compliment. "You should be flattered that it seems longer to me."

"And you, madame, that I have kept such accurate count."

A gentleman had drifted up. Amélie included him. "Monsieur de Sartines, let me present the Chevalier d'Amond of Holland." And to Richard, "I can think of no more valuable acquaintance for a novice in Paris to have. As you know, Monsieur de Sartines is our Lieutenant General of Police. He can resolve any difficulties with a wave of his hand. I commend you to him."

So this, thought Richard, was probably the clue to Amélie's behavior. De Sartines, of course, knew all about him and had been watching them both. What did he know, or what did Amélie fear he knew, about her? Richard found some balm for his ruffled feelings in that uncertainty. At once he was very much on his guard. General Yorke in The Hague had warned him that Sartines would be his chief danger; that he had untold informers to depend on, that he would suspect Richard of espionage; and that any sign of it would mean not only the failure of the latter's mission but likely enough the Bastille.

The Minister of Police did not choose to hide his claws. "Ah," he said graciously. "I have heard of Monsieur d'Amond, who comes so well recommended. Indeed, sir, as it happens, only yesterday the Duc de Choiseul spoke of you in my presence and desired me to show you every attention. He awaits the pleasure of receiving you at the Palais Bourbon."

Richard bowed. "I shall hasten to pay my homage to the Duke, as I have now the honor of paying it to your Excellency."

"Monsieur's politeness," smiled de Sartines, "is most obliging. Meanwhile, I hope you find the Hôtel de Luxembourg more to your taste than the inn at Beauvais. Somehow it reached me that you had trouble with post horses there."

"A slight disagreement," Richard said easily, though he took good note of the hint. "Is your Excellency omniscient?"

"Oh, no, monsieur, but I am well informed."

"And here," Amélie ran on in the smooth manner of a perfect hostess, "is one who needs no introduction. Like me, he shares the pleasure of your acquaintance, Monsieur le Chevalier. It's a small world . . ."

Engrossed with de Sartines, Richard had been only half aware of someone who had come up behind him. He looked now — and managed to control a start — into the handsome, debonair face of Marcello Tromba.

"Mon cher Monsieur d'Amond," Tromba bowed, with the expression of a man uncertain that he will be remembered, "you may recall that we met in Bath when you, the Comtesse des Landes and I, were all visiting England."

It took adroitness to interpret this. That it was intended for the benefit of de Sartines could be assumed. The latter, of course, knew about Amélie and Tromba in Bath, but possibly he did not know too much.

"Mon cher Marquis," returned Richard, "could I ever forget that honor!"

The man at the door was on the point of announcing the personage who had arrived behind Richard. Amélie excused herself. "For the moment, messieurs, I entrust the Chevalier d'Amond to you. Will you present him to the company?"

The flunkey intoned, "Monseigneur le Maréchal de Richelieu."

Amélie's curtsy to the tall, slender old gentleman was almost as deep as if he had been a prince of the blood. Grandnephew of the famous Cardinal, the most distinguished roué of the age and one of its leading soldiers, he occupied a special position. When he made his bow, she beckoned to a lackey. "Hurry, Michel. Pray inform the Comte des Landes that his Excellence is here. — Ah, Monsieur le Duc," she went on, "nothing less than your presence will tempt the Count from his den."

To Richard, drifting along with Tromba and de Sartines, it was all as real or unreal as a play. Treating it as such, he felt at ease. If nothing else, one could admire the art of it, which seemed almost artless. Exquisite amiability. Charming manners. None of the English haughtiness and chill. The give-and-take of talk, spiced with wit, subtle as a toccata. Artifice that had become nature. Richard's cynical old friend Monsieur Coco, gorgeously ruffling on his perch — even a couple of the ladies' lapdogs, curled and perfumed, sniffing each other on the floor — belonged to the cast.

It was a mixed salon, chiefly aristocratic and political, but with a seasoning of letters. As he was gradually taken around, Richard, who had been well coached by his father, knew most of the names and something about them: Madame de Boufflers, for example, the bewitching and adored mistress of the Prince de Conti; or the equally celebrated Madame du Deffand, once mistress of the Regent, now in her sixties, but managing herself so well that one hardly supposed she was blind; or, a little younger, the still spirited Madame de Luxembourg, wife of the Marshal; or the still lovely Madame de la Vallière; or the gay and newly married Madame de Broglie; or Madame de Crussol, Madame de Cambis, Madame de

Caraman . . . Some old, some young, but all great ladies and adepts of savoir vivre that set the tone and served as model for social Europe. They and the gentlemen surrounding them were the defenders of that last ideal of aristocracy, the religion of good breeding. To anyone they recognized, all the doors of fashion were open; and anyone they rejected remained outside.

But, for the moment, they included Richard as one of themselves. He was soon aware that the fiction of the Chevalier d'Amond was already an open secret which they found piquant. They had all known Lord Marny and were well disposed toward his son, while politely accepting the latter's incognito. Marny, indeed, had written to one of these gentlemen, the Comte de Saint-Florentin, who cordially welcomed Richard to Paris, referred, with a twinkle, to his illustrious father, the Comte d'Amond, and asked for news of The Hague. And here was a Monsieur Prud'homme, the confidential secretary of the Duc de Choiseul, who seemed to be no less well informed. There were many allusions with a double meaning, in which the ladies joined. Richard could feel that his debut had been successful. He heard Madame de Boufflers remark (perhaps for his benefit): "Ce jeune homme là me plaît."

Meanwhile, tactfully guided by Tromba, who seemed popular here as elsewhere, he moved from group to group. This handsome, vivid man who greeted him so civilly was none other than the world-renowned d'Alembert; and that odd, whimsical gentleman, the wit and dilettante Pont de Veyle . . . At the end of the room he became suddenly aware of his old acquaintance (if he could call him such) the Count des Landes, who stood talking with the Marshal de Richelieu.

In this connection, he heard one of the younger men near by observe to another: "Tiens! There's something new. The master of the house himself! I don't recall seeing him here before."

"You could hardly expect to, mon cher. He has other interests. Besides —" the speaker's glance rested on Tromba, who, at the moment, was chatting with Madame de Crussol — "I understand he detests the amant en titre."

"Jealousy? Incredible."

"Don't be absurd. Not jealousy — antipathy, mon cher . . ." The two moved away, leaving Richard in the depths.

Yes, that accounted for the reception he had had, Amélie's smiling indifference. It had not only been play-acting for de Sartines. He had been conscious of something more, of Tromba's possessiveness and leading role in the salon. And no wonder, if Tromba was now her accredited lover. At a stroke, Richard found Paris savorless. Besides, what of his mission . . .

But it was no time for brooding. Aware of Monsieur de Sartines's speculative eye, he joined him.

"Can your Excellence tell me," he asked, "if the Marquis de Tromba-Corleone has some employment in Paris? When I last saw him, he was very much a man of leisure."

"Indeed?" said de Sartines. "You know, I find it hard to imagine that so ingenious and active a man as Monsieur de Tromba could ever be so qualified. I'd have supposed that he had always had a number of irons in the fire. Certainly it's the case here. But, to answer your question, he is officially employed as a director of the state lottery, which was established several years ago to defray the cost of the École Militaire. I believe, too, he's engaged in private lotteries."

"Successfully, I hope?"

"Ah," shrugged de Sartines, "I hope he is. I'm a child when it comes to finance, monsieur. You knew him well in England?"

Richard could shrug, too. "As one meets another socially."

"He left under something of a cloud, I'm told." De Sartines was obviously probing. "A duel, wasn't there?"

Richard nodded. He wondered how well informed the Lieutenant General of Police actually was. "Now that your Excellence mentions it, I believe I did hear of a duel."

"What caused it?"

"Ah, as to that, monsieur . . ."

"You can trust me, Monsieur d'Amond."

"Indeed, your Excellence inspires confidence. But as to that, the Marquis himself is a more reliable source. No doubt it was some point of honor. I heard that Monsieur de Tromba is very scrupulous in such matters."

De Sartines smiled. "*Scrupulous*, no doubt, is the word that best describes him." And, with another smile, "You're discreet, Monsieur le Chevalier. I admire discretion."

They both handled their snuffboxes amiably and with mutual esteem. Neither had been able to pierce the other's guard.

The two young men who had been discussing des Landes came up with a show of eagerness.

"Now," exclaimed one of them, the Comte de Coigny, "we'll consult the Oracle in person and settle this matter. For what Monsieur de Sartines doesn't know about opera girls isn't worth mention."

"Yes, if he'll commit himself," put in the other. "Oracles seldom do."

"He will this once for my sake. Isn't it true, Monsieur de Sartines, that you write something lush every day about these dear creatures of the Opéra for the special delectation of His Majesty and Madame de Pompadour?"

"Is that the subject of debate?" fenced de Sartines.

"No, it's to prove your competence; it's to show Monsieur de Tessé here that oracles do commit themselves."

"Gentlemen, you flatter me with such a title. What shall I say? It's true that the King is informed about *all* his subjects through various channels."

"You see!" chuckled de Tessé.

"But what," de Sartines added, "was the matter you wished to settle?"

"Wait," said the Count — "have you seen La Tour's painting 'Venus Receiving the Apple'? There are plates of it in all the stalls. What a parade of charms!"

The Minister of Police nodded. "Yes, superb! Devastating!"

"Isn't it? Cela fait sauter les boutons, eh? Now the question is this. I claim it's a portrait of the danseuse Mademoiselle Allard. De Tessé denies it. He says the face is unlike —"

"Ah, ça, messieurs," de Sartines interrupted, "it isn't the face one recognizes in such a painting."

"Exactly!" triumphed de Coigny. "As I told him. Ce grain de beauté sur la cuisse. Cette petite fossette . . . It can only be l'Allard. And *he* suggested la Venier!"

Richard's ears burned. He forced himself to gaze indifferently across the room.

"They have the same figure," de Tessé put in. "I find la Venier's more attractive."

"But, Monsieur l'Oracle," challenged the other, "which of us is right?"

De Sartines could see no reason for hedging on such a point. "*You* are, Monsieur de Coigny. Aside from the well-known features you mention, I talked with La Tour. The painting is of Mademoiselle Allard, at the command of her patron, the Duc de Mazarin. He has it now in his bedroom."

"Voilà!" de Coigny gestured, "And de Tessé owes me twenty-five louis. He can have his Venier."

Richard asked casually, "Are you gentlemen referring to Mademoiselle *Maritza* de Venier?"

"Yes. Do you know her?"

"We have met. How is she regarded at the Opéra?"

The others exchanged glances. It was evidently a debated subject.

"As for me," said de Coigny, "I find her detestable."

"And I, ravishing," said de Tessé.

"And I," said de Sartines, "a superb artist. But that, Monsieur d'Amond is not enough. She has the worst possible reputation. And, therefore, she has no future."

Forgetting his manners, Richard exclaimed: "Bon Dieu, your Excellence! I can't believe it. A reputation for what?"

De Sartines shook his head. "Chastity, monsieur," he said in a low, troubled voice. And at Richard's change of expression he added, "No, I'm quite serious, though I blush for our age. In her profession and in a clearinghouse of gallantry like the Opéra (you know we call it the *Magasin,* where one shops for girls) to be known as chaste is to be disreputable and, still worse, grotesque. It's the unforgivable vice."

"Now, come," put in de Tessé, taking up the cudgels, "the late Mademoiselle Sallé had a similar reputation, and you can't deny that she was one of the leading ballerinas of her time."

"No," the other agreed, "I don't deny it. I could point out that her greatest success was in England and that she left the stage early. But, mon ami, one swallow, account for it as you may, doesn't make a summer, and great exceptions usually prove the rule. Who else can you mention?"

De Tessé looked nonplused.

"There you are," de Sartines waved. "I admit that the Venier dances well. But what of it? Is she protected by the Duc de Mazarin? Is she painted by La Tour? Is she the talk of Paris? Do her escapades amuse the King? In the name of heaven — or, rather the other place — what future can she have?"

"Perhaps," leered de Coigny, "it isn't too late! Perhaps she'll repent. Mon cher de Tessé, for the sake of the devil, convert her in time to give Monsieur de Sartines at least one gay paragraph for the eyes of His Majesty."

De Sartines joined in the laugh. "Yes, her career depends on it. And while there's life, there's hope."

Excusing himself, Richard looked about for his hostess. He had made the round. Besides, he felt oddly sick of the place.

Finding Amélie, he took his leave. She remained only charming and impersonal.

He walked a little frozenly toward the door, and, happening to pass the Count des Landes, who was still in talk with the Marshal de Richelieu, bowed civilly before moving on.

The old gentleman, in the act of refreshing himself with a drink of brandy from the decanter on a side table, gave a cough and a start, then called out after Richard. "Hey, monsieur! Dammy! One moment!"

And when Richard turned, the Count stood regarding him with a glassy expression. The Marshal, too, seemed equally disturbed.

"Yes, monsieur?" Richard prompted.

Des Landes cleared his throat. "Mon ami," he said to Richelieu, "remember the dream I had in Italy that I told you about? Well, I'm not drunk now. Do you see what I see?"

"Diable!" said the Marshal. He looked like a handsome old greyhound and spoke in a dusty voice. "Hm-m, Milord himself. — And I'm not drunk either. — Monsieur," he said to Richard, "I ask your pardon. Will you be good enough to tell us your name?"

Aware that he was again being taken for his grandfather, Richard smiled. "D'Amond, monseigneur."

"Yes, yes . . . of course," muttered the Duke. "D'Amond, de Marny. Same thing."

Des Landes put in, "Look here. I don't believe in ghosts. Please explain yourself, monsieur."

398

Richard feigned surprise. "There's little to explain. I am Richard d'Amond of The Hague, spending some time in Paris." He addressed the Marshal. "Your Excellence spoke of de Marny. As it happens, my grandfather was the Baron de Marny. I am said to resemble him."

"So *that's* it!" The Duke's face cleared. "*Resemble* him? Good God, you gave me a turn. For if there's any man would be restless in his grave it's your venerable grandfather. The Comte des Landes and I, monsieur, were intimate with Charles de Marny in the old King's days. When we were young, d'you see . . ." He gave a reminiscent cackle. "Lord! If you resemble him in character, my young friend, you'll have a devilish good time in Paris."

"And, by God," put in des Landes, who, though visibly relieved, was still a trifle confused, "isn't it plain he's having it! He always had a penchant for his friends' wives. So you meet him first in my wife's salon. Dear old Charles!" He made an effort. "Where are you lodging, monsieur? . . . that is, I mean, if you're lodging anywhere."

"At the Hôtel de Luxembourg."

The Count nodded. "Yes, I recall you always stopped there. I'll wait on you tomorrow, Milord — I mean, Monsieur d'Amond. You're a godsend. You'll renew my youth. Some cards, eh? As for wenches, I'll bring you up to date — that is, I'll acquaint you with Paris."

"On that point," interrupted the Marshal, "I think I know more than you, mon vieux Hercule. Pray include me. I need some renewing myself. You know, I find it cursed amusing to step back into the past this way. Monsieur d'Amond, please consider me very much at your service. I've never had a more congenial friend than your grandfather. Anything I can do . . ."

Watching from across the room, Monsieur de Sartines itched to overhear the conversation. How did a newly arrived young Englishman happen to be on such cordial terms with two legendary rakes of Paris like des Landes and the Duke? But before the Minister of Police could edge over to them, Richard had bowed himself off and left the salon.

Downstairs, a lackey summoned Monsieur d'Amond's fiacre, bowed him in, and asked for his destination.

On the spur of the moment, Richard decided against returning to his lodgings. After the ache of the past hour, he felt an odd longing to see Maritza again.

"To the Opéra," he said.

LVIII

THE Royal Academy of Music, to use the official title of the Opéra, was then, and had been long, established in the eastern wing of the Palais Royal. Built originally as the private theater of the Cardinal de Richelieu and later occupied by the troupe of the great Molière, it became still later the scene of Lully's musical triumphs, sustained now by the masterpieces of Rameau, and enjoyed a fame in Europe out of proportion to its size and old-fashioned appointments. Repeated fires and subsequent changes would obliterate it and would completely alter the aspect of the palace itself, together with the expanse of as yet unenclosed gardens behind. But on this May evening Richard's fiacre deposited him in the courtyard of a building which had changed little in the past seventy years.

"Down that way," said the driver, indicating a passage between walls, which served as a public access to the Opéra. "We can't drive in there."

It was after five and not long until curtain time. A poster announced that Rameau's ballet *Les Paladins* would be given. But, consulting it, Richard could not find Maritza's name among the ballerinas advertised — nor Marie Allard's, for that matter — only such veterans as Lyonnois and Vestris. However, since the presence of understudies was required in case of accident, Maritza would probably be in the theater.

Joining the trickle of early arrivals, who would fill the unreserved pit, Richard followed them to the end of the passageway. Accustomed to the splendor of Venetian theaters, he was struck by the modest approach to this world-famous place. And yet, dingy as it was, its glory made up for it. One might contest the preeminence of French music or singers — there were two schools of thought about that — but here certainly was the pinnacle of European ballet. No other opera house in the world had such a history of great names: among many, the ballerinas Prévost, Sallé,

Camargo; the dancers Lany, Noverre, and Gaetan Vestris. Just as other countries took their directive in fashion from the Rue Saint-Honoré, so with respect to dancing they followed as best they could the lead of the Paris Opera. That Maritza Venier, with no other aid than her talent, had already made a place for herself on this stage seemed to Richard a considerable achievement.

Skirting the entrance, he found his way to the stage door and walked boldly in, to be stopped at once by a sergeant of the Gardes Françaises on duty there. Long experience had made him an adept in such dealings. Though most theaters had rules for excluding the public, they were seldom proof against a lordly manner and the right tip. Richard now used both with the air of a man who took admission for granted, and asked to be shown the dressing room of Mademosielle de Venier.

The man stared. "Did Monsieur say *Mademoiselle de Venier?*"

"Certainly."

"With all submission to Monsieur," urged the sergeant, "take my advice. Do not attempt it. Do not cause another incident. So many have tried. She is inhuman, monsieur. Why, only last week an officer of the Gardes Suisses who desired to pay his respects was bitten in the leg . . ."

"Now, come!" put in Richard. "What do you mean?"

"The truth, monsieur. She has a ferocious dog. If you get past the dog, she has a dragon in the form of a woman who watches over her. If you get past the dragon — which no one has ever done — you have Mademoiselle Spitfire herself. I ask you, monsieur, is all this worth while? There are so many of the girls who would value Monsieur's attentions. For example, Mademoiselle Damiré has no one at present in her dressing room . . ."

"No," Richard insisted, "it must be Mademoiselle de Venier." He could not help adding: "I have fifty louis on it. As a sporting man, Monsieur le Sergeant, you would not wish me to lose without an effort?"

The other shook his head. "No, but it is my duty to warn you. Remember, monsieur, that Mademoiselle had the law on her side. The ladies of the Académie Royale have a right to their privacy if they desire it. God knows, most of them don't . . ."

He beckoned to a soldier (there were some forty policing the

401

Opéra) and directed him to guide Monsieur to the dressing room of Mademoiselle de Venier. The words created a stir among several bystanders; and as Richard set out with his guide, two or three followed at a short distance.

Like all backstage premises, these were dim, dusty, and cavernous. They were alive, too, with the bustle that precedes the rise of the curtain, a racing up and down stairs, an occasional figure in costume, injunctions to hurry, the remote tuning up of fiddles in the orchestra. Richard decided that his friend the sergeant must have gathered a harvest in tips that evening. There were plenty of fops dangling at the doors of dressing rooms and masculine voices mingled with titters from inside. This was especially true of the larger rooms that contained the figurants.

Apparently the news of his undertaking accompanied him; for by the time he had scaled a couple of stairways and threaded a few corridors, he had quite a retinue of idlers tagging along. They were in the high spirits of people bent on excitement.

"Two to one," hissed a voice.

"Agreed!"

"Ah, le pauvre benêt! Qu'il fait pitié, celui-là!"

Another exhorted Richard, "Courage, mon héros!"

"Hush!" warned someone. "Here we are. Give him a chance."

Richard's guide paused. "Yes, monsieur, here we are. And if Monsieur had any small contribution in mind —" he let the suggestion hang and murmured — "better now than afterwards."

Richard gave him a coin. The sound of footsteps and voices had evidently been heard in the dressing room, for a deep-throated growl, rising in cadence, answered through the door. The group of followers stepped back.

"Who shall I announce?" the soldier hesitated.

"I'll announce myself."

Richard knocked. The growl took on volume. "Coss'è?" challenged the voice of Anzoletta in its sharpest tones.

He answered in Venetian. "A friend, Sior' Amia."

"Va al Tuco! What friend?"

"Richard, whom you —" he caught himself in time — "whom you met in Bath."

There was a moment of dead silence, then a hurry of footsteps, another voice, "Richard? — Milòr?"

402

"Ma certo."

And to the openmouthed amazement of the spectators, the door flew wide. The unapproachable ballerina, half dressed, threw her arms around the caller's neck, kissed him on both cheeks, kissed him again.

"Caro ti! *Caro ti?*"

Then the dragon embraced him, too, while the big yellow dog twitched its tail, though with a look of suspicion.

Anzoletta turned a stream of Venetian on the idlers, who melted away.

But this was something tremendous. This was something ten times better than the row they had expected. A sensation! An event to set the Opéra in a buzz, to be reported in the gazettes. Grand Dieu! La Venier had a lover! La Venier, after all, was no monster of chastity. She had simply been faithful to an unknown gallant, this Milord or whoever he was. That made sense; that was creditable. Une vraie affaire de coeur. Une grande passion. But perhaps he was her husband? Absurd. Or brother? Ridiculous. No, messieurs, those kisses were not wifely or sisterly. She had ceased to be a reproach to the Opéra. But who was he? The gossips could make anything of this they pleased . . .

Meanwhile, in the cluttered dressing room that Anzoletta had not yet had time to tidy up, exclamations and questions darted about. The strain and constraint of their last meeting in Bath was gone.

"But, Richard! . . . Tell me . . . How does it happen . . . Gran' Dio . . ."

Maritza hurried into a dress that Anzoletta held over her.

He took the occasion to put in: "Is this our Bapi, this huge beast?" and held out his hand to the dog, who sniffed, then wagged decisively and let his head be scratched.

"Beast? Not at all," she said, emerging, "he's an angel. But you couldn't hold him in one hand any more, Richard. Sior Rubini of the Italian Theater brought him to me from Turin. He's been my protector ever since. — And now . . . now . . . you've so much to tell . . . Canada? . . . the war? . . . How long have you been in Paris? . . . What are you doing? . . ."

"Maritzetta, wait. You haven't told me about yourself, your father. How is his Excellence?"

The sudden empty look on her face and Anzoletta's warned him. After a moment, she said: "No, of course, you couldn't have heard . . . Sior Pa're died six months ago . . ."

Anzoletta turned away.

"No," said Richard, deeply moved, "I hadn't heard."

"He was ill a long time," Maritza went on. "He often spoke of you . . . I think at the last he imagined he was home in Venice again . . . He wanted you to read his poem . . ."

"It was finished?"

"No . . . not finished . . ." The muffled sounds of the overture drifted up from the main hall. She seated herself absently in front of the mirror. "I'm not on tonight, but we're supposed to be ready."

"Maritza cara, I wish I could say . . . I wish I could tell you . . ."

"I know." She nodded at his reflection in the mirror. "There's nothing anyone can say — nothing at all." She turned and held out her hand to him. "Richard! I'm so glad you're here. At first, Anzoletta and I . . . But you can imagine how it was . . ."

Yes, he could imagine . . .

Anzoletta planted her fists on her hips. "One has to face things," she said. "That's what the gist of life is. Mostly one has to face them alone. So — we managed. Now tell us about you . . ."

Later, the three had supper at the Café Foy that opened on the gardens of the Palais Royal from the Rue de Richelieu. The theaters were over at nine; and on a soft May evening such as this, tables everywhere were filled, and people strolled here or in the neighboring gardens of the Tuileries. A drift of colors under the lanterns, the vast murmur of voices, an orchestra playing somewhere, the sound of carriages on the streets, the magic of a spring night.

By this time, after a fashion, the present had been linked to the past: Canada, Maritza's season in London, her months in Paris. They found it easy now to talk about everything — or nearly everything. Time had subtly altered their relationship, though Richard could not have defined what it had become. Mellower than once and more perceptive; an acceptance rather than a challenge; warmer than friendship, cooler than love. Friendship tinged with love was perhaps the nearest he could come to it; but a friendship haunted by what had been between them.

"So you won't tell us," she smiled, "why you're now Monsieur d'Amond of The Hague?"

"I'd like to, madonna. But it isn't my secret. State business. You can be assured that it's open enough. The French know who I am."

She nodded. "I won't pry, and I'll be discreet. It doesn't matter as long as you're here. I can guess, though, that Lord Marny's pleased. But to help me to be discreet — there are Italians, and some Venetians, at the Théâtre des Italiens, friends of mine." She lowered her voice. "You'd rather not meet them, I suppose?"

"Better not," he agreed, "after what happened in Venice."

"I heard from your mother in Bordeaux when Father died," she went on. "Does she know about you?"

"Yes, and disapproves because of Lord Marny." A shadow of the old ache, the old division in himself, returned. "I'm sorry. But I hadn't much of a choice, Maritzetta."

"I know," she said, and returned to the present.

He was relieved to find that she and Anzoletta were in not too difficult circumstances. As one of the promising ballerinas, she had a salary of fifteen hundred livres from the Opéra; and there was something left over from the sale of the mortgaged palazzo in Venice. They lived sparingly but not in want.

"And you're still glad you became a ballerina?" asked Richard. "You still care for dancing as you used to?"

"More than ever. Why, Richard caro, think of what's happening now. The whole art's changing, growing. One has to be an actress as well as a dancer — in pantomime, of course. But the ballet's becoming a real part of the opera, not just thrown in as an interlude." She ran on about the great dancer Noverre and his innovations. "You see, Richard, this is all happening in Paris. It's the beginning of a new ballet really. I can't tell you how exciting it is . . ."

Anzoletta, the realist, threw in: "That's all very well, but it isn't enough — not for a woman anyway. Do you think it takes the place of a husband and children? Not in the end, it doesn't, not when you're old. Your mother was a great ballerina, but she got married. You're too choosy —"

"Please!" flushed Maritza.

"No, I don't please. Do you know, Milòr, the Count de Tessé made her an offer of marriage in writing? As men go, he's better than most. She could be a contessina now if she wished. But she had to pick flaws —"

"Listen!" Maritza brought her hand down sharply on the table. "I intend to be première danseuse at the Opéra. That may not be a great thing, but it's what I've worked for. And I don't care for the Count de Tessé — in fact I care nothing at all. And now let's drop this, cara."

Richard half teased, "But look at Mademoiselle Allard and the Duc de Mazarin."

She said gaily: "I've always told you, Milòr, that the public will be my patron. Some night, I'll have a really big chance, and then you'll see. Besides, I do have a patron, or, at least, a patroness, and a very fine one. Do you remember the Countess des Landes at the Villa Bagnoli? You were much taken with her."

"Yes," said Richard uncomfortably. It occurred to him that Maritza had not met Amélie in Bath and perhaps did not know she had been there. "Yes, of course." And deciding to avoid as much hypocrisy as possible, he added: "Strangely enough, I called today at her salon. She's a friend of Lord Marny's."

"Did you? Really? Well, after I was invited to Paris by Messieurs Rebel and Francoeur — they had heard good things about my dancing in London — Madame des Landes looked me up. You see, she recalled meeting me at the Villa. She's been very kind, has had me often to her house, and, I'm sure, has helped me at the Opéra. She spoke of you once. Of course, I told her what happened in Venice and that you had disappeared . . ." Maritza broke off. "It's strange. If she's a friend of Lord Marny's, she probably knew all about you. I suppose she was testing me . . ."

"Perhaps," Richard nodded. He did not intend to keep up unnecessary pretenses. "She did know, as a matter of fact. You see, we met in England."

"Really? . . . Then I wonder why . . ." Maritza's voice held a note of suspicion.

"No wonder at all," he explained. "She knows that Venice has to be forgotten. She couldn't know how much you knew. She was trying to find out . . ."

"Yes," Maritza hesitated. "I can understand."

Conversation drifted clear of the reef. Richard had something to wonder about, himself. Why the devil should Amélie have favored Maritza except on his account? And, if so, how did that modify her recent cool reception of him? Strange, unaccountable Amélie! . . .

Supper over, he escorted Maritza and Anzoletta home to their lodgings near by on the Rue de Richelieu. He must come, they urged, for dinner on Thursday when there was no performance at the Opéra. They promised real Venetian minestra and roast sausage. Afterwards they would drive out to the country. How they would look forward! . . . So, a rivederti, a rivederti, caro! . . . E grazie! Mille, mille grazie! . . .

It was after ten by now; and the city, constrained by darkness and police regulations, had closed up. Not finding a fiacre on the streets, which were empty except for private coaches, Richard engaged a *falot* or lantern bearer to attend him back across the river to his hotel. There was prudence in this as well as the advantage of light and guidance, for his fine clothes were an invitation to roughs and prowlers. Indeed, except for safety, he could have dispensed with the man in that quarter of Paris, where the overhanging street lamps, though dim enough, were adequate in most places. And yet, even so, he had the uncomfortable impression of being followed along the narrow Rue Saint-Nicaise, that then led to the river, and during the rest of the walk downstream to the Pont Royal. He heard a sound of footsteps echoing his and glimpsed a vague figure momentarily under the street lights. When finally he stopped at the entrance of the hotel, the footsteps behind him stopped too, as if the darkness at last had blotted them out.

Paying the falot, Richard could not help observing with a nod upstreet, "That individual seems inquisitive."

"Ah," shrugged the man, "Monsieur is a stranger. Monsieur will find that curiosity is a custom of Paris. Certain people make it a business to know about strangers."

"The spider's web, eh?" Richard grinned.

"I do not understand."

A concierge had opened the door. The falot drifted away. It was not improbable, thought Richard, that the lantern bearer would report to someone up yonder in the shadows.

"Monsieur has a caller," said the concierge, closing the door. "He insists that he is an old friend of Monsieur and would not be turned away. I took the liberty of showing him to Monsieur's suite ten minutes ago."

Richard at once thought of Tromba. "Tall? Dark? Bold features?"

"But no. Short, good-looking. I should say one of the military, for he wears a mustache and boots. He's evidently of the best tone, or I would not have taken the liberty . . ."

Wondering who it could be, Richard climbed the stairs to his rooms. It was perhaps some emissary of Choiseul's. Since the defeats of the past year, peace with England eclipsed every other concern of the French government.

A cloaked figure rose, as he came in. The candlelight showed a young man still wearing his laced hat. Richard had never seen him before. A bulky dispatch case lay on the table.

"Yes?" he said. "I don't believe I've had the pleasure . . . I regret that Monsieur has had to wait . . . My excuses."

"I don't accept them," returned the officer in a low voice. "You should have been here when I called. Please close the door."

"But, monsieur —" snapped Richard.

The caller put in, "I asked you to close the door."

Richard, on the point of anger, complied. Turning back, he stood spellbound. The hat and mustache of his visitor were gone. The very familiarity of the face confused him.

"Amélie!"

She exclaimed: "Mon petit Noiraud! Enfin!"

The next moment she was in his arms.

LIX

"HOW I pity men!" she was saying several minutes later.

"Why?"

"Their frightful clothes! Boots! Mon Dieu! Clump, clump! These silly breeches! This absurd waistcoat! This choking cravat! And buttons, buttons, buttons! What inconvenience! What delays! Whereas, women . . . Ma foi, c'est vite fait. I don't see why you men endure buttons. Think of the Golden Age when you wore tunics and togas. Délicieux! You can see how much I love you, Richard. I wouldn't suffer like this for anyone else."

"But you haven't explained —"

"You haven't given me a chance. Admit I acted my part well this afternoon."

"Too horribly well. I still can't see the reason for it. After I'd been counting the days for months . . ."

"Had you — really?"

"I'll prove it to you . . ."

"No, please, Noiraud . . . not yet . . . we haven't much time, and I've so much to tell you."

"At least you could have given me a hint, while you were freezing me."

"Yes, mon cher, and that hint might have ruined everything. Remember, I had to make you act your part, too. There were sharp eyes on both of us."

"Of course I understood about de Sartines. But after all —"

"After all," she caught him up, "I don't think you understood about Marcello Tromba. That's more important."

He had half forgotten Tromba. Now the chance remark he had overheard that afternoon came alive again like an inflamed tooth.

He stiffened. "Yes, I'm not up to date. Apparently everyone else there understood, though."

"What do you mean?"

"I heard him called your amant en titre."

She nodded brightly. "That's true; he is. And therefore he's jealous, and therefore his eyes are twice as sharp as Monsieur de Sartines's. So you see how necessary it was . . . What's the matter?" She bit her lip, then burst out laughing, the familiar little wrinkle across her nose. "I just love you when you're fierce and dark. You're so sweet. It's wonderful to tease you. I can understand why the French ran away at Quebec. But remember our agreement that time when we first became lovers? About telling the truth? I didn't promise to be faithful, did I?"

He seethed, "I'm not accusing you of anything."

"No, you're just sulky. And for no reason. Think! In eighteen months, I've only had two affairs — well, three perhaps. Three in eighteen months! Little trifles not worth mentioning. Poof!" She blew away imaginary feathers. "I wonder at my own virtue. And you sulk! What did I promise in Bristol?"

He was still unreconciled and shook his head.

"I promised to love you, that's what. And I do. And these bother-some clothes prove it. Fun isn't love, mon Noiraud. So there — stop frowning at me."

"The devil!" he burst out. "You can't puff away Tromba. Is he your third affair or a fourth?"

"Oh, Marcello . . ." she smiled. "You see, he isn't an affair at all —"

"I like that! Your amant en titre! Your recognized lover!"

"Please don't interrupt. He's not an affair, he's an investment. — Though I won't deny that he's attractive. But here it is. I've loaned him money to float a private lottery. — Heavens! I hate to think how much. He's in love with me, and, of course, would like to snap me up at one bite. But what would happen then? No, I have to play carrot, just in front of his nose and just out of reach. That way, he keeps hopeful; he exerts himself for the lottery. I let him have the title of lover; but, believe me, he'll get no more for the present. I can be practical sometimes." Her eyes teased. "Does that satisfy you, Othello? Give me a kiss."

"Little rascal! Suppose I gave you a spanking?"

"No! . . . no, mon adoré . . . Please! I haven't finished telling you about Tromba. And we must lay our plans . . ."

"Must we?" he grumbled, releasing her. "Well?"

"You're so rough. — Where were we?"

"Still with Tromba."

She grew serious. "I didn't put on this masquerade for the pleas-ure of it. To go back a moment. In the salon today there was, of course, de Sartines, who mustn't guess that we were too intimate in Bath. If he thought we had been, your business here for Mr. Pitt would be hopeless; and it's already difficult enough. But, I say again, Marcello Tromba's the real danger. He guards me like a watchdog. He endures no rivals. I'm sure he's bribed all my serv-ants to keep a watch on me. Peste! He thinks he's so clever." She smiled. "He thinks I'm on his hook. Poor Marcello! Men are such idiots. But I have to consider you. If he suspected for one moment that I love you and that we are lovers — what an explo-sion! You can imagine what would happen."

"Vaguely," Richard grinned.

"On the other hand," she went on, "he likes you well enough and

410

could be of great service to this mission of yours — especially if you made it worth his while. Say, ten thousand livres. He can always use money — as who can't?" She smiled again. "So, there we are."

"You mean —"

"I mean that's why I took such trouble tonight — hunted up this old costume, gave my maid the evening off, and slipped out through the garden. It was luck finding a fiacre on the Chemin de la Justice. I suppose Tromba will hear about it, but it won't do him much good."

"And de Sartines? I imagine this hotel is being watched."

"Of course it is," she nodded cheerfully. "I knew that before I came."

"But when you go out —"

"Mon pauvre Noiraud," she laughed, "don't be so simple. They'll expect a man to come out, and they'll keep on expecting him. They won't pay attention to a woman." She pointed to the dispatch case. "I brought a dress along. By and by you can help me change. Now let's finish with business. We mustn't forget Mr. Pitt and Lord Marny."

She withdrew to the end of the sofa. "Listen. Of course I've been well instructed by London. You'll be meeting the Duc de Choiseul and will report to The Hague whatever he chooses to tell you on the subject of peace. Also, you'll suggest this and hint that to him as coming from Mr. Pitt. Good. On the other hand, your real object here is to secure definite proof that Choiseul, while suing England for peace, is stirring Spain up to an alliance for war at the proper moment. There's your game. Am I right?"

"Perfectly."

"Well, then, mon cher, it won't be easy. I have no doubt that Monsieur de Choiseul writes interesting letters to Monsieur d'Ossun, our ambassador in Madrid. But you'll find it difficult, if not impossible, to get copies of them. And I can think of no other proof than that. However, there's one lead — Monsieur Prud'homme, the Duke's secretary. You met him today in my salon. I've been cultivating him, with you in mind. You could do the same."

"No," said Richard, recalling the shadow that had followed him from the Rue de Richelieu. "I don't believe Monsieur de Sartines

411

would approve of that. I think Marcello Tromba is the one to cultivate him and earn the fee you suggest. Perhaps Prud'homme has a weakness for gaming; perhaps he has a mistress —" He broke off at Amélie's odd, probing expression. "What's wrong?"

"Nothing. I believe I *have* heard of a mistress, a Mademoiselle d'Argencourt. Prud'homme's quite mad about her."

"Very well, he may be in debt, he may need money. He gives the impression of a showy little man. — But, chérie, there *is* something wrong."

"No, I was only wondering at the progress you've made. I didn't think of de Sartines nor of how to corrupt Prud'homme. I take it all back: you're not simple at all. You've learned a great deal. You're almost one of *us*."

"Doesn't that please you?"

She shrugged. "You must tell me all about Canada. Lord Marny wrote you were very clever. — Mais pour revenir à nos moutons, you're right about Marcello. He's an archcorrupter. If Prud'homme has a weakness, he'll know how to exploit it. Of course, you'll need patience. It will take time."

Richard agreed. "Mr. Pitt is aware of that. Meanwhile, how about correspondence with London? They told me at The Hague that you would advise me."

"I was coming to it," she said a little absently. "Of course, whatever letters you wish to have read and reported to Monsieur de Choiseul should be sent or received through the Dutch embassy here. The Duke, as well as Mr. Pitt, has every means of intercepting letters."

"Yes," said Richard, "but I take it you use a different channel."

"Sometimes. It all depends on what you want Monsieur de Choiseul to believe. Naturally he doesn't believe all he reads, so you make allowances for that. But to answer your question —"

She dipped into a waistcoat pocket and brought out a finely chased gold snuffbox.

"Here's a little present for you. Come close." Her voice dropped to a whisper. "Look. You press here . . . then here. Then slide out the bottom. You see there's room for at least two sheets of thin paper between this and the real bottom. But I defy anyone who doesn't know the springs to find out that it isn't just an ordi-

nary little box. I had it made for me by a watchmaker in Geneva.
— Now, then. Like everybody else of fashion in Paris, you'll have
your snuffbox filled at the sign of the 'Civette' at the Palais
Royal. Simply hand it to the demoiselle at the counter. Her name's
Lenoir. If there's any message for you from England, she'll insert it; if you wish to send one, she'll slip it out. She's perfectly
reliable."

"You're sure?" said Richard, trying the springs of the box.

"Qu'est-ce que tu penses!" she retorted. "Would I take the risk if
I wasn't sure? Do you know how they kill people who are guilty
of treason? It's very horrid. And I'm not a martyr. No, you can
count on the Demoiselle Lenoir. She's well paid. Aside from that,
she hates France. Her father was broken on the wheel."

"What does she do with the messages? How does she receive
them?"

"Oh, there are business men traveling between here and Holland, men of confidence." Her eyes probed him again. "What did
you think of me, Richard, when you heard that I was a spy for
England?"

He took her hand, turning it over and back again, before answering.

"I was sorry to hear it."

"Were you?" Oddly enough, she sounded pleased. "Why?"

"Because I was a simpleton, I suppose . . . old-fashioned ideas."

"I love you when you're a simpleton. What would you say if I
told you that I'm also a spy for France — and for the same reason?"

"What reason?"

"Money. One has to live — at least what I call living. Two pay-
masters are better than one. Does that shock you?"

"You're being cruel, Amélie."

"And how do you know," she went on, "that it wouldn't serve
my interest to betray you to Choiseul? How did Lord Marny
know? He's not a simpleton. I'm sure he suspects that if I warned
Pitt of de Conflans's sailing, I probably warned Choiseul of the
armament against Quebec. As a matter of fact, I did — regiments,
size of the fleet, and all. No doubt Marny reckons that on balance
England profits. But why shouldn't I make a good thing out of you,
mon cher? You're here on dangerous business. No one could blame

413

me if you disappeared. And God knows I need cash. Yet here you are, putting your life in my hands, with Lord Marny's blessing. Aren't you terrified?"

He raised the hand he was holding to his lips, more aware of its perfume and softness than of her question. "No," he said.

"Why not?"

"Do I have to answer?"

"No. You'd just be gallant. It's because you and Lord Marny think I love you and so I can be depended on. And of course you're right. He's very shrewd. It was a good stroke, choosing you for this affair in Paris." She snatched her hand away in mock anger. "You're so assured. I wish I could teach you a lesson. But I can't. I have to go on loving you, and all the while you sit there despising me as a hard, mercenary little spy —"

"What would you call *me?*" he put in.

"Well, I wouldn't call you that at least. You're an envoy of sorts. You're expected to find out what you can. You aren't doing it for money. Come, be honest. Say you despise me. Be honest."

"You know I adore you."

"Then you ought to be ashamed of yourself. You *have* become one of us."

"Because I love you?"

She looked up at him, unsmiling. "That's very dangerous, Noiraud. But what's the use? You won't believe me, and what would I do if you did! So, we'll just drift along. How drab life would be except for the devil, wouldn't it? That's what the mouse said about the cat." She leaned closer to him. "Speaking of the devil, what on earth have you done to Monsieur des Landes?"

"Nothing, I hope. Why?"

"You've enchanted him, that's all. He's excited as a girl." She tapped her forehead. "He seems to mix you up with some old crony of his and de Richelieu's. He told me if you're my lover, he's delighted — as a good joke on us both. Wicked old thing! Who are you supposed to be?"

"My grandfather, the Baron de Marny. There seems to be a likeness."

She stared. "The Black Baron? I've heard of him. He was a byword in Paris. So! You're like him. I hope not. At the same time, it makes me feel better."

414

"What do you mean?"

"Well if you are, at least I'm not corrupting innocence. You know, Richard, this gives me an idea. Monsieur des Landes is the next thing to Satan. He was a friend of Bernis, whom Choiseul supplanted, so he hates Choiseul. Apparently he dotes on you. Perhaps you could use him. From all I hear, Prud'homme's mistress, the Argencourt woman, is the kind he knows how to deal with better even than Marcello does. She's really a franche putain. We'll see what we can do."

"Very well," he agreed absently. "But haven't we talked enough business? You said there wasn't much time, and I'm an expert on buttons. A propos, how are we going to meet after this, if, as you say, Marcello keeps such an eye on you?"

"Oh," she smiled, "it's a point of honor with me to fool him. I've a little house in Passy he doesn't know about. We'll meet there."

"But wouldn't de Sartines know of it?"

"Ne t'en fais pas." Her eyes danced. "Pretty soon he'll have a brilliant idea and never suspect where it came from. If he wants to keep watch on you, what better agent could he have than your mistress? Don't forget I'm in his pay. He thinks he owns me. Poor Monsieur de Sartines! My house in Passy will occur to him. He'll persuade; I'll have to consent. C'est tout simple."

Getting up, Richard made her a deep bow. "Sheer genius, Madame de' Medici! — And now what about the buttons?"

L X

IT was the public boast of Antoine de Sartines, Lieutenant General of Police, that he had his eye on everyone in Paris. And most of Paris believed it. From his offices in the gloomy old Châtelet near the Pont-au-Change, he directed an army of thirty thousand agents, exclusive of the watch and other law-enforcement units. He oversaw both the policing of Paris and the secret service, which was largely political, though concerned too with the supervision of foreigners and the combating of foreign spies. But, as an able man, he was privately aware of his own limitations. He knew well enough the crookedness of the world he dealt with and that the all-seeing eye missed too much of it. The knowledge kept him alert, unsatisfied and disillusioned.

Take, for example, the dossier of Richard d'Amond, alias Hammond. During the past six months, constant reports from that gentleman's valet, his coachman and footmen, waiters at cafés, ushers at playhouses, other more expert informers, such as the Countess des Landes, had made quite a volume of it. It revealed nothing except that d'Amond was a young man of wealth, amusing himself for the most part, but adroit, too, in presenting to Choiseul or the Spanish ambassador, Massones, the quibbles and evasions of Mr. Pitt, who was clearly resolved to spin out the war. D'Amond's instructions from, and his dispatches to, England, duly intercepted and copied by de Sartines's agents, amounted only to a routine correspondence. They reflected Pitt's arrogance and the young envoy's tact but contained nothing valuable. Certainly they gave no hint of espionage. On the social side, d'Amond was equally correct. He appeared in various salons, dined at various tables, was credited with charm and good manners, lost or won pleasantly at cards, had a box at the Opéra and perhaps an affair with the danseuse Maritza Venier, attended the races, spent an occasional night (with de Sartines's blessing) at a certain elegant little house in Passy, had been adopted by the Duc de Richelieu and the Comte des Landes. No doubt, with such mentors as these, he might be going to the devil; but that did not trouble de Sartines. On the whole, a complete and inoffensive dossier of a normal young man about town.

And yet, reviewing it one rainy morning of early November at his desk in the Châtelet, the Minister of Police, uneasy and skeptical, felt almost inclined to toss it into the wastebasket. He suspected its bland innocence from beginning to end. His instinct, more convincing than the record, jeered at him. The all-seeing eye, indeed! Bah! At any rate he did not flatter himself.

Consultation, perhaps, would either sharpen his mind or reassure it, and he ordered an attendant to fetch Monsieur Marais, one of his chief inspectors, who was responsible for the Hammond case. Waiting, he drummed with his fingers on the desk. After all, something more than his innate distrust of appearances fretted him at the moment. His thought kept sniffing around the suicide of the

Duc de Choiseul's confidential secretary Monsieur Prud'homme day before yesterday . . . No apparent motive . . . A foggy business . . . Nothing pointed to any connection with d'Amond. But Prud'homme was in a key position. If he had been tampered with . . .

The few facts of the case drifted through de Sartines's mind. Because of his close connection with the Duc de Choiseul, Prud'homme had been kept under surveillance by the secret police. Two days ago, Saturday, he had left the Palais Bourbon at approximately four in the afternoon. He had gone directly to the apartment of his mistress, the Demoiselle d'Argencourt, on the Rue des Fossés-Montmartre and had spent the night there. Next day, he had returned to his own lodgings on the Rue Gaillon. There had been a caller, someone unidentified by the agent on watch. When the caller departed, Prud'homme had sent his valet on an errand across the city. While the man was away, Prud'homme had hanged himself. That was the jist of it, and nothing further had developed. He seemed to be well off. There had been no quarrel with his mistress. The Duc de Choiseul's papers were in order; but this meant nothing because copies could have been taken . . .

". . . Ah, Marais . . ."

"Monseigneur desires?"

De Sartines waved his subordinate to a chair beside him, Marais was a sallow, unimpressive man, with features hard to remember and therefore helpful in his work. But he had the sharpness, flair, and cunning of a veteran city rat. The shape of his nostrils, darkened with snuff, and his long fingernails recalled the same beast.

"Does all this," said de Sartines, with a flick of his hand toward the familiar papers, "satisfy you, Marais?"

The other added to the smudge on his upper lip with a pinch from his box.

"Frankly, no, your Excellence. It never has."

De Sartines nodded approval. "Why not?"

"Because, for one thing, it runs pretty shallow. And my belief is that Monsieur d'Amond runs pretty deep. Voyez, monseigneur? It doesn't fit him. Almost but not quite."

"What do you mean by *deep?*"

Marais answered with a question. "Does your Excellence really

417

believe that he has no other correspondence with England than the letters we open? Don't they read like letters meant to be opened? Well, then!"

"You mean he has a secret contact, eh?"

"Of course he has. And we'd know more about it if we knew who that caller of his was six months ago on the night after he reached Paris." Marais showed a glint of teeth. "Good God, what a fool's mate! Think of that blockhead La Mouche waiting outside there! Lord!"

De Sartines's grave Spanish face (he was a native of Barcelona) looked bleak. "Well, we've been over that enough. We have to write it off, unless," he added with a glance, "you've hit upon something new."

"Not exactly," Marais shuffled. "It's a mere thought, a notion. I ask pardon in advance. Has the thought of Madame des Landes ever occurred to your Excellency?"

De Sartines's eyes narrowed, but he did not show the displeasure that Marais feared.

The latter added: "I know that Monseigneur has the utmost confidence in Madame des Landes —"

"Pooh!" de Sartines interrupted. "You know nothing of the sort. I haven't much confidence in anyone, mon vieux Marais — not even in you or myself. What about her?"

"Well, then, with Monseigneur's permission, it could be suggested that the Comtesse des Landes and the Chevalier d'Amond knew each other in England, that he is Milord Marny's son, and that she and Marny are old acquaintances. I have established the fact that on the night in question, contrary to her custom, she dismissed her maids early. She could have left the Hôtel des Landes by the garden exit. In other words, there is that much possibility."

"Anything else?"

Marais shook his head. "Nothing. Of course I'm aware that Madame des Landes, though not in my department, was of service to France in England and that, with Monseigneur's knowledge and approval, she *pretends* to serve England here. She has been useful in betraying various English agents. But . . ." Marais spread his hands.

"You're suggesting that instead of betraying d'Amond, she collaborates with him. Why?"

"A woman isn't always logical, your Excellence. I repeat: He's Milord Marny's son."

De Sartines's lips curled. "I don't think that would weigh very much with her."

"A big sum perhaps?"

"Too dangerous, and she knows it. We hold the trump card there, Marais."

"What card, monseigneur?"

"Her life. She has too clear a head to risk losing it."

The Inspector, running short of possibilities, murmured, "Une affaire de coeur?"

"Vertudieu!" barked the other. "You're going sentimental, my friend, which is more, I believe, than Madame des Landes is capable of. She enjoys herself, yes; but the seat of pleasure with her is in a different region from the heart. Come now, you pride yourself on a keen eye for people; have you ever known a more superficial woman, I mean emotionally, or one more set on her own advantage? She's charming, of course; but underneath — Peste! I thought better of you."

"Yes, I admit," Marais conceded. "I admit. And yet . . . there's Passy. I know your Excellence proposed it. But —"

"But you don't know what difficulty I had or how indifferent she was until — well, frankly, until I made it worth her while. I withhold the figure."

Marais chuckled in admiration. "There's a smart woman!" His theory about Madame des Landes had seemed plausible but he acknowledged defeat. He sighed. "I wish we knew more about her relations with d'Amond in Bath, though. She took maids with her from Paris. I suppose Monseigneur has had them questioned."

"Impossible. She didn't bring them back with her. They entered the service of her relatives in Ireland."

Marais's interest revived. "Comment diable! And that doesn't seem odd to your Excellence? Isn't it clear they knew too much?"

To his surprise, de Sartines laughed. "Of course it's clear. They knew too much for the Marquis de Tromba. Listen, Marais. I'm in the confidence of Madame des Landes — up to a point. I don't think you realize her problem with Tromba. Nothing could be less sentimental or more cynical." He explained the business of the lottery to Marais. "So, my friend, she leads him by the nose and

419

cannot afford servants who know her too well. As clever and hard a little piece as any in my experience. And yet you credit her with a love affair against her own safety and interest! No —" de Sartines glanced back at the inspector's suggestion — "it won't do, Marais. Interesting but too thin. Madame des Landes isn't the channel to England which, I admit, d'Amond probably has. — Have you considered Mademoiselle Venier? That's more likely."

"You'd think so." The other lifted his thin shoulders. "Her season in London and so on. Have I considered her! My God! She's cost more hours of shadowing than anyone. And with what result?" Marais rounded his thumb and forefinger to form a zero. "That much. D'Amond's footmen have reported their conversations when they drove to the country or the races. I've had waiters beside them at every café. Her lodgings have been repeatedly searched. Our agents have tapped her dressing room at the Opéra. I can honestly say that she and her woman have been covered, monseigneur, and I mean completely. But nothing, nothing at all!"

"Gallantry, I suppose?" de Sartines grunted.

"No, your Excellency, not even that. It sounds incredible. It is incredible. For they're evidently fond of each other. You and I know that they must be having an affair. But there's no sign of it. They take remarkable precautions. Talk of *running deep!* The Chevalier d'Amond is too deep for me."

"But, in God's name, man, what do they do, then? They spend hours together."

"Conversation," Marais gloomed. "D'Amond seems to have been brought up in Italy. They knew each other there. Old days — that sort of thing. Her dancing and prospects at the Opéra. She and Mademoiselle Allard. His experiences in Canada, as Madame des Landes reported to your Excellency. Why, they even read poetry together, some old thing written by her father . . ."

De Sartines raised both arms. "Enough! Let's get on. Here's another possibility — the Marquis de Tromba. D'Amond sees a good deal of him. I don't trust that charlatan. Except for his service to the state lottery, he'd have been sent packing before this. As an adventurer, he's second to no one."

Marais agreed. He sat silent a moment, his long, sharp nose

420

twitching. He said finally: "I think we're close to something there, monseigneur. Don't imagine he isn't being watched. Monsieur de Tromba is one of my favorites. I have two others: the Maréchal de Richelieu and the Comte des Landes."

"Precisely," de Sartines approved. "There's another odd business. Why should two old rakes concern themselves with a young man like d'Amond? I know: they were friends of his grandfather; but it makes no sense."

Marais said: "It makes more if one remembers that they are both enemies of the Duc de Choiseul. And that isn't all." He broke off. "It's a little uncanny. As Monseigneur will have noted, every report states that with them d'Amond seems a different man. As if he became someone else. A Regency buck, one of the old sort. He may be playing a role with them, but I'm not sure. In any case they dote on him, treat him to their little suppers à la Satan. And in that connection it grows interesting. We pick up the scent of the late Monsieur Prud'homme's mistress, the Demoiselle d'Argencourt."

De Sartines straightened up. "What do you mean?"

"I've just learned," Marais said, "that on the night following Prud'homme's suicide, she danced — you can guess how — for the Maréchal and old des Landes at a maison close they patronize on the Rue du Mail. No, d'Amond wasn't there. I believe she hadn't yet heard of Prud'homme's death. Perhaps it would have made no difference; she's a prostitute of the worst sort. But observe the sequence: Prud'homme, this woman, the Maréchal and des Landes, then d'Amond."

"Possible," nodded de Sartines. "I'm glad you bring up the Prud'homme affair. It's much on my mind. He's seemed prosperous lately. I hear he refurnished the Argencourt's apartment for her. Nothing would be easier for him than to sell copies of secret papers to whomever they concerned. And yet he had the reputation of an honest man. Monsieur de Choiseul deeply regrets him. I tell you, Marais, if you can find out why he committed suicide, it may go far in drawing the net on d'Amond. Prud'homme's recent expenditures . . . I note, too, a set of trinkets for his mistress. Does that give us a lead?"

"Yes," said Marais, "to a lottery ticket, to a tip at the races, to a lucky evening at cards."

"Nothing unusual, then."

"Except this, monseigneur. The ticket was in Monsieur de Tromba's lottery. Monsieur de Tromba won on the same horse. Monsieur de Tromba has a share in the gaming rooms where Monsieur Prud'homme played. A coincidence to be noted."

De Sartines noted it, but shook his head. "Difficult to prove."

"As to the reason for the suicide," Marais went on, "I believe it was fear. Nothing else accounts for it. Prud'homme must have known he was under observation. Suppose he believed that he had been discovered. No wonder he hanged himself!"

The supposition ran parallel to de Sartines's own thinking.

"You have an alert out for the man who called on him that afternoon?"

"I'm not a novice, your Excellence. But the man may not be easy to find. After what happened, he'll lie very low. Still, we have a good description of him. — And now, with all submission, may I ask Monseigneur two questions?"

"You can ask them, Marais. Perhaps I won't answer them."

"The first is this. If the Chevalier d'Amond causes such anxiety to your Excellence, why is he permitted to remain here? He can be sent home. What need has Monsieur Pitt for a secret envoy in Paris? He makes no concessions. He scorns Spain as much as he scorns France. He intends to make the most of his advantage. Why, then, do we put up with the annoyance of a spy?"

The Minister of Police shrugged. "Because we have no evidence of anything but the most harmless conduct on his part. Monsieur de Choiseul finds him sympathetic. We cannot afford to affront Monsieur Pitt out of mere suspicion. That, first. The next reason is that George II died last month. We hear that Pitt is less solid with the new King, that a peace party under Milord Bute gains ground. In that case, the Chevalier d'Amond may have better terms to transmit. What's your other question?"

"Tromba."

"Ah, mon vieux Marais, why are adventurers tolerated everywhere? Because of our sins which they flatter and feed on. Because of the dry rot which they bore into. We live in a crumbling house, mon ami. Get rid of the woodworms, and you risk toppling it down. This fellow Tromba is clever in finance; so, we use him. Meanwhile he bribes here, pimps there, makes himself influence, is favored by Madame de Pompadour, lingers on till the day when he stinks too much to stand. There you have it."

Marais bowed to realism. The interview being at an end, he got up.

"In all this business, monseigneur, I'm troubled by one thought. It must have occurred to you that the Chevalier d'Amond may be only a blind. The real secret agent may be someone else. Perhaps we're beginning to smell Tromba or the Maréchal himself or old des Landes."

Pessimistically, de Sartines observed: "No, I think all four of them together. Keep on their traces, Marais. I depend on you."

The Inspector made his bow and departed. But almost at once he entered the room again.

"There's one less to bother about, your Excellence. News has just come that the Comte des Landes died early this morning. Heart or a stroke. His last supper with the devil seems to have been too much for him."

L X I

MARCELLO Tromba had word of the Comte des Landes's death a little earlier even than Monsieur de Sartines. It was brought to him in his splendid apartment on the Rue Saint-Dominique by La Flèche, a young, sharp-eyed underfootman at the Hôtel des Landes, who expected a reward for good news. At the moment, Tromba, having passed through the hands of his valet, had just entered the bureau next to his bedroom, where he transacted some of the lottery business and gave ear to tradesmen or humble callers waiting in his anteroom. There were standing orders that any communication from the Hôtel des Landes should be brought him at once.

"I value your promptness, La Flèche," he commended from behind his handsome desk. And, drawing out a gold coin, he sat clicking it on the table surface. "How did Monsieur le Comte die?"

"He returned night before last from supping with the Duc de Richelieu. I understand they were at a certain house on the Rue du Mail. He seemed in excellent spirits; but then, while being undressed, he had a seizure. The physicians bled him in the morning. He recovered his speech and lingered through the day, but died in the course of the night."

Tromba clicked the coin. "Rue du Mail, eh? Any particulars?"

I gathered from Monsieur le Comte's valet Julien that Monsieur le Comte spoke of being diverted by several of the ladies, notably one named Argencourt, who did a danse en chemise."

"Ah," observed Tromba, his black eyes only a trifle sharper. "Anything else you think would interest me? The Countess, I imagine, is inconsolable?"

"No doubt, monseigneur. Her women tell me she is already in complete mourning. Further dresses have been ordered."

"I grieve with her," said Tromba. "I suppose Madame des Landes did not attend her husband on his deathbed. Too painful for a woman of her delicacy."

"But no, she attended Monsieur le Comte at his request. They were together at least an hour."

"The devil you say!" exclaimed Tromba. "Have you any idea what they talked about?"

La Flèche hesitated. "Julien overheard something. He waited outside to be on call . . ."

"With his ear to the keyhole, eh?" Tromba nodded. "Well?"

"Ah, Monsieur le Marquis, is it proper — I submit the question — for a servant to reveal the deathbed confidence of his master? Is it correct?"

"For two louis, it is," the other laughed, adding a second coin to the first and rubbing them together, "But let me tell you this. What I hear has to be worth while. Now, then?"

"Of course, Julien expects something . . ." breathed La Flèche, his glance hungry.

"Share with him, if you please. It's up to you." And, as the man still demurred, Tromba added in another tone, "Have you the impudence to trifle with me?"

La Flèche cringed. "Julien could hear very little. It seems that Monsieur le Comte gave a paper to Madame — for the Chevalier d'Amond. He said it came from Monsieur Prud'homme."

"Tiens!" Tromba muttered.

"Only, he was confused, and called the Chevalier d'Amond sometimes Baron and sometimes Charles. Madame corrected him, but he said it was all the same devil and not to trouble him about names. He said the paper would cancel some debt. Julien did not catch that part of it."

"And then?"

"Why, Monsieur le Comte asked for brandy, which the doctors had forbidden; and when Madame denied him, he cursed her into fetching the decanter."

"And then?"

"Julien said Monsieur le Comte's mind wandered. Old recollections, assez grossiers. It shocked Julien, the way he insulted Madame."

"As to what?"

"Her conduct. He told her that, except for age, he and she had been well matched. Madame laughed."

"Did he mention me?"

La Flèche looked embarrassed.

"Speak out, man. I'm not sensitive."

"Well, in that case . . . I believe he regretted that he had not assassinated Monseigneur."

"He spoke of no one else?"

"No. Madame suggested a priest. But Monsieur le Comte refused and bade her instead to fetch him the parrot, Monsieur Coco. So, Madame, gay as ever, had Monsieur Coco brought in and then took her leave. Monsieur le Comte finished the decanter. When he was too far gone to know of it, she sent for the priest."

Tromba gave the coins to La Flèche. "Voilà. If you snap up anything else of interest, be sure to inform me. I shall leave my card this afternoon at the Hôtel des Landes. I suppose that Madame will receive no visitors today."

"No, monseigneur, she has directed the doorman to make her excuses. — Again I thank Monseigneur . . ."

When the man was gone, Tromba did not immediately turn to the day's routine. Instead, he sat enjoying the shining prospect that the news had brought him. The Comte des Landes had offered no check to his amorous ambitions; but with Amélie a widow, the situation changed. She would no doubt remarry. And, after all . . .

Why not, after all? He was getting on. A few more years would slow up his wanderings, dull his capacity for pleasure. By God, he would be middle-aged. Amélie tempted him even as a wife. What had begun as a casual pursuit — one more bird for his bag — was now an infatuation. No other woman had coquetted with him so long and remained so desirable. Besides, the lottery had turned out well. He could hand her back a good profit, expect her gratitude, and recover the money by marriage.

It was odd, he reflected with a pinch of snuff, how at certain times everything worked together for good. What with Prud'homme's suicide and the uncertainty attending it, he had been on pins and needles. Now, after hearing La Flèche's report, he could breathe easily. The ticklish business for which he had been paid by Richard Hammond was unexpectedly over.

Unlike Monsieur de Sartines, Prud'homme's suicide presented no mystery to him. During the past six months, his contact man, Ambrose, a smart undercover agent, had purchased from Prud'homme copies of most of Choiseul's letters to the French ambassador in Madrid. But, so far, the trouble had been that these letters, while indicating a rapprochement between France and Spain against England, had provided nothing that Mr. Pitt could use as a shocking proof of French perfidy. Such a letter, Prud'homme had hinted, would be forthcoming; and he had finally stated that it could be delivered. With this in view, day before yesterday Ambrose had called at Prud'homme's apartment on the Rue Gaillon, where, instead of the promised letter, he found the secretary in despair.

At the thought of it, Tromba again took snuff. Ambrose's report had been frightening indeed. Prud'homme, on the point of handing over the letter, found that he did not have it. Somewhere between that moment and his departure the day before from the Palais Bourbon, the paper had disappeared from his wallet. To the terrified man, the inference was plain, and so, too, it had seemed both to Ambrose and Tromba. The letter could only have been taken by some agent of the police bent on establishing Prud'homme's guilt. Whether his mistress Mademoiselle d'Argencourt had sold herself to de Sartines, or whether it was some other agent, made no difference. The fat was in the fire. Ambrose had left Paris in hot haste even before the news of the suicide. Tromba, not too confidently, awaited developments.

Now he could smile at so much panic. His quick mind at once traced the links between Prud'homme, Argencourt, des Landes, and the paper delivered to Amélie for Richard. It was obvious that the old Count had meddled independently. So, after all, the paper was safe; the business, concluded; and no torture could wring any confession from a corpse. Talk about luck! . . .

Tromba's callers that day found him unusually gracious.

Early in the afternoon, he summoned his coach and drove solemnly to the Hôtel des Landes to leave his condolences. Other coaches on the same mission rolled up and departed, though, for the most part, only a footman got down to deposit the card or note of sympathy. Tromba, however, as a very intimate friend, did not let it go at that but stepped out for a word with the impressive Swiss at the door. He desired his card to receive special notice. La Flèche was by no means the only servant at the Hôtel des Landes whom he kept well tipped.

He found the entrance hall festooned in black and the porter wearing a crepe badge. If the late Count had been a saint instead of a devil, his house could not have looked more steeped in mourning. Silence everywhere, and *pompe funèbre.*

"Joseph," said Tromba to the doorman, "I hope you will see to it that my card is at once presented to Madame la Comtesse with my warmest expressions of sympathy. You will assure her of my personal grief, and that I shall call again at her earliest convenience."

"Monseigneur's most devoted servant," Joseph bowed, accepting the card with an accompanying gratuity. "I know how deeply Madame will value Monsieur le Marquis's message."

But on the point of withdrawing, Tromba stopped. His sharp glance, that rarely missed any detail of interest, had caught sight of a gentleman's cloak and hat on a stone bench in the shadow of the stairway.

"I take it," he hinted, "that there's no chance of my seeing Madame for a brief moment?"

"Alas, no. In the sorrowful circumstances . . ."

"And yet," Tromba persisted, with a nod at the cloak and hat, "it would appear that someone is calling."

Whatever Joseph may have thought of the careless lackey who had not removed such evidence, he remained inscrutable. "Yes, the Chevalier d'Amond. Madame asked him to come on an urgent matter. Otherwise, she has seen no one."

Since Tromba could easily guess that the urgent matter involved delivering the copy of Choiseul's letter to Richard without delay, and since he had a part in the espionage affair, he smiled pleasantly and swung off his cloak.

"Ah, d'Amond," he said. "I'm sure that Madame and he, if they knew I was here, would desire me to join them. I'm familiar with the business in question and can perhaps be of use."

"But, monseigneur, my orders —"

"If they do not apply to Monsieur d'Amond in this case, they do not apply to me. Have no concern, friend Joseph."

Under Tromba's masterful stare, Joseph meekly took charge of the proffered hat, cloak and cane. He had received too many coins from the Marquis and knew the latter's position with Madame too well to offend him.

"I must stay by the door . . . Let me ring for someone to announce Monseigneur."

"Don't bother. I know my way. Madame will be in the little salon, I imagine?"

Still smiling, Tromba walked upstairs. It would be pleasant to give Amélie the news about the lottery at once. He knew that would please her. Of course, unless she and Richard told him of the recovered letter, he could not even hint that he had learned of it from La Flèche. But doubtless they would announce it, and after mutual congratulations, young Hammond would know enough to take his leave. Tromba resolved to press today's luck to the utmost.

He followed the hallway to the door of the little room that communicated with the more formal salon, and knocked but received no answer. Listening, he heard nothing from inside. At last, having knocked again, he opened the door . . .

LXII

BETWEEN Amélie and Richard, the faintest convention of regret with regard to des Landes's death would have been an affectation. On the other hand, the shadow of death in a house is sobering and it would have been equally false to make light of it.

Amélie, glancing back, remarked: "At least it can be said of Monsieur des Landes that he died as he had lived. He was all of one piece. Not like you and me. — However," she added, producing the small sheet of paper that the Count had given her, "this is why I asked you to come. I should think that would make your fortune, mon cher. Mr. Pitt will be pleased. He ought to be. It cost a suicide and several betrayals."

Scanning Prud'homme's now familiar handwriting, Richard could see at once the value of the letter. It meant the complete success of his mission. It contained definite proof that behind the peace proposals, Choiseul had in view a counterstroke of war in alliance with Spain. This time he made specific offers to the Spanish King. It would give Pitt the argument he needed for combating the blandishments of peace until after complete victory.

Richard put the letter in his wallet. "Yes, Mr. Pitt will be pleased. I'm most grateful, though I'm sorry for the complications."

"Do you know," Amélie put in, "what reward Monsieur des Landes offered the Argencourt for stealing that paper? It's been all arranged through the Duc de Richelieu. She'll give her dance at the Parc aux Cerfs for the private entertainment of the King. And they call Mr. Pitt the conqueror of France. Do you think he has much to do with it? But that's a dull subject. I suppose this means you'll be leaving Paris soon to collect your laurels in St. James's Square."

"No sooner than I can help," he answered. "You ought to know that. Of course I'll have to wait for instructions. They're not apt to arrive short of a month. — Parbleu, you look adorable in black, Amélie, and with no powder on your hair. How long will you wear mourning?"

"The rule," she said, "is a year and six weeks: four months and a half, this estamin stuff; four months and a half, crepe and wool; three months, gauze and silk; six weeks, semi-mourning. But you know how I feel about rules — at least in private." She gave a twitch of her dress that showed a flash of scarlet garter and diamond buckle. "I haven't your simple tastes; I like color. — And after you're gone, what shall I do with myself?"

"Please!" he retorted. "Isn't that understood? I thought you had promised. Do I have to beg all over again?"

"No . . . I suppose not." They had drifted over to the deep bay window, almost an alcove, that overlooked the naked November garden. His arm crept around her; she leaned against him. "Remember? We were standing here when you first asked me. But it was August, and everything in flower. I forget what I said."

His arm tightened. "Some nonsense. The point is you accepted me."

"No," she said, "I don't forget at all. I told you I'd be a fool not to marry you if I could, and that you'd be worse than a fool to marry me. It's still true, Richard. Don't you see how true it is?"

He smiled. "Don't you see what nonsense it is?"

"No, it's the plain truth that you won't accept. I'll be marrying the Honorable Richard Hammond, M.P., whom I'm in love with, favorite of Mr. Pitt, slated for the Foreign Service, son of the rich Lord Marny, who offers me a settlement of twenty thousand pounds. Wouldn't I snap that up! You'll be marrying your mistress, whom you know like an old glove, a woman of no scruples and with no intention of mending her ways, who couldn't even promise to be faithful to you. Don't tell me it isn't the truth."

"With one point left out," he said — "that I love you."

She looked up at him. "Perhaps Monsieur des Landes was right after all in confusing you with that old friend of his. He was uncannily sharp at times. He kept saying that we were born for each other. I want to believe it. I couldn't have believed it once. But the truth is, too, Richard, that you've changed; you've become more like me. I'm glad, because that way, perhaps, I'm the sort of wife you should have."

He kissed her. "There, my divinity, you're talking sense at last. In the spring, we'll be married in Holland. Lord Marny —"

There may have been a sound behind them, or perhaps it was an instinctive awareness that stopped him. They turned sharply to find themselves confronting Marcello Tromba.

He stood a pace or so off, his lips compressed, his eyes two black slits, one hand on the hilt of his sword. He looked so menacing that Richard, with no time even for surprise, braced himself and took a step forward.

But the deadliness was momentary. Tromba smiled; the tense hand relaxed; his eyes widened, though he could not conceal the

430

lingering fury in them. He bowed, perhaps a trifle deeper than usual.

"Apparently—" he began.

Too quick to give him the advantage of the first word, Amélie blazed: "Apparently you forget the custom of knocking, Marcello."

"Not at all," he said gently. Richard had heard the silken tone of voice before. "Not at all, madonna. I knocked twice, as a matter of fact. Believing that the room was empty or that you had not heard me, I looked in to make sure. When I saw, indeed, that you had not heard me, wasn't it natural to rejoin two old friends? I beg forgiveness if I startled you, madonna."

The iteration of the Italian word gave an odd feline rhythm to the voice.

Her eyes, so practised in reading men's faces, read his, and the finality in it. No coquetry or ruse would serve now, only war.

She said dryly: "Nothing of consequence. You're always welcome, Marcello, even when I leave orders below to admit no one, or when I have matters to discuss which do not necessarily concern you."

He did not intend to be put on the defensive. "I thank you, madonna. You have encouraged me to believe that I am always welcome. As to the orders you mention, when I learned that young Richard here —" he paused on the word *young* — "was with you, it occurred to me that the matters under discussion concerned me as well. We have been collaborating together in a ticklish affair. Am I wrong, Richard?"

So far, he had played coolly. It was too bad that passion got the best of him at this point and gave a glimpse of his hand. "It reached me," he went on, "that the virtuous Mademoiselle d'Argencourt and your lamented husband, madonna, were together on the night following Monsieur Prud'homme's death. A valuable paper had been lost. I could not help wondering if it had been found. I thought I might venture to inquire."

Yes, war, thought Richard. He knew Tromba well enough not to underrate the danger. But times had changed. He was not the novice of two years ago and could meet the challenge on even terms.

"Quite right, Marcello," he said. "Only, as you took pains to learn, we were occupied with something very different. It gives me

431

pleasure to confirm what perhaps you did not quite overhear. Madame des Landes has consented to marry me. Being such an old friend of us both, I'm delighted that you're the first to know of it."

"And the first to congratulate you," bowed Tromba, more silken than ever. "There could be no happier way of repairing the loss of a husband — even before his funeral. Subtle madonna! Clever Richard! For I gather this charming announcement has had a long and intimate prelude. Devil take me! And all the while I was kept dangling. If I couldn't help showing surprise a moment ago, it's the measure of my simplicity and your finesse. Ma foi, I can't adequately express my admiration."

He smiled from one to the other, the tiger in him not yet decided how to strike. In the agony of his hurt pride, he was capable of anything.

"From an expert like you," said Richard watchfully, "such praise is memorable. You have so many triumphs to your credit that you can afford to be generous. Madame des Landes, I'm sure, values your congratulations as much as I."

Tromba arched his brows. "At least they have the merit of being sincere, my dear boy. We know each other very well, don't we? I flatter myself that I've had some part in your education and should, therefore, take pride in being overreached by you. Let me predict that you'll have a brilliant career, if you live long enough to exercise your talents. It's only the uncertainty of life that need trouble you."

If this hinted at a duel, Richard thought, it might be just as well to get it over with. A duel would be the cheapest way out. At the salle d'armes where he and Tromba fenced, there was now little to choose between them.

"Yes," he agreed, "there's always that, of course. My hand shows a long life line, though. Does yours, Marcello?"

"No, it doesn't," said Tromba, opening his palm. "And the devil I care. But now that we've exchanged the proper amenities, may I revert to that lost paper? Was my guess correct? Has it been found? I think my long services, Richard, in this affair of yours, justify an answer."

Amélie did not wait for Richard's reply. "Of course they do,

Marcello. If the paper you mention had been found, you would be the first to hear of it. Though why you imagine it should turn up here, I don't understand."

"I was asking Richard, madonna. I'm more apt to learn the truth from him. He's very discreet, but he hasn't quite your finish."

"Is that an insult?"

"No, a tribute. Will you be good enough to answer me, dear boy?"

But if Tromba hoped to gather anything from the other's expression, he was disappointed.

Richard merely looked puzzled. "I can only echo Madame des Landes's assurances, Marcello, and her surprise that you should have such a notion. Do you suggest that the Comte des Landes stole the paper?"

For an instant, Tromba's suppressed passion shook him. Then he turned it into a shrug. "No, but I'm suggesting that it's apt to turn up soon in the wrong hands. It's a dangerous paper. I sought reassurance — to no purpose, it seems. Well, every man for himself, eh? It's always been my guiding principle. And so, mes chers amis, I leave you to discuss the future. My deepest apologies for the interruption."

"One moment," put in Amélie, serene as usual. "I'm expecting good news from the lottery, Marcello."

On the point of leaving, he turned back. "True, I'd forgotten. Let's discuss that another time. There may be some difficulties, cara madonna."

The latch clicked behind him. They heard his footsteps recede along the hall.

Amélie's unrouged face turned scarlet, her eyes like blue flint.

"Bandit!" she snapped. "As if we'd put ourselves more in his hands than we are by admitting anything! Still, he knows about that paper, and it's easy to guess how. We'll see, Monsieur Tromba! I think I can read your game. We'll see who wins the last trick. But we haven't one minute to lose, Richard. Give me back the letter."

"Why do you want it?" he asked, opening his wallet and handing her the paper. "What game do you mean? He can only send me a challenge, and I'm not too much afraid of that."

"He's no fool," she answered in the same cold voice. And, crossing the room to a little Chinese cabinet that could serve also as a desk, she selected a quill, trying the nib on her finger. "It won't satisfy him to risk his own life. He'll denounce us to the police."

"You forget I have his receipts for the money I've paid him."

"And a good thing, too. But that won't help us if he turns state's evidence. To Monsieur de Sartines, we're bigger game than Tromba. We must be beforehand with him at the Châtelet."

She was busy copying the letter. Her pen raced across the page . . . "I'm glad you can read my handwriting . . . In any case, you'd have had to recopy Prud'homme's script on the thinner paper . . . There!" She sanded the sheet hurriedly and held it out to him. "You can have that; I'll keep the original."

"I don't understand."

"Then you're very stupid, mon cher Noiraud. You forget I'm a trusted spy of the French government. I must see Monsieur de Sartines at once and give him this. Then, let Monsieur Tromba denounce us. The laugh will be on him. And something more than a laugh. Because I intend to give Monsieur de Sartines another letter."

She opened the cabinet, removed a drawer, and evidently touched a hidden release. From inside, she drew out a piece of paper.

"See, Richard. There's some advantage in having pleased the King."

It was a blank lettre de cachet signed *Louis R.* It directed the immediate arrest and confinement in the Bastille of the unnamed person above. Said person was to remain there at the King's pleasure.

Dipping her pen again, she wrote in boldly the name *Marcello Tromba.*

"His Majesty," she explained, "has a sense of humor. I wheedled this out of him once to use against Monsieur des Landes, but then thought better of it. I'm glad I did. Our furious friend will have leisure to cool off." She looked up, once more radiant and enchanting. "What about the last trick now, Richard? At least you know what kind of wife you'll have. — And now to the Châtelet. À bientôt, mon coeur."

Then, having rung for a servant, she bade him order her coach.

434

LXIII

NO one who caught sight of Tromba's imperious face through the windows of his carriage as he drove back to the Rue Saint-Dominique would have noted anything unusual about him. He looked as always the perfect model of a grand seigneur. Nor did Monsieur de Sartines's agent who drifted along in a fiacre at a safe distance behind observe any change in the Marquis's expression. It would have taken keen eyes indeed to pierce the mask he had so long cultivated. The mask had reached a point of independence from the mind it concealed and only now and then betrayed a glint of his inner mood. But if the seven devils that now possessed him could have shown themselves, they would have caused some panic in the quiet streets of the Faubourg Saint-Germain.

Having arrived at his house, he ordered the coachman to wait and mounted the stairs to his apartment. Then, behind closed doors, he took to pacing back and forth, though pausing at times to gaze at some pattern on the rug or to finger an object on his worktable. Once he stopped to open a case of small pistols, and, selecting one of them, spent a concentrated minute or so loading and priming it. But when this was done, he left the weapon lying and resumed his hot meditation.

Finally, with a sharp nod, he reached a decision, again made sure of his pistol and slipped it into a convenient pocket. Then, resuming his cloak and hat, he walked downstairs to his carriage. In his passion, it did not even occur to him to give a false destination and afterwards change it en route. An apparent idler, leaning against a nearby lamp post, caught the address, the Hôtel de Luxembourg, Rue des Petits-Augustins; and, when the coach had driven off, proceeded by a short cut, through narrow alleys, in the same direction. Using agility, the man reached a bookstall across from the hotel and was gazing at titles through the window, when the carriage drove up, and Tromba, getting out, dismissed it. Not long afterwards, the Chevalier d'Amond's man l'Esprit left the hotel, with his hat on, and sauntered beyond the corner of the Quai Malaquais, where the amateur of books joined him.

"What's doing, l'Esprit?"

The valet shrugged. "Why, Monsieur d'Amond isn't home yet,

and the Marquis de Tromba brought me a message from him to fetch a new coat he's had made at André's on the Rue Sainte-Honoré. Meanwhile de Tromba is waiting for him."

"So, you're off?"

"Hardly. I couldn't refuse to go out. But my job is to keep an eye on the Chevalier d'Amond and not to run fools' errands. It's clear Monsieur de Tromba wants to see him in private. I must know when the maître gets back and how long they meet."

The other scratched his chin. He was a couple of steps higher in the service and could give l'Esprit orders.

"No, I'll take over. You inform headquarters and then come back. Since this morning, Monsieur Marais is as much interested in the Marquis de Tromba as he is in d'Amond. He wants to know at all times where to find him. It's worth Monsieur Marais's while to hear that he's now in d'Amond's apartment."

Then the agent strolled back to the bookshop, entered it, and began turning over volumes, though he glanced more often through the window.

Meanwhile, Tromba, his ear alert to any sound of Richard's coach in the street below, conducted a deft but hurried search of the rooms. One weakness of his position, which he did not overlook, was the fact that Richard had shrewdly enough exacted receipts for the money paid in connection with the bribery of Prud'homme. Tromba's scheme demanded the recovery of those receipts one way or another. He hardly expected that the search would yield anything, for Richard would know that de Sartines's men combed his apartment from time to time and he would probably keep such papers well hidden. But there was always a chance of finding something, and Tromba did not miss the occasion.

It turned out that he had plenty of time, too much time, as a matter of fact; and he began to fear l'Esprit's return from the trumped-up errand. He had reasoned correctly that Richard would not at once drive back to his lodgings after leaving Amélie. That would look too odd from the standpoint of the secret agents by whom Richard knew that he was being shadowed. He must make the call at the Hôtel des Landes seem conventional, one of other calls or an incident of a normal afternoon. But surely he would not delay his return any longer than necessary. He would be on fire to dispose of the paper he had received from Amélie. And yet, Tromba began to doubt his calculations, could see that he had acted too much on impulse. He had come prepared for anything except failure to confront Richard. Now he would have to invent another approach.

His search came to nothing. Perhaps it would be best to withdraw and strike late that night. But so much depended on facing Richard at once, before . . .

A coach stopped in front of the hotel. Glancing through the window, he saw his prey descend from it. And, triumphantly, he at once took cover behind a door which stood open at the entrance of the next room. If this served to conceal him, so much the better; if not, he was ready. Then, between door and wall, hand on pistol butt, he waited.

Richard had called on Madame du Deffand in her fine apartment at the Convent of Saint-Joseph and then had chatted a half-hour in the salon of Madame de Cambis. This seemed to him long enough to remove any singularity from his call on Amélie. It was important now to copy Choiseul's letter on the thin paper used in his secret corresponednce with England and then, having concealed it in the hidden compartment of his snuffbox, proceed at once to have the box refilled at the sign of the "Civette." After that, he could relax; his work in Paris was done. As to the recent scene at the Hôtel des Landes, he would have felt a little sorry for Tromba, if the latter had been the kind of man one could pity. But, in the circumstances, the Bastille was an effective and necessary solution.

It did not surprise him too much to find his rooms empty and l'Esprit out. Though an excellent valet, the man had a way of slipping off at odd intervals, which Richard rightly enough ascribed to the service of Monsieur de Sartines. On this occasion, he welcomed his absence, since he would otherwise have had to invent an excuse to get rid of him. So, having rapidly glanced through the rooms, he locked the entrance door, seated himself at his writing table, and drew out Amélie's copy of the letter, which he now studied sentence by sentence.

No, Mr. Pitt would never have anything more to the purpose

than this. As usual, it was addressed to the Marquis d'Ossun in Madrid. It ran in part: "The situation is extremely serious, and only violent measures can remedy it. The one I am about to propose would strike a real blow at England. It is to attack Portugal. That Kingdom may be considered an English colony; and on this score alone it is the enemy of France, aside from the fact that the King of France has serious reasons for discontent with the King of Portugal.

"Considering this, as well as the necessity of making a strong diversion against the designs of England, we propose in the greatest secrecy to His Catholic Majesty" (the King of Spain) "to inform us if he will contribute to the conquest of Portugal and Brazil with a view to the complete annihilation of that power and to its absorption by Spain. If His Catholic Majesty approves this idea, its execution will be easy, provided the secret is kept; and the King of France is willing to furnish fifteen thousand troops, who will cross Spain for the invasion of Portugal, as well as to furnish the number of ships which His Catholic Majesty deems proper for the conquest of Brazil . . .

"Another proposal would be to invite Holland to join with France and Spain . . ."

A sudden voice across the table observed, "Yes, a valuable document."

Richard looked up with a start at the height of Tromba, looming over him.

The masklike features showed a faintly humorous wrinkle between the black, arched eyebrows; a half-smile under the hawk nose. Only the steady smolder of Tromba's eyes betrayed the relentlessness behind them.

"It's strange," he went on, "how handy small skills are — for example, the ability to read handwriting upside down. Besides, I'm familiar with that handwriting. By God, I didn't expect such luck as this. A valuable document indeed! It could cost your future wife her head, my dear boy."

Maneuvering for time, Richard said: "You seem to have learned the skill of ghosts, Marcello. You never taught me how to walk through locked doors."

The half-smile did not change. "It was no trick at all to get rid of your man and wait for you here. — Now hand me that paper. I

want, too, whatever receipts I gave you. Hurry. We haven't lon
before your servant gets back. I say hurry."

It was, of course, crystal-clear to Richard that, however unfortunate might have been the surrender to Tromba of Prud'homme's
original copy, the possession by him of this letter in Amélie's handwriting was infinitely worse. In the hands of the police, it meant
nothing less than her death warrant. Snatching it up, he thrust
it into an inner pocket.

"Neither that nor the receipts, Marcello. How do you propose
to get them?"

"Keep seated," Tromba rapped, his lips showing a glint of
teeth. "Don't move . . . I propose to get them this way." Like a
conjuring trick, his hand held the pistol. At the same moment,
he drew back its hammer. "Now think fast, Richard. Don't imagine
that I'll hesitate to blow your brains out, no matter what happens
to me afterwards. And don't imagine that your foolish death would
help Madame Amélie. The letter will still be there in her handwriting."

"May I ask," returned Richard, his eyes on the other's steady
hand, "what you intend to do with these papers?"

"Yes, and I'll tell you. They deserve a high price."

"What price?"

"Madame des Landes, for one thing, and as much money as I
choose to demand of you, for the next. I say think fast. You have
only one life, my boy. There are other women in the world —
your little Venier for instance — and you have money enough. Hand
me that letter to begin with."

The hand was steady as a rock. In his present mood, Tromba
meant what he said. Without knowing of the *lettre de cachet,* he
had rendered it useless.

"Be sensible, Marcello. We can reach an agreement about the
money. As to Madame des Landes, she must decide."

"She'll decide soon enough."

"But, listen . . ."

"I'm counting ten," said Tromba, "and I've already started."

How fast was he counting? Richard sat focused on the black
point of the muzzle three feet off, his hands gripping the table
ledge.

"Nine," Tromba said.

439

Perhaps it was instinct, perhaps thought transference — Richard suddenly ducked and at the same instant flung up the edge of the table as a kind of shield. The movement coincided with the pull of Tromba's finger on the trigger. The shot splintered the edge of the table an inch above Richard's head. It filled the room with thunder and a brief fog of smoke. But at once reversing his weapon, Tromba, though still hampered by the upturned table, clubbed down at the crouching figure on the other side. In the haze, the heavy butt missed its aim and landed harmlessly beyond Richard's shoulder. A second blow fell too late. Richard was on his feet and out of range.

"Now," he breathed, "unless you have a second pistol, Marcello . . ."

With an imprecation, Tromba rounded the table and leaped forward, clubbing again, but found his wrist in the other's grasp and a powerful arm about his waist, though the force of the charge carried both men reeling against the wall. There, for a minute, they stood locked in a stalemate, equal in strength, the younger man fighting for his life, the adventurer reckless of anything now but his hatred and his passion — locked together, staggering here and there. But in this sort of struggle, Tromba's experience was apt to have the best of it.

Suddenly he dropped the now useless pistol, and with a quick, whirling movement wrenched himself free; then, as Richard tried to close again, he shot in his fist to the other's chin.

Only the wall, against which he found himself, kept Richard on his feet. And at that moment, Tromba whipped out his sword.

"I'll settle with you," he panted. "By God, if it's my last act . . ."

There was no time for Richard to draw, even if he had been capable of it. Dizzy from the blow, his eyes half blinded by patches of darkness and light, he could see vaguely Tromba's poised sword.

And then incredibly . . .

Someone, gripping Tromba from behind, pinioned his arms. Another joined in, and another, the valet l'Esprit. But the new assailants had indeed caught a tiger, and, in spite of the odds, for several moments it looked as if Tromba would break away. Then at last, disarmed and held by men on each side of him, he stood rag-

440

ing. Even the reiterated command *In the King's name!* did not at once quiet him.

Engrossed by the fight, neither he nor Richard had heard the negotiation of the lock by a master key from outside. The door had been opened only in the nick of time.

Coming partially to his senses, Tromba roared: "In the King's name, is it? What's the meaning of this? . . ."

"The meaning of it," said a nondescript, sallow man, "is that you are under arrest, Monsieur le Marquis."

"Who the devil are you?"

"Jean Marais, an inspector in the Ministry of Police, at your service, Monsieur le Marquis." But the suave reply was sarcastic rather than polite.

"Then, for God's sake," Tromba stormed, "loose me and arrest that fellow!" He glared at Richard, who had now regained his poise and stood facing him. "An English spy! I came here to apprehend him!"

"And you were yourself apprehended," said Marais. "How droll!"

"It won't be droll for you, rascal, when I report your stupidity to the King."

"Pray do," Marais returned, "if you can report anything from a cell in the Bastille. And, while you're about it, report that my stupidity consists in carrying out His Majesty's personal commands."

"The *King's*? You're mad!"

"If so, monsieur, it's a madness shared by Monsieur de Sartines, who has a lettre de cachet in your name signed by His Majesty."

"But . . . a thousand devils! . . . for what reason?"

"The King does not have to account to you for his reasons. I suggest —" Marais glanced about the disordered room, sniffed the powder fumes, eyed Tromba's still naked sword in the hands of one of the guards — "I suggest that His Majesty may not care for jealous assassins, may wish to prevent their crimes, which a certain noble lady in his service could have warned him of. But that is merely a suggestion. There may be other reasons."

Knowing Amélie, Richard could very well reconstruct her interview with de Sartines. She would have established herself more solidly than ever in the Minister's confidence by handing over the Prud'homme copy of Choiseul's letter. She had recovered it, she

441

would say, after her late husband's death. She would have hinted of his antagonism to Choiseul. Then she would have presented her lettre de cachet. Tromba, she would say, had discovered the rendezvous between herself and d'Amond at Passy. He was insanely jealous. There may have been other hints. Tromba would not help his case at the moment if he showed too much knowledge of stolen documents.

Richard could not refrain from smiling. "You see, Marcello, the lady in question has made her decision."

"I demand justice," Tromba raged. "I tell you to search this fellow. I tell you —" The words died on his lips. A trace of prudence came to his rescue at the last moment. A man could leave the Bastille, but no one condemned as a spy ever left the grave. Vengeance might be sweet, but it was hardly worth torture and death.

"Why search him?" Marais prompted.

Tromba said nothing. However, he stared, when Richard put in: "At your service, Monsieur Marais." The letter was in a secret pocket at the back of his coat and not likely to be found. "If you have any doubts . . ."

"None, Monsieur le Chevalier," Marais bowed, "unless the prisoner cares to explain his remark. I wonder if he knows anything of a certain letter stolen from the late Monsieur Prud'homme which is now in the hands of Monsieur de Sartines."

The blow which had landed on Richard's chin was no more dazing than the effect of these words on Tromba. His startled eyes shifted from Richard to Marais and back again.

"Christ!" he muttered at last in a tone of deep admiration.

"Eh?" prompted the Inspector. Do you know of it?"

Tromba shook his head. "How should I know of such a letter?"

"Very well, Monsieur le Marquis —" Marais smiled over the title — "this way then."

But Tromba hung back. The mask was once more in place. "Farewell, my dear boy," he said. "I'm convinced now that the Bastille is saving me from a much worse fate. You're welcome to it. And you can tell the lady so with my compliments. Gran' Dio! What a woman!"

Alone with l'Esprit, Richard felt that the occasion merited a

442

pinch of snuff, and he inhaled it with gusto. But the sight of his box recalled the still unfinished business. Tromba might decide to talk after all; there was no time to lose.

Having dispatched the valet to a pharmacy in search of ointment for his bruised chin, Richard copied and burned Amélie's telltale paper, then added a few personal lines to Lord Marny. He would attend the Opéra that evening and have his snuffbox refilled at the sign of the "Civette" in the Palais Royal.

L X I V

A MONTH later, Richard's recall arrived formally through the channel of the Dutch embassy. It stated that, in view of the French insistence upon terms of peace unacceptable to England, the King, though sensible of Captain Hammond's zeal and industry, did not find any useful purpose to be served by his continued residence in Paris and directed him forthwith to return to London. Upon arrival there, he would report to His Majesty's Secretary of State and receive the latter's instructions.

At the same time, his snuffbox, filled for him by the Demoiselle Lenoir, contained a short but ecstatic communication from Lord Marny. Even this was in guarded terms, but it left no doubt as to the reception awaiting him at St. James's Square.

The Earl wrote: "Needless to inform you, my dear boy, that a certain Eminent Person finds your last dispatch very much to his taste and is warm in your praise. Whether or no the conclusive evidence you send will be enough to turn the political tide in his favor remains to be seen. But that is not your affair. You have succeeded admirably and completely. You may expect the shining recognition you deserve. — As to the personal good news with which you favor me, you know in advance how fully it gratifies my own desires and meets with my warmest approval. Indeed, may I not claim some credit for this happy consummation? Though young, Madame des Landes is as old as Lilith in those worldly arts which assure success at any court and among people of fashion everywhere. Pray commend me to her and convey my paternal blessing, as well as the renewed assurance of the twenty thousand pounds, which I shall be delighted to settle upon her on the occasion of your wedding. She will agree with me that true love is all the firmer when coupled with material advantages . . ."

Richard showed this communication to Amélie when he next called at the Hôtel des Landes.

"Do you agree with him?" she asked, handing back the letter.

"Why, yes. — Human nature being as it is. — What are you smiling at?"

"Your progress as a man of the world, mon cher. Then, too, it reminded me of a recent talk I had with the Marquis de Chabrillan . . ."

Since the death of her husband, Amélie, though officially in retirement, had not sacrificed pleasure unduly to mourning. She did not receive, to be sure, in the crepe-hung grand salon but entertained the favored few at discreet suppers or at small card parties in the less formal rooms. Selected gallants still superintended her toilet in the mornings and brought her the gossip of Paris. It would have been scandalous to be seen in an open box at the theater, but screened boxes were always available. In fact, she enjoyed herself too much for Richard's peace of mind, and he had begun to look coldly at the young Marquis de Chabrillan.

"In what connection?" he asked, trying to keep his voice casual.

"Why, to be frank, Noiraud, I believe Monsieur de Chabrillan would propose to me, except for those material advantages that Lord Marny recommends."

Still elaborately casual, Richard asked: "I suppose you haven't informed him of our relations?"

"Of course not. Nothing could be more dangerous until I'm across the frontier and you meet me in Holland next spring. Wasn't it understood —"

"I didn't mean that. I mean our relations as lovers. What Monsieur de Sartines knows, de Chabrillan might as well know, too — and the Comte de Coigny and the Comte de Tessé and the Marquis de Monteynard and all the other coxcombs ogling you, now that they aren't afraid of Tromba's claws. By God —"

"Now, now," she soothed. "You were doing so well. Don't be grim. Whatever you feel, Richard, always smile. It's the essence of good breeding. If you wish to proclaim yourself my preferred

444

lover, I won't contradict it. But I wish you wouldn't. You'll be leaving in a few days. And what of me in the long months till spring? The gentlemen you mention are really quite engaging. I simply can't endure solitude."

Her eyes flashed in mock anger, then melted again to their usual heavenly blue. She smiled, slightly wrinkling her nose. He found her as always irresistible. She had to be accepted on her own terms.

But he could not help a sigh. "The eternal tease, m'amour."

She nodded. "Of course I'm teasing, but you force me to it. You would like me to give everybody up and keep only you as the pièce de résistance. It's what makes marriage so forbidding. It simply wouldn't do for a gourmet like me. I must have my hors d'oeuvres, my entrées, salads and desserts. I wish you'd stop confusing such trifles with love!"

"I'm doing my best," he smiled.

"It will come," she encouraged him. "You're almost there now. And, after all, didn't I fall in love with you because you were you? I'm such a contradiction."

She had acquired a new lap dog, all fluff and perfume, languid eyes and aristocracy, which she now caught up to kiss.

"Pas vrai, Tonton? Que ta petite maman est drôle! Ah, salaud. Va-t'en avant que tu fasses pipi."

The little dog, released, strutted across the floor and looked up with a yawn at Monsieur Coco, who dropped a seed on him and remarked, "Fils de putain!"

"I didn't tell you," Amélie said, "that I've had news of Marcello in the Bastille. I sent him some books and a letter, in which I hinted that the sooner he pays what he owes me from the lottery, the sooner he'll get out. The rascal! I've heard that my share is thirty thousand livres. But he wrote back: freedom first and money afterwards. He doesn't seem to trust me, Richard. They say he's cooled off a good deal and is writing his memoirs. I'll wager they're amusing."

"How would you get him out?"

"Oh, that's easy — an appeal to the King. After you're gone, I'll arrange to see Marcello and come to terms. You'll leave me the receipts he gave you. It's always good to have a curb on his bit.

445

He'll rot in prison, though, unless I get my thirty thousand livres. The old pirate!" She turned to a servant who had appeared at the door. "Yes?"

"The young person from the Opéra, whom Madame has received at various times, Mademoiselle Venier. Will Madame see her?"

"Of course." Amélie flashed a smile at Richard.

The man lingered. "She is accompanied by a big, ugly dog. Perhaps the animal should remain below because of Monsieur Tonton?"

"Not at all. One does not reject the dogs of one's callers. Tonton must learn savoir-faire."

"As Madame wishes."

Amélie hastily slipped on a black outer gown and covered her hair with a crepe scarf. "This tiresome mourning! But we mustn't shock the poor child. I wonder what brings her."

Richard wondered himself. During the past months, Amélie had continued to favor Maritza in small ways — a word to the directors, Rebel and Francoeur, a puff here and there. She and Richard had sometimes discussed Maritza's future at the Opéra, of which Amélie took a dark view because of the rising star of Mademoiselle Allard. Today's call at the Hôtel des Landes meant something out of the ordinary.

But, with this in mind, Richard was unprepared for the impression Maritza made upon entering the blue and gold of the little salon. It was as if the focus of the room shifted at once to her. In the artificial surroundings, she alone seemed real.

She was evidently in the highest spirits. Although she had learned to speak French after a fashion, she always preferred Italian with Amélie.

"Contessina cara," she began, after a hurried curtsy, "I couldn't wait —" And then, "Richard! I've just been past your lodgings. Your servant told me you might be here. — Sioria, I couldn't wait to tell you both the good news. Think, tomorrow night — Bapi! Ah, maledetto!"

The reaction of Monsieur Tonton to Bapi had not been favorable. He abhorred the ruffianly intruder's smell and mean appearance. His languid eyes kindled. Accustomed to jasmine and violet, he found this vulgarian insufferable. On the other hand, Bapi felt only bewilderment as to what the animated fluff might be and ap-

"Oh, everything. I've had all the luck. I wanted her to glory over me. It smooths out the past."

They mingled in the kaleidoscope of the foyer and drifted upstairs to the box, where they were joined presently by the Marquis de Chabrillan and the Comte de Tessé, whom Amélie had invited. Richard could well have dispensed with them, but more than one gentleman in public attendance was essential to the Countess. Waiting for the curtain, she ordered candles lighted, proposed cards, and sat down to picquet with de Chabrillan, while de Tessé looked on. Richard, more interested in the audience that Maritza would have, studied it, lorgnette in hand, through the open screen of the loge.

Though small, in view of its national importance, the interior of the Opéra made a rich enough impression with its amphitheater, its circles of gilded boxes, the great canopied loges of the King and Queen, hung in blue velvet with golden fleurs-de-lis, to the right and left of the stage. Their Majesties, who were entertained at their private theater in Versailles, rarely appeared at the Paris Opéra. But their loges symbolized them and lent a royal character to the theater not to be found in many of the other places of entertainment.

Richard could see at once that there would be a full house. It was Friday, the fashionable night. Many who cared nothing for music would attend in order to see or be seen. Then, too, the *Indes Galantes* by the leading French composer Rameau was justly an old favorite, and had been often revived since its first production twenty-five years ago. As a ballet opera, it gave scope to the peculiarly French skills in dancing, costume, and stage settings. In the minds of the audience, it was associated with the famous ballerinas Sallé and Lyonnois. Maritza had therefore a great chance and a great challenge.

The pit, where people stood crowded together between the seats of the dress circle and the musicians of the orchestra, was already full; the boxes were filling. A sudden burst of acclaim from the pit drew Richard's attention to one of the lower boxes, which had just been entered by Maritza's rival, Marie Allard, in company with her patron, the Duc de Mazarin. That she, except for her accident, would have had the lead in the ballet this evening was of course well known. Her beauty and her escapades had made her a favorite with the public, and nothing could be more natural than a tribute of admiration and sympathy from the pit. But Richard, attuned from his childhood to the demonstrations of theater audiences, felt a sudden misgiving. This one was too organized, too prompt, as if at a word of command. It sounded like a claque. Standing at the front of the loge, her fine bosom and many diamonds in evidence, Mademoiselle Allard waved a gracious acknowledgment to her admirers, then seated herself with an air of pleased expectancy.

"What's happening?" Amélie asked, glancing up from her cards.

Richard explained, and de Chabrillan, intent on his hand, said absently: "Yes, I've heard reports. The Allard isn't happy about being replaced. Monsieur de Mazarin would do anything to humor her. It may be interesting . . . Your play, madame."

Uneasy for the first time, Richard again examined the audience. Perhaps it was nothing. The Duc de Mazarin might have dropped a word here and there that Mademoiselle Allard would appreciate recognition when she entered the box. But he could also have packed the pit against Maritza. In that case, her task would be doubly hard or even impossible. What would the Duke care about her blasted hopes as long as he satisfied the spite of his mistress? Still, such a maneuver was improbable, did not need to be assumed. Marie Allard had no reason to fear competition. As Maritza had said, there was room at the Opéra for both of them.

And yet, alive now to a possible danger, Richard detected, or thought he detected, signs in the pit that he did not like: an exchange of grins and nods in certain groups, a look of humorous understanding, like schoolboys up to a prank. There seemed to be ringleaders to whom they referred. Richard's anticipation of the evening turned to a fever of suspense, the worse because he was entirely helpless. He could picture Maritza in her dressing room, keyed up to this great occasion.

Then the overture began; the hum of the audience lessened; and he sat forward, tense.

"Your round, Monsieur de Chabrillan," said Amélie, shifting her chair for a better view of the stage, "but I'll have my revenge later. I'd much rather win your money than listen to music. Operas are always too long. Don't you agree?"

"They have that failing, madame."

"Then remember it's my deal next. We'll watch the ballet in between rounds. Monsieur d'Amond, you're not sociable tonight."

Richard answered with a phrase or so. The Comte de Tessé remarked: "If Mademoiselle de Venier had shown as much favor to me as to d'Amond, I'd be absent-minded myself. As it is, I'm at ease. Who was it called the opera a spectacle gravely comic and ridiculously serious? I confess . . ."

The curtain rose on the prologue, and with it a murmur of admiration from the audience. The scene designer had surpassed himself. It was the palace gardens of Hebe, goddess of youth, and the famous Sophie Arnould herself began the dramatic screaming that passed for song on the French stage, and that Richard, trained in Italy, could never distinguish from recitative. But neither Sophie Arnould, nor the slight plot, nor the magnificent staging made the least impression on him. At the invitation of Hebe, the lovers from four nations, France, Spain, Italy, and Poland, in splendid costumes, gathered to revel in her gardens. The stage filled with the ballet, who, after a polonaise, dissolved into the two opening minuets. There at the center was Maritza.

He had never seen her so lovely as tonight, in a fanciful Italian costume — all lightness and grace. The talent she had of interpreting the mood and meaning of a dance had never been more evident. She incarnated youth and pleasure, lending to the formal and somewhat rigid minuet enchanting overtones. But, since this was an ensemble, and the humor of the audience with regard to her could not yet be determined, Richard remained tense until the first pas seul.

And now Bellona, goddess of war, disturbed the revels with a fiery appeal to glory, while Amour descending in a winged chariot urged the lovers to flee with him from strife-torn Europe to the blissful East dedicated to beauty and love. So ended the prologue, and in the concluding dance Maritza briefly appeared alone.

It was too slight a figure to justify a verdict of the audience one way or another — only a few steps. But the pit at once exploded in boos and catcalls which ended as soon as Maritza again merged with the ranks of the ballet.

Richard felt sick. The intention of the claque was plain beyond

451

any doubt. As the opera progressed, the bullying would grow louder. No sense of pity or fair play would restrain it. It had been paid for. And the sniggering Duke in his loge, with the triumphant Allard beside him, was there to see that he got his money's worth. Maritza's great night had been doomed at the outset. It had become the night of her execution.

"By God!" Richard exclaimed, springing up. "I've got to see her. This mustn't go on. She mustn't dance . . ."

Amélie shook her head. He was half aware that she felt more disturbed for him than for Maritza. "What a pity! Yes, tell her not to dance. There's no use exposing herself to that kind of humiliation. Give her my love . . ."

In a daze of concern and anger, Richard found his way outside, entered the stage door, climbed the well-known stairs to Maritza's dressing room, pushed past the agitated Anzoletta, and found Signor Collalto of the Italian Theater expostulating with Maritza.

"No, fia mia!" he was saying. "A thousand times no! I'll see the director and explain. I'm sure he'll agree. Your understudy will do — any understudy. Only don't go back on stage. It's impossible . . ."

"Niente!" She was standing rigid in the center of the room, her eyes hard with the pain in them, her head tilted back. "Niente! I'll go on to the end. You'll see . . ."

Richard burst out: "Maritzetta cara, don't give them that satisfaction. You can't win against a pack of bullies. If you don't appear, Mazarin will have spent his money for nothing. You'll have another chance later. If you go on stage now, it will be the end. I beg you —"

"Niente!" she repeated. "I won't cringe to them. I won't be driven from the stage because of them. I'm not a coward. They're only a few. The rest of the house will be for me in the end. You'll see —"

"The curtain, mademoiselle," said a voice at the door.

"I'm coming," she said and walked out, head up and smiling.

Richard returned absently to the loge.

"Well?" asked Amélie.

"She's going on with it."

De Chabrillan took snuff. "Tant pis pour elle."

"Yes," Amélie nodded. "I think we'll be seeing a crucifixion.

452

Tiens! That's a droll idea! A dancing crucifixion. I don't know that I care to look at it. Cards, Monsieur le Marquis?"

She had used the right term for what followed. The entr'actes were short at the Opéra. As scene followed scene, now an island in the Indian Ocean, now the Peruvian Andes, or a Persian garden, or an American forest, with most ingeniously devised effects and tuneful music, the harrying went on. Maritza played into the hands of the claque, exerted herself to win the audience in spite of it, danced as never before, only to be isolated by the horseplay that made her efforts look absurd.

The claque was skillfully managed. It applauded the mise en scène, the singers, those parts of the ballet where Maritza did not appear. It avoided stirring up the wrath of the house by spoiling the evening's entertainment. Its shafts were only for her. Gradually, it added to the general amusement by clownery that made people laugh. The applause, which at first could be heard above the ridicule, died away. The house was obviously waiting to see what kind of witticism her next appearance would prompt and began, indeed, to join in with its own witticisms. After all, why be considerate of a little-known Italian dancer, when it was such good fun to bait her? Who could expect good dancing from an Italian, anyway, as compared with a product of the French school like the glorious Marie Allard? It would teach the directors to keep such parvenus out of leading roles.

And, across the expanse of heads that separated him from the stage, Richard could sense the progress of Maritza's heartbreak. She did not flinch before the personal jibes shouted up at her. He could guess what increasing courage it took to meet the next outburst of derision at every new entrée. But her dancing grew more mechanical. Slowly, from act to act, the animation in her faded, leaving only the force of will and professional training to carry her through.

Richard sat staring at her across the intervening space, wretched and yet absorbed. However, there were long stretches of sight and sound between her appearances. He did not see or hear them. Gradually, he found himself involved with his own thoughts. He became absorbed not only in Maritza but in the problem of Richard Hammond.

He did not think logically, of course, much less abstractly. It was rather a pelting of detached memories.

Maritza in the Villa garden, or on the roof of the old palazzo, or beside him on the lagoon — the sweetness and freshness of those days — and now here, beaten but undefeated. Glorious, really. How could he have ever dreamed that he loved anyone else!

And there were other recollections apparently unconnected yet somehow pertinent. Canada. Wolfe. The smell of autumn forests; the intimations of American vastness . . .

Or, as counterpoint, the frigid indifference of great houses in London. Flights of stairs. The perfumed closeness of Parisian salons and boudoirs. Himself with the Maréchal de Richelieu in the stony splendor of Versailles as Louis XV, the bored Apollo, passed between ranks of bowing courtiers. Himself servile to the King's mistress, the great Pompadour, who held France in her hands. Himself in every way currying favor here and there in the interests of his government, gaming, flattering, bribing, restless, his eye alert to the main chance.

Certain it was that if God existed, He did not rule here nor in terms of the Black Mass offered to Lord Vanity . . .

A drift of faces, all with the same stamp on them, the stamp that showed in the portraits of Baron Marny at Marny House and now in Richard's own mirror.

But, after all, why should he delude himself that he still had a choice? He was engaged to Amélie. It was too late. He had made his bargain with open eyes. He did not have the right to break it.

Amélie's voice brought him back. "Quelle veine! I win, Monsieur de Chabrillan. Ten louis. Not bad, eh?"

"Madame always wins . . ."

The house was applauding the mise en scène of the last act. Richard grew conscious of flower-covered arbors, lighted with crystal chandeliers and extending apparently into the distance. They centered on a fountain mid-stage and were on two levels, the ballet, as Persian odalisks below, the singers above. It was the supreme effect of the opera. In this act the great Sallé had scored one of her most distinguished triumphs, when a rose tree, opening, revealed the ballerina representing a rose, surrounded by other animated flowers. Maritza had looked forward to it as the climax of the evening. One could imagine what the claque would make of it.

Amélie got up. "Messieurs, I think I've had enough. Cruelty bores me in the long run, and so does useless courage. Vive Monsieur de Mazarin, with his whore and his canaille! À bas Mademoiselle de Venier of the brave heart! Let's be going. I'm sure the Chevalier d'Amond would second the motion if he hadn't lost the use of his tongue. — My cloak and mask, Lisette."

Apparently the claque had reserved its finest effort for this scene. As the gazettes reported it, no personalities were this time directed at Maritza, but practically the entire pit turned its back on the stage and acclaimed her rival.

Leaving the Opéra in advance of the crowd, Amélie and her escort could hear the muffled roar of voices.

"Marie Allard!"

L X V I

"HOW often have I told you, Noiraud," Amélie remarked after a moment of silence, as they drove back to the Faubourg Saint-Germain, "how very often, that, whatever your feelings, you should never show them in public! It's not done in good company. You should continue to smile even with the toothache."

"No doubt," he said absently.

"But you pay no attention. Tonight you were utterly hopeless. You moped like an owl. Couldn't you see that our friends were laughing at you? And tomorrow everybody will be laughing at the poor Chevalier d'Amond, who pouted and sulked to no purpose. Won't that add to de Mazarin's gaiety? When, instead, it's you should have laughed. You should have sparkled with bon mots; and then later, on some quite different pretext, you could slip your sword through de Mazarin with a final bon mot. As it is, you cut a sorry figure."

"I'm sure," he agreed. "Does it shock you that I don't much care?"

She smiled. "Bad as that, is it? Allons, gai, Monsieur le Philosophe! I beg you to consider that in spite of Allard's triumph and Venier's failure, the world will go on spinning for a long time."

"Yes," he shrugged, "it has that habit."

"Naughty Amélie, keep quiet," she said, and sank back in her sables.

They reached the door of the Hôtel des Landes.

"I suppose now you'll be driving back to the Rue de Richelieu," she said. "In the circumstances, Mademoiselle will cancel the party."

"Of course," he nodded. "But I have to go whether she sees me or not. I can have a word with Anzoletta. I want them to feel that I care. You see how it is."

"Quite. Only give her time to get back from the Opéra. And give me a few minutes. Have your coach wait. I must put you in better spirits, mon ami, or you won't be much of a comfort to anyone."

The fire and the candles in the gilded little salon had been lighted. A servant appeared with wine and a tray of delicacies. When Amélie had slipped off her furs, and the maid was gone, she seated herself at one side of the small hearth and waved Richard to an opposite chair.

"Do you know what this reminds me of, mon cher? Guess."

"I haven't an idea. Bath, perhaps?"

"That's it — Bath. And you look exactly as you did that night when we came back from hearing Monsieur Wesley. It's the first time I've seen you that way since then. Remember how touched and solemn we both were? Bon Dieu! And then we had a wonderful night together. Quelles délices! But, heaven knows, Monsieur Wesley didn't preach this evening. What makes you look as if he had?"

"Maybe the same kind of thoughts."

"What thoughts?"

He made an effort. "Oh, about life in general. You'll have to admit that the recent sample of it wasn't pretty. If I look solemn, that's the reason. But why dwell on it? Didn't you promise to cheer me up?"

"And so I shall." She absently turned one of her hands this way and that, watching the sparkle of the diamonds. "When I last went to confession — it's long ago — I felt wonderfully light afterwards. Tell me what's on your mind."

"No," he said. "I choose to forget it. Remember, on that famous night you mentioned, how you said it was the last time you would be troubled by any such compunctions — the last flutter, you called

456

it. Well, I feel that way tonight. Good company forever! You'll have no cause to scold me again."

She stared at her ring. "Yes, I did say that. I'm not very consistent. I still have qualms at times. Rarely, I admit. But sin's no fun if one hasn't. So, you see, I can sympathize with you — still. I can even tell you, since you won't tell me, what you were mulling over at the opera."

"Clairvoyance?" He smiled. "You hardly need it. What would anyone have been thinking who had half a heart?"

She shook her head. "I didn't mean Maritza. You said *life in general*, didn't you? No, your thoughts went further. They rebelled, they longed, they despaired — just as once in the galleys. Am I right?"

She was so right that he found nothing to answer, but sat intent on the fire.

"They even included me, didn't they?" she went on. "But I won't embarrass you by revealing them. The jist of it was that you could escape from the galleys except for me."

Her shrewdness startled him into denial. "Nothing of the sort."

"Yes, very much of the sort, Richard chéri." Turning, she poured herself a glass from the decanter at her side, tasted it, and held up the amber-filled crystal to the light. "Let me remind you that the one feature of our relationship which has been most precious to me, because it's so rare, is the openness we've used with each other. If that's lost . . ." She shrugged. "You see, Richard, I know you so well."

He could only answer: "In that case, why force me to speak? Words seldom express what one means. They imply too much or too little."

She tasted her wine again. "Yes, you're in something of a dilemma, aren't you, mon pauvre? You urged me to marry you in spite of all my warnings. I gladly agreed. You're a man of honor. So, it's the galleys."

"Amélie —"

"No, wait. As you say, words imply too much or too little. Perhaps I can help you. First of all —"

"Listen," he interrupted. "I think I know you, too. I think you'll understand, whatever the words. It's not you. It's a way of life.

457

The sort of thing we watched tonight — all that's behind it, all it means. The stupid heartlessness. The stupid code. That, and the cursed, empty career I'm saddled with. The damned falseness of it. Year after year. Until —" He broke off. "Do you see at all what I mean?"

She put her glass down and leaned toward him. "Until what, Richard?"

"Why, until it seems natural. Until you forget that there is any other kind of life."

"Where?" she put in. "What would you do?"

On the spur of the moment and yet with no sense of improvising, he said: "I think I'd go back overseas. It isn't Paradise there. It isn't the sort of thing Monsieur Rousseau writes about. That's nonsense. But it's so big and new that a man has more of a chance to be himself."

"Canada?"

"No, Virginia. It interests me somehow. Of course I couldn't keep the property Lord Marny gave me. But there's land to the west. I have an acquaintance there. He was in the Royal Americans. Come with me, Amélie."

Her lips were parted, her eyes, distant. Then she gave a smile, that was half a grimace, and leaned back. "Now, *that's* nonsense. Talk about Monsieur Rousseau!" She laughed. "Amélie des Landes returns to Nature! What a thought! Imagine Messieurs Coco and Tonton in the big new world, being themselves. They wouldn't have a worse time of it than I. No, for me, the old, little world, with its wickedness and comforts! I haven't a trace of the heroic. Dear Richard, how absurd you are!"

She looked so amused that he stiffened a little.

But she turned serious. "No, I didn't mean that, either." She sprang up and seated herself on the arm of his chair, looking down at him. "Not absurd, just considerate. You promised to marry me. You'll keep your word. I know how it is . . . Only I'm a part of the life you're tired of. And there's no use wishing I wasn't. I'm simply what I am, a woman of fashion and not transplantable. Now, if I were Maritza Venier —"

She stopped suddenly. He could see her eyes widen and her expression alter. Standing up, she faced him from the hearth.

458

"What a humbug you are," she breathed, "and what a fool I am!"

She had changed so abruptly that he rose in his turn. "Will you explain what you mean, Amélie?"

"Your talk about a way of life!" she went on in an odd, sultry voice. "I ought to have known that a man in his senses isn't prepared to give up wealth, position, a career, a not unattractive marriage, except for one reason. So that's it! You're in love with Maritza Venier. I was silly enough to believe that was over." And when he said nothing, "Well! Do you wish to cover it up with more finespun excuses?"

"I wasn't aware," he said, "that I was covering up anything. Until tonight, I believed like you. Now I know that I've always loved her. That doesn't make me false to you. Perhaps it makes me false to what you say you're a part of. Maritza belongs to a faith I used to have and turned my back on. That's all. I'm tired of good company, as you call it."

"It's rather late to be tired of it, Richard."

His voice matched hers. "Do me the justice to remember that I implied that to start with. It's too late, indeed. You insisted on bringing up these things."

She disregarded him. "And of course you assume that she loves you. I suppose you have good reasons to be very sure of it."

He grew colder. "What do you mean? I assume nothing. I have no reasons at all."

"Bon Dieu!" she exclaimed. "I really think you've lost your mind. What's the point of this folly?"

"I thought you would understand," he said. "I thought we knew each other well enough for that."

He was unprepared for her sudden volte-face. She looked down. "Yes, I understand." Then, after a moment, "I wonder if you understand me. I don't myself." She drew closer to him. "Can you understand why I'm really glad . . . Why now I love you and shall always love you — now that we may never see each other again? I don't, and yet it's true. Mon bien aimé, I suppose it's because you give me yourself again, I mean what I loved in you and what we both would have lost. Mon bien aimé . . ."

Her arms were about him, her lips, against his.

459

"For once be proud of me as I am of you."

Then she slipped away from him and added after a short pause: "Now I won't keep you any longer. It will be easier for both of us if we don't meet again. You and I are only human. Tonight I see clearly how dreadful it would be if, instead of ending this way, we spun life out until nothing was left. But tomorrow . . . Desire is so plausible — yes, and common sense. You agree, don't you?"

He had the sensation of a vast emptiness. The rebellion which had fired him began to seem unreal and a little fantastic.

"I suppose so," he answered.

She caught the indecision in his voice. "Don't think, Richard. Don't balance one thing against the other. Follow your heart and not your head. The heart is usually right."

Transparently, she reverted to her accustomed manner. "I suppose, in any case, you'll be returning to England now."

"Yes. I owe a report to Mr. Pitt. I must explain, if I can, to Lord Marny."

"It won't be pleasant."

"No," he shrugged. "But you, Amélie? What —"

"Ah, mon cher," she interrupted, "the last thing in the world you have to be concerned about is me. I'll attract a husband if I want one, material advantages or not. Then, too, I'll amuse myself with Marcello Tromba. He and I are really very congenial. He deserves some amends for the Bastille."

Turning, she found her glass of wine on the small table and emptied it.

"Of course, you'll let me know about your marriage with Maritza. You'll write now and then. I'll send you the gossip of Paris and whet your appetite for the big new world. Frankly, I wonder how long our old, little world will last. They say His Majesty has the vapors about it, speaks of an end and prophesies a deluge. Think of Amélie, Coco and Tonton in a deluge! . . ."

She filled her glass and then another.

"Do you remember the toast we drank two years ago in Bath? It was to Cythera, wasn't it? Now that the voyage is over, we ought to drink at parting. What shall it be? The future?" Her voice shook suddenly. "There isn't any for us together. The past? No, we mustn't turn back. What toast is left, Noiraud?"

He felt as he had that morning of cold and mist at her sailing from Bristol — the moment of farewell.

"Only one," he said. "This hour!"

"Yes," she said. "It doesn't belong to time. I can drink to that . . ."

LXVII

IT was not yet ten when Richard's coach stopped in front of Maritza's lodginghouse on the Rue de Richelieu. Looking up at the third floor, he could see a faintly lighted window. It confirmed what he had assumed. The gay little supper she had planned for her friends of the Italian Theater had, of course, been impossible. Maritza would have retired. Anzoletta was probably still up, on the chance that someone who had not heard of the evening's disaster might yet call, or perhaps expecting Richard himself.

Feeling the need of a walk later, he dismissed the carriage and then trudged up the dim flights of stairs. He felt already divested of the trappings of Richard Hammond, as if he had crossed back over time into his earlier obscurity, as if his coach and servants, the fine clothes he wore, no longer belonged to him. But it was not the same as once. That, after all, had been a familiar world. He found himself alone in a kind of void, dedicated to an uncertain quest.

"I knew you would come," Anzoletta greeted him at the door. "Ah, fio mio, God grant that I never have to live through such a thing again!" She drew a rough hand across her eyes. "What a blessing that his Excellence . . . Come in, come in. I need someone to talk with."

"Maritza?" he asked in a low voice.

"She won't see anyone, not even me. Of course it won't last. But I'm frightened, Milòr. Not a tear. Nothing. Nothing. Just blankness. If she could only pour her heart out . . ."

They were in the small parlor of the lodgings. Richard glanced at the closed door to Maritza's room.

"You don't think I could have a word with her?"

461

Anzoletta hesitated. "No. But wait. Perhaps it will do her good to hear us talking." She laid a finger on her lips and, crossing to the bedroom on tiptoe, silently raised the latch, so that the door stood a little open. To Maritza, it would easily seem that the latch had been insecurely fastened. Then, crossing back, the woman prompted, "You were saying, caro ti . . . ?"

Richard took pains to speak clearly. "Just that I wanted to thank her for what this evening meant to me, Sior' Amia. She showed me how blind I've been and what I've lost. She taught me how very much I love her — more than anyone or anything in the world. Tell her that from me, Sior' Amia. Tell her . . . Tell her that I've no role to act any longer, that I've quit the stage."

He could not know whether Maritza heard him or not. He kept his eyes on the door. As long as it did not close, he could still hope.

Anzoletta, amazed, faced him across the table where they had seated themselves. She had forgotten her own ruse. "I don't understand, Richard mio. What do you mean?"

"Maritza will know," he said. "After what happened tonight, I'm through with Paris, through with Europe. I intend to see what I can do in America. And I wondered if Maritza . . ." he could not find the words and paused . . . "if it was still possible for her to care for me . . . if she could forgive . . . it would be all I want in life. Tell her that, Sior' Amia."

"But what . . ." the woman faltered. "I still don't understand. The Contessina? We supposed . . ."

"No, I've told her how I feel. She's been very gracious, but we shall not see each other again."

"And Milòr Marny? And the great Mr. Pitt? You were telling us . . . Fio mio, what has happened?"

He explained to Anzoletta and to the unclosed door. The hours of the opera. What they had brought home to him. And the greatest revelation of all. "Remember to tell her this, Sior' Amia. You have always been good to me. I depend on you to help me now. Tell her how much I worship her . . ."

He became aware that Anzoletta's face, so careworn at his arrival, had become radiant. But her answer and tone of voice contradicted it. "Alas, caro ti, I wish I could help you! I'll do my best.

462

Only you know her Excellence, how proud she is. She'll say that she doesn't want pity because of tonight —"

"Gran' Dio!" he burst out. "Pity? Cara Anzoletta! When I can't express how magnificent she is! When I put my life in her hands! Surely . . ."

He received a profound glance from across the table. It was not a wink but it implied one.

"Then, too," said Anzoletta, "she no longer cares for you in that way. She esteems you as a friend. Besides, she'll be more stubborn than ever now to make a mark for herself. There's Dresden and Vienna. There's St. Petersburg. Ah, Richard mio, I'm afraid she's grown very hard and ambitious. It would be wrong to encourage you."

Uncertain as to what answer was expected of him, he said honestly: "I see. Of course it was foolish to imagine that one can ever turn back the clock. I was only thinking of myself and of my love for her. If she married me I would have nothing to offer her except myself — beyond that only uncertainties. Life in America isn't the same as here. I was selfish to propose it."

Anzoletta looked in higher spirits than ever.

"Yes, I think you were, fio mio. And I'm sure her Excellence would not consider it for a moment. After all —"

The door opened, and a passionate voice exclaimed: "Anzoletta! How can you be so wicked? When you know how much I love him! I never expected to hear such words from you!"

Maritza had not undressed and was in her usual plain street clothes. But, far from blankness, her face showed more animation than ever. He thought at once of Venice, as if no time had intervened.

"You *heard?*" exclaimed Anzoletta in mock horror.

"Yes . . . No . . . I mean, I'm not sure I heard. I want to hear it again, except what you said, desgraziada. Richard, I don't believe . . . Caro ti!"

He caught her up in his arms. "Reina mia! Piccina mia!"

At last she turned back to Anzoletta. "How can I ever forgive you, serpente! *Proud,* am I? As if I cared whether he pities me or not, as long as he loves me! *Hard,* ambitious . . . Thank God, I've danced my last chaconne! Thank God for tonight! I want to be a

463

woman, not just a dancer. I want the New World, I'm so sick of the Old . . . And you had the falseness to say . . ."

Anzoletta was not a good actress. She looked too triumphant. Maritza broke off and suddenly smiled.

"Ah . . . So, that was it! I ought to have known . . . Richard, just for that, I'm going to make you propose all over again — right now — and not through a crack in the door. I'm going to make you propose twice a day until we're married. Now you know."

"*Every* day?"

"Every single day."

"But, Maritzetta, how many days are there until tomorrow? . . ."

L X V I I I

IT was not to be expected that a man of Lord Marny's impeccable self-control would betray any weak or womanish emotion upon receiving the letter that reached him from Holland on December twentieth. Mr. Jean Martin, the Earl's secretary, often referred to it as a notable example of his lordship's polished and impenetrable composure. It was all the more impressive because the news came as a sudden reversal of his most confident hopes.

During the past fortnight he had awaited the announcement of Richard's arrival in Holland, which in turn would fix the date of sailing for England, and he had shown a smiling impatience at the delay. But, indeed, the winter roads were foul everywhere. Then, too, Richard would find it hard to tear himself away from his enchantress in Paris. Meanwhile, it was gratifying to elaborate plans for the future. He had his eye on a handsome house in the neighborhood of St. James's Square which he believed would meet with Amélie's approval. He could not resist dropping a hint here and there of Richard's approaching marriage with so distinguished a woman of fashion as the Countess des Landes.

"Well, at last, eh, Martin?" he said, when the secretary handed him the letter. "Our young rogue finally deigns to let himself be heard from. And at length, too," he added, prying up the seal, "to judge from the weight of it. Eh bien, tant mieux. He owes it to me."

Since, from the outset in Venice, it was Martin who had superintended Richard's change from Morandi to Hammond, and since,

464

with regard to Richard especially, he enjoyed the Earl's confidence, he did not retire but stood waiting while Marny read the letter.

He noted at once the contraction of the brows, the intent expression, the tightening of Marny's lips. Then, even these indications yielded to impassiveness. It was a long letter. Apparently the Earl read more rapidly toward the end; and, having finished, he tossed the sheets onto the side table next to his chair.

"Incredible!" he said in a dry voice.

"Not ill news, I hope, my lord?"

"Why, as to that, Martin, he's in good health and married. He hopes soon to present himself with his bride and craves my blessing."

"But, sir, I thought that the marriage with Madame des Landes could not take place at earliest until May."

"True, very true. Only his bride isn't the Countess des Landes. He has married the ballerina you know of, Maritza Venier. Yes, quite incredible."

Martin stood thunderstruck. "My God, sir! I can't express . . . But, my lord, I would put a harsher word to it than that. I couldn't have believed Mr. Hammond capable of such duplicity or ingratitude."

For a while Marny said nothing, but then observed in the same colorless voice: "No, those terms, as a rule, imply self-interest, not suicide. For that's what it amounts to. He's resigning his commission. He rejects any thought of a public career. He insists on returning me the deeds to the Virginia estate. As far as I can gather, he intends to plunge off somewhere into the American wilderness and set up for himself. Preposterous, eh?"

"My lord, it sounds like madness."

Again the Earl fell into thought. "Yes," he conceded, "for a truth, it does. And yet 'tis a connected letter, not straying from the point, nay, exceeding well written, and couched in terms of affection for me. I discover no marks of frenzy about it, save that what he proposes is lunacy."

Martin suggested, "Is it possible that he quarreled with Madame des Landes and has taken this course as a result — the petulance of youth, my lord?"

"No, it appears not. They parted amiably. One would have supposed that Amélie des Landes would not have let twenty thousand pounds slip through her fingers. But who can depend on a woman? He reminds me that this — this Mademoiselle Venier was his first love, as if he considered it important."

"And yet, sir, he must have some reason beyond whim for renouncing such a career and such advantages."

Marny shrugged. "Aye, reasons enough — if you can find any sense in 'em. He writes me that his entire life has been torn between *being* and *seeming*, *belief* and *make-believe*. He will endeavor to choose between *honesty* and *sham* and to live accordingly. He holds that the career he has been following makes this impossible. There are the reasons. 'Tis to be noted that he and Mrs. Hammond have just paid a filial visit to his mother in Bordeaux — much, I conceive, to the latter's contentment. She has always entertained similar notions. — Here, read the letter yourself."

And he sank back into frozen abstraction.

Martin read gravely. "A sad case, indeed, my lord," he said, finishing. "But perhaps —"

Marny interrupted. "Suppose I had made the same choice once. Egad, I was tempted. She was very appealing, very beautiful. I have never loved any woman since as I loved her. Suppose, then, we had married . . ." He fell silent a moment. "But I put that folly behind me, although the choice seemed hard, and I did well. I chose realities, Martin. With what result? This." The wave of his hand included the handsome room and the splendor of Marny House. "This. With all it betokens. A degree of reputation and power, pleasure, too, of a sort. What more's to be had in this silly world? Certainly not the humbug of happiness. I had hoped that Richard would share my view of it and keep sentiment where it belongs, in the chapel. I should have enjoyed wagering on his game. As it is — snuff out the candles." He gave an abrupt laugh. "I said I put that folly behind me. And yet here it is in the person of my son. Jeanne wins in the end, and I lose. That's the moral."

"But perhaps," Martin persisted, "your lordship takes too dark a view of the matter. I own 'tis disturbing but not irreparable. Mr. Hammond's wife is of noble birth. He may be brought to reconsider —"

"Bah!" put in Marny. "It is irreparable on every count. He has made his bed; now let him lie in it. You will answer the letter,

Martin. I have no heart to do so. You will apprise him from me that, though shocked by his decision, I will receive him and Mrs. Hammond, if they choose to call upon reaching London; that I esteem the propriety of his conduct in returning me the Virginia deeds, and I shall be glad to accept them at his convenience. You need not add that I wash my hands of him, but you may imply it."

"Does your lordship desire me to write at once?"

"Immediately."

While the secretary set himself to work, his master took several turns through the room and then came to a halt in front of the wide window overlooking St. James's Square. It was a cold, damp winter day. The soot-laden mist veiled slightly but did not conceal the imposing house fronts opposite, stony, massive and inscrutable. The little park in the center looked shriveled and frozen. Absently for some time, Marny stood gazing out.

Then, he crossed back to the fire and extended his hands toward the glow of the coals.

"Will you see the letter, my lord?" Martin asked, laying his quill down.

"Aye, let me have it."

But when Marny had glanced over the page, he dropped it upon the grate and watched the flickering turn to ashes.

"It does not meet with your lordship's approval? I endeavored to convey the sentiments you expressed."

"You conveyed them well enough. It won't do, Martin. I'll write him myself." The Earl continued to warm his hands. "I shall make him welcome here, nay, both of them welcome. I shall not accept the return of the property I gave him. That's certain. If Richard's a fool, he need not disgrace me in Virginia as a pauper. Even he may condescend to that much sense."

"I'm happy," said Martin, "that your lordship is more kindly disposed. After all, Mr. Hammond's young."

"Nay, sir," replied the other in a low voice, and still intent on the fire, "after all he's my son. I can't help loving him, fool or not. He loves me, too, in a measure — or so I hope . . . so I hope. Perhaps, sir, love is less of an illusion than I once believed." He half turned. "Pray oblige me by calling one of the servants. The fire sinks. It would be well to replenish it."